189

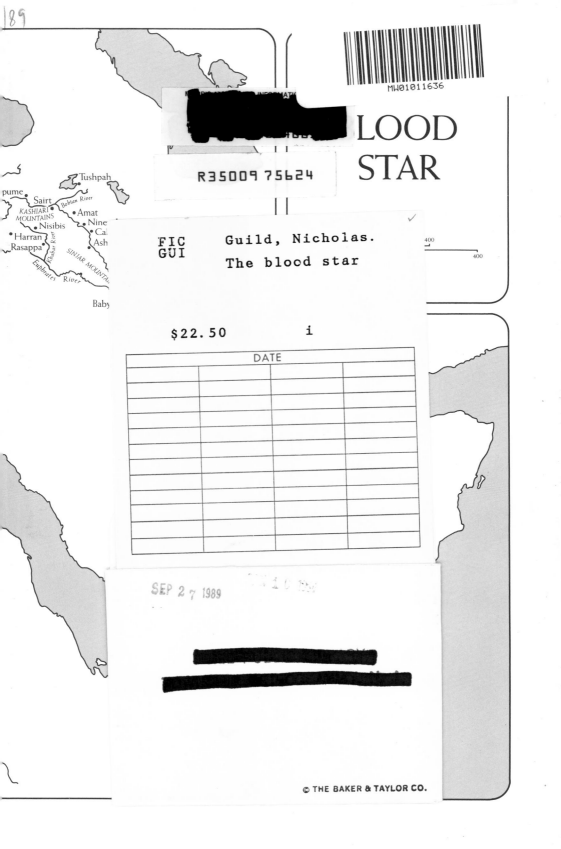

LOOD
STAR

FIC
GUI

Guild, Nicholas.
The blood star

$22.50   i

Tushpah
pume Sairt
KASHIARI
MOUNTAINS
Amat
Nisibis Nine
Harran Cal
Rasappa Ash
Euphrates River
Baby

400
400

DATE			

© THE BAKER & TAYLOR CO.

THE BLOOD STAR

THE
BLOOD STAR

NICHOLAS GUILD

ATHENEUM
NEW YORK 1989

Atheneum
Macmillan Publishing Company
866 Third Avenue, New York, N.Y. 10022
Collier Macmillan Canada, Inc.

Library of Congress Cataloging-in-Publication Data
Guild, Nicholas.
  The blood star/Nicholas Guild.
    p. cm.
  ISBN 0-689-11898-8
  I. Title.
PS3557.U357B57 1989   89-18   CIP
813'.54—dc19

10 9 8 7 6 5 4 3 2 1

Printed in the United States of America

This book is for my friend and agent,
Al Zuckerman

ὅπερ γὰρ ὁ Δημοσθένης ἐπὶ τοῦ κοινοῦ τῶν
ἀνθρώπων ἀποφαίνεται βίου, μέγιστον μὲν εἶναι
τῶν ἀγαθῶν τὸ εὐτυχεῖν, δεύτερον δὲ καὶ οὐκ
ἔλαττον τὸ εὖ βουλεύεσθαι, ὅπερ οἷς ἂν μὴ παρῇ
συναναιρεῖ πάντως καὶ θάτερον . . .

Longinus, 3

THE BLOOD STAR

I

THE WESTERN LANDS—THE PALE SUN WHICH WARMS MY face, the soft blue sky, the wind and the shining water, these are the gifts of their openhanded, childlike gods. It is a place of vines and fruit trees, of stone farmhouses and earth that turns black under the plow's iron blade. It is a place a man might love if he did not chance to dream of his distant home. If he were not a sojourner in the midst of another's garden.

I am such a one. As a boy I did not know the taste of olives or the murmur of the wine-dark sea. Yet, although I was not born here, it seems certain here I will finally die. And that time is not far distant, for I have grown old in this place of strangers—I, the son and grandson of kings, rulers of the wide world. Yet that grandeur is past. The story I tell is of my own life, which even now the god cradles in his hand.

Ashur, god of my fathers, he who is called by many names, who is lord of heaven, the master of this world and the next, he whose will is fate has chosen this path for me, and I take up my pen again that his glory may be known, that his purposes may be seen and understood by men. I am Tiglath Ashur, the god's servant, whose name was yoked with his in the hour of my quickening, who survives perhaps as the last to honor him.

Though she be but a shadow in my own brain, a poor dream of memory, once more my eyes fill with the sight of mighty Nineveh, envy of the world, queen of cities. I am five and twenty. What have I not known already of glory, wealth and power? What have I not known of emptiness, of despair, of jealousy, of the bitterness of lost love? My brother, who is king now in our father's place, turns his face from me. Esarhaddon, who was once my friend, has pronounced my sentence of banishment, that I will be forced to wander in the distant places of the earth, forever a stranger, forbidden to return lest I die for it. Nineveh, which once held all that I loved, now I must flee from you like a slave guilty in his master's sight.

"Let him pass forever out of the Land of Ashur, and all the lands where the might of Ashur's king is felt." So spoke my brother, the mighty king, lord of the earth's four corners. *"Let him hide himself in the dark lands beyond the sun. Let him be taken from my sight!"*

The guards escorted me away. I did not resist them. They took me by the arms and led me stumbling from the king's presence, for I hardly had wit enough left to walk by my own will. My mind was dark. It seemed to me that I had already died.

They took me to a room in my father's palace—my brother's now, as now were all things under the bright sun—and servants stripped me of the silver robes which were marks of my princely rank and I was given a plain soldier's tunic. I put it on, hardly knowing what I did. I sat down. Someone brought me a cup of wine, but I did not drink from it. Does a corpse drink the wine offerings meant to quiet his restless soul? I had no taste for wine, no more than if I were dead and the clay had stopped my mouth. At last the soldiers returned and led me away again.

Where would they take me? I knew not. I was no longer one of the Lord Sennacherib's royal sons—I was a stranger here now, and his heir and successor hated me. Perhaps they took me to my death. It hardly seemed to matter.

But it was not death which awaited me. Instead, I found myself in the palace gardens, where I could hear the sound of the swift-flowing Tigris, mother of rivers, where I had so often seen my father, grown old, resting upon a stone bench as he fed bread crumbs to his birds.

The soldiers departed, without speaking. I was alone. It did not oppress me—I had spent many days alone, in an iron cage in the dungeons of my brother's palace. What weighed upon my heart were the memories stirred within me by the sight of this place.

My father, the king, struck down by an assassin as he knelt to pray before the Lord Ashur. We had avenged that, my brother Esarhaddon and I, and then we had turned one against the other—or, at least, he had turned against me. And only because my father loved me and would have had me succeed him as king, even in defiance of the god's will. Yet I would not put myself up against the god and my brother both. I made my submission to Esarhaddon—let him have the glory of a king's crown, I thought—and for this he could not forgive me.

For this, and for other things.

It was the month of Nisan, when winter begins slowly to die and the world is reborn. Still, it was a bleak world. The flower petals had long since been swept away, but snow still hid in the shadow of the wall. There was no moon, no stars overhead, only the dull black of a cold, cloudy night sky. One needed only to look about to believe that the world had stopped forever. Perhaps it had. I would not have been surprised, or even sorry.

I sat down on the bench, merely because I had grown weary of standing. I cannot claim that I was waiting for anything—or expecting anything. I did not think of the future, not even to the next quarter of an hour. The future had been annihilated for me.

The past, however, would not allow itself to be pushed aside. It kept rising before my mind's eye, unbidden, of its own will, or perhaps because I seemed to belong to it so completely.

My father, sitting on this very stone, old and defeated, knowing that all his hopes for me had come to nothing. How he had hated Esarhaddon, and for no sin of his own. Old men make mischief when their hearts are dark.

And love. Esharhamat, my brother's wife. I could see her face, the tears in her eyes, and hear her voice . . .

"Have you not made my heart a widow?"

"I would be king for your sake," I had told her once, while we still knew hope. *"For your sake, and to change the world."* And she had answered, *"Would you, my love? But the world will not allow itself to be changed."*

And other voices . . .

"You will be great in the Land of Ashur," my mother had told me, since the first days of my youth.

"Do not think that happiness and glory await you here, Prince, for the god reserves you to another way." The counsel of one wiser than my mother.

Words—words that filled my mind and made it ache like a wound in cold weather. I had seen so much, heard so much, and I had been made blind and deaf.

But perhaps not so blind at last.

Gradually, as happens sometimes with a memory that forces its way into the center of one's brain, I became aware that I no longer had the garden entirely to myself. I shared it with another visitor, someone as out of place there as I had become myself. I glanced about, wondering who this intruder could be—perhaps, finally, an assassin sent by my brother to ease his mind by slipping a dagger in under my rib cage? I was almost disappointed to see merely a small boy in a soiled loincloth, his hands clasped behind his back as he watched me through large, intelligent, untrusting eyes.

He stood beside an arbor covered with dead and withered vines—it struck me that the boy must be cold, but if he was he gave no sign of it. He was perhaps six or seven years of age, one of the army of raw little urchins who hung about the docksides and the wineshops of the city, turned loose by parents who could not afford to keep them, scratching out a livelihood from begging and running errands. It was a life that doubtless taught many hard but useful lessons. I was not offended that the child regarded me with such suspicion.

"What do you want?" I asked him—presumptuous of me perhaps, but I had difficulty believing that this ragged boy had merely blundered into the sacred precincts of the king's palace.

"Are you the Lord Tiglath Ashur?" he inquired in his turn, as if the idea seemed unlikely enough to him, "he whose palm is crossed with the blood star?"

"I was until a few hours ago."

"Show me."

I opened my hand, holding it out to him. Even in the dim light of a moonless evening the birthmark was visible, dark red and lurid, as if it were a glowing coal—the god's indelible brand upon me.

"Then this is for you."

He stepped forward and at arm's length held out to me a strip of leather, rolled tightly and tied with a thread. I undid it and spread the strip out across my knee, squinting at it in the darkness. I was not even surprised. The message it contained was written in hasty, slanting Greek, in a hand with which I had long since become familiar.

"Dread Master, your guards have been bribed to bring you here. Be pleased to follow where this child leads and it is possible we may both find deliverance from the king your brother's wrath."

My former slave Kephalos, a fat, luxury-loving rogue, a thief and a coward, a scoundrel upon whose word neither man nor woman could rely. And yet, for all this, my friend, the one soul in all the winding labyrinth of Nineveh in whose love I had any confidence.

I rose from the stone bench, my knees stiff with the night cold I had not until then even noticed, and wrapped my cloak about me.

"Then you shall be my guide, boy," I said, attempting to smile but no doubt making a bad job of it—the little urchin stared at me with cynical astonishment, as if he thought perhaps my wits had gone rancid. "Come, let us depart. There is little enough to hold me here."

A door stood in the garden wall, concealed behind a vine arbor. I had never noticed it before, nor had my father ever mentioned such a contrivance, but perhaps, since even kings must have secrets to keep, it had served some purpose he did not care to have known. In any case, the boy knew of it, and now so did I.

He pushed the door open and we entered into a tiny courtyard that had the look of having been long since forgotten. We stole across it as silently as thieves, and then through a warren of little alleyways filled with trash and broken oil jars until, quite suddenly, we were somewhere down by the water.

The place was deserted and dark. The pale moon had drifted behind a bank of clouds. I heard no murmur of voices, only the whisper of the swift-flowing Tigris, and there were no lamps throwing pools of yellow light onto the brick street. These were the docks, at night as quiet and empty as any mountain waste.

And then, all at once, not ten paces from where I stood, there was the scrape of flint against iron and then the crackling sound of a pitch torch coming to life. As it burned brighter it revealed the shape and at last the face of the worthy Kephalos.

My former slave was one of those who seemed to acquire riches the way other men do bad habits. His wealth would have done credit to the king himself. He kept gold and silver with the merchants of distant cities. He probably owned the very docks upon which we stood. And yet now he was dressed in the faded, dust-stained green-and-white tunic of an Amorite caravan driver, and his great brown beard, usually combed and perfumed like a harlot's nether hair, was a greasy tangle. His broad face was creased with dirt and worry. He had the eyes of a man who had not slept for many nights.

He looked at me, somewhat mournfully I thought, and then turned his attention to the boy, whom he motioned toward him. The boy extended his hand and Kephalos dropped five copper shekels into it, slowly, one after the other, and then, at last, when the boy did not move but still held out his open hand to him, he grunted, as if he expected no better from the wanton world, and added a sixth. Instantly the hand closed into a fist and the boy disappeared into the darkness on naked feet.

"Come, Master, we must leave at once," Kephalos murmured. "There is no honor among outcasts, and that lad, if he is half as wicked and clever as he looks, is this very moment on his way to sell our lives to the king's watch. We cannot be gone too quickly."

With a suddenness of which I would not have imagined him capable, he was on his feet, and before I knew what was happening he had his arm through mine and was leading me, almost dragging me, along the quay.

"I have chosen a boat for us to steal," he whispered tensely, almost through his teeth, as we hurried along. "This out of neither poverty nor avarice but because I feared betrayal if I attempted to purchase one openly. The Lord Esarhaddon is greatly hated in Nineveh, but he is even more greatly feared, and there are spies everywhere. Come—here it is. It is a poor thing and thus the crime is less likely to prey upon your conscience."

"A poor thing" hardly described it. It was barely even a boat at all but that flimsiest of all river craft, known as a *gufa*. Kephalos and I—and he the size of two—were to make our escape on a circular platform of bundled reeds held together with twine and bitumen and supported around the sides by some ten or twelve inflated goatskins. I was reasonably certain the currents would tear it to pieces before we were out of sight of the city walls.

Yet what was that to me? If I drowned, and my corpse were carried downstream by the tumbling water until, bloated and unrecognizable, it came to rest in some tangle of riverbank reeds, why should I care? Yes, I would as soon meet death this way as any other.

I shook off Kephalos' grip on my arm and stood there on the pier, looking about me, trying through the darkness to fill my eyes with the sight of all that I must now leave behind forever.

"We have until sunrise," I said—my voice sounded hollow, even to myself, like the murmur of an intriguer overhead at a distance. "My brother says I have until then to be gone from the city. How many hours has the night left to it?"

But he did not answer. He only watched me, as if waiting to have his worst fears confirmed.

At last he shrugged his shoulders and allowed his hands to drop to his sides in a gesture of resignation.

"My young fool of a master, have you not yet learned from life the folly of expecting all men to be all that they seem and to act in conformity with their words?"

"My brother would not . . ."

"No—but it would be greatly to the Lord Esarhaddon's interest if you could be prevailed upon to disappear forever from the world of men, and you will recall that the king has a mother. And the Lady Naq'ia has pledged her word to nothing and, as you have reason to know, fears neither god nor man. My Lord, let us be gone from this place!"

Esarhaddon, Naq'ia—they were merely names belonging to some life I had left far behind me. They could do me no harm, even if they took my life, so I had nothing to fear from them. I was too caught within myself even to understand what fear meant.

Yet it was easier to yield than to resist. To resist meant to make choices, to act, to behave as if life somehow mattered, and I was still too hidden inside my own mind for any of that. So I allowed Kephalos once more to take my arm and lead me down the stone steps of the quay to where our little boat was bobbing in the water like a piece of tethered cork. I sat down in the front, facing away from the river, and watched as my former slave, now my accomplice in flight, untied the rope. The current took us at once and we began drifting away, out onto the bosom of Mother Tigris as we left the shore.

An hour later, in the first pale gray light of dawn, I could just distinguish the outlines of the watchtowers. My last glimpse of Nineveh, I thought. It had actually happened. I had fled the city and was now an exile, a man whom no land welcomed, who must learn to forget that he had ever belonged to one place.

For three days we let the river carry us. On the first day, late in the afternoon, we passed under the walls of Calah, where my brother had lived as *marsarru*, as the king's first son and heir, his mind slowly poisoning with distrust and fear, and on the second we saw holy Ashur herself, city of the god, mother of the race.

"You will speak 'farewell' until your tongue sickens of the sound," Such had been the *maxxu*'s warning, and it had all come true. It had come true long since.

And at night, since Kephalos was in mortal terror of capsizing in the dark, to be swept away by the black water, we would drag our *gufa* up onto the shore and build a small fire. Then Kephalos would bury himself under a pile of reeds and fall asleep, snoring like a water ox, while I sat by the red embers of the fire, tormented by dreams that held sleep at bay like prophecies of death.

Dreams? Worse than dreams. One wakes from dreams. Memory is not so easily dismissed. A dream is a phantom—or, perhaps, at best, a warning from the gods. It can be turned aside. But prayers cannot prevail against what has been done and seen and heard and is therefore fixed and solid as the earth itself. The past is unalterable, and memory, its image, will not yield even to our most pious supplications. Memory catches us in its net like fish.

At night I could not sleep. Only in the daylight, with the shoreline floating by and the sun shining in my face, could I close my eyes and, as I listened to the lapping water, sink into the arms of weariness. And while I slept my soul was at rest, for I did not dream.

Thus we lived for three days, drinking the cold swift water of the Tigris and eating out of a bag of dates Kephalos had been wise enough to buy in the bazaar. It was left to him to do everything—I merely slept and ate and stared back toward Nineveh, as if I still hoped to catch one last glimpse of her. I hardly spoke during that time—except to curse Esarhaddon, and myself, and the malevolence of the god who, it seemed, had abandoned me. These were the themes around which my every thought seemed to revolve, like a kite circling in the air above a wounded animal, waiting for it to die.

"Helpless . . . my hands empty . . . nothing—no defense, no answer. What else could I have done? That was the worst . . . What else could I have done? I would kill him now—I would . . ."

A fair sample, perhaps, of my muttered ravings. I would sit before our campfire, staring into the flames, addressing myself as much to them as to anyone, hating my brother for having lacked the courage to kill me, hating myself for lacking the decency to die. Above all, hating the god for having shown me favor only to render my exile the darker. I had been called "he whom the god loves," and I had struggled, even against myself, to be his servant. Yet he had made a joke of my devotion. It seemed to me sometimes that I could hear his laughter.

Kephalos, who feared that my brain might have been curdled by misfortune, attempted from time to time to draw me forth, to distract me from these bitter reflections, but his words were no more than the buzzing of flies in my ears. I hardly even heard them. At last he gave up and left me in silence, since I seemed to have decided to bury myself alive—if ever in my life I have been mad, deserted by reason and lost to the world and myself, it was then.

But the race of men would have died away long ago if their sorrows could hold them forever, and so it happens that, when at last it is healed and ready, the mind is called back to itself by the small, thin voice of some trivial emergency. It was thus with me when, the fourth morning of our flight from my brother's wrath, the sky lightened to reveal that our *gufa* had disappeared.

It was a common enough sort of catastrophe. As she is wont to do at that time of year, when the snows in the northern mountains have already begun to melt, the river had risen during the night—this we could see plainly, for her shore was now within three or four paces of our cold campfire—and, silent as the hand of death, had carried away with it our little reed raft.

Perhaps I had fallen asleep without knowing it, or perhaps I had been too distracted in my mind to notice, but this turn of our fortunes was as much a surprise to me as to Kephalos.

"We shall have to walk," I said, perhaps a little startled by the sound of my own voice. "If we follow the river we must come to a village, or perhaps a farmhouse, where we can purchase horses. I assume, my friend, that you were wise enough to provide us with money?"

I smiled at him, but he only stared at me as if at a conjuring trick. I almost laughed out loud, for suddenly I felt the return of hope and life. We were marooned in the midst of Esarhaddon's realm, where my life was forfeit should I be recognized and taken, but this was merely one more difficulty to be overcome, which was, after all, no more than the business of living. I had almost forgotten. I was glad that the *gufa* had been carried off, for now I remembered that I had blood in my veins and not river water.

"Money, Lord? What . . . ?"

And then I did laugh, and then Kephalos, slapping his thighs with relief, saw the joke and laughed with me.

"Yes, Lord, plenty of money—all the money in the world!"

And we laughed and laughed, rich men stranded on a muddy river-bank. We laughed until we had to hold each other up, for we would be well enough now.

Even though we stood on the river's western shore, I had but to glance about me to know where we were. I had passed this way many times, a soldier in the king's army on the way to Khalule or Babylon or some other place where men left their bones to bleach white in the sun. The Tigris has a different look after she is joined by the Lower Zab, as if somehow she has grown lazy on her journey south, as if she misses the sight of the mountains she is leaving behind and does not care how sluggishly she creeps along towards the lands of Akkad and of Sumer, mud-brown and flat as a threshing floor for as far as the eye can carry.

"Yesterday, did we pass a city by the left hand? Did it have walls of red-painted brick, and were the watchtowers close together like vine stakes?"

"Yes, Lord—an hour or two after midday."

"Then we have left Ekallate behind already." I looked downriver, with my left hand shading my eyes against the rising sun. "It is well. The garrison there is full of soldiers impressed from Borsippa and Dilbat, and they think they have found their champion in Esarhaddon. I would not care to hazard showing my face there, but in Birtu we will be safer."

"Soldiers are soldiers—I do not see . . ."

Kephalos made a despairing gesture, as if he thought I must still be unsteady in my brain to speak of safety under the eyes of the king's army. I could not blame him, yet safety is always a relative matter.

"I know the commander," I answered. "I do not believe he would betray us. It is best not to tempt him, for in times like these all Esarhaddon's servants are anxious to prove their new loyalty, but Zerutu Bel was always an honorable man. At least in Birtu we can buy whatever we need. And, if my brother has seen fit to keep his word, we are still a day or two ahead of the riders from Nineveh."

"How far to Birtu then, Lord?"

"Two days' march, if we set a good pace."

"All of that, and on a few dates rattling around in an empty bag?" My former slave sat down on the pile of reeds that had only lately been his bed and covered his face with his hands. "Two days' march, and I a man of education and culture—Kephalos of Naxos, sometime physician to the royal house of Assyria! May the gods curse the hour that tied my destiny to that of a dust-stained soldier."

For several minutes he would not be consoled, nor could I induce him to begin our journey on foot, but he continued as he was, chewing his nervous way through our depleted supply of dates. It was only when they were almost gone that, having breakfasted himself into a better humor, he consented to rise.

"Well, if it must be, then it must," he said, stretching himself like an overfed cat. "I expect to die of exhaustion before nightfall."

Kephalos did not die, of exhaustion or anything else, but neither did we set a good pace and reach Birtu within two days. For this the blame is as much mine as his for, if he was fat and unaccustomed to the rigors of a forced march, I had spent most of the past month in a cage in the royal dungeons, waiting for my brother the king to decide what to do about me. By sundown there were blisters on my feet as well, and I imagined, as I plastered them with the river mud to take away the soreness, that perhaps I had crippled myself for life.

Still, when the dawn came and we awoke to a spring morning that still felt cold enough to be winter, it was better to be moving than to stand still. And in an hour, when the stiffness had at last left our joints and we could feel the heat of exercise in our bodies, for a while even Kephalos stopped complaining.

It was late afternoon of the third day, the sixth since our flight from Nineveh, when finally, with weary limbs and empty bellies, we came within sight of Birtu, a market town hosting a small garrison of soldiers, with mud walls that were hardly more than a formality—no enemy army that had penetrated so deeply into the homeland of Ashur would have been stopped by them, but it had been over four hundred years since one had even tried. This was not a place accustomed to alarms, nor did the intrigues of the king's court have much meaning here. In the evening, just at dusk, we passed under the main gate, in a crowd of city folk and foreign traders and farmers with their goats and their oxcarts so that the guards in their watchtowers probably did not notice so much as our existence.

"Let us find a tavern," I said, "where we can buy a basin of hot water and space on their floor for a sleeping mat."

"Yes, and where we can eat fresh-killed goat and drink wine, and where the harlots are pretty." Kephalos smiled in anticipation. "I doubt if tonight I could do any woman justice, but there will be tomorrow—and it will give me something agreeable to think about while I grow bloated on food and drink."

"Better if the harlots are not pretty. Better a humble place where even common soldiers would be ashamed to go. I have no wish to run afoul of some old campaigner who would know me by sight."

"Rest assured, Lord. Your servant, as always, considers your good above all else and has hit upon a contrivance which will prevent any such unfortunate reunions."

He smiled, seemingly unwilling to enlarge upon his plans, and touched my shoulder to guide me into a side street—Kephalos had a nose for such places of resort; we had not walked a hundred paces before he found as pleasant a wineshop as ever I had seen, even in Nineveh.

As we entered, our legs covered with dirt, brushing the dust of many days' travel from our garments, the mistress of the house was less than welcoming. A foreigner from the look of her—my own guess was that she had been born in Musri or Tabal and brought here as a slave by some caravan, for her face had the sullen cast one sees in those races—she was well past her youth and wore no veil, but the corner of a shawl covered her hair to show that she was or had once been some man's concubine and must therefore be respected over the tavern girls carrying wine and food to men who felt free to caress them in any manner they liked. She crossed her arms over her huge bosom and regarded us from beneath heavy, lowered eyebrows, as if prepared to bar a pair of obvious vagabonds like us from intruding any further on her hospitality or the freshly swept tiles of her entranceway.

But Kephalos, who understood every refinement of this sort of negotiation, was undismayed. He merely took his hand from a secret pocket in the bosom of his tunic and allowed a shower of tiny silver coins to fall through his fingers to the floor below. In an instant the woman was on her knees making her obeisance before this mighty lord who, for reasons best understood by himself, chose to be disguised as a beggar and, at the same time, gathering up his bounty with a single deft movement of her right hand.

"A clean room, woman," he said, in Aramaic—so his conjecture about her origins had been close to my own—"and hot water for my servant and I to bathe in, and fresh clothes, and food and such wine as can be had in this doghole. Are we to be kept waiting forever?"

"Yes, Your Excellency—I mean, no!" She scrambled to her feet and immediately took Kephalos by the arm, leading him through a curtained doorway as delicately as if he were an invalid as well as rich. I, largely ignored, was left to follow if I would.

A few minutes later, stripped naked and lying on a pair of thick, sweet-smelling reed mats, we were sponging our faces while four giggling harlots in flimsy linen tunics busied themselves with rubbing fragrant oil into our backs and limbs. There was a pitcher of cold Lebanese wine on the floor between us and I could already detect the scent of cooking meat.

"I have a razor in my bag," Kephalos said, inclining his head toward me confidentially—why I cannot imagine, since he spoke in Greek, which certainly these women had never heard before in their lives. "That is my contrivance. We will shave off our beards. A man is unrecognizable without his beard and, since a smooth face is not the fashion here, everyone will take us for foreigners. In my case, of course, it will be no more than the truth, but they will believe it just as quickly of you—do not take offense, Master, but the fact is, half Greek as you are, you have not truly the look of an Assyrian."

One of the harlots, all smiles and dimples, a chubby little thing who was massaging Kephalos' massive rump, tittered as if he had made a joke. He reached back and pinched her knee and she laughed all the louder.

"You see, Lord? It is a great protection to be a foreigner."

"Yes—I can see that plainly."

"Then it is settled about the beards, though I shall hate to part with mine. It was ever a great attraction for the women, but perhaps I have reached the age when I should begin to grow indifferent to such things."

While he was thus resigning himself, our hostess entered with a bowl of pomegranates, red as blood, and behind her a servant carried a large plate heaped with chunks of roasted lamb on a bed of millet. She smiled at Kephalos, giving the impression she would have found him a tasty enough dish by himself, and, after waving away the dimpled girl, herself squatted down on the floor beside him to stroke his hair with the tips of her heavy, ring-laden fingers. These attentions seemed to please Kephalos.

"Your Eminence must forgive our poor house for misjudging appearances and not seeing the lord beneath the muddy rags. Your Eminence met with some misadventure?"

"We were set upon by robbers who stole our horses and pack animals," he replied, rolling over onto his back and thus displaying, in the size of his erect manhood, that such comforts as her "poor house" could provide had not been lost on him. "They were as numberless as flies in summer, the coarse, cowardly devils. It was nothing except our stout resistance that kept them from stripping us of our lives—and discovering, when they searched my corpse, that they had in fact missed the greater share of their spoils."

"The brave man is safe in any danger." She knelt down and lowered her mouth to kiss him upon the brow. She was a fool if she believed him, and I do not think she was a fool. Yet this seemed to matter not at all. "You honor us, Eminence. All that we have is yours. My name is Kupapiyas, should you have need of me. I was born in the Land of Hatti, where women are taught what value must be put on a lord's comfort."

So—at least I had been correct on the one point, for the kings of Hatti had ruled in Musri and Tabal for as long as men could remember.

"Do you enjoy much custom from the garrison, Lady?" I asked.

It was the first time she had heard my voice, and the sound of it did not seem to please. Kupapiyas of Hatti, proprietress of a wineshop in the mud village of Birtu and therefore a gentlewoman whose refinement of feeling was not to be trifled with, twisted her head to look at me, her eyes narrowing as if she fancied herself insulted in being addressed by one as low as myself.

"My servant is doubtless thinking that we will need horses," Kephalos added quickly, intervening on my behalf. "Perhaps, since we are strangers here, you could tell us whether the commander would regard it as an affront if we approached him on the matter. I have heard men mention the name of one Zerutu Bel . . ."

"The *rab abru*? Hah!"

She sat up suddenly, and her great backside settled on the floor to spread out like a split grain sack.

"You will need to go farther than you might find convenient to do business with him—his throat was cut by command of the king in Nineveh and his body left outside the walls to be eaten by dogs. That was nearly a month ago. There is a new *rab abru* now, a rogue named Dinanu, who would sell you his mother if you wanted her. Speak with him if you have need of horses."

I cannot claim it was not an unpleasant shock to hear of the death of Zerutu Bel. He had not been numbered among the rebels at Khanirabbat, nor, so far as I know, had he had any hand in the conspiracies of my royal brothers Arad Malik and Nabusharusur, but it seemed that mere innocence was no protection in the reign of Esarhaddon. His throat cut and his corpse left to the dogs—that a brave man and loyal soldier should suffer such a death at the hands of his own king was as shameful a thing as I could imagine.

Yet why should I have been surprised? I too had kept faith with Esarhaddon—and with far greater provocation to contest his right to our father's throne than could have heated the imagination of the *rab abru* of Birtu—yet I was now a fugitive, a man whose life was forfeit even to the meanest of my brother's subjects. Had I been fool enough to suppose that Esarhaddon's wrath would reach down no lower than myself?

I had been a month languishing in the royal dungeon at Nineveh. Who could say how many had been purged in that time? What would I have heard of them?

Zerutu Bel was a skeleton which the crows were picking clean outside the walls of Birtu. To the king in Nineveh my head was worth its weight in silver shekels, and every soldier in the garrison would know it. There was no one here whom I could trust as a man of honor—not if the reward for honor was the fate of Zerutu Bel.

Kephalos and I must be off as soon as possible.

The next morning was a market day, so I was up early, early enough that the mistress of the house, Kupapiyas of Hatti, was still snoring quietly next to Kephalos. I washed my face in a basin of water—last night, in conformity with his plan, my wily servant and I had played barber to one another, and now it felt strange to be rubbing my hands over a naked chin. I found myself considering if I could find a bronze mirror somewhere to see how it changed me, thus wonderful is a man's vanity, driving all else from his mind, even in the extremity of danger.

I heard a grunt behind me and saw that Kephalos too had roused himself. He sat up, loudly cleared his throat, and rubbed his eyes with his fingertips—he too, when he felt the smooth flesh of his jaw under his hands, seemed startled.

There had been a girl on my own sleeping mat last night. She woke quickly enough and with a bright smile, as if mightily pleased with herself and all the world, inquired of me if our eminences would care for breakfast. I sent her off in search of raw figs, bread and beer.

"That one will not be so agile," Kephalos said, pointing back towards his sleeping mat after the girl had gone. I could believe him. Kupapiyas, with her backside rising like a mountain range and her thick cheek pressed against the floor, never stirred. "I put something in her wine at dinner. It was not only courteous but also wise of me to go into her last night. The thoughts that find their way into the mind of a spurned woman are dark, and ours is not a situation that allows us to invite much scrutiny. Yet I did not anticipate finding her companionship so amusing that I would wish very much of it. Look at her, dreaming of youth and beauty—as ugly and mean-tempered as a brood sow. What is it in me, I wonder, that such women find so fatally attractive, even without my fine, handsome beard?"

"Let us be gone from this place, Kephalos—I feel danger."

It was a moment before the lover of Kupapiyas could be summoned back from the pleasure of his own reflections, but at last he fixed me with a frowning stare, as if I had suggested something indecent.

"This haste is most unseemly, Lord. We have been many days exposed to all manner of hardships—we need to recover ourselves."

"Kephalos, we are in the midst of a garrison of soldiers, and their commander is a dog who begs scraps from Esarhaddon's table."

"Yes, but we are safe enough within these four walls . . ."

"These are the walls of a wineshop, dolt! Soldiers come to wineshops, to drink and to gossip with the harlots. Do you imagine we can remain undetected for long?"

"Yes but, Master—a day. One single day? I am tired. My bones ache, and I have need of a little comfort!"

He was begging me. His eyes pleaded for that one day, almost as if he would die without it. And had he not saved me in Nineveh? Had he not stayed behind to rescue his ruined lord when he could so easily have fled to safety? And did I not owe him this small thing?

"One day then. And we leave tomorrow morning, as soon as they open the gate."

"Yes—yes! I will prepare everything against tomorrow morning. You will be safe enough if you stay inside this room. I will do everything. I will purchase the horses . . ."

"You will do nothing of the sort. Kephalos—what do you know of horses? Some farmer will sell you his broken-winded old mare, and you will pride yourself on your guile, thinking you have robbed him. No, it will not do. I will purchase the horses."

"As you wish," he answered, shrugging his shoulders, happy enough, I think, to have carried his main point. "I will attend to the provisions, and I need to find a few items for my medicine box. The horses will be left to your more expert eye, but perhaps it would be well if they remained your one task outside this room—no one will know me in Birtu, but the Lord Tiglath . . ."

"Your wisdom is not lost on me, Worthy Physician."

It was not until the girl had returned with our breakfast, and we were nearly finished with it, that our hostess, the Lady Kupapiyas, at last returned to life. Eventually, after a few groans and several clumsy, strengthless attempts, she was able to sit up, her elbows resting on her knees as she stared straight ahead, seemingly at nothing, an expression of the most malignant resentment upon her face.

"I will provide a remedy," Kephalos murmured to me, mixing a greenish powder into a cup of beer and stirring the whole with his finger.

"Here you are, my little river swallow! A little something to return the twinkle to your bright eye. Drink now . . ."

With hands that seemed to have forgotten how to grasp, she finally took the cup, Kephalos guiding it to her lips lest she drop it. The effect was astonishing. In less than a minute our hostess was nestled next to her great lord, smiling and cooing like a fifteen-year-old virgin, stroking his arm as he skinned a fig for her.

"And now, my little duckling, you must enlighten my servant here concerning how best to proceed in the matter of horses . . ."

Dressed in the clothes Kupapiyas had found for me, I ventured out into the streets of Birtu. I had never felt so much a stranger anywhere. The very dust under my sandals seemed strange.

Birtu was like a thousand other towns within the borders of Ashur's empire. It was like Amat, where for four years I had been garrison commander and *shaknu* of the northern provinces. Yet as I looked about me, I found myself hardly able to believe that I was here and that this was what the world looked like. It seemed as unreal as if it belonged to another order of existence. Perhaps it did. Perhaps I had only just now entered into the human race.

I kept expecting people to stare at me in astonishment and fear. They did not. As I walked along, men brushed by me, hardly noticing my existence. Why should they? I was no longer a prince. I was not even the king's soldier. I might look like the servant of a Lydian merchant, but even that was a lie. For the first time in my life I was required to face the world stripped of rank and position, alone. I had become no one. I was now merely myself. It was an odd sensation.

The bazaar was busy and noisy and as anonymous as an ant heap. Everything was for sale: melons, rugs, jewelry, live geese, great mounds of dates and onions and dried fish. Scribes wrote letters and copied deeds for local farmers and merchants from Lebanon and Egypt. A physician was treating a patient for an eye infection under a tavern awning. There was even a slave auction, although the three or four girls who sat around disconsolately on the block were not comely and attracted few bidders. I stopped by a stall displaying pottery drinking cups—there was no reason for it; I merely stopped for a moment, and perhaps glanced at the wares—and a woman in a green tunic and wearing a tattered black shawl over her hair began plucking at my sleeve, threatening me with a lifetime of regret if I did not buy something. I moved away and she shouted after me, cursing me for a fool and a miser. It was like being stoned with handfuls of sand. I could hardly restrain the temptation to break into a run.

At another stall there were weapons for sale, a common-enough thing in a garrison town. Javelins, bound together with a string like a shock of wheat, were leaning against the reed-mat wall. I motioned to the trader to show me one—it was sound and straight and had good balance, and it was tipped in shining bronze.

"Your honor has been a soldier?" he asked, smiling, showing me a mouthful of stained teeth. He was a wizened little creature, as old as the world, and his hands moved tentatively about as if of their own volition, like spiders feeling their way in the dark. Yet if he had made this, he understood his craft.

I rolled the shaft between my palms, watching to see if the point would twist and betray a kink in the wood. It did not.

"No—I want them only for hunting. My master and I travel the caravan routes, and a little fresh meat is a blessing. I will take six of these, and a leather quiver for them. And that sword over there, provided the blade is not hacked. How much do you want for all that?"

"Five silver shekels, if Your Honor pleases?"

The pouch Kephalos had given me bulged with coins, and I was on the verge of paying the man what he asked until I remembered that I was supposed to be the servant of a traveling merchant, who would be expected to bargain.

"I will give you two," I said.

"Your Honor beggars my wife and small children. I could not sell so much for two silver shekels, for that is a fine sword—an officer's sword—and you will not find such javelins even if you were to go to Nineveh for them. Yet I will part with them for three silver shekels, although my children will go hungry and my wife will curse me."

I let him wait for an answer. His eyes begged pity of me.

"Two silver shekels," I answered at last. "And six of copper."

"Your Honor is cruel to a poor man. Yet I need money to buy food for my babies. Two silver shekels then, and eight of copper."

I walked away, carrying my weapons with me, wondering by how much the man had cheated me.

In the town's central square, in makeshift stalls fashioned of hemp and reed mats, were the livestock that were to be sold that day. There were some ten or fifteen horses, most of them half dead, not even fit to limp along in front of a plow, but I saw two I thought might serve: a pale brown gelding with good legs, and a stallion, black as death, made nervous by the crush of people—the man who held its halter looked as if he feared to have his arm torn from its socket. I would buy those two and, since our lives might depend on them, I did not care what I had to pay.

I feared it would be no small sum, for there were others who were interested. One of them wore the uniform of a *rab abru*.

I could not remember ever having seen Dinanu before, although that meant nothing. It was possible we had been in the same room together a dozen times, since in recent years Esarhaddon and I had not been on such good terms that I would have paid any great attention to the members of his entourage. Yet there was no mistaking that this was he, sent down from Nineveh with the king's commission to assume command of the garrison and to visit a shameful death upon Zerutu Bel. He seemed the type for such work.

He was standing with five or six of his junior officers, a squat, thick, clumsy-looking man with heavy eyebrows and a face that seemed to narrow to an edge like an ax blade. His hand was on the black stallion's fine arching neck, attempting to calm it—without noticeable effect it seemed, since the beast capered and snorted, as if it could hardly wait to trample him into paste beneath its hooves.

It would have been wiser simply to withdraw, but that was not possible. I could tell, from the way Dinanu looked at it, he meant to have this horse and no other, and I could not allow such a thing. This animal did not like him and would surely, one day, leave him with his neck broken. The prospect did not disturb me very much, except that they cut the throats of man-killers. So for the stallion's sake, and for simple spite, I would do the *rab abru* a kindness he would never understand and save his life.

"This one will serve very well," he said—in Aramaic, since he was treating with a foreigner. "I will give you ten silver shekels for it. Have it sent around to my headquarters by midday."

"My master will give you twleve silver shekels—unless, of course, you have already closed your bargain."

Dinanu glowered at me from beneath his massive black brows, his eyes burning like hot coals. Yet I do not think he recognized me—if he did, he did not show it.

At last he turned to the horse dealer, who wore the elaborately curled beard of an Harrian, men notorious as sharp traders. The horse dealer's nostrils were flaring slightly as if at the scent of unexpected profit.

"I think you have hit upon a stratagem," the *rab abru* said to him, seeming, for the moment, to have dismissed me from existence. "I think you have hired this villain, that he might bid against me and drive up the price. If I find this to be true, I will order your right hand to be cut off as an example."

"My master is not this man. My master is the caravan merchant Hugieia of Sardes. Having lost his own to bandits, and trusting my judgment in these matters, he instructed me to purchase him a mount suitable to his wealth and dignity."

I stepped forward and placed my hand upon the horse's nose. I have a way with horses, and at once the great stallion quieted down.

"It would appear I have found something worthy." I smiled at the *rab abru*, as if to annoy him. I was a crafty foreign servant, out to wrest my little victory from one of the mighty of the earth. "It only remains to be seen which of us has the heavier purse."

"Let me see the color of your money, slave."

He put his hand on the hilt of his sword and, although I was carrying one myself, I thought it more prudent simply to take the bag of coins from my belt and open it for him. Dinanu's mouth tightened when he saw the glint of so much silver.

"These foreigners are all rich," one of his officers said in Akkadian. "They are all—what is this?"

The man reached out and grasped my wrist, yanking it toward him so that the bag slipped from between my fingers and fell with a soft clink to the earth. He held me so that my palm was up, and they could all see the birthmark there, red as blood and shaped like a star.

"It is not possible! It can't . . ."

"No, it is not possible."

Dinanu stooped down and picked up the bag of coins, returning it to me.

"The king's traitor brother is in a dungeon in Nineveh," he went on in Akkadian, speaking only to his officers. "Either that, or he is dead by now. Look at this one—he is no prince. Any man may have a mark upon his hand.

"It seems you have bought a horse." The *rab abru* looked at me with cold, appraising eyes. "May you ride far on it, and never return to Birtu."

He turned on his heel and walked away.

"Twenty silver shekels for the stallion and the brown gelding, both— quick, man, yes or no?"

I grabbed the Harrian by the neck of his tunic and shook him, for he seemed to be in a dream.

"Yes or no!"

"What?—yes, Excellence. Twenty silver shekels, yes!"

I counted out the money for him, took the horses by their lead ropes, and went on my way. I wanted to find Kephalos. I did not trust to luck.

I had not gone a hundred paces from the main bazaar before I knew I was being followed.

It was perhaps two hours to midday. People flowed past me on their way to the shops. I had two horses in tow and thus trod cautiously along the center of the street.

Three times I had glanced back and seen him, always the same distance behind me—his back to me as he paid a vendor for a cup of beer, turning abruptly into an alley, now idling in the doorway of a brothel. His face was in shadow, but he wore the tunic of an officer and I was sure he had been one of those with Dinanu.

There was a public stable near the main gate. I took the horses there rather than back to the wineshop, where Kephalos would be waiting. The garrison at Birtu had no business with Kephalos, whose existence they did not even suspect. There was nothing to be gained by leading them to him.

The stablekeeper showed me his stock of bridles and saddle blankets—I took my time choosing. I had yet to make up my mind what to do about this second shadow I had acquired.

And when I turned to go, there he was, standing in the doorway, no longer even attempting to conceal himself. He was waiting for me.

I stopped when I saw him. We stood staring at one another for a moment and then he glanced about, almost seeming to fear that someone might have been following him, and then approached me as warily as if I had been an adder.

"What do you want of me?" I asked.

"You are the Lord Tiglath Ashur," he said, as if this constituted an answer. "You need not dissemble—even without the god's mark on your hand, and though you have shaved off your beard and dress now like a foreigner, I would still have recognized you. I saw you once when I was still a boy. You came to Arbela, where my father was an omen reader at the shrine."

He was hardly more than a boy now—perhaps sixteen, perhaps younger. Perhaps as young as I was when I first went to war and put my boyhood behind me forever. He was still as beautiful as a girl, and his eyes were large and dark. He had yet to learn guile.

"I ask again. What do you want of me?"

"Not to betray you, Dread Lord. I was sent by the *rab abru*, who is a man without respect for the gods, to follow behind and see where you dwell. He plans to wait until after dark and then come and arrest you—he will not take the risk in daylight, for he fears a disturbance if it became known that you . . . Also, he does not trust his own soldiers. There are many in the army who believe that you are he whom the Lord Ashur loves, the true king."

"Esarhaddon is the king."

"He wears the crown—yes. But the god has always put wise and noble men to rule over us in the Land of Ashur, and you would never have turned your face from your brother as he has from you."

What could I have said? Nothing, in that moment. My heart was too full. I felt humbled by the unsought loyalty of this stranger, for in those whom they would follow men always see what is finest in themselves.

"What do you want of me?"

"To do your will, Dread Lord. Whatever you require of me I will do, even to the forfeit of my own life."

He meant what he said. I could see it in his face.

"Do you know the wineshop of Kupapiyas of Hatti?"

"Yes."

"Then tell the *rab abru* that I dwell there—it is the truth, so you will have fulfilled your commission. Yet you might wait a few hours before you tell him."

"It shall be as you say, Dread Lord. You had much business in the bazaar and were a long time about it."

"What is your name?"

"Ishtar-bel-dan, Lord—named for the patron goddess of my city."

"Ishtar-bel-dan. It is a name I will remember all my life."

There was no more to be said between us. He turned, as if to go, and then came back to kneel before me, taking my right hand in his and touching it to his forehead, as if I were the king in truth.

Then he rose and left. I never saw him again, but I will not forget him until I am dust.

And there were but a few hours left in which to purchase my life.

I did not return to the wineshop of Kupapiyas—there was nothing to prove that Dinanu had no other eyes with which to watch me. But the stablekeeper had eyes only for the silver I counted out into his hand. He was willing enough to carry a message for me.

"Find me a fat Ionian who will know you are from me when you say it was the son of Merope who sent you. Tell him to come back here quickly, as he values his life. Tell him not to leave anything behind."

The stablekeeper hurried off, promising he would be back with my Ionian before the day was a quarter of an hour older, but the time seemed to stretch on endlessly. I bridled the horses and put blankets over their backs and then went up to the hayloft, where I could watch the street. It struck me as an even wager which I would see first, Kephalos or a patrol of soldiers come to carry my head back to Nineveh in a jar.

I sat there, the loft door open the width of three or four fingers, listening and watching. I had my sword and a javelin—I had not the slightest intention of allowing myself to be taken alive. And I would not sell my life cheaply. No one would ever say that Tiglath Ashur died like a cornered rabbit.

I could hear the sounds from the peddlers' stalls and the low, busy murmur of a thousand voices. All of that would be hushed if the soldiers came. I would hear that stillness long before I saw them, or heard the tramp of their sandaled feet. I waited for that.

But it did not come. Only Kephalos came, almost running but not quite, bustling along as fast as his bulky dignity allowed. I went down to meet him.

"My Lord, if this is some prank I will not be amused—by the time that ruffian barged in affairs had reached a very delicate state between myself and the lady . . ."

"They know I am here—they know it, Kephalos."

If it is possible to change in an instant from wrath to fear, as a man may be living and then dead, with no line between that the mind or eye can see, this is what happened in Kephalos' face. The truth did not come creeping into his brain like the sunlight at dawn, first slate, then pearl-gray, then pink like blood in water, but in one flash that revealed everything. Not a muscle altered in his face, yet he seemed stricken, as if all strength had left him. I put my hand on his shoulder lest he fall, but he did not fall. He was still as death.

"I must flee," I said. "You will be safe, my friend, if you will but stay behind. Yet do not return to the wineshop, for they will search for me there. I only could not leave without saying good-bye."

"There can be no thought of my staying behind, Lord—I have not come so far as this to abandon you to your own foolish whims. We must be gone at once."

With a leather strap I tied together his bag and his medicine box—all the luggage we had between us—and threw them across the neck of the black stallion. Then I held its bridle, waiting for Kephalos to scramble onto its back, but he was not eager.

"It is a fearful-looking beast, Lord, and, as you know, I am no very enthusianstic rider. Perhaps you—and it—would be better pleased if . . ."

"You are a wealthy Lydian merchant," I answered impatiently. "Would you mount your servant on a better horse than you rode yourself?"

"Yes. Of course—what is so . . .?"

"Get on, Kephalos. Throw your leg over its back and let us leave this place?"

I mounted the brown gelding, clutching the quiver of javelins under my arm. No one stopped us in the street. At the city gate the guards let us pass unchallenged. Even as we headed west, away from the main southern road, the dust kicked up by our horses settled quietly behind us. We rode until the walls of Birtu sank from sight behind us, and we saw no one. There was no sound but the whispering wind.

An hour passed, and then two. We slowed our horses to a walk. It became possible to think of something besides the fear of death. The afternoon grew hot and quiet. The wide plain stretched empty around us, and I began to believe we had made good our escape.

Yet what does a man escape in his life? As the sun began to slide down toward the western horizon, and Kephalos and I felt the first hint of the night's cold, I glanced over my shoulder and saw behind, just far enough back that the sound from their horses' hooves failed to reach us, a troop of cavalry, perhaps ten riders, coming up at a trot.

I pulled the gelding to a halt.

"Look."

Kephalos looked, and his heart died within him.

"We have at least a quarter an hour's start on them," he said. "Perhaps more. It will be dark in two hours—perhaps, if we can lose them then . . ."

"There is no escape. This gelding of mine will be no good against army horses, and the stallion is made for speed, not distance. It would wear its wind out before you had gone half a *beru*. I would as soon die here as anywhere, and I will not be chased down."

It was the wisdom of my ancestors that a man meets his *simtu*, his fate, the end of his days, when and where the god wills. This he cannot evade. I thought then that perhaps the Lord Ashur had not meant for me to be driven from the land that bore his name but to lay down my bones there. If it was to be, then let it, I thought. I got down from the gelding and allowed the reins to drop to the ground. I took a javelin from the quiver and weighed it in my hand. Let them come, I thought. Let them come.

"They are not interested in you, Kephalos—they will not pursue if you escape alone, and it is a fool who throws away his life for nothing. Be off now."

"Lord, this is madness! This is . . ."

I did not wait for him to finish, but struck the stallion on the rump with the tip of my javelin, yelling fiercely. This was enough to make it bolt forward at a gallop, with Kephalos, in terror, hanging on to its neck like a leech. They would go far together before that horse could be brought to a halt, and by then my business would be finished.

It is astonishing how calmly a man can wait to die. I was not afraid. I was even, in a curious sense, relieved, as if some conflict within me were finally resolved and I could at last act with the perfect freedom of a mind untroubled by doubt or hope. I waited, standing well away from my horse so the inevitable shower of arrows would not kill it as well. I watched them come.

It was not the first time I had faced mounted soldiers with a javelin in my hand. It had been just so in the first battle of my life, on the plains at Khalule, when I was but fourteen years old and first knew that ecstasy which makes a pleasure even of fear itself. Yet I did not feel ecstasy now—only a cold resolve to meet this too with honor, and to avenge my own death.

"If you must turn your thoughts to death, Prince, let it not be your own but theirs," his voice said—perhaps nowhere else but in my mind. "Did I not ever instruct you that a soldier's first duty is to kill his enemies? Death comes of itself, so you need not invite it into your heart."

I was almost tempted to look behind me, so real did that voice seem. Tabshar Sin, who had taught me the craft of a soldier, dead these three years, killed by a Median lance and buried in the rock-filled ground of the Zagros Mountains.

"I hear you," I said, aloud—perhaps he only spoke to me because now I was almost a ghost myself. "I am not afraid."

"I believe you, yet fear does not enter into it. I speak of wrath. And of my own shame if I raised you up to forget you are a Man of Ashur."

The troop had seen me by then, of course. They knew they had me and were in no hurry. Perhaps it had not yet crossed their minds that I would fight back. So I waited while they made their leisurely approach. I waited for the lead rider, wearing the blue uniform of a *rab abru*, to come within range. I did not have to be told that he was Dinanu, whom I would kill because I would avenge Zerutu Bel—and myself—and because he was not the king my brother and could therefore be killed without impiety.

They came, it seemed, with no suspicion in their hearts, believing that death was theirs alone to dispense, like copper coins to beggars. I would acquaint them with their folly.

"You shall witness, Tabshar Sin, that I brought no shame upon your ghost."

"No, *you* shall witness, Prince—which is more to the point."

At last, when they were close enough, I swung back my arm and then let my body uncoil like an adder striking. The javelin flew from my hand—it seemed to have its own life.

If ever the god was with me, and gave strength to my arm, it was then. I knew, even before my fingers had opened, that the dart would find its mark. It rose, arching through the air, higher and higher, and then dropped like the hunting falcon.

Dinanu was a corpse even before he pitched backwards over his horse's rump. My javelin had taken him square in the breast—he did not even have time to try to shield himself. It was not a man that fell to the earth, but a load of carrion.

I took a second from my quiver and steadied myself for the throw. I had enough for a few more before they rode me down and cut me to pieces. They would charge now . . .

But they did not charge. Dinanu's men reined in their horses and then, after what seemed a few moments of confusion—I could see one or two of them making excited gestures in the air—they retreated the fifty or so paces that carried them out of range.

What were they waiting for?

Perhaps they did not know themselves. I could see them pull together into a tight little circle—it appeared they felt the need to parley concerning what they should do now. I could not hear them across the wide emptiness of the plain. I would have to wait and see what they decided about the manner of my death.

There was no wind. There was no sound. There was only the oppressive silence.

Enough, I thought. Finish this. Let us have our fight and make an end of it.

They forced me to wait. That was the hardest thing, the waiting.

Let me embrace my death, I thought.

But they did not take up the challenge. In the end they rode away, without hurry, as if nothing had happened, leaving their commander's body where it had fallen in the dust.

II

DEATH SEEMS TO TAKE ALL MEN BY SURPRISE. THE EXPRES-
sion on Dinanu's face, as he lay sprawled on the plain, the wind quietly
covering him with dust, suggested that it was the last thing he had
expected. His eyes, already clouding over, were filled with outrage, as if
he felt himself insulted to have met his *simtu* thus. His mouth was open
and his teeth bared, implying that he had died preparing to tell me so.

His horse stood with my gelding not far away, picking the leaves from a
bush with a deliberate, self-absorbed delicacy, seeming to ignore the
corpse of its master as one might a drunkard's tasteless jest at dinner. In a
leather bag strapped to its withers I found a mattock, no doubt the one
with which the *rab abru* had expected to chop off my head, and with it I
began to dig up the soft, stoneless earth for a grave. I would not leave
Dinanu to the birds, as he had Zerutu Bel; I would not for mere spite
abandon any man's ghost, not even such a man as he, to wander eternally
on the comfortless winds.

"A mere three handfuls of earth," came a sudden voice—I turned and
saw my former slave, covered with dust and sweat, leading the black
stallion by the reins—"enough to hide him from the sight of the eternal
gods, Lord. Nothing more is required."

"Doubtless the *rab abru* would not have agreed. He was not a Greek,
and neither am I."

"I think, by now, you had best think of becoming one, my witless
young master, since it seems you are no longer welcome in the world as
an Assyrian. I am pleased, by the way, to discover you are still alive—how
did such a thing come to pass?"

I made a gesture toward the corpse. "In this case, all the venom was in the snake's head. The others lost interest as soon as their commander fell."

Kephalos grunted approvingly, as if he imagined I had planned that outcome from the beginning, and then sat down on the bare earth, watching with interest while I dug. The stallion, by now placid as a dairy cow, wandered off to join the two other horses.

When I had hacked out a suitable hole I threw the mattock to one side, placed one foot on Dinanu's chest, and pulled my javelin loose. It came away with a sickening sound.

"Give me a hand with him."

We picked up the *rab abru* by the arms and legs and dropped him into his final resting place. In Birtu, Kephalos had purchased a wineskin, which he carried slung from his shoulder; I took it from him, poured some of the wine out into my hand, and scattered it over the dead man's face and chest to calm his ghost. Then we covered the corpse with enough dirt to keep the jackals from digging it up again.

"I think we would do well to be gone from here now," I said, wiping my hands on my tunic, glad to be done with this piece of work. "Whatever made them quit so suddenly, there is nothing to guarantee that the *rab abru*'s men will not find their hearts again and renew the chase. Let us fetch our horses and be away from this place."

"Good—it is almost nightfall, and I have little enough desire to sleep beside a grave."

We rode far into the black night, until the moon had risen to the top of the sky's vault. Then we tethered the horses, gathered brushwood for a fire, and tried to forget that only one day had passed since we had slept on clean reed mats, our bellies full and our hands closed over the breasts of soft-bodied women. With the cold wind blowing at our backs, we would not sleep so well tonight. It seemed almost pointless to try.

"There is one consolation at least," Kephalos said, as he tried to stir the embers of our fire into some kind of life. "I do not imagine we will have much to fear from pursuers."

"Oh? Why is that? Is Birtu such a pleasure garden that the soldiers of the garrison will not be able to tear themselves away?"

He stared at me in reproving silence for a moment, as if, under present circumstances, he had little taste for hearing the comforts of that place disparaged.

"No, Lord. Yet I believe that the patrol you encountered this afternoon, whatever their reasons may have been for abandoning the chase once you had killed their commander, will have little enough reason to brag about the exploit. Dinanu, if he was a cautious man—and all those who curried favor with your brother during his years as *marsarru* would have learned to be cautious men—kept his intentions to himself when he set out after you, and doubtless his soldiers will wish to preserve the secret. They must assume by now that you have eluded them, and they will not be eager to report a failure of this kind to Nineveh. They will concoct some lie to explain the *rab abru*'s death, and they will keep silent about you. Thus we will be left in peace. They will not care to risk the king's wrath."

Not many minutes later I heard him snoring peacefully, his dreams undisturbed, it seemed, by any suspicion of danger, and it occurred to me that, as usual, Kephalos had spoken as a good physician and diagnosed our condition correctly. Esarhaddon's temper was as uncertain as a bull's in springtime, and no one would be eager to tell him that I had been seen at Birtu and then allowed to escape. Kephalos, that rogue, as usual had seen deeper into the hearts of men than I—perhaps because, as a rogue, he had less to cloud his eyes.

Still, as a precaution, for the next several weeks we kept to the wilderness, away from the paths of men, living off the land, always watchful for the cloud of dust that would signal to us our pursuers. They never came, and gradually we began to imagine ourselves forgotten.

Our wine ran out after three days—a grief to Kephalos, who grew fond of saying that a life barren of luxury was hardly worth the inconvenience of living—but otherwise we were well provided for. There was fresh water and good hunting, and this far south the date palms grew wild. For myself I was perfectly content. Like every soldier, I had only to compare this with the rigors of campaign to feel myself in a paradise of ease and comfort, and, provided I could forget that there was a world beyond—a world where my brother was king and I an outcast and a fugitive—I was quiet in my mind. I felt as if I would have no cause to consider myself ill-used by fate if I should continue thus forever.

Yet, as the man who dreams he is a soaring bird must finally awake and find himself tethered to the earth, so at last the world forced me to remember it and I was drawn back into the life of men.

It happened on a day when we made our camp beside the source waters of the Tartar River, where it flows from a lake I have never heard given a name. It happened when, during the night, we discovered that we had a caravan for neighbors.

"Master, I am weary of this savage existence," whispered Kephalos. We sat on a bluff, watching the light from their campfires reflected in the black water. "I sicken at the smell of wild game cooked without spices, and I know not what crime I would commit for a mouthful of beer—even beer, Lord! for to such I am reduced by privation. And, most of all, I long for the sound of an unfamiliar voice. I want to hear the gossip from distant cities and be reassured that the world has not been redeemed from its wickedness. Most Merciful Lord, say that we might break off this pastoral idyll, this living as if we were the first men the bright gods made—say that we may rejoin the living."

And truly, I must own, I felt the force of everything he said, for I too, almost from that moment, had grown tired of pretending to be one among the beasts of the wilderness. Everything Kephalos said of himself applied to me as well, for men were made to live among men.

"We will go down among them at first light," I said. "Let us catch them when they are still half asleep and less likely to be treacherous."

"Good—men will believe anything at that hour. And let us do something about the mark on your palm, lest it betray you again as it did at Birtu."

In the morning, before we set off to try our luck among the caravan drivers, Kephalos wrapped my right hand in a long linen bandage, so that I seemed to be wearing a glove with the fingers missing.

"Should anyone inquire, you burned yourself." He smiled at his own cunning as he tied the final knot, just at my wrist. "You are a clumsy, stupid sort of servant and only yesterday morning had an accident while trying to bake the last of our flour into bread. You ruined the bread, which caused me, your master, far more anguish than the ugly blister you raised across the palm of your hand. I called you many terrible names and threatened to sell you if ever we reached a town big enough to have a slave market. I said you would end your days making mud bricks with your own urine. That, I think, is a nice touch to the story, the sort of detail that makes men believe all the rest, since every slave reproaches his master with such lack of feeling. Repeat it often."

"And, for your part, let us settle on a name and a history, since it would be embarrassing were we to be caught in a disagreement on this point. In Birtu I styled you "Hugieia of Sardes" to Dinanu—will you agree to that, since it seems to have been a lucky choice?"

"Hugieia?" Kephalos considered the matter, stroking the month-old growth of beard that now adorned his chin. "Yes—well enough. At least it will be easy to remember, since health is all that a physician can claim as the end of his skills. Yet I am not as happy with Sardes, since I have never been there and, in any case, have no great admiration for the Lydians. Let us compromise a little with the truth that I may be Hugieia of Naxos, since every man should honor his birthplace if he can. Hugieia, yes. It was clever of you—almost clever enough to convince me that you might make a Greek yet. And what of a name for yourself, Lord?"

"I am Lathikados from nowhere in particular, as befits a slave. That too is a compromise with the truth."

Kephalos nodded in silence, understanding the bitterness of my jest, and thus I took the name by which my Greek mother had known me in the king's house of women. "He who banishes grief," she had called me—and now I was banished myself, and the name had been turned upon its head.

And before the sun had well and truly risen, while the sky was still pale gray, we mounted our horses and rode from our own encampment to that of the caravan drivers. It was no very great distance, no more than a man might walk in a quarter of an hour, but it marked the longest journey we had traveled since leaving Birtu, since it carried us back across the frontier of the race of men.

We entered their circle of tents even while the breakfast fires were still cold, and the few who were already awake stared at us in silence, blinking as if they could hardly believe their eyes.

On the other side, there was little enough for us to marvel at. Perhaps twenty men, allowing a tent for every two of them, with perhaps twice that number of pack horses, their trade goods bundled up in stout leather pouches that lay in a heap in the center of the camp. The horses, tethered in a line beside the lake's edge, looked half starved and as if their ribs were made of rotten wood, the men as if they might have found a life of brigandage more to their taste. Doubtless, of course, we appeared no better to them. A month of sleeping on the hard ground will rub the respectability off any man.

No one welcomed us—no one even spoke—but neither did any among them hint at offering to attack us. None of them, it appeared, wished to take the responsibility for attempting either. They seemed merely perplexed to find us among them. We stayed on our horses while the impasse dragged on, waiting through several heavy moments of silence.

And then, at last, a tent flap opened and another of them stepped out into the cold morning sunlight. It was easy to see, from the manner in which the others glanced at him, with that mingling of relief and dread I had seen so often in the eyes of my own officers and men, that this one was the leader here.

I could well believe it. He was not a tall man, but he had a way of carrying himself that made him seem as wide and solid as a wall. His narrow, smiling eyes and pointed beard suggested that this was one for whom life held no more unpleasant surprises. He stood with his head cocked a little to one side, seeming to mock at all the world. I had known many like him, men who had run away to join the king's army while yet boys and had risen to the rank of *ekalli* for perhaps even *rab risir*, who could never be trusted with command of more than a hundred men but would know well enough what to do with those, who cared nothing for strategy or the statecraft of war, holding these things in derision, honoring only courage and cunning and plunder, but who were virtuous in their way and understood every detail of a soldier's life. The caravan leader, I suspected, was just such a one.

"Whose camp is this?" shouted Kephalos, wisely seizing the initiative. "What route do you follow, and to what destination?"

"The camp and all within it are mine—Hiram of Latakia," the caravan leader answered, in the most villainous Akkadian I had ever heard. He crossed his arms over his chest in a way that implied the mere sound of his name should strike terror into our hearts. "We carry metal to Babylon, which the new king of these lands, who does not care how much treasure he spends, is rebuilding to appease the Lord Marduk. I expect to make good profit out of the god's wrath. I have finished ingots of copper and iron. And now, what of you?"

"I . . . ?"

Kephalos, that master of self-presentation, dismounted his horse with all the dignity of a great general taking possession of a conquered city. He looked about him surveying the tents and the wretched, slat-sided pack horses and the men themselves as if he had been offered the whole lot in payment of a debt and was sure he was being swindled. At last he fixed his gaze on Hiram of Latakia and smiled a tight, not-quite-disdainful smile.

"I am Hugieia of Naxos—physician and adventurer, scholar and man of affairs, counselor to the great of many nations, sometime trader, sometime shareholder in the trading schemes of others, presently the victim of a cowardly attack by bandits that has left me . . . as you see. I would be grateful for the opportunity of traveling with you some distance along your way, since two men alone are seen as all the world's natural prey, and I am not without means of manifesting my gratitude."

The expression on Hiram of Latakia's face as he listened to all this was not one to inspire much trust. He seemed very pleased with us, the way a cat is pleased with the bird under its paw.

"As you say," he began, "two men alone—"

The words caught in his throat when he saw that I had drawn one of the javelins from their quiver and was balancing it in my hand in a way that suggested it might not stay there forever. It was a moment in which no man's intentions were clear, which was perhaps just as well, since caution has saved more lives than strength and daring put together. After a while he switched his glance to Kephalos, who merely smiled a trifle broader.

"Yes—my servant." The daring and formidable Hugieia of Naxos—just then I could almost myself believe there was such a person—shrugged his heavy shoulders, as if at the intricacies of life. "He speaks no language except his own, which makes him suspicious in foreign lands. And, it must be granted, recent experience has confirmed him in his distrust. As a friend I would advise you to tell your men that they had best tread carefully around him."

Suddenly the crisis, if such it had been, was passed. There would be no blood spilled this day. The rule of civilization, that delicate counterbalancing of fear against violence and avarice, that web of tenuous, insinuated threats had once more, if only this once more, prevailed. We were safe enough in the camp of Hiram of Latakia. He had seen the wisdom of not attempting to cut our throats.

He uncrossed his arms and made a wide gesture of welcome, as if to acknowledge the fact.

"You may travel with us as far as Babylon," he said.

"And, of course, you will gratify me by accepting my contribution toward the expenses of the journey." Kephalos reached inside his tunic and produced a small leather pouch. "Shall we say—some twenty shekels of silver? Ten now, and ten when we reach Babylon. I trust that seems reasonable to you?"

All men despise a foreigner. If his habits are dissimilar he is without manners, unclean, uncouth and savagely indifferent to the feelings of others. If he cannot speak their tongue it is because he is as mindless as a beast. To be unlike others is to be less than human. Such is the prejudice of every nation, which men carry with them even into lands where they themselves are the foreigner.

That day, traveling with the caravan, we set our faces to the south. There was no risk of our losing our way. We would follow the Tartar River and then, when it disappeared into the spring mud, ride on until we reached the Euphrates, where it forms a great eastward loop into which we could not help but be drawn. That night, when we camped, Kephalos dined with Hiram, and I, the slave, was suffered to eat out of the common pot of horse drivers who scorned me as their inferior because they were free men and had been born in the Land of Hatti and could not begin to comprehend my Ionian gibberish.

Yet I was tolerated around their fire, if only grudgingly and in silence. No one mocked at me or tried to strike the food bowl from my lips, for I carried a sword. Their contempt, like their master's, was tempered by a reasonable fear.

It is instructive to listen to the conversations of men who imagine they speak among themselves without being understood. I sat next to them on the bare ground, and they talked, in Aramaic, of me and of my good master, as if I were as insensible as a log.

"This Hugieia of Naxos, the fat rogue; I, for one have never heard of a place called 'Naxos' and do not believe it exists."

"This one—by Mother Kamrusepa, how he stinks! Tomorrow we must remember to sit downwind of him" murmured a great oaf with one eyelid stitched shut over an empty socket. 'I will be just as glad when Hiram catches him asleep in his tent and puts a knife under his ribs."

He glanced at me furtively from time to time, peering around the bridge of his nose as if he were concealed behind the corner of a building, but could not be brought to look me straight in the face.

"I cannot imagine why he hesitates, since we are many and one man with a sword and a few rabbit-stickers is yet but one man."

"A scorpion, even when you crush it under your heel, still has a sting. Hiram knows his business."

There was a general hum of agreement around the campfire.

"Doubtless he wishes to discover where the Ionian conceals his money," the man went on, licking the grease from his fingers as he finished eating. He had the longest arms I think I have ever seen on a man, and the muscles in them wobbled loosely. "It would be a nuisance for him if he killed the great sow and then couldn't find it, eh?"

He smiled, revealing teeth as rotten as year-old tree stumps.

I said nothing. Whoever spoke I did not look at him, but maintained an appearance of uncomprehending indifference. When it was time to sleep and I went to the tent Hiram had loaned us, I told Kephalos everything I had heard.

"I am not surprised," he answered. "Having had dinner with him, I would not be surprised to hear that as a child he had sold his mother into a brothel. I would not be surprised to hear that he never had a mother.

"What of the others—do you think we have anything to fear from them?"

"No." I shook my head. "Hiram of Latakia keeps none but toothless dogs. He is the only one here with the courage to knife a man in his sleep—if it were otherwise he would be dead already himself."

We lay there in the darkness, neither of us speaking, the leather walls of the tent enclosing us like a grave vault.

"He will wait a while," Kephalos murmured at last, almost as if he were speaking to himself. "I told him I have money with the merchants of Borsippa, implying that the sums ran to many hundreds of shekels of silver—I was far gone in drink, you understand, and inclined to brag, yet I am convinced he believed me. A sum like that would set up such a man for his lifetime, so he wants to believe me. He will ponder for a few days how best to rob me of it."

"Nevertheless, one of us had best keep awake through the night."

"As you will, Lord." Kephalos yawned violently, for, indeed, he had drunk a good deal that night. "An attitude of caution is perhaps the wisest thing. Let us do nothing rashly."

"In that case, if you think it best, I will delay killing him until tomorrow."

My former slave laughed softly, perhaps imagining that I was in jest.

"I am glad you agree," I said, keeping my voice cold that he might understand I took the matter seriously. "In the morning, then—as soon as he is up. I will make a public act of it, that his men may understand we are not to be picked over like a corpse."

"By the gods, Master . . ." He sat up and leaned toward me in the darkness, his head almost touching the peak of the tent. "What has become of you that you show so little pity and so little sense? Would you really kill him, just like that, between rising and breakfast? No, Lord, it would never serve."

"What would you suggest? The man plans to—"

"What the man plans is beside the point! It is better to have one enemy at our throats than many. I can control Hiram of Latakia, and, should it prove necessary, you can always kill him later. The fact remains that we are safer traveling in a large party than we would be on our own."

He took a deep breath—I could hear it in the darkness, like the wind over ice.

"My Lord," he went on at last, and in a calmer voice, "I submit to you that if we leave this caravan, there is no shortage of brigands between here and the borders of your brother's realm, most of them worse than

Hiram because they have not heard my tales of the wealth I have waiting in Borsippa. We are better as we are, with a known evil. Leave this rapacious villain to me, for I understand the baser passions better than a noble soul like yourself. It will be well—after all, even a viper is harmless enough if you know to stay away from the sharp end."

I had long since learned the wisdom of submitting of Kephalos' judgment in these matters, so I rolled over and closed my eyes, pretending to sleep. In fact, I did not sleep. I stayed awake all the night, listening to the worthy physician's contented snoring and waiting for the sound of the footfall in the darkness that would mean Hiram's greed had overcome his patience.

But it never came. The camp was quiet until dawn. It seemed that Kephalos, once more, had seen more clearly than I and that we were safe enough, for the moment.

For three days we followed the wanderings of the Tartar River until at last it disappeared into a tangle of irrigation canals in which the slow water glistened heavily under the pale spring sunlight. We were traveling through farmland now, and almost every hour we met some peasant on his way to the fields, his naked legs covered to the knees with mud. They watched us without curiosity and without suspicion, for the Land of Ashur was a place where kings ruled and, in the settled places at least, men had little enough to fear from strangers.

On the evening of the fourth day we camped near a village, a circle of mud huts some distance from the closest water—these were folk who spent their whole lives within sight of a single river and knew better than to trust it in the season of flooding—and Kephalos and I, as it had been some time since we had tasted any meat but the stringy flesh of game animals, walked over to buy a goat.

In the end—such being the generosity of my countrymen—the headman invited us to feast with him and his sons, with which, it seemed, since they appeared to occupy nearly every hut in the village, the god had graced him almost beyond counting. He would roast the goat we had purchased from him, along with two more of his own, and he would acquaint us with the many excellences of his wife's beer. The invitation was extended to Hiram and his men and accepted by them with almost indecent haste.

Nor, it seemed, was our presence the only cause for celebration among the villagers, nor we the only recent arrivals. The headman had a cousin, the son of the son of his father's elder brother, a man who had been a soldier for many years and at last had retired on his share of the booty from Esarhaddon's sack of the city of Tishkhan, which had sided with the rebels in the late civil war.

This cousin, whose name was Tudi, was now almost an old man. His beard was full of gray, and he was glad to be out of the king's army and still in full use of all his limbs. He was now rich, being possessed of some fifty shekels of silver, disposed to take a wife young enough to bear him children, and to live out the rest of his life on the earth that held the sacred bones of his fathers. Yet for all this, for all that Esarhaddon's fury against the rebels had brought him wealth and ease, he was not comfortable in his mind about the new king, who he said lived under the god's curse.

I sat leaning my back against the wall of the headman's hut, whither Kephalos and Hiram had been invited to shelter themselves from the night cold. The hearth fire was a bed of smoking coals, my belly was full almost to bursting, and I was drowsy with too much beer, which had been as delicious as the headman had promised, even if one had to drink it through a hollow reed to keep from swallowing the husks. I was also a foreign slave, to whom the Akkadian of these farmers was as the chirping of crickets, so no one would have thought it impolite of me to fall asleep. Yet I did not sleep. Instead, with my eyes half closed, I listened to Tudi telling his cousin and his cousin's guests the story of my own life.

"The king walks in wickedness," he said, wiping his beard to clean the goat grease from his fingers. "He offers sacrifice at the idol of Marduk, which his father carried in chains from its temple in Babylon. He claims for Marduk the lordship of the gods, when all pious men know that it is Ashur who reigns in heaven."

"A man may choose to honor what gods he will—is this not so?" Hiram of Latakia shrugged his shoulders, like one to whom all gods were but a childish illusion. "Is not a king as free as other men? And if the Lord Esarhaddon is pleased with Marduk, what is that to anyone else?"

"In this land, Ashur is king," said the headman, and the eldest among his sons, some five of them, who had been invited to dine with his guests, nodded their heads, muttering in agreement.

"The king affirms no less when he is crowned," he went on. "The fruits of the land, the land itself, the men on it, all belong to the god—the king more than any. When the king is impious, he involves us all in his sin. Already there are stories of the births of monsters, and other omens yet more terrible. It is the cry of heaven against the king's wickedness. Ashur will not long allow himself to be thus slighted, and he will make known his wrath."

"They say the mud walls of Babylon rise higher every day. They say the king's desire is that it shall be a mighty city yet again, and thus shall Marduk's anger be turned aside." Once more it was Tudi, the old soldier, who spoke. He spat into the fire. "No more than that have I regard for the anger of Marduk!"

Hiram laughed, as if he were politely acknowledging a joke.

"You are a brave man then," he said. "Braver, it seems, than your king. Yet the rebuilding of a city is a thing not to be despised, since there will be money to be made from it."

"Money—yes, money for foreigners. Power for the Babylonians, the black-headed folk, and those who love them. Misery and disgrace for the men of Ashur."

There was silence for a moment. The headman looked embarrassed, as if afraid his cousin's words had offered an insult to his guests.

"And that it not all," Tudi went on, looking only at the fire, speaking as if with some inner voice. "The king has set his heart against his brother, the Lord Tiglath Ashur, whose name all men know, who is a brave and blameless man and much loved by the gods. I say it is an evil thing when brother turns against brother and the king in Nineveh is unrighteous to one whom the gods favor."

"Men have heard of this—even here," said the headman, clucking in disapproval. "Then has the king slain his brother?"

"No. This he feared to do, lest he be consumed by the god's wrath. He banished him. He made him to wander, a nameless man among strangers. Yet all may know him from the sign of the blood star upon his hand, token of Ashur's special favor."

I cannot hope to describe the sensation these words produced in me. I could feel my hand, still wrapped in Kephalos' bandages, curling of its own will into a fist. The mark with which I was born seemed to burn on my palm. I did not dare to look at anyone out of fear that I would find them staring at me. I could not have met their eyes. It seemed to me that everyone must know my secret, that it must be written across my face as it was across my bandaged hand.

Yet I could not stifle the flush of pride that welled up in me like new blood. To these people I was a figure of myth—beyond death and weakness and the corruption of time. And as such I might live forever, forever the god's favorite, forever the shadow in which the king my brother must live his life. With their muttered stories the men of this village, of villages up and down the Land of Ashur, took from Esarhaddon that which I was forever powerless to take for myself—my revenge.

"I saw the Lord Tiglath at Khalule," Tudi said, sitting up a trifle straighter, as if he had uttered a boast. "It was his first battle, and he no more than a boy, yet he killed great numbers among the enemy and received many great wounds. *There* was a soldier!"

His eyes fell on me as he spoke these words—whether because he noticed some resemblance or because a man must look at something while he speaks, I could not have said. Not then, at any rate. I merely glanced away, wishing I were back in my tent, asleep and dreaming of the dead past.

"Many say it was the god's will that the Lord Tiglath be king, that there was treachery," said another finally, breaking a silence that threatened to grow awkward.

"Yet Lord Tiglath honored his brother's claim and stood aside, though he loved his brother's wife, the Lady Esharhamat, beautiful as the dawn."

So they knew all this—all that Esharhamat and I had struggled to keep hidden in our own hearts. What fools we had been, when all our secrets were known even here, in a cluster of mud huts at the edge of the empty earth!

"Yes—he stood aside. He paid public homage to his brother on the steps of the king's own palace. And what was his reward?" Tudi looked about him, as if daring anyone to be impertinent enough to answer. "Banishment. His brother cast him out of the land like an unclean leper. The prince was set to wander, every man's hand turned against him for the price in silver shekels the king has put upon his head."

"Yet few, I think, will hazard the attempt to collect it."

The headman reached out his hands to take the beer pot from one of his sons. He stirred its contents with the reed straw and then took a long pull while everyone waited respectfully for him to have done.

"You think, then, this Lord Tiglath has gone where none will find him?" Kephalos asked at last. It was the first time that evening I had heard him speak.

"It does not matter where he goes," the headman answered, looking from one to another as if to have his opinion confirmed by everyone present. "He lives under the protection of the god, who has given him a mighty *sedu*—as the impious Dinanu learned to his sorrow."

"Dinanu? You mean the garrison commander at Birtu?" Hiram of Latakia appeared suddenly to come awake. His eyes brightened as he seemed to wait to hear something amusing. "I know him—he is a thief and scoundrel but not bad company when he is drinking. Has something happened to him?"

"Yes—has something happened to him?"

Kephalos glanced about, his expression all innocence, for the subject was not to his taste and fear made him uncautious.

But the headman did not regard him. His mind was elsewhere as he considered the might of his god.

"It is said that the Lord Tiglath was seen in Birtu," he said, "and that Dinanu, his heart blinded by greed, pursued him into the wilderness. He would have stripped the prince of his life, such was the wickedness he had learned from our king, but that Ashur, in his wrath, surrounded his favored one with a *melammu* of divine fire so that none might harm him. A wise man would have taken this warning and departed with his life, but the *rab abru* was not wise. Ashur, who is mighty and just and suffers no man to trifle with him, struck the fool dead, shattered the heavens with his war cry and pierced Dinanu's breast with a bolt of lightning. To this hour his corpse lies unregarded on the ground, and not even the crows will touch it."

"What is a *melammu?*" Kephalos asked me later, when we were alone together in our tent. "I have lived fifteen years among the Assyrians and have never heard that word. What does it mean?"

"It is an aura such as surrounds the bright gods, and sometimes the heroes they most favor—the thing the Greeks call a *nimbus.*"

"No wonder then that I have not heard of it, for life has not brought me into contact with many heroes—with, of course, the obvious exception of yourself, Lord."

"Do you mean to mock me, Kephalos?"

"No, Lord—of course not. How can you think it?"

He was quiet for a moment, as if considering the question.

"But is it true then? Did this *melammu*, this cloak of fire, cover your shoulders when you stood against Dinanu?"

"If it did, I did not see it."

"Which of course does not mean that it did not."

"He was an old man speaking rubbish. The god may have aided me—I do not deny it—but Dinanu fell before my javelin and not a bolt of lightning. And his corpse does not lie neglected on the plain. I buried it with my own hands. You saw me."

"Yes, that perhaps is embellishment. Perhaps no one went back to look, leaving each man free to assume what he most wishes to believe. It is what men *wish* to believe that matters, Lord. Those soldiers—that was why they rode away and left you unmolested. You killed Dinanu, whom none loved. It is a rare thing to cleave open a man's breast like that, and at such a distance. They saw the hand of their god in it and, like pious men, withdrew. Who is to say they were mistaken?"

Within a minute or two, I could hear him snoring. Yes, perhaps that had been it after all.

And I too was free to believe the god had saved me. I did believe it. I will believe it until I die.

The next morning, while I was building the breakfast fire and Kephalos was struggling to warm himself by the first tentative wisps of flame, Hiram strolled by and, seemingly surprised to find himself among us, stopped to exchange a word of greeting.

Kephalos, who had not yet grown accustomed to rising early, and who was always out of sorts until he had had his breakfast, could barely manage a civil grunt but huddled closer than ever to our weak little fire, as if afraid this intruder might rob him of some of its warmth.

The caravan leader, for his part, smiled his jolly brigand's smile, cocking his head to one side so that he seemed to be aiming the point of his beard at Kephalos' chest.

"It is a fine morning, eh?" he said, in a way that suggested he himself could hardly be bothered to notice. "And, for a change, we dined well last night, although I confess I have little enough desire to linger among these dung-caked Assyrian farmers with their beer that smells like garlic and their never-ending fables about the wrath of Ashur. I put it to you—who could believe such tripe? Dinanu, if I understand anything of the matter, was probably killed in some tavern brawl. I knew the fellow and, take my word for it, he was not the type on whom any god worth the name would waste a thunderbolt."

"They are a religious people," answered Kephalos, speaking with a tone almost of rebuke. "And all the Assyrians, even the humblest villagers, are greatly enamored of their princes. I have lived among them for many years and have learned the wisdom of a respectful silence."

"Oh, I would not dream of interfering—and who would wish to tamper with a man who walks about cloaked in fire?"

He glanced at me and smiled again. Then he excused himself, saying that he had business with his horses.

"Do you think he suspects?" I asked, when Hiram was out of sight. Kephalos shrugged his shoulders.

"It would not surprise me, but it changes nothing. He will whisper nothing of his surmises to his followers—why should he? what would he gain? So we are left where we were, a choice between the one enemy we know or the many we do not. I see no reason to alter our plans."

I will report only one more incident from that journey. It happened after we had broken camp, when the sun was still cool and we had mounted our horses and had found the way south. As we passed that cluster of mud huts where we had been entertained the previous night, we saw that the headman, his cousin Tudi—the old soldier who had seen me at Khalule—and all the men of the village were there lining the road, come out to watch us as we departed. They did not speak. They offered no salute. They merely stood there in the dust and kept their vigil as we passed by. Yet in its way it was an occasion as solemn as the feast of Akitu, when the god is carried from his shrine to greet the new year. I felt their eyes upon me, like the weight of a pledge, and knew that they knew, had known all along, and that this honor was intended for me.

"I would not dream of interfering," Hiram of Latakia had said, smiling his smile of mockery. "And who would wish to tamper with a man who walks about cloaked in fire?"

III

THERE IS AN ANCIENT PROVERB THAT THE ROAD TO BABY-lon is paved with corpses. Even now, nearly a lifetime later, I have only to close my eyes and think of the southern lands, the most wicked place the gods made, and dread floods my soul. My nostrils fill with the odor of death. I hear the cawing of crows as, their bellies heavy with carrion, they flap their black wings above the bodies of the slain. How much stronger were my memories in those days when, at five and twenty, I rode with the caravan of Hiram of Latakia along the banks of the Euphrates, most hateful of rivers.

In the land where I first drew breath the men of Ashur may stand at the edge of the cold, swift-flowing Tigris and see mountains in the distance. The gods, it is said, love to dwell in high places, so we felt ourselves always to be living under their gaze, as does the child under the eyes of his parents. It is not so in the Land of Sumer, where the dusty brown earth stretches flat for as far as mortal sight can reach. There no one loves the gods, though all fear them, and the minds of men grow dark with treachery.

I had first come to this place as part of the army the Lord Sennacherib, my king and father, had raised to punish the Elamites for murdering his son, Ashurnadinshum, whom he had made king of Babylon, and for stirring the southern lands to rebellion. We stood against our enemy at a place called Khalule—may its name disappear forever and the very ground perish. It was a terrible battle, where countless good men died, where for me the illusion of glory perished with them, but it was only the first of many horrors I saw in that long war.

We sacked many cities, leveling their walls and the houses of their great men, burning their grain stores that the survivors might perish of want before the next harvest. We laid siege to Babylon herself for over a year, drying up the river that watered her, starving her people so that few were left to die by the sword. And at last, when we took her, for five long days we murdered and pillaged, for pity had died in our hearts. Words pale before the wickedness that was done at Babylon, and in the name of our just vengeance. We were like beasts, believing that since we had suffered much so should we cause our enemies to suffer—this, it seems, is ever the way in a war that has gone on longer than men can bear.

Thus, had I no other reason, I could have hated the Land of Sumer and all who dwelled in her, for what my sojourn there had forced me to see within my own breast.

Not that these thoughts alone occupied my mind, for I studied my part as the Lord Hugieia's surly, brutish servant with great care, encouraging Hiram's men to shun me, closing my mind to everything spoken in my presence, speaking myself to no one except Kephalos. And I felt the strain of it, as one must who cannot permit himself even to relax the muscles of his face without hazarding his life. Yet the mask must slip now and then, even if I was never aware of it. As the days wore on, Hiram seemed to find me an increasingly interesting object of scrutiny.

His men, however, paid us no heed but went about their business and saw to their own comforts as if Kephalos and I did not exist. One night two of them quarreled over the settlement of some wager. One stabbed the other in the arm, and his friends seered the wound closed with a hot iron, apparently having forgotten that they had a physician traveling with them. Five days later the man's arm suddenly blew up like a waterskin and he died after a fever that lasted two nights and a day. This time, without waiting to be asked, Kephalos attended him and tried to ease his suffering, but he told me it was already too late to save his life. Even after the man was buried, no one thought to offer thanks to Hugieia of Naxos for his compassion. This did not trouble us. We welcomed their indifference. It was a measure of our comparative safety.

Although I can think of no reason why it should be so, it has always been my experience that a caravan makes slower progress even than an army on campaign. These Hittite barbarians could be expected to take no notice of the month's five evil days, during which men who fear the gods dress in rags, abstain from their wives, and neither work nor travel nor eat any food cooked in a pot, yet a commander serving Ashur's king would have flogged to death any soldier who dragged along as they did. Hiram made no complaint, however; he seemed to accept the slack pace of his drivers as normal. It was eight full days before we watered our horses in the Euphrates, and still, I heard the drivers say, we would not reach Babylon before a month had closed its door behind us.

The evening we made our first camp on the bluffs overlooking the Euphrates, I took a leather bucket and went down to the river to fetch water for our cooking pot. There were ducks among the reeds and I thought, If I but had a net . . .

But I did not have a net. I sat on the bank for a long while, merely watching them, pleased with the bright green feathers along their backs and the way their yellow feet kicked in the air as they struggled to dive for roots from the muddy bottom. Finally I was glad I did not have a net. I filled my bucket—carefully, lest I frighten them—and made ready to go.

Just as I stood up, a stone struck the water and the ducks scattered, their wings thrashing at the river's surface as they called out their alarm. I turned and saw Hiram standing on the bluff above me. He was grinning, as if he had achieved some victory.

"You are annoyed? I have disturbed your little reverie?" he asked, precisely as if he expected me to understand his words. "You are an odd one. If you were my property, I would have you whipped for loafing about like this. A slave with a taste for private reflection is a nuisance. And perhaps a danger as well.

"The burn—it heals slowly, does it?" He pointed to my right hand, which was still wrapped in a strip of soiled bandage. "Does it not give you pain to carry such a heavy bucket?"

He was right, of course. I resisted the temptation to switch the bucket to my other hand. He spoke in Aramaic; I was supposed to be ignorant of that tongue. I would not betray myself any more than I had already.

Without a word, I climbed up the bluff and pushed past him as if he were merely an object in the way. As I walked back to camp, I could hear his laughter behind me.

I was finding that it is a vexatious thing to be a servant. Kephalos always insisted, and with some justice, that the water of the Euphrates is not fit to wash one's face in until it has been strained several times through a wool cloak. Yet no matter how many times I performed this operation, inevitably he would wrinkle his nose at the first sip and comment that the foul stuff was still so thick with mud that a man might be tempted to make bricks with it.

"The next time you can fetch the water, and strain it through your own cloak—which, by the way, is no cleaner than my own."

"And I put it to you, Lord, how would that seem to our friends?" He sat back, bracing his hands against the bulging waist of his tunic as if I had profaned myself before the bright gods. "I, Hugieia of Naxos, doing a slave's work for him? Have some respect for appearances, and let us not bring scandal among these honest thieves by outraging the usages of the world. There is a distance between master and servant which must be respected—did you hear me complaining when, as a boy in the house of war, you set me to clean the dust from your sandals?"

"Yes, and bitterly."

"And what of it? Even a slave has a right to grumble."

"Grumble was all you did—grumble and play at dice with the soldiers. I never had a decent day's work out of you."

"And did I not always give you your fair share of my winnings? Did I not through my labors make you a rich man in the Land of Ashur? Are we not this moment making our escape with the treasure that I and I alone was wise enough to lay aside for such an emergency? And have I not, in my wisdom and care for you, deposited great wealth with the merchants of Egypt, that your life in exile will be such that even a prince would not disdain? Have I not done all this? Besides, a slave's life was not to my taste. I was not born to it."

"Neither was I, so you need not upset yourself thus. And cease complaining about the water."

"Oh, very well."

He sat watching me for a moment, like a physician at the bedside of a child, stroking his beard as if it were a cat's back. Then he nodded, apparently satisfied with the results of his meditations.

"You are annoyed with more than my poor self," he said at last. "Has something happened this morning about which I remain uninformed? You are the prey perhaps of unpleasant reflections?"

"I had an encounter with the worthy Hiram, not an hour ago, down at the river. He knows all about us. He seems almost to make a joke of it."

"He may guess much, but he knows nothing."

"In the end he will sell us to Esarhaddon."

"In the end, yes—if any of us are privileged to reach the end. But first he will try to squeeze what he can from me, and that gives us more than enough time to safeguard ourselves against future troubles. Be at peace, Lord. Do not be apprehensive over distant evils."

"I still believe it would be wisest to kill him now."

"Would you so willingly pollute your soul with murder?" He raised his eyebrows in astonishment. "Besides, as I have pointed out before, at present the caravan master serves our purposes as well as his own. We have nothing to fear from him until we reach Babylon."

"Babylon . . ."

I rose and walked away, my heart too bitter to bear the sight of any living creature.

Babylon. We could see her walls, still broken in places, even after all that time, three days before we reached her gates, but distance lent no charm. She rose up from the flat brown earth like a ruined mountain, the stronghold of some god long since cast down from heaven. My guts clenched at the sight of her.

At night, the priests of Marduk were busy. In the center of the city the fires atop the great ziggurat burned with black-red flames, offering sacrifice of blood and fearful pain. We saw them, camped three days' ride away. Anyone with eyes could see them.

I could remember other flames. I had seen the whole city burning. I had helped to set the fire in Marduk's temple and, not many months after, I had watched Mushezib-Marduk, once lord of Babylon, a wicked king indeed and the author of much suffering, boiled alive in a bronze jug, over a fire fueled by the corpses of his queen and children. These things were done in time of war, the works of war's cruel passions, but those passions still heated the blood, even after years of peace. The Babylonians had not forgotten, and neither had I.

Long after the cooking stones had grown cold I sat wrapped in my cloak, watching the distant, pulsing glow of that sacrificial fire, knowing the priests did their work at Esarhaddon's command, wondering what ghost within himself he hoped to quiet with all this spectacle of pious terror.

Esarhaddon was a born soldier. The man had not yet opened his eyes who could frighten him. Cheerfully he would pitch himself into the worst of the fighting, heedless of death. While the battle was fought no misgivings clouded his mind, but as soon as he lay down his sword demons began flapping their silent wings over his head. He feared the gods, naming each of them in turn as he quaked with horror. He feared the omens of their wrath and saw them everywhere. He feared the ghosts of the unquiet dead. He feared the spirits without number that claim to dwell in every corner of the wide earth.

And as king he had too much time to listen to the mutterings of priests. Since the voice of Shamash, Lord of Decision, had named him to succeed our father, he had not had a quiet hour. I could have pitied him had he not turned his hand against me. It was not in me to pity one who would have hunted me to my death, yet I could have pitied him, for the gods had played him an evil trick to make him king.

For he was the king, and it was at his word that the priests were busy and the sacrificial fires lit the night skies over Babylon. The gods of the south found their hearts stirring once again, and all manner of wickedness was let loose in the world.

Babylon, city of wickedness, city of turning minds, glory and curse of men.

On the day we came under the shadow of the Ishtar Gate, in the first hour before noon, slaves past counting, their legs caked with mud, their knobby backs bent beneath the weight of bricks hardened almost to stone in the pale winter sun, were trudging up the long, ragged stairway of a wall shattered by the king my father and the will of Ashur, rising now once again to please the king my brother, that the will of Marduk might be done. Slaves as gaunt as corpses, hardly bleeding from the great gashes on knees which a hundred times had buckled under their burdens— theirs was a living death; a few months, a year perhaps of toil and suffering before they starved, or their lungs burst, and their souls left their unburied bodies to flutter off into the barren night. No bread or wine would comfort these ghosts. Forever would they whirl about the wall they had built with their misery, cursing all those who dwelt within.

Wicked, wicked city. Place of darkness and shame.

"It rises—you see? In two years it will be as it was in the days of the great kings. Hah, hah, hah!"

Hiram of Latakia laughed like a jackal, as if this city, where he had not been born, which could be nothing to him, constituted some personal triumph.

"Yes," Kephalos answered, drawing in the reins a little to trim his horse's pace. "So it is feared in the north."

"Let them fear what they like in their mud villages. I will retire to raise grapes in the Lebanon, a rich man thanks to Marduk's anger. Then let them wash the ground with their blood for all I care. Hah, hah, hah!"

I rode just behind, my hand closed around the shaft of my javelin, wishing I could bury its point under Hiram's ribs.

Half an hour later we were in the central market and Hiram was sitting on a carpet, drinking date wine with a short, wide-eyed little man much given to sudden movements, who was one of the overseer's supply agents. They were haggling over the load of iron and copper ingots the caravan had fetched from the lands by the Northern Sea—the price of four months' labor was settled in a few moments' hard bargaining.

The thing was done. The pack horses were unloaded and Hiram's men were paid off from a bag of silver shekels, money that would be spent in the wineshops and brothels even before Hiram had bought the bales of embroidered wool cloth, the arsenic and spices, the tin and pressed dates he would sell in the west to buy more iron and copper for the rebuilding of Babylon. Kephalos and I watched for a time and then led our horses to the stable of an inn hard by the temple district, where a man could be sure of every luxury.

"I have invited that thief with a pointed beard to dinner," he told me. "Amuse yourself in the city until then. Buy clean clothes and drink wine. Spend your seed in a woman. Stay quiet and draw no attention to yourself, and be back by the first hour of darkness."

"You wish me out of the way then?"

"Yes." Kephalos nodded, as if admitting to a fault. "Hiram will not let me far out of his sight today, and I do not wish you to tempt him into any rash act against his own best interests. I wish him to think of my gold in Borsippa, and not of the gold the king your brother would pay to see your head mounted on the point of a stake."

So he counted out money into my hand, over a hundred shekels of silver—"Remember," he said, "without money even a prince is a beggar. Beguile the time with wanton pleasure, as befits a wise man who stares at the future with blind eyes"—and I found myself dismissed. Lathikados, the slave from nowhere, off on a holiday.

The last time I had walked the streets of Babylon they had been carpeted with the slain. I had seen the corpses of young girls, hardly more than children, lying in doorways with their throats cut, their thighs covered in blood from the attentions of our warriors of Ashur. Old men had their heads beaten to pulp before the eyes of their wives and daughters. Buildings were burned with their occupants locked inside. In places the narrow alleyways were clogged with bodies, such had been our pitiless wrath. It had been an appalling slaughter, a stain upon the soul even of those who merely witnessed it. It did not end for five days.

Yet the guilt for this rested not only with the men of Ashur, for the siege of Babylon lasted many months, and mercy dies in the hearts of men who have had to suffer war too long. Hate grows in its place, like lichens in a dead tree. I and all the vast armies of my father the Lord Sennacherib learned to hate Babylon and all it held, until the word itself was bitter in our mouths. The king of that city, fearing a death he could not have hoped to avoid, would not surrender and thus abandoned his people to ruin. It could have ended no other way.

And even all those years later the hate still burdened my soul.

Babylon, city of wine and plenty. City of shining faces.

Esarhaddon had taken the grain trade for three days' ride in any direction and placed it in the hands of the Lord Marduk. This my brother did that the wrath of heaven might be turned away from his care-creased brow. The god must reign in Sumer and his temple vaults must creak under the weight of his gold—a peasant with fields along that branch of the Euphrates could have his feet chopped off for selling his harvest to any but the priests. There would be famine in the countryside next winter, but the people of Babylon would not starve. The wineshops would dance with laughter while the chill, unforgiving wind whistled through farming villages emptied by death.

Babylon would not starve—not until once more her gutters ran with fresh blood.

Even Nineveh, Nineveh the beautiful, city of my birth, capital of the wide world, even she was never so crowded as was Babylon on that afternoon as my shoulders rubbed against her multitudes. The murmur of a hundred thousand voices shuddered against my ears, the shouts of traders and the high, sweet laughter of harlots and the gossip of twenty different tongues, and my nose was filled with the smells of roasting lamb and spices and barley as it simmered in copper brewing pots. I was hungry. I bought meat and cooked rice and a piece of flat bread to wrap them in and ate it all leaning against an ocher-colored wall, a stranger in the midst of strangers, unregarded and safe. Once done, I wiped my fingers on my travel-stained tunic, grown stiff with dirt, drank a pot of beer, and asked directions to the nearest sweating house.

For the next hour I reclined on a cedar bench in a tiny, steam-filled room, drowsy with pleasure. My clothes had been washed and were drying before a fire somewhere. There was a small boy sitting in the doorway, polishing my sword with handfuls of sand. A woman, grown too old to sell her body to strangers, rubbed mine with a wet linen cloth, scraping away the months of living in the open. Warm and clean, my weary muscles loosening beneath her hands, I lay there half asleep and completely content. I loved her. She was mother and wife to me. She made me happier than I could have been with the prettiest tavern girl. When I was ready to leave I gave her three silver shekels, around which her fist closed like a trap.

The old crone had burned the binding that covered my right hand—"It is filthy, paugh! so that only the fire can purify it. I wonder you have not poisoned yourself by wearing such a thing so close to raw flesh." Yet in this city of strangers I would be safe enough until Kephalos could bandage me again. Here, so far from Nineveh, the blood star across my palm would be merely a birthmark.

Kephalos had instructed me to amuse myself. I would find a tavern somewhere, one frequented by such as would not resent the presence of a foreigner in travel-faded clothes, and I would drink wine and perhaps take a woman. Yes—the pent-up seed felt ready to burst my groin like a pomegranate left in the sun. I had been too long without a woman.

The Red Lizard, on the Street of Damkina, was in one of those uncertain districts, almost equidistant from the river quays, the army garrison and the temple complex, where men of all conditions are accustomed to mingle freely. Household slaves in linen uniforms bore the sedan chairs of the mighty past the oxcarts of farmers and soldiers' horses, while humbler men made their way on foot. Everyone had money here, since it was a place where purses were expected to be open, and if a poor fool of a slave wished to squander half a year's earnings he was welcome to do so.

It was a large building, with three stories. Wealthy patrons might solace themselves above, but the ground floor was filled with soldiers, shop-keepers, foreign merchants of the meaner sort, and such as myself. The walls had once been white, but the smoke from generations of braziers had long since painted them a pale yellowish gray. The floor was covered with wine stains, like dried blood, and the air was thick with the smell of food and sweat and—yes, it took me a moment to recall—women. An Amorite flute player and a drummer from nowhere in particular were making music in one corner, but they were drowned out by the laughter and loud talk of men whose notions of pleasure held little enough place for music. I took a place at the end of a crowded bench.

There were perhaps twenty or twenty-five girls working in the tavern, and all, to ply their trade the easier, were naked. Most served wine and sat with the men who drank it; some few danced with varying degrees of skill to the all-but-inaudible music; and some, their sleeping mats spread out upon the crowded floor, provided other entertainments. This was a common enough sight in the lands between the great rivers, where a man unburdens his lust in public with as little sense of shame as a Greek might feel pissing against the city wall.

"Your honor will take some refreshment?"

She was comely enough by the standards of the south, where they favor dark, fleshy women. Her face and body were shiny with oil and her breasts were as round as melons. The hair between her thighs was heavy and matted, like the fur of a cat.

"Wine," I answered, looking up nearly to impale my eye on her nipple, rouged pink as a cherry blossom. "And perhaps the pleasure of your company while I drink it."

She smiled, suggesting that was the answer she had been waiting all her life to hear.

I am compelled to admit that I grew tolerably drunk that afternoon, and without much waste of time. I must have been drunk, for I was uncautious enough to allow Penushka—that was her name, Penushka—a glance inside my purse. Almost in the same instant that she saw the quantity of silver shekels it contained I found myself being dragged upstairs, by force, or very nearly, with the tavern proprietor supporting me on one arm and Penushka on the other, to one of the private rooms reserved for gentlemen of means and fastidious tastes.

"Your Lordship must excuse . . ." the proprietor kept muttering, ". . . we had hardly expected . . ."

I offered no resistance. I was affability itself, as a man generally is when he is showered with unexpected comforts. The room contained only a single low table; its only other furnishings consisted of such a plentiful variety of pillows and cushions as I had never seen before. Who was I to object to such luxury?

I rolled about on the cushions, laughing and trifling with Penushka, who fed me grapes and pieces of cooked meat and suffered me to drink wine from the hollow of her navel or from the cup she made by pressing her round breasts together. I went into her and loosened my seed, but the lust accumulated over many weeks is not spent in an instant—no more than I would she have it so, saying that she found more pleasure in a lover the second time, when he was not in such a hurry, and very quickly she teased my manhood back up again. We had a comfortable enough time in that room and cleaved together many times. It became a kind of game to see how many times, but I have since forgotten the precise number. A harlot, who knows that the men whom she takes between her legs are with her but a time and then are gone, such a woman is sometimes bolder than the wife of one's heart, who must cook her husband's breakfast in the morning and live all her life within the sound of his voice. A harlot does not fear to offend and thus does not offend, for no man but a fool believes there is any truth in her smile or credits what she says or cares what she may think of him. I was not offended when Penushka, playing with my hand, pushed open the fingers and traced with her nail the outline of the birthmark that the god had written across my palm.

"Such things are omens," she said, allowing her eyes to grow round, as if at a sacred miracle. "Perhaps you are destined by the will of heaven to be a great man, powerful and rich."

Her lips parted in a smile as she said it, as if the glorious future she contemplated were her own, but perhaps she only mocked at the idea that a slave, even one such as me, with a few shekels in his purse, should ever be anything more.

"All the wealth I care about is here," I said, taking her breasts in my hands and kissing them. "And all the power that matters you have drained out of my loins."

She smiled even more widely and let her fist close lightly around my manhood.

"Perhaps there is still a little left—do you think . . . ?"

After a time one becomes conscious of one's excesses. I had drunk too much wine. This woman no longer pleased me. Desire was gone, and I felt only resentment that I lay in the arms of a Babylonian harlot and not with the woman who had led by heart away in bondage while we were yet children in the king's great house. I longed for Esharhamat, my brother's wife.

What had happened to Esharhamat and me? Why had the god turned his back on us?

"I must go," I said. "My master awaits my return."

She did not plead with me to stay—why should she, when I was finished with her and she with me?—but rose to her feet and began helping me back on with my clothes.

"Will you come again?"

"I do not know."

I shook my head and offered her a thin smile, for there are decencies to be observed in these matters and who was I to ignore the feelings of Penushka the harlot simply because I had exhausted my interest in her?

"Perhaps, if the gods will it. But I serve a master and I do not know his plans."

"We all serve one master or another," she answered, smiling. I liked her better for that smile.

We had only just reached the foot of the stairway when one wearing the tunic of a common soldier pushed his way through the door—there is no other way to describe his entrance, for he was a large man, not tall but wide and solid, and his bulk so filled the doorframe that he seemed to squeeze past it like dough through a baker's fingers.

"Penushka!" he brayed, like a man entering his own house. I disliked him. Of course, the situation precluded any other reaction, but I was close to hating him for the way his eyes turned first to her, then to me, then back to her, as if dismissing my existence. "Show me your backside, girl, for I am an impatient man. Here, girl!"

He reached for her, as if to do her some injury, and without thinking I stepped forward and slapped his hand aside—it was an impulse, nothing more. A moment of angry revulsion.

"Who is this?"

We stood facing one another and after a moment the soldier wrinkled his nose, as if at a bad smell.

"A foreigner, Penushka? He shook his head, seemingly unable to believe such a thing. "Even a donkey mare will not suffer a dog to mount her. Penushka, have you come so low that you must spread your cheeks for every monkey that crawls in from the western deserts, stinking of onions and cow dung?"

A foreigner. *I* was a foreigner. This one's Aramaic was as thick as river mud—from what mountain cave, forty days' march from here, had he crawled to enlist? I wondered.

"Lashu, if you . . ."

Penushka, poor girl, did not know what to do nor where to look. This, apparently, was a regular client, and I had just given her four silver shekels. She only wished to offend no one, so the words died in her throat and she merely smiled like a witless child and tried to disappear into the wall.

She needn't have concerned herself. She was hardly even a party to the quarrel.

Because a quarrel it must now become—Lashu had seen to that, for with his bellowing voice he had summoned the attention of the whole tavern. Everyone stared. The flute player put down his instrument, realizing that he had lost his audience. No one could have ignored us. No one wanted to ignore us, for men come to such places to be diverted and there is nothing quite so amusing as a fight.

He realized this, did the mighty Lashu. He looked around at the gaping faces and grinned, delighted to be the center of interest. He would give them a show. I could see the idea coming together in his mind like the pieces of a child's puzzle. It amused him. The muscles under his thick, heavy face, full of unintelligent cunning, twitched with pleasure.

He would make a great spectacle of humiliating this uncouth barbarian. Perhaps he would wound or maim me, perhaps kill me as an added entertainment. Who would stop him? Who would object if he spilled some of my blood onto the floor? I might, but would that matter? I carried a weapon, but so did many men—many more than had any idea of using one. And, after all, he was a soldier, trained in butchery and accustomed to it. There was little enough risk. And no one would speak up for a dead foreigner, not against Lashu, soldier in the king's army.

His hand dropped down to his sword, and the fingers closed about the hilt.

"The king your master must be desperate for soldiers," I said, not caring what I said, since my only object was to goad this ox into losing his temper—anger, like fear, makes a man hasty and prone to error, and an insult does not have to be eloquent to do its work.

"I would have thought the Lord Esarhaddon could have chosen better than one fool enough to call another man 'foreigner' when he himself was probably born under a blanket in the hind parts of the world."

I heard a woman's nervous, high-pitched giggle, and one or two men were incautious enough to laugh. Lashu's forehead creased with annoyance.

"Where are you from, Mighty Warrior? Is that how they pick their soldiers, these masters of the world—if it can walk on its back legs it must be a man? Where did they find you, scampering about, covered with nothing but your own fur?"

I showed him my teeth in a smirking grin. He was not quite ready to fight yet, but he was close enough.

"Dog!" he shouted. "Unclean pig! Son of a leprous harlot!"

"Pleased to meet you. And I am Lathikados the Ionian."

This was too much for him to bear. In a single movement he drew his sword and, with his arm locked straight, reaching for my belly, swung it at me in a wide arc. I had only to draw back a little to avoid the stroke, but Penushka, pinned against the staircase wall, was not so lucky. Even as it slowed to a stop, the point of Lashu's sword cut across her naked breast, slicing it open, covering it with her bright blood. She screamed and fell to the floor as if she had been knocked down.

If Lashu noticed, he gave no sign. He merely grunted in vexation that he had missed his chance to kill me. And then something else attracted his attention.

For as I stepped back I had raised my hand—whether to pull it out of the way or to ward off a second blow, I could not have said. I raised it, nevertheless, and with that unconsidered gesture exposed the palm, with its mark of the blood star, for Lashu to see.

And he saw it. Perhaps no one else in the room save he, but he saw it. I did not have to ask if he knew what it meant, for his eyes, wide and staring, told everything.

"You!" he whispered, so that none but I—and perhaps Penushka, whose attention was engaged elsewhere—could have heard. "It's you!"

"Yes. It is I."

In that instant we understood each other perfectly. We both knew that this petty squabble over the attentions of a tavern girl had at once become a fight to the death. He had to kill me now, or I would surely kill him. He knew the secret that must spell my death, so I would have no choice. Now neither of us had a choice.

And yet for an instant Lashu the soldier could not move. He had been taken by surprise—nothing had prepared him for this—and he hesitated. It was time enough. I drew my sword, and made it an even contest.

His eyes narrowed, for he saw that he had made a mistake, and once more he slashed out, this time aiming the blow at my head. I caught his blade on my own and, nearly wrenching my shoulder from its socket, managed to turn him aside. He was a strong man, and it was not easy.

I am not gifted with the sword, but I was a king's son and had had years of practice on the drill fields of the house of war, the garrison at Nineveh. I, at least, had been taught its use. Lashu was a plain man who had somehow become a soldier; no one had taken many pains with his training, but he had long arms and knew how to slash. And he was strong. We were a match for each other.

He cut at me again, more in control of himself this time. It was a shallow jab, not meant to reach me—he was only testing my reactions— and I let it pass harmlessly by without even raising my sword point.

We faced each other, each looking for that tiny opening in the other's defenses, waiting to strike.

On the floor between us, leaving a little trail of bloody handprints, Penushka had come to her senses enough to have begun crawling out of harm's way.

From one instant to the next, Lashu began a furious attack, hacking at me like a madman. The close air of the tavern rang with the sound of iron striking iron as I blocked and parried. Crowded against the stairway, I had hardly any room to retreat. I could only fend him off and hope he tired, or made a mistake.

And then, just as suddenly, he stepped back. His face was streaming with sweat, but he was not weary. He grinned at me with ferocious pleasure—I belonged to him now, he seemed to say. I was not without skill, but he was the stronger. He would wear me down, and then . . .

He rushed at me again. There was the clash of our swords, like the sound of ice splintering in the spring thaw. I could hear him grunting with effort as he tried with each stroke to break through and cleave my skull open.

He eased a bit—only for the space of a few fast heartbeats—but it was only a feint, a trick to catch me off guard. Before I could draw a breath he stepped forward again, and his sword whistled through the air as it slashed at my chest.

I turned the blow aside, but this time, as he attempted to recover, Lashu seemed to lose his balance.

His foot had slipped. He had stepped into a pool of Penushka's blood, and had slipped.

It was enough. I came in low, under his sword, and drove up. I caught him just under the rib cage, and my blade buried itself nearly to the hilt. I pulled it free and jumped back, tense and waiting. A man can kill you even while his life deserts him.

But I do not think he had time enough even to be surprised. I think he died in that very instant.

There was not so much as a cry—not a sound, not even a whisper of pain. Lashu simply collapsed. All at once he lay on the floor, staring up at me with dead, reproachful eyes.

This fight was over.

Suddenly I became conscious of the sounds of the crowd around us. All this time, it seemed, they had been holding their breath, but now they buzzed with that uncertain wonder men feel in the presence of death. I turned to look at them. They were all staring at me, waiting.

"Remember who struck the first blow," I said, surprised at the loudness of my own voice. "I had no choice—he would give me no choice."

They continued to stare. Naked women, men surprised in the midst of their pleasures—one, I remember, an old fellow, his beard shot through with gray, fingering his chin with strengthless, uncertain fingers—not knowing what to believe. Knowing only that I had killed a man and still held the sword in my hand. Prepared, perhaps—I could only hope—to believe anything.

"I am innocent of this man's blood. I did not seek his end. He brought death down upon himself."

I waited. I could feel the blood coursing through the veins in my neck.

And then, slowly, as they looked around among themselves, I could see they accepted what I had told them. It was the version they would tell when the soldiers came. It was what would pass for the truth when I was gone—my absence, and their unwillingness to stop me, would create of it what they had to believe.

I must make my escape now.

I heard a whimper somewhere behind me. It was Penushka, huddled on the floor, still bleeding. I bent down beside her for a moment and saw that the gash on her breast was a clean cut, too shallow to be dangerous.

In a sense, she had saved my life.

"You will be well," I said, almost in a whisper. "A physician will come and close the wound. In a few days you will have nothing but the scar to make you remember."

Her face tightened with grief, and her eyes filled with tears. It was only then that I remembered that, for harlots, scars were a discouragement to trade.

"Time to retire," I said. I put my arm over her shoulder. "Time to find some good man and take the veil of marriage. Here—accept this for your dowry."

I reached into my cloak and took out the purse full of silver shekels Kephalos had given me, pressing it into her hands. It was probably more wealth than she had seen in her whole life. She could hardly believe it.

"Forgive me, Penushka—and kiss me good-bye."

She raised her face, and I brushed her lips lightly with my own. Then I rose and hurried away.

In the street I kept waiting for the sounds of shouting behind me. There was only the busy hum of ordinary life. I broke off into an alleyway that led to another street. I did this several times before I began to feel myself safe.

"Safe." That word had little enough meaning for me. How safe could I ever be when every common soldier knew me on sight? I would never be safe until I found a place where no one had ever heard of the mighty race of Ashur. where "Tiglath" and "Esarhaddon" were only empty sounds in the dull air. Until then, every man's hand would be turned against me. I would not be safe until I had hidden myself in some land my brother had never even dreamed of.

It was nearly dark before I returned to the inn where Kephalos was waiting for me.

"There is blood on your tunic," he said. "You have had an adventure? No. Do not tell me of it now. Change your clothes. No—I knew you would not remember, so I have purchased new ones for you. They are in that hamper. Have you dined?"

I did as he instructed, throwing open the lid of the wicker chest that stood against the bare wall and taking out linen undergarments and a richly embroidered tunic of green wool. It was scented with jasmine. I felt quite the dandy in it.

"Yes. I have dined."

"Good—then that is at least one thing you will be spared."

I turned around to look at him. He was seated at a long table, such as the inn might supply against a feast. The only object on the table was a cup half full of what looked like cloudy water. The expression on Kephalos' face did not suggest that he was finding much refreshment in it.

"I told you, did I not, that our benefactor the noble Hiram is to be my guest tonight." The worthy physician put a hand on his stomach, as if his digestion troubled him. "He is now at liberty to discuss terms, he tells me—the terms on which he will allow us to escape the king your brother's wrath. I entertain no doubts concerning his sincerity, since I know he will sell us to the garrison here no matter how liberally I bribe him. The characters of some men are as plain as their footprints in the mud.

"But you will oblige me by entertaining no idea of murdering him, since he will be our guest and the gods always punish such breaches of hospitality. And you will play the good servant, say nothing, and not think to take food or drink in the presence of your betters. Have I made myself clear?"

"No, but it shall be as you say. I have already killed one man today and have not the bowels to kill another—nor much taste for revels."

"Then I was not mistaken in my surmise. Yes, well . . . We will speak of it later. When we are safe."

He picked up the cup and, after a pause in which he seemed to be gathering his courage, bolted down its contents. A drop slid down his chin, glistening like oil.

"You will leave this matter to me, My Lord?"

"I will leave it to you."

"Good, then—just remember to be Lathikados the slave and not Tiglath the prince, and I think I can promise us a good outcome."

"If it depends on no more than that, we will live forever."

The thin smile that flickered over Kephalos' face, like a shadow in the fire, suggested he was less hopeful.

We waited in silence. Slaves came in to prepare the banquet, setting out bowls of flowers and scented water and a brazier to keep off the night chill. There were jars of wine that had been left to sleep all day at the bottom on the river so they would be sweet and cold. Oil lamps were lit.

The cook appeared to receive her final instructions. At last we were left to ourselves again.

It was already late before we heard the sound of Hiram's sandals on the stairs.

"Good! You have not begun without me," he said. Like Kephalos, like myself, he was dressed in new garments. He wore a bright yellow turban fastened by a pin set with blue stones. His beard had been freshly trimmed and shone with oil.

He sat down heavily, his eyes glittering. He had been drinking.

"No, I waited. After all, you are the guest of honor."

Kephalos smiled and nodded to a slave, who broke the seal on one of the wine jars, poured half into a great bronze pitcher, and then mixed in three cups of water, one after the other, from a silver jug that stood at Kephalos' elbow.

"No more than that!" Hiram protested, a shade too loud. "Too much water and a man cannot grow suitably drunk—hah, hah, hah!"

"Too little and a man risks becoming sick," Kephalos observed, smiling again, dismissing the slaves that his guest might not disgrace himself in front of them. He seemed in a temper to humor this oaf, who he had said would surely betray us. Or perhaps he still thought there was room for compromise.

The dinner was brought in—rice and millet, cooked vegetables, roasted lamb, even honeyed locusts. Kephalos, whose appetite I had never known to fail him, ate even more voraciously than usual, but Hiram hardly touched his food. He seemed only interested in wine.

"Do you feel so starved after a few months on the caravan route?" he asked. "Or do you wish to show me that I have nothing to fear from poison—hah, hah, hah!"

He shared the joke with no one. Kephalos did not laugh, and I, who sat behind him, still less. This seemed to annoy Hiram of Latakia.

"I see your slave eats nothing," he announced glumly.

"He shows respect," Kephalos answered. "He is a good servant."

"Perhaps not so good a servant to his last master—now, who would that have been?"

This time he did not seem to care that he laughed alone.

At last, and as if the subject had been forced on him, Kephalos shrugged his shoulders.

"I've no idea. I know nothing of his history."

"Then perhaps he was a foundling, stolen by wicked genies. Perhaps his father was some great man—perhaps even a king."

"It seems unlikely enough to be true."

With his own hand, Kephalos poured more of the wine into his guest's cup and his own. Hiram drank it off in almost a single swallow, and Kephalos filled his guest's cup yet again.

"This is good wine," Hiram said, as if he had just made the discovery. Already his speech was becoming slurred.

"The best that this city can offer, the proprietor tells me—and I have no doubt that in Babylon the best is very good indeed."

Hiram shook his head, and then set the cup down. He seemed to have forgotten all about it. He was staring at me, frowning. He seemed to hate me.

"Yes, I do believe it," he murmured finally, almost to himself. "I do believe his father might have been a king."

His eyes narrowed, as if he were having trouble seeing.

"You should light another lamp, Physician. It has grown confoundedly dim in here."

Kephalos nodded, without speaking. Then he reached across the table and took Hiram's cup from between his unresisting hands. It was only then that I began to understand what was happening.

"Come, Lord—help me with him."

Even as I rose from my seat, Hiram was beginning to sag in his chair. He was staring at us, his face expressive at once of the fear growing within his soul and the change, whatever it must have been, that had robbed him of all strength. He tried to speak, but his voice failed. He did not resist as Kephalos and I picked him up by his legs and arms and carried him over to a sleeping mat laid out in one corner of the room.

"Look at his eyes," Kephalos murmured. "This slackness will not last long."

I looked, and the pupils had contracted down almost to nothing. I did not know what it meant.

"The doors of sight are nearly closed, as you see. It is no wonder he thought the light grown dim."

Kephalos took him by the wrist and raised his arm. When he released it, the arm hung suspended for a moment and then, only very slowly, sank back down to Hiram's side.

"He is already becoming rigid," Kephalos said. "Excuse me, Lord."

He went into the next room, and I heard the sound of retching. When he came back, his face was pale and he seemed exhausted.

"I lined my guts with oil, and made certain there was plenty of food in my belly to absorb the poison—a recipe I learned years ago from an Arab colleague of great learning. It was in the water with which we tempered the wine and it acts on the muscles, causing them to contract. It is like a cramp of the whole body. I am well enough, however. I have a headache but nothing more."

Then he squatted down beside the sleeping mat where Hiram lay, unable even to move now, and spoke to him.

"Listen to me," he said. "I have given you something to keep you quiet while my Lord Tiglath and I make good our escape, but it will not kill you unless you are very foolish. You are deprived of the power of motion, and even of speech. You must accept that. If you allow yourself to grow frightened or excited, there is a chance you will throw yourself into a convulsion, and you will be unable to breathe. Your own body will strangle you from the inside. Do you understand that?"

It was impossible to know whether Hiram understood anything, since the only sound that came from him was a faint clicking inside his throat.

"In three or four days, this paralysis will begin to wear off. You will be returned to the full enjoyment of health, but you must remain calm. By then we will be far, far away and out of your power to do us any harm. Remember, Hiram of Latakia, your life is in your own keeping. Stay quiet and you will recover."

Then Kephalos stood up and turned to me.

"Take only your sword and javelin, Lord," he said. "We must leave everything else—we must allow the proprietor to believe we have only stepped out for a little air. I have seen to everything. There is a boat waiting for us by the great bridge. Hurry, Lord—there is no time for reflection!"

As we fled that place, I cast one glance back at Hiram, his lips trembling in a meaningless palsy. Perhaps it was all lies. Perhaps he would die—he looked like a dying man—and then my secret would have claimed another victim.

IV

"MY GUEST HAS DRUNK HIMSELF INTO A STUPOR," KEPHA-
los told the proprietor of our inn. "I have left him to sleep himself
sober—you would do well to advise your household slaves not to disturb
him, since wine seems to make him quarrelsome and he will have a
tender head when he wakes up. It is a great pity that some men grow to be
worse than beasts for want of a little moderation, is it not?"

The proprietor nodded sagely, stroking his beard. He was a man to
recognize good advice when it was given to him. The walls of his inn were
not thick and the doors no more than curtains, and yet he had heard
nothing to suggest violence, not even the sound of raised voices. And he
knew all about men like Hiram of Latakia. The Lord Hugieia of Naxos
and his slave were taking the evening air to be out of the way of a
troublesome drunkard—what could have seemed more natural? Besides,
Kephalos had been wise enough to pay our reckoning for three days in
advance.

We walked calmly into the street. Babylon, like all the great cities of the
east, never sleeps, so even at that hour of the night crowds engulfed us.
We had not gone a hundred steps before we were lost in that multitude
beyond any chance of discovery. We had made good our escape.

"But did you kill him?" I asked.

"Who?"

"You know perfectly well who."

Kephalos slowed his pace a little and glanced at me, his face puckering
with annoyance.

"And what if I have? Is the life of Hiram of Latakia so precious that it would be a great grief to the world if I ended it? You tell me yourself that you have slain a man today—what if I have slain another?"

"Then have you?"

"My foolish young master, I am a Greek," he replied, almost as if he expected this to be sufficient answer. "The farther we travel from Nineveh, the more forcefully I remember that I am, indeed, a Greek—a man born in the lands of clear sunshine, within hearing of the wine-dark sea. A Greek prizes his intelligence, he prefers cunning to violence, and he walks in fear of the gods. With each day of our journey I think more and more of my own gods, and of their horror at the deeds of men. No, I would not kill a guest at my own table, no matter how much he may have deserved it. Hiram of Latakia will recover to cause more trouble in the world."

"I am delighted to hear it."

"A man such as yourself, who has been a soldier, should be less dainty about the spilling of blood."

East and west, Babylon is divided by the width of the Euphrates River. Near the great bridge that spans it, famous for its stone pillars, like the legs of storks, we found a barge loading bales of oxhides. It was some forty cubits long and had a crew of five men. I saw Kephalos' medicine box sitting on the pier, as if waiting for him.

"I made all the arrangements through a leather merchant whose shop I noticed across the street from a brothel I happened to be patronizing—he robbed me, but I could hardly come down to the docks myself to buy passage. I was quite certain Hiram was having me followed.

"We will travel thus to Ur, which is as far south as your brother's hand can reach after us. How we shall proceed from there I know not."

Neither did I, but, like Kephalos, I was content for the moment simply to be at liberty and thus willing enough to let the future look after itself.

Kephalos introduced himself to the scribe who sat on the pier, making marks upon a clay tablet as each bale was loaded on board, and it seemed we were expected. The scribe, a eunuch with thin arms and the manners of a woman, sent his servant for beer, and we refreshed ourselves as the work progressed. It was nearly morning before the barge, resting low in the water, was ready to depart.

So near its end, the Euphrates runs wide and deep, and its coils are as many as a serpent's. There is hardly any current—one simply drifts—but the boatmen are not afraid to travel at night because they have only to keep to the great central channel to avoid running aground. Thus we were six days between Babylon and Ur, never once setting our feet on the dry land.

Yet it was a pleasant journey. A fugitive does not feel constricted by the instrument of his escape, and the boatmen of every nation are entertaining company, full of stories and gossip from distant places—although I doubt if any of these had ever been beyond the waters of this one river. Nobody inquired into our histories, except to listen to Kephalos' tales of Sidon and Tyre and the great cities along the Northern Sea. The wrath of kings seemed far away. It was as tranquil a six days as I have spent in my life.

Ur is a famous city, but I remember hardly anything of it. We were there only a few hours—long enough to drink more wine than was good for us and then steam it out in the sweat baths. Long enough to hire another boatman who undertook to carry us to our destination, our only hope of safety, the last place on earth.

This time it was my task to strike the bargain, for the fellow understood only the thick, tortured Akkadian of the southern lands, a dialect to which Kephalos' ears could not seem to grow atuned.

"You want to go to the Great Water, then?" the boatman asked, screwing his eyes tight, as if looking into our faces were no different from looking straight into the sun.

Our destination was a point that needed to be settled, but he had no curiosity beyond it. He was a man who had lived long enough to learn the virtues of minding his own business.

"Can one find ships there?"

"Oh yes, many ships."

He nodded—if we wanted ships we could have them, for it was nothing to him.

Kephalos and I exchanged a glance. Yes, of course. He was an ignorant fellow, his skin long since tanned to leather, who would know nothing beyond his own little stretch of the Euphrates, but he could only be talking about the Bitter River that flows around the circumference of the world. From there we would be certain to find places on a trading ship that would carry us to Egypt.

"Then take us there. How long a journey is it?"

"If we leave now, I will be back to sleep with my own wife tomorrow night. And we will leave now if you will pay me now."

That seemed all the answer we were going to receive.

"Then we will leave now," I said, counting out the agreed-upon number of shekels into his hand.

Kephalos began to say something and then seemed to think better of it. His eyes fixed on the boat, which floated on the sluggish water like a dead leaf. He was not enthusiastic.

I could not really blame him. The boat was hardly even a boat at all, merely bundles of huge reeds tied together and coated on the outside with bitumen—a little wider in the center and fitted with narrow wooden benches that a few men might sit down in her, but for the most part seeming as slender and insubstantial as a blade of grass that the wind had carried into a puddle.

"We will be all right," I told him. "The river is quiet, and I imagine not even your weight will be able to sink us."

"My Lord is pleased to jest," he replied, smiling sourly as he stepped aboard with the greatest possible caution. "I trust he will find equal occasion for mirth when the fish are nibbling at our bloated corpses."

The boatman sat in the rear and pushed away from land with his oar. It was already evening, and behind us the lamps in the city watchtowers flickered like a warning. As the light faded, as the darkness became as tangible as the black river and the solid shore dropped away and out of sight, I began to share Kephalos' sense of unease—it was as if we had separated ourselves forever from the ordered world of men and returned to that chaos that reigned before the gods first divided the sky from the dry land and the water from both.

Thus we traveled, in silence, for many hours. There was no sound except that of the boat scratching its way across the blank face of the river. I closed my eyes and tried to sleep, but I could not. I felt almost as if I had died, or were about to be born.

At dawn the sun rose like an old woman getting up from a nap. I cannot remember ever welcoming anything as much as those first few pale streaks across the night sky.

Yet what they at last revealed was very far from anything we had expected or hoped.

What had my imagination conjured up for me? A trading port perhaps, her shores as busy as an ant heap and her waters crowded with great wooden merchant vessels fresh from places I had never dreamed of. What I found was a village, the houses made of reeds, with a few reed boats pulled up on the beach, most of them smaller than the one that had carried us hither.

The "Great Water" was no more than a lake. A vast lake, vast enough that its opposite bank was shrouded in purple mist, but a lake for all that. I scooped some up in the palm of my hand and tasted it—it was fresh. This was not the Bitter River that flowed around the girth of the world. This was not our avenue of escape.

Our boatman looked unconcerned. He had fulfilled his commission and cared not if we were satisfied with our bargain.

"What is this place?" I asked him.

"It is the end of the world."

"Then what is there?"

I pointed to where the lake's other shore was hidden in mist. He followed my gesture, his eyes registering no interest.

"Nothing—only reeds, an endless wilderness of reeds. There is nothing there."

"You said there were ships."

"Look about you."

Drawn up on the beach were perhaps twenty reed boats, all built after the same pattern as the one which had brought us here. A few might have been capable of carrying eight or ten men. Along the beach there were poles stuck in the sand with nets strung between them. This was a fishing village.

It was useless to protest. In the world that this man understood, these were ships. And a village one night's journey from his own hut was the end of the world. He had not intended to deceive us, for he had not comprehended what we required.

"I will take breakfast with the daughter of my mother's brother, who married a man of this village," he said. "If your business allows you to return with me then, I will ask for only half the sum you paid to be brought here. If you are detained, then you will easily find another to row you back to Ur."

I said nothing.

"By the bright gods, what doghole is this?" Kephalos asked, as he woke from what seemed a deep and tranquil sleep.

"The end of the world, he tells me."

"I can well believe it."

I helped him out of the boat, and the boatman dragged it up onto the beach and left us to take his breakfast.

"And where is the Bitter River?" he continued, looking about him. It was easy to see that he was beginning to grasp there would be no great merchant ships to carry us away from this place.

"There, in the mists, beyond this frog pond and whatever lies beyond that. He says there is nothing but a wilderness of reeds, which can only mean that we have reached the Sealand."

"The what?"

"The Sealand." I made a despairing gesture, for I had grasped by then the real character of our predicament. It was something I should have seen from the first. "It is a huge area of marshland that marks the joining of the Tigris and the Euphrates. The boatman called it a wilderness,

and he was right. It is a place I had only heard about—I had not realized . . ."

"Perhaps we can hire another boatman. Surely, living so close,
someone from this village will know his way."

Kephalos looked hopeful, but I could only shake my head.

"It is a place of terrible danger," I said. "More than one of the world's
great armies have gone in there to conquer it and then simply disappeared forever. It is the ancient home of a race called the Chaldeans, a
savage people, as they would have to be to live in such a wretched land. I
think, however, not even they love it, since for hundreds of years now
bands of them have been making their way north, bit by bit subduing the
towns and cities of Sumer and making themselves masters there."

"Yes—I have heard of the Chaldeans."

"Everyone has heard of the Chaldeans. They have fought against the
men of Ashur since the reigns of the first kings. I do not think we would
be very warmly received among them."

We walked up the beach, following the boatman's footprints in the
sand toward the little circle of reed huts that was almost the only sign of
human presence in this lonely place. Naked children came out to stare at
us, running away as we approached. Obviously, it was not a village much
accustomed to strangers.

Finally the parents of those children, first the men and then the
women, came out of their dwellings to witness for themselves the
remarkable sight of two visitors who had come so far to be among them.
The women dressed in plain linen tunics that reached to their knees and
the men wore nothing more than twisted loincloths. These were poor
people to whom, even in our travel-stained clothes, we must have seemed
like kings in a fable.

They said nothing. They made no show of welcome. They only
watched us with wary, measuring eyes.

At last our boatman stepped out from among them—I had not even
noticed him before that moment—and came toward us.

"I am going now," he said. "And I cannot take you back to Ur with me.
You must stay here."

He loped back toward his boat, kicking up the sand with every footfall,
before I had even presence of mind to ask him why.

"Into what have we betrayed ourselves this time, I wonder," Kephalos
said, when I had made him understand the boatman's words. "I am glad
you have your sword and javelin by you, that these creatures may be
made to comprehend they may not kill us at their pleasure."

"I think they have no such idea," I answered, looking about at the fifty or sixty silent faces. "I think they are even more afraid of us than you are of them, my friend."

"I, afraid . . . ? I? Ridiculous!"

Yes, of course it was ridiculous. In the lands between the rivers, village people respect the rights of strangers and the laws of common hospitality. As a rule we would have been greeted with bread and beer and the headman would have asked us to unroll our sleeping mats in his own hut—a man is not to be turned away like a cur with the mange. Nothing but fear could have robbed these fisherfolk of their manners.

I motioned to Kephalos to stop and we waited there until it should please the inhabitants of this village to explain themselves. We had time enough. We had nowhere else to go.

At last a man well past the middle of life, with shocks of gray mixed into his black beard, separated himself from the crowd and came toward us with all the dignity of bearing one who is near naked can manage. He presented himself and bowed—something for which I was not prepared. Something which, under ordinary circumstances, even the headman of such a paltry village as this would have felt to be beneath his dignity.

It was to me that he bowed. He seemed to ignore Kephalos' very existence. It crossed my mind that, once more, my identity had somehow been revealed, but this turned out to be but halfway to the truth.

"My people are not much used to visitors," the headman said, for that was who he was. "Your Honor must excuse them. The first frightened them with his words, and now you have come—as he said you would."

"Then you have had another visitor?"

"Yes, Your Honor."

"And he spoke of me?"

"Yes, Your Honor. He said you would come among us five days after he had left us, and today is the fifth day."

"Your visitor was a diviner then?"

"Yes, Your Honor. He wore the yellow robes of a priest, but he was not a priest. He was an old man, Your Honor. A holy man. A *maxxu.*"

I cannot possibly describe the sensation that ran through me at the sound of the word. A *maxxu.* In all my life I had only met one, and he had . . .

"And this holy old man—was he blind?"

"Yes, Your Honor."

"And yet he seemed to see, as if the world were but a shadow?"

"Yes, Your Honor. He said you would know him. He said you would come on the fifth day, and you would know him."

"Yes, I know him."

A man may feel the god's fingers closing around his heart. His chest seems ready to burst open, and he cannot breathe for the pounding of blood in his ears. He knows he is not his own anymore, that his path has been chosen for him. He is not free. I felt all of this.

And more. For I knew now that I was not deserted, that the Lord Ashur, the god of my fathers, still held me in the hollow of his hand.

"And he left no message for me?"

"No, Your Honor."

No—his presence here he would have understood to be message enough.

It was a cold morning. The women of the village built a fire on the beach and brought us food and drink, but no one offered to take us within their walls, and no one, saving only the headman, spoke to us. This was the *maxxu's* doing—such was the awe he had inspired in these simple souls that I, the stranger whose coming he had foretold, was to them like the image of the bright god himself, the evidence of his presence among them, to which no man may dare to raise his eyes.

I had been set apart, yet once more. For what purpose, I could only guess.

"When will Your Honor go from amongst us?" the headman asked, squatting on the sand some four or five cubits away from me, as if apprehensive lest I suddenly burst into flame and he be consumed with me. "Without disrespect, my people do not understand the god's purpose in this matter, and they are filled with dread. When will Your Honor go?"

"I too do not understand the god's purpose. When I do, I will know how to answer your question. Tell me—are there any among you who can take me through the Sealand to the Bitter River, which lies beyond?"

I pointed to the other shore of the lake, that he might understand my meaning.

He shook his head.

"No, Your Honor. There are none who can find their way through the reed wilderness except such as were born there—and to such you would not wish to entrust your life."

"You mean, the Chaldeans?"

"Yes, Your Honor. They come sometimes to pillage and to carry off our women—not often, for we are poor. They are a cruel people. They respect not the gods."

"We will speak again when Ashur has revealed himself to me."

He nodded—he understood that my words concealed no boast, merely the acknowledgment of a mystery which involved us both. He left to rejoin his people, and to explain it all to them as best he could.

"We should go back to Ur," Kephalos announced, as soon as we were alone. He had eaten most of the millet and cooked fish that was our breakfast and was now at liberty to consider other matters. "We can join a caravan . . ."

"And put ourselves into the hands of another Hiram of Latakia?" I shook my head.

"We could find one heading west. We could be gone from your brother's kingdoms in a few days."

"Kephalos, there is nothing west of here except desert. The caravans follow the Euphrates north and then west to the Lebanon."

"There is nothing south of here except reeds."

"There is the Bitter River—somewhere."

"Then what are we to do?"

"We?"

I glanced up at him with what amounted to surprise, although why the idea should not have occurred to me before I do not know.

"Perhaps it is time for our paths to separate," I said. "You can return to Ur and join a caravan. You will be safe enough—Esarhaddon can have no interest in your movements if I am not with you. I must do as the god bids, whatever that may be. I think it the best thing if we part."

"No, Lord." He made a dismissing motion with his hand, as if driving away a troublesome fly. "I have become so accustomed to saving you from your own folly that it has grown into a habit. I could not desert you now. I would spend the rest of my life wondering how it had all finally ended with you."

"If you stay, the rest of your life may not be very long. You had better go, Kephalos my friend, and with my blessing."

"No, Lord. It is impossible."

What reply could I make? My heart was full, and we were both embarrassed.

"Then I must pray to the god," I said at last. "I must pray he reveals his will for both of us."

"And I will pray as well—that your god is wiser than you are, my foolish young prince."

We both laughed. There are times when it is better to laugh than to speak.

There was no sweating house in the village, so at dawn the next morning I bathed in the cold waters of the lake, purifying myself as best I could with the soft, tallowy roots of the hyacinths that grew all around the shore. I had no holy mountain nearby this time—the southern lands are not plentiful of mountains—but I felt sure the Lord Ashur would guide my steps to some spot pleasing in his sight. I set out as soon as the sun had dried my body. I took no food. I wore nothing but a loincloth and carried nothing except a sword.

The earth, stoneless and flat, was soft beneath my unsandaled feet. The direction I had picked, away from both the river and the lake, was as blank and featureless as the sky above me, empty of clouds. I walked until the sun was within an hour of setting. When I turned about to look, the lake at my back was no more than faint smudge of the horizon, as if the god were an artist who had seen fit to mar the symmetry of his creation by drawing his thumb across that one part of it.

When it became dark, and at last the stars were visible, I found I had been walking in the direction of Ashur's star, which sat low on the horizon, as if waiting for me. I took this for a propitious sign.

The cold oppressed me. My joints seemed as rusty as old hinges. I was faint from lack of food, and thirst shriveled my belly.

The first light of morning found me walking still. How far had I come? Eight beru? Ten? How far can a man walk in the space of one day and night? I knew not.

I walked on through the next day, through the still, quiet morning, through the afternoon, when the wind choked me with dust and I could hardly bear to open my eyes. My steps slowed to hardly more than a clumsy shuffle. With the coming of night I saw, still ahead of me, Ashur's star.

I do not remember stopping. I do not remember sitting down upon the cold ground, my arms resting on my knees, my head a weight I could no longer support, yet it must have been so. At last I became conscious that my journey had reached its end, if only because it was not in my power to go on.

I took my sword and buried its point in the soft earth. The sword is Ashur's sacred symbol, and this one, purchased from a stall in the marketplace at Birtu, would serve me as his altar.

Sick with hunger and thirst, tormented by the cold, my legs numb with weariness, I did not think I could sleep yet knew not how to keep awake. Did I sleep? Or did my giddy mind simply go blind to the world that Ashur, Lord of Heaven, Master of Destiny, might fill my sight with his wonders? I know not.

I remember the night wind, cold and harsh, heavy with sharp sand, whispering through me as if my body offered it no resistance. It was like being scourged with a bronze whip. It was agony, and most because my whole self was laid bare to it—the pain entered and left me as I might walk through a shadow.

The god requires this of me, I thought. This penance belongs to him. I must humble my pride before him that I may become his instrument.

Did the wind blow? Did it happen thus, or was this too part of the vision the god sent me?

I know not.

Would that the life might escape my body, I thought. Would that I were free of this suffering.

But there was no escape. Perhaps that was the lesson the Lord Ashur required me to learn—that there was no escape. Not from him, not from myself.

My eyes burned in their sockets until I believed they would melt. The black night became red as fire. My brain ached.

I think that I wept for the pain, but I cannot know for certain.

And then, slowly, I did not so much cease to suffer as to lose all sense of myself as one to whom such things, either of pain or pleasure, might belong. I was not of this world. I could almost witness the agony of Tiglath Ashur as if of someone else. I felt not even pity for him.

I became pure as the hottest fire. I burned white-hot yet felt nothing. Was this what the god knew? Was this what it meant to be he, passionless and empty, able to see into any mystery, all wisdom and knowledge, and yet touched by nothing? Free, even of death? Had he made me like him, if only for a moment, that I might understand?

Some questions do not have answers.

And then I was a man again, and he opened my brain to dreams. Or to visions. It did not matter which.

A flock of white doves covers the ground. They pace about in that preoccupied way peculiar to birds, picking over the earth with their beaks. Suddenly, with a great throbbing sound, they burst into flight. The very air turns white with their beating wings—what has alarmed them?

And then I see. It is a serpent, a creature of black and red and gold, with a red mark, like a burst of flame, on his black head. He coils and uncoils, seemingly to no purpose. He is not interested in the birds. They do not exist for him.

And then, slowly, he finds his path. The ground the birds have left behind is as white as they. It is a harsh place. It is a field of salt. And above swarm five eagles, circling overhead, swooping down one at a time to torment the serpent. I notice a strange thing: each of the five eagles is missing a talon from its left foot. There is only the stump, dripping blood.

Each of the five falls through the air, shattering the silence with its screams, trying to catch the serpent in its claws. One after the other, they tear at his poor flesh. Yet at last they are gone—they simply vanish— and the serpent makes his way across this waste. His body leaves a slithering track behind as he crosses the salt-covered earth. He seems almost to swim through it, and behind him the wind fills in the marks of his progress.

At last he is free. He has left the white salt behind him. He rests, curling himself about the base of a tree. It is a strange tree, with green boughs that mass themselves in great horizontal planes. And on a branch of this tree, falling heavily through the air, lands an owl. The branch sways under its weight, and as it comes to rest it looks about and blinks, as if the light hurts its great yellow eyes.

The tree, the owl, the serpent—all dissolve into the gray light of morning. The dream has ended. I am awake. My body aches. I am cold and hungry and my throat is parched, yet I am awake and alive in the bright world.

My sword was still buried point-first in the earth. I did not attempt to retrieve it—I would not have dared. I left it where it was. It was time to go back.

I had not walked an hour when I saw before me a patch of earth that seemed bleached white as old bone. As I approached, they started up into the sky in front of me—a vast flock of doves, the beating of their wings seeming to make the very air tremble.

I was the serpent, the mark of the blood star upon me. It was as the dream had foretold.

V

I HAVE LITTLE MEMORY OF THE NEXT FEW DAYS. I HAVE been told that some children found me a quarter of an hour's walk from the village and that I was carried the rest of the way on a blanket.

I lay on the floor of a reed hut, listening to the voice of my murdered father.

"You see, my boy? Eh? It is vanity to imagine we understand. I had to die before I could grasp even so much as that—this is how the god sports with us. I wanted you to be king after me, but the god denied it and set your brother the Lord Donkey upon the throne. Now he has some other destiny for you."

"Do you know it, Father?" I whispered, through parched lips. "Do you see what must come?"

"Yes, my son. Yet I may not tell you."

What then? Only silence.

My next clear recollection is of drinking some sort of broth. It tasted of fish and I could hardly keep from gagging. I was ashamed of this, since it seemed an insult to the kindness of the old woman who was attempting to feed me.

My mind was drained. I knew no fear, nor uncertainty. I understood nothing, yet this did not seem to matter. The god would make all things clear, of this I was sure. I would suffer or prevail, die or live by his will. The outcome did not matter to me. I was not even resigned. I felt only a great weariness that killed thought. The mysteries that lay behind and ahead meant nothing. For the moment I was content to sleep and to take fish broth at the hands of an old woman.

When I woke up again, Kephalos was there.

"You will be perfectly well in a few days," he told me. "You are only weak from hunger, and your guts are dried out from lack of water. I am thankful my gods are not so demanding as yours."

"If they were, they would not be your gods for long."

He laughed, although it was a feeble enough jest. Perhaps he was only pleased that I could make one at all.

"I will be leaving this place soon," I said, no longer in jest. "Think again if you wish to come with me, for the way will be a hard one. This much I know."

"Which way will it take you?"

"I have yet to discover."

"Your way is always a hard one, but I will come. I have said as much, and I will not change."

"A wise man alters his course if there is danger. And there will be danger. Think again. If you decide not to come, I will only judge you to be a prudent man. Perhaps, if I am spared, we can meet again in Memphis, or some other place."

"I will think again." His brow furrowed, and he looked as if he might be ready to weep. "I will think again, if you wish it."

"I wish it. Now send the village headman to me—I have seen things in my mind which I do not understand, and perhaps he can explain them to me."

The headman was with his men on the lake, where they cast their nets for fish to sell in Ur. He did not return until an hour after sunset, but when he did he came straight to me. He stood in the doorway and bowed.

"Did you see the god, Your Honor?" he asked.

I could not answer—I was not sure what would be the truth.

"Do you know the farther side of this lake?" I asked.

"A little, Your Honor. We must go there eight or nine times in a year to cut reeds for our boats and our houses."

"It is a long journey. I am surprised your people have not chosen to settle there."

"The water on that side—and into the reed wilderness as far as any of us has gone—is brackish. The river keeps the water sweet on this side."

"Thank you," I said. "As soon as I am strong enough to travel, I will trouble you no more."

He bowed again and left me. Doubtless I had given his whole village cause for rejoicing.

The water on that side is brackish. They were salt marshes, far into the reeds. The serpent's track had closed behind him, as the water closes behind a boat. It had passed through a track of salt. Now at least I knew the direction my journey must take.

The next day I felt strong enough to rise from my sleeping mat and walk about a bit. And within four days my strength had returned. It was not until then that I explained my intentions to Kephalos.

"I suppose any attempt to dissuade you from this folly would be pointless," he said. When I did not answer at once, he merely shrugged his shoulders. "If what these fisherfolk say is even an approach to the truth, you are embracing your . . . What is it you always call it? Your *simtu*. You know as much?"

"My *simtu*, whatever it is to be, was written on the god's tablet long ago. I do not think he means for me to die until I am beyond the salt marshes."

"I could wish your god would offer me a similar assurance, but if this folly is to be your end you might as well have two deaths on your conscience as one."

"You have decided, then?"

"Yes."

I was glad, yet I dared not trust myself to say so. For many minutes I dared trust myself to say nothing.

"These will probably be the last hours I will spend in the lands my father ruled in the Lord Ashur's name," I murmured finally, conscious that I was attempting to explain the inexplicable. "The Lord Sennacherib called himself 'king of the earth's four corners'—is this collection of reed huts not at the very edge, in the very farthest corner of that world? In the places beyond, his name is nothing but an empty word.

"The god has been pleased to draw a line in the dust, and to say to me, his servant, 'Go. Cross this line and find what the world your father never dreamed of holds.' Kephalos, my friend, I know not what else I can do except to obey."

"I know. And that is why I am obliged to accompany you—because this god of yours means nothing to me, and I cannot abandon you entirely to his whim."

That evening I spoke again with the headman. I told him we would need a boat, goatskins in which to carry fresh water, and food for several days. I offered to pay him for these, but he shook his head.

"I am a poor man," he said, "but I respect the gods. All that you wish you shall have, but no one in this village will take your silver. We do not choose to profit from a business such as this."

I understood his mind and knew that he intended no insult.

The next morning our boat waited on the shore. It was a good six paces from end to end, and we had water and dried fish. Even my javelin was aboard.

As we pushed off, and our oars cut the quiet surface of the water, the villagers stood on the beach and watched.

We had rowed for perhaps an hour, and the shore behind us was no more than a dark brown line against the water, before Kephalos, who sat forward of me, showed signs of tiring. Finally he lifted his oar out of the water and placed it across his knees.

"My palms are beginning to blister," he said.

"I should have thought all these months would have toughened you," I said, hoping, I think, to shame him a little. I should have known better.

"It is different for you," he answered, somewhat petulantly. "You are a soldier, born to a life of adversity. I am not a soldier and have not a soldier's calluses. I am a skilled physician and a gentleman—I am not accustomed to handling anything except money and the breasts of harlots."

I could not help but laugh, and then Kephalos laughed. And then he opened his medicine box and took out some salve for his hands and then wrapped them in layers of linen bandages.

"There—I think that will serve," he said. "Give me some of that dried fish, for I am hungry from my exertions."

He made a face when he tasted it.

"This is disgusting. It is better to starve than to eat such trash."

"You have only to wait until your belly collapses like a leather tent in a rainstorm and it will taste good enough."

"On your advice, therefore, I shall wait until then."

He threw the piece of yellowish dried fish away from him. It landed in the water with a faint splash and disappeared from sight.

It was nearly nightfall before we reached the other side of the lake.

In truth it is misleading to speak of the lake as having another "side" at all. There was no shoreline. The water seemed just as deep. At first there were only widely scattered patches of reeds—little islands, some of them no more than a few paces across, that seemed anchored to nothing, as free as we were in our boat. These gradually increased in size and frequency, some of them appearing to link together, until at last we found ourselves in a maze of channels. Was this where the Euphrates exited the lake? We had no way of knowing. There seemed to be no current.

And these were reeds such as I had never seen. In places they grew out of the water to three or four times the height of a man, bowing under their own weight, so thick that I could not have slipped my hand between them. One could not help but feel trapped by them. They were like walls, blocking out the sunlight of late afternoon so that we found ourselves in unbroken shadow.

"I think we had best tie up and wait for morning before venturing into this fearful place," Kephalos said.

"I think you are wise."

"I am not so much wise as frightened," he replied. "Sometimes to be one is to be the other."

"And let us sleep in the boat tonight rather than trusting ourselves to these reed islands, these phantoms of dry land. The river waters have been rising every day."

Kephalos nodded vigorously. "By all means, let us sleep in the boat."

So we moored to one of the largest of the reed islands, but it was not a particularly restful night for either of us.

The noise began almost as soon as the first stars were out, and with a terrific splash close enough to us that I found myself spattered with water. Almost at once the birds, doubtless, like us, settled down for the night, started screeching with ferocious indignity. Startled awake, I sat up—the first object that greeted my eyes was Kephalos, at the other end of the boat, also bolt upright, blinking like an owl.

"What was that?"

The boat was rocking frantically, and we had only to turn our heads to see the source of the disturbance—a large, dark animal was swimming ponderously away from us, making its oblique way towards another of the islands.

"Some beast," I said. "We must have disturbed it."

"And it decided to return the compliment—I suppose we should offer thanks to the gods it restrained itself from jumping square into the boat with us."

We watched it—or, rather, we watched the glistening, moonlit trail it made in the water—until finally it seemed to disappear beneath the surface. All the while the birds kept up their querulous, monotonous racket.

"You . . . you are quite sure it *was* an animal, aren't you?" Kephalos wiped his eyes with his sleeves, looking genuinely distressed. "It couldn't have been a demon—or . . ."

"It was an animal. If you were a demon, would you live in a place like this?"

"Demons, one imagines, are not so particular, but what you say makes admirable sense."

Finally the birds quieted again, yet there seemed always to be something. A breath of wind would set the great reeds, tall as date palms, rubbing against one another, making a noise like river frogs that had swallowed the god's own thunder. The unearthly howl of jackals echoed across the water, making one think of the torments of the unburied dead. Several times I heard something that sounded for all the world like the snarling of some great cat. Things were forever crashing through the undergrowth and there were always the birds, alive to every little disturbance.

And, of course, there were also the insects—mosquitoes and black flies the size of wasps. It was a cold night, but they swarmed up out of the stagnant water and feasted on our exposed flesh, even getting under our tunics. At last we had to scoop up mud to smear over our faces, our arms and legs, or they would have devoured us.

The swamps, it turned out, were a busy place after dark.

The next morning, covered with itching, red welts, our backs sore from lying in the water at the bottom of our boat, we woke to a breakfast of water and dried fish. Neither of us was in perfect temper.

"Life is bitterness," Kephalos said at last. "I have but one complaint to make against the mother who whelped me, and that is that on the day of my birth she did not leave me exposed on a mountainside, to have my guts torn out by eagles before I was old enough to know the harsh world. The gods love none but those whom they allow to perish young."

"I think it possible we may perish ourselves before long," I answered, hating him for speaking the words of my own heart.

"You think so? Then Ashur is more merciful that I imagined—by the gods, my head splits! What I would not give for a cup of wine."

But there was no wine. There was only the empty sky and the water and the reeds. Was Ashur merciful? Would he deliver us from this, or had he been jesting with me?

That day, and the next, and the day after that, we navigated by the sun, always heading roughly south. As the water became shallow, we shipped our oars, finding it more convenient to cut down a few of the great reeds and pole our way through the labyrinth of channels. The heat was terrible, so we rested while it was at its height, finding what shade we could. We had plenty of food—Kephalos raised no more objections to the taste of dried fish—but we had to be careful with our sweet water, for the marshes were indeed brackish. I cherished the hope that this meant the headman had been mistaken, that the reed wilderness was merely the final barrier between us and the Bitter River, but it was no more than a hope.

One afternoon, high over our heads, we saw cormorants swooping down through the blank sky—they were fishing. We came close enough to hear them splashing into the water of a great still pond, almost a lake, which for some reason the reeds had not choked off. We had no net, so we could not hope to catch them. We could only listen and dream of their muddy-tasting flesh cooked over an open fire. Yet it was a rest from the terrible sameness of the marshes. I was almost grateful to them. With the sun to our left, we headed our boat back into the channels, which quickly swallowed us up again.

Thus we went, day after day, sleeping as best we could at night, struggling by day to preserve strength and faith as we journeyed through this waste of reeds and sluggish, wandering water. I do not know how long we had been thus before we found we had at last intruded into the realm of the Chaldeans.

The sun had not descended more than two hours from noon, and we were preparing to resume our hunt for a main channel to the Euphrates, when, silent as death, another reed boat slipped from beyond the far side of an island and came into view directly in front of us, crossing from left to right. There were three men aboard, one sitting in the middle and two at either end, poling her along. These two wore tunics that hung to the middle of their thighs and carried curved knives stuck into their belts, and all three covered their heads with a piece of red cloth held in place by a rope headband.

We lay on our bellies in our own boat and watched, praying to every god we could remember that no one should think to glance in our direction.

In the space of perhaps ten heartbeats they were gone. It was much longer before either of us remembered to breathe.

"Did they see us?"

"No." I shook my head. "I think not. I think if they had seen us we would already be dead."

Suddenly it occurred to me to remember that men do not live where they will die of thirst. I scooped up a little water in my hand and tasted it—it was sweet. We had passed beyond the brackish water that I had hoped would mark the entrance to the Bitter River. Now one direction meant as little as any other.

We were lost and surrounded by enemies—had the Lord Ashur meant me to come to this, or had I misunderstood his signs? I was filled with a wild despair.

As if in answer, almost as a rebuke, a huge serpent, black as death and thick as a man's arm, slid out of the reeds and swam a little way before disappearing once more around the corner of an island. No, perhaps I had not misunderstood. All of this had been intended from the beginning. The god fulfilled his own purposes, not mine.

Yet we were lost for all that. We waited another hour before we resumed our wanderings—aimless, it now seemed. We pushed out into the open water, listening for the slightest sound, but for the rest of that day we saw no more signs of human life.

Yet men were somewhere about. One had only to listen. Men are jealous of their dwelling places—they drive out all competitors and impose their will so that even the birds will not nest near their dwellings. That night the silence was almost oppressive.

It was in the morning that I most sensed the nearness of our danger. I awoke with a sense of foreboding, an almost tangible feeling of menace for which I was unable to account. What had altered since yesterday?

And at last it came to me—the bird cries had changed.

I could hear them echoing through the reeds, a call and then an answer. Another call, from yet somewhere else, and yet another answer. These were not birds, but men.

"Quietly, Kephalos my friend," I whispered. "I was mistaken—they did see us. We must try to find some place of safety. They are hunting for us."

We picked up our poles and shoved away from the island that had been sheltering us, our boat lifting its prow and then, as smoothly as a knife cuts the air, moving out into the empty water. We allowed her to drift for a moment, listening for the murmur of voices that would mean we had betrayed ourselves. There was nothing. Yet we knew the Chaldeans were close around us. They were there somewhere, pulling the net tight, narrowing the gap through which we had to slip if we hoped to escape.

We made our way, soundless, moving our poles so quietly that they pierced the water without so much as a splash, our hearts dying in our breasts with every turning of every narrow channel. At intervals we would stop and listen—the birdcalls would fall silent and then, after a time, begin again. It was almost as if they could track us through the water that closed behind our gliding boat.

On and on we went. A pause to listen, and then on again. How many were there pursuing us? Six boats? More? They seemed everywhere. The sun rose to noon, but we did not stop to rest and avoid the heat. We did not dare.

I rested on my pole for a moment. The sound of an egret floated on the heavy air. It was far away. At last—or was it merely an illusion born of anxious fear?—at last I had a sense that they had fallen behind us. An answer came, equally faint, and then silence. Then the calls became more frequent, as if our pursuers also were beginning to doubt they had us in their grasp.

No, they were falling back. I knew it now. Now was the time to make for deeper water, and then run like the wind.

We raced for the mouth of a wider passage, making the sluggish water race by us. We swung round an island, and I could see pieces of reed frond floating past, carried by the almost imperceptible current. We were in a main channel now. I could feel the blood in my veins. Was it possible we had escaped?

And then we saw them.

Three boats, turning the corner together, like the horses pulling a chariot, men standing in the prows, as calm and steady as if their bare legs stood on solid ground, the spears in their hands already brought up to the shoulder.

I turned, my guts clenched with dread—it was the same behind us. We were trapped, as neatly as rabbits in a baited snare. They had led us here, and we were trapped.

My javelin was lying at the bottom of our boat. I picked it up. I would not sell my life for nothing.

"By the bright gods, Lord—no!"

It was Kephalos' voice. I looked down and saw him, his hands clasped in supplication, his face a mask of terror.

"They will slaughter us, Lord," he said, only a little softer. "Stay your hand from this rashness. I beg you."

In an hour, I thought—perhaps less—we might wish they had slaughtered us. Yet he was my friend. I had led him to this. His life was not mine to give away.

I let the javelin drop from my hand.

I sat down to wait. There was nothing else to do.

The boats drew near, and someone in one of them threw a grappling hook over our prow and took us in tow. They hardly glanced at us, their eyes looking past us. The red cloths with which they protected their heads from the sun framed faces as dark and seamed as old leather. They said nothing, these men. They showed no sign of triumph, as if our capture brought them no more merit than if we were oxen being herded home to be penned up for the night. Perhaps they were merely disappointed in us. Perhaps we had been too easy.

This is defeat, I thought. This is what it is like. This is what the Medes felt when I humbled them in their own mountains. This bitterness was what Mushezib-Marduk felt when my father led him from Babylon in chains. And now it has come to me. My god has deserted me, and my *simtu* will be a shameful death at the hands of my enemies. What I felt was almost like remorse.

"Forgive me for this, Kephalos," I said. "It seems I have brought you to your end."

"Lord . . ." He moved his shoulders in a despairing gesture. "Regret nothing, for I do not."

Not even he believed it. Yet I was both touched and appalled. He had risked everything for my sake, and I had as good as murdered him.

For an hour they dragged us through the water. I could hear the insects buzzing, as monotonous as death. My heart was black within me. I cursed my own folly, the blindness of my heart, and I cursed the Lord Ashur.

At last we came to a village—a village of reed huts, floating on an island of reeds.

Our captors, throwing lines to others who waited on the shore, shouting orders at them in a tongue of which I understood not one syllable, prepared to moor their boats. Women, old men past any use, hard young warriors, and children barely old enough to be left alone—they all stood about, talking and making incomprehensible gestures, like people at a bazaar. It was hardly the reception I might have expected from this fabled race of warriors. We could as easily have just returned from a fishing expedition.

One man, at last, stepped forward, resting his hands upon his hips, grinning in obvious triumph through his great dark beard. In this wild place, his black tunic was shot through with silver. There was a glittering sword in his red sash and rings of gold and precious stones on his fingers, but these were not what made him so striking a figure.

He was no taller than his fellows, nor was there any unusual grace to his person or beauty in his strong, broad face, crowded with sharp and irregular angles. A lump, the size of a grape, appeared over his right eye—his one distinguishing feature. Yet even this somehow only enhanced the general impression of a man with perfect confidence in his own powers. He had the bearing of a king.

"Prince Tiglath Ashur," he shouted, in only slightly accented Akkadian, and raised his arm. "I am glad you have arrived among us at last, Lord. I was afraid that in the marshes you might have come to harm."

VI

THE *MUDHIF* OF MY LORD SESKU, WHO STYLED HIMSELF King of the Halufids, although he was no more than a tribal chief, was perhaps eighty paces in length and fifteen in width. The ceiling and walls, which consisted of several layers of reed mats, were held up by eleven great arches, the columns consisting of bundles of reeds, each as wide as a man's shoulders, roped together and bound at the apex. The whole structure, in fact, had been built of nothing except reeds, as was everything else in the village, for there was neither stone nor wood to be found in the marshes, and even mud for bricks would have had to be dredged up from the bottom of the channels. Reeds, on the other hand, were everywhere.

This was not the king's home, for he lived in a humble dwelling no grander than that of his poorest subject. Except perhaps to sleep there for a night or two, no one lived in the *mudhif*. This was where Sesku received guests and petitioners, where he dispensed justice to his people, where he held banquets to honor his victories in war and the festivals of his gods—and, as it happened on this occasion, the arrival of an important visitor.

"You were surprised I knew you, Great Prince?" he asked as we sat cross-legged on the reed-mat floor, drinking buttermilk together. It was an agreeable drink after the huge meal—I had been served first, and then Sesku's retainers in strict order of precedence, and only last did one of his servants bring Sesku himself a small plate of lamb and rice, for it would have been unthinkable for the king to have eaten before all of his guests were seen to.

Poor Kephalos was pegged down on the cold, damp ground by the boat landing, his fate still unsettled. As, indeed, was my own.

"My Lord, I am surprised even to be alive," I answered.

This made Sesku throw back his head in laughter. His retainers, when he repeated my answer to them, laughed too, beating the ground with their reed canes in sign of appreciation, although what I said had not been intended as a jest but merely as a statement of fact.

"Great Prince, there is nothing to be surprised at in that," he said finally, wiping his eyes with his sleeve. "The king in Nineveh, who is your brother, has driven you from his lands and desires your death. Word of this has reached us even here, for the Lord Esarhaddon has caused riders to be sent in every direction, and I have my spies, even in the great city of Ur. Your brother is a rash man who will doubtless come to a bad end someday. He hates you, and thus, as he is my enemy, he makes you my friend. My people are poor, but their king is not a savage who kills against his own interests. No—I would spare your life if only to annoy the Lord Esarhaddon, but that is not the only, nor even the best reason."

He made an expansive gesture with his right hand, seeming to invoke the whole world as his witness.

"No, Prince Tiglath, that is not the reason."

"Then what is?"

"We have met before."

He opened his tunic and, pinching up a fold of skin over his rib cage, displayed a ragged scar, as long as a man's finger.

"You gave me this," he said, grinning like a demon. "At Khalule, when we were both no more than boys."

He paused, as if waiting for a reaction, but I made no answer. I did not wish to—what could I have said?—yet I am not sure I even had the power. The blood was running through my heart as cold as melting snow. In my mind formed the words to the ancient prayer: "Lord Ashur, deliver me from the vengeance of my enemies . . ."

But Sesku merely laughed again, bringing his hand down sharply against his knee, relishing the jest.

"You took me clean off my horse," he cried merrily, reaching across to jab with his fingers the corresponding spot on my own breast. "A boy just come from the marshes, I dare say I wasn't much of a rider. I fell straight back over the damn beast's tail. At first I thought I had only been thrown, but then I saw that lance of yours sprouting up out of my chest like a bulrush—by the gods, what a moment! I can remember lying there on the ground, staring up at the cloudless sky, half convinced I must be dead already—such was the end of all *that* day's glory—hah!"

He leaned forward. He even put his hand on my shoulder to draw me towards him. It seemed he was about to impart a confidence.

"You see, I had run away to join King Kudur-Nahhunte's army as a mercenary. My father, the Lord Hajimka, was a jealous fool who hated me for not being a weakling and favored another of his sons to succeed him because he took pleasure in the boy's pretty voice, the old . . . Ah well, perhaps it is best to speak as little ill of one's ancestor as possible, hey? So, I planned to cover myself with glory among the Elamites. I saw one battle, and got skewered like a rabbit for my trouble, yet I returned to my father's *mudhif* a hero. A man's reputation is the greater for having illustrious enemies—this wound was the making of me, I promise you. When the old king died, I cut the throat of that effeminate nightingale my brother and took his place as heir. No one voiced the slightest protest. So, you can see how it was. Had not the mighty Tiglath Ashur, son of Sennacherib, terror of the bright world, so exalted himself in the world's eyes that day at Khalule, it might have been me left smiling from underneath his jawbone. I can hardly make myself responsible for the death of one who has done me so singular a service—you saved my life, Great Prince. You are the foundation of all my prosperity! Hah, hah, hah!"

Once more his retainers joined his laughter and once more the reed mats covering the ground danced under the blows of their canes, although but few could have had any notion why. It was expected of them, and so they laughed.

I did not laugh. To laugh would have been unseemly and, besides, my memories of that battle were perhaps less agreeable.

"And yet," I said, pausing to let the laughter die away, "and yet you sent out men to capture me, as if I were a quail to be snared in a net."

"Yes, of course—you must not be offended, Great Prince." With his own hand he refilled my cup from a goatskin bag that rested beside him. "These waterways are a maze through which you might have wandered until the hour of your death. And I could not simply have left you to your own devices, even if your fate had been a matter of indifference to me— a king must be seen to be a king in his own domain. You will appreciate it was a question of prestige."

"So you had me dragged to your camp like a captured woman and now, having asserted yourself, you can afford the luxury of mercy."

"That is it precisely. I see, My Lord Tiglath, that you are truly a king's son, for you understand the arts of rulership."

"Then I hope your mercy will extend to my companion."

"No—he will die." He said this quite calmly, not even glancing at me. "You have committed a trespass, and someone must be punished for it or my people will imagine me weak."

"Did you not see the notch in his ear? He is a slave, my property, and I sit at your feet as a guest. Your people will imagine nothing except that you know what is due to a visitor in your house."

"There is no notch in his ear."

"Out of vanity he keeps it hidden with colored beeswax, but it is there."

"You permit a slave vanity?"

"He is also my friend."

Sesku watched me through narrowed eyes, as if he did not quite believe me, and then shrugged his shoulders dismissively.

"Very well—it shall be as you say."

He clapped his hands to command attention.

"Let the Ionian dog be brought in and fed," he shouted, his voice registering the slightest trace of resigned annoyance. "It seems our guest the Lord Tiglath puts some small value on his life."

When they dragged Kephalos inside, a hemp noose still dangling from his neck, he stumbled forward as if his knees had turned to water. His face was a pale gray and his eyes glittered with terror. I was certain he would have collapsed if Sesku's retainers had not been supporting him by the arms. Perhaps he imagined they had decided to amuse themselves with his death, for the fear of mortality was surely upon him.

They led him to the back of the *mudhif,* among the children and servants, and when at last they released him, he dropped down to his hands and knees, gazing about like a caged animal. They put food before him, but he merely stared at it as if he had forgotten its proper use.

"You will pardon me," I said, rising, "but I must speak to him."

Sesku dismissed me with a bored wave and I made my way among his guests, who sat in tangled knots on every available cubit of the reed-mat floor, until I could crouch beside Kephalos. I put my hand on his shoulder. He glanced up with a start, as if surprised to see me.

"You must not be afraid," I murmured in Greek. "These savages have no idea of killing us. They have decided that we shall be their honored guests."

"Then they have peculiar notions of hospitality," he answered finally, when at last the words no longer stuck in his throat like splinters of bone.

"Take some food—it is wisest not to offend them."

He looked at the bowls of rice and cooked lamb before him and at last picked one of them up only to set it down again, his hands trembling, his face, if possible, even a shade paler than before.

"I am afraid I might gag on it," he said. And then, as if an idea had just occurred to him, he clutched my arm. "You are sure they will not murder us?"

"For the moment they are disposed to friendship, yet men who are a law onto themselves can be fickle. Eat the food they offer."

I began to rise, and then remembered something.

"I fear I was forced to make you a slave again," I said. "I beg your pardon for it, but it was only on such terms that their king felt inclined to spare your life."

Kephalos reached up and plucked out the little triangle of wax that filled the notch in his ear, throwing it to the ground like the discarded husk of an orange.

"Think nothing of it, Lord. At least they are respecters of property—I will find what safety I can in that."

Immediately he took a bowl of rice and began scooping the contents into his mouth with his fingers. I knew then that he would be well enough.

I returned to Sesku.

The feast continued until nearly dawn. The Halufids were not a people much given to drunkenness. Indeed, the cheapest date wine, or even beer, was enough of a luxury among them that even a king would hesitate to offer it to every guest who entered his *mudhif*, and thus, because it is only a pleasure to grow flushed with drink when all partake of it, and there are no sober witnesses to disapprove, the celebration of our arrival was a relatively decorous affair. There was much music and singing, but no one started a quarrel or staggered off to some corner to vomit or fell asleep or otherwise disgraced himself. Perhaps that was why their revels could wear out the night.

As a special treat, Sesku had provided for professional entertainment, in the form of a *dhakar binta*, a boy from another village who had acquired great local fame for his dancing. He was indeed very skillful, almost more an acrobat than a dancer, but I found his performance, for which he was dressed as a woman, even to padded breasts, rather repulsive. He wore his hair to his waist, had painted his face, and his gestures were those of an expensive harlot. Indeed, as Sesku informed me, the boy would offer his backside to any man who could meet his price.

Kephalos, I noticed, watched the dance with great interest. I remembered Ernos, the boy who had once been a slave in his house, and wondered if perhaps the *dhakar binta* had not found a new patron.

Yet Kephalos himself, as it turned out, was an object of much admiration. Several hours into the evening, an enormous woman wearing a red tunic, with gold bangles tinkling from her heavy arms and a gold ring in the side of her nose, entered the *mudhif* and sat down next to

Sesku. Her presence somehow changed the whole atmosphere of the feast. Gaiety appeared to die away as men who had been singing and laughing only the moment before fell into uncomfortable, murmured conversation. No one seemed to wish her to stay, not even Sesku, and yet no one seemed possessed of the courage to send her away. She seemed both aware of the constraint her presence had imposed and, at the same time, indifferent to it—or perhaps she took even a smug pleasure in this oblique acknowledgment of her power. It was only after she had come among us that I noticed the absence of other women from the feast.

She was of sufficient years to be considered elderly, although, from her manner, I rather suspect she would have resented being called such.

"My mother, my father the king's most beloved wife, the Lady Hjadkir," Sesku announced, by way of introduction—almost, it seemed, by way of apology. He then spoke to her in her own language, and at last a faint smile crossed her heavy face as she nodded. Had I been presented to her as anything less than a foreign prince, I doubt I would have received even so much as that.

"She enjoys the gift of prophecy," he said, turning once again to me. "She is foolish, like all women—more foolish, perhaps, than most, for even my father was hard pressed to control her. Yet sometimes the gods are pleased to speak to her through dreams, and this blessing must be respected. I have been saved from disaster more than once by listening to her warnings. And, of course, she is my mother. My Lord, what reverence does a man not owe to his mother?"

I made some reply, enough to satisfy my host that I did not think it a weakness in him thus to honor the Lady Hjadkir, and the matter was allowed to drop.

And gradually, as it will in the presence of even the greatest evil, the natural cheerfulness of men reasserted itself. Sesku's retainers apparently decided to ignore his mother's intrusion, as no doubt they had on other occasions, and they took delight once again in the music of the flute and drum, the dancing of the *dhakar binta*, and each other's company.

Gradually, however, I became aware that the Lady Hjadkir and her son were having what sounded like an argument, and several times I saw her point toward my servant. At last Sesku turned to me to explain.

"My mother wishes to know for what price in silver shekels you would sell that slave of yours," he continued, fixing me with his gaze almost as if he dared me to laugh, yet at the same time admitting to the ludicrousness of this infirmity in one of his own family. "He has caught her fancy and she wishes me to buy him for her."

His eyes narrowed slightly—some question of family prestige was involved here, but of what sort I could only guess. It was a difficult moment.

After a time I found courage enough to make the only possible answer.

"Were he in honor mine to dispose of," I said, "I would take pleasure in making your lady mother a present of the rogue. But he is not. He has served me faithfully since I was a boy, and has made my exile his own. He must serve me or serve another only as his heart pleases."

The king of the Halufids translated my reply for his mother and, strangely, it did not seem to anger her. She appeared to consider the matter for a time, and then her gaze returned to Kephalos, who of course was unaware of the impression he had made. As she studied him her eyes glazed over with passionate longing.

Again she whispered something to her son, and then she rose and left us. As soon as she was gone, Sesku began to laugh.

"You are to send this slave to her tomorrow night," he told me finally, when his laughter would allow it. "She says, as she is a woman, he will never again leave this place of his own will. For all that he is only a slave, I pity him—and yet, what would I not give to witness that evening's entertainment. Oh, it will be a delicious thing, hah, hah, hah!"

Thus began our sojourn among the Chaldeans.

"You cannot reach the Bitter River while the season of flooding is upon us," Sesku told me. "There is so much water that even parts of the desert are covered. And there are storms that appear without warning—it is a bad time. Besides, I must make arrangements with the kings of other tribes that they grant you safe passage through their lands. Be patient, and when the floods subside I will send guides with you all the way to the Arab trading ports, if that is your wish. But no one would be so foolish as to guide you now, and alone you would die among the reeds."

But in the meantime we were accepted quite as if we had lived among these tribesmen all our lives. I was honored as their king's friend, and no restraints were placed on our movements.

Unlike the Aryan of the Zagros Mountains, the Chaldeans hardly yet thought of themselves as one people. So far they had not found a king like Daiaukka, a man to tell them it was their destiny to rule the wide earth, and they still worshiped the humble gods of their ancestors, praying to these for luck in battle or for a good rice harvest. So when they cast their eyes north to the Land of Sumer—and this they had done for hundreds of years —they saw not the empires they might build there one day but only such plunder as a man might carry home with him after a raid, to be a rich man all his days.

Not yet, for the armies of Ashur were still too strong, but one day, when we seemed to falter, this savage people would find its will in the voice of some great leader and they would pour out of their marshes like a plague of locusts, devouring all before them.

But for the time that I was with them their world was the Sealand, that vast tract of marsh formed by the conjunction of the Tigris and Euphrates, a wilderness of reeds and water, of huge lakes and twisting, narrow channels and floating islands, as changeful and capricious as a woman, a landscape with no fixed points, where a summer storm might so alter the face of things that a man could lose his way and perish within a two hours' boat ride of the village where he had been born.

And if the legends speak true that the god Ashur, like a potter laboring at his wheel, shaped men from the river mud, then the Chaldeans were molded from that of the Sealand, for only such a place could have made a people so full of extremities and contradictions as they. Cruel and arrogant, yet generous, bravely contemptuous of death and yet, in the face of the first reverse, quick to lose heart and slink away, sudden in anger and yet in friendship steadfast even to their dying breath, virtuous and cunning by turns, they seemed to know no law but the word of their chiefs and the impulses of their own giddy natures. Like all savage races they believed themselves to hold exclusive title to every human perfection, and indeed I found much in them that was admirable. Yet there was never a moment when I felt, as I had among the Scythians, and even the Aryans, that, yes, these men were the seeds of a great nation, rightly destined to take its place among the mighty of the earth. If the Chaldeans should ever rule in the lands between the rivers, the children of the gods will crack their breasts in lamentation.

That misery, however, is still to come. Perhaps it will be postponed forever, yet no man can pretend to read the gods' will. For centuries— perhaps, if the annals are to be believed, even in the days of the first great Sargon, who reigned in Akkad some eighteen hundred years before the time of my grandfather, his namesake—these tribes had been slowly filtering their way north, sometimes in small groups, raiding parties of a hundred men, sometimes as a conquering army. They arrive with no object except plunder but then fall under the spell of the settled life, coming to rest in the cities or on the rich land, taking foreign wives, learning a new tongue, establishing dynasties of kings and forgetting within a generation that they ever knew another way. Thus the lands around Ur, even stretching east to the Tigris, have long been known as Chaldea, but the people have turned their backs on the old habits.

None can blame them for this, since life in the marshes, their ancestral homeland, is a harsh business. A man with five oxen and enough arable land to grow rice for his family is called rich, and only the chiefs, to whom all pay tribute and serve with their lives in time of war, can lay claim to splendor.

Sesku called himself king of the Halufids, yet he was not this—at least, not as my brother Esarhaddon was king in the Land of Ashur. Esarhaddon was king by the god's will, but Sesku, though he claimed descent from a long line of rulers, was master only so long as his people would obey him. He had not been the first-born of his father's sons, but the Halufids had chosen him because he was noble and brave and strong and his elder brother was a weakling. If he faltered, and the tribe lost faith in him, they would choose another to put in his place. It was entirely a question of personal prestige.

It was thus with everything that was thought and acted in the marshes, where hatred and love governed all of life. Men embraced when they met and sometimes wept for joy, but they carried on mortal feuds that often lasted for generations, not only between rival clans but even within the same family. These not the chiefs themselves could settle, for hatred was stronger than loyalty or even the fear of death, and the raids and counter-raids, the ambushes and treachery would continue until at last one side begged for peace, offering cattle and gold and women as payment of the blood price, or until all were dead.

Sesku's own family had become involved in such a feud. A cousin, the son of his mother's sister, a man named Kaliphad, had married a woman from another tribe and, displeased with her, had sent her back to her father's house. This, of course, was his privilege, but he was a man noted for miserliness and had neglected to return the woman's household goods, purchased by her father out of the bride price, which, in any case, Kaliphad had had no right to expect returned. The insult was strongly felt, and within a month, having disappeared two days before, when he told a brother that he was setting out to net ducks, Kaliphad was found dead in his boat, the water at the bottom stained red with blood. His throat had been slit and his manhood cut off and stuffed into the money pouch he always carried on a leather thong about his neck.

This put Sesku in a difficult position. Like everyone else, he had disliked his cousin and felt that he had been in the wrong in the matter of the household goods—the woman's relations could hardly be expected to ignore such a thing—yet Sesku had his own position to think of and could not simply pass over the murder of a kinsman in silence. He offered a compromise: he would accept a blood price of five women and a like number of oxen, along with two talents of copper, from which he would subtract the value of the household goods belonging to the bride whom Kaliphad had rejected and return it to her father. It was a reasonable, even a generous offer, and perhaps for that very reason, because it was interpreted as a sign of weakness in the king of the Halufids, the woman's family rejected it. In the three years since, there had been seven more murders among Sesku's kinsmen, one of them his only son, a boy of thirteen, and I know not how many among the kinsmen of his enemies. Had the two tribes not been separated by a four days' journey over the water, doubtless there would have been many more deaths. How it would all end none but the gods knew.

The night after our arrival among the Chaldeans, Kephalos did indeed visit the Lady Hjadkir in her hut—we hardly found ourselves in a position to refuse our hosts anything—and when he returned the next morning to the *mudhif* where, as Sesku's guests, we were being quartered, he lay down on the sleeping mat next to mine, dragged his cloak over him, even covering his face, and drew his legs up to his chest, as if he wished to occupy as little space as possible.

"That woman is worse than a demon," he said finally, in a voice that sounded ragged and hoarse. He said no more for several hours, until, when the sun had already declined an hour past noon, he woke again and sat up to take the bowls of rice and buttermilk I brought him. Even then his face was lined and haggard, and there were dark pouches under his eyes.

"Was it as bad as all that?" I asked. He scowled, as if it was in his mind that I mocked him.

"Yes—it was as bad as all that."

"Eat then, for you will have need of your strength."

Taking my advice to heart, he began scooping up the rice with his fingers. When he was finished he took a sip of the buttermilk and contemptuously dashed the bowl to the floor.

"Have these people never heard of wine?" he asked, scandalized. "What do they bring back with them when they plunder the villages of Sumer, jars of muddy water? How can they bear to be so uncouth? My Lord, we find ourselves among savages."

"Perhaps, but at least our corpses are not stretched out over an ant hill somewhere. We are alive."

"You are alive—I am dead." His arms lying along his thighs, he sagged under the weight of so much misery. "I am dead. That dreadful old hyena bitch has killed me already. Like an olive press, she squeezes the seed from my loins so that I ache there as if I had been kicked. In all honor you must admit it, I am not to blame if all my life many and many such as she have loved me so that I have known no peace. She says that, having found me, she will never let me go, but I will die in her arms, her kisses taking the breath from my body. May the gods know I curse them that they made me a snare for all the lustful weaknesses of women!"

"You are perhaps not aware, My Lord, that the king in Nineveh has dispatched assassins after you?"

"He has put a price on my head, if that is what you mean."

"No, that is not what I mean."

Sesku, king of the Halufids, fell silent for a moment. He was sitting in front of me in his war boat as we were rowed back to his village, so I could not see his face.

"I mean that he has sent men to all the distant corners of the earth and that these men will be your death anywhere they find you, even beyond the distant seas where no man knows the name of Esarhaddon, king in the Land of Ashur. Of this my spies in the great city of Ur send me reports."

"Well, if it is only rumors . . ." I could allow myself to laugh, although I felt little enough like jesting. "Many among the common people dislike Esarhaddon and are willing enough to believe anything against him. Stories circulate, even in Ur."

"Nevertheless, a man speaking in the accents of the north made inquiries there after a Greek physician and his slave. He got as far as the fishing settlement by the Great Fresh Water, where, it is said, the villagers slit his throat and rowed across to our side with the body that they might hide it under one of the floating islands. You are safe enough from him, but I doubt he was the only one whom your brother sent this way."

"Esarhaddon is not a man to send assassins. Besides, if he so much wanted me dead, he had his chance in Nineveh."

"Really? Perhaps he has come to regret his mercy. Moreover, do not imagine that you understand him so well, even though everyone says you and your brother once loved each other well. Power coarsens a man, making him capable of anything."

The next month passed away in a kind of unfocused suspense as we watched the flood waters slowly recede and the summer sun grew merciless to man and animal alike—even the fish, floating in the tepid water of the canals, even when they saw the shadow of the fisherman with his spear, could hardly summon the energy to move.

I had almost given up thinking about the future. I had become quite skilled in the management of boats, and I spent much time away from the village, exploring among the reed islands. I snared ducks in my net. I fished and sometimes hunted for wild pigs, which the Chaldeans hate almost as enemies in a blood feud because they trample down their crops.

So matters stood on a hot, sultry afternoon of a day in which all anger was forgotten and no man raised his voice, when the village dozed in a sluggish quiet, when even the children had crawled into the shade of their mothers' huts and waited for the first stirrings of the evening breeze. The cooking fires were still and nothing moved in air so stagnant that it was almost too much trouble to breathe. I lay on my sleeping mat with a damp cloth spread out over my face, feeling myself ill-used because the cloth was rapidly drying out and soon I would have to go to the trouble of wetting it again. There was no sound save the croaking of the frogs along the reed banks. Why then, I wondered, was I listening for something?

And then I heard it—the slap, slap, slap of sandaled feet on the bare earth. Someone was running, and in this heat. It seemed almost unimaginable.

The curtain over my hut's door lifted, admitting an unpleasant shaft of coarse white sunlight. It was blocked out again almost at once by the broad shape of my former slave.

"Kephalos!" I announced with surprise. "You are the last person I would have expected to see violating the calm of this grisly heat. I hope you have remembered to steal some wine."

"No wine, My Lord, for which I entreat your pardon. I come bearing news—or, if you will, prophecy."

He crouched down on the ground beside me, his face and arms streaming with sweat.

"Yes?—what?"

"A moment, My Lord . . ." He held up his hand as a sign that I must first allow him to catch his breath, for indeed his chest was working like a bellows. But at last he was calmer.

"It is no more than this, Lord: it seems that the drunken old vulture on whom I am condemned to waste the vigor of my manhood has been visited with a dream."

He had a sudden fit of high-pitched, almost hysterical-sounding laughter, as if the idea had all at once struck him as a rare jest. It was possible for an instant to believe that the sun must have touched his mind.

"The Lady Hjadkir?" I asked, hoping to pull him back to the point.

"Yes—the Lady Hjadkir. That lecherous, wheezing old hag, with her slack breasts and her wrinkled belly, she awoke, not half an hour ago, starting out of her wine-fogged slumbers with a shriek like a demon frightened of the dark. How she trembled—and in this heat!—her flesh as gray and lumpy as that of a plucked goose. She screamed and screamed, still lost in her phantom world for all that her eyes were wide open. A dream, I thought—yes, merely a bad dream. A thing born of too much wine and a lifetime of wickedness. Only that."

"And now you think perhaps it was something else?"

The worthy physician shrugged his shoulders, as if in the face of the unknowable.

"Who can say? She has a great reputation among her own people as a seer, yet I would not have troubled either of us, except for . . ."

"Except for what?"

"A doubt, My Lord," he answered, smiling out of one side of his mouth, like one who knows he speaks folly. "And the natural caution of one who has lived long in the shadow of Prince Tiglath Ashur and therefore knows that the gods speak in strange voices. Why else would that old bag of carrion, who hardly remembers the faces of her grandchildren, have sent me to you?"

"You are sure it was me to whom she sent you, and not her son?"

"Yes, Lord—it was you she meant. The Lady Hjadkir is not of a conversational bent and, beyond a few which delicacy forbids me to name, I have learned hardly any words of her strange speech. Yet she is not without resources for making herself understood. When she dismissed me with her message she pointed first to her own eye and then to mine, then to hers again and then back to mine, repeating this until she was sure I had grasped the distinction she intended. Then she motioned me away, pronouncing the word *shikan* many times. Is is not clear enough? She calls her son *shikan*, so I must conclude it is some title of respect. And you, My Lord, are surely the only person in this village, of whatever rank, who shares with me the distinction of having blue eyes."

"Yes, it seems clear enough." I nodded, wondering to myself if anything would ever seem clear again. "What is this 'message' of which you spoke?"

"This," Kephalos answered, holding up his left hand, the fingers splayed wide apart, and then pressing it into the earth in front of where he was sitting. When he pulled it away there was a clear impression in the dust. "And then, using her thumb, she erased the fourth finger—as I do now."

When he was finished the handprint showed only a stump where the smallest finger had been, as if it had been taken off at the joint.

"And you are quite sure it was the left hand?"

"Yes, Lord. The left. Do you know what it means, or was it only too much wine?"

"No, I do not know what it means, but it was not the wine."

His eyes narrowed for an instant, almost as if he expected that I might be concealing something from him, and then he shook this perplexity from him with a shrug of his shoulders. It was all the same to him if the Lady Hjadkir and I shared secrets, he seemed to imply.

"Really, Kephalos, I cannot guess what is intended. I know no one who is missing his fourth finger. There was nothing else? Only the maimed hand?"

"Nothing, Lord. Except that the lady seemed no more pleased with her vision than if she had seen the face of death itself."

"Then it is a mystery. I can only pray the god sees fit to enlighten me before it is too late."

"Pray well then, for the gods are capricious creatures."

He got up to leave, rubbing the dust from his knees, no more satisfied with me than before, it appeared.

"Kephalos . . ."

"Yes, Lord?"

"Where do you sleep in the Lady Hjadkir's hut?"

"In her arms generally—what makes you ask such a question?"

"Offer some excuse why you must leave her alone tonight, and make your bed somewhere away from the royal compound. Sleep in the *mudhif*, among the travelers who shelter there. The safety of a guest is respected by everyone among the Chaldeans. You will be better off there for one night."

"I will take something to give myself the wind," he said, grinning. "You will scarcely credit it, but the old hag has a sensitive nose."

He left me then and I sat in my hut alone, studying the handprint in the dust.

In the evening, when the sun smoldered on the horizon like a live coal, I went down to the river to wash the sweat from my body. I felt rimy with salt, and it burned in my eyes and in every crevice of my face. I would take a swim and then I would feel better. The enigma of the old woman's dream remained intact.

The village was beginning to come awake again. I heard the laughter of children and there was the smell of smoke in the air as women kindled their cooking fires. I had been among the Halufids for nearly two months now, and no one paid the slightest attention to me as I walked behind the line of huts to the eastern and less populated side of the island, whither I went because there would be more shade and the water would be colder—I wanted to submerge myself up to the chin in the dark canal and float quietly while I felt my legs turn numb. It would not happen that way, not in the midst of summer, but it was a happy idea.

As I approached the bank I met a group of young boys who must have had the same thought, for their hair was still wet and shining as they raised their arms to me and shouted, "Shala!" "Shala!" I said, returning their greeting—it was the one indispensable word among the Chaldeans, for it meant "peace."

The canal was almost as dark and cold as I had hoped, and after I had bathed I climbed out onto the bank to let the lowering sun dry me, listening to the reeds creak in the faint evening wind, trying to think of nothing. Yet even the pleasant heat of the sun seemed an illusion, for as soon as I had shivered myself warm again the old dread turned the heart in my breast to ice. I had the sense of inhabiting a world of appearances, where nothing was itself but merely the symbol of something else, yet of what? Once more, it appeared, Ashur, lord of earth and sky, god of my fathers, was amusing himself at his servant's expense, setting riddles for me to solve if I hoped to live. A hand with one finger missing—what could it mean?

And then, of course, as if out of pity for my stupidity, the god made clear his purposes.

It was the thing of an instant. All at once a shadow raced soundlessly over the face of the water. I glanced up and saw a great bird rising out of the lowering sun, red as blood. Its wings were set and it glided easily through the dead air. An eagle, I thought, but at that distance, there was no way to know.

It was several seconds before I remembered.

In the wilderness, dreaming or awake, I had seen myself as a great serpent crawling through the white salt waste. And above me had been five eagles, swooping low for the kill. They had torn my flesh.

And each had had a talon missing from its left claw.

I wondered how I could have missed anything so obvious, yet all becomes clear when the god wills it. And until then shrouded in impenetrable mystery. Soon one of these five eagles would dive down on me from some place of concealment—this was the warning contained in the Lady Hjadkir's dream.

This was quite an open threat. I was not afraid of treachery. I was not afraid that someone from among the Halufids would make an attempt against my life. Yet if there was danger there was no reason to imagine that I would be its sole and specific target. It seemed unlikely that a lone assassin would make his solitary way to this village, with no object except to cut my throat. There would be an attack, and I might die in it, but my death might be no more than incidental. It was not as if Sesku had no enemies of his own.

Doubtless it was no more than my imagination, but even walking back to the village I felt as if hostile eyes followed my every step. Sesku would have to be told—and in such a way as to compel belief—or the Halufids might end by being butchered while they slept. These people had shown me nothing but hospitality, and I did not want their innocent blood on my conscience.

As it happened, I found Sesku less difficult to persuade than I had imagined. He was waiting for me outside the door of my hut when I returned, carrying a lamp, since it was already dark, and, without speaking, with only a gesture of his hand, he bade me enter before him. When we were inside he sat down on the floor, drawing his legs under him and folding his hands in his lap. His manner was very formal. I had the impression he wished to be taken seriously and was not sure this wish would be gratified.

"My mother dreams of one who has lost a finger," he said, in a confidential voice, leaning a little toward me as if afraid of being overheard. "By itself, the dream means nothing—or, rather, its warning is too vague to profit us. I know of no man afflicted in this way. Do you?"

"No one. And you are quite right—by itself, the dream means nothing."

He raised one eyebrow at my slight shift of emphasis. For a moment I could not tell if perhaps he thought I mocked him.

And then, it seemed, the question was decided in my favor.

"You are aware of something which might . . . ?" A real urgency came into his face, and he reached across to grasp me by the wrist. "Speak, Prince. Everyone has heard the stories of your *sedu*, how you stand under the protection of the gods. If you know something, by the mercy of your own Holy Ashur, then I beg you not to keep it hidden from me."

"My Lord, I too . . . I hardly know how to say it." I could only shrug my shoulders, since the whole business seemed as fantastic to me as, doubtless, it would to him. "I too have received certain signs. All my life—dreams, omens, things the truth of which I sometimes saw only after the event. The god's voice speaks in whispers. Yet sometimes he makes his purposes clear. I will not tell you why—accept it, if you will, as no more than my opinion—but I believe that this village is in some danger."

"An attack? When, do you think?" It seemed it did not occur to him to doubt me.

"Perhaps tonight. The god gives his warning in good time."

"Yes, in remarkably good time. But then of course you could not know—the Sharjan have within these last five days chosen for themselves a new chief. You may be confident I believe everything you have told me." He released my arm and leaned back, considering the matter. "Then let it be tonight, if that be the gods' pleasure. When the wind blows, a wise man pulls his boat up unto the shore. I will give the necessary orders."

After he had left I found myself wondering how he would couch those orders, what reasons he would give for throwing his village into such a state of alert that tonight men would sleep with their swords next to them instead of their wives. And few enough, probably, would sleep at all. How would Sesku explain it to them? All men wish to believe their commanders are both fearless and full of wisdom, and the truth of this case might make a doubter of anyone. Who, after all, would wish to serve a leader who starts at shadows?

Still, I thought, that was not a matter which concerned me. And the king of the Halufids was a plausible enough rogue to think of some story that would keep him from looking foolish if all was for nothing and neither the Sharjan nor any other enemy thought to bring mischief to this collection of reed hovels. Someone else would answer for it, but not he.

Yet I did not believe that Sesku or anyone else need worry about a quiet night. I took down my javelin and felt the point with the ball of my thumb, wondering how much blood it would spill before the sun rose tomorrow—wondering if I would be alive to know.

I went to look for Kephalos and found him not at the *mudhif*, as I had expected, but sitting disconsolately down at the water's edge, where the villagers left their boats tied up like cattle in a stall. His head almost between his knees, he was amusing himself by tracing the Greek alphabet in the dirt.

"The withered old hag has thrown me out," he said, without even glancing up to see who it was. "I did not even have to feign indisposition. She chased me from her hut with no more ceremony than if I had been a limping cur nosing around after scraps. And these savages will not even allow me to enter the *mudhif*, such is my disgrace. They laugh and make obscene gestures, and then throw things at me. Imagine, if you can, the indignity of it."

"She is probably afraid. She senses that what is to come has more to do with me than with the Halufids, and you are my servant. She wishes to keep the danger at a more comfortable distance."

"It is not very comfortable for me, I can tell you. Lord, allow me to sleep in your hut tonight."

"That is the last place you should wish to be. Sleep here, among the boats, if you must, but as you value your life stay away from anywhere men might look for me."

For a moment his face assumed an expression of the most appalled horror, which with only the greatest difficulty he was able to quell. At last he returned to drawing letters in the dirt.

"You must preserve yourself, Master," he said quietly. "You must not leave me here to die alone in this desert."

The hours of waiting are the hardest part of any battle. The enemy has no face. He is the shadow that threatens to engulf one, the dark specter of death. How does mortal flesh and bone fight a shadow? Who can teach a man not to be afraid? It is the lesson each must learn for himself.

The village was held in the center of a web of waterways and tiny islands, and Sesku had his men out in their boats for two hours in any direction. As the fly cannot touch a strand of silk but the spider senses its presence, so no enemy could enter into the territory of the Halufids without their knowing it. I could hear their bird cries trembling in the night air, a call relayed from the gods knew what distance but understood and answered almost within the drawing of a breath. I stood with Sesku, my javelin in my hand and a borrowed sword thrust into the belt of my tunic. There was nothing to do except to wait.

"It must seem strange," he said, his quiet voice as startling as a handclap in that silence. "To go into battle thus, with no soldiers under your orders, with no one to answer for except yourself. I do not envy you—without the distractions of command, death seems to stare one straight in the face."

"Yet it is not the first time."

He nodded, and then turned to me and smiled. Like me, he was thinking of Khalule, where, without even knowing of one another's existence, we two had each hoped to be the other's end.

At last the low, quavering birdcalls became more frequent and seemed, in some way impossible to define, to take on the urgency of men whispering in the dark. Sesku closed his eyes for a moment, as if to listen even more closely.

"You and my lady mother were right, it appears," he said, his eyes coming open with a snap. "They are coming, perhaps twenty boats of them. They will attack the island from two directions, side and rear, and before this hour is finished. There is no doubt they are Sharjan."

It was almost a relief to hear the words.

"The main party will come from the rear. They hope to marshal there and reach the village before we even know they are upon us. Then, when we are fairly engaged, the rest will land and catch us between them like ducks in a net. This, however, is precisely the fate which we have prepared for them. The think to show us no mercy, so they can hardly expect any."

The idea of slaughtering his enemies gave him an obvious satisfaction, yet I could not find it in me to blame him. He was afraid. His life and the lives of his people were threatened, and pity did not live in his heart.

"Where will you wait for them?'" I asked.

He answered by pointing back through the village to the spot where hardly six hours before I had been swimming in the cool black water.

"Then I will wait there with you."

It was a simple enough plan. The Sharjan had chosen a moonless night, gambling everything on surprise. So did we. Sesku and some two hundred of his men, myself among them, would wait, sitting in long lines in the darkness, our weapons resting on our knees. The enemy would come in from the marshes, slipping through the Halufid war boats without ever even realizing that they were there, and once they had drawn their own boats up on the shore—once there was no turning back for them—we would rise up and unleash our arrows and javelins, aiming into the blank, unseeing night, with no targets but their murmuring voices. We would kill enough that way to sow confusion among them, and confusion is the mother of defeat. Then we would light our torches and butcher the rest at our leisure. The few who might survive to escape into the marshes would find that the trap had closed behind them. In their panicked flight they would run straight into Sesku's boatmen, waiting to spear them like fish.

The same death would await the second, smaller party. When they heard the sounds of battle they would either run their boats ashore, thinking that their strategy had prospered, or they would flee the way they had come. It did not matter if they died on the solid land or in the water. In the morning the crows and the fishes would glut themselves on their corpses.

That was the plan—and easy victory over men who would find their surprise turned back upon them. It only had to work to be perfect. We would know before we were a quarter of an hour older.

It began, as it always does, with sick fear lying in the belly like a lump of bronze. We could hear the enemy. We could hear their voices and the sounds of their feet splashing in the shallow water. We listened, waiting. We heard the scraping noise of boat keels being dragged up on the reed-choked bank. We heard the rasp of metal against metal. They had come, and they suspected nothing.

"Now," Sesku whispered, crouched beside me. And then, in his own tongue, what had to be the same word, shouted as no less than a challenge—"NOW!"

In answer, the war cry of the Halufids, repeated from two hundred throats, then, at almost the same instant, the whisper of two hundred arrows sliding through the black, empty air. The night seemed to tremble with the sound, crashing over us in a great wave.

Someone lit a torch. Then another, and another. The grass was set afire, and in the lurid yellow flames we could see the enemy, not a hundred paces away. The corpses of their dead lay on the ground, and we would hear the cries of the wounded. Those still on their feet seemed paralyzed with astonishment. They did not awaken from their trance until the second volley.

Not desiring to squander my opportunity, I had held my hand until then. I chose a mark, a man standing in the midst of the Sharjan—a good, brave, soldierly sort of man, I thought, one who seemed little disposed to turn and flee—and my javelin made a clean arc through the air and caught him full in the chest. The blow seemed to carry him back with it, and his lifeless body pitched over onto the ground.

He was not alone in finding death. Some twenty or thirty more fell with him, and it was only then that the Sharjan, the hundred and fifty or so who were left alive, remembered that they had not come to this place to be cut down like barley. First one, and then another, and then all of them together, took up their war cry, shaking their weapons at us in defiance, and charged us straight on.

The collision was like the shock of hammer against anvil. It was a brave contest there in the flickering light of the grass fires, but it was short and, for the Sharjan, hopeless. They were in confusion and disarray. They never recovered from that first surprise and thus had no plan except what was in each man's heart—to do battle and, if need be, to die a brave death. The Halufid, keeping their lines formed and fighting with discipline, hacked them to pieces. We suffered few losses. For us it was what every boy, who has never seen one, dreams that war will be like—quick, unequal, and glorious.

We fought with swords only, cut and thrust, in close combat against a desperate enemy. I received but a single wound, and that a trivial business. The point of a Sharjan dagger opened the skin over my shoulder muscle and spilled enough blood to stain my arm red, but it was no more than a gaudy-looking inconvenience.

Afterwards I was very glad, because the dagger had been meant for Sesku's back. We were standing only a few paces from each other, just as the Sharjan were beginning to break and run. I had only that minute slain one of the last with the courage to stand against us, and I glanced over toward Sesku and saw that another, not caring if he lived or died, had managed to come in behind him.

His hand was filled and he was ready to strike—Sesku did not even know he was there. I shouted a warning and charged the attacker, catching him just under the rib cage with my sword.

I shall never forget the expression on his face. He seemed to snarl like an animal, hating me for having ruined his last chance at revenge. With his dying strength he swung his dagger toward me, cutting my shoulder open just before the weapon fell from his lifeless hand. Even as he lay dead, he seemed to stare at me with hatred.

It was only then, it seemed, that Sesku became aware of his danger. He turned and looked down at the dead man, and then up at me. It was the blood on my arm that made him grasp what had happened.

"I had no idea Khalule weighed so heavily upon your conscience," he said.

"It was a point of honor—if I cannot have your life, then I would prefer you to be immortal. I will concede the honor of killing you to no one else."

He laughed, and then pointed to my wound, as if he had just remembered some trivial detail.

"You will live, I trust?"

"A small thing, of no consequence. I doubt, in six months' time, I will even have a pretty scar to show for it."

We could stand there, speaking thus, because the battle was over. The Sharjan had fled to their boats, leaving only the dead behind them, and already I could see the distant shimmer of torchlight upon the water and hear the screams of men who knew they had forfeited their last hope of escape. The Halufid boatmen had been waiting for them.

But for us the fighting was done. Some of Sesku's men were looting the corpses of their enemies, cutting the throats of any survivors, but the rest simply milled about, still too excited to stand quietly.

"We have conquered, my people!" the king of the Halufids shouted, as if the fact had just occurred to him. From one instant to the next, he seemed beside himself with exultation.

"The heavens make manifest their favor. They fortify our hearts with omens; they deliver the enemy into our hands—"

Sesku's last words were almost drowned out by the shouting of the victorious Halufids, who crowded about us, raising their weapons over their heads in triumph.

Then he touched my arm and held up his hand to show off the fresh blood of my wound dripping from his fingers. The Halufids, mad with joy, shouted their approval, although I think, in that moment, they would have applauded anything.

We walked back to the village together, where I went in search of Kephalos that he too might rejoice in our deliverance. I found him asleep aboard a reed raft that had been dragged up onto the shore, his arms wrapped protectively around his medicine box.

"You look as if you need the services of a physician," he said when he saw my arm. "By the wisdom of Apollo, what a lot of blood! But it is just as well, for blood is purifying."

When he was finished with everything else, Kephalos stitched my wound closed with a thread drawn from the entrails of a rabbit. I did not find that part of the operation very amusing.

"Will you come then and share my hut?" I asked. "I hate to think of you lying out here in the mud."

"No, Lord—you gave me good advice before, and I will follow it. A cautious man lives long enough to enjoy the memory of his follies."

"As you will."

There would be singing and celebration all night tonight in the *mudhif* of my Lord Sesku, but I was weary and, besides, it was not my victory. I would be glad to close my eyes against the morning. I would sleep like a corpse in the earth.

I was perhaps fifteen paces away when I thought I saw the blanket covering my doorway move.

Of course. In the excitement I had nearly forgotten. The god had sent his warning not to Sesku, but to me.

But perhaps I was merely imagining it all. I raised my torch to look about me. There was nothing. Then I happened to glance down and saw a sandalprint in the dust.

It was not mine, and it was not Kephalos', which I knew almost as well. And the Halufids did not wear sandals, not even their king. I found myself in the presence of an enemy who was as much a stranger here as I.

And he was waiting for me inside the hut.

Well, I would not oblige him. I would not step through that doorway, ducking down as I did so because it was built too low for me, and let this man hack through my neck like a housewife cutting her husband's meal from a block of cheese.

I still carried the sword Sesku had loaned me, and the torch that had lit me home still burned hotly. I threw it up on the hut's roof, which, being nothing but dry reeds, caught fire in an instant.

Within a quarter of a minute the roof was blazing and ready to collapse. I would not have long to wait.

Nor did I. With a cry of panic he came rushing out, clawing aside the blanket over the entrance, no thought in his mind except escape. He ran straight into my sword, taking the point just under the navel. I drove it up and at an angle so that it pierced his heart. The dagger he had been carrying dropped harmlessly to the ground.

A dead man lying at my feet, so astonished that it had ended thus. Who was he? I had never seen him before. His tunic could have been from anywhere, but he did not have the look of a Chaldean.

He had died clutching at his wound so that his left arm was under his body. Thus he lay on the ground. I put my foot on his shoulder and rolled him over.

It was then I saw that the last finger of his left hand was missing.

VII

"HE IS A STRANGER TO ME."

Sesku crouched down and grasped the dead man's left arm by the wrist to examine the hand. The flames from my hut still burned bright enough that he had no difficulty seeing.

"Yet clearly this is the one my mother beheld in her dream. You can understand now why I tolerate so much from her—it is a rare gift to read the future. We must find out what he was doing among the Sharjan."

"How will you do that?"

"My boatmen captured some ten or twelve who preferred the hazards of surrender to a quick and honorable death. In the morning, after they have had a few hours to sit in the dark wearing a prisoner's noose, we will put the question to them."

I saw them that night when I went to the *mudhif* to sleep. They were sitting in a little circle facing out, all bound together at the neck, with their hands and feet tied. Captured men always look just the same—tired, dirty, and hopeless. Sesku had set a watch, but these hardly seemed worth the trouble of guarding. They knew well enough what awaited them, for the Chaldeans are a cruel race, and doubtless they had reason enough to regret that brief failure of nerve that had prevented them from forcing a quick end that would forestall all future suffering. Yet they seemed empty even of the will to save themselves. They seemed almost dead already.

I was too weary, however, to pity them, and the memory of the assassin's dagger was still too vivid in my mind. Let them die, I thought, in any manner which shall be pleasing to the Halufids. What should it matter to me? I slept untroubled that night.

The next morning, when I awoke and came outside, the boats had already returned. Sesku's men had been out catching vipers.

"When the dawn breaks they lie on the reed banks, warming themselves in the sun. They are sluggish then, and one can pick them up easily enough with a hooked stick. They make quite a sight, do they not?"

They did. The boatmen had carried them back in wicker baskets, which they emptied into a copper urn the size of a war drum—it could not have held less than a hundred serpents, colored dull red to muddy brown, tangled together in a grotesque, ever-changing knot. Sesku thrust his walking stick in among them, stirring them up. He did not seem satisfied with the results.

"They are still half asleep," he said. "When the sun has heated the sides of the urn they will grow more alert. They need the warmth before they can even move, but too much of it makes them evil-tempered."

He withdrew his stick and held it out to me that I might see where a few of them had left the marks of their fangs in it.

"My Halufids have selected these with great care," he went on. "Their bite is painful, and a man does not die of it too quickly. Yet none recover. It is not an end anyone would choose for himself."

We waited another hour, and the twisting mass inside the urn grew more and more agitated. Sesku stirred them again with his walking stick, and this time I could hear the series of angry snaps, like stones falling to a cobbled floor, as they struck out at it.

"Now they are ready," he said, and then turned to one of his retainers to give an order.

The prisoners had of course been watching with great attention, their eyes large and grown yellow with fear—as he waits for death, a man's faces takes on a peculiar grayish cast, as if he were already becoming part of the lifeless earth.

The Halufids selected one among them, took the noose from his neck, and cut the bit of hemp that bound his ankles. They had to help him to his feet, for his hands remained tied behind his back. I think they would have had to help him up in any case.

He began to scream uncontrollably as soon as he saw what was about to happen to him.

Two men held him by the arms while another used a hooked stick to reach into the urn and, one at a time, lift out some ten of the vipers and drop them into a leather bag a littler larger than a water bucket. Then the two men holding the prisoner forced him to bend over at the waist and the bag was slipped over his head, the drawstrings at the top pulled tight and knotted. Even as this was done he stamped his bare feet on the ground, seeming to dance in an agony of terror.

When his arms were released he straightened up at once, and the bag over his head did nothing to silence his cries. He limped about, hopping from one foot to the other, blind and helpless, his shoulders hunched as if he entertained some hope of thus drawing his head out of that mortal darkness. After a time he went down to his knees, his loincloth by this time soaked with urine, and at last toppled over onto his face. He lay there, still twitching in the dust, for several minutes. It was impossible to say whether he was still alive or not.

They removed the bag from his head—with all possible care, as the vipers had by no means exhausted their poison—and the sight he made was not one I am likely to forget. His face was covered with tears, each the center of a dark bruise, and his tongue, which protruded from his mouth like something on which he might have choked, was black and swollen. The vipers had bitten it as well, and had punctured one of his eyes so that a thick, bloody syrup ran down his cheek. Sesku used his foot to turn the corpse over, and it had already gone quite rigid.

I have seen many men executed by torture, and I know that one can die more slowly and in greater pain, yet there is something in the mind itself that revolts against such a death as this, making it terrible out of all proportion to the agony of mere flesh. Sesku was right—it was not an end anyone would choose for himself.

"Now they have all seen how we can treat an enemy," he said to me, as the dead prisoner was hauled away by a rope around the foot. "I will now inquire of these Sharjan if they know anything of the man with a finger missing. We have no shortage of vipers, nor of captives, so I think we will find one among so many who will prefer a sword under the ribs to putting his head into that bag. Go and enjoy your breakfast in peace. When I see you again I will have something to tell you."

I went away gladly enough. At least in that I followed Sesku's advice. My appetite had failed me, although I am not cursed with a delicate stomach. I wanted only to sit quietly somewhere and wait for the impression of what I had just seen to wear off a little.

Such scenes are best not witnessed sober. Once, during the second year of his campaigns in Sumer, I sat beside my royal father as he presided over the flaying alive of a king who had rebelled against him. To watch a man's skin stripped from his body, to smell the blood, to hear the screams of agony was not pleasant, yet my father, the Lord Sennacherib, sat with his hands on his knees through the whole of it, never turning his eyes away and betraying no emotion. I did the same. My father, who understood all the arts of kingship, had first seen to it that we were both so besotted with date wine that very likely the executioners could have gone to work on either of us without our being greatly inconvenienced, or perhaps even noticing. I would have given much, crouched alone by the water's edge, to be as drunk as I had been that day in Sumer.

"Have you seen, Lord, how these savages amuse themselves?"

It was Kephalos, looking white and shaky, as if he had just emptied his belly into the canal. He sat down beside me, holding one hand inside the other in his lap.

"How many have they killed so far?" I asked.

"Four—five perhaps, by now. I saw only four corpses. They are taking their time. They will be at it all morning."

"I think not. When they have what they want, I expect they will gut the rest like fish."

He glanced at me with an expression of the most profound distaste.

"And for what, then, are they looking?"

"Information." I shrugged my shoulders, like a man forced to admit something shameful. "About the man who tried to assassinate me last night. A courtesy, if you will—although I expect Sesku has his own reasons for wishing to find it out."

Suddenly, and for no obvious reason, I was overcome with a most dreadful grief. Life seemed a misery beyond bearing. I felt ashamed for the breath under my ribs. I could only hide my face in my hands and weep, for I was helpless against the force of this terrible affliction into which the gods had turned my existence.

"Dread Lord, I . . ."

Poor Kephalos, what must he have thought as his voice trailed away in perplexed embarrassment? At last, as my fit of despair began to pass, I became conscious that he was standing some way off. I looked behind me and saw he had his back turned, and then I heard him make a sound as if to clear his throat—a signal perhaps that my solitude was about to be broken in upon. I reached into the canal, took a double handful of water, and threw it in my face. At almost the same instant I heard Sesku's voice behind me.

"Our inquiries have met with some small success," he announced—there was nothing in his tone to indicate he had witnessed any part of my lapse. "It seems our friend with the missing finger entered the marshes from the direction of Lagash, on the Tigris, and bore an offer of 'tribute' from the king your brother if the Sharjan would help him in relieving you of your head so that he could carry it back to Nineveh—imagine it, the Ruler of the Earth's Four Corners demeaning himself to offer 'tribute' to a race of brigands; I am ashamed for him. The precise amount seems a trifle vague, which is not to be wondered at considering that the Sharjan are all beggars and can hardly imagine sums greater than a handful of copper shekels, but I gather it was enough make some impression. The villain's name, by the way, was Mushussu."

I threw back my head and laughed. I laughed until the tears flooded my eyes and I could hardly breathe. No doubt I was still a trifle hysterical, for Sesku stared at me in the most shocked manner.

"Are you quite well, my friend?" he asked, crouching beside me on the canal bank. He even put his hand upon my shoulder, as if to steady me. "Did you know him then?"

"No, I did not know him, and now neither will anyone else." I washed my face yet again and was at last able to see the joke without losing control of myself. " 'Mushussu' is not a name—or at least not one that any mother would choose for her son. It is the word for a kind of demon, an avenger, sacred to the god Marduk and made by him from equal parts of lion, snake and eagle."

My bowels went suddenly cold as I remembered the eagles of my dream. It was as if the earth had suddenly collapsed beneath my feet.

Yet it did not collapse, and Sesku remained there next to me, one hand on my shoulder, the fingers of the other thoughtfully rubbing the lump over his eye, as if the answer he sought were to be squeezed out of it. Finally he shook his head, frowning with perplexity.

"I do not understand the blasphemies in which you northern races indulge yourselves," he said as he rose to his feet. "I am at a loss to comprehend how you can mock at your gods thus—and why they do not burn you to ashes for your impudence. It is a wonder that you have reigned so long over the nations of the world. I had always heard that the Lord Esarhaddon was a man most scrupulous in his piety."

"So he is. No man ever feared the gods more than my brother. And Marduk is his particular devotion."

"Then it is most wonderful."

"Yes."

Sesku did not linger, but returned to direct the execution of the remaining prisoners, who, as he had promised them, would die by the sword, and that quickly. I was not sorry to be parted from him, for at bottom he was still only a tribesman, delighting in savagery, and I began to find his company an oppression of the soul.

"We must leave this place," I said to Kephalos as we walked back toward the village. We had allowed a suitable interval to pass, hoping, at least for the rest of this day, to avoid the sight of blood. "We must depart from the Sealand and enter into the nations that lie beyond the Bitter River. We must not rest until we find a place where my brother will never find us—where the god himself cannot reach. Yes, I would flee from Ashur. I would forget him and the dreams he sends. Always in my mind I hear the words of the Lady Esharhamat: 'Your god, he plays with us. A child pitching stones at a bird's nest could not have less pity.'"

But before Kephalos and I could leave the marshes, there must be an end to the blood feud between the Halufids and the Sharjan. And this Sesku determined he would purchase not with cattle and gold and women, but with the sword.

All that day and the next there was a brisk traffic in war craft at the village dock, and on the third morning after the raid we set out with perhaps seven hundred warriors and perhaps a hundred boats of every size. We traveled fast, sacrificing stealth to speed, since it was obvious our enemies would begin to expect an attack as soon as their own men failed to return after their time. The journey to the territory of the Sharjan took four days, and there were more than a few great battles, bloody, cruel and one-sided, before we ever came within sight of their main settlements, and many a bloated, water-logged corpse was carried along on the slow currents of the canals, for a whole people does not easily resign itself to death.

Yet the Sharjan were a doomed nation—even they seemed to sense it. The best of their warriors had already been killed, and the rest fought with the courage of hopelessness. The Halufids simply crushed them, almost thoughtlessly, like a boulder rolling down a mountain.

What happened when we reached their villages cannot be fairly described as war. War, even such war as I have seen, does not admit of such horrors. The young men were gone, either killed or fled, leaving behind only the defenseless. Most of these were slaughtered. I saw children hacked open before their mothers' eyes, and old men, white-haired and trembling, had their feet and hands chopped off and were forced to creep about on their bellies, begging their tormentors for death. Over and over it happened—within an hour of our landing the air was rank with the smell of blood, and only a few among the women, the virgins and the young wives whose breasts had never been swelled with milk, were left alive. These would be roughly divided into two categories and either roped together by the neck to live as chattel or to be raped repeatedly, and with such brutal violence that some even died of it, and then stripped naked to be driven into the water, where the Halufid boatmen bludgeoned them to death with their oars, a traditional punishment for unchastity.

Nothing was spared. Animals were slaughtered and the village was put to the torch. The dead were thrown into the water and the living led away. Sesku put no limit on his vengeance.

"I will leave the Sharjan nothing, not even their lives," he said. "I will hunt them down until I have butchered the last one—no man's son will survive to carry on this feud. I will see that their very name dies from men's lips."

He was as good as his word. In a month of campaigning he made the marshes into a grave.

And then we returned. The women, some three or four hundred of them, were divided among his followers. Sesku, although not a lecherous man, kept some twelve of the best for himself, as he still lived in hopes of a son, and I was offered my pick, but I did not expect to stay much longer among the Halufids and therefore declined. Within a few days the whole episode seemed forgotten, like something which has happened in a dream.

After Sesku had secured safe passage for me from the chiefs of all the tribes along my way, and after a great banquet during which he called me his friend and brother, he loaned me his own war boat, four of his best paddlers, and his nephew Kelshahir to act as my guide and interpreter and sent us on our way. I will always remember the sight of him, standing on his pier, waving us off. We had not even disappeared from sight before he let his arm drop and began walking back to his *mudhif*, as if dismissing us from existence.

Our journey occupied more than a month. It was late summer and still very hot during the days, although night provided some relief. The sun's light glared off the water, which made it wearisome to the eyes. Both Kephalos and I experienced leg cramps from sitting in a boat for so many hours together, although I do not believe Kelshahir and his oarsmen were so affected.

Yet I have always found pleasure in traveling, and even in the marshlands, as monotonous a place as it is possible to imagine—all reeds and heavy, stagnant water—each day had its rewards. Sometimes we would stop to hunt for wild pigs or to net ducks, or simply for the happiness of a few hours on solid ground. Once we watched a great male lion swimming from one island to another—he looked very comic and uncomfortable with his huge mane, and when at last he climbed up onto the bank he roared loudly at nothing in particular, out of sheer vexation it seemed. And of course each evening, as we dragged our boat on shore and made our campfire, there was the pleasure of remembering that we were one day closer to the Bitter River and the great world beyond.

As we traveled farther south we began to enter the territories of other tribes. Everyone recognized the war boat of the Lord Sesku, and many seemed to know Kelshahir by sight, so everywhere we chose to stop we were received with the greatest shows of hospitality. In populated areas we would pass two or three little villages every day, and always the same dialogue would take place:

"Peace by with you, Lord Kelshahir," someone would shout from the shore. "Come and feed with us."

"Thank you. We have fed already, may the gods be praised."

"Then may the gods protect you on your journey, My Lord."

If it was near dark we would stop to dine and spend the night in the local chief's *mudhif*. Kephalos and the oarsmen would be given their food and then largely ignored. Kelshahir would be received with cringing respect, and then he and the village elders would hold a long parley—these being, I suspect, the real reason he had been sent along with us, although I never had any inkling what these conferences were about.

At last we began to leave the marshes behind. The main canal grew steadily wider and acquired a noticeable current, which meant that we had once more found the Euphrates. Kelshahir took the empty skins from the bottom of the boat and filled them with water—a useful precaution, as I saw soon enough. One morning, after we had been underway about three hours, he touched me on the shoulder and grinned.

"Taste," he said, dipping his fingers into the river.

I leaned over and scooped up a handful of the water—sure enough, it was brackish.

"Before this day is finished, we will reach the Bitter River."

It was true. That night we built our campfire on its hard, muddy shores, and for the first time in my life I heard the crashing of waves against the land's edge. The paddlers lifted our boat up onto their shoulders and carried it perhaps a hundred paces, to the shadow of a reed-covered bluff, before setting it down. When I asked Kelshahir the reason, he smiled, as if I had made a joke, and pointed back toward the water.

"It will rise," he said.

"Why should it rise? The season of flooding is past."

"It rises every morning, and every night—of its own. Its god is mighty, caring nothing for the rivers and swallowing their floods as if they held no more than an old man's bladder. It cares nothing for seasons. You will see."

I did. By the time our fire had died down to embers, the water was less than twenty paces away.

"Will it not come up the rest of the way and drown us?" I asked.

"No. It only reaches all the way to the bluffs in the spring, before the floods come. Now it stops and goes back, leaving the upper shore dry. I think the hot weather makes it lazy."

Thus I first learned of tides, which the Greeks say are caused not by a god but by the pull of the moon. Yet I was taught that the moon is the face of the Divine Sin, patron of Ur, whom the Babylonians call Nannar—different races use different names, yet the moon is still a god for all that—so I think it comes to no more than which god one chooses to invoke. Thus Kelshahir's explanation seems to me no less probable than that of which the Greeks are so vain.

The next day and the next we traveled east, following the coast but staying well offshore where the swells did not make paddling so difficult. On the morning of the third day we turned our boat away from the land and straight out into the Bitter River. I thought perhaps Kelshahir had gone mad, but shortly before noon we sighted a distant haze of land.

"Is that the farther shore?" I asked.

"No. That is merely an island, called Afesh. There is no farther shore."

This announcement filled me with dread, confirming as it did what I had already begun to suspect: that the Bitter River, which seemed to have no detectable current, was not a river at all but some sort of vast sea stretching possibly to the limits of the world. I began to wonder if we would ever again behold the haunts of men.

Thus it was with some relief that I saw, as we came closer, that there were many fine ships, the smallest of them larger even than the great war galleys of the Urartians, anchored along the shore.

"This is a trading post," Kelshahir volunteered, even as I was about to phrase the question. "It is convenient to the river traffic through Elam, so the Arabs maintain it as a permanent settlement and as a stop-off along the routes to the Eastern Lands."

"Will these Arabs give us passage to Egypt?"

"An Arab will do anything if you pay him enough."

I caught Kephalos' eye and he looked pleased, for greed was a language he understood. In his medicine box and on his person he carried some eight talents of gold, enough to keep us like rich men for the rest of our lives—enough to get us to Egypt certainly, even if we had to buy the ship that carried us.

"What tongue do these men speak?"

Kelshahir shrugged his shoulders, suggesting that he held no very high opinion of this race of merchants.

"The same," he said. "If a water ox could speak Chaldean, he would pass for an Arab."

He was able to laugh very hard at his own joke. He translated it for the benefit of the oarsmen, and they laughed too.

We landed shortly before the setting sun spilled a trail of blood into the blue salt water, tying up along a pier anchored in the mud with massive wood pilings—an uncommon enough sight in that treeless part of the world. We climbed up the heavy plank stairway to the dock and in a few steps passed from the solitude of the empty sea to the busy world of men, for this was a port as crowded with life as any I have seen in a lifetime of travels.

"I will arrange your passage at once," Kelshahir said, looking around him with some uneasiness. "I will not stay but must return to the mainland tonight. My men are afraid to leave the boat for fear someone will steal it."

Before I had a chance to answer, he had disappeared into the shouldering mob. There was nothing to do except to wait, and to look about us in wonder.

For a man could well fill his eyes with all that was to be seen on that dockside at Afesh. I might have imagined myself to have blundered into a congregation of princes, since never in my life, not even in Nineveh, had I witnessed such evidence of wealth among common people, nor so great a variety of costumes and races. Surely these had been gathered here from corners of the world of which my fathers had never even dreamed.

I saw men with faces the complexion of bronze or dark wood or freshly hammered iron, some wearing nothing but a loincloth and some dressed in long robes of a material that glittered in the light like colored fire. One wore a great green stone in a hole cut in the lobe of his ear, and the nostrils of many were pierced with silver and gold pins. Some had shaved their faces and even the crowns of their heads—many of these, I suspected, were probably Egyptians—and some wore only a thin ribbon of beard around the line of their jaws and over their upper lips. I saw but few with the full plaited beard in fashion among the men who dwell between the rivers, and these, from their dress, were clearly Elamites.

And such a confusion of tongues! By this time I had learned some two or three hundred words of Chaldean, and I recognized its cadence and forms well enough, but along with this there was a clattering of speech of which not a single syllable that came into my ear was familiar, and among so many voices hardly any two seemed to speak as to be understood by the other.

Yet business was being done here, that was obvious. All along the docks there were booths selling cloth, weapons, precious stones and jewelry of copper, gold and silver, fruits and vegetables, most of which I had never seen before, wines, cooked meats, live chickens and even eels pulled out of a water jug with a hook, carved wood and ivory, mirrors, combs for women's hair, sandals, powders of red, yellow, white and green, some so precious they were purchased in little folded scraps of leather. I saw scribes busy writing on clay tablets and Egyptian papyrus. Old women were reading fortunes in the palms of young ones. Barbers and surgeons were plying their trades in the shade of stall awnings. Within a few hundred paces of where we stood, there seemed nothing that was not for sale.

"Dread Lord, do you smell it?" Kephalos put his hand on my arm and shook it as if to wake me from a trance. "Can it be food, or is it incense from a temple? By the gods, I am starving! I think my belly has shriveled down to nothing since we have been among these savages. As soon as they can be prevailed upon to leave, I will drink a bucket of wine to toast their departure."

"Then you will not have long to wait. Kelshahir tarries only to arrange a ship for us. He says he is afraid to leave his boat overnight for fear it may be stolen."

"Nonsense. He is merely ashamed. Look about us. Who among all this multitude would condescend to steal a reed boat? He may be the king's successor among the Chaldeans, but here he is no more than a ragged beggar. He wishes to creep back to his marshes where he can still believe himself a mighty man."

Yet Kelshahir did return to us quickly enough to suggest a certain anxiety to be gone. He brought with him a short, plump little man dressed in a green-and-white linen tunic that would not have embarrassed my friend the worthy physician in the days of his splendor but whose hand, when he offered it to me, was as hard and callused as a carpenter's.

"This is Ishmahel, the master of the *Jinnah*," he said, pointing back toward a great, black-sided ship about halfway down the docks—Ishmahel, hearing his name pronounced, smiled and made several quick bows, addressing himself to me in a few muttered words of which I understood not one. "He has promised to carry you as far as the great cities of the south, from which it is possible to travel wherever your will takes you. This he undertakes to accomplish for a price of one hundred shekels of silver or five of gold, which I tell you now because, like all Arabs, he is a thief and will try to cheat you later. The ship sails with the dawn winds, so you had best be aboard before sunrise. Have I done well, My Lord Tiglath Ashur?"

"You have done very well, my friend, and I thank you."

"Then I will say farewell to you now, for I would be gone before the darkness comes."

He touched his forehead in salute and walked away even before I had a chance to thank him once more. I do not know what became of him after that, for I never saw him again.

And thus we were alone on the dock with only Ishmahel, master of the *Jinnah*, for company.

"At dawn then, My Lord?" I asked, turning to him with what I hoped was a confident smile. "We leave at dawn?"

He made another little speech, as incomprehensible as his last, and bowed a few more times, pointing frequently back towards his ship. This exchange of courtesies went on for several minutes.

At last he left us, having apparently satisfied his sense of the proprieties and made sure of his hundred silver pieces, and, as the sun sank into the western sea, Kephalos and I were left with nothing to consult except our own inclinations.

It is astonishing how well one can make oneself understood with only fifty words and enough coins in one's purse to assure an audience for them. Within a quarter of an hour we had purchased new garments, more in keeping with our position as wealthy travelers than the rags in which we had arrived. The old woman who sold them to us, and who seemed to understand that the men of all nations ultimately wish to spend their riches on the same things, kindly directed us to a wineshop in the next street, indicating with a really astonishing vocabulary of gestures the delights we could expect to find there. She did not deceive us, for upon our arrival, and by the simple expedient of Kephalos' holding up a pair of gold shekels for the proprietor's scrutiny, we were shown into an upstairs chamber, provided with hot water for bathing, also with food, wine, and an ample choice of naked women to minister to our comforts—and these in a such a variety of shapes, ages and colors as to appeal to almost every possible taste. To avoid any impression of either bravado or effeminate weakness, we settled on three.

"Ahhh," sighed the worthy physician, lying on a clean mat after he had cheered himself with hot food and an excess of wine. "My Lord, never forget that drunkenness is the first blessing of civilization, for it murders shame and allows one to enjoy without embarrassment having one's limbs scrubbed clean by pretty women. Look at this one, will you? She has hardly more fuzz on her cleft than you could find on a ripe peach. Do you suppose she could be a maid?"

"I doubt it, not unless she found employment here this morning."

"Are you a maid?" he continued, addressing the girl now, quite as if he had not heard me. "It would be a great inconvenience if you were, My Delight. Perhaps we should just see . . ."

The girl, a pretty little creature, slight as a boy, with laughing black eyes and skin the color of wood smoke, giggled as he slid his hand in between her thighs—doubtless she had had this highly diverting trick played on her before.

"No, Lord, you were quite right. She is still tight, but most definitely not a maid. I think, unless of course you fancy her for yourself, I will entertain myself with this one, since a man must begin somewhere. She will make such a change after the Lady Hjadkir."

"I wish you every joy of her, since I see she prefers you mightily."

"Ah, the wise child. Come, my little dark flower."

Kephalos sat up and then, with his arm over the girl's narrow shoulders, rose to his feet and staggered off behind a screen with her. Within a few moments I could hear laughter and then the moans of feigned passion and then, at last, the gentle sound of snoring. It seemed probable he would both begin and end with just this one.

But there had been no Lady Hjadkir to make demands of my strength, and I had not spent my seed in many months. Of the two remaining women—and I decided there was nothing that forced me to a choice between them—one was pale-skinned with small, firm breasts and eyes like a cat, and the other, who had by this time brought me to a fine hardness by the gentle, dexterous employment of her tongue, was possessed of a belly as burnished and smooth as the outside of a copper cooking pot. I went into her first, requiring but two or three quick thrusts to achieve my climax. After a few minutes' rest and a cup of wine I climbed between the other's thighs and, if the flush that came into her face and throat were any indication, managed to please her as well as myself before going as limp as water.

Yet if I imagined I would be allowed to cease there, I was mistaken. The lady with the copper-colored belly was not to be cheated out of what she took to be her fair share of my attentions and, with much trouble and skill, contrived at last to return me to some show of vigor. I labored over her for possibly as long as half an hour, at the end of which we were both covered in sweat and my manhood felt as if it had been tied in a knot.

I do not think I had been asleep more than a few hours when Kephalos woke me by pulling on my foot. We were alone. He had paid off the women and sent them away. The only light was from an oil lamp resting on the floor.

"How long until dawn, do you think?" I asked, simply to prove to myself that I had truly come awake. Kephalos shook his head.

"Not long I think, Lord. I hear people moving about on the streets, which in a seaport town means that the ships are being made ready. Perhaps two hours, but no more."

"Two hours is an eternity. Time enough, at least, to get drunk again, if nothing more."

We laughed at this and—the god be blessed for his mercy—found after a short search that there was indeed one last jar of wine that had survived with its seal intact.

"Do you think this one is a maid?" I asked, and we laughed once more as Kephalos broke through the clay stopper with the hilt of his knife. The first gray light of morning found us fuddled as owls, our arms over each other's shoulders to keep from falling as we walked toward the docks, singing the Greek version of an obscene song about a harlot and her soldier lover I had first heard when a boy in the Nineveh barracks.

The *Jinnah* was waiting for us, and with it the world beyond.

Even after the lapse of so many years, it gives me pleasure to recall that first sea journey aboard the *Jinnah*. Yet I will not dwell on what, at the time, seemed the supreme adventure, since all which gave it such novelty for me is so monotonously familiar to every Greek born within sight of the curling, wine-dark waves, that my grandchildren and their children after them will think their aged sire who wrote this chronicle of his life must have been a tedious old fool to have found excitement in memories of the smell of the salt wind and the sun's dance upon the water. So I will let it all pass and content myself with stating that our voyage was without incident and carried us within a month and a half to the city of Cana in the kingdom of Hadramaut, one of several nations that divide among themselves the southern coast of the land called Arabia.

From Cana we traveled with a spice caravan to Maudi in the kingdom of Saba. These caravans of Arabia have been wearing away the stones over the same tracks of desert for a thousand years. The paths they follow were laid down by necessity, for to the north is the Rub' al-Khali, the "Place of Emptiness," a waste of sand and rock at once vast and unforgiving, where no man wanders long if he hopes to live. Even in time of war there is truce along the caravan routes, since all depend on them and no one can do battle at once against both man and the desert.

The journey from Cana to Maudi was some hundred and twenty *beru* long and lasted for thirty-two days, the heat being such that men and camels rested from an hour before noon until three hours after, leaving only seven or eight good hours for the march. The Arabs would not travel at night for fear of demons, called—like Lord Ishmahel's ship—*jinnah*. It did not seem an empty fear, for the land was such as evil spirits might love.

Kephalos and I walked, as did the caravan drivers, who saved the camels for beasts of burden. At least, we walked for the first few days. Finally Kephalos, whose mode of life had not prepared him against such hardships, could go on no more, so when we met another caravan traveling in the opposite direction he purchased two of their camels and we attempted to ride these.

It was an interesting experience. A camel's hump, padded out with blankets, is not an uncomfortable place, but the animals walk in such a way that one is pitched about as if one were aboard a small boat in a storm. One can, I suppose, become accustomed to it, but I soon decided that I preferred to walk. Kephalos, whose knees would no longer support him and whose feet were raw with broken blisters, had not that option. He merely hung on as best he could, green in the face, so sick he was unable even to eat until we had stopped each night. Never have I seen a man so wretched. The caravan drivers could not be persuaded to halt for a few days, and in this they were probably wise—the desert makes little enough provision for human weakness—but the thought did sometimes cross my mind that Kephalos might find his *simtu* out there.

In Saba I was warned that if we traveled to Egypt, the wisest course was to go with a caravan up the spice trail north to the Hebrew city of Gaza, where we could take a ship to the mouth of the Nile and then south to Memphis. The water route up the Red Sea—so they called it—to the Egyptian city of Myos Hormos was hazardous because of storms and also the presence of pirates, renegade Arabs and Egyptians who honored no law but that of their own cruel purposes. I conveyed this advice to Kephalos, who received it without enthusiasm.

"It is a fearful thing to risk drowning or murder," he said, clutching a wine jar to his bosom as he sat on a corner of his bed—it was perhaps time for us to leave, for the alternating spells of privation and luxury imposed by our journey through the Arab lands seemed to be having a bad effect on him. "Yet these are merely risks. I feel morally certain that another such trek as we have experienced would mean my death, and no very pleasant one at that. Camels and I share a mortal antipathy for one another. I have only to be in their presence and I grow quite sick and doubtless they feel the same, for you will recall how last time that great gray brute tried to bite off my ear. If you wish to kill me, then by all means let us go by land, for you are my master and I obey you in all things; but consulting only my own pleasure, I would prefer to have my throat cut by a pirate, since it would at least be quicker."

The ship on which we booked passage was called the *Bootah*, which means "duck," and carried a cargo wrapped in bales of wool—I never knew what it was. She was a small craft, some thirty paces from end to end, and did not inspire confidence. This impression was increased as soon as we left port, when master and crew assembled on deck to sever a goat's jugular vein with a sword, drain the blood into the water, and then throw both sword and goat overboard. Almost at once the sea on that side appeared to boil , and I could see quite clearly that a school of fishes, some of them as long as a man, were swarming over the carcass, tearing it to pieces as the red stain spread out in the water. Kephalos watched for only a moment and then retreated to his cabin.

"Sharks," the master told me, grinning as if my servant's distress amused him. "They can smell blood—it puts them into a frenzy. See? That goat is nothing but fragments now, but they will churn about in the bloody water for another hour. Now that her children are fed, the sea will give us fair passage to Myos Hormos."

But she did not, and ours was an unlucky voyage. Two days out of port we were becalmed—the wind simply vanished; we could not even catch the land breezes to stir our sails. Our ship floated in the water like a basking turtle, and there was nothing for us to do except to lie about on her decks and watch the sun. This last for six days.

And then, as suddenly as it had disappeared, the winds returned. We sailed up along the western coast, sometimes coming within sight of men with glistening black bodies in boats made from hollow logs, fishermen paddling through the surf, but for the most part our journey was past shorelines that looked as if their sands had never known the impress of a human foot.

"Is that Egypt?" I asked.

"No, that is not Egypt. That is nothing." The sailor shook his head, as if the sight of the blank, dun-colored bluffs made him sad. "Egypt, though, is not much different—such of Egypt as can be looked at from the sea. Egypt is the Nile River, and a strip of green on either bank no wider than a man could walk across in two hours. The rest is desert, just like that."

"And the port of Myos Hormos?"

"An oasis, of sorts. A few date palms, a well with fresh water, a scattering of mud buildings. Then the road through the desert to Keus on the Nile. I traveled it once when our ship foundered. The Nile is a sweet place. A man could stay by her banks all his life and die content."

So passed eight long, pleasant days, each followed by a night of sleeping under the winking stars, listening to the water as it lapped against the wooden hull.

On the ninth, even while the morning air was still gray and full of sleep, the wind began to rise in a steady moan, as if lamenting the world's old age.

"A storm, the first of the season—and early by half a month!" The captain seemed delighted, although I think his excitement had its source in something else. "Have no fear, however. We will let it carry us, and the sea is wide here. It will blow itself out before it runs us aground."

They ran up their sails and the wind bore us east, away from the shores of Egypt—for we had reached Egypt by then—out into the empty sea. The sky never lightened, so that for two days we seemed trapped in perpetual night, and no man slept or rested while we bailed the deck and tried to keep the ship straight and running with the wind.

I had no idea where we might be, for the sun was always hidden, and Kephalos, who alternately execrated his gods and begged them for mercy, did not care where he was but only where he could have been had we taken the spice trail like decent men who cared for their lives.

"I am a coward and a weakling and have been all my life—this is your fault, Lord, for listening to my entreaties, and may it be a just punishment for you that we shall both drown like cats. One who was almost a king should have known better than to hearken to the snivelings of a bondsman."

But we did not drown. At last the storm blew itself out, just as the master had said it would, and we found ourselves once more becalmed within sight of land.

When the sun set that night it set over the land, which was thus west of us. Yet the land was not Egypt, for the fierce wind had carried us east, away from Egypt, for two days and two nights.

The master, when approached on the subject, expressed himself with surprising hostility, as one might who feels himself hedged about by enemies.

"It is a wedge of rock," he said, "jutting out into the sea, pushing itself between Egypt and Arabia. It is empty. It has no name. Not even the *jinnah* would consent to live there."

It was just such, as I would discover for myself.

For the sea was not as empty as the land. The next morning we sighted a ship and I watched how all hands cursed heaven and prayed for wind, as if the storm were on them again, more terrible than before. Suddenly I understood everything.

The ship was long and narrow, sleek as a fish, and painted black. It ran without a sail but was propelled by oarsmen, which over short distances gave it the advantages of speed and also maneuverability in these shallow, calm waters. I had seen such ships, called galleys, manned by the Urartians upon the Shaking Sea—they were warships, not merchant-men. This was a pirate craft.

Glancing down at the water, I saw a black fin cut the surface like a knife through fine linen. Could they smell the blood already? I wondered.

The master issued his crew with weapons, short swords, almost like daggers, and pikes with copper points to repel boarders, but I could see by the way they handled them that these were not men much practiced in the use of arms. He gave swords to Kephalos and me as well, but Kephalos instantly let his fall to the wooden deck, as if its touch had burned his hand.

"I am no soldier," he shouted, panic-stricken. "I have no skill with weapons. Does the fool think I will encourage them to cut my throat?"

And he was right. We were but eight men—two passengers, the master, and a crew of five—and even at this distance I could count at least fifteen oars on either side of the pirate ship, dipping into the water and then rising up again, as regular as the pulse in a man's veins. To resist was to invite death.

"The poor wretches who man those benches are slaves," the master stated in a calm voice as he reached over to pick up the sword Kephalos had let drop. "Men taken from plundered ships, chained to an oar and forced to pull it until their lungs begin to bleed and they are thrown to the sharks. Each must do as he thinks best, but I for one would prefer having my throat cut here and now to such a lingering death."

Yes. This too was no less than the truth. And the master was a brave man thus to stare it in the face.

We had nothing to do except to wait. The pirate ship came ever closer—in an hour, no more, it would be upon us. There was not a breath of wind, so nothing except the faint tidal currents moved us and these dragged us ever closer to shore, where we were sure to founder. The sun glared down upon us like the god's burning eye, and we could only stand silently in its light and hope to die like men.

The pirate ship had archers crouched in her prow, and these let fly at us with arrows dipped in burning pitch. Two sailors were killed in the first volley and the rigging caught fire. In the second, the captain was hit in the belly so that he screamed like a devil. I did not blame him, for I would have done the same. Three men dead and the sail blazing like a torch. It seemed enough—perhaps they were shorthanded on their rowing benches and looked to take us alive. They did not loose their arrows upon us again.

We waited by the ship's rail, my former slave and I, while the three sailors who were left scrambled to pull the sail down and get it over the side—it seemed to burn as quickly as if it had been woven of straw, and tattered fragments, winking like fireflies, drifted in the stale, still air. This would be our last chance for a word. It was time to say good-bye.

"I am in debt to you for my life, Kephalos, more times than I can number, and there is nothing you can do for me. You are no fighter, and they will gut you in the first rush—or spare you for a time, a short time, to pull an oar. When I tell you to, jump. Swim for shore. I will hold them here while I can. If you reach the land, you may have a chance."

"The water is full of sharks, Lord! By the gods, have you not seen them? I feel their teeth in my flesh already! Kill me yourself if you must, but—"

For the first time in all the years we had been together, I struck Kephalos. Hard, full in the face. He was so surprised he forget even to be afraid.

"Do not be such a coward as to open your arms to death, fool! If your belly is ripped open by a shark or by a sword, mine or another's, it comes to the same thing. When I tell you, jump."

There were tears in his eyes. He looked so bewildered I knew not what he would do, but I owed him this one chance. Even if he did not choose to take it.

I turned away from him, for the pirate ship was closing on us fast. I went to join the sailors and found them arguing among themselves over the wisdom of surrender. It seemed to be two against one in favor.

"The worst life is better than the best death," one of them said, even as he threw his sword in the water.

Another, a narrow-shouldered man with pale eyes, said "yes, yes" several times. He seemed excited almost to the pitch of madness.

"Perhaps they will let us join them, but in any case a slave always lives in hope of escape."

"Escape to where? To that?"

This, followed by a gesture toward the shore, full of contempt and hopelessness—what had I done but to condemn Kephalos to a slow death by drought and hunger?

"There is only the desert, the sea, the pirates—or death," he went on. It was the sailor who had spoken of Egypt, where a man might die content. "I choose death. It comes to the same."

"Then choose death. Now!"

The pale-eyed man stabbed him, pushing his point in under the rib cage. His victim cried out and clutched at the sword that pierced his belly, so that his hands were cut through to the bone when the pale-eyed man pulled it loose. Thus he died.

Why? I wondered. Perhaps he did not even know himself. Men do strange and bitter things when fear seizes them.

I too was afraid, and suddenly full of rage. The pale-eyed man turned to me—the gods alone will ever know what was in his heart—and I raised my arm and struck, so that my blade bit halfway through his neck and he fell at my feet, twitching wildly and spraying blood everywhere.

Good. Let him die, I thought. I have done him a service.

The other man, the last of the crew still alive, his sword at the bottom of the sea, fled from me with a cry.

The pirate craft raised its oars, slowing so that when its prow struck us obliquely there was only a faint shudder. I seemed to be alone in the middle of the ship, holding a bloodstained sword in my hand. I could see the pirates standing along the rail, their arms folded across their chests, almost as if our ship were deserted and harmless, waiting for the grappling hooks to draw us together. A few of them watched me, and grinned.

"Jump, Kephalos!" I shouted, not looking behind me. "Jump—now!"

The pirates were almost ready to board, so I turned my eyes and my swordpoint to them. Perhaps twenty men prepared to leap across from ship to ship. Behind me, I heard some object strike the deck with a heavy, muffled thump and then, surprisingly a loud splash.

He had done it, after all. That was something at least. Now I could try to purchase him a few moments' grace so that no one would impale him with a spear as he floundered clear of the ship.

I glanced back and saw what had made that thump. Kephalos' purse lay beside the rail. He had abandoned it, fearing perhaps that its weight would sink him. It gave me an idea.

A few steps and I had it in my hand. Yes—it was heavy enough to carry a man to the bottom like a stone. There were pirates on the deck now and two or three of them thought to rush me, but I slid the point of my sword through the purse strings and swung it out over the side. These thieves understood well enough, and stopped.

"There is enough gold in here to make ten men rich all the days of their lives," I shouted in Arabic—who could know what tongue such as these would speak? "A step, a move, and it goes to the fishes. Stay back!"

What could they do? I had only to let the sword slip from my fingers and the gold was lost in the sea. A pirate should, I thought, be a great respecter of gold. Let them consider the matter carefully.

There was silence. I could hear splashing in the water behind me— Kephalos was making good his escape. A few minutes and he would be safe from these. The sharks might kill him, or the nameless desert that stretched back from the shore, but not these. I waited.

"Your life, Lord—for the gold, we give you your life."

Did they think I was so foolish as that? I laughed at them—I was not even afraid. Strangely, a man on the point of death hardly ever is.

The splashing faded. Good. I would keep my implied contract, even if they did not. They could have the gold, and I would show them how Tiglath Ashur, Son of Sennacherib, could die.

I swung my arm around that they faced the point of my sword. With a twitch, I cut the strings and Kephalos' purse fell to the deck. The pirates jumped back, as if I had attacked them.

"Now—come," I said, quietly, between my teeth. "See how many will make the journey to death with me."

The war cry broke from my lips of its own will. I charged the knot of men that stood closest to me, cutting at them as if they were a stand of wheat. One I caught on the arm, and the bright blood poured from his wound. The rest stumbled back, astonished—afraid.

I laughed. The laughter boiled inside of me at these women, who feared death—I . . .

Something happened. I felt a shock—no pain at first, just a shock, as if the earth beneath my feet had all at once shuddered with dread. Nothing more.

And then the pain came, welling up behind my eyes. I felt suddenly as if I were made of iron. I sagged under the weight of my own body. The light failed—sunset, as the air turned red as blood.

And then blackness. More than blackness—emptiness. I was falling through the empty black air. And then . . .

Nothing.

VIII

"I STILL THINK WE SHOULD KILL HIM—NOW, WHILE HE IS quiet. He is dangerous. He fights like an animal."

"You are only cross because he opened you up. Why waste such a man? With those shoulders he will do very well on the oar benches. He might last a year, this one."

It was not this, but the sound of screaming that brought me to myself.

I cannot say precisely how long I was unconscious, but it could not have been more than a few minutes. I awoke with my face against the deck, my head feeling as if it had been split open. Everything hurt. I did not want to move. My left eye remained resolutely shut, sealed up like the door of a crypt, and I felt little enough inclination to force it open. What would there have been to look at? There was a taste in my mouth as if some small furred creature had crawled inside to die.

Gradually, as I lay there, as still as a corpse, I became aware that something warm and sticky was trickling over my ear. It was probably blood, I thought. Probably it had crusted over my eye and that was why I couldn't open it.

"Look at the mark on his palm!"

Someone had hold of my right arm. He was pulling back my fingers as if displaying the claws of a dead lion. I wished he would leave me in peace.

"Yes. That makes a difference."

And always, somewhere in the background, there were the screams. Who was screaming? And what were they talking about, these men? Yet it seemed too much trouble to find out. All I wanted was to lie there quietly and think about the pain in my head.

And then I felt myself being pulled over onto my back. It hurt such that I thought I would be sick.

"Throw some water in his face—get him on his feet."

The water was a blessing. It shocked me back to life, and as I rubbed my face I discovered that my left eye was now willing to open. There was a deep cut in the scalp over my ear and the salt made it burn, but even this had the effect to reducing the pain in my head to something like normal dimensions.

Getting to my feet was another matter. My captors tried and I tried, but it was hopeless. My knees simply would not lock. Finally we all settled for my sitting up and supporting my head in my hands.

A wave of nausea passed through me and I started to cough. At last I spat up a black clot of something, about the diameter of a copper shekel, after which I felt better.

It was then that I was able to observe where all the screaming had been coming from—the pirates were amusing themselves. They had tied one end of a rope around the surviving sailor's waist and the other end to our ship's mast. The game was to kick him into the sea, where the sharks could get at him, which had probably been attracted to the spot by the smell of blood, since the deck was clear of corpses. After a few minutes the pirates would pull him out again, give him a few minutes to rest on the deck and contemplate how much flesh was missing, and then throw him back. It seemed they had repeated this process several times already because the poor creature had grown remarkably tattered, with great pieces pulled loose from his legs, particularly his right thigh, and one foot completely gone, so that the deck was stained red with his blood and he hardly seemed to know what was happening to him anymore. He might even have been dead already.

I watched with no particular emotion. I did not even feel pity. Why should I have? In a short time I would probably be taking my own turn at the end of that rope.

"We do that to the ones who don't fight," one of the pirates said, crouching beside me and showing me a smile full of yellowed, broken teeth. He had a long scar that ran from his right temple straight down into his beard, as if someone had tried to hack him open with a mattock. "The ones without enough spirit even to fight aren't worth the trouble of sparing. Generally they don't last a month on the benches. You, on the other hand . . ."

"That mark on your palm—where did you get it?"

Another, the one who had rolled me over, grasped my wrist and held my hand up before my face, as if he imagined I had never seen it before.

"I was born with it," I said, wondering what difference it could possibly make.

"He is no good to us then," he said. "Some god has put his mark on him, whether for a curse or a blessing no man can tell. But it is wise to be prudent. It is a pity."

This respecter of prudence and of the gods was remarkably thin, with glittering black eyes and a face pitted over by the ravages of some disease. His beard consisted of no more than a few irregularly scattered tufts of hair growing at peculiar angles. In all he made an unpleasant impression, so that I had little confidence in his mercy.

"Then let us throw him overboard," suggested my friend with the scar. "Perhaps the sharks will get him or, if he lives, the desert; yet either way his god must hold us blameless of his death. That is the best way—give him an empty waterskin that he does not sink at once, then let the sea have him."

This idea met with such approval that it was immediately put into execution. I found myself being picked up by the arms and legs and carried to the railing, where I was pitched over like the dead goat that had been sacrificed at Mauza. I could hear the pirates' laughter behind me even before I hit the sea.

The waterskin struck me between the shoulder blades as soon as I came back to the surface and I turned over and grabbed it, clutching it to my breast with strengthless arms that I might not slip back under and drown. They laughed still—I saw them, standing at the ship's rail above me, watching the sport—but I paid them no heed. They were not important now, for I had remembered that I wanted to live.

A few seconds to catch my breath and I kicked out awkwardly, trying to swim. The shore seemed far away, part of some other world, out of reach forever. I kicked again, and again, but without any sensation of moving. Again I tried, attempting to sustain the effort, and when I stopped to rest I found I had moved at least out from beneath the ship's shadow—perhaps it was merely that the current had carried me a little. I let myself drift and then tried again. By degrees it became easier.

It was fear of the sharks that drove me, even more than the fear of death. I did not want to be rent to pieces, to end as a few torn fragments floating in a cloud of blood until the sea disbursed me to nothing. It seemed horrible beyond imagining to die thus, unburied even by the thoughtless, wind-blown dust. If I could make the land I would stretch out my bones there with an easy mind, though my ghost might wander over this barren place forever.

Yet even fear has its limits, and when I grew weary enough not even the sharks frightened me.

At last, as I floated helplessly, my arms stretched across the waterskin, which had just air in it enough to keep my face above the surface of the water, a single black fin approached from the left, wandering this way and that, as if it could not decide about me, yet coming ever closer.

All I felt was annoyance. What am I to do about this? I wondered. The shark rose a little in the water, so that its back was visible, and very tentatively approached.

"Where shall I bite you?" it seemed to be asking. "On the belly or along the ribs? Shall I take your arm?"

The creature was so slow, almost leisurely, that I actually felt insulted. At last it began to swim straight for me, turning a little on his side as it drew close. In a passion as much anger as fear, I lashed out, striking the thing on the point of its snout with the back of my fist. It stopped abruptly, turned straight about, and carved a deep trench in the water as it sped away.

"Lord Ashur, my protector," I whispered, "hold me in the hollow of your hand that my life may be spared. Forgive me that ever I turned my back on you."

Perhaps my prayer was answered, for I saw no more sharks. Perhaps all the rest were sated on the corpses of the *Bootah*'s crew, yet whatever the reason I did not meet with another.

Still, my strength had failed me at last. I could only drift, waiting until I lost consciousness and the sea took me. It was like being dead already—there was no fear, no . . .

Then, suddenly, I heard a great commotion somewhere nearby. There was the sound of splashing, as if the water were being torn apart, and then I felt a pair of arms about my waist.

"Master—bless the gods that you live still!"

It was Kephalos' voice. Somehow, it was Kephalos, pulling me to shore. All at once my heart swelled within me, so much that I wanted to weep.

Kephalos has told me how, even as he dragged me to shore, I could not be persuaded to let go of the waterskin. It was well, for we discovered that, though swollen with air, it still contained three or four cups of water, enough to wash the salt from our throats and give us hope of life for that day at least.

"How did you make it to land?" I asked him, when rest and a few sips of water had returned me to myself. "I half expected you to drown, or for the sharks to make a meal of you."

We were sitting on the sandy beach, just under a bluff that provided a few handspans of shade. Kephalos picked up a pebble and threw it contemptuously at the hissing sea foam.

"As I seem continuously to be reminding you, Lord, I am a Greek, and an island Greek in the bargain. Even as a child I could swim like a porpoise and, although it has been many years since I have exerted myself in that way, fear is a wonderful stimulus to effort. If any sharks thought to pursue me, no doubt they were left far behind. That cut on your head is a nasty business, but fortunately the seawater has washed it clean. I wish I had something with which to stitch it closed."

"I am pleased enough simply to be alive. I will not tell you what happened, knowing such stories are but little to your taste."

"Please do not—by the gods, look! They are burning the ship!"

And so they were. We could see the smoke and, at last, pulling out from behind it, the pirate craft.

"They must have all that they want of her," I said, with some bitterness. One grows attached to a ship, as to a woman, and it was not pleasant to see this one abused thus.

We watched for a long time. We watched the pirates disappear over the horizon as the hull of the abandoned *Bootah*, trapped now in the tidal currents, floundered helplessly. It was a mournful sight.

After perhaps half an hour, the smoke thinned almost to nothing. The fire, it seemed, had burned itself out.

Yet the hull was still intact above the waterline. An idea was beginning to form in my brain.

"The currents will carry her ever closer to the shore," I said, suddenly filled with wild hope. "She must run aground somewhere, and then perhaps we can swim out to her."

"Lord, recall what you yourself have said," Kephalos answered, clearly not enthusiastic about the idea. "The pirates have doubtless already taken everything of value. And, lest you have forgotten, there are still the sharks."

"There may be much aboard of no value to the pirates but of use to us. She has a shallow draft, as I recall her master complaining while the storm carried us. Doubtless she will hang up somewhere close to shore.

Besides, alone in this wasteland, with no water nor means of sustenance, what other chance have we?"

He was forced to agree that in our present helpless circumstances, with nothing between us and death but a few mouthfuls of stale water, we had little enough to lose by indulging this whim of mine. Thus we followed the ruined *Bootah* all that day and even into the night, for there was a full moon and we could see her very clearly. Towards dawn it became clear that she had stopped drifting.

We waited until the tide had gone out, thus saving us a few score paces of swimming and grounding the ship all the firmer on whatever sandbar held her, and then started out for her. We found it was possible to wade much of the distance, for she was in water not much deeper than the height of a man. Kephalos was the first to reach her. He clambered aboard easily enough, for she was heeled over so that her deck on that side was only a few cubits higher than the waves.

Kephalos helped me aboard and we looked about us. The ship was a forlorn sight, with her mast charred and her rigging burned away—her deck was scorched in places, but one had the impression the fire had never really taken hold. Part of the rope from which the last sailor had made a feast for the sharks was still tied to her railings, but hacked through with a sword when, presumably, the game had at last ceased to be amusing.

A stranger, seeing her like this, might have wondered what disaster had overtaken the *Bootah*. We knew.

"Let us not tarry here overlong," Kephalos said. "She may pull loose when the tide changes."

It was very good advice, and we made haste.

And we were lucky. The cargo, whatever it had been, was gone, but my javelin was still where I had left it, leaning against the wall of our cabin—I cannot imagine why the pirates did not take it, since it had a fine copper tip, except that perhaps it was not a weapon of much value to sailors. I also found a sword, with the blade badly hacked, which perhaps they had left behind for a better one, and several knives. There was a little dried meat to which the sea had done no harm and, most important, four skins of sweet water. Of these we took two, the limit of what we could carry, and started back for shore. Once there, we made a good breakfast of the meat. It left us feeling like different men.

"I lament having abandoned my purse," Kephalos said at last. "I feared it might sink me—were I a braver man I might have had more faith in my own powers and we would not now be beggars."

I had no choice but to laugh, remembering the use I had made of his gold, but I thought it prudent not to share the joke.

"On what would you spend it here?" I asked instead. Kephalos looked about him and nodded.

"My Lord is wise. Besides, if we live to reach Egypt we will be rich beyond the dreams of greed."

"True. Let us hope that thought sustains us through what lies ahead, for we have but a few days' supply of water and know only that Egypt lies somewhere to the north and west of us—how far, and what stands between, the gods keep hidden. By all means let us remember that we will be rich men in Egypt."

"My Lord Tiglath has an unfortunate way with the truth. Let us also remember that yesterday we expected by this time to be corpses. By the gods, what an adventure! Never again in my life will I speak ill of a camel."

"My Lord Kephalos is wise."

We both laughed, for it is impossible to lose hope entirely while one's belly is full.

"Perhaps we should follow the seacoast," he suggested, when we were disposed once more to consider serious matters.

I shook my head.

"No. If this sea is anything like a river, its banks will have more coilings than a snake. What might be only fifty *beru* in a straight march can be made a hundred if one follows the wanderings of water. We will choose our direction and stay with that, until we either find our way out of this place or die in it."

"Again I could wish that my Lord would learn to soften his expressions, but I see there is something in what you say. Tomorrow, when we have recovered somewhat from our ordeal . . ."

"Today, while there is still food in our guts. Rise, Worthy Physician, for every hour we linger here is an hour closer to death. You see those mountains behind us? I intend that we should be on the other side before the light fails—come!"

And he did, although not willingly, for the mountains to which we now turned our faces were as ragged and barren as any the gods ever made, as if hacked out of naked rock only the hour before.

Did anything live in this place? Could we? One had the sense of being an unwelcome stranger, an intruder between the sun and the land that burned in its embrace like a woman made numbly wretched through surfeit of her lover's passion. The wind seemed to carry her fitful, half-mad moan. Beyond was only hostile silence.

When traveling long distances by foot, it is best to set a slow, steady pace and to stop for nothing. Neither hunger nor thirst, nor blisters nor the sheer weariness of the flesh—nothing. Perhaps, if we could have managed thus, we might have crossed the mountains in a single day, but it was not possible. First because Kephalos was still not hardened to such journeys and found, particularly since our path led constantly uphill, that he had to stop and rest every few hours, and second because the heat along those rock-strewn trails was like nothing either of us had ever experienced. I am forced to confess that when Kephalos sat down in the shade of some overhang, there to rub his legs and complain that the god must surely have been in a black humor when he made this place, which men would not even honor with a name, I was happy enough to sit down beside him and listen.

In fact, as we discovered, for the first two or three hours after noon the sun was simply more than a man could bear, so when the night dropped like a curtain at the end of that first day we found we were no farther than about six good hours from the sea and so were forced to spend the night only a few hundred paces down from the summit of the first pass, where the winds were bitterly cold.

Yet what I remember most vividly from that night—and all the nights to follow while we wandered through that bitter, lifeless landscape—was the moon, vast and beautiful, that seemed to bathe the whole world in its chill white light. Save for the strange shadows it threw across the twisted rock of those mountain trails, changing the face of every object, making a strange and haunted place of ground over which your feet had passed but a few hours before, you might have imagined the day was no different from the night, that nothing held you where you rested, that the path lay open before you. Probably more than one traveler in this desert had perished of imagining thus, and had ended at the bottom of some ravine with his head smashed.

The moon was sovereign in that land, more even than the sun—or so it seemed to me in the ghostly night. The Great God Sin, I fancied, must love this place that he pours down his light thus. And thus it became, for me, the Place of the God Sin, and thus I named it in my private heart, calling it Sinai after the usages of my own tongue. And thus, one day, through the strange turnings of fate, would all men come to know it—Sinai—the land of the moon's god.

It took us four full days to cross the mountains, and by then our water was nearly exhausted and so were we, for the cold had hardly allowed us any sleep. Beyond the mountains we discovered only a great plain, a place of limestone and sand that seemed to stretch on endlessly without relief or variation. It seemed the end of hope.

"It is now nearly sunset," I said, when we were within an hour's walk of this plain. "I suggest we go straight on until the heat of the day tomorrow, for in a land as featureless as this the moon gives enough light to see by without fear of falling and I would as soon walk and stay warm as let the cold harden my sleepless limbs. Also, we will use less water if we travel by night."

"Ah, Master, you make of my life a misery and a bitterness. What is amiss with you that you have no fear of demons, which all pious men know haunt the night as their special time?"

I glanced at him and saw that the tears had started already in his eyes—yet I did not think he wept for fear. I thought, in fact, that he gulled me with his talk of demons, trying to turn me aside from my purpose.

"I am more afraid of death than of demons. Remember, Kephalos, this is a land which shows little mercy to weakness."

"Yes, I concede it, Lord—it is an admirable plan," he said, sighing with resignation. "Except that I am so weary one foot will hardly consent to go before the other. But two hours of rest, I beg you—then it shall be as you see fit."

To this I consented, and then we set out across the great plain of the Wilderness of Sin—a place I was to know again, many years later, but then that was hidden from me. The moon lighted our way and the stars guided us, and we walked from darkness to first light, when we rested one hour only, and then until the noon stood in the center of the bright sky.

There was no shade, so we took off our tunics and covered our heads and backs with them, sitting on the hard-packed limestone dust in nothing but our loincloths, the nearly empty waterskins stretched across our knees. I was weary enough, but Kephalos was a spent man.

"These will run dry before the day is gone," he said miserably, laying his hands flat over his waterskin. "By tomorrow, probably, in this heat, we will be dead."

"Do not take so dismal a view of it, my friend. By tomorrow it may be we will only wish we were dead."

It was a weak enough jest, and certainly one I should have kept to myself. Kephalos hardly even seemed to hear—and then, all at once, his breast began to heave with great sobs.

"I wish it already." He lowered his head to his arms, and his shoulders shook under the weight of this terrible grief. "Were I dead, and the birds had picked the flesh from my bones—if there be birds in this wilderness—then my misery would have found its end."

I could not answer. What could I have said, since most probably he was correct and both of us would be corpses within a day or two? I felt helpless and ashamed. There was nothing I could do except put my arm around him for comfort and wait until his fit of despair should pass off.

And at last it did. He was calm once more, as if resigned. We rested for two hours and then stood up, took a swallow of water each, resumed our tunics, and started out again on our journey to death.

It was perhaps an hour later when I noticed an odd shape against the horizon, like a rain cloud hovering just above the ground.

"Do you see that?" I asked. Kephalos shaded his eyes with his hand and peered in the direction I indicated.

"What?" he replied, as if annoyed. "What is there to see?"

"I can't be sure."

I lied, for I did not wish to say what was in my mind. We walked on. We stopped again, and looked again. This time I knew that we both treasured the same hope, yet we did not speak it. Half an hour later we could see it quite clearly.

It was a clump of palm trees.

"Dates," Kephalos whispered, with profound reverence. "If there be dates . . . We have not eaten in two days and more."

"A tree cannot grow without water," I said. My heart seemed to be melting in my breast. "I would settle for that."

We did not reach it for nearly two hours, and there were no dates. But there was water.

"This is fine," Kephalos sighed, bathing his face in the warm, stagnant pool that fed the trees. "This is luxury. Now if a man could be spared but a single morsel of food . . ."

But there was no food to be had. There were not even any animal tracks around the muddy banks of the water hole, so we refilled our skins and set out again as soon as the sun was down.

Several hours later, in the darkest part of the night, we halted again, stretching out on the dusty earth and falling asleep as if in our own beds. There was no wind, and the ground kept the sun's heat, and we were weary. I have never slept so well as I did during those brief rest stops in the Wilderness of Sin.

Perhaps an hour before sunrise I was awakened by a most peculiar sound—a sound familiar enough to all save those who have spent their lives in cities, but one I never expected to hear in this desert. I did not even recognize it at first. It was the throaty cooing of birds.

I lay quiet, listening. I could not believe it. Then, as the gray dawn broke, I saw them—quail, hundreds of them, wandering about on the sand, searching for food.

I sat up, expecting them to take wing in alarm, but they did not. A few of the closest scurried away, but the rest seemed to ignore me. They had probably been migrating from one watering place to another and exhaustion had forced them down—that was why they did not fly. Like us, they were starving.

"Kephalos, wake up." I put an arm across his chest and covered his mouth with my other hand, lest he start awake. "Wake up. Your prayers have been answered."

As soon as he had grasped the situation we stripped off our tunics and, after weighting down the sleeves and hems by knotting them around small stones, used them as nets to catch the helpless quail. With every throw we would capture two or three, then wring their necks and try again. Even in this extremity, the birds could hardly summon the strength to run more than a few paces, and it was a simple enough matter to keep them from scattering too widely. Before we were finished we had some fifty of them.

Kephalos, resourceful man, took pieces of flint and iron from a small leather pouch he carried by a string about his neck. We had merely to skin and gut the birds, gather enough dry brush for a fire, and roast as many as we could eat—together, we managed about thirty. Their flesh was full of oil and very good, but I think we were hungry enough to have eaten discarded sandal leather with relish. When we were sated, we roasted those that were left until the carcasses were quite dry and hard. These we put in a sack made by pulling off one of the sleeves of my tunic and knotting both ends. They would last us for three or four days at least.

"A wise man could live forever off the bounty of this paradise," Kephalos said, as we set out again. "There is food and there is water, and one learns the vanity of luxurious pleasure. I fancy I will be much improved, both in body and spirit, for having made this journey—always assuming we do not perish before we find the next oasis."

We laughed at this for, with food and water to last even a few days, we imagined ourselves invulnerable to death, as if we had won a victory over this Wilderness of Sin and held it as our private garden, even if, finally, it did conquer us. Thus wonderful is the folly of man.

Yet we had not the place quite as much to ourselves as we imagined, for it was the very next day that we encountered the golden-haired giant.

The morning sun had already risen high when, after climbing over a long line of sharp-edged boulders that crossed the desert like a scar that had been left to heal of itself, we looked down and saw what could only have been described as the site of a small battle. On the plain below us were scattered the bodies of some five men, their swords lying uselessly nearby, and near as many camels. Some of the camels were still alive, and screaming in their death agony, but the men were corpses, split and bleeding, hacked open from shoulder to crotch. They made a messy sight.

The battle, it appeared, had been fought to something like a draw, for a few hundred paces farther off, still mounted on their camels, rode three more men who wore the dress of the nomads I had seen in Arabia's Place of Emptiness, pacing nervously back and forth as if uncertain what to do next.

And in the center of the plain, squatting in the sand to catch his breath, holding in his hands a monstrous double-bladed ax, rested the obvious author of this carnage, the most enormous man I have ever seen.

"Wait here while I see what this is about," I said. Kephalos obeyed willingly enough, and I proceeded down the rock-strewn slope to level ground.

At first this giant's gaze never left the ground in front of him. He seemed not to notice as I approached, as if too weary to care, or too lost in his own musings. His bare arms, for the coat he wore had no sleeves, were as thick as another man's legs and streaked with blood from wounds there had been no time to see to. Then, when I was still some distance from him, his eyes snapped up and he rose to his feet. He raised the ax, held like a wand, and scowled his defiance. I thought my last moment might be upon me.

As I am taller than most in the Land of Ashur, by so much was this one taller than I. But his great size was not merely a matter of height, for his chest and shoulders, even his neck, were thick with heavy muscles that showed quite clearly beneath the skin. Never, it seemed to me, had there been a mortal man with such huge hands. He might have made three men, and had the strength of ten.

His hair grew long and was swept back and, like his beard, was precisely the color of wheat, so that it resembled the mane of a lion. His eyes, shining narrowly in his strong, tanned face, were blue, and with them he watched me, not moving, silent.

This wild giant was such an arresting sight it was several seconds before I realized that, stretched out on the ground behind him, was the corpse of another man, clearly not one of his nomad antagonists. The dead man's arms were folded over his breast, as if for burial, and he was dressed in a rich tunic of blues, reds and yellows, made after the Tyrian fashion. He might have been a wealthy merchant, although I do not think he came from Tyre—he too had wheat-colored hair, although resembling his companion in nothing else, and the men of Tyre are dark.

The names and conditions of these two men, and how they had come to be in his place, were a mystery, and a mystery they have remained to this hour.

My intrusion, for some reason, seemed to embolden the men on their camels. While I was still some distance from the giant and his dead companion, one of the nomads broke away from his comrades and began to ride toward me, first at a walking pace, as if to test my reaction, and then, as I stopped and waited to see what he would do, gradually faster.

When he drew his long, curved sword he made his intentions plain enough. I was the easier victim, a man on foot, armed with nothing but what might have looked to him like a walking stick—my sword, hardly a cubit long, could count for nothing—so he would try his luck with me. It was so pathetic a mistake that I could almost have pitied him.

I allowed him to come well within range, then dropped back with my right foot, raised my javelin, and let fly. It arched and fell, like a bird of prey, and caught him full in the belly so that he slid from his camel with his hands still tangled in the reins. He took little enough time pouring his blood out onto the thirsty ground, and then he was dead.

I ran over and pulled my javelin from his guts. Had I been a bit quicker in my wits I might have caught the camel, which would have been worth something, but it bolted and ran before I could come near.

That was all the dead man's friends needed to see. They turned and rode away, leaving the field to me and the silent colossus who had watched it all with cold, measuring eyes. I approached him now, feeling no more confident of my reception.

When we were some fifteen or twenty paces apart, I stopped—it was as close as I cared to venture. I pointed to the corpse of the man behind him.

"Was this your master?" I asked, first in Arabic and then in Aramaic, and at last in Akkadian. In no case did my question elicit any response.

Barring Sumerian, which in any case would hardly have served, I knew only one other tongue, so I asked once more, this time in Greek: "Was this your master?"

To my intense astonishment, the narrow blue eyes flickered in recognition, and he put his left hand on his chest and bowed.

"Then you are from the western lands," I said, merely stating the obvious.

The giant once more silently indicated his assent.

"What has brought you so far from your home?"

My question was answered by a gesture toward the dead man—this, it seemed, was judged sufficient.

"Can't you speak, or do you not choose to?"

But I might have saved myself the trouble of inquiring. He merely continued to look at me, as if I were no more a living thing than the very stones.

"Then we shall leave you now. I bid you good fortune."

I gestured to Kephalos, who made a wide circle around us, and we continued on our way. I tried to dismiss this strange adventure from my mind. A few hours later, Kephalos touched my arm.

"Look, Lord—see what he has done!"

I turned around, and back in the distance were visible the smoke and flames of a great fire.

"The giant savage seems to be burning the corpse of his master," he went on. "He must have spent all this time collecting the dry brush to do it."

We watched for a while, and I confess I found the sight inexplicably moving. I did not understand why, but I felt as if I had discovered something about myself.

It was Kephalos who suggested the probable origins of so strange a being. That night, while we halted to rest for a few hours, I told him everything that had happened.

"And you say you spoke to him in Greek, Lord?"

"Yes, in Greek. I tried all the other languages at my command, and Greek was the only one which would serve."

"Oh—well then." Kephalos leaned forward, planting his hands upon his thighs as if to consider the matter. "It follows he must be a Macedonian."

"What race, then, are these Macedonians?" I asked. "Do they have a land to call home, or are they wanderers like the Scythians?"

"No, they have a land, Master. It is to the north of the main Greek peninsula. Good farming country in the mountains, I am told, but an inhospitable climate with bad winters—that, you know, will mark the character of a people."

Kephalos' eyes wandered about in the moonlit darkness, as if wondering who might be listening.

"They are a primitive nation, the Macedonians," he went on. "They have a king, who calls himself lord of all, but each tribe has its own king as well and men owe their first loyalty to him, who lives among them and can claim a blood tie. I would hazard the guess that this one was a fairly typical specimen, although certainly on a larger scale. The people there tend to hardiness.

"He did not strike me as a congenial companion, so I am just as pleased we have seen the last of him."

But Kephalos was mistaken. The next day, even as we searched for a place to hide from the noontime sun, we crossed a ridge and, looking back, saw that a lone rider was following us. I did not have to guess who it might be.

That night we took turns keeping watch—I half expected him to come down on us in the darkness, and the memory of that ax did not make me anxious for such a visit. But he did not come. The next day, an hour or so past noon, we again caught a glimpse of him, less than a *beru* behind us. I decided we had played this game long enough.

"We will stop here, and we shall await his pleasure. Whatever he wants of us, let us find it out sooner rather than later."

Within an hour, he came into sight. I took my javelin and stuck the copper point into the ground.

"If he comes in peace, all is well," I said. "But if he feels himself somehow offended, then he will learn that, big as he is, he too can die."

At last the great golden giant was close enough that we could hear the sound his camel's padded hooves made against the dusty ground. He dismounted, tied the reins around the head of his mighty ax, and left his camel tethered thus while he came on foot.

We stood facing one another. His face showed nothing and he did not speak. Then, suddenly, he knelt before me, and I understood.

"You would follow us, then?"

He shook his head. Finally he pressed the fingertips of his right hand against my breast, and his eyes held their own question.

"You would follow me, then?"

I had my answer, without a word spoken.

"Then so be it," I said, gesturing for him to rise. "Have you a name? By what do men call you?"

He shook his head once more.

He is like the great beast man in the legend, I thought. "The locks of his hair sprouted like grain, and all who saw him were numb with fear, for he was mighty." He is like the companion of great Gilgamesh.

"Yes—Enkidu," I said out loud. "You must be called something, and that is as fine a name as any."

And if ever destiny showed itself in a name, it did in that one, for, while I was no hero of legend, Enkidu, whose voice no man ever heard, followed me through many adventures in many strange lands and was my friend and my preserver to the very hour of his death.

We were many more days in the Wilderness of Sin, time enough to form some more definite impression of this strange colossus who now answered readily enough to a name from legend. It became apparent that he was no less quick in his wits than other men, for all that he could not or would not utter a syllable. Yet there was no denying that he was set apart, not only by his silence and his great size and strength, but by an almost feral apprehension—not the slightest sound nor the most distant object escaped him. If there was a spring of fresh water about, he would find it. If the dead earth held anything that might sustain life, he knew where to look for it. Once when we were close to starving he discovered a riverbed, dry perhaps for years, and cut a hole in the stone-hard mud. From this he pulled a nest of snakes that fed us for two days. He understood all the arts of survival. In this he was like the wild beasts. One might have supposed he had lived his whole life out of sight of plowed fields and the dwellings of men. I will always believe that without him we should soon have perished in that terrible waste.

He was, so far as I was ever able to determine, a being empty of carnal passions, tenacious of life yet utterly without fear of death. The fixed and ruling principle of his character seemed to be loyalty, and that as absolute as the god's own purposes. I never knew the tie by which he was bound to the man whose corpse we found him defending that day in the Wilderness of Sin, nor do I know why he then chose to transfer his ceaseless vigilance to me—perhaps it was nothing more than that I was the first to happen by and to show myself not an enemy—but after that it never wavered.

And best of all, Enkidu had put us in possession of a camel.

"It is a pretty creature, is it not?" Kephalos asked, grinning. "I will keep my vow, and you will never hear me speaking ill of this or any of its race. My Lord, I think now we may flourish."

And flourish we did, for a camel places a comfortable distance between a man and his own death, and that was the only conception of prosperity the desert allows a man to hold. When our own water ran out, we could force a stick down the beast's throat and make it disgorge that which it kept stored in its belly—rank and nasty stuff, but still drinkable even after five or six days. We had recourse to this extremity before we finally escaped from the Wilderness of Sin.

Beyond the main plateau there were first ravines, vast, deep and empty, some of which obliged us to follow their course for many hours before we discovered a crossing, and then there were mountain ranges, one before the other, like waves upon a troubled sea. These were many times so sheer that we had to look for passes, and more than once we found ourselves confronted with a blank wall of stone, or a chasm the bottom of which was hidden in darkness, or some other obstacle that forced us to retrace our steps and search again. We were ten more days, resting infrequently, eating and drinking little, and traveling as much as possible by night, before we saw another sign of human presence.

And then, suddenly, there it was, no more than one long day's march ahead of us: a tiny settlement of stone buildings beside an oasis. Even at such a distance, we could just make out the shapes of men walking about in that calm, random way that implies carelessness of danger. They appeared to us very little less than gods.

Really, it was only then that our many days of suffering seemed to weigh on us, and I remember wondering if my legs could possibly be made to carry me all the way to this distant paradise. My strength seemed to drain away at the mere sight of it.

That final day was the hardest. Yet at the end we were rewarded with fresh water and the sound of a strange human voice—and a sight of the most extreme human misery. We had arrived at a copper mine, manned by slaves and run by a small contingent of Egyptian soldiers, a group of whom watched us silently as we stopped beside the oasis' water hole.

Finally one of them approached and addressed a question to us in a tongue I had never heard before. I answered him, first in Arabic and then in Aramaic, with which, as it turned out, he had a halting familiarity.

"Have you any food?" I asked.

"Yes, and wine too. Have you the means to pay for them?"

"Yes—trade goods. You will not find yourself poorer for your hospitality to us. What is this place?"

"The oasis at Inpey, a bad place."

"I have seen some that were worse."

He regarded me for a moment through narrow, inquisitive eyes, as if he did not believe me. He was a dark-skinned man who looked as if he was accustomed to shaving his face and scalp but had neglected to do so for four or five days. His face was pinched and suspicious and carried a few scars which, from his general appearance, I would guess he had acquired in tavern brawls. He was wearing what must once have been a uniform of some sort. I did not like him very well.

"Who are you?" he asked finally. "Where have you come from?"

"We are travelers, shipwrecked by pirates," I answered, not really expecting to be believed. "That was five and twenty days ago, I think, but perhaps I have lost count."

"You have been five and twenty days in the desert?"

"So it seems."

He laughed at this. It was not a pleasant laugh.

"Then you have done well to stay alive. Men have died out there in three. Pay me first, and I will bring you wine and bread and the flesh of a goose killed only yesterday."

Among the items for which the nomads had murdered Enkidu's former master was a silver cup, well worked and weighing not less than ten shekels. I gave it to our host.

"We will stay here a few days," I said, "until we are replenished and fit to go on. This should compensate you for our support until then. What is the way to Egypt from here?"

"North, to the fortress at Tufa. Beyond that is a port where ships stop before entering the Duck's Foot. They will take you anywhere upriver you wish to go."

"What is this Duck's Foot?"

He laughed again, as if I must be a fool not to know.

"The many legs of Mother Nile—they spread wide before the sea tickles her, for she is an old harlot."

"Thank you. Now, if it pleases you, we would eat and drink."

The wine was watered, and the whole jug would not have cost two copper pieces in Nineveh. The bread was plentiful but stale. The goose had died of old age long before yesterday. Yet we were more than content and thought ourselves very well provided for. Such is the effect of deprivation.

That evening, when we had rested and washed our sunburned limbs, delighting in the coolness and the abundance of water, the slaves began filing out of a stone hut built over the opening of the mine where they had labored all day. A long chain shackled them together at the wrist, but this precaution seemed unnecessary. I have never seen men in a more abject state—starved and listless, their skins grown pale as limestone from months of working underground, far from the sun's sacred light. They walked, hardly troubling to lift their feet, but they seemed less alive than the dust caked onto their legs.

"What have they done to be punished so?" I asked.

"They are criminals," was the answer. "They have angered Pharaoh and must be punished for it. A year in this place will finish any man, so they will not suffer long. No need to pity them."

They had angered Pharaoh—the name the Egyptians give their king, whom they believe to be a god. In the Land of Ashur only prisoners of war and traitors would have been punished thus, but in Egypt a farmer can anger Pharaoh by not being able to pay his taxes in a year of bad harvests. A poor man who runs afoul of a priest can end his life in the mines. I understood what the soldier had meant when he called this 'a bad place.' In a few days, when our strength had come back, we were glad to leave.

"The fortress at Tufa is but two days from here. The trail is well marked, and there is water."

"Will we be received kindly there?"

"That is between you and the commander. You will have to offer him a substantial bribe, for he has many officers under him with whom he will be obliged to share it. Otherwise, he will decide you are up to some mischief and feed you to the vultures."

"Leave this commander to your servant," Kephalos said to me, as soon as we were on our way north. "I understand such men better than you. All will be well."

Traveling at night, we set a better pace than, apparently, the Egyptians did, so we arrived at Tufa midway through the morning of the second day. The fortress walls were made of sandstone, no more than three times the height of a man, and enclosed an area anyone might walk around in an hour. I guessed that the garrison was probably two hundred strong and that they did not live in much dread of attack—we were within half a *beru* of the gates before a rider came out to challenge us. As he escorted us inside, I saw that the walls were hung with corpses left dangling head-down from ropes tied round their ankles. It was not an encouraging sight.

"Leave all to me," Kephalos said. "Stay behind with the Macedonian and do not let him kill anyone. I will speak for us all."

So Enkidu and I waited on the parade ground, under the bright sun, surrounded by soldiers who perhaps were merely curious but looked as if they were anticipating the pleasure of hanging us over the wall with their other trophies.

It was an hour before Kephalos returned.

"The commander does not believe that we could have crossed the desert from the Red Sea," he said, quite calmly, as if relating a trifle. "He affects to believe we are spies, yet he is willing to lay aside his suspicions since I have written a letter under my own seal to a business acquaintance of mine, one Prodikos, a merchant of the city of Naukratis, who will come here to vouch for us—bringing with him two talents of gold, which will speak to the commander far louder than Prodikos ever could. The commander is a practical man and realizes that no spy has such a sum at his disposal."

"And this Prodikos, you are sure he will come?"

"He will if he is still alive, and he was two years ago when I deposited many more than two talents of gold with him. If he is dead, then the commander will have us killed, but the journey is at least ten days in each direction and we are thus safe enough for a while. The commander will treat us well, for two talents of gold is more than he could have hoped to see in his whole life—he finds great merit in having been born the son of a scribe attached to the royal granary, so his notions of wealth are modest enough."

And it was true that while we awaited the arrival of Prodikos we were not on the footing of prisoners but were treated with the courtesy which is normally extended to diplomatic hostages. Since there was nowhere within two days' journey to which we could have escaped, we were left unguarded and enjoyed the liberty of the fortress. After the Wilderness of Sin, it was an agreeable enough place.

For the first few days there, I had the curious sense of having ended one life to be born into another. I had evaded death so many times since my flight from Nineveh that I started to entertain the hope that the Lady Ereshkigal, Mistress of the Dark Realm, had at last forfeited her claim to me and that I might now begin once more, as someone else. Tiglath Ashur, son of Sennacherib—the world I was about to enter knew nothing of him. I could be as other men in that world. I could begin to think myself safe.

Thus do I bear witness to my own folly, for there is no greater fool than he who assumes that the gods have grown blind to him.

The fortress at Tufa afforded little in the way of amusement. One day I reached such a pitch of boredom as actually to be driven to playing the old soldier and inspecting the fortifications. Like the spy the commander pretended to believe me, I measured the height and thickness of the walls, climbed into the watchtowers to see how well they covered the surrounding area, and satisfied myself as to the water supply and the size and location of the storehouses. In short, I learned all that would be needful to me to know should I ever command an army laying siege to this place.

But a siege appeared to be the last thing the garrison at Tufa expected. Indeed, at this outpost of the mighty Kingdom of Egypt, a land of wealth and power, fabled for a thousand years as the mighty sovereign of the west, the dry rot of inactivity had taken such firm hold that the men there seemed almost to have forgotten they were ever meant to be warriors.

I had seen such garrisons before—indeed, I had once commanded one, at Amat, among the northern mountains in the Land of Ashur— places on the borders of empire where men are sent as a punishment, men whom no officer wants in his command. All the same symptoms were present at Tufa: the slovenly uniforms, the parade grounds littered with refuse, the watch details who spent their time gambling. I did not inquire, but it would not have surprised me to learn that harlots lived and plied their trade in the barracks and that every month one or two men were killed quarreling over them. It was a disorderly place, full of monotony and festering hostilities, where the soldiers, trapped by long enlistments and no hope of transfer, forget they can have any enemies except each other.

Such was the garrison at Tufa, guardian of the eastern approaches to Egypt. Given ten days, I decided, five hundred good men could crack it open like a pea pod—and this took no account of the fact that it was garrisoned by Egyptians, who did not seem a race very gifted as soldiers.

Their talents seemed rather to lie in cruelty, an impression formed at the oasis at Inpey and confirmed here at Tufa. Even the men of Ashur, whom all the world feared, would not have thought to adorn their own city walls with the corpses of their victims, and yet on my tour of the fortress perimeter I counted no less than fifteen hanging from the walls, some quite fresh and some rotted almost to skeletons.

Who were they? I wondered. And what crimes had they committed to be punished thus? Perhaps some had been thieves or murderers or spies, or perhaps this was how the Egyptians punished serious breaches of discipline among their soldiers. One or two wore the tatters of what might once have been uniforms, but the rest gave no clues to their identity.

Save one. Hanging from the northeast corner of the fortress wall was the body of a man who, from his general condition, looked as if he had been dead no more than a month. There was a wind that day to carry off the stink of putrefaction, so I had no hesitation in venturing quite close—one will take an interest in anything if there is little enough else to do. I had a good look at him. It was difficult to tell for certain, but he might have been fairly young when he died. His head was shaved, like an Egyptian or, perhaps, one of my own countrymen who has taken a vow of atonement to some god.

On his left hand, the last finger was missing.

IX

IN MY DREAM THERE HAD BEEN FIVE. FIVE EAGLES SWOOP-
ing down for the kill. But now three were dead, and I was still alive. That
left but two. Where were they waiting for me?

I now understood the vanity of imagining I could escape this. The
dream would assume flesh and find me out—it did not matter where I hid
myself.

This time I made no inquiries. I spoke of it to no one. The corpse
hanging from the fortress wall at Tufa would remain that of a nameless
traveler executed for an obscure crime, or perhaps merely because he was
suspected. There was nothing the Egyptians could tell me I did not know
already.

I tried to turn my mind into other paths.

Fifteen days later a supply train arrived from the coast, and with it
traveled Prodikos, merchant of Naukratis, carrying with him several
leather purses filled with gold and silver coins, a cedar chest containing
new garments of the most elegant linen, a large basket of fruit preserved
in honey, a calf just weaned for fresh meat, and two vast jars of the finest
Lebanese wine.

This Prodikos, though he shaved his head and face and dressed after
the Egyptian fashion, even to painting his eyelids, was a Greek, born in
the City of Megara, who as a young man had settled in one of the Greek
colonies in the "Duck's Foot"—which he called the Delta of the
Nile—and there made his fortune in the dye trade between Egypt and
Phoenician cities of Tyre and Sidon. Although very fat and much
troubled with the gout, he was an active man with a happy temperament,
a lover of money and luxury, and, in his youth at least, a great traveler

who had been west as far as Carthage and east to Meskineh on the upper reaches of the Euphrates. They had never met, being known to each other only through business correspondence, but he and Kephalos fell in together at once, as if they had been intimate since childhood.

"The dealings I have entered into on behalf of Master Kephalos and yourself have prospered exceedingly," he told me at dinner that first night, when he had grown a little drunk and thus was disposed most generously to let that intimacy embrace me as well. "So much so that the few talents of gold you will distribute among the soldiers here, that they may buy their way out of Pharaoh's army and set up with a wife and a hundred *plethra* of muddy land and thus consider themselves rich men, are as nothing. You will be like a great noble, living in a palace with fine gardens, with slaves beyond numbering and pretty, fair-skinned women for your bed.

"Only follow the advice I give you as if you were my own son and always study to keep yourself clear of the intrigues of these Egyptians. Sleep with their wives if it amuses you and let Master Kephalos tease them out of their money, for they are a light people, without morals or wisdom. Live only for your own amusement and you will die an old man full of pleasant memories. But do not meddle with their priests or interfere with their statecraft, for these are troubled times along the Mighty Nile and not all the crocodiles are in the river."

"Then perhaps I should make my home in one of the Greek settlements of the Delta."

"No, My Lord, for you would find it a constraining existence. The merchants who abide in a foreign land may hoard up great wealth, but they live modestly lest they excite the envy of their neighbors. Such is not for you, who was born to another way. Were I a young man, with such wealth and liberty as blesses you, I would dwell in Memphis, which is perhaps the greatest city in the world and contains all that can bring joy to the heart of youth. There will be little enough to hold you when you tire of the place, but every man should taste of Memphis while the appetite for pleasure still abides in him. Visit Memphis and gorge on it. Afterwards, have a good vomit to purge your bowels of such follies and then continue on with the rest of your life."

"Very well then, Master Prodikos, it shall be as you say."

And so it was. Kephalos saw to bribing the garrison commander and even distributed small sums of money to the common soldiers, in case any man should feel himself ill-used through our having escaped execution as spies—a fugitive from a powerful king, he argued, must take elaborate precautions.

When the supply train set out on its return journey, we accompanied it, arriving three days later by the shores of the Northern Sea, which the Greeks call merely "the Sea," as if there were no other. From there we took ship to the second mouth of the Nile and then upriver to Naukratis, altogether a journey of some eight days.

We traveled under sail, since the winds blew quite steadily from the sea and the river seemed to have almost no current. At that time, at least, I cannot claim to have been much impressed with the Mighty Nile, which was narrower in its banks than the Tigris and slower than the Euphrates is even in midwinter. I had to remind myself that this was only one of many branchings and that to be fair I would have to reserve judgment until we broke out of the Delta and encountered the main river on our passage up to Memphis.

Still, it was pleasant enough to stand in the prow of our little ship, which was carrying wool from Joppa, and to watch the countryside floating by. Egypt seemed a rich land, a land of date palms and thick green fields, a land of sunshine and water. I remembered the words of the Arab sailor, who had said a man might live all his life here and die content.

Yet even here there were indications that we had not left the world's cruelty behind us. Crocodiles, sunning themselves on the riverbanks, were a common sight. An envoy of Pharaoh, knowing my father to have a taste for all manner of freaks and curiosities, had once presented him with one, its belly stuffed with straw and red glass in its eye sockets. As a child I had marveled at its beautiful scales and its cruel teeth, shuddering to imagine there could be such a creature in the world. And that one had been no longer than a man's arm, while these, basking along the shoreline of black mud, looked as big as the reed canoes from which the fishermen threw their weighted nets. Once I saw an ox, which must somehow have gotten loose, wandering into the water up to its belly. The crocodiles, which seem to be cunning brutes, came in behind it, cutting it off from the bank, and within a few minutes there was nothing left but a red stain on the water.

"Not all the crocodiles are in the river," Prodikos had said.

Naukratis, where we arrived in the middle of the afternoon, was a busy mud-brick town, very hot and swarming with flies. Our ship tied up barely long enough to let us off and then was on its way south again, as if there could be nothing in such a place to hold it.

Yet, as my travels among the Arabs had taught me, the outward signs of wealth are not everywhere the same as at my father's court in Nineveh, and it was obvious that vast quantities of money changed hands along this crowded harbor, where cedarwood, bales of cloth, crates and wicker baskets of every size—and containing the gods and their owners only knew what treasures—almost crowded one back into the river. Here there was the shouting of many voices, but loudest and most often in Greek. And every word of the tongue I had first heard from my mother's lips quavered with the excitement of unsatisfied greed, for the purses of merchants, it seemed, are never crammed quite full.

"That man has tired of life who says, 'Yes, I have enough,'" said Prodikos, smiling with pride as with his arm he made a gesture that seemed to take in the whole wharf. "Whether he seeks pleasure or land or wealth or glory in battle or knowledge of the world or simply of his own nature, no Greek is ever entirely satisfied. That is our glory and our curse, My Lord Tiglath. That is what separates us from the other races of men—as doubtless the promptings of your own heart have brought you to understand. Come, let us make our way to my poor house, where at least I can offer you a decent dinner and a comfortable bed after our journey."

And indeed it was a very decent dinner, consisting of wine from a place called Buto, reputed to possess the finest vineyards in all of Egypt, fruit, emmer cakes and pork roasted in honey—"Enjoy it while you may, My Lord," Prodikos told me, "for you will have nothing like it in Memphis. The Egyptians regard pigs as unclean and will neither eat their flesh nor allow them to be slaughtered or cooked anywhere within the walls of their cities. Fortunately the authorities do not attempt to impose such restrictions on us here in Naukratis, for a man might go slack-witted attempting to remember all the strange customs and foolish prejudices of these people. I have lived among them the best part of my life and have found it wisest not to let myself be thus inconvenienced."

Our meal was a leisurely affair. We ate reclining on couches, after the Greek fashion I had first learned in Kephalos' house in Nineveh—all except Enkidu, who crouched in a corner and, when invited to join us at the table, answered our host with a mute glare, as if he hated him. Prodikos, of course, had by then grown used to the outlandish ways of my follower and merely directed one of his serving girls, a pretty, dusty-skinned little creature with fine breasts, to provide him with food and wine in proportion to his great size.

This she did, at first with some show of reluctance, but at last, recognizing that she was in no danger and convincing herself that this great golden-haired giant was merely a man like other men, she began favoring him with becomingly timid smiles. Perhaps she took his mirthless indifference as a challenge, but in any case it was not long before Enkidu had absorbed all her attention and the rest of us were in danger of starving.

"Iuput, you lazy slut!" Prodikos shouted at last, "shall we be left to perish of thirst while you disport yourself with the Lord Tiglath's servant? Be about your duties, girl—I trust you can wait so long as the conclusion of our meal before you entice that great wad of muscle to your sleeping mat?"

The girl, with many blushes and murmured apologies, hurried to us with her wine pitcher and then rushed off to the kitchen to bring more plates of meat and fruit.

I do not believe, however, that our host could have been of a jealous temper, for that night, when I retired, I found Iuput waiting in my bed—perhaps this was her punishment, for Enkidu, as usual, slept stretched across the doorway to my room. Yet, as I had not had a woman since leaving Arabia, I did her more than justice and she seemed pleased enough with the exchange.

The next morning, at breakfast, Kephalos announced his intention of journeying on ahead to Memphis.

"There is much business which needs my attention," he said, dipping a piece of flatbread in honey. "You are now, My Lord, a man of princely wealth, and the merchants to whom you have advanced gold with such generosity must be called to account—you they will cheat, but me never. Also we must purchase a house, which I prefer to do myself, since I do not share your soldierly disdain for comfort. And then, of course, there are the household slaves to be selected and various officials to be bribed and many other matters to deal with, for which your upbringing has left you ill equipped. Remember, the Egyptians, like all men, judge from appearances. We must have a decent regard for your position as a man of substance and importance."

After Kephalos had left for Memphis, and the Greek quarter began to seem as cramped and stifling as a prison, curiosity and boredom combined to drive me out. At first cautiously, and then with the confidence of greater experience—yet always with Enkidu, like a dog that does not trust its master with his own safety, only a few paces behind—I began to venture into the Naukratis of the Egyptians, where I learned my first lessons about that land upon whose shore Shamash, Lord of Destinies, had set me down as lightly and carelessly as the sea does a piece of driftwood.

Their writing is impossible, yet a man may learn to speak the Egyptian tongue quickly enough. Within a month I had some few hundred words, although I hardly needed them. I rarely met anyone who could not stumble through a little Greek, and this, so Prodikos led me to understand, would be the case everywhere except the dustiest village—"Here they are used to doing business with us, but even in the great cities upriver, Greek is quite the fashion. Poor simple souls, it makes them feel part of the world."

Yet men may dwell together in something smaller than a world and not know it for the same place. Even this little town, built upon an island in one of the lesser channels of the River Nile, the Egyptians knew by a different name, calling it Piemro, and there they lived as separate an existence as if they had raised their houses beyond the dome of heaven.

At first I imagined I must have come among a race of women, for the men are slight and smooth-limbed and shave their faces and even their heads, preferring to wear wigs rather than their own hair. A beard, prized by all other races as the symbol of manly authority, is regarded with disgust, as both unclean in itself and a disfigurement to the beauty of the face. As a mark of rank sometimes a high official will wear a false beard, a few strands of hair glued to the chin, or perhaps only a lacquered wooden box to represent one, but even this very unwillingly. And all, men and women alike, paint around their eyes—this not only from vanity but as a sovereign protection against infections, which are common among them; yet it surprised me, since in the lands between the rivers it is a thing practiced only by harlots.

Although the weather in Naukratis was not as warm as it would have been even in Nineveh, the Egyptians of the upper classes covered themselves with few garments, for both sexes are mightily proud of their dainty bodies. The men usually wear only a short skirt of thin pleated linen, and the women frequently go about with their breasts uncovered, painting their nipples a vivid red. They decorate their arms with gold and sometimes silver bracelets—the silver, which is more highly prized, is brought in by the Greeks from Thrace and Macedonia—and their wigs, which they trim with gold, are often dyed bright blue.

Only the priests, it seemed, covered themselves from shoulder to foot, which was perhaps well done since many of them were astonishingly fat. The priests of all nations, I have observed, tend to corpulence, but nowhere more so than in Egypt. They are also arrogant and greatly hated for this and also for their greed, which is insatiable, the gods in Egypt being richer even than Pharaoh. The priests do not wear wigs, but their shaven heads glisten with oil.

Yet the priests, though hated, are powerful, and this because no people are more in awe of their gods than the Egyptians. The gods own Egypt, Pharaoh being but one among them, and no master ever held his slave in such bondage than they do the people of that land. No farmer opens his irrigation sluices without first offering sacrifice to obtain the water god Sobk's approval. The harlot prays to Mut, consort of Amun, before she visits her first customer, and the warrior promises to sprinkle the altar of Hathor with blood—unless his grandfather was a Libyan, in which case he is more likely to favor Neit. In the land of my birth, and even among the Greeks, the gods are imagined as having the shapes of men, but the Egyptians represent theirs with the heads of jackals, hawks and crocodiles, making them seem fearful and revolting creatures, which, far from being an insult, is taken as the special mark of their holiness. Yet for all this, the Egyptians seem to live on the best of terms with their gods and take a childish delight in honoring them. Every month has almost as many festivals as days, when shrines are carried through the streets of every city and village and their way is strewn with flowers. The gods dwell among men, making a paradise of the Land of Egypt, and for this reason the Egyptians regard themselves as blessed above all other peoples, both in this life and the next.

And the reason for this foolish confidence is not difficult to discover, for the chief of their gods is the great river itself, which has nourished the Egyptians and framed the terms of their lives since the foundations of the world.

The Nile is nothing like the Tigris, to whose rushing waters I had listened all my life. A man who grows up by the Tigris understands the tenuousness of his hold on existence, for the floods may come suddenly and sweep him and all he cares for into oblivion—or they may not come at all, that he dies of want. These are the facts which govern his tenure on the earth and shape his understanding of what it means to be alive. Thus in the east the river-dwelling people trust neither to the future nor to the mercy of their gods.

But the Nile is a sluggish, predictable, good-hearted river, and as a consequence the Egyptians are more cheerful and weaker than the men of Ashur. They believe that all is for their good because their river is kind to them, and thus they commit the folly of believing in the benevolence and wisdom of their gods and even of their king. Their language has no word for "fate," as does the Akkadian of the east, and they do not understand its blind and capricious power. They are like children in a world they believe filled with their own toys. It is possible to pity them, but not very much, for the gods seem to smile on their folly and have blessed them with an empty history.

Egypt is a land famous for its magicians, many of whom practice their art for the entertainment of any who might stop in the street to watch them. Once I saw an old Numidian who could cause what looked like an ordinary river reed to turn into a serpent and then back into a reed again; I tried to buy the reed from him that I might discover how the trick was done, but he would not sell it, explaining that such reeds were only to be found in the place where he had been born, which was many months' journey to the south, by a great lake which is the Nile's mother.

Thus might a man spend many hours filling his eyes with wonders and delighting his senses. During the day there was the bazaar and at night there were the brothels where every taste could be satisfied, for the harlots of that city, both in the Greek and the Egyptian quarters, are noted for their beauty no less than for their skill.

The country people of the Delta are usually willing enough to sell their daughters into slavery for a few pieces of silver, enough to pay their taxes to Pharaoh that year and perhaps leave them with a little with which to celebrate the Feast of Osiris, but the Greek brothels are forced to import their women. In every city in Egypt, yet nowhere more than in Naukratis, there is a brisk traffic in girls between the ages of perhaps eight or nine and fifteen years of age—a harlot has a short career, and a good one, like an acrobat or a musician, must begin her training early if her master is to have his profit out of her. Thus it was that Selana entered my life, while she was yet a child, before love and a woman's beauty had awakened within her.

The man who wishes to keep his illusions should stay away from the docks while the slaves are being unloaded. I had come down that day from the house of my friend Prodikos because Kephalos had written that he was expecting the arrival of several boxes of medicinal herbs from Byblos and wished me to give the galley master directions for having them sent on to him in Memphis.

The galley arrived just as the morning wind had begun to subside. Enkidu and I met it, and I showed the master, a Corinthian named

Strophios, the letter that Kephalos had written. He recognized Kephalos' seal, but the rest was a mystery until I read it aloud to him. Strophios the Corinthian listened sullenly, nodding now and then, his eyes fixed on Enkidu as if he expected mischief from the great iron ax with which my servant was scraping a blob of pitch from the bottom of his sandal.

"Yes, it is very well," he said, as if indulging me in a whim. "It shall be as the Lord Kephalos wishes and he shall have his cargo as soon as we reach Memphis, four days hence."

Having dispatched this business, I was ready to make my way back to the Greek quarter when suddenly, with even more than the usual commotion and shouting, a ship some thirty or forty paces down the wharf began to disgorge its wretched female cargo.

The girls were pale as ghosts and some of them raised a hand to fend off the sun, blinking with astonishment at the light—how many days, one wondered, had they been locked away below the decks of that cramped little ship? Wearing only filthy rags, their hair and skin streaked with dirt, an utter weariness in their faces that made them look like withered old women, although few of them could have been old enough to be fairly described as women at all, they were too defeated even to weep as they filed down the gangplank, bound together at the ankles by a length of hemp the burn marks from which they would probably bear on their flesh forever.

Yet otherwise the slave traders were careful enough of their goods— scarred faces and backs only drove down a harlot's price. In place of whips these considerate merchants used staves of polished wood, about the thickness of a man's wrist, to urge their little girls forward with blows which no doubt were painful enough but would leave no mark more permanent than a bruise.

There were perhaps twenty altogether, still only children but already impossible to imagine ever having known the love and safety of parents— or indeed any life but as slaves. Perhaps they had been born into bondage, but perhaps not. Had I not heard from my own mother's lips how a child, the daughter of a family, may be sold like a jar of oil to pay her father's debts? Slowly they assembled in a little knot on the wharf. The brothel keepers, who had been waiting since the ship's arrival, did not linger over formalities but began at once to examine teeth and to pull aside tattered garments to see if underneath there might perhaps be hidden something a man might someday want on his sleeping mat. The slave traders, however, merely stood about, leaning on their staves, as if they had lost interest in the transaction and could think only of a few nights in the taverns and then the voyage home.

"It is a bad business," Strophios murmured, as if he were afraid of being overheard. "I know not why any decent man would trade in women when there is almost as much profit in wine—after a year or so you can't clean the stink of them out of the cargo hold and the whole ship has to be burned."

I turned aside, disgusted and somehow faintly ashamed, wishing Kephalos might have seen to his own affairs and that I could have been somewhere else on this particular morning.

Fear, danger, wrath—these are things we can sometimes sense in the air, even while the settled calm of the ordinary seems still undisturbed. They are like the flash of lightning caught in the corner of one's eye just before the thunder breaks.

Thus I knew, even before I heard the shouting, that something had happened. I looked back to see. Otherwise I might never have become involved.

There had been an escape. Two of the slave traders, bellowing with anger, had started to chase after a half-naked little urchin like a pair of barking dogs after a rat. One of them, grunting with effort, took a swing at her with his stave and missed by no more than a handspan—he was in a rage now and the blow, had it found its mark, might have killed her.

They were big men and the wharf was narrow, but she was quick, a flash of bronze-colored hair dodging between her pursuers, cutting back and forth, staying just beyond their reach. Yet this could not go on. She was only a child, and there were two of them.

I could hear her naked feet slapping against the planks. It seemed the only sound in the world. One of the men began to close on her, but in the last instant her hand caught the lip of an empty oil jar and she pulled it over behind her so that it fell straight across his knees. He went down flat, like a falling tree, but it was only a brief reprieve—the other man was running her down and there was nowhere else to flee. Surely in a few seconds he would have her.

She must have known that too. A glance in my direction—our eyes met. I think I understood what she would do almost in the same moment she did herself.

Suddenly she dived at my feet, almost knocking me over. Her arms locked around my ankles, and in her gasping voice she pleaded with me for the mercy she would surely find nowhere else.

"Please, Lord—don't . . ." she panted out, as if every syllable had to be squeezed out from her breast, ". . . don't let them . . . please . . . beg you."

The words were in the wide, flat accent of the Peloponnese, but it was

Greek. She clung to me as if she would drown, hiding her face against my leg so that I could see nothing except her hair, the color of bronze new from the forge. Something stirred within me, as if a long closed door had all at once come open.

The slave trader, ignoring me, reached down to grab her by the neck, as he might have pulled her loose from a rock. I put my hand on his shoulder to stop him, but he knocked my arm aside.

After that, everything happened very quickly. In a sudden flash of anger I struck him across the face with my clenched fist—I think I must have broken his nose, because almost at once there was blood on his upper lip. He was as tall as I and broader, with the coarse strength of a laborer. I had no weapon, no way to defend myself. When he realized this he raised his stave to strike me. He could not have made a worse mistake.

The wind went out of him in a rush—Enkidu, ever watchful, had seen it all coming, and the flat side of his great ax caught the man square in the belly, taking him right off his feet, so that the next instant he was curled up on the wharf in a tight little ball of pain, trying to remember how to breathe.

The combat was finished. Enkidu strode over and put his foot on the slave trader's chest to force him over onto his back. He held him like that, the ax still in his hand. The man glared up at him in stark terror, but Enkidu's eyes were on my face.

What shall I do with him? they seemed to ask. This one, who has dared to raise his hand against you, shall I strike off his head here and now?

"Let him live," I said.

It was not what he had hoped to hear. With great reluctance, Enkidu raised his foot and allowed the slave trader to crawl out from under it. At the last he could not restrain himself from driving the rogue off with a kick that would have broken most men's ribs.

"There is still the question of my chattel, Majesty."

The master of the slave ship was a squat figure and unpleasant in his aspect. Although a Greek, he shaved his head after the Egyptian fashion, and the top of his right ear was missing. His small brown eyes looked as lifeless as if they had been painted on. He stood, just beyond Enkidu's reach, with his heavy arms folded across his chest. I hadn't even noticed his approach.

"The girl, Majesty. I purchased her in good faith and have an investment to protect. I am not in this trade for my amusement, Majesty."

The girl, whom this toadlike creature had purchased in good faith, was still huddled at my feet. I knelt down and placed my hand on her head—yes, the hair was the same color.

"Get up," I said, as gently as possible, for even as I spoke I felt her arms tighten around my ankles. "Do as I bid you. Get up."

At last she was persuaded to rise. She was trembling. She stood close enough beside me that I could feel this. She would look neither at me nor at the master, as if she trusted neither of us.

"From whom did you purchase her?" I asked. It did not matter, and I did not really care, but I needed time to consider what must be done.

"From her mother and father, Majesty—who could possibly have a better right? They were peasants from a village near Amyclae, and I paid for her in silver. I have also had the expense of feeding her this half month."

The villain was practically inviting me to buy her.

"From the look of her, you cannot have spent much on that."

This was the first time I had really noticed her appearance, and it did little enough to recommend her. She stank, for one thing—Master Strophios had been right on that point. Her cheeks were dirty and scratched and her hair looked as if nothing could ever untangle it. Her broken fingernails were encrusted with black ship's tar. And she was thin and ungainly, with hands and feet too large for her body—but she was only a child, and starved in the bargain, so no one had any right to expect she would be a beauty.

I put my hand under her chin to have a look at her face. The skin was as white as parchment from all those days in the ship's hold, but it was a strong face. She had a short, slightly tilted nose and large intelligent blue eyes and they held mine now with a certain defiance, as if she had decided that I was no better than the rest of mankind and didn't care if I knew it.

"How much did you pay for her?" I asked.

"One hundred and fifty drachmas—"

"You liar!" she shouted, pulling violently on my tunic to call my attention to such a gross untruth. "It is a cheat, Lord—neither my mother nor my father could even *count* so high as a hundred and fifty drachmas!"

"And then, Majesty," he went on, just a shade too quickly, "there has been the keeping of her, as I said, and a reasonable profit—"

"You are lying." I put my hand on the girl's shoulder, as if to establish my claim of ownership. "For one hundred and fifty drachmas I could probably buy all the children in Greece. I will give you no more than thirty silver shekels and call you a thief at the price."

The master must have thought me a great fool, for he accepted at once, and I counted out the money into his open palms.

As soon as he had left the girl took my hand in her two and, before I could stop her, bowed down to kiss the thumb in token of submission. Not wishing any repetition there on the wharf, I made a sign to Enkidu, who caught her by the wrist and dragged her along behind us as we threaded our way through the narrow alleys that led to the Greek quarter. I did not even trouble to turn around until I heard her stumble and cry out.

"My lord, please . . ."

We stopped. She picked herself up and with impressive fury kicked Enkidu in the shin, as hard as she could. If he even noticed the attack he gave no sign, but kept hold of her wrist as if she were a bag of onions.

She, however, immediately let out a howl and fell down again to the paving bricks, where she sat cradling her foot in her free arm. The tears, whether of rage or pain or both, streamed down her face—I felt sorry for her but not so sorry that I could keep from laughing, for she made a comical sight.

"It will be a good lesson for you," I said finally, when the fit had subsided a little. "Pick the targets of your wrath with greater care, for my servant is not of a disposition to be vexed by such as you. You might as well have leveled your blow against a stone idol as Enkidu."

With remarkable self-possession, she forced herself to stop weeping. She glared at me for a moment, as if she had never hated anyone so much, and then, quite suddenly, smiled as sweet a smile as I have ever beheld.

"My Lord does well to reprove me," she said in a low voice. It was clear she had already had title to a woman's cunning.

This time I did not laugh, although I was tempted.

"And there is little enough need for such wiles, child, since you are not fated to be my property any more than that repulsive brute of a slave trader's. Enkidu, release her!"

She snatched her hand away from his grasp and then stuck out her tongue at him—she was such a bold little savage that I found myself beginning to like her exceedingly, enough almost to make me regret parting from her. But, of course, there was no place in my life for a slave who was still only a child.

I opened my purse and dropped twenty shekels of silver into her lap.

"Here," I said. "Now you are rich. You own yourself, by report worth one hundred and fifty drachma, and now you have nearly half that sum entirely at your disposal. Run along. Enjoy your prosperity."

Her kness snapped together like a trap, capturing the shower of coins, but she was merely being practical. She was not at all pleased with me.

"Then why, Lord, did you buy me in the first place?"

"A whim," I answered, lying even as I told the truth, "and the fact that I had taken a dislike to your masters and did not wish to appear a fool before them. It was an expensive mistake, and you are the beneficiary. Now be off."

Yet it was I who abandoned the scene to her, for all at once I could not get away fast enough. I hurried down the street with what I cannot deny was cowardly and indecent haste, not even looking back.

The bazaar was crowded and the day hot. An hour after noon I purchased bread and wine and two skewers of cooked meat, and Enkidu and I took our midday meal under the awning of a wineshop. I had by then almost erased the morning's unpleasantness from my mind, so quick are we to forgive our own follies and weaknesses. It was not until I had finished eating that Enkidu touched me on the arm and pointed toward an alleyway across the square.

The little slave girl with the bronze-colored hair was hiding in the shadow, watching us.

"Has she been following us all day?" I asked.

Enkidu nodded. I did not inquire why he had neglected to point this out to me before, since I would have received no answer.

"She will tire of the game soon enough."

Yet in this I was mistaken, for all that afternoon I had only to turn my head to see her, stalking us like a cat after barn mice. At last, thinking to be rid of her, I visited a brothel and stayed to play at dice with the harlots even after my seed was spent. For some reason it did not occur to me how demeaning it was to hide thus from a child. I tarried until the lamps were lit, until it was night outside and it was time to return to the house of Prodikos.

I did not see her again on my way there, so I pleased myself with the reflection that probably she really had tired of the game—either that or had lost track of me in the dark.

This, however, was a vain hope, for the next morning, when I went outside, I almost tripped over her in the doorway. She was asleep, having spent the night there.

"What do you want?" I shouted at her, once I had shaken her awake. "What is it you want that you pursue me thus?"

"Why will you not accept me into your service?" She rubbed her eyes, frowning with resentment at the morning sunlight. "I could make myself of use in the kitchen, and in a year or so, when I have my growth, you can take me for a concubine—if last night proves anything, you are of a lecherous disposition."

"How old are you, child?"

"I will finish my tenth year six days after the next Festival of Maia."

"And when is that?"

"What Greek does not know the Festival of Maia?" she asked in astonishment at my stupidity.

"I am not a Greek."

"Of course you are a Greek—what else would you be except a Greek?"

"Then let me be a Greek, but one who does not know the Festival of Maia."

She shook her head, seemingly unable to grasp that such a thing could be possible.

"Are you sure?" she asked finally, her eyes narrowing with suspicion.

"When is the Festival of Maia, child? Require me to ask again and you will regret it."

"In the month of the last harvest before winter."

"So you are not even ten years old?"

"No, Lord," she answered, lowering her eyes as if it were a thing to be ashamed of.

"Then you are entirely too young to know anything about the matter. 'You can take me for a concubine'—I do not rut on children, nor am I so anxious for the supply of harlots that I will raise them up for my own use like pomegranates."

"Then what am I to do?"

"That is for you to choose. You are free—no man owns you—and I have given you silver. Leave me in peace."

"It is very well for *you*, Lord, to say 'leave me in peace,' but what of *me*?" She jumped to her feet, her blue eyes flashing, ready, I fancied, to serve my shins as even she had Enkidu's. "How am I, a child as you call me, to live in this strange country, where I know no one and do not even speak the tongue? How long do you think it will be before I am caught by one like my late master and sold into a brothel—who will know or care then that you have said no man owns me? But perhaps that will not happen. Perhaps some bold robber will cut my throat for the sake of the silver you have given me, which, unprotected as I am, is little better than a sentence of death!"

"Then perhaps it can be arranged to have you sent home to your parents," I said, sagging inwardly, conscious that I was engaged in a hopeless struggle.

"My parents! Oh, that is wise, My Lord, wise and merciful. My father and the man to whom he sold me are as alike as a pair of hands, and my mother makes a third. What am I to hope for from parents who would sell me to be a harlot—and for seventy drachmas!"

She burst into hot, angry tears, and as she stood there weeping I felt shame, for everything she had said was perfectly true. She had won, although perhaps she did not know it yet.

"What is your name, child?"

"Selana, Lord," she answered, and smiled at me through her tears. Yes, of course she knew she had won, for what man is a match for any woman—or even any girl, though she would not be ten years old until after the Festival of Maia?

X

PRODIKOS' COOK WAS FIRM THAT SHE WOULD NOT ALLOW "that filthy child" into her kitchen, not even to eat breakfast, so I purchased Selana a bowl of cooked lamb and millet from a street peddler and she ate it greedily as we walked to the public baths. I also bought her a pair of reed sandals—the first she had ever owned, as it turned out—a comb and, most important, a new tunic and loincloth, since by then even the rag merchants would have disdained her tattered Greek homespun, unchanged and unwashed during half a month in the hold of a slave ship.

I hired an elderly bath woman, charging her, as this was a desperate case, to have no mercy.

"Aye, Your Worship, you can depend on it that I shall scrub her down until she shines like a new copper pot," she answered, smiling toothlessly.

As I lay in the next room, drinking wine while a harlot rubbed oil into my back, I could hear Selana's howls of protest. The results, however, justified my severity.

"That old crone held me down and rubbed me all over with sand," she said, crouching on the tiled floor in a posture of extreme wretchedness. She was still naked and her flesh gleamed a bright pink. "My hind parts are so sore it will be days before I can even sit down again. I feel like a skinned rabbit."

"At least now no one will mistake you for a water rat. That, at any rate, is an improvement."

In her misery, which seemed to go beyond even tears, absently she pushed her fingers through her bronze-colored hair, still damp and shining now with oil so that it was quite beautiful. She was too thin—her ribs showed and her hips and shoulders seemed all bone—and her childish awkwardness had not left her, but I could see why the brothel keepers, with their eyes to the future, might have found her interesting. She had a pretty, impudent face, and childhood is a disease that cures itself.

"You are not as ugly as I thought, Selana. In a few years, when you are grown a little, perhaps you will find some man who wants you."

"Then you can make me your concubine."

"It would be better if we found you a husband—then at least I would be rid of you."

"I do not want a husband," she answered, her gaze quite steady on my face. "My mother has a husband and is every bit as miserable as she deserves to be. I would rather be your concubine, since you seem less of a villain than most men."

She could smile now, for she was as the generality of her sex—a few words of praise, even such as mine, repaid her for much discomfort. She knew she had found favor, and for the moment that was enough.

Still, I wondered, what was I to do with her? I could not decide.

But she was an intelligent child and managed to make herself useful in the house of my friend Prodikos. She served me at table and helped in the kitchen with so much willingness that the cook forgave her all past sins. Gradually, and with my hardly being conscious of it, Selana managed to install herself in my life as a fact. It seemed there was nothing left for me to decide, for she had decided it all herself.

Even Enkidu she finally won to her will.

At first she appeared frightened of him, as if it were somehow my whim to keep by me a great gray wolf, a creature that might turn savage at any moment. But Enkidu did not seem to notice; he hardly even glanced at her. In fact, she might have been the footstool in my sleeping chamber for all that he seemed conscious of her existence. Perhaps it was this very obliviousness she found so intimidating. Perhaps it amounted to no more than her anxiety lest he might absent-mindedly crush her under his heel.

But gradually, as the strangeness wore off, she stopped being quite so careful to stay out of arm's reach, and when at last she had decided that "the one who is the Lord Tiglath's shadow," as she sometimes called him, was no more than a man like any other, she knew well enough how to deal with him.

Enkidu was my servant and the guardian of my life. His loyalty he proved many times over the years, yet I never understood in what it found its root. What was I to him? I never knew, nor could I even begin to guess. Sometimes I thought it was his heart which had no voice.

Yet if he loved anyone, I suspect it was not me but Selana—not perhaps as a man loves a woman, for I never saw anything to suggest this, but as no man is so hard but that he must cherish someone. She was the object of his special protection. If I whipped her as punishment for some small sin, his mouth would harden and his eyes grow black, as if in warning that I, even I, must not carry this thing too far. No one else, I think, would have been suffered to live—the cook hardly even dared to scold her. When I would send Selana to the marketplace on some errand, Enkidu, silent as death, always accompanied her. Sometimes, if I happened to glance out a window, I would see her returning, her Macedonian watchdog walking three steps behind her and with all her parcels gathered in his huge arms.

Thus was the pattern of our domestic life when I received a letter from Kephalos, saying that all was prepared against my arrival in Memphis and that he had sent conveyance thither. I was to expect its arrival within a few days.

Yet nothing could have prepared me for the sight of Kephalos' "conveyance." The craft on which my royal fathers had journeyed down the Tigris to holy Ashur, mother of cities, was as a reed raft to this: a pleasure barge some fifty cubits long by twenty wide, with thirty rowers manning its oars and a great square sail, dyed red as fresh blood, that might have been pitched as a tent over the house of my host and friend Prodikos so that none dwelling within could know if it was day or night.

"It is a royal barge," Prodikos announced, with something like awe, when we went down to the wharf to look at it. "I have seen it before and know if for the property of the Lord Nekau, Prince of Memphis and Saïs, mightiest of the rulers of Lower Egypt, second only to Pharaoh himself in wealth and power. Master Kephalos must have impressed him deeply with tales of your greatness that he would extend such a courtesy to a stranger."

We dined on board that evening, for Kephalos, with his infallible sense of how all such matters should be managed, had equipped the barge with every luxury. There was wine in copper jars, sealed with pitch and kept cool in the mud at the bottom of the river, fruits, fresh meat, a large brazier and a cook to operate it, a pair of boys to stir the stagnant air with large ostrich-plume fans and five pretty women to play the lyre and dance and to serve at table.

We became very merry, and more than a little drunk, and Prodikos attempted to go into one of the women—a plan to which she was in no way averse but which, at last, he found he had not the vigorous force to bring to a satisfactory conclusion. Afterwards he fell asleep. It was a warm night and he slept on the bare planks of the deck, his tunic rolled up under his head for a pillow, snoring like a hippopotamus. In the morning I bid him a most fond farewell, urging him to visit me in Memphis whenever his affairs should allow it, and set out on my journey south.

We were on the water twelve days, for the wind very often failed us and the men had then nothing but their arms with which to defeat the river's feeble yet nevertheless unremitting current. At night there was no choice but to stop. During the day they would row four hours and then tie up and rest one.

One night I had too much wine with my dinner, which made me low-spirited. I kept thinking of the pain of exile, and of my own father, who lay in his tomb in holy Ashur, murdered by one of his own sons. I in my turn would wander the earth until I found a hole hidden enough to bury me in. Life seemed an empty business.

I sat in the prow of the barge, looking down into the black water. If I became drunk enough, perhaps I would topple in and the crocodiles would eat me. The idea gave me a certain pleasure.

"But you see it is not so great a thing, my son. Life is empty and death is even less."

Suddenly there he was—an old man, the streak of silver in his hair at least four fingers wide, unchanged from the last time I had seen him alive. He was sitting beside me, peering into the Nile's secret darkness, as real as any man of flesh and bone. For fear he would leave me, I had not courage enough to speak.

"The dust covers us all, and the glory of kings is a phantom. Do not burden your heart with the past, my son, but turn your thoughts from the Land of Ashur and all who dwell there. The god will summon you to him in his good time."

"The Lord Tiglath's belly is as tight with wine as a tick's with blood," came the thin, child's voice.

My father had vanished and it was Selana who knelt by my side gathering in my cup and wine jar that they might be safely out of my way. I had not even heard her approach.

"What will happen if you drink more? Will you grow wrathful and beat your women, or will you begin weeping over the sorrows of your youth, or will you merely be sick into the river and have to be carried snoring to your sleeping mat? I have seen my father do all these things, but I had not expected them from you. It seems that all men, the mighty and the low, are just alike."

"I do not choose to be reprimanded by an infant, Selana. Go find your bed and leave me in peace," I said, feeling more abandoned now than ever. Why had she come to break the spell?

"It would be better, Lord, if you found your own, where your harlots are waiting to try whether any strength remains in your loins, or if you are as empty as your bladder is full."

I turned to her with anger, but when I met her eyes, large and knowing, no more afraid of me than if I were a kitten baring its claws, my anger vanished and I began to laugh. Suddenly I felt much better, although nothing had altered. Life was still barren, but it no longer seemed to matter so very much.

"Selana," I said, when at last I had recaptured my voice, "you must tell me when the Festival of Maia comes, that six days after I may purchase you a slave of your own for a birthday present. I will find you a girl three or four years old, who can torment you as you do me."

"I still find it difficult to understand that a Greek would have to be told when comes the Festival of Maia."

She smiled, having apparently forgiven me—and why should she not, since she still retained custody of my wine jar?

"I have told you that I am not a Greek."

"A duck does not bray like a donkey. Neither do its jaws bear teeth. You look and sound Greek, therefore how can you not be Greek?"

"My mother was born in Athens, but I was born in my father's house, by the River Tigris in the Land of Ashur. It is a long way from here."

"And what does that make you?"

"An Assyrian," I said—the word sounded strange on my tongue. "As was my father, so am I."

Do not burden your heart with the past, my son, he had said—my kingly father, the Lord Sennacherib. Once ruler of the bright world.

"Yet you live among Greeks as one of them. Perhaps at last you will become a Greek. Or will you go back someday and become an Assyrian again?"

"For me, to go back is to embrace death."

She shook her head, as if she had caught me in a lie. As if to find me thus false made her sad.

"I see my Lord Tiglath chooses not to answer," she said.

Two days later, at the hour before sunset, we arrived in Memphis.

I can only assume that Kephalos had lookouts posted downriver, for he was waiting for me at the docks, surrounded by a crowd of servants who were busy strewing flower petals into the water in token of greeting.

I hardly recognized him at first, for he had shaved both his head and beard and his eyes were outlined in black paint after the Egyptian fashion. As the barge pulled up he made a low bow and shouted something, yet I could not hear him over the noise of drums.

It seemed that the barge, with all its luxury, had been but a foretaste of my reception—there could not have been less than a hundred souls assembled there on the wharf. As soon as I stepped ashore, horns let out a deafening roar as if to mark the end of the world. Kephalos, dressed like a great lord, with a heavy gold necklace pressing against his bosom, prostrated himself before me and embraced my ankles. A herald read a little address in Egyptian, so filled with archaisms and rhetorical ornaments that I could not understand one word in ten, and then I was conducted to a sedan chair, canopied with ostrich feathers and covered with hammered silver so that it hurt my eyes to look at it. When I had sat down four slave women began to wash my feet with scented water, after which we set off to another blare of horns, Kephalos himself assuming the place of one of my bearers—in a purely symbolic fashion, to be sure, by taking up a cord attached to the end of one of the carrying poles.

I was carried through the city in no less state than if I had been Pharaoh, a progress that required over an hour to complete and left me feeling extremely foolish.

"There will be a banquet tomorrow night," Kephalos said, having conducted me to a room where dinner was set out for us. "Everyone of any importance in the city will be there, including the governor himself, for, as you know, wealth attracts curiosity as quickly as spilled honey does wasps. It was from the governor, by the way, that I had the barge. I paid him almost as much as the thing must have cost to begin with, but he is in great need of money and it is always worthwhile to have friends with influence."

So Prodikos had not been far wrong. I was not in the least surprised, so perhaps Selana was right and I was becoming a Greek myself.

"Eat, My Lord," Kephalos went on, waving his hand over the table, which he had furnished with his usual opulence. "You are still lean from the desert and need to gain more flesh. If the food appears strange to you, know that the cook is an Egyptian and I can do nothing with him. They are a curious people, fastidious and prejudiced, but if we are to live among them we must accept some measure of hardship."

Yes—without doubt Kephalos was right to speak of hardship. The wine was potent and sweet and every course of the meal delicious. We were attended by eight serving women, their eyes black and smiling and their naked bodies gleaming with oil. I dwelt in a palace, surrounded by every comfort and pleasure, and I was rich. Life in Egypt surely would be an ordeal.

"By the way, Lord, you would do well to adopt this fashion," he announced, running his hand over his freshly shaved head. "It is unnatural I know, but the Egyptians will suffer no one to be different from themselves. Even a prince they think no better than a dog if he does not make himself like them. I will send a barber to you in the morning."

"As you think best, Kephalos, and while I assume one disguise, perhaps I might as well assume another. I think it will not profit me much to be a prince in this land."

"My Lord wishes to live as a private man then?" he asked, raising his eyebrows as if the idea had taken him by surprise. "Very well—this is doubtless wise, since it is close to my own thoughts. I have let it be understood that you are a rich Greek who has quarreled with his family and for this reason chooses to dwell abroad. It is only a little at variance with the truth and thus will offend no one's honor."

There was a small plate of figs in front of him. He picked one up and examined it, holding it delicately with his fingertips. Then he set it back down and seemed to forget all about it.

"You have grown cautious, Prince," he said, in an altered voice. "Has anything happened since we parted in Naukratis?"

"Nothing, my friend. I am only conscious of having enemies and wish to be prudent."

"Was it prudence, then, that prompted you to acquire the little bronze-haired slave girl?"

I had known Kephalos most of my life, and through all the shifts of fortune which had accompanied it, and yet never had I seen such an expression on his face. Was he angry or annoyed, or merely amused? I was not meant to know—I was not sure he knew himself. This was not merely my wily servant who concealed his purposes, for whom guile was as natural as breathing—I would have been familiar enough with him. He smiled, yet there was a tightness to that smile that made it like a mask. He was hidden behind it. I did not recognize him.

"It is a question who acquired whom," I answered, shrugging my shoulders as if I could dismiss the matter thus easily. "And whether she is a slave or a freedwoman is also a debatable point—I tried, believe me, to send her on her way, at liberty and with silver in her purse, but she insists she is my property and will not leave."

"Then it is even worse than I had feared." Kephalos rested his hands upon his thighs, frowning.

"Why do you attach such importance to this child? She makes herself useful and has wisdom enough to stay out of the way."

"And do you think she will always be content to 'stay out of the way'?" he asked, raising his eyes to peer into my face as if he suspected my brains had gone softer than a rotten apple. "And do you think it is the child which concerns me? She will be a woman soon enough, and perhaps, Dread Lord, you have not noticed the way she looks at you. Have not women brought enough misery into your life but that you must store them up for the future like jars of wine? Besides, do not imagine I am so naive as not to grasp why you suffer her presence near you. Has the resemblance escaped you? Hers is the most dangerous claim any woman can make on any man—you look into her face and see your mother's."

I was as surprised as if he had struck me. Why I know not, for what he said was plain enough. It was simply that I had never framed it thus to myself before.

"Alas, I am the most wretched of men, since my master is a blind fool. Had you hidden it from yourself, then?"

It had gone beyond a jest, for there was real anguish in his voice. He made a gesture of hopeless dismissal.

"This house, as you perhaps *have* noticed, is well supplied with women. I know your tastes in such matters, Lord, and have seen to it that you will find nothing wanting. A round brown belly and a pair of firm breasts—or, better yet, a proper harem full of such—will sate your appetites and leave your heart untroubled. Let me drive this child from among us before she is old enough to be more to you than merely a shadow from the past."

"This I cannot allow, Kephalos. She has a claim to my protection which I am not at liberty to ignore. Leave her as she is."

"I feared as much—it shall be as your will commands, My Lord."

He quickly turned the conversation to other things, yet a constraint remained. He drank too much wine so that his gaiety became stumbling and hectic and at last the serving women had to help him to his bed. At last I could only wonder at the source of this secret grief.

The house that Kephalos had purchased was on the outskirts of the city, some distance from the river but supplied with water by a system of irrigation canals that would have made the farmers of my native land cringe with envy. My private quarters occupied several rooms but could only be entered through two doors, one of which allowed access from the house itself—in the antechamber behind this Enkidu slept—and the other opened into a private walled garden.

The garden was a great blessing, for the house was full of women, eight of whom had no other duties but to attend upon me as servants and concubines. Women under such circumstances, when all compete for the attention of one man, become restless and, finally, something of a nuisance. By forbidding them the garden I was able to preserve my tranquility.

Whether it was willful mischief or, as he later claimed, a wholly excusable misconstruction concerning my intentions, Kephalos at first placed Selana among this private garrison of harlots. The first morning I went to wash myself I found her at the bathing pool, quite naked but with her hair most cunningly arranged and her scrawny little body gleaming with scented oil—the other women seemed to have made something of a pet of her and she appeared most satisfied with herself.

I was less pleased and drove her out with a good thrashing and the excellent advice that she had better not expect to grow up in my house as a lazy slut of a whore. I gave instructions that she should be given employment in the kitchen. A few days later I went there to see her and at first she would not even speak to me.

"Go ahead and rut on your fat Egyptian cows," she said at last, weeping hot tears of anger and mortification. "If such women amuse you, then I suppose there is nothing more to be said—if they can open their legs wide enough to receive a man they think they have mastered all the arts of pleasing. All they ever talk about is how best to remove the hair from their bodies and what shape to cut their nails. I am surprised you do not fall asleep over them out of pure boredom."

"Then do not lament so bitterly that I have taken you from among them. You are right to disdain the life of a concubine. I hope some more respectable destiny awaits you."

"I do not wish to be some dung farmer's wife!"

I left her there to master the craft of plucking quail, troubled in my mind as to what would become of her who seemed suited neither for the one life nor the other.

But if Selana was not pleased with her apprenticeship to the kitchen, at least Kephalos was. Afterwards, he seemed to have fewer difficulties reconciling himself to the new situation.

"Yes—let her clean fish," he said, with a venom which by then had almost ceased to surprise me. "Let her come to stink of poultry guts, and may her hands grow as hard as flint from scouring the floor. This once, Master, you have shown wisdom."

And then he went on to describe to me his arrangements for the forthcoming banquet.

I had been a soldier in the Land of Ashur, and that not so long since that I had not spent most of my life up to that point in the company of soldiers. My father, though a king, had also been a soldier, like most of the nobles of his court in Nineveh, and soldiers, as everyone knows, are somewhat unpolished in their amusements—garrison banquets are rowdy affairs, with much drunkenness and noise and occasional assaults upon the entertainers. Thus it may be said, and not without justice, that I was little accustomed to refined company. I must own that the society of Memphis took me by surprise.

The great banqueting hall of my new home held perhaps as many as two hundred people, and Kephalos seemed to have invited about that number of guests. In keeping with my place as host, I went around to all the couches and tables to introduce myself with a few sentences of halting Egyptian, and more often than not I found myself being answered in flawless Greek.

I had also not expected so many ladies to be present, nor for them to be so forward in their manners—many held out their hands to me, expecting to be kissed upon the palm or the inside of the wrist, a familiarity from which any respectable eastern woman would shrink with something like horror. Yet the ladies of Memphis were prepared to flirt in the most shameful ways, and this directly under the eyes of their, apparently, indifferent husbands.

"My Lord Tiglath could make us wish all our men had been born foreigners," one of them told me, punctuating the thought with a forced giggle. My own mother was no older, but no consideration of the dignity belonging to age could prevent this lady from smirking like a girl. "Such rough, strong fingers—you must sit here next to me and relate all the history of your life."

The gentleman beside her kept staring off into space as if he chose not to hear anything his wife said. I thought it wisest not to accept the invitation.

"Does the climate of our country agree with you?" another asked. "I hope it has not had a dispiriting effect." She smiled, and ran the tip of her tongue along her upper lip in a most provocative manner, such that I found myself wondering, Are all the women of Egypt harlots, lifting their skirts for any stranger who happens by?

Yet there is no denying that the presence of so many ladies has a softening effect upon men's manners. No one attempted to mount any of my serving women and, while many became drunk, they did so without riot, slipping back on their couches in quiet insensibility. Until experience taught me that the Egyptians always conducted themselves thus, I was convinced my banquet could not but have been a failure.

I cannot speak for other cities, but at least in Memphis it is not the custom that an invitation to dine binds anyone to a fixed schedule. Hospitality is a relaxed affair, and guests arrive when they will, are fed when they arrive, and then depart when it suits them. Throughout the evening I was obliged to welcome new guests, who occasionally seemed surprised that I would take the trouble. It was thus well past the fourth hour after sunset when Lord Senefru appeared at my door, accompanied by his wife, the Lady Nodjmanefer.

The Lord Senefru, who was perhaps forty years of age when I first met him, was a man of wealth and a member of a family that could trace its origins back to the first Seti, the great warrior Pharaoh of Egypt. He was also reputed to enjoy great influence with Nekau, Prince of Memphis and Saïs, although he played no formal role in government. In appearance he was tall and thin to the point of uneasiness, with large, handsome black eyes which never seemed to rest. He hardly ever smiled, and he had the look of one who takes pleasure in nothing. I had heard him called a vain man, and I could well believe it—not vain in his dress or of his possessions or style of life, although he lived like a man of rank, but eaten up with pride for his ancient lineage, his position in the world, and his own intelligence, which was of a very high order. He was also vain of his wife, who was as beautiful a woman as I had ever beheld.

I must now speak of the Lady Nodjmanefer, although even after all this time the thought of her still gives me pain. I close my eyes to see her the way she was that first evening, and I know what a fool I must have been not to have anticipated everything that happened after, for her great beauty seemed to carry with it a sense of sadness, as if she knew somehow that her life must be short and full of sorrow.

"My Lord Tiglath, I present my wife."

She was her husband's niece as well as his consort—the Egyptians have no scruples about such alliances, their kings frequently marrying their own sisters and even daughters—and I suppose she was a year or two older than twenty.

She was a sight to take the breath from under a man's ribs—if he be not dead as the earth he must be stirred by her. She was small, hardly taller than a child, yet she possessed a woman's body, with a waist I could enclose in my hands and high, round, perfect breasts. Her mother's mother, she told me once, almost as if it were a secret, had come as a bride from Lydia, which perhaps explained why Nodjmanefer so little resembled the other women of Egypt. The Egyptians are a dark race, but her skin, flawless as water, was almost the color of gold and appeared to glow from within, as if she burned—yet it did not, for her flesh was cool. Her face was what a sculptor might see in his dreams, with high cheekbones and delicate pink lips. Her eyes, almond-shaped and seeming always to catch the light, were as green as the sea.

She touched the tips of her fingers to her bosom and bowed to me, and Senefru led her away. I yet remember the smell of her perfume as it lingered in the still air.

I could not keep my eyes from her. Throughout the evening my glance would steal in her direction, but she seemed always occupied with her husband and his friends and never had a look to spare for me. The Lord Senefru and his lady stayed for a few hours and then departed. I did not have a chance to speak to them again. I never even heard the sound of her voice.

The evening was otherwise a dull affair. Kephalos had done all things admirably; everything ran smoothly and the food and wine were excellent. The musicians played well and the dancers moved their comely, well-oiled bodies in perfect time. My guests, I think, were pleased enough, but I was bored almost beyond endurance.

I walked about, holding a gold wine cup I hardly touched, listening to gossip, paying and receiving compliments, telling lies about myself and being lied to in turn. The smile on my lips seemed frozen in place, something I would eventually be obliged to have removed by force.

Nekau, Prince of Memphis and Saïs, came very late. Kephalos introduced us and we spoke for a few minutes while Nekau picked over the food on his plate as if he expected to find a scorpion concealed beneath it. He was not a large man, yet he looked fat, as if there were nothing under his skin except jelly. He seemed nervous, almost frightened, like one anticipating some vague disaster. I had the impression he was very far from being a fool. He did not stay long, but this, I was told, was the etiquette.

And at last, just before dawn, it all came to a merciful end. The last guest was carried home in his litter and the slaves set about cleaning up. I found my bed.

My women, like good slaves, were still waiting for me, and it was just as well. I felt strangely alert for one who had not slept—it was like the nervous edge I had known so often before a battle, when I knew I might be dead in the next hour but had almost ceased to care, as if fear itself had become a kind of pleasure. I felt like that.

Each profession has its wisdom, and a concubine knows when her master is close to his lust. I sat on a stool while my women sponged me with hot scented water, and one of them knelt between my knees and, covering my manhood with her lips, brought me dexterously to my full power. I went into her, rolling her over on her back like a turtle.

Afterwards I drank a cup of wine to restore myself and wondered why I had felt so little pleasure in the act. This little fever of fleshly passion was still with me, as if I had touched no woman in days. I remembered the Lady Nodjmanefer and experienced a giddiness between desire and grief—this would never do, I thought, being both unnatural and un-manly.

I retired to my pillow with a wine jar and two more of my women, thinking to burn myself to ashes. They were both glad enough to crawl to their own beds by the time I had done with them, my body washed in sweat and my groin and back aching. At last sleep closed my eyes to bitterness.

"A man has appeared in Naukratis who makes inquiries after our young friend. He seems to speak no tongue but Aramaic, so he is not one of us. I think he must come from the Eastern Lands. There is nothing to distinguish him, except that the smallest finger of his left hand is missing. What am I to tell him?"

This was contained in a letter Kephalos received from Prodikos just three days after my arrival in Memphis. It seemed so inevitable that I was almost relieved.

"How shall I instruct him?" Kephalos asked, his brow creased with worry—he knew as well as I what that missing finger meant.

"To tell the truth," I answered. "Half the Greek colony in Naukratis knows I have settled in Memphis, so someone will reveal it. I do not think this is a man to be trifled with, and I would not have Prodikos put himself at risk for my sake. I cannot hide from him, Kephalos, for it is scratched on the god's tablet that he shall find me. Let Prodikos tell him where to look that our business may be settled quickly."

"As you wish, Dread Lord, but I think you have gone mad."

He left me, shaking his head in dismay as he walked back to his own quarters. No doubt he did think me mad.

Yet it was not my intention to wait passively for a stranger to put his blade between my ribs. I would set a guard around my house. I would have the docks watched. I would discover the identity of this man who had been sent to murder me, and I would make him understand that the ground would stain as red with his blood as with mine. If he could be brought to accept reason, perhaps I might not have to kill him, but I would not shrink from it.

But for now I would put the matter from my mind, for I had other business. I too had received a letter.

"Come and dine with me tomorrow night, one hour after the sun has set." It was written in the Egyptian script; I had to show it to a scribe at the bazaar to know what it said. The papyrus was sealed with wax bearing the scarab of Lord Senefru and brought to me by one of his household slaves, who did not even wait for an answer, as if it had not crossed his mind that I might refuse.

Why should he wish to make so quick a return on my hospitality? I had only to accept to find out, and I did not even care very much. All that mattered was that I might once more fill my eyes with the Lady Nodjmanefer. That seemed reason enough to go.

Senefru lived close to the temple complex, since, like most high officials of state, he was a priest of the god Amun. His house was made of limestone and very large. A slave holding a torch met me on the stairway and conducted me through a wide central passage, past dark rooms—our footsteps echoed in that empty space—and then out to the gardens, shimmering and mysterious in the light of what seemed like hundreds of tiny oil lamps.

The slave, who had not spoken, left me there, withdrawing in silence. I was alone. My host did not come to greet me and there appeared to be no other guests. I thought it strange.

The light made a trail to the center of the garden, so I followed my eyes there. I found a few women waiting attendance, hiding discreetly in the shadows, a table spread for a feast, and, on a couch covered in gold, the Lady Nodjmanefer. She did not even smile.

"My husband will not join us," she said.

XI

IN MY ARMS SHE WEPT, WHETHER FROM PASSION OR GRIEF
or something between the two, I could not know.

My mouth wandered over hers as her pointed tongue, sweeter than
nectar, sought mine, and she whimpered with pleasure. Her lips seemed
parched of kisses. She would die if I turned from her. She would perish of
want.

The vague light of the oil lamps played across her golden body,
shadowing her beauty, making her seem not of this life and world. I was
haunted by her. As I forced my way inside her, she seemed to enter my
soul.

A man and woman, almost strangers, alone at night in a garden, know
that rapture of the senses which is the common property of all. Was it no
more than that? Yes, it was more.

"I have had many lovers," she said. "I have loved no man save
you—this moment. Now."

I believed her. It was simply not possible to doubt.

"I had imagined love as dead within me. I had thought my heart had
turned to dust. Yet I am alive now. I live under the weight of your body.
Your touch is all that quickens the breath in me."

I believe her still.

The dawn was no more than an hour away. Already the sky seemed to
shine darkly over the earth. I heard the tap, tap, tap of a dagger blade
against stone, letting me know that someone had begun to stir within the
Lord Senefru's great house. It was Enkidu. How, I wondered, had he

known to find me here? A door opened in the garden wall, letting in a few rays of feeble light. It was time to leave this place.

"I must go," I said. "I do not wish to, but I must."

Her arms tightened about my neck, but she was wise and knew she could not hold me long.

"The day is a tomb," she said. "It will hold me lifeless until you are with me again. I will close my eyes and die now."

I kissed her once more, but her lips seemed cold, as if she really were dead. I stole away from her, not daring to look back.

It was a gray morning, and a cold wind blew in from the river. Memphis, like an old woman with a chill in her bones, was waking up cross—the cries of the river porters, like a complaint to the gods, echoed up from the docks. Peddlers were setting up their stalls near the temple gates. The proprietors of wineshops and brothels swept their doorways, already glum at the prospect of a slow morning's trade. A few weary souls, looking as if the night had taught them bitter lessons, made their way home. Doubtless other eyes saw me as one of these.

Yet for me youth and passion and the hot flame of life had come back. Happiness and hope, which end being much the same, so swelled my breast that I hardly seemed able to breathe. I had found a goddess, and she had called me her beloved. It was enough to make me glad that I had escaped yet a while longer the dark oblivion of death.

When I returned to my house I found Kephalos waiting for me.

"Prodikos is dead," he announced. "I had word last night from Naukratis, in a letter from his kinsman. They found him in his warehouse eight days ago, with his throat cut. It must have happened the night before, even on the very day on which he had written to me."

He still held the letter in his hand. He held it out to me, as if offering proof of what he said, but I did not need proof. I only wondered why the man with the finger missing from his left hand should have found it necessary to kill Prodikos, who had meant no harm to anyone.

"A murdered man does not rest quietly," Kephalos went on. "I will offer millet cakes and wine to appease his ghost."

"And I would give him his murderer's blood to drink—I pray to Holy Ashur that the one who did this wickedness may be delivered into my hands."

"Be not rash, My Lord, for death follows upon the lust for vengeance, like a sore head after a night of wine. You are not to blame that Prodikos was killed."

"Am I not, Kephalos?" I smiled at him, though my liver was full of wrath. "Am I not?"

That day and the next night and the day and night after, I kept to myself. When my women attempted to come near I drove them off with curses. I would see no one. I sent no word to the Lady Nodjmanefer. I stayed in my garden, even in the dark. I ate nothing, but I drank wine, and enough that my remorse never lost its sharp edge. As a mother cradles her child, thus did I cherish this bitterness in my heart.

Some sins a man is powerless to avoid. Prodikos had been my friend—and for that he had been killed. From this pollution I could not cleanse myself.

I did not wish to. Only more blood would wash it away. I would find this murderer. I would strip him of his life, and then . . .

It seemed so simple.

At last I grew ashamed of sulking. I went into my house, slept, ate, and turned my steps toward the city. Only now, when I ventured beyond my own gates, I wore a sword.

People stared at me—they said nothing, but they stared. The Egyptians did not carry weapons. Yet had they no eyes? There was more here to make men afraid than just one assassin bent on the life of a stranger.

Smiling Memphis, clutching to her bosom a dagger of her own. City of menace. Did no one else see what I saw? Were they all blind that they walked thus among snares? Memphis, with its temples and its broad streets, as peaceful as a cobra sunning itself on a flat stone.

And one did not have to look far to search out the dangers. The docks were lined with beggars, and along the city's outskirts had grown up squalid camps filled with those whom starvation had driven in from the countryside. Memphis was crowded with misery, and misery can quickly translate into violence.

A people settle by a mighty river. She is generous and feeds them. Yet if they will grow numerous and strong, becoming a great nation in the world, they must make the river obedient to their will. This is not the work of a day or a year or even a lifetime, but of centuries. Canals must be dug, and levees erected that the waters may be controlled. A whole system of irrigation must be constructed, and all this must be maintained by ceaseless labor. And the people must put a mighty king over them to see that the labor is performed. Hence the kings of Ashur and of Babylon. Hence Pharaoh.

Yet in Egypt the canals were filling with silt, and the dikes were left unrepaired. And the people starved. And in their hearts they blamed Pharaoh for their wretchedness, for he was no longer mighty.

Or so it seemed to me, for no one said so aloud.

And today the city was crowded, because Pharaoh had arrived from Tanis, and everyone hoped for a sight of the blessed god-king.

I had wondered why the bazaars were so deserted. Soldiers had come through and closed the stalls, for it was considered sacrilege to do business on the day when Pharaoh would issue forth from his palace (Prince Nekau's house, taken over for the occasion) to be carried on his chair of state to the great temple, there to do honor to the god Ptah, patron of the city, sacred potter on whose wheel was turned the egg from which the world hatched. The street that ran between the two, guarded on both sides by rows of stone lions, had only that morning been freshly sprinkled with white sand from the western desert, and now, even as the drums pounded, announcing the approach of Egypt's divine ruler, naked girls scattered flower petals along the route and the priests jangled cymbals and recited prayers. I stood with a crush of people near the obelisk of King Amenemhat, waiting to behold this miracle.

Times beyond counting I had seen my father, the Lord Sennacherib, honored with such processions. The people would cheer him, shouting "Ashur is king, Ashur is king!" and would throw gold coins in his path that the shadow of his chariot might pass over these and bless them. The people of Ashur loved their kings.

Yet the Egyptians stood in silence, watching the approach of their pharaoh as if he were a criminal on his way to execution. As he passed they lowered their eyes. One might have supposed they were ashamed.

They did not love him, it seemed—not as the crowds of Nineveh or of Calah had loved my father. Perhaps it was simply that my father had never claimed to be a god.

I did not lower my eyes. I wished a look at this god who was not stone or wood, but flesh and bone like any man. I wished to see Pharaoh Taharqa, Lord of the Nile Valley. I did not know why, but it seemed important, as if our paths might someday cross again.

They would, many years later, yet this was the only time I ever saw him.

There is little enough one can tell about a man sitting on a carrying chair, rigid as a block of granite. His arms were crossed over his chest and in his hands he carried a whip and a shepherd's crook. The crowns of Upper and Lower Egypt were on his head, and strapped to his chin was a little black box to symbolize the beard of authority. Thus has every pharaoh appeared in public since the Scorpion King united the two lands two thousand years ago—or so the story goes.

Taharqa himself was not an Egyptian. His dynasty had come out of the Land of Ethiopia less than a hundred years before. He was tall and strong-looking and his skin was black, so that he looked as if he had been carved from obsidian. I never heard any Egyptian express an opinion of him—Pharaoh is sacred, even when he is a foreigner—but I would learn many years later, and from personal experience, that he was a man of energy and ability and a good soldier, a better ruler, perhaps, than his people deserved.

I could not but wonder what was in his mind, this man who, for such occasions of state, allowed himself to be turned into an idol, a living statue, rigid as death. What was behind the still face? What did the eyes see when they looked out at the sullen multitude? What was the world like in which Taharqa lived?

If he was still Egypt's god, he was not its ruler—not as the pharaohs of old had been.

Taharqa hardly even possessed title to the double crown, since it was not he but Mentumehet, Fourth Prophet of Amun and Prince of Thebes, who ruled in Upper Egypt. The priest was called the Living God's deputy, yet he it was whose word was law in the ancient seat of pharaohs and who worshiped at the most holy of shrines, the Temple of Amun. And it was not much different in the Lower Kingdom.

Pharaoh controlled Tanis and the eastern towns, and the army—mostly Libyans, since no Egyptian will enlist for a soldier unless he is starving—owed its loyalty to him. The rest of Egypt paid him tribute, called him "Lord," and dreaded his interference in their affairs, but it was with the local princes that the bulk of the power lay. They bickered among themselves, yet they would all resist if Pharaoh tried to make good his claim to absolute rule.

The time for being great in Egypt was over.

He passed before us, this god-king, carried on a golden chair to the Temple of Ptah, and behind his procession the street became once more clogged with ordinary humanity. The flower petals were trampled beneath the sandals of barley merchants and weavers, beggars and slave dealers and prostitutes and scribes. It was over.

Yet perhaps not.

I was preparing to leave—the sun was hot and I entertained thoughts of a cup of wine. I had dismissed Taharqa and his dreams from my mind, since who was I to care about the ambitions of princes?

Still, at the last moment and for reasons hidden from me even at the time, just before the thickening crowds would have blocked him from view, I turned back and caught sight of a man sitting in an alleyway on the other side of the street.

There was little enough to distinguish him save that the lightness of his skin showed him to be a foreigner, and Memphis was filled with those. His skull was covered with a tight-fitting leather cap, and he wore a black robe with sleeves long enough to conceal his hands. I might never have noticed him had his eyes not been locked on my face—he wanted me to notice him. Our gazes met and he smiled a tight, uncomfortable little smile, as if everything were understood between us.

He was Prodikos' murderer. He was the man who had inquired after me in Naukratis. Nothing had ever been so clear to me in my life.

And then, of course, he disappeared behind the moving crowd.

The street was perhaps twenty paces wide, yet there were people everywhere now and to fight one's way through them was not the work of a moment. Yet I must hurry or I would lose my chance.

A soldier angrily swung his arm after me as I dashed past him. My foot caught on a basket full of figs and they went tumbling onto the ground. An old woman darted in front of me. I caught her in my hands just in time to keep her from falling, and she screeched at me like a hawk. Her cries rang in my ears—probably they all thought I was a thief in flight—but I did not stop.

I reached the alley. He was gone. There was a street beyond, but I had a glimpse of a man's shadow against the alley wall. His? By now my sword was drawn, but he was gone. I followed one street and then another, but he had escaped.

Yes, of course—he planned it thus. He only wanted me to know he had found me.

Yet I could not find him. The man in the black robes seemed to have vanished from Memphis. Kephalos employed spies and paid out a fortune in bribes to brothel keepers and porters, and still he uncovered no trace of a foreigner with one finger missing from his left hand.

"He is gone, Lord," he said. "How can he possibly have eluded our search, a stranger with such an obvious disfigurement? He has fled for his life."

Yet I was not so sure.

I made a point of spending part of every day in the bazaars and among the dockside taverns, places where, if someone were watching out for me, he would not have much trouble finding me. I kept Enkidu with me, as I did not relish a knife in the kidney as I walked along the crowded streets, and also because the man in the black robes would certainly know about him and would be watching his own back—it might make him feel a little safer if my Macedonian giant was right out in plain sight.

I spent days and days thus. I never saw the man, never found the slightest trace of him, yet I felt his presence. It is a strange feeling, to be watched in secret. It preys upon the nerves.

Enkidu sensed him too. Enkidu, whose eyes and ears nothing escaped, would now and then bolt away, only to come back a few minutes later, shaking his head and frowning. The man whose quarry I had become was very cunning if he could elude Enkidu. I did not find this a comforting reflection.

Yet it all might have been nothing more than a delusion. I had seen a man who had taken flight when I pursued him—there was perhaps nothing more to it than that. A man may run away for other reasons than because he is an assassin. Perhaps, since I had chased him, he was the one afraid of being murdered.

I tried to drive the matter from my thoughts. It seemed that the man had left the city. I was safe enough. There was a guard posted around my house, so at least I would not have to worry about having my throat cut while I slept. What more could I do without becoming a prisoner of my own fears? If one man desires to kill another, he will always find his chance.

And, remembering the murder of my friend Prodikos, I wished him all speed, for his chance would also be mine.

"I will kill him," I said to Enkidu. "This is a madman, who murders for pleasure. I will not hesitate. One does not hesitate with a rabid dog—one kills it."

Pharaoh's arrival in Memphis was the occasion for a ceaseless round of celebrations and banquets. The great and powerful of the city vied with one another in the costliness of their jubilees, and this even though Pharaoh himself came to none of them—it would have been unthinkable for the god-king to mix thus with his subjects, as a man among other men.

Pharaoh, indeed, was merely the pretext, for the Egyptians will make a festival of anything. No one really cared about Pharaoh. The revels continued even after he had left.

I was invited everywhere. My presence was desired at every feast.

Indeed, I was part of the entertainment, like the musicians and the acrobats, for I was a novelty and the Egyptians are like children in their love of novelty.

Besides, the harvests had been bad that year and hardship was everywhere. While the peasants starved in silence, the landowners looked about for new means of financing their extravagances. Many a brightly colored bird found itself pecking at the dry earth, and most of these seemed to end by coming to Kephalos for a loan. Very shortly it seemed that everyone, from Prince Nekau down, owed us money—I say us, for I was graciously allowed a share of the profits. It was a pattern to which I had long since grown familiar. Sometimes the thought struck me that if we only traveled widely enough, my former slave would end by owning the whole world.

At any rate, great wealth acts as a sovereign guarantee of one's place in society.

The fashion that year was for river parties. A barge, strung with colored lanterns, would be anchored in the middle of the Nile and guests to the banquet would have themselves rowed over in their own little pleasure boats, similarly decorated. Sometimes there would be two or three such barges on the water and people would float from one to the next, carried along by restlessness and the languid current. The twinkling lights made a pretty enough sight from the shore, so it is possible the people in town enjoyed these diversions as much as anyone. For myself, I grew quickly bored with this folly and would have stopped attending had it not been for Nodjmanefer.

For the month following our first encounter I was hardly ever able to speak to her alone. Yet as her husband's power and her own beauty recommended her to the world, I could at least see her. For our paths to meet I had only to accept enough invitations.

She would glance in my direction and smile and turn away, having forgotten, it seemed, that I was alive. Had she? I wondered. Had it meant so little to her? And was I touched by this deeper than in my vanity? I did not know. I only knew that my gaze longed to dwell upon her face, and that I did not care very much if I was making a fool of myself.

One night the Lord Senefru did not accompany her. She sat with a group of her friends, wearing a red wig trimmed in gold and looking lovelier than the dawn. I was not far away and could hear her laughter, like the tinkling of bells. The sound at once thrilled me and made me wretched, for I was sure by then that I had lost her.

The banquet lasted longer than usual and the river wind had started to turn cold. People were beginning to leave. I stood near her, just a pace or two behind, as we waited for our boats to pull alongside and take us home. She had not even looked at me that evening.

"Oh, dear," I heard her say.

It was something of a jest, really. Her oarsmen had gotten drunk and were asleep in the prow of the boat—I remember how one of them lay with his arm over the side, his fingers trailing in the water. Neither of them would be good for anything before daylight.

And then she turned back to me with a smile of amused perplexity on her lips. Not to anyone else, but to me. We might have been alone there.

"Perhaps My lady will allow . . . ?"

She held out her hand to me, and the thing was settled. I would take her home. We would not reach the shore for perhaps half an hour. For that time, at least, I would have her to myself.

The Egyptians are good boat builders, but their pleasure craft are slow and cumbersome to handle. The passenger lies under a canopy in the stern, and two rowers are obliged to stand in the front, plying their oars through locks placed inconveniently forward. This is no doubt intentional, since they must thus at all times keep facing front and cannot intrude upon the privacy of their masters. After all, no one is in a hurry.

Certainly I was not. Nodjmanefer lay beside me. I could smell her perfume in the still, moist air, and her breasts shone in the moonlight like polished brass. My heart seemed to choke me, but I did not care if we never finished this journey.

"I thought you had forgotten me," I said, touching her face with the tips of my fingers, almost as if I had to reassure myself that she was there. "Perhaps you had."

"I am here because I could be nowhere else. It would have been better for us both if we had never met, but at last it shall be I who suffers more for it. Men do not love as women do, and you, I think, will never love me."

"I love you already."

But she only touched her brow to my cheek and was silent. I kissed her and slid my hand across her breasts, and she breathed in long, ragged sighs that would suddenly catch in her throat. If I had tried to go into her she would not have resisted, but I did not. I would not treat her like a harlot.

"Senefru will have your oarsmen beaten when he hears," I said. I could not understand why I spoke of such things—except, perhaps, to punish her for making me care that she was not a harlot.

"He will not punish them because he will not hear. The wine was drugged."

"Then you planned this?"

"Yes. Did you think I could wait forever?"

There was a tavern near the waterfront, the sort of place where the sleeping mats smell of pitch. We went there and I gave the landlord three silver coins for a room and a jug of spiced wine. He did not seem surprised to see us, but doubtless he did a brisk trade in high-born ladies and their lovers, and where in Memphis do such things surprise anyone?

A woman's pleasure in the flesh is greater than a man's. Perhaps this is why in all nations Love is a goddess.

Yet I had not meant to speak of love. I did not love Nodjmanefer. She was right in that, but women are always wiser than men. Love and passion, though tangled together, are not the same. Save for my mother, I have loved but two women in my life, and Nodjmanefer was not one of them. I did not understand this then, however.

Still, passion can carry the burden of much tenderness, until it is so nearly like love, as tears are like seawater, that no man can tell one from the other. No *man* can, but women are not so easily deluded.

Thus, when I think of us as we were in that little tavern room, my heart swells with pity for Nodjmanefer, who had a claim to more than simply my lust, even if in that moment I believed I withheld nothing.

"You have come here before?" she asked, almost playfully. She put her arms about my neck, her face buried in my chest. "You have been here with other women?"

"Never to this place, but to others not much different. And never with a woman like you."

The thought of Esharhamat, precious as life, came into my mind of its own will. Esharhamat, whom I loved and never hoped to see again—I wondered if Nodjmanefer grasped that I lied to her.

"I have been here before. Other lovers than you have brought me here."

"Why do you speak to me of these things?"

"That I would hide nothing from you. And that later, after I have lost you, you may regret our parting less."

"Am I just one among many, then?" I asked, since I would rather hear her speak of her lovers than of our parting—of anything rather than of our parting.

"You are not one among many. You are only you. Understand that I am not so blind I cannot see how you are different."

I listened, but the words seemed to mean nothing. I wanted only to feel the comforting weight of her body against mine and to listen to her slow breathing, so slow that she almost seemed to be asleep.

"I have tired of other men, but I will never tire of you," she went on, as I have heard men whispering prayers to themselves, to comfort their dying. "That is how I know I will lose you, for whatever has brought you here will take you away again."

Love is a goddess—if her name is Ishtar or Aphrodite or Inanna or Saris or Hathor or Isis, she is the same. And if love is a curse, as the Greeks will have it, then it is one which falls more heavily upon women than upon men.

Nodjmanefer loved me. It would be her undoing—this she knew—yet she loved me.

In the Land of Ashur they call the Lady Ishtar mistress both of love and war. All perish before her might.

Yet all seemed to follow smoothly. I met with Nodjmanefer when I could and saw her often, alone and in the company of her husband.

The Lord Senefru was not an easy man to fathom. I had no doubt, then or later, that he knew I was bedding with his wife, yet, although he did not give the impression of one easily to forgive a slight, it was as if this matter did not touch him. His manner to me was cordial, even friendly, and I was a frequent guest in his home, as was he in mine. He spoke to me often and at length, even seeking my opinion on matters which no doubt he understood better than I did. He seemed to court my good opinion.

Yet he was not a base man. It was not from hope of gain that he tolerated me—more than tolerated me—for he never sought either gift or favor.

Perhaps, I thought, he has grown weary of his wife. Perhaps he has ceased to care. If ever I allowed myself to believe this I committed a grave error, but it was nevertheless true that Senefru sought me out, making me his friend and the confidant of his secret thoughts. Or so I imagined.

He owned an estate on the fifth channel of the Delta, a place where he went when he wished to escape from life in Memphis, and because the hunting and fowling were good there and he had a taste for such sport. He rarely invited anyone to this retreat, so it was all the more remarkable that I should have been his guest, not once but several times. His country house there was large, and he maintained apartments separate from those of his wife. Under the circumstances it was easy enough to find my way to her sleeping mat. It was almost as if the husband had become the lover's confederate.

"He will not surprise us together," Nodjmanefer told me. "He would never do anything so clumsy and direct."

"He knows, then?"

"He has said nothing, and his manner to me has not changed, but he knows. I am sure he knows. I beg you, Tiglath, put no trust in him—I feel sometimes as if we were living poised on the blade of a knife."

She would speak no more of it. If we were alone and I chanced to mention him, Nodjmanefer would turn the talk to something else. It was as if her lord were merely a painful memory, but, perhaps closer to the truth, the three of us had become trapped in our own silence.

During the day I was much with my host, in pursuit of game. The Nile is thick with waterfowl, which common men snare with nets, but among gentlemen it is considered great sport to hunt ducks with nothing but a curved throwing stick. We would float down the river in a tiny reed boat and, when we came close enough, stand up and shout to startle the birds into the air. To hit a rapidly moving target with nothing but a stick is no insignificant feat, and men would starve to death if they depended on this means of supplying their bellies. Senefru was considered quite skilled and never killed more than one or two birds a day. My own average was much worse.

"But I fear the sport does not interest you," he said finally. "In truth, one has to have hunted thus all one's life or it is simply a great nuisance. My overseer tells me that hippopotamus have been seen just a short way downriver—I shall direct that a hunt be organized."

Thus the next morning, an hour and a half before sunrise, we set out in four boats, Senefru and I with two paddlers in one and the three others carrying provisions.

Senefru and I sat facing each other in the front of our boat, sharing out a breakfast of bread, goat cheese and wine—the journey would occupy us until shortly before noon, so there had not been time to eat before leaving. On the river neither of us wore anything expect a twisted loincloth, and thus there was nothing to distinguish the great man from his meanest servant. Perhaps this was the release he sought from these expeditions, for he was always more relaxed and open while hunting, a changed man from the Lord Senefru of Memphis, whose merest word had almost the force of law.

"You will enjoy this," he said, wiping his fingers on the scrap of linen in which his breakfast had been wrapped. "Seth, our god of chaos and disaster, called 'great of strength,' sometimes takes the form of a hippopotamus, and with good reason. They are unpredictable beasts and it is dangerous sport to hunt them, but the scars you carry on your chest reveal you as a man who does not shrink from danger. If one may make so bold as to ask, how did you come by them?"

"In war, for the most part. These from a lion, when I was too young and foolish to think anything could kill me."

He smiled, and then nodded, as if something had just occurred to him.

"That surprises me, for I have never heard there were lions in the Ionian lands," he said, in Greek—he raised his eyebrows as if to glance over my shoulder, a reminder that we were not alone. "But perhaps, in truth, you are from some other place."

"I was raised in the river lands of the east," I answered, also in Greek, conscious that there was probably very little about me that this man did not already know. "There are lions there, but they are not so large as the ones in Egypt. This one, however, seemed large enough at the time. I let him catch me alone and on the ground."

"Yes—it is a frightening thing to face so savage an adversary on such nearly equal terms. But, since you are still here and not in the Land of the Dead, I must assume your lion had the worst of it."

I nodded, acknowledging the compliment, wondering why this conversation seemed to be about something else.

"I myself have never hunted lion," he went on, shrugging his shoulders in resignation. "They dwell only in the desert and I am not a man of the desert. My ancestors hunted them, for my family came from Karnak, far to the south, in the Upper Kingdom. It is a different place, the Upper Kingdom. The Duck's Foot is rich, but all that made the old Egyptians noble and strong found its source in the Upper Kingdom."

He paused, and I waited, almost holding my breath. It was one of those moments when one realizes that something is about to be revealed—it becomes inevitable from the simple momentum of a man's ideas. Senefru would speak, not because I was his friend, for in secret he probably hated me, but because he must, because he had no choice. Because he suspected that I might understand.

"Yet it is all ended now. It is over—Egypt, me, everything. I am almost thankful to be the last of my line, for I would not envy a child of mine who will live on to see what the future holds for this land where my fathers are buried. Where I shall be buried. Pharaoh wears the double crown, but by now that is no more than a tired jest. We are a broken reed,

My Lord. Perhaps the house of Senefru and the long history of Egypt shall end together."

He smiled grimly, as if the thought gave him a measure of cruel, joyless satisfaction.

"Egypt, they say, has lived for three thousand years," I said, wishing, for reasons unclear even to myself, to deny him this self-mortifying pleasure. "Perhaps, since neither are dead yet, both it and the noble line of Senefru will go on for another few thousand before the Nile dries up and the earth turns to dust."

The smile tightened, becoming almost painful to witness, and then he shook his head.

"Egypt may continue for a time, like a sick old man who cannot summon the resolve even to die, but my line, I am quite certain, will end with me. I married the Lady Nodjmanefer when she was fifteen and it has proved a barren union—the fault doubtless is mine, since neither have any of my concubines enriched me with children.

"But, as I say, My Lord, I do not regret this . . . extinction. Only look at Egypt as she is now and you will understand. The land grows poorer every year, so the farmers starve and nurture hatred of their betters. Yet the nobles, men of my own class, are indifferent to the suffering around them and care for nothing except their golden toys. And the princes, whose duty it is to rule, they squabble among themselves like little boys. You have met Nekau, and thus you know what he is like—well-meaning but powerless. The Egyptians are not one people anymore, for nothing unites them except their hatred of the foreign Pharaoh.

"But I am speaking treason. I blush to guess what you must think of me, My Lord."

"I think only, My Lord, that you have been honoring me with your confidence."

A strange expression came over his face, and I knew he believed himself to have achieved some manner of victory of me. An instant later it was gone, as if it had never been, but now we understood each other perfectly.

"You see what children we are," he said, slowly closing his eyes and then opening them again, like someone waking from a dream. "Even I, thought a clever man, have never learned discretion. The Egyptians will be the end of Egypt. We are like sheep who imagine there are no wolves in the world."

Suddenly, even against my will, I remembered Esarhaddon, now king in the Land of Ashur, once my brother, who had dreamed all his life of conquering Egypt. I wondered what he would have made of the Lord Senefru. Would he have guessed, as I had, that such men, even when they are defeated, will not be held long in subjection? Sacred Pharaoh did not wear a cobra upon his crown for nothing.

Another three hours on the river and we entered a marshland of wide, seemingly bottomless pools, shaded by huge stands of papyrus reeds. Crocodiles sunned themselves on the narrow mud banks, not even troubling to slip away at our approach. There appeared to be no current to stir the water, and the air was steamy and rank. I would not have cared to live my life in such a place.

"The hippopotamus dig these bathing holes out for themselves," Senefru told me. "They can sink to the bottom like lead weights and stay there for a quarter of an hour at a time—they can even sleep there. Have you ever seen one?"

I shook my head.

"Then you are in for a shock," he went on, laughing as if he had had his little joke on me already. "The gods never made an uglier brute."

This turned out to be not far from the truth, for a few minutes later a gigantic object, gray as mud, bobbed to the surface and began snorting ferociously, spewing plumes of water in every direction. It was much larger than I had expected, being at least twice the size of any horse I had ever seen, and looked like a monstrously bloated pig with a huge square head and the jaws of a crocodile. I will not attempt to describe it further, since I never saw one out of the water and, in any case, I have no hope of being believed.

The beast was perhaps fifty cubits distant from the closest of our boats and remained quite calm, wiggling his short ears back and forth and regarding us with what seemed more like curiosity than fear—indeed, what should he have found fearful in us, who were such paltry creatures beside him?

One hunts the hippopotamus with spears not unlike the harpoons I have seen the Greeks use against dolphins. The lance point is attached to a hemp rope and, once the barb finds its mark, the shaft of the spear comes away so that the hunter has a line well anchored in the beast's flesh.

These creatures have hides as thick as a man's thumb is wide and tough enough to be much prized by the Egyptians as shield covers, and beneath that is a layer of heavy fat. Against such protection—united with the fact of their great size—a spear has little chance of inflicting a fatal wound. The heart is simply out of reach and, although a lucky thrust may sever one of the great veins, an animal of such vast bulk will take many hours to bleed to death.

Pain, however, and the pull of the line, fill the brute with terror and it dives to the bottom of its pool in hopes of escape. Yet in the end it must come up for air, and then the hunt has the chance of planting another dart. Finally, worn down by its exertions, by panic and by loss of blood, it can no longer resist. It rises to the surface one last time, too spent to struggle further. A rope is tied around its neck, it is dragged to the shore where its head is cut off with an ax.

This, at least, is the hunter's plan. In fact, a hippopotamus is as likely to attack as to flee, and if it swamps the boat, a thing it can manage with very little difficulty, and its tormenters find themselves in the water, then what chance does a man have against a beast twenty or thirty times his size, with jaws like a pair of grindstones? And such work as the hippopotamus leaves undone, the crocodiles will finish. It is dangerous sport for an idle afternoon.

I sat in the reed boat, my spear balanced between my knees, sick fear weighing heavy in my belly. I could remember no quarrel I had with this placid creature, huge as an island, that rocked back and forth in the quiet pool, noisily blowing water out of its nostrils as it inspected us with trusting, cowlike eyes. It seemed to me that we had come on a foolish errand.

"As my guest, you have the honor of the first throw," Senefru murmured behind me. "When we approach he will begin to turn from us. Aim for the roll of flesh just behind the ear, and strike deep."

I stood up. I could feel the boat rocking beneath my feet. I wished myself somewhere else—anywhere else.

The paddlers, soundless on their oars, pushed us slowly forward, shortening the distance to five and forty, then forty cubits. The hippopotamus twitched its ears violently, as if warning us off, and then, precisely as Senefru had foretold, began to turn away.

The line was laid out in wide loops on the bow in front of me, one end tied to my lance point and the other to the prow of the boat. I had only to remember not to step on it—or to let a loose coil catch me around the ankle, for thus, when the beast dives, a man can be dragged to his death—and to think of nothing else except my mark. I brought the spear up to my shoulder, took a breath, held it an instant, and let fly.

"Well thrown!" Senefru shouted. The point lodged deep in the thick neck, the shaft came away, and with a bellow of indignant surprise the beast threw up a wide sheet of water and dropped behind it into the dark pool.

The line sang as it was pulled under. There was blood on the water and a great churning, as if the whole pond were being turned over from the bottom. At last the line pulled tight, dragging us forward, the boat's prow so low that we had to sit far back to keep it from going under.

"Not long now and he will come up again. Then I will have my chance!"

I turned around to glance at Senefru, and his face was lit up with excitement. He was afraid too, but it was the kind of fear men delight in. The hunt seemed to have brought him to life.

At last the boat began to slow. Then it stopped. Then the line went slack. The water was black and empty below us. We waited.

The paddlers watched the surface of the pool, now clouded with mud, anxiety contracting their faces.

"How long can he stay down there?" I heard myself asking.

Senefru, as if in answer, was already readying his spear and laying down the coils of line.

"It is an odd thing," he said, glancing in my direction but hardly seeming to see me, "how the only true peace of mind seems to come hand in hand with hazard and the threat of death. I have never been a soldier, but this is how I imagine I would feel before a great battle. You would know, My Lord—is it the same thing in your heart?"

"Yes. A strong desire to run away."

He laughed, perhaps imagining I had made a joke.

He is mad, I thought, to speak of death and peace of mind in the same breath. Or is life so bitter for him that he finds escape from its pain only in the grip of fear? And is this not a measure of how much he must hate me?

At last the hippopotamus rose again to the surface, snorting loudly, blood streaming from its neck. The beast was clearly tiring and rocked from side to side in the water as it struggled to pump air into its lungs. We could watch its back swell and then sag with the effort of breathing. For the moment, at least, it was too preoccupied with its own physical distress even to notice us.

We were about five and twenty cubits off, and our quarry had its back to us. Senefru made his throw—a shade too quickly, I thought—and his point buried itself in the animal's shoulder blade.

"Blast!" he muttered. "I should have—"

But the rest was lost as the hippopotamus swung around in the water and gave voice to the most appalling scream. I have heard horses wounded in battle scream just that way, but this was many times worse. It seemed to shatter the air.

And then it went under again, throwing up great waves. At first the thick smear of blood that leaked to the surface marked the progress of its dive, but this finally dissipated in the foul, muddy water.

Senefru raised his arm to signal one of the other boats to draw near. He seemed annoyed.

"We shall have to give over these two lines," he said. "We must be ready when it rises again, although the gods alone know what will happen then. I pulled my throw, I think. My point must have struck bone and gone shallow—probably the beast will scrape it loose on the reeds and be little the worse for it, except in a rage now."

A perfect stillness settled over the pond. Even the water birds were quiet, as if waiting . . .

It happened with such suddenness that I did not at once grasp the extremity of the danger. At first I was only aware of the shock, for there seemed to be no sound. This impression lasted only an instant. Then I turned and saw what was taking place—the hippopotamus had come up directly under the boat, which was breaking in half as it was lifted out of the water.

The paddlers screamed in terror—I think we all must have been screaming, but I only remember the high-pitched, panicked cries of those two poor wretches. We seemed to be high above the water, balanced on the creature's great square head. Then the boat snapped like a rotten twig and we fell, back into the wild, swirling water.

The thing appeared poised above us. It was bellowing with rage, like an ox with a voice of bronze. The huge jaws opened—I could have reached out and touched its eyes; it seemed to be looking straight at me—and then it crashed down, shattering the surface of the pond as a hammer might a clay pot. I thought my ears would burst with the sound. I thought . . .

I know not what I thought, for it seemed the monster had killed me. I was sure I was dead.

The rest is empty turmoil—I have no memory, not even the memory of a dream. Nothing.

I woke up, and I was lying on the muddy bank. My arms and chest were covered in blood.

So it has killed me, I thought. My body ached, as if every bone had been separately broken. I closed my eyes again, despairing of life, almost indifferent to it. I felt sure I would never open them again.

"Your gods must love you, my friend," came Senefru's voice. "I do not know how otherwise you are alive."

I looked in the direction of the sound and there he was, sitting beside me, streaming with water. Almost at our feet lay the corpse of one of the paddlers, looking half buried in the muddy pond—his whole chest was torn open, and the expression on his face, what I could see of it, suggested a death of unspeakable agony.

"Where is the other?" I asked.

"Dead. The crocodiles got him—just as well, for it kept them too occupied to trouble about us. You were unconscious."

"Did you pull me out?"

"Yes," he said, grinning like a demon.

Fool, fool, fool that I was! Could I not see? Could I not guess? What was my life to him?

I could not even ask. Something kept me silent, yet I knew not what. The question formed on my lips, but I could not bring myself to ask it.

Why?

XII

I DO NOT THINK THAT I AM NATURALLY STUPID, SO PER-
haps it was merely the self-absorption of youth that caused me so to
misunderstand the Lord Senefru—perhaps I can excuse myself as easily
as that. I was perhaps not blind, but I saw no more than I wished to see.
And he was not my only mistake.

There was a banquet in my house, a birthday celebration in honor of
Prince Nekau, which Kephalos had decided would be a politic excuse for
the distribution of certain expensive presents—if Pharaoh had not been
so far away in Tanis, doubtless Kephalos would have found a means of
bribing him as well, for Kephalos bought rulers the way another man
might buy a cloak, as a protection against the weather.

In any case, to me it was merely another banquet, another crowd of
wealthy parasites who had to be fed and entertained and provided with
suitable pretexts for their various indiscretions. The Lady Nodjmanefer
was absent, having departed the city three days before to accompany her
husband on a trip to Saïs, so even this last prospect of pleasure was denied
to me.

Yet I performed my duties as host. I listened to gossip that did not
interest me and laughed at jests that were not amusing and smiled at
foolish women and spoke with their husbands about the merits of various
well-known courtesans and whether slave girls were not, in the long run,
a better bargain.

By the second hour after midnight, with my eyeballs as glazed as a
pottery water jug, I decided to retreat to my own quarters for a moment
and wash my face in cold water until it would unclench enough to allow
me to stop grinning. I would be safe for twenty minutes or so. No one

would notice my absence or, if they did, would regard it as any breach of manners. They would merely assume I was busy consolidating a triumph over some one or the other of the ladies, such being considered among the principal purposes of these gatherings.

On my way back, my shoulders squared and the creases pressed out of my face, it occurred to me to say something to my steward Semerkhet about the wine, which I noticed had grown weaker as the evening wore on—guests who are never allowed to grow properly drunk, I wished to point out to him, only piss against the wall and return to their tables, never thinking of their own sleeping mats at home.

Thus I skirted around the dining hall by a back corridor that led to the kitchens. It was here that I found Selana, near a half-open door, watching the banquet from behind a screen of empty water jugs.

"What do you mean by this?" I hissed, pulling her up by the back of her tunic. "What are you doing here? You should have been in your bed hours ago!"

Screeching like a peacock, she twisted around and attempted to bite me on the wrist. I swung the door shut—this was not a scene I wished my guests to witness—and dropped her, giving her a kick in the backside that sent her sprawling.

Once was enough. When she regained her balance she did not continue active hostilities but instead grew quiet. She sat up, drawing her knees in under her chin and glaring at me, leaving me to wonder why all our recent encounters seemed to end in brawls.

"What are you doing here?" I repeated.

"What difference should it make to you?" she answered—if a look could kill I would have died that instant. "You made me a kitchen slave, remember? I should be beneath your notice. You would not punish one of the household cats for stealing a peek at your silly friends."

I went back to the door, opened it a crack, and looked out. She was perfectly right. They were silly.

"They are not my friends," I said. "I hardly know most of them."

"Then why do you invite them to your house? They drink your wine and eat your food—perhaps you have become a tavern master."

She stuck out her tongue at me.

"Why are you angry with me, Selana? You are a child and should be in your bed. I repent that I struck you."

"Oh—I don't mind that."

"Then what do you mind?"

Her only answer, after a long pause, as if made under compulsion, was a curt gesture at the door to the dining hall.

"You resent these people, Selana? Are you jealous of them?"

"Jealous of them? Why should I be jealous of them?" she asked hotly, straightening her legs with a snap. "I am a Greek and better than that rabble of mud-colored Egyptians! Jealous of them!"

"Go to bed, Selana—what am I to do with you?"

"I know not, Lord. I know not."

There were tears in her eyes. She got up from the floor and went back to the kitchen.

What *was* I to do with her? Over the next few days I considered the question from several different vantages and could arrive at no conclusion. In another three or four years, when she had grown to womanhood, what would become of her? Certainly she had never been destined for life in my kitchen—if I kept her there she would probably run off one night and end up in the brothels, or in the gutter with her throat cut. Something else would have to be found for her.

"What do you think, Enkidu? She should be taught to read and to do sums. Then, when she is old enough, we can give her a dowry and marry her off—in Naukratis, to some young man with his way to make in the world. She can be a merchant's wife. She is no fool and would be a great help to him."

The Macedonian, who was eating his breakfast at the time, merely glanced at me for a moment, as if he thought I had gone a little mad.

"Well—*someone* must have her. Sooner or later, someone."

He growled, exactly like a large, bad-tempered dog that resents the interference.

"I suppose I shall have to do it myself—I mean, teach her to read."
But Enkidu had lost interest.

That evening I told my steward that I wished the girl Selana to be taken from the kitchen and given her own room. I did not explain why, so the gods alone know what the man thought.

The Lord Senefru returned from Saïs, and with him Nodjmanefer. I saw her again the night of a festival honoring the god Set, and the next afternoon she lay in my arms.

It was soon generally understood in my household that the master was involved in an intrigue and, since no man can long hope to keep anything secret from his slaves, doubtless many knew the identity of the high-born lady who had become the Lord Tiglath's mistress. Certainly Kephalos knew.

"Every man must take an interest in something," he said. "And, since now you may no longer pursue a soldier's glory, and have never displayed any appetite for wealth, a fashionable woman, safely provided with a husband, is a harmless enough pastime. This one is no Esharhamat and will not disturb the tranquility of your mind."

"Kephalos, how can you know what she is?"

"I receive the confidences of your serving women, Lord, and, since you continue to go into them with a healthy and pleasing regularity, I can guess well enough what she is *not*—at least, to you. Beyond that, the question concerns me but little."

I could not even make pretense of being offended, since he was so delighted to have found me out.

Another matter, however, seemed to give him much less satisfaction.

"I am informed, Lord, that you removed that wretched infant from the kitchen."

"You refer to Selana?" I asked, secretly gratified at being provided with the means of avenging myself upon him. "Yes—she was not happy there and, besides, we must give some thought to her future. I have decided to have her instructed in the calculation of sums, and I myself will teach her to read and write the Greek script."

"Teach her to *read*! Have her instructed in *sums*!"

Kephalos swept his hands back across his shaven head as if this latest of my follies would be the end of him. For a moment he seemed too vexed even to speak, but this could not last.

"My Lord, think what you do," he managed to gasp out at last. "She is the daughter of a Doric pig farmer—*read*! She was born, at best, to be the concubine of a drunken tavern keeper and to have her backside rented out by the quarter hour. Teach such a creature to read and you will make her the curse of any man stupid enough to have her under his roof—and such men will not be plentiful, since, for all her bronze-colored hair, she is a repulsive little toad. Hearken to the wisdom of age, Master. Practical knowledge may be one thing, but a woman who has learned more letters than those which make up her own name is a burden upon mankind and good for nothing but to promote the misery of the world."

Nevertheless, I went ahead with my plan. I hired a scribe from the marketplace to come every second day and open to her the mystery of numbers, and on the alternating mornings I sat down with her after breakfast, a wax tablet across my knees, and began to teach her the alphabet.

At first, at least where writing was concerned, she seemed to be of Kephalos' opinion.

"What would you have me read?" she asked, with some asperity. "To do sums is of use, but I can tell the difference between one coin and another without having to read it."

"And if you should receive a letter?"

"I know no one who can write except you and Master Kephalos. *He* would sooner cut off his hand and a letter from you would only be full of lies. I think I would be foolish indeed if I ever trusted you far enough away from me that we would have occasion for letters."

"I am not your property, Selana."

"No—I am yours. Can the Lady Nodjmanefer write?"

"I doubt it, as the Egyptians have as many letters as words and she is not a scribe. What has she to do with it?"

"With writing, if you speak the truth, not a thing; but with you, much. Teach her to write, since she is often gone from you. I am not so foolish as she."

She snatched the wax tablet from my knee and hurled it across the room, so that it hit the wall and shattered.

"She is a great lady and I am only a slave, but you will tire of her first!" she shouted. "Remember, love is a punishment from the gods, but what is your property you have forever."

She then cursed me furiously and ran away. I promised myself I would have her beaten, but I did not. I did nothing. Two days later she returned, kissed my hand in submission, and said she would learn letters if it was my will.

"Why have you changed your mind?" I asked.

"I remembered that I am a slave in your house and must learn obedience."

"Do not mock me, Selana."

"Very well then. I will learn to read for the pleasure of annoying Master Kephalos."

"And what grievance have you with him?"

"None. In fact, he has recently done me a great service—he has set my mind at ease. You cannot guess how, can you, Dread Lord." She smiled in the manner of an accomplished harlot, mocking me. "No, you cannot guess. For it is true what your concubines say, that men are all great simpletons. Yet if Master Kephalos is not jealous of the Lady Nodjmanefer, then *I* have nothing to fear from her—and he still hates me. I am comforted."

"You speak in riddles. Do not vex me, Selana. Why should Kephalos hate a child like you? And if he did, what comfort can you take in it?"

"Dread Lord—my witless Lord," she said, putting her hand on my cheek, as if I were the child. "Who could claim your heart without provoking the hatred of Master Kephalos? Someday, if you have pity on him, you will go to the slave market and buy him a dark-eyed boy with a face as pretty as a woman's. But until then, should he ever cease to be my enemy, I will know I have lost you forever."

For this I did beat her, because I remembered the boy Ernos, and the young dancer, the *dhakar binta*, in the *mudhif* of my Lord Sesku, and I knew she spoke the truth. For this I could not easily forgive her, for she seemed to dishonor my friend.

Yet it was not Kephalos' jealousy which most directly concerned me just then, for I had not forgotten the expression on Senefru's face when he told me he had saved my life. The same question echoed in my mind—why? Why would he have tarried even an extra minute to keep me from death?

"It is his vanity," Nodjmanefer told me. "He spoke of it himself, that same evening: 'It would have been so unseemly a death for one we both hold dear—to be ground up in the jaws of a hippopotamus, with the crocodiles getting whatever was left. I should not like it said that I allowed such a thing to happen to a friend.' You could not be permitted to die by accident, not before he has enjoyed his revenge."

We were walking in her garden, just at twilight. She had taken me out to show it to me, just as if I had never been there before. Guests would be arriving for a banquet soon, but for the moment we were alone. The Lord Senefru, with his customary tact, was attending to reports on the poor state of the barley harvest.

"Has he ever spoken to you of revenge?"

"No." She shook her head, and then her beautiful sea-green eyes fastened on me, and she smiled. "No—he has never suggested that there exists any pretext for revenge. He speaks of you as his friend, and acts to me as if he trusted his wife beyond all other women. Perhaps, in his way, he even does."

Her gaze dropped, as if she had admitted to something shameful. Was she ashamed? I knew not, for her life with the Lord Senefru was closed to me. She never spoke of her marriage—at least, never of those things that might have allowed me to understand her feelings. It is even possible that in some way she loved her husband, but no more than possible. Over all that she had drawn a veil.

"If he does not speak of revenge, then let us not speak of it either," I said. "There is no way we can forestall him. We can only wait and see. Perhaps at last he can even be persuaded to let you go. Would that please you, My Lady? Then, if you are fool enough, we could marry."

The sad smile returned to her lips, but she did not look at me. Perhaps she imagined I had been jesting. Perhaps I had been, at first.

"Would that be your wish?" she asked.

"Yes—of course. Why should it not be? If you speak the truth when you claim to love me."

"To you, I have never spoken anything except the truth."

"Then, with you as my wife, how could I be anything but happy?"

"Have I made Senefru happy?" She clutched my arm, holding it to her. "In any case, he is unlikely enough to consent."

"You know best, My Lady. But think if it would not be wise to ask him."

"Not now."

"As you will."

The garden was turning cold. We walked back toward the house in silence. I do not know what I had expected, but somehow I had the sense of having been rejected.

Perhaps she did not love me. Did I love her? Perhaps not—perhaps Kephalos was right that she was no Esharhamat—but if it was not love, it would do.

Senefru was waiting at the top of the steps. When he saw us he smiled one of his rare, unconvincing smiles.

"Lady, the servants require your calming hand or we may all be left to starve," he said, and then turned to me. "My Lord Tiglath, be so good as to accompany me to my study. It shall take but a moment—I have a favor to ask of you."

The lovers of other men's wives pay for their transgressions with a thousand little moments of remorseful dread. I was aware that I wronged the Lord Senefru and was coward enough to feel my guilt—had he been anyone but Nodjmanefer's husband I would have thought of him as my valued friend, so I was denied even the consolation of disliking him.

I wondered, as together we walked down the great corridor of his house, if this could be the moment he had chosen to confront me.

A scribe in the robes of a priest of Amun was arranging scrolls on a large table. When he saw us he bowed to Senefru, who waved him away. When we were alone, Senefru sat down behind the table, indicating a chair for me as well. He picked up a clay tablet, holding it delicately by the edges, and handed it to me.

"What can you tell me of this?" he asked.

I looked at it and discovered it to be nothing extraordinary.

"It is a diplomatic letter," I said. "It is from Ishpuinis, the king at Tushpa, to Adad-Nirari, king in the Land of Ashur: 'Be warned, my royal brother, that my fathers did not plant villages on the great plain to be places of resort for your soldiers, that the women of the land already have husbands among their own people . . .'"

I set it down again on the table, not knowing how much he would wish to hear or what his purpose might have been in asking. Senefru, who seemed to have been listening closely, glanced up.

"Is there more?"

"Yes, there is more," I answered, "all in the same style. The Lord Ishpuinis is angry and threatens war. May one ask how you came by it?"

"It was brought to me—such things are from time to time, My Lord. In what tongue, then, is it written?"

"In Akkadian."

"Akkadian?" He raised his eyebrows, as if trying to remember something, and then nodded. "Prince Nekau follows the events in foreign places with great attention. Do you think I ought to bring this information to his notice?"

"I imagine not," I said, hardly able to smother a laugh. "This tablet is at least a hundred years old, since both kings had long been dead when my grandfather's father was still kicking in his mother's womb."

"My Lord, you astonish me."

Senefru, resting his chin on his knuckles, studied my face as if he had never seen me before. Finally he shrugged and allowed his hands to drop back into his lap.

"I doubt if there are a hundred people in Egypt who could have read these scratchings—we here by the Nile are too quick to think the rest of mankind mere illiterate savages. Yes, I had recalled your saying you were born in the lands of the eastern rivers. You know the area then, its history, its kings?"

"I was born there—yes."

"And you know the Greeks too, who consider you one of them."

"Yes, I suppose I am a mongrel dog."

At this, as if at a great jest, he laughed—it was the first time I had heard his laughter and there was that in the sound, like rusted iron, which suggested long disuse. It made me profoundly uneasy.

He stood up, bidding me rise as well, and took my arm.

"A mongrel dog, are you," he said, laughing again. "Yes—well, a man is the better for having two souls. It lets him choose which is the more agreeable to live in. Yet one must live in one or the other, for a homeland is not simply another place, the dust of which one can wipe from his sandals whenever he will. In all important ways, one never leaves it."

"Then, if a man has two, he is in an odd predicament, for two souls fit uncomfortably inside the same skin."

"That you would know better than I, My Lord—but, come, I cannot keep my guests waiting . . ."

It was so often thus with the Lord Senefru that I had almost ceased to be troubled by it, this sense of a conversation being at the same time about different things, as if he were the one with two souls. I am not a diviner and cannot fathom mysteries, so I did not think much on the matter, either then or later.

A few months later, however, he returned to the subject.

"We hear rumors, My Lord Tiglath—disturbances in the east, rebellion among the petty northern kings who pay tribute to Nineveh. It is said the gods do not love the new king of Ashur, and that the people are stirred against him. To us here in Egypt these are distant matters, yet one would like to know the truth of them."

"It is always difficult to judge the truth of a rumor, My Lord."

He looked at me speculatively, perhaps trying to decide whether I could be concealing something or was merely stupid. The moment lasted a long time, and then he put it aside, opening and closing his hand as if to free some thought he had been holding tight.

"Alas," he sighed, shrugging his shoulders, "alas, more difficult for some than for others. For myself, nearly impossible. For you, perhaps not quite. You have experience of that remote place and it may chance can guess more wisely. What is the character of this new king of Ashur, this Esarhaddon? Is he wise or a fool, strong or weak? If the Phoenician cities do rebel, how do you think he will answer them? Men's minds circle around these questions—here and in other places."

"Other places?"

"Yes. In Tanis, for one. Pharaoh's eyes are always fixed on his eastern border. We are all servants of Pharaoh, My Lord. Do you know anything of King Esarhaddon which might prove of use?"

"That he is a good soldier. That he will punish rebellion with fire and sword. That he will pile the heads of his enemies before the gates of their cities."

"All this?" Senefru pursed his lips in seeming astonishment. "Then you know him well."

"I know only that he is king in the Land of Ashur, and that all the kings before him have known how to command armies and make conquered peoples feel their weight. Esarhaddon will not hide himself in Nineveh while the empire his fathers built breaks up like mud drying in the sun."

I stopped, realizing that I had spoken with more heat than I had intended and thus revealed too much. Yet the Lord Senefru, if he sensed any of this, gave no sign.

"You see I was right," he said, after an instant of silence. "A man never quite wipes off the dust of his homeland—some loyalties we cannot ever quite escape. Yet you speak wisely and we are not without influence in the north. Perhaps it would be best if our ambassadors urged a policy of caution."

"Best for whom, My Lord?"

"Best for Egypt—I do not think that Pharaoh would sleep easy with Esarhaddon and his soldiers in Judah, where nothing separates them from the Nile but a few leagues of sand. I thank you, My Lord Tiglath. You have served me like a friend."

Yet my thoughts had not been of Senefru, but of the Land of Ashur, for he had spoken truly about the dust of one's homeland—even now I could not bring myself to speak against Esarhaddon, and not because he had once been my brother but because he was still my king. I could not harm him, or even his name, for to abandon him would have been to abandon myself. There was no escape.

Over time, Senefru asked me many questions, the answers to which I would not have been surprised to learn he already knew. Clearly he was testing me—to what end I could not guess—and I seemed thus to rise in his esteem. Less, I suspect, for my knowledge than for the dexterity of my evasions.

Yet all this while I thought little on Senefru, for my life was elsewhere. In his wife's arms, when I had the chance. When I had not, in the delights of Memphis.

The Egyptians are the most charming people on earth. They have beautiful manners and are as light-hearted as birds. The gods granted them every grace but did not equip them to live in any world harsher than a banqueting hall.

The fashionable ladies of Memphis kept cats and thought themselves as seductively predatory, and half the young men of the city wore the elegant uniform of the princely militia, which had not fought in a war for three hundred years—Pharaoh was no fool and did not think of cutting stone with a wooden ax. An officer's whip or a woman's lovers, these were playthings, toys in the hands of rich and idle children living in a dreamy paradise of pleasure and intrigue.

It was my paradise as well, except that with time it grew less and less amusing. I, after all, had been the conqueror of the Medes, the Scoloti and the Uqukadi. I had thrown open the gates of Babylon to my father's armies and had treated as an equal with the kings of many nations. Once I had almost held the crown of Ashur in my two hands—how long was I to be diverted by feasts and the empty flattery of empty people? In short, I was growing bored with an existence that served only to teach me the distinction between pleasure and happiness.

A banquet held in the house of one Nekhenmut, priest of Khonsu and first cousin of Prince Nekau: a swallow has somehow found its way into the room and, dazzled by the light, flies about from corner to corner, dropping and soaring in a perfect ecstasy of panic. It is a great game—the women squeal like rabbits, covering their wigs with their arms, and the men are beside themselves to catch this dangerous intruder. Finally someone thinks to fetch a net from the servants' quarters and the swallow, at last subdued, is fed to a cat belonging to the Lady Hennutawi, whose breasts, it was said, had been kissed by every man in Memphis and who was the wife of My Lord Siwadj, judge in the princely courts and a renowned author of erotic verses.

I remember the incident for the way it made Nodjmanefer laugh and because of my own misery that night. It had been three months since our return from Senefru's hunting estate in the Delta and still she had said nothing more about asking her husband for a divorce. I did not feel able to raise the subject myself, and I began to fear that for her our love was perhaps after all no more than another in a long succession of such entertainments. Was she really no different from all the rest of them? Sometimes I could not help but wonder.

No, she was not.

"A woman is tied to her husband by other things than love," she said. "I cannot leave my lord unless he releases me—I cannot."

"We could quit this place," I said. "There is more to the world than Memphis, more than Egypt. We could find a refuge somewhere beside the wine-dark sea of the Greeks and be happy together."

"I would ask for no more than this," she said. "I would go with you into the Land of the Dead. But I cannot leave my lord, even for you and the white sand beaches of the Northern Sea, if he will not let me go. I know you cannot understand, but perhaps with time you will learn to forgive."

No, she was not like the rest of them.

So I waited. And I lived my life—her life, the only life this brothel called Egypt held for either of us—forgetting there could be any other.

Until the day I was reminded.

In Egypt, the desert is never far away. A hour's ride from Memphis and the green valley of the Nile seems as unreal as a memory—it is a world of sand and ragged mountains the color of buckskin, which the hot, unforgiving wind has carved from solid stone. Here the ancient Pharaohs yet reign, hidden in the quiet of their secret tombs. Here time seems to have lost its meaning. Here I came now and then, to hunt the gazelle and the lion, to forget the world for a while, and to be alone.

Yet never quite alone, for there was always Enkidu, his feet almost dragging the earth as he rode thirty paces behind me on one of the swift, strong Libyan ponies which the whole world admires. He was as constant as a shadow, and as silent. He was not a companion so much as a presence, like fortune or the favor of the gods. It was much the same as being alone.

I had ordered a chariot built for me—the Egyptians make good chariots, smaller than those of the east but agile—and when I grew weary of even the sound of my own voice I would hitch up my pair of fine Arab horses, a present from Kephalos and swift as darting birds, and I would drive off into the emptiness of the desert.

It was here, where I thought myself safely out of reach, that death almost found me.

On hunting days I liked to rise at least two hours before dawn, bathe in cold river water, and breakfast lightly, for a man feels more alive when there is not much lying in his belly. At first light I made sacrifice to Ashur, Lord of Heaven and Earth, to Shamash, Giver of Destinies, and also, after my encounter with the hippopotamus, to Seth, Full of Strength and Master of Lower Egypt—this from simple caution and also the sense that a traveler in strange lands should not ignore their gods. Then I mounted my chariot and drove off with the rising sun at my back.

It is a wonderful thing to feel the horses' strength through the reins, to hear the clatter of their hooves and know that the sand rises in plumes from beneath the wheels. That morning I felt the dry desert wind in my face and I rejoiced in life. I felt as the immortals must—full of breath, mighty, invulnerable.

In the midst of the desert there is a valley, hedged by bluffs, accessible through a single narrow pass, like a notch cut through the hills that shelter and conceal it. Here there is shade and sometimes water, the runoff from the highlands all around. Here there is nearly always game. here I went to test my luck.

It was good that day.

The pass ran over uneven ground, and I had to proceed slowly to keep from breaking an axle. Besides, for some reason the horses were skittish that morning. They seemed afraid of the place, as if they smelled a lion. But there was no lion.

At first I thought it was the sound of thunder. I glanced up, yet the sky was clear. Then I saw the dust and the first fine spray of stone, and I understood.

It was an avalanche—it was coming straight down almost where we stood.

The horses by then were mad with fear, but the pass was too narrow to turn round in, and there was no time. They tried to bolt—they would have run straight into the path of the slide. I yanked on the reins, struggling to hold them back, but they only reared in panic and starting trying to scale the steep sides of the pass to turn back. I could not hold them. I could not. I was nothing to them. They did not even know I was there.

They were hopelessly tangled in their runners now, trapped and helpless. Still they reared, snorting and neighing, beside themselves with terror. Their hooves tore at the walls of the chariot—the platform shook beneath my feet. At last, just as the stones reached us, they flipped the chariot over. They seemed to be trying to climb across it. I felt something strike me in the chest, taking the wind out of me with a rush. The horses would tear me open with their hooves—I was being buried. I felt an unbearable pain in my left arm. I couldn't breathe. The darkness closed around me . . .

How long had I been unconscious? Not long, I think. I awoke to find myself under the chariot, pinned down by one of the horses—he still stirred a little, but he was nearly dead. I felt such pity that I almost wept, though my whole body was like one long bruise. He had shielded me, and probably saved my life—for a time. I could not see the other.

Was I dying? Everything hurt. I felt as if I should be dying. I discovered the fingers of my right hand still moved, and the arm with them. I tried the left, then the two legs. My head, I found, only felt shattered. By a miracle, I had been spared.

If I was not crushed beneath the weight of a dead horse. Could I get free? It seemed not.

Where was Enkidu? He would have to dig me out. With his great strength . . .

But when I turned my head to look back, I saw that the pass was blocked. Almost the whole mountain had come down behind me.

He would be hours reaching me through all that. Probably he would assume I had been killed. I was thrown back on myself.

Yet I did not feel real despair until I heard the voices of men.

"He must be dead," I heard one of them say, in Egyptian.

"Yet you will look," another answered. "You will not be paid until I have his right hand, with the mark of the bloody star upon the palm. That is the proof that it is he and no other."

"Oh, very well. But we will be all day clearing away this mess."

I could not see them. I knew not how many there were. They were coming down to find me, to cut off my hand for a trophy.

I had to get out from beneath the chariot.

My ribs felt broken. I ran my hand over them and found they stung like a nest of scorpions—a rock had scraped the skin raw. Better that, I thought, than that they should be caved in like rotten barrel staves.

I tried pushing against the chariot, although there was hardly any room to move my arms. Nothing—it was useless.

I tried again. No, useless. No—yes. Perhaps yes. This time it seemed to stir a little.

My left elbow was badly swollen, but the joint, though sore, was unbroken and I could still work it. I pushed once more against the weight of the chariot and managed to lift it perhaps half a span from my chest. I filled my lungs with air and pushed again.

A large, irregularly shaped rock rolled loose and hit my arm, just above the bruised elbow. I felt a sharp twinge of gut-wrenching pain that forced me to drop the chariot. When I had stopped cursing I realized that the platform no longer lay on my chest, that the rock was holding it up. I could crawl out from underneath now. Somehow I felt like apologizing.

I could not see my attackers, but from the noise of their progress they seemed to be about a third of the way down from the summit of the bluff. I had no more than a few minutes.

I had been carrying javelins, a bow and a quiver of arrows. And of course my sword was still in my belt. As soon as I was out from beneath the chariot I reached back and retrieved the bow and the arrows and one of the javelins—the other two were broken.

The air was full of dust, and rocks were still settling into place. I stayed low, crouching behind the body of one of the dead horses. The men coming down to collect my hand had not seen me.

But I saw them. There were five of them, as ragged a tribe of bandits as you could imagine—it was almost an insult to be ambushed by such as these.

They wore gray tunics that did not even reach to their knees, and dangling from their belts were the long curved daggers worn by soldiers—that was probably what they were, runaway soldiers who lived by robbing graves and the occasional piece of villainy. Their heads and beards showed half a year's absence from the razor, which in Egypt meant that they were outlaws, cut off from the decent part of humanity, little better than beasts. Three of them carried war spears and one had a bow in his right hand. The last had no weapon and appeared to be the leader. I decided he would be the last to taste death.

My horses lay dead, spattered with blood, their bellies ripped open and their backs broken. I was alive only through the power of my *sedu*, the favor of the Lord Ashur. Anger burned in my bowels, for I would be avenged. I did not care if there were five or five hundred—they were corpses.

When they were halfway down, and within range, I stood up. I let them look at me, that they might know I was not afraid.

But they were. They stopped short—this they had not expected. I strung my bow, selected an arrow, couched it, took aim, and let fly. The man who was closest, the man with the bow, took my point full in the chest and dropped dead with a groan.

One summoned the courage to throw a spear, but it fell short. I raised my bow and killed him. My arrow found his guts, that he might suffer a time before he died.

The other men had seen enough. They turned and ran, clambering over the rocks like mice.

Two of them I did not care about—they could wait until I had leisure to think of them—but the leader, the one without a weapon, him I wanted, and alive. I aimed low. The first arrow missed him, whining as the iron point glanced off a stone, but the second buried itself in the calf of his right leg. Blood streamed down. He screamed, looked down to see what had happened, plucked out the arrow and threw it aside, then turned and hastened on in his flight. Yet he was not so agile now.

The others outstripped him, leaving him to die. He called to them, but they did not answer or even look back. His leg was stiffening now. I myself was bruised and in pain, but he would not escape.

With hands and feet I crawled over the rocks. The more I worked my body the stronger I felt, but the other man, his wound bleeding thickly, was slowing. His friends were gone and I was behind him. In his heart he must have known he would soon feed the crows—I hope he suffered. When I was almost upon him, I could hear him whimpering with ignoble fear. A slave would have faced death with more dignity.

Finally I had him. The distance between us closed, and at last I could reach up and grab him by the ankle. With a weak little cry of terror he tried to pull himself free, but he lost his footing and fell backwards.

I had him. And then, all at once, I did not. He struggled, he slipped on the loose ground and fell. Suddenly he was rolling down over the rocks like a log, unable to stop himself. All I could do was to watch.

When he reached the floor of the pass he lay still.

"You greasy dog," I thought, "if you have escaped from me into death . . ."

But he was not dead, not yet. Even as I made my way down I could see him stirring. With luck, he would live long enough for my purposes.

He lay there amidst the stones, his face and arms coated with the pale desert dust. His eyes were wide and shining with pain or fear or the gods knew what, and his mouth was open as if to speak. Yet he did not speak. As I approached he raised his left arm, perhaps in supplication.

I saw at once that the smallest finger was missing.

I knelt beside him. He tried to clutch at my sleeve, his hand opening and closing, but angrily I brushed his arm aside. I hated him worse than bitter death itself, for I could see he was slipping away from me.

"Who sent you?" I shouted, grabbing the neck of his tunic and shaking him, as a dog might a rat. "Who will give you money if you bring him my hand? Who sent you?"

"Wa—" He stopped, drew a breath, and tried again. "Water."

"Curse you, may the dry sand stop your mouth before I give you water! Who sent you?"

But I was already too late. The light faded in his eyes and his life fled from him. He would tell me nothing.

I sat there beside the dead man for a long while. My whole body seemed to ache and my mind was dark. I felt surrounded by enemies. The world was a bitter place.

Finally I picked up his hand and looked at the stump where his finger had grown. The edges of the wound were pink, as if they had just healed—this was no old injury.

He had been an Egyptian, this one. Light-skinned, but still an Egyptian. And he had not known who I was, not really. A man who asks for water with his last breath speaks in his own tongue, not one he has borrowed. This man had never lived beside the twin rivers.

He was not the one. Someone wished me to believe he might be—perhaps only if he failed. This was not the one who had been sent from Nineveh.

At last I heard the sound of leather sandals climbing over stone. A shadow fell across the ground. I looked up and saw Enkidu. He was carrying his ax and there was blood drying on the blade. I did not have to ask what had happened to the two who had escaped me.

He looked at me, and at the dead man, and I heard a low growl.

"No," I said. "He is not the one."

XIII

WITH ONE MOUNT BETWEEN US, WE RODE AND WALKED by turns, until at last I could walk no farther. I returned to Memphis clinging to the neck of Enkidu's horse; hardly able to keep from falling off. My elbow had grown so swollen that I could no longer bend it—Kephalos said later that when he lanced the bruise nearly four *kyathoi* of blood drained out in a gush. I must accept his word, for by then I had already fainted.

Kephalos insisted that I keep my bed and refrain from women for the next two days, and I felt but little inclination to disobey him. Yet I was not seriously injured and within four days was walking about out of doors, feeling sore and bad-tempered but not otherwise inconvenienced. By the sixth day my chief complaint was boredom, even with my garden, and I was very glad to receive a visit there from my Lord Senefru.

"I have been informed you suffered a hunting accident," he said, sitting down at the opposite end of a couch on which I was sunning my various bruises. "No—you need not lie about it. When I received word that your servant had brought you back, I thought to myself, What misadventure would cause the Lord Tiglath to leave both chariot and team behind when the whole world knows how fond he is of his fine horses? Thus I sent a man into the desert to discover the truth. What he found there you know."

He paused, waiting perhaps for an explanation. When he did not receive one, he shrugged his shoulders in resignation.

"No doubt you were justified, My Lord. Such brigands as those you may slaughter in their hundreds and the citizens of Memphis will look upon you as a benefactor. Besides, since clearly you did not bring that rock slide down upon yourself, one can only assume you were the victim of a murderous attack—such is the conclusion I reached in the report of the incident I sent to Prince Nekau."

"Then your call is in the way of business, My Lord?"

"How can you think it?" he asked, his face contracting as if from some inward pang. "The prince's only interest in the matter is with your safety. He was concerned that in his province so honored a guest, whom he looks upon as a friend, should have been set upon in this manner. For myself, I only wanted to be satisfied that you had sustained no lasting injury—and to be able to take that assurance to my Lady Wife."

We exchanged a nod which, under the etiquette governing our somewhat peculiar relationship, amounted to my apology and his acceptance of it, and for several seconds we waited together in silence, as if to see if a shadow would pass.

"I suppose they intended to rob you," he continued at last, his face innocently blank, for he supposed nothing of the sort.

"Of what?"

He raised his eyebrows inquiringly.

"Of what would they have thought to rob me?" I asked, as if the simple amplification would make everything plain. "I was out hunting. I had nothing with me of any value except a chariot, a pair of fine Arab horses, and my life. They wrecked the chariot and killed the horses. It was my life they wanted, and that is not robbery but murder."

Senefru's eyebrows dropped suddenly. He was less than pleased.

"You astonish me, My Lord," he said, not at all astonished. "It seems a grotesquely cumbersome way to murder someone—an avalanche. In Memphis, people are murdered every day with much less fuss."

"Perhaps it was intended to seem an accident."

Of course, had the assassins succeeded in their intentions, no one would have been deluded into imagining my death an accident—the missing hand would have been too difficult to explain. I saw fit, however, not to mention this detail to My Lord.

"Yet why should anyone go to the trouble?" he asked, answering my answer with a question. "Unless you have offended someone here in Memphis, who wishes to avoid a scandal." He smiled thinly, in silent acknowledgment of my right to suspect him.

"There is no one in Memphis so foolish or so base as to hire men such as those to roll stones down upon me from the top of a desert bluff. And no, My Lord—the man who did hire them wishes me dead not for any wickedness I have done. I offend him merely by living."

It seemed to gratify Senefru that I did not think to lay this deed at his feet, for such a mode of revenging himself would certainly have struck him as, at the very least, somewhat undignified. Perhaps that was what gratified him, for he gave the impression of being satisfied. Thus, at any rate, the reckoning between us drew a little closer to even.

"Then you must learn to be careful," he said, "for someone has a long reach."

Flesh heals faster than most things. Within half a month of the attack I had nothing by which to remember it except a few yellowing bruises. It was not much longer before I did not even have those.

I followed the Lord Senefru's advice and learned to be careful, yet after a while it began to seem that my caution was unnecessary—a month passed, and then two, and then several, and still no further attempt was made against me. With time the danger began to seem a trifle unreal, and gradually, if I did not quite dismiss it from my mind, it became like the stories of the gods which in childhood once made such a vivid impression, still believed but later without much conviction. This is the work of time.

It is of time, whom the Greeks recognize as one of the oldest of the gods, that I must now speak. Yet if he is a god he is also a magician, not very different from those one saw every day in the streets of Memphis, for his power lies chiefly in the creating of illusions, making what is false seem true, what is wicked pure. This is the magic which time worked on me in Egypt, for I lived there three years and learned to think I was happy and beyond the reach of evil.

Certainly I was fortunate. One of Senefru's neighbors died, so I bought the house and moved into it. It was smaller, so Kephalos almost choked on a fury of injured pride, but the garden adjoined Nodjmanefer's—now nothing separated us but a wooden gate in the wall.

Senefru made no objection. Indeed, he declared himself pleased that we should all thus see so much more of each other. The three of us were now so much in and out of each other's houses and company that we seemed almost to be living together. For practical purposes, Nodjmanefer and I almost were.

Yet if I imagined myself content, if I thought myself prosperous and happy, Egypt was not similarly deceived. For the common people those were hard years. The Nile flooded less and the barley withered in the fields. The ground cracked and turned to dust and in the countryside men and women slaughtered their oxen and then their girl babies because there was nothing for any of them to eat. The cities became crowded with those who fled the land, but the price of food had risen until ordinary working people could hardly afford to buy it—once I saw pressed dates being sold for equal weights of silver—and those without employment could afford nothing, not the poorest broken millet.

Sometimes riots broke out, and these were truly dreadful. They begin with some trivial disturbance when, for instance, a peddler, selling vegetables beneath a canvas awning, at last is made impatient by the heat and worry and weariness, and perhaps by a pity he cannot afford to indulge, and too roughly turns away a beggar, of which were are always too many.

The beggar objects, and onlookers take sides. Some say the beggar is a thief, but most the peddler, who is resented for being rich enough to have something to sell. Soon a mob forms. The peddler's stall is torn down and looted. Perhaps the peddler is even killed—surely he is killed.

All at once people who for as long as they can recall have known nothing but misery now know power and the thirst for revenge and blind rage. The mob is like a mad animal—it plunders and destroys. To be outside is to invite death. No one's life is safe. There is blood on the cobblestones and the white sand in the streets drinks it up.

Then, suddenly, things have gone too far. The rich, behind the stone walls of their houses, feel threatened—someone might presume to plunder not a vegetable peddler's stall, but them. The soldiers are called out. There is a massacre as innocent and guilty alike fall before the swords and the chariot wheels. Screams rend the air into tatters. By sundown the river is filled with bloated corpses and the crocodiles gorge themselves. For days the vultures walk along the muddy banks, too heavy with carrion even to fly.

Thus was Egypt in the time I lived there, and each year it grew worse.

"Soon they really will begin murdering respectable people in their beds," Prince Nekau complained to me while sitting at his dinner table, peeling the skin from an apple with a silver knife. "This quarter alone I have had to spend seven hundred thousand *emmer* from the public treasury, and it has hardly bought half as many bushels of wheat, for some of it must be brought from as far away as Judah. Soon I shall be obliged to impose new taxes, which the rich shall have to pay because the poor are already squeezed nearly lifeless. Of course they will all write to Pharaoh in Tanis, complaining that I rob them. As if I were responsible for the famine. They would do better to ask Pharaoh's aid in petitioning his fellow gods for a high flood next season."

"And will he not petition the gods without their asking?"

The prince laughed a short, bitter laugh and shook his head.

"No, My Lord, he will not. Pharaoh is a god and therefore, of course, pure, but the men who have his ear are neither. They welcome these hard times, as they would welcome anything that brings discredit upon me. They want only an excuse to hang me by my heels from the city wall that Pharaoh might rule in Memphis directly. They wish the old days of Egypt's glory brought back."

"And you do not?"

"They will not come back, My Lord—they are gone."

He shrugged his shoulders, as if so easily the weight of these troubles could slide from his back, and went on with his dinner. Afterwards he spoke of his scarab collection, justly famous among connoisseurs of such things, and of his delight in a slave girl he had recently acquired from Nubia.

But if Prince Nekau saw only dimly, and through the window of his own interests, his subjects among the noble houses of Memphis saw not at all. The famine was merely a nuisance, a temporary constraint upon their incomes, something which would pass soon enough and leave their lives and fortunes restored to what they had always been. They closed their eyes to the suffering around them, and to what it might finally come to mean.

"I hardly ever go into the city anymore," I once heard a woman lamenting. "There is hardly anything amusing to be found in the marketplace these days, and the *smell* . . . ! Of course trade is bad, but who wants to take the trouble to visit the bazaars when things are so unpleasant? All I have to say is that if people are hungry, then the prince should put them to work clearing away the corpses."

No one even laughed. It was as if they hadn't heard.

Yet is is possible their blindness was deliberate, and not quite the folly that it seemed. What could they have done, a few hundred wealthy aristocrats with no power—given away their jewels, opened their private granaries to the starving, and then wandered into the desert to live as hermits? What would that have changed? There might have been a few fat and merry days in the poor quarters of Memphis, and then famine would have tightened its grip again. The rich were not rich enough to make a difference.

And no man embraces suffering willingly. So my fashionable friends drew the curtains of their carrying chairs as they passed through the city—what they did not see did not exist. Thus it was still possible to be happy and to sleep soundly at night.

The vogue for river parties had been forgotten, perhaps because these days there were too many corpses in the water, and thus for two winters in a row the desert was in high favor. Fowling became something of a craze and expeditions would be organized so that men and women could cast nets for birds brought specially for the purpose, quail and partridge carried out from the city in wooden cages, their wing feathers clipped so as not to place too severe a strain upon anyone's abilities—after all, whatever would be the point of sport if it had to be taken seriously?

This would all happen in the late afternoon, when the sun was no longer so oppressively hot, and then, after we had all chased around like children—and full half the birds had escaped into the wilderness—our cooks would roast those even less agile than their pursuers and we would lie about on carpets spread over the sand and enjoy a lovely banquet by the light of huge, picturesque bonfires. Usually we would even spend the night in linen tents, and ladies would conveniently manage to lose their way.

As he had told me more than once, Senefru was not a man of the desert, so he rarely joined these entertainments. I shared his distaste, for the hunting was poor stuff, but I never failed to attend. I could put up with an afternoon of foolishness if at the end of it I was sure of sleeping the night through with Nodjmanefer in my arms.

"I do not like the desert," she told me once, while we took a walk through its long twilight. "It frightens me. It is full of silence, like death."

"Yet its silence allows us to be alone together," I said, smiling, trying to make her forget her mood. I put my arm around her shoulders and drew her close.

"Yes, that is something. But it makes me think of all the vast time when we will be alone separately." Her tiny hand pressed against my ribs. "I wish we were back in Memphis, Tiglath—I do not desire to think of anything except the few hours we can be together."

"There is nothing in Memphis except Senefru."

I knew, even as I said it, that I had made a mistake. I could feel her grow rigid within the circle of my arm, as if she had suddenly felt a chill.

"Yes—death is everywhere, not simply here. I have been talking like a simpleton. Forgive me."

We lay together that night. Her thighs opened to receive me and her mouth pressed against mine. The commerce of the flesh happened as it always did, but only the flesh found any happiness. She seemed to be there for me only as flesh, as if somehow I had lost her. We seemed divided from one another, as if I had been blinded and only she had eyes.

There is nothing in Memphis except Senefru.

There he was, sitting behind the long table in his study, reading over the papyrus scrolls that appeared to cover it. He was always there, and when he was not he was in Saïs or Tanis, about some secret business which he never mentioned. The years had made Senefru an important and powerful man.

Nodjmanefer was his wife, and he called me his friend. When we returned he would rise from his chair and greet us, and we would all three dine together, and he would listen in an absent-minded way to whatever the news might be. He did not seem to care. He seemed to have dismissed us from existence—or perhaps merely to have forgotten that we were in the world.

It is difficult with such a man to remember that you are wronging his bed. There were long periods when I did not remember it, when the unnatural character of our relationship did not appear to me. Yet I do not believe that Senefru ever lost sight of it. Nor did Nodjmanefer. It was this knowledge, perhaps as much as anything, which united husband and wife.

That last year the floods came late, and when they had come and gone the old men in the villages were consulted, and these pronounced that never in living memory had the watermarks on the steep banks of the Nile stood so low. The temple records which the priest kept said the same. For yet another year there would be famine in Egypt, and worse than before.

One morning, at breakfast, Kephalos presented himself to me. He did not seem particularly pleased.

"As you know, Lord, I do not often trouble you with business," he began, nervously fingering the hem of his tunic and glancing about him as if he found the sight of food oppressive. "Yet I wish you to consider whether it would not be for the best if we began to think of leaving Memphis—of perhaps returning to Naukratis, although I think it would be better if we quit this nation altogether."

I regarded him with frank astonishment, and after a moment of silence he raised his hand in a dismissing gesture.

"When there is trouble, Lord, foreigners are never popular, and the trouble in Egypt becomes worse each month. It is time to go. Two years ago, when prices were better and when you were foolish enough to forgive some of your tenants their rents, I saw the way of things, with Egypt and with you, and began selling off your land and sending whatever I could convert into gold and silver out of the country. Most of it is deposited with merchants in Sidon. There is nothing now to hold us here."

"Kephalos, I have made a life for myself here," I said, all at once seized with an absurd panic, as if I feared there might be men waiting behind the door to carry me off by force. "I cannot simply leave—I have attachments . . ."

"My Lord, be reasonable." He smiled sadly, apparently believing there was little enough chance of that. "Life here is fast growing intolerable—I can hardly pass through the front gate for the beggars who collect there, and all because you have given orders that no one is to be turned away with nothing. You are not hard enough to live in such a place in such a time.

"And besides, you and I both know you think only of the Lady Nodjmanefer, and there is no reason why she should be an obstacle. A woman is as easily carried downriver as a bushel of wheat. If you ask it of her—and make it clear you will go in any case—then she will come away with us. If she will not, then you will know she is not worth the staying for."

Yet he was right to doubt me, for I did not wish to know which way she would answer. I had not the courage to put her to such a test. Still, it would have been better for both of us if I had, even if she had let me go.

"You must do as you think best," I said, "but for myself, since I must die in some strange land, this one will do as well as any other."

Kephalos, who understood but was ever my friend, recognized the futility of argument. He withdrew in silence. I did not see him again for several days.

Yet if his voice was not raised against me, another's was. That night, over the western desert, there was a lightning storm such as the Egyptians had not witnessed in a hundred years. It was visible from every rooftop in Memphis, and people said that the very stars dripped bloody fire.

I did not see it—I would not see it, but stayed in my rooms—but I believed then and do still that they spoke the truth.

I could not hide from this warning, even if I would not listen. The Lord Ashur must have me know that I did evil under his very eyes.

XIV

THE NIGHT OF THE BLEEDING STARS, AS IT CAME TO BE called, marked the beginning to a season of calamity. The gods had given warning of their displeasure—this was what the priests said—and now all of the Land of Egypt lay under a curse. Prophecies of fearful disaster were whispered about, and the people of Memphis were not kept waiting long to see them fulfilled.

It is said by the Egyptians that if the sun grows high enough it spawns vermin from the Nile mud, which splits open to let them crawl out through the cracks. I do not doubt it, for the sun was blinding that final summer, and even before the long grass had withered yellow and brittle one had only to walk down to the river to watch hoards of rats crawling over the banks and each other, chattering in their high-pitched voices, loathsome and rapacious. Soon after they reached the city, plague broke out in the poor quarters. The people, weakened by famine, perished in their own doorways.

There is no answer to plague except fire. The prince ordered entire streets burned. Gangs of soldiers went about torching rows of reed-mat hovels, sometimes with the corpses of whole families still inside, and the smoke from these, mingled with the ever-present smell of death, left a permanent stain upon the air.

On the first day of the Feast of Opet, which traditionally lasts for four and twenty days but which this year the people of Memphis were too poor to celebrate for even one, Prince Nekau led the procession of the god Amun and was cursed by onlookers and pelted with cattle dung. Members of the crowd were arrested, apparently at random, and these had their hands lopped off and were then hanged, but the scandal did not end there. Such a thing, such an insult to the god, as well as to the prince, had never happened before. For a time people were hardly able to speak of anything else.

Wild rumors floated about. Pharaoh, it was reported, had fallen ill—I read in letters from Naukratis that he had only turned his ankle while hunting—but soon everyone seemed to believe that he must be dead. After all, to most people Tanis probably seemed almost as far away as the Field of Offerings.

One man told me that he had heard that Pharaoh had been assassinated by foreigners, another that the gods had recalled him to them that the Land of Egypt might be destroyed.

Not many days later Prince Nekau was forced to issue a public denial that the city grain supplies had been poisoned by the priests, who were now more unpopular than ever and many of whom had been murdered in the streets. I do not know how many believed this denial, but certainly many fewer cared; the poor, if you offered them bread, would simply eat it, whether they believed it was poisoned or not.

And then, of course, there were the riots, which now took place every few days, almost as if someone had established a schedule for them. Sometimes, when they were dispatched to quell a disturbance, small contingents of soldiers joined in the looting and had themselves to be put down. The gardens of wealthy houses were ransacked and the trees stripped of their fruit. Several people hired guards, which sometimes almost amounted to inviting the thieves inside the walls, and no one ventured into the city without an armed escort. This after a man I knew slightly, a certain Pa'anuket, tempted the gods by visiting the bazaar— which, in any case, was nearly empty—was cornered by the mob and then torn to pieces. His wife did not get enough of him back even to bury.

Thus the Egyptians, who only a few years before had affected to despise such things, now openly carried weapons.

I was not such a fool I could not see by now that Kephalos had been right, that it was time to leave Memphis. Things were safer in Naukratis, where the harvests had been better and, in any case, foreign grain was easier to come by, so I thought of withdrawing my household to that city and then deciding if finally it might not be necessary to depart from Egypt altogether. It required only the consent of my Lady Nodjmanefer, for I had no intention of leaving without her. Yet in the end I never had to ask her. My request was forestalled by a visit from her husband.

The Lord Senefru was as a rule quite scrupulous in all matters of form. He gave the impression of detesting surprises, or anything that suggested cunning. He considered it only polite to give notice of his intentions. So I was surprised when, late in the afternoon, an hour or so before I was engaged to join him for dinner, I glanced out the window of my study and watched him open the gate in the wall that separated our two gardens and walk through.

He knew he had been observed, no matter that the shutter remained half closed. He raised his eyes to me and made a curt gesture inviting me to join him. I found him studying the fountain, dried up now and the flagstones around it drifted over with fine sand—it had seemed an indecent luxury to keep a fountain running while farmers struggled to find water for their crops—frowning as if he had discovered some secret flaw in my character.

"You will forgive this intrusion," he said, without looking at me, his attention apparently still held by the fountain. "I did not care to send a servant ahead to announce me. I did not wish to give the impression . . . You will understand, I wish this meeting to seem quite casual, a matter of the merest chance."

I nodded, although I was not sure if he noticed. I waited, without speaking, for what seemed several minutes but was probably only as many seconds, until he chose to continue.

"My Lord Tiglath, my wife the Lady Nodjmanefer has asked me to divorce her."

He turned to me at last, smiling his tight, meaningless smile.

"I see I have surprised you," he said. "You and I have always treated this matter with a tactful silence, assuming that each knew the other's mind and that, finally, there was nothing to be said. Yet now all is changed, and I must know, My Lord, whether this news is agreeable to you or not."

"It—yes, it is agreeable," I answered, hardly knowing where I found the words.

"Then I am prepared to release her—provided, of course, that the two of you leave Memphis and undertake never to return during my life. I will mourn the loss of you both, but you must understand that otherwise matters would grow awkward . . ."

"Yes . . . of course."

"And there is one further condition." He smiled again, as if at last he had closed the trap on me. "My Lord, I would have a favor of you."

"Anything—I . . ."

Even as the words left my tongue I could hear a warning whispered in my secret soul, yet I would not listen. If the man wanted my arm at the shoulder he was welcome to it, provided I had Nodjmanefer in return.

Yet I knew, even then . . . Knew what? I could not have said, except that there was no innocence.

"My Lord, you are not blind," Senefru began, turning away from the fountain and pointing to the sky above the garden's northern wall, where a cloud of gray smoke was gathering. In the distance, if one listened carefully, it was just possible to pick out the murmur of human voices—raised, it seemed, in panic. "The people are not content to starve quietly. It seems something must be done."

"I gather something is being done," I said, my voice sounding flat and harsh, even to myself. "From the sound of it, the militia is out clearing the streets again. I wonder how many corpses the crocodiles will have to feast upon tonight, and if they will ever again be content with any other diet."

We both listened for a moment. Yes—it was unmistakable. Not four hundred paces from the street where we two lived, prosperous gentlemen, safe from the wrath of the world, there had risen a settlement of miserable reed huts, the refuge of potbellied children who by now could hardly stand and women with withered breasts—farming families, driven from the land by want—driven out now again, it seemed, only this time the goad was smoke and fire and the sharp edge of a soldier's sword.

"Yes." The Lord Senefru spoke quite calmly, like a priest explaining a point of ritual. "The prince has adopted a new policy of burning all the encampments within the city walls, even if plague has not yet broken out. These beggars can set up their hovels by the riverbank, where they will not have such easy access to the bazaar squares. He hopes thus to reduce the rioting, as well as the outbreaks of sickness."

"And do you share this hope, My Lord?"

Senefru turned to me speculatively, as if I had said something remarkable, but at last he only shrugged his shoulders.

"The hope, perhaps, but without much confidence. Yet he must do something, for if he does not Pharaoh will come with his armies. And the blood that will be spilt then . . . You see, Pharaoh has sent word that he has heard what his priests have suffered at the hands of unruly mobs and that in his realm he will tolerate no disrespect for the gods—it is a pretext only, but I fear it will serve. Pharaoh wishes to remove the prince, saying he cannot keep order in his own city. Yet how is he to keep order while people are starving?

"No, I fear the only thing that can save us from disaster—and that for perhaps only a brief time—is bread. When the people's bellies are full there will be peace once more in Memphis. At least for a while. Lamentably, the prince has no more silver with which to buy grain."

"If he wishes a loan from me, My Lord, he shall have it."

"A loan, yes, but not from you." Senefru put his hands upon his knees and looked up into my face, squinting as if the light hurt his eyes. "The prince knows you have been sending your wealth abroad—for which he does not criticize you, My Lord, since as a foreigner you must be careful and such precautions are wise in a time of trouble. Besides, the sums he requires are beyond the powers of any one man. What the prince wishes is to avail himself not of your purse but of your good offices. You have many friends among the Greeks of Naukratis—he wishes you to go there and to secure pledges, in his name, for at least five million emmer of silver."

I was stagggered, I admit it. Such a sum took my breath away—it was enough to beggar a king. For the moment I could not think beyond it.

And perhaps the Lord Senefru took my silence for reluctance.

"The prince will, of course, secure the loan in whatever manner your friends think fit." Having spoken thus, he retreated a little into his natural dignity, like a man who expects to be rebuffed.

Yet he needn't have worried, for I knew what answer I must make.

"And to show my confidence in him," I said, "I will pledge my house here in Memphis and whatever else I can raise. I cannot guarantee success, My Lord, for I cannot speak for others. Yet if it depends solely on my voice, the prince shall have whatever he requires."

Senefru rose and placed his hands upon my shoulders, as if he meant to embrace me. This he did not do, however, but turned away, as if in embarrassment.

"I ask no more," he said. "Yet remember that in these matters appearances are all. It would be as well if your friends in Naukratis received no exaggerated accounts of conditions here. And say nothing of Pharaoh, for their tenure in Egypt depends upon his patronage. Prince Nekau would have money to buy grain, that his people might not perish from want. So much is the truth—and as much of the truth as the Greeks need hear.

"Nor must word of this reach Pharaoh. At present, no one except you, myself and the prince have knowledge of your commission—let it remain so as long as possible. Let it be thought that you journey to Naukratis on private business, and once there speak only to men you trust—and to no one before you arrive. I have come to you privately, and so must you go to them. Make haste, that all this may be settled quickly, and use cunning. I think you may have a talent for that, My Lord."

He did not even wait for my answer but turned away, planning, it seemed, to return to his own house. Then he paused, and stood not quite facing me.

"I do not reproach you because of the Lady Nodjmanefer," he said, raising a hand to forestall any reply. "I do not reproach you."

He departed in silence, the gate swinging closed behind him.

"I think you have gone mad, My Lord. The summer sun has baked your brain as soft as fresh camel droppings."

"Nevertheless, Kephalos, I wish you to hire a barge with a team of strong rowers. I wish to leave for Naukratis before dawn."

I did not keep my appointment to dine that night. Instead, I went to my former slave and told him all that had passed between myself and the Lord Senefru. He was not pleased.

"My Lord, you have lived in safety here in Memphis these three years. Here no one would dare raise his hand against you. When we leave this place, let us go with a proper retinue. I would not have you slinking off like a thief, exposing yourself to every danger—or have you forgotten you have enemies?"

"My friend, I will be well enough. I go only to Naukratis."

"Have you forgotten what happened to Prodikos in Naukratis? Be so good as to furnish me with a towel."

Kephalos, naked and gigantic, was standing in water up to his knees in the center of the great green stone tub in which he was fond of bathing. I had chased his women from the room, so there was no one else to attend him.

Hanging on a hook near the door was a piece of heavy linen which would have served some fisherman quite well for a sail. This I took down and held out to him. He snatched it angrily out of my hand and wrapped himself in it, its edge trailing in the water as he stepped out onto the floor.

"You have no consideration," he stated flatly, sitting on a stool to dry his feet. "I had not even had my back oiled yet—do you have any conception how irksome the sun of this country is to me? How my skin cracks like old leather unless it is kept properly oiled? No, I thought you had not. I suppose it is a mark of your princely rank that you are mindful of no one's convenience except your own."

"Kephalos, my friend, what is the danger? If I leave at once, while darkness still covers the face of the earth, who will regard it? No one knows of it except Prince Nekau, my Lord Senefru, and now you."

"My Lord Senefru?" He looked at me sidewise, raising his eyes from his foot, which rested on his left knee, to my face. His mouth was a crooked, disdainful line. "Your mistress's husband, and you trust him? Where have you lived your life, My Master, that you have grown into such a fool?"

"Kephalos, will you arrange the barge?"

"Yes, of course. But take Enkidu with you."

"And Selana—I do not want her here if real trouble should come. I will say I take her to Naukratis to find her a husband."

"An excellent idea. And along the way, be sure to take pity upon the crocodiles and drop her into the Nile."

Selana herself was less enthusiastic.

"I have told you, Lord, I will not be married off to a ship's clerk. If you force some man upon me, I will only run away. If I cannot escape, I will school myself to make his life a misery."

"Why should you not wish to be married? You are old enough—almost."

I hardly believed it myself, seeing her as she stood before me, a thin little figure in a linen tunic that hid nothing while it showed how little there was to hide. She would be thirteen that year. Half the girls in Egypt were married at thirteen, but perhaps not Selana.

"I will not trade a master who is a prince for one who deals in hides, that is all. Your sleeping mat, at least, will not smell of onions and ox tallow. When it is time for me to spill my maiden's blood, I will let you know and we will settle the matter between us."

She crossed her arms over her meager chest, her eyes narrowed, daring me to try to compel her to anything.

"Then I will strike a bargain with you," I said, knowing in advance that I was defeated. "I ask only that you bring yourself to reason. I will force you to nothing. Come to Naukratis with me. If we find no man there who pleases you, we will let the matter drop for another year."

"I have found already the man who pleases me, and in Naukratis. It is *he*, and not I, who must be brought to reason. Yet is is clear you serve some purpose of your own in going to Naukratis, and I will go as well if it is your pleasure."

Did this child really find me as transparent as that? So it would seem.

"It pleases me," I said, pretending to be the master. "Go and ready your things."

She left my presence, and when I opened a window I found it was dark night already. In a few hours I would be on the river, setting out to free Nodjmanefer from the entanglements that held her from me. Yet now it was dark and cold and the hours were empty. I felt a strange sense of desolation. I went up to the roof of my house to look out over the quiet world and find my peace again.

In the northern quarter of the city there were still fires burning with a reddish light, revealing little except black smoke that boiled thickly skywards like mud stirred up from the bottom of a quiet pond.

To the indifferent stars this must seem a wretched place, I thought. More barren than any desert, a scene of suffering and little else.

Some said the wicked suffered thus when they died, in a world the gods had reserved for their punishment, but I did not believe this. Men suffered enough in the world they knew, wicked and good alike.

Yes, I was sick of Memphis. What had Prodikos said? *"Go to Memphis and gorge on it. Afterwards, have a good vomit to purge your bowels of such follies and then continue on with the rest of your life."*

He had given me good advice. I was ready to leave Memphis—to leave Egypt. It was no longer enough.

It was perhaps a feeling that comes to all exiles. I was weary of living as a spectator, of being amused by the folly of other people, of being wise at their expense, of risking nothing, of caring for nothing, of being empty. In Egypt I felt myself hardly human.

And there was Nodjmanefer—this twilight existence with her, this stealthy love affair which everyone pretended to ignore, it was a game that was no longer amusing. I wished to marry her. Whether I loved her or not I hardly knew—it hardly mattered. I wished to marry her.

And so much, at least, was within reach. It was in Naukratis, waiting.

Below me, under the cold summer moon, I could see the Nile glistening in the distance. And between us was Memphis, destroying itself by degrees. The night made everything visible, and by the simple device of hiding what did not matter.

It was still dark when we made our way down to the river, where a barge was already provisioned and manned—I do not know how Kephalos had managed everything so quickly, but he had.

It was a small pier, used only by pleasure craft and well away from the bustling stretch of deep water where the trading vessels tied up. At that hour it was quite empty; the loudest sound was that of the frogs croaking down at the water's edge. Kephalos had insisted on accompanying us with an armed guard, but in the quarter hour's walk from our house near the temple district we had encountered no one except a beggar woman asleep in a doorway, who had been astonished when Selana woke her with a little purse of silver coins. Otherwise, we were quite alone—Memphis was too weak and weary to trouble herself about us.

I felt like a criminal escaping on the very eve of his execution. Behind us the city seemed deserted—a doomed city awaiting the final catastrophe. Perhaps this was what it would be if I could not persuade the Greeks of Naukratis to lend Prince Nekau the money he needed, but I had to admit that my own motives were private and selfish. I did not care about Memphis. Greek silver was the price Senefru demanded for his wife, and I would get it for him if I could.

Enkidu stood by the gangplank, waiting to leave. Beside him, hardly reaching as high as his belt, was Selana. They both seemed to be wondering why I still lingered behind. I could not have told them.

Then I knew. In the darkness I heard the slap, slap, slap of naked feet, the short, quick steps of men carrying something. Then I saw them—first a yellow blaze of torchlight, then four slaves wearing the livery of my Lord Senefru and carrying a sedan chair. They set it down on the pier and a hand opened the curtained door. It was Nodjmanefer.

We had little time and no privacy. In front of so many people there could be no embrace, only a word or two.

"I will be back as quickly as I can," I said. "There was no opportunity to send you notice."

"I know this—from Senefru. He told me as soon as he had seen you. It was only that . . . I could not let you go in silence."

Her eyes were shining. Screened by my cloak, our hands touched and joined. It was all the farewell we would have.

"Does he mean to let you go? If he does not, if he has lied to me, I will come back and kill him."

"He will let me go," she said, her voice little more than a whisper. "He will—now. Tiglath, my belly is heavy with child."

I cannot describe what I felt then. I do not even remember clearly, for the recollection is stained with too much grief. But my bowels melted with tenderness and a kind of pity, I know that. And I know that if ever I loved Nodjmanefer, it was in that moment.

"Are you sure?" I asked, quite unnecessarily. Was it not the question every man asks?

"Yes, I am sure. It is your child—I am sure of that too, and so is Senefru. This is why he will let me go."

And then, with no word spoken, she turned from me and left. The curtain closed around her chair and her slaves carried her away. I waited until I could no longer see her, until I could no longer see the light of her torch, and then I remembered why I had come to this dark, still place.

I embraced Kephalos, who admonished me one last time to be careful with my life, and then I climbed up the gangplank to the barge, where Selana was waiting, standing behind Enkidu's leg as behind a wall, scowling at me.

"Is *she* the reason you go to Naukratis?" she asked bitterly, having already guessed the answer. "Then certainly you are a fool."

Another time I would have beaten her for such insolence, but not then. I only threatened it, and told her to find a place to unroll her sleeping mat. I could not have been angry—I was even fool enough to be amused.

We would make good time to Naukratis. The current was with us, so it would not be necessary to tie up every night. I was full of hope as Ashur's sun rose over the eastern mountains. Everything I wanted seemed at last within reach.

In the gray morning light I watched a monkey scrambling about on the bluff above the riverbank. He seemed greatly pleased with himself as he capered back and forth, eating a piece of green fruit which he held in his paw—where he had found it in that barren landscape I cannot guess, so perhaps he had a right to be pleased.

Suddenly, out of the sun, an eagle swooped, its wings folded back, dropping like a stone. I saw, but the monkey did not. Not until the eagle struck, snatching away life with its cruel talons, did the monkey drop his prize.

The eagle circled back and plucked up the dead monkey from the ground, carrying it higher and higher until both were lost in the sun's bright disk.

XV

"FIVE MILLION EMMER! TIGLATH, MY DEAR YOUNG FRIEND, such a sum! I could not raise five hundred on Prince Nekau's name, not if he offered Memphis and Saïs together as security. I fear you have come on a fool's errand, for everyone in Egypt knows that that well has long since run dry."

Glaukon, who had lived in Naukratis for thirty years and yet, out of contempt for the Egyptians, had never shaved off his iron-gray beard, sat in his counting house, a small room with bare plastered walls where every day bargains were struck involving enough to keep a man in wealth forever. His elbows rested on the table and his hands were neatly laced together to support his head. Prodikos had been his partner in trade and closest friend, and from him he had, in a sense, inherited a benevolent interest in my affairs. His had been the first name to occur to me— Glaukon will know how to manage this business, I had thought. He will not fail me. I was bitterly disappointed, but probably I deserved to be.

"No, do not look at me thus," he said, frowning and leaning back in his chair. "Have the grace to know that what you ask is simply impossible. I could as easily swim from here to Cyprus and back as persuade the merchant council of Naukratis to loan the sum of five million emmer to Prince Nekau, who has squandered the wealth of two of Egypt's richest nomes, who does not own so much as a linen loincloth for which he is not already in debt, and whom Pharaoh, if this were not enough, has decided to hang by the heels from the city walls. Five million emmer! All the Greeks in Egypt are not worth such a sum. We are rich, but not that rich.

"I am sorry, my friend, but the prince is a bad risk, and we cannot afford to offend Pharaoh."

His hands came apart and he held them out to me, palm up, as if to suggest how utterly the matter was outside his control. As far as he was concerned, it seemed, there was nothing more to be said, and if I could not understand the obvious then explanations would be in vain.

All at once an idea seemed to enter his mind. His eyes narrowed and he cocked his head a little to one side.

"Tell me, if you can—if you will, my friend—was it the prince himself who approached you in this matter, or some other?"

"It was my Lord Senefru," I answered, since to do so violated no confidence. I was surprised, in fact, that Glaukon had needed to ask.

"Senefru, you say!" He pursed his lips, as if that had been the last name he might have expected to hear. "He is a cunning old dog and knows how the land lies—I would have thought . . . Yet in these questions of statecraft even a clever man is sometimes blinded by hope or ambition or old loyalties. Sometimes there is no accounting for how things fall out."

"Yet I cannot return to him empty-handed"—very well, I thought, if I am a fool then at least I will be a stubborn one—"I know that Kephalos has been employing you to send my wealth out of the country. How much is left that I can collect at once?"

"A hundred thousand emmer, give or take . . ." He shrugged his shoulders, as if we were discussing trifles.

"Then be so good as to collect it for me, to be held in Prince Nekau's name until you receive instructions. And my house in Memphis, how much will that bring in a quick sale?"

"With the houshold slaves?"

I nodded.

"Perhaps another twenty thousand. Yes, of course, I will undertake to guarantee that much."

"Then prepare the agreements."

I rose to leave, my heart filled with resentment which I knew even then was foolish, for why should I think myself ill-used if Glaukon, to whom this was all purely a matter of profit and loss, refused to oblige me by ruining himself? Yet I did think myself ill-used, and perhaps it showed. And perhaps Glaukon saw it.

"Let us not part in bitterness," he said, putting his hand upon my arm, as if afraid I might break and run. "It is not my doing, or even the Greeks'—it is Pharaoh. Do you imagine he did not foresee this? And his agents have made it clear that whoever gives aid to Prince Nekau forfeits his patronage. We are strangers here, Tiglath. We *need* Pharaoh."

"I understand."

And I did, truly. How were little men like Glaukon and his friends to stand against Pharaoh, who with a word could ruin them? And what motive had they to try? Pharaoh had chosen to destroy Prince Nekau, and had selected the famine as his instrument. The matter was settled.

"And, Tiglath . . ." He glanced furtively about, although there was no one except ourselves in the tiny room—it was merely a reflex, the sort of thing which betrays a man's true state of mind. "It is whispered, my friend, that Pharaoh means to act quickly. He already has his agents in Memphis, who will provide him with a pretext, so it will not be long. Take my advice and do not return. Send word to Kephalos to remove your household, but do not go back yourself. The city will be in turmoil, and at such times everything goes a little mad. There are those who say you have made powerful enemies. Any mischief is possible."

"I thank you for your warning, Glaukon, but I must go back. I have no choice."

He nodded, smiling the way one does when confronted with a willfulness one is helpless to move. Thus we parted.

I was staying at a tavern near the waterfront, but I did not return there at once. The morning coolness had not yet fled, and it was pleasant to be outside and out of sight of the river. Besides, I did not wish to return to Enkidu and Selana, neither of whom knew of my business or would care if they did, and hide my sense of failure from their indifferent eyes. For a few hours, at least, I wished to be among strangers.

It struck me as a measure of Senefru's desperation that he would send me thus on what he had to have known would be a fruitless search. He probably better than anyone must have realized that the prince would find no allies in Naukratis, but there were times when a man will grasp at the most slender hope. So, at least, it seemed to me.

Now there was nothing. Disaster seemed to have achieved its own momentum, like water falling over a cataract. Pharaoh would come to Memphis and the crocodiles would feast again. Whether at last that would be good or bad for Egypt was unknowable, or perhaps beside the point. Did anyone care what was good for Egypt? Did Pharaoh? Did Nekau? Certainly I did not. I cared for Nodjmanefer, and my mind was haunted by visions of bloated corpses floating in the Nile.

That was what I had come to Naukratis to prevent. It had not been my first consideration, nor even Senefru's, but perhaps finally it was all we could hope for. I could return to Memphis with silver with which to buy grain—perhaps not very much, perhaps only what I could buy with my own hundred and twenty thousand emmer—but at least a few less people would perish of want. If they perished under the swords of Pharaoh's soldiers, that would have to be on his head.

I wandered into the bazaars and discovered that Naukratis had not changed so very much in three years. There was less to buy, and the price of food had increased perhaps ten or twentyfold, but matters were not as desperate here in the Delta as they had become upriver. In Naukratis, this was merely a time of adversity, and as such could be counted on to pass away.

A cup of wine was five pieces of silver—and that was watered. I drank three cups to cool my belly, since it was good for little else, and went back to take dinner at the tavern.

"Someone called for you," Selana told me, even as she held the bowl in which I washed my hands. "A man—a stranger."

"What was his business, then?"

I dried my fingers on a bit of linen. Probably, I thought, he was some acquaintance from a previous visit—yet why hadn't he waited and taken dinner with me?

"I do not know. He spoke to the landlord, who told me. The landlord said he was a foreigner. Not a Greek, something else. He dressed like an Egyptian, but he spoke the tongue badly."

The landlord's wife came in with my dinner. She was perhaps sixteen and pretty, and she had been married only a year. She liked to flirt, but her husband, who was forty, was besotted with her and took it as a great compliment that men found her attractive. He hardly ever beat her, and in such a place there was little else to encourage her to virtue. I asked her how the landlord had known the stranger was not Greek.

"In Naukratis, if a foreigner speaks Egyptian no better than this one, he speaks Greek."

"Then where do you think he came from?"

"If they are not Greek, one foreigner is like another," she said, shrugging her fine brown shoulders. Like most women in her class, she wore only a loincloth and a short linen skirt that did not even cover her thighs, so with every movement her breasts stirred enticingly. "Khonsmose thinks he was from the Eastern Lands."

Khonsmose was her husband, and when Egyptians say a stranger is "from the Eastern Lands," it only means that he is not black, not a Libyan, and not a Greek.

"Had he a finger missing from his left hand?"

"If he had, Khonsmose did not mention it."

The subject clearly was without much interest for her, but that did not matter. She smiled, showing me her small white teeth. She liked the way I had been looking at her.

When dinner was over, Selana poured me another cup of wine, as if she thought I had not grown drunk enough.

"The landlord's wife will visit your sleeping mat tonight if you give her twenty silver pieces," she said.

"And how is it you know that?"

"Because she promised me I would have two if I told you."

"I was in the bazaar today. A cup of wine there costs five."

"I think the landlord's wife should regard herself as fortunate if she gets ten. Her backside is too big, and she smells of onions."

"Perhaps she has to give half to the landlord."

"I think the landlord, and you, and all men are great fools."

She was angry now, coiled up inside like a little viper. I was considering how best to praise the landlord's wife—after all, how often did I have such a chance to annoy Selana?—when I found that the subject had been abruptly changed.

"The foreigner said he would be back this evening," she said, taking back the wine cup while it was still half full. "He said it was a matter of business. He said it was important."

"If then it is business, he had best not find me in the company of children. Go to bed, Selana."

She scrambled to her feet, leaving the cup and the wine jar behind her.

"And what of the landlord's wife? Will you sleep with her? She is certain to ask me."

"I might—if only that you can earn your two silver pieces. I will decide about that after I have spoken to the foreigner."

This answer was not very agreeable to her and she fled the room in a high rage, making me feel a certain pity for the landlord's wife.

Not half an hour had passed when Khonsmose, a great lump of a man with huge, muscular arms and incredibly hairy shoulders, presented himself at my door, bowing meekly.

"Begging your Honor's pardon, but the foreigner has come again," he said, his sad eyes seeming to acknowledge that he must accept the full measure of blame for this intrusion—since for all his obvious size and strength, it was clear he was one of those whom the gods mark out to be the victims of the whole human race.

When he saw I was not angry, a faint glimmer of hope lit in his eyes.

"Shall it please Your Honor that I send him away?"

"No—I will see him now."

Disappointed yet again, Khonsmose shuffled off. He did not return, but a minute later another man appeared in the doorway—light-skinned, spare of build, in stature a little under the average for that part of the world, his head and beard shaved and his eyes painted after the Egyptian manner.

Khonsmose had been right, however, for he was "from the Eastern Lands," from Sumer, I would have wagered much, although how I could have been so certain I could not have said.

"I am in the presence of the Lord Tiglath Ashur?" he asked, in Aramaic—it was not merely a good guess, since my name, if nothing else, marked my origins. He smiled, as if we shared some secret.

"Then we have not met?"

I did not rise, but gestured for him to sit. Neither did I offer him wine, for I did not like this stranger.

"No." He shook his head—why did I imagine he was lying? I would almost have said I knew his face from somewhere, but that is a common enough mistake. "I have not had that honor. Had our paths crossed before this, I would have remembered."

"And certainly we are both a long road from home," I said, in Akkadian.

There was just an instant of hestitation, and then he cocked his head a trifle to one side and regarded me questioningly. It was perhaps even possible that he had not understood me—could I have been mistaken?

I repeated myself, this time in Aramaic, and he smiled again.

"I am a Hebrew," he said, as if in answer to a question. "Born in Jerusalem, but raised up in Tyre. Egypt is an uncomfortable place for a foreigner—yes, sometimes it seems a long road home."

It was a safe story, for who in the wide world knows anything of the Hebrews? A man might be from anywhere and make such a claim.

"You have lived here long?" I asked, letting the matter pass. After all, who should understand better than I that a man may have very good reasons for wishing to make a secret of his birth?

"Only a few years, in Saïs until now. This is my first visit to Naukratis."

During our conversation he had sat with his hands folded in his lap, the right over the left, but suddenly he raised his right hand and smoothed down the breast of his tunic with it. There seemed no particular reason for the gesture. Then his hands returned to his lap, the left once more hidden by the right.

Yet I had seen that none of his fingers was missing.

"It is from Saïs that I have come, My Lord. And with no purpose but to see you."

There was a certain tension in his face, but I had a sense it was probably habitual with him—all sharp lines and abrupt angles, it seemed the sort of face that never relaxed. I had the impression he was waiting for some reaction, as if I should have known from the beginning what he wished of me.

When at last I said nothing he made a small dismissive gesture, perhaps to indicate that he claimed no virtue from the journey.

"I have come with another man, a noble of great wealth who in this instance has entrusted me to speak for him," he went on. "It is my lord's understanding that you are in quest of loans on behalf of Prince Nekau. Is such the case?"

"If it were true, I would hardly declare the fact to a stranger."

I smiled, without much warmth, wondering why this man and his rich and illustrious patron should interest themselves in my mission for Prince Nekau—and, more immediately, how they had found out about it. There were only a limited number of possibilities.

There was a faint flash of anger in his eyes, instantly controlled. He knew I was baiting him. He was not a fool.

"You wish to know the source of my patron's information. Your caution is admirable, My Lord; however, in this instance it is also misplaced. It only matters that he does have such knowledge and that he is prepared to make such a loan to the prince. Nothing else need concern us. We have only to discuss the terms and the rate of interest."

"And, of course, the amount of the loan," I said, struggling hard to keep down a rising sense of excitement—Glaukon, I thought. He has arranged this somehow. I should have guessed.

"Yes—of course." The man drew back his lips in an unconvincing grin, as if I had made a joke. "The amount—whatever the prince requires, I should think."

"The prince requires a great deal."

"How much would that be?"

"Five million emmer."

"Five million. As much as that, you think?"

"Yes."

He pursed his lips, but no sound escaped them. He seemed to be considering the matter.

"My patron may wish to limit himself to three million," he said, raising his eyes questioningly to my face. "Would that be acceptable, or will only the full five million serve?"

"It is possible that even five million will not be enough, but the prince was licensed me to borrow as much as I can, and on whatever terms I find reasonable. I will be happy to discuss this matter with your patron."

This pleased the man who claimed to be a Hebrew from Saïs, who might be anyone from anywhere. Nevertheless his eyes narrowed slightly, as if the conversation had suddenly taken a painful turn.

"There are, of course, certain matters which must be agreed upon in advance of any such meeting," he said. "The prince's credit is not very high—and of course my patron, as a nobleman of Saïs, is his subject and understands quite well the embarrassment of his circumstances. Any loan made to the prince would naturally require that there be certain guarantees. You would of course have to offer your own fortune as security. The rate of interest, by the way, would be two parts in three of the whole—to be paid back within the year."

"My wealth is now almost entirely invested abroad. Nor does it approach such a sum as three million emmer."

"My patron is aware of this, and has factored the risk of default into his requirements by way of return."

"That risk is very great," I said. "Your patron must know what everyone in Egypt knows: that Pharaoh plans to move against the prince. If that happens, or if there is another year of famine, or if the prince finds himself too pressed by his creditors and simply repudiates the debt, I would be left with nothing."

"You must decide for yourself, My Lord, how much you wish to interest yourself in the prince's affairs. I can only repeat my instructions."

Still, it was clear that those instructions were not entirely displeasing to him. We had taken a dislike to each other, I and this man whose name I did not know, whose origins I could only guess at. We might find ourselves doing business, but the animosity would remain permanent.

"I shall need time to consider the matter," I said. "I will give you my answer at this time tomorrow evening, if that is convenient."

"It is quite convenient, My Lord. I shall wait upon you then and, if we can come to an understanding, I shall arrange a meeting with my patron."

"Does your patron have a name? Do you?"

"My patron wishes, for the present, to remain anonymous. My own name is Ahab."

"And your patron would not by any chance be missing the least finger of his left hand?"

Ahab of Jerusalem looked perplexed for a moment, as if he wondered whether some insult was being offered.

"My patron is an elderly gentleman, Lord," he answered finally. "He is plagued by many infirmities, yet such a loss is not among them."

"Then I bid you good night," I said. "I will see you again tomorrow evening."

"Yes, My Lord."

He bowed and departed. I was left to consider the matter in solitude.

Ruin—that was what it would mean. I had no faith in Nekau's chances in this crisis. And even if somehow he did survive, he was not a man to have any scruples about abandoning his friends. Should the prince default, I would not have enough for bread to eat.

Could I face that? I was the son of a king. All my life I had been surrounded by wealth and power. I had abandoned power—could I abandon wealth too? True, Kephalos and I had been poor enough at times on our long journey to Egypt, but we had been fighting for our lives and poverty means little in the face of death. It is nothing to die a beggar, but could I live as one? I did not know.

And then there was Nodjmanefer. I had to think of her as well.

Glaukon had brought this upon me—I was sure of it. I was half angry with him, although certainly he had acted as a friend. Knowing that no one in Naukratis would give me decent terms, he had come up with this Ahab of Jerusalem. If that was who he was.

I did not believe he had come from Saïs only to discuss this matter with me, as he claimed. Glaukon had seen me only that morning, and Saïs was a day's journey. The man must have been in Naukratis to begin with, but why lie about it?

Nothing made any sense.

I sat in my tiny room drinking wine, I do not know how long. Certainly the street had been dark for some hours, and the tavern must have been closed, when the landlord's wife entered my doorway. In her hand was a small papyrus scroll, sealed with wax.

"A sailor brought this for you, My Lord," she said, offering it to me. "His ship landed only half an hour ago, he told me to tell you. He came from Memphis."

I took the scroll, broke the seal, and read:

Tiglath, my love, there are terrible disorders in the city. A mob broke into our house this morning, and Senefru had to call soldiers to disburse them— many wretched people were killed. Senefru is half distracted in his mind and utters many frightful threats of what will happen if Pharaoh comes. Please return soon and take me from this city of death. For the first time I am really afraid.

The writing was Greek, but the name at the bottom was that of Nodjmanefer.

So at last, it would seem, I was to have no choice. Suddenly the future stretched before me as a black, empty pit. A grave.

"Will you require anything more, My Lord?"

At first I did not even realize that she had spoken. Then I looked up and saw her smiling at me—she was thinking of twenty silver pieces. No doubt I looked a favorable chance, for I was drunk enough.

But in that instant I hated her with a blind rage.

"Be gone, harlot!" I shouted, throwing my wine cup at her so that it shattered not a handspan from her head. "Go and sleep in your husband's bed for a change!"

She screamed in fright and ran away. The whole house must have heard her scream—it seemed to echo in my mind as if it were trapped inside me. At last I covered my face with my hands to make it stop.

XVI

IN THE END, WRATH IS ITS OWN PUNISHMENT. I SLEPT but fitfully that night and woke up with a bad conscience and a worse head. In the morning Selana brought me breakfast and a small jug of very cold wine.

"Drink this first," she said, pouring me a cup. "No—I do not care if it does taste like pond water. You must drink yourself sober again before you will be fit for anything. You should be content to live a strictly temperate life, Master, for you always pay much too dearly for your debauches. The landlord's wife, by the way, has been in a fearful rage all morning."

"I have no doubt of it."

The very smell of wine produced in me an almost overpowering impulse to vomit, but when I managed a few swallows I really did feel better. It was several minutes, however, before I could even look at the food.

"It is safe to assume, then, that she did not collect her twenty silver pieces?" Selana raised her eyebrows in mockery. "I can almost pity her, since it must have been a great shock to her vanity. But at least I am consoled by the knowledge that I am not the only one whom you punish with your disdain."

"Damn you, you little bitch."

This, however, only made her laugh. I reached into my traveling chest and pulled out a small purse of coins.

"Here—pay her her twenty pieces of silver. Pay her thirty. Tell her anything you like. Tell her I will sleep with her tonight if it pleases her. Better yet, tell her that as a boy of six I fell astraddle a wagon tongue and have been of no use to women since. Give me some more wine, Selana, and kindly school yourself to witness my discomfitures without such obvious relish."

She swept up the purse and disappeared, perhaps before I could change my mind. I had to pour my own wine, as it turned out, but by then it no longer tasted so evil and I was able to manage an enthusiastic start on breakfast.

I felt better, and not only in my head and bowels. Perhaps that was more Selana's doing than the wine's, for she had the trick of reminding me that life was not all misery and darkness.

And one's affairs never seem as hopeless in the morning as they did the night before. I had other friends than Glaukon among the Greeks of Naukratis. I would consult with them—at the very least they might be able to tell me something of this deliberately mysterious Ahab of Jerusalem. If the man was to impoverish me, I owed it to myself better to make his acquaintance.

The day's inquiries, however, left me much as I had begun. No one was prepared to lend Nekau, Prince of Memphis and Saïs, the price of so much as a single measure of wheat.

"Tiglath, you are a fool if you imagine he will spend any of what you give him to buy bread for the poor or peace in his own realms. It will all go to harlots and luxury, see if it does not. Pharaoh is wise to topple him, and his people will be the better for it."

"His people will not be the better for starving to death, or for being gutted by Pharaoh's Libyan soldiers. And I will guarantee that the money will be spent wisely—you may count on me to have enough sense for that."

"Nevertheless, if it is Pharaoh's purpose that in Memphis they starve or perish by the sword, you will find no one here in Naukratis willing to oppose it."

Questions about Ahab of Jerusalem were just as fruitless.

"His is not a name I have heard, but it is possible he may be in earnest. The Hebrews are a nation of poverty-stricken goatherds who understand nothing of statecraft or commerce."

This seemed to settle the matter. All doors were closed to me save one, and behind that one lay a threatening darkness.

Still, I had no choice but to open it—how could I not?

Yet I continued to visit my increasingly impatient acquaintances among the Greek merchants.

Word traveled quickly in Naukratis, and by the middle of the afternoon I began to detect a certain reluctance to be seen with me. I would meet someone in the bazaars, he would greet me effusively, and then, when I mentioned business, he would break in on me with, "Come to my office tomorrow, my friend Tiglath, when we will have time—you must know any interest of yours I will embrace as my own." This followed by a hasty retreat. Everyone, it seemed, had heard that I was entangled in some mad scheme of Prince Nekau's, and no one wanted any part of it.

Even Enkidu was growing impatient with me. Usually he squatted in my interviewer's doorway, as if he thought it might be necessary to bar the man's escape from his own premises, calmly sharpening the blade of his ax with a small whetstone. He was silent, apparently indifferent, like an adult witness to the amusements of other people's children. Gradually, however, I noticed him sometimes glaring at me with a look of the most intense vexation—he saw, if I did not, that mine was a futile pursuit, that I was simply making a nuisance of myself. I was finally obliged to agree.

All that summer the sun was fiercely hot, and in the Delta the air was thick with water so that one seemed to live in a gray cloud, making each breath like lifting a weight, sapping one's strength, even one's will. I was glad at last to surrender my empty quest and embraced defeat almost as a blessing.

"What do you think, Enkidu? I will turn over my pledges to the prince and take my Lady Nodjmanefer away, perhaps to the Greek isles, where I will follow the trade of my mother's father and make sandals. A soldier can always make a decent pair of sandals, so perhaps we will not all starve. Do you fancy my Lady Nodjmanefer will enjoy being a cobbler's wife?"

Enkidu's only answer was a low growl. I was talking nonsense again, and he was not amused.

"I am not jesting, my friend. It will probably come to some such thing, since it seems I must close with this fellow Ahab and his mysterious patron. Well, it is at least a wide world, in which a man can always find a place where no one knows him."

We went back to the tavern, and I shut myself in my room to lock out the din of Selana's quarrel with the landlord's wife, which gave indications of having been simmering through the full length of the day. Even among the Egyptians, normally the most placid of races, the heat was beginning to fray tempers.

About an hour after sunset, Khonsmose made his customary apologetic entrance. This evening, however, he seemed unusually satisfied with life—he was smiling like a felon who, having confessed his crimes and repented of them, has been pardoned, given Pharaoh's bounty, and once more finds himself turned loose upon the bright world.

"Your Honor will be pleased to give his instructions concerning dinner?" he asked, even making so bold as to smile.

"Nothing," I said. "Only wine—I am expecting a guest."

He appeared not to hear me but continued to stand there, grinning, in an apparent stupor of bliss.

"Are you quite well, my friend?" I finally felt compelled to ask.

"Yes, very well, Your Honor, I and my wife both."

"I am delighted to hear—and everything prospers between you, I trust?"

He nodded vigorously, not at all taken aback by such a question, delighted to have found someone to whom he could confide the secret of his felicity.

"Yes, Your Honor. My wife makes me the happiest of men."

Looking at him, I could well believe it. So it appeared that someone at least had profited from the distresses of the previous night.

"Good. Then when the foreigner who was here yesterday comes again, will you bring him to me at once?"

"Yes, Your Honor."

Still he remained, regarding me expectantly—was he waiting to render me a more complete account of his felicity? Perhaps a detailed history? I could very well imagine it all for myself.

"Well then . . . Please give your wife my most sincere respects."

"Yes, Your Honor."

We continued in silence for several seconds more, and then at last Khonsmose seemed to recall something.

"If Your Honor will excuse . . . ?'

"Yes, yes . . ." I dismissed him with a wave, watching him disappear through the doorway. In the end his wife would make his life a misery, but perhaps he already knew that—perhaps, today at least, he did not care. It was possible to envy him. I did not envy him his wife, but the fact that he loved her.

My mind kept returning to Nodjmanefer and the child she carried in her womb. I had a son already, at home in Nineveh, but I could never acknowledge him—his mother was lady of the palace, so the king my brother must be his father. I had never even seen him.

But there would be no one to stop me from owning this child as mine. I would take mother and child both and find someplace where we offended no one by being together. I was now eight and twenty years old, no longer

>> 249 <<

young but still vigorous, and I would find a means of supporting those who depended on me.

I would have a chance at real happiness. Was that not worth the surrender of all my wealth? It seemed so to me.

Then perhaps I would no longer envy Khonsmose the tavern keeper, with his pretty wife.

Several hours had passed before I raised my eyes and saw the face of Ahab of Jerusalem, who smiled at me as a cat might at a mouse. This time I did offer him wine.

"My patron has considered the matter," he said, almost without preamble. He sat before me, motionless, his hands hidden in the long sleeves of his dark-brown tunic. "He is prepared to loan the full five million emmer, but the additional two million must fetch a return of four million when the whole amount falls due."

"So at the end of a year Prince Nekau will owe nine million emmer. It is a considerable sum."

I paused and took a sip of wine, as if the matter did not concern me. In fact, it hardly did, for why should I care if the prince defaulted on nine million rather than five?

"My own liability, however, must be limited to the sums presently deposited in my name with merchants both here and in Sidon," I continued, smiling. "That includes virtually all my wealth, but you cannot extract from me what I do not have, and I will not tolerate that my family and household should be sold into slavery for no better reason than to reconcile your patron to having struck an unprofitable bargain."

"My patron will agree to this. After all, he is a reasonable man and would have no motive to avenge himself upon you."

"Where money is involved, men are very rarely reasonable."

He nodded, as if he appreciated my point. I had the sense, however, that profit and loss were not really the issues here, for Ahab's patron must certainly have understood that he could not emerge from these dealings the winner. I could only assume that statecraft, and not wealth, was the object of this contract, that what was being bought with five million emmer was not the chance at nine million in a year's time but a claim on the future of Egypt.

Yet, as it seemed to me, these were not my concerns. In a year, I would be far away. I should have been wiser.

"How do you wish the five million?" he asked, as if he were a shopkeeper taking an order. "In silver or in grain? My patron has access to large stores of wheat and millet and can give you an excellent price—

three million bushels, delivered to the docks at Memphis within ten days."

"Very well then, I will take the grain."

"Then would you be prepared to put your seal to the undertaking tonight? My patron is prepared to meet you this very hour."

"Yes—of course."

It was not until we were standing that I noticed he had not touched his wine.

At the door of the tavern we met Enkidu. Ahab of Jerusalem glanced at him, shook his head, and then turned back to me.

"You will understand, My Lord Tiglath Ashur, that these are sensitive matters," he said, with a faint shrug. "My patron takes a considerable risk of . . . shall we say, embarrassment, if his involvement becomes known in Tanis. His position, his very life might be put in jeopardy. What I am trying to say is, he will not tolerate a witness at your meeting—not even a mute beast such as yours."

I smiled, a mirthless grin.

"You are fortunate you speak in Aramaic, my friend. He is mute, but he is far from a beast. Yet I will tell him to stay behind."

I did, and Enkidu fixed me with his cold blue eyes, as if to say, *You are a great fool to trust your life out of my keeping.*

The hour of midnight was just past. The streets of Naukratis, which at other times were crowded with people, were now almost empty. We could hear our own footfalls as we walked together through the maze of little alleyways that led toward the river. Ahab of Jerusalem offered no directions, save to touch my arm now and then when we reached a turning. I had thought I knew the city well, but very soon I lost my way in the darkness.

As was usual on warm summer nights in the Delta, the mists were heavy. The very walls of the buildings appeared to sweat. I could not see the stars. Common noises, the yapping of a stray dog or the frogs croaking on the muddy riverbanks, sounded distant and muffled. On such nights the world seemed slightly blurred, as if the everyday solidity of existence had given place to phantoms. As in a dream, it seemed impossible to be sure of anything.

Thus I was prepared to believe myself mistaken when I began to suspect that someone was following us.

But even this is making the impression more precise than it was. I had no clear sense that there was one man, or three, or five. And he—or they—were perhaps not so much following as staying abreast of us, and always just out of reach. It was all very vague. What I saw or heard, or thought I heard, was always so at the edge of my consciousness as to be only a little more than nothing at all. It was simply that we no longer had the night to ourselves, that someone—or more than one—was there because we were there.

Did Ahab know? Had he known from the beginning, and did he know because he had planned it thus? Did they intend any harm, these companions of the darkness, or were they simply another precaution of Ahab's mysterious patron?

And did they even exist? I had no confidence about anything.

At last we reached a warehouse, a crude wooden building, simply boards nailed over a frame. It was perhaps slightly larger than the main room of the tavern where I was living, and the door stood open.

Ahab motioned for me to enter first.

There was an oil lamp hanging by a chain from the ceiling, but otherwise the warehouse was nearly empty, with only a few bales of canvas resting against one wall. The lamp was burning—otherwise the appearance of the place suggested no one had been inside for many months.

When we were both inside, Ahab closed the door and slid the crossbar shut. He reached behind one of the canvas bales and withdrew a sword. I knew at once that he intended to kill me.

"What is this about?" I asked, turning to face him, strangely calm, almost as if I had expected something of the sort—almost as if I welcomed it.

"It is about your death, Prince," replied the man who had called himself Ahab of Jerusalem but who spoke now in Akkadian, in the accents of Babylon. "It is about the debt you owe to Marduk for having defiled his temple and his city. It is about the hatred of one royal brother for another. And do not think to cry out, for no one will hear except my own men, who are outside guarding our privacy."

His mouth was stretched into a tight grin, a ghastly thing that distorted his face into a mask of hatred. He waved his sword in the air, as if he wanted me to admire the way it caught the light. He held it in his left hand and I noticed that he grasped it in a peculiar, clumsy grip, as if at some time he had injured his hand. Probably I had not yet fully realized my danger, for I was still placid enough to notice such things.

And, of course, this was the man I had seen in Memphis, on the day of Pharaoh's procession. How was it I had not recognized him before this?

I carried no weapon of my own, nor had I since leaving Memphis—

somehow, in Naukratis, it had seemed a trifle foolish. Perhaps it had been. Perhaps, had I not come unarmed, Ahab's shadowy followers, now suddenly so real, would already have killed me in ambush. As it was, he seemed content to do the work himself.

"Then I take it your 'patron' will not be coming."

It sounded almost like a jest, but I wanted to keep him talking, if only to give me time to think.

"My patron waits in Nineveh for the return of your head—I am free to leave the body where it falls, but I cannot return without the head. I have sworn I would not."

"Sworn?"

"Yes." The grin outstretched a shade tighter. "Does it surprise you? I took an oath—we all did. All five of us."

"An Oath? To whom?"

"To Marduk. To the Sixty Great Gods of Akkad and Sumer. To the true king. We sealed it with our blood, with the sharp blade of the sacred knife. But what does that matter now? I will be the one to return to Nineveh with your head wrapped in a cloak, and there I will receive my reward. I, and no other—the god's servant, Mushussu."

The five eagles, each dripping blood from the stump of a missing talon. The prophecy was fulfilled and its meaning revealed. But, as usual, too late.

Mushussu—I should have known.

There were no more than three or four paces between us, and suddenly he cut at the air with his sword, missing me by the width of a few fingers. I jumped back out of the way, which was what he wanted. He wasn't yet ready to kill me.

"I always knew I would have to deal with you myself," he said, sounding almost as if he were out of breath. "In the desert, that was a cowardly mistake, and the gods will not be served by half measures. All these years I have had to wait until I could lure you out of Memphis!"

He flourished his sword again, as if daring me not to be afraid. He needn't have troubled himself—I was afraid now, but the fear only seemed to make my mind more agile.

I was perhaps the taller by a span. I had all the advantages of height and reach, but he had the sword. I would have to find a way inside its arc if I was to reach him.

He managed his weapon with reasonable skill, suggesting he might have been a soldier once. If his grip was clumsy it was only because he clutched the handle with only three fingers, the last sticking out from his grip as if he had broken it at some time and the joints had frozen straight. I did not stop to consider the question further—he was too dangerous for that.

I threw a quick glance about, but there was nothing anywhere I could have used as a weapon or a shield. There wouldn't have been. He would have seen to that. There was only the oil lamp swinging from its short chain, and even that was out of reach. It threw eerie shadows across my attacker's face and his sword caught its light.

"It was Senefru," I said, a bit startled at the sound of my own voice. "He told you I was coming, and why."

"Yes—he found me out where you could not." He laughed, as if glorying in his triumph. "He searched a long time, but he found me out. It seemed you make enemies wherever you go, Prince."

He laughed again. It was cruel, mindless laughter, in its way as terrifying as death itself.

He is mad, I thought to myself. He is quite mad. Feeding on this one obsession, his mind has sickened.

He crouched forward a little. The time for explanations was over now—I could see that. Now he meant for me to die.

He cut at me again, swinging from right to left, and this time I was not quite fast enough and the point skimmed across the palm of my left hand, slicing it open. I felt the blow, nothing else, but even in the wavering yellow lamplight I could see the spray of blood.

Then the pain came, a surge of it, as if the nerves were being violently twisted. It poured straight up my arm and into my chest. For a few seconds, there was nothing else in the world but that pain.

He could have finished me, but he did not. Another man would have—I would have—for no enemy is safe until he is dead. But this one was enjoying himself too much. He wanted to kill me slowly, to shave off pieces of my life one at a time.

I have allowed myself to go soft, I thought. He cuts my palm and I am ready to faint like a woman. If this one kills me, it will be no one's fault but my own.

I have to get inside the arc of his sword. I have to fight the man and not the weapon.

I clenched my hand into a fist to slow the bleeding, trying to remember that a man is not invincible simply because there is a sword in his hand.

We faced one another, each of us slightly crouched, like cats ready to spring. He seemed more careful now. The point of his sword danced in the lamplight and he took a cautious step forward, making me back away from him. I let him do it—I let him think I would run like a rabbit were there not a wall behind me. I had to give him back his confidence, so he would make a mistake.

Another step. Another. He tried another slash. His blade whistled through the air and I was only just able to pull myself back beyond its reach. My balance was bad and I almost stumbled, but his was worse. He did not know it, but if he had extended himself just a little farther, I would have had him.

We both recovered. He felt better now because he was on the attack once more.

I could see him readying himself to try again. This time it was a thrust, and as I stepped away from it the point snatched at my tunic, just brushing against my rib cage. But I had parried the attack, which gave me an opportunity too tempting to resist.

My kick caught him just below the knee. He grunted in surprise and pain and almost went down—almost, but not quite. He cut at me with his sword, driving me off.

It seemed I had made an error.

"You think you are clever," he said, panting for breath. "You think you are clever and brave, but now I will kill you—NOW!"

He made a rush, screaming, his sword slashing wildly. But he was slower now and I could get away. He paused for a moment. Then he rushed me again.

I waited, dancing out of reach, backing away. He lunged again, but he was tiring and each time the sword swung in a wider arc. Each time he took an instant longer to recover.

At last, just as the sword swept by, I threw myself at him, catching him full in the chest with my shoulder.

But I could not hold him. He broke from me, throwing himself back until he slammed into the wooden wall behind him. The impact seemed deafening in that small space.

Then something strange and terrible happened. He stood against the wall, an expression of the most profound surprise on his face. He did not move. Slowly, his arms fell down at his sides. The sword dropped from his hand. I started towards him and then stopped. He was shaking his head, back and forth, back and forth, as if to warn me away.

And then, very slowly, his knees gave way and he slid down. Then I saw.

There was a broad red smear on the wall, just where his head had been. And in its center an ax blade was sticking through the wood. It was wiggling back and forth, back and forth, as someone worked to pull it loose from the wall.

Mushussu—I must call him something, and I never learned his true name—was lying crumpled on the floor, the blood welling freely from a deep notch in the back of his skull. He did not move. He would never move again.

I cannot say I understood at once. Then I heard a low growl from outside, like a dog warning away intruders. I went to the door of the warehouse and lifted away the crossbar. When I pushed the door open I saw Enkidu. There were still traces of blood on his ax.

I will never discover how he found me, nor how he knew when to strike with his ax against the wall, or what became of Mushussu's men— although on this last I can at least make a guess. I did not care how. I only cared that he had saved my life.

Yet he gave me no opportunity to thank him but swept past me to where the dead man lay. Enkidu crouched beside the corpse, grasped the left arm and held it up for me to see, glaring at me impatiently.

"I don't understand," I said.

His answer was to take the smallest finger and pull it off. It came loose with a snap. He threw it on the floor at my feet. I picked it up and looked at it under the light of the oil lamp. It was wax.

The hand, on close examination, showed only a stump where the original had been cut away. The scar had long since faded to a white line. Like the street magicians one saw everywhere in Egypt, Mushussu had tricked me with an illusion.

It was only then, for some reason, that I grasped the enormity of what had happened.

"You will take Selana downriver to Buto," I said. "I am in your debt, but this time do as I ask. Here she is still within Senefru's reach, but she will be safe with you in Buto and you must stay with her there. I will join you when I can."

I knew from the way he looked at me that this time he would obey. *Where will you go?* the eyes asked.

"I must return to Memphis. It is possible that even now I may not be too late."

XVII

I LEFT THAT NIGHT, STOPPING AT THE TAVERN ONLY long enough to pay my reckoning, bind up the wound to my hand, and write a letter of instructions to Glaukon. He was to turn whatever money he held for me over to Selana and to arrange passage downriver for her and Enkidu.

I did not reveal to him my intention of returning to Memphis— probably he would assume as much without any word from me—but I did tell Selana. She listened, without interruption or protest, and gave me her promise to do as she was bid. She understood, I think, how futile would be any attempt to stop me.

Khonsmose had a horse, a brown gelding, no very fine specimen, which he sold to me for three hundred pieces of silver. It was not worth a hundred, but that was what he asked and I payed it. If he had asked a thousand he would have gotten that—I only wanted to be away, and traveling upriver a man alone can move faster on horseback than by boat. I have wondered since if perhaps he did not later come to realize how he had wasted his opportunity and also to convince himself, perchance, that I had ended by cheating him instead of the other way about.

By the time the sun rose, I was already three hours south along the river trail.

Had Khonsmose's horse only known how to walk on water I could have been in Memphis in two days. The distance from Naukratis is not so great, but the Nile, which has only seven mouths, has many channels. I had to cross the river eleven times, and each time I had to find a village, hire a boat and a man to row it, tie the horse's bridle to the stern and then hope the crocodiles didn't get the poor jade before we made it from one side to the other. Thus the journey took five full days, during which I stopped only when the horse began to stumble from weariness.

During all that time I knew no rest. Even when I stopped for a few hours because the horse would not go on, even when I had every intention of sleeping, I hardly seemed able to close my eyes.

Thus I cannot be sure if what happened that last night before I saw Memphis again, while I sat holding the horse's reins, my back against the trunk of a date palm, my mind stunned with fatigue, I cannot know if it was real or merely a dream. But perhaps, if it was a dream, it was no less real for being such.

Dawn was yet three hours away in that, the blackest part of the night. There was no moon, but the stars glimmered angrily. I could just hear the soft whisper of the Nile, like an old woman dreaming of her youth. There was no other sound except, now and then, the cry of some water bird. My brain ached from simple exhaustion. I felt myself alone in the world.

And then, all at once, I was not. Tabshar Sin, my grandfather the Lord Sargon's old *rab kisir*, who had trained me up as a soldier in the house of war, was there beside me, squatting on the ground just at the limit of my field of vision. Somehow I did not find this strange, although he had been dead for seven years, killed in the war we had fought together against the Medes and buried on the field of battle. I did not think about it.

For a long time—or what seemed a long time—he did not speak and neither did I. I was glad for the companionship, on any terms, and it occurred to me he might vanish if by breaking the silence I admitted I knew he was there.

I needn't have worried, however.

"You are beginning, Prince, to depend too much on that great mute of yours to mind your back," he said finally. "Ah well, I suppose you might have been able to deal with the Babylonian alone, but it was a close thing. You were a fool not to have seen the trap."

"I am aware I was a fool," I answered, perhaps a little tartly. "Recently I have been a fool with breathtaking consistency. I am probably on my way to be a fool again—is that what you have come to tell me?"

"No."

For a moment he seemed to have lost interest in the conversation. He gazed out at the invisible horizon, in the direction of Memphis, as if he wished to measure the distance. Absent-mindedly he rubbed the stump from which a Nairian horseman had taken his left hand some twelve years before I was born.

"No, it is not folly that a man should seek to turn aside danger from that which is precious to him. What is folly is to imagine he can use his own life as the shield. Who knows how things stand in Memphis just now? Has Pharaoh come with his armies, or is there still peace? If Senefru sold you to the Babylonian, he will sell Nekau to Pharaoh."

"Yes—I had thought of that."

"Had you, Prince? If so, I congratulate you." He looked at me disdainfully out of the corner of his eye, as he had a thousand times on the parade grounds when as a boy I made some mistake in my drill.

"But why then have you not thought of its consequences for whatever plans have hatched in your moldy brain? Probably Senefru already has the blessing of Pharaoh to rule in Nekau's place once the city has fallen. Have you thought of that? He thinks you are dead—he hopes you are dead—but if you come riding through the gates with a sword on your hip he will discover his mistake soon enough. What do you think he will do then? And what use will you be to the Lady Nodjmanefer once the crocodiles have finished with you?"

"I will find a way. If Senefru plots against Nekau, one imagines he has many things on his mind besides me."

"Has he? His mind doubtless was sufficiently employed before, but he still found time to hunt up your Babylonian friend and then send you scurrying off to meet your death in that warehouse. Do not count too heavily on the Lord Senefru's preoccupation with affairs of state."

He ceased, and once more the silence closed around us like the walls of a tent. Somewhere in the distance I could hear a jackal barking, a lonely sound, one which the Egyptians take as an omen of death.

Tabshar Sin gave me good counsel—but that had always been so.

"What, then, would you have me do?"

He laughed, as if I had made a jest.

"Prince, I was never anything more than a soldier, and the only wisdom a soldier knows is to try to stay alive. You are descended of kings and have the arrogance to believe you will always find favor with the gods of your fathers, but the gods are not always kind to those whom they favor. I can only warn you of what you cannot hide from yourself, even now. Memphis is this day one of the dark places of the world, and for you darker than for most. If you enter its gates, a part of you will never come out."

"Will I die there, Tabshar Sin? Did you ever teach me to run from death?"

"It is not of death I speak, but of life."

"Yet you know I must go."

"Yes . . . I know.'

I turned to look at him. There was a smile on his lips, even as his image faded into the black night. Before I could even speak, there was only the smile. And then, nothing.

The next evening I came within sight of Memphis. Black, heavy smoke boiled up and mingled with the night sky. Within the walls whole sections of the city were burning themselves out, and along the waterfront the flame seemed to stain the Nile with blood. In the light of the fires I could just distinguish the corpses that were hanging head-down from the city walls, and I wondered how many of them I would have recognized. Tabshar Sin had spoken well to call this one of the dark places of the world.

And it seemed his judgment was widely shared, for I was not the only one using the road. There was a flood of people streaming away from the city in both directions, their way lit by torches as they escaped to the north and south and even into the western desert, it seeming better to them to starve in the barren countryside than to stay in Memphis and be burned alive in their hovels or be butchered or trampled to death in the streets.

About three hours from the city gates stood a ruined village, abandoned in the first season of famine but crowded now with those who had fled from Pharaoh's wrath. There I gave up my horse, which, as soon as I had dismounted, the refugees promptly swarmed over and slaughtered, cutting it up for pot meat, fighting among themselves over the scraps. No one asked my leave—these people were too desperate with hunger to stand upon ceremony. I think they would have eaten me had I not been armed. Within half an hour there was nothing left of Khonsmose's three hundred pieces of silver except a few strips of tattered hide and a skeleton gleaming in the light from a hundred campfires.

Seeking to disguise myself, I also traded my last bag of pressed dates for a peasant's woolen overcoat, worn and dull brown with age but sufficiently loose to hide the fact that I carried a sword in my belt. Everyone around me, I noticed, seemed to be barefoot, so I kicked off my sandals as well. I had not bathed or shaved my face or head for five days. If anyone in Memphis was on the watch for the arrival of the wealthy and illustrious Tiglath Ashur, friend of princes and counselors, I doubted he would trouble to look very closely at me.

"What is going on over there?" I asked the man from whom I had bought the overcoat, making a curt gesture toward the fires just visible on the horizon—I tried not to appear too interested because the common people of Egypt dislike inflicting disappointment on a stranger and I did not wish to be lied to.

He shook his head and, when he had cleared his mouth of my dates, grunted savagely.

"It is bad, Your Honor," he answered, apparently assuming that if I spoke like a foreigner and was rich enough to trade food for an old overcoat, it was probably wisest to treat me with respect. "The Libyan soldiers are killing everyone they find and half the city is too hot to walk through. No one will dwell in Memphis for a hundred years, I think."

If the soldiers were Libyan, it meant they were from Pharaoh's army—and so it had begun. I wondered how long since, but it seemed an unwise question.

"Is there still sickness?" I asked instead, but my informant only shrugged.

"When so many are dead, who asks what they died of? If there is none now, there will be, for there is no shortage of corpses. For myself, I hope to get far enough away that at least when I die the vultures will not have so easy a time finding me."

"And Prince Nekau, is he still alive?"

"I know not, Your Honor—is he some friend of yours?"

He looked at me so quizzically that it was obvious he had no idea of whom I spoke. Pharaoh's soldiers were wetting their swords with his subjects' blood, and Nekau, the object of his divine wrath, was not even a name to the victims, nor, probably, to the Libyans who were killing them.

Thus I set out on the last leg of my pilgrimage, against the tide of travelers, since, even in the still of night, when the world seemed to have ended forever, the road remained crowded with those who would escape what I sought. It was yet more than an hour before dawn when I reached Memphis.

My first problem, getting past the sentries and into the city without attracting attention to myself, was the most easily solved. It appeared that Pharaoh's soldiers had begun to be concerned about the spreading fires, which presumably they themselves had set, and were therefore drafting into work gangs anyone they could find. I merely had to join—or allow myself to be impressed into—a rather dazed-looking crowd of some two or three hundred people, mostly peasant men and women, but with the usual small contingent of sleek merchants who must have annoyed someone by offering too small a bribe, that had been collected to fetch water. We stood about until we were each given a pair of leather buckets and then herded first down to the river to fill them and then back up and through the gates. I bent low under my carrying stick as I passed the guards, yet I do not think I need have worried because they did not even glance at me.

Soldiers were stationed here and there but widely spaced, as if it hadn't occurred to them that this starved, dispirited mob of unarmed townspeople could pose any threat. I emptied my buckets against the fire, which in that section was hardly even smoldering any longer, and then, on my way back to the river, took the first chance that presented itself to drop them and run.

I heard someone shouting behind me, but no one offered to give pursuit—I was simply too easy to replace to be worth the trouble. After that it was no very complicated matter to disappear into the narrow and anonymous streets of the poor quarter, or as much as survived of it. It was only then that I grasped the full dreadful scope of what must have happened in the days prior.

As a youth I had been at Babylon when the armies of the king my father sacked the city and rained slaughter down upon those who dwelt within her shattered walls. Thus I was hardened to the spectacle of carnage, but only as seen through the eyes of a conqueror. I had never before experienced its danger, as distinct from its squalid horror. I had never known what it was to hide myself from death, which was as undiscriminating as a sandstorm and just as difficult to keep clear of.

Unless soldiers are kept under the strictest discipline after they have taken a city, there is always an orgy of killing, and it was obvious the armies of Pharaoh had simply been allowed to run wild, like hunting dogs that have slipped the leash. As I walked along the Street of the Cobblers, which was in a district where the fires had been less devastating, there were still so many corpses lying about that here and there they had had to be piled up against the sides of buildings in order to clear a path.

And these people had not been burned to death nor had they perished of sickness—they had been massacred, many of them hacked to pieces. I saw the trunk of an old man with the head and arms missing and even the legs cut off at the knees.

But, as is usual in such circumstances, it was the women who had suffered most. Everywhere there were the bodies of women with their breasts and bellies slit open as if they had been butchered for market. Many of them were covered in enough blood to suggest that they might have lived for several minutes after being attacked—the fact that these were usually hamstrung confirmed the impression. They had been mutilated and then allowed to flounder about, helpless, until shock and loss of blood put an end to the entertainment.

Libyans, who made up the bulk of Pharaoh's armies, were hated in Egypt. I had heard it said many times that they were a race of brutal savages, lost to all human feeling and decency, and, had I not been at Babylon with the soldiers of Ashur, Memphis doubtless would have persuaded me to believe it. Now I know that, given a license to be so, we are all brutal savages. Evil is the ground of our existence. One of the punishments for a long life is to learn that all men are wicked.

It was still only gray morning and already the heavy, stagnant air swarmed with black flies grown fat on so much carrion. One could hardly breathe for the stink of death, and I was glad I had not eaten in a day and a half. I did not linger but struck out for the wide streets of the temple district. I wanted to find Nodjmanefer.

Most of the corpses had been cleared from the great public squares, but the sand in the streets and sometimes the walls of the very shrines were still stained with blood. The first orgy of killing appeared to have subsided, but clearly there continued to be danger if one ventured out into the open. Here and there I heard screaming. From the shadow of an alleyway I saw a soldier on a horse ride down a man, a peasant wearing nothing except a grimy loincloth, and spear him to death. I made my way carefully.

That part of the city where the wealthy lived seemed to have been untouched by the recent violence. There were soldiers about—in greater numbers, in fact, than elsewhere—but none of the buildings were burned or looked as if they had been looted. Except for the patrols the streets were empty, for my wealthy neighbors knew enough to stay within doors at such a time.

To avoid the soldiers I made my way through alleys and around the backs of houses, climbing over the low plaster walls when I could not find a gate. Since I knew the district well I made good progress. Only once was there any difficulty. A woman came out onto her porch to catch me walking along the gravel path of her garden. Not more than a few paces separated us, and suddenly she began shouting in an excited, high-pitched voice: "Thieves! Help! Murderers!" I ran back the way I had come. Even at a distance I could still hear her, for she was nothing if not persistent. I was already in the next street before I was aware that I had recognized her. She was Mutemwia, the wife of Pesyenwase, whose family had prospered by controlling the stone quarries of the western desert, and I had been a guest in their home many times. Since that day I have often wondered if later, having regained her composure, she ever guessed the identity of her intruder.

At last I stood at the rear of Senefru's house. It was still the first part of the morning and there were actually birds singing in the trees of his garden—I remember that quite distinctly, since it struck me as such an odd sound to hear in this ravaged city.

The door that opened from the back of the great receiving hall was unlatched and slightly ajar, and no one challenged me as I entered. The place seemed abandoned.

I went straight through the house, from back to front, and did not encounter anyone. All the servants had doubtless fled. The front doors had been forced from the outside—the crossbar was on the floor, snapped and splintered in the center as if a giant had broken it over his knee—and there was a chair overturned in the reception hall, but otherwise nothing looked out of the ordinary. There was no sign of looting. When I went into Senefru's study I discovered that all his papers lay on his desk, precisely as they had the last time I had been in that room. Somehow the sight of them filled me with dread.

"Nodjmanefer!" I shouted—the sound of her name echoed through the deserted house. "Senefru! Nodjmanefer!"

There was no answer.

I went back out to the entrance hall and looked again at the front doors, which stood open to let the bright morning sunlight fall across the stone floor. It would have taken perhaps eight or ten men working in concert to force them; they would have had to use a battering ram. Yet, on the ground floor at least, very little had been disturbed. They could not have been looters, and if they had come to arrest Senefru they would have taken his papers with them.

Just off the entrance hall was an alcove opening onto the main stairway. As in most homes of the Egyptian nobility, the first floor rooms were used for entertaining and business while the family lived their private lives on the floor above. In this alcove there had always stood a small bronze tripod supporting a pottery jar full of flowers. The tripod was still there, but it had been overturned and the jar lay on the floor, broken into five large pieces. The water had evaporated and the flowers were wilted. It was a narrow space, so there was no difficulty imagining the scene—a body of men, doubtless in a hurry, going up the stairway of a strange house, could have knocked over the tripod easily enough. I did not have to wonder how it might have happened.

The means of its happening was not, however, what preyed on my mind. Senefru was not a man to lose his nerve. For one thing, he had too much pride to die like a frightened servant. Pharaoh's soldiers, if that was who they had been, would not have found him cowering in his sleeping chamber. He would have met them, and his death, at his front door. Yet there was no sign of that. What, then, had they been looking for upstairs?

Of course I knew the answer even before I could bring myself to frame the question. They had not come for Senefru. They had come for Nodjmanefer.

I did not have to search long. I found her in her sitting room, lying curled on her side by a wall. Here too there were hardly any signs of a struggle—the curtains around her bed had been pulled down on one side, but that was all. The men, whoever they were, knew their business and had been very efficient.

I think she had probably been dead about five days. There was a thin stream of blood, long since dried black, running from the corner of her mouth, but the only wound that showed was low on her belly and had been made by a sword with a blade about three fingers wide. It looked as if it had been angled down, killing not only her but the child she carried in her womb. Her face was partly hidden in the crook of her arm—I was glad I did not have to see her eyes.

They had come up here to her private rooms and had murdered her—that was what had brought them, the only thing they had wanted: to kill a woman who had offended no one but her husband. It might have happened just about the time I was supposedly meeting the same fate in Naukratis. Had Senefru told her that? Had he stayed to watch? After it was all over, had he been the one to depart through the door to the garden, leaving it slightly ajar?

And she had lain here ever since, alone, with no one to comfort her ghost. The Egyptians entertain great hopes for the life after death, but Senefru had left her to rot.

Why had he done it? Was the thought that she wished finally to leave him, that she was going to have a child by another man, so insupportable? Had he loved her after all, or was the wound merely to his vanity? And why had he chosen this means—had he wished the world to believe his wife had perished in a random act of violence, just another horror in a season of horrors?

My mind spun with such questions, to which there would never be any answers. Senefru, by this act, had made himself as impenetrable as a stone.

I wrapped her corpse in the pad from her sleeping mat, tying it tight with whatever linen I could find—I used one of her gowns, I remember.

Then I carried her out to the garden, where I found a spade, picked up a few of the great flat stones around the fountain, and buried her there. Then I replaced the stones and covered every trace of my work. No one would ever suspect. She would lie there forever, safe from her husband's wrath, unknown to all save me.

XVIII

I HAD NO CONSCIOUSNESS OF TIME AS I SAT ON THE STONE bench in Nodjmanefer's garden, but I must have been there several hours. When the sound of the garden gate swinging shut brought me to myself with a start, I could see from the length of my own shadow that it was already late into the afternoon.

"So she is dead, is she," Kephalos said in a soft, expressionless voice. "I can see she is. I can read it in your face, Master. I had rather thought she would be."

"What happened here?" I asked, surprised at the way my own voice seemed to catch in my throat. All at once I was shaking with emotion, as if I had only just discovered my own feelings—as if, until that moment, I had been listening for the sound of her voice and only now realized that I would never hear it again.

Kephalos sat down beside me, resting his hands on his knees like a man who has at last finished a long day's labor and can afford the luxury of weariness.

"I hardly know. The soldiers came to your house first, and I escaped with the servants. The servants have not come back, by the way. The gods alone know what has become of them by now."

"In that case I wish the gods joy of their wisdom. When was this?"

"Five days past—six, really, since it was late enough at night that I had to flee for my life in a sleeping tunic. I hid in the cellar of the house my Lord Userkaf is having built on the Street of the God Bes, and I do not envy him the accommodation since it is only half finished and already has rats. I came back the next morning and have been awaiting your return ever since. We are safe for a time—this is probably the safest place in the city, since they have already been here and, in any case, do not often invade these precincts. Pharaoh, it appears, has extended the divine grace of forgiveness to the wealthy and confines his wrath to the starving and the homeless. Perhaps that too is a mercy, for most of them are certain to perish anyway."

"Then it was Pharaoh's soldiers who came?"

"Yes—without doubt. They are the only soldiers in Memphis, for Prince Nekau's militia melted away like frost at the first word the Libyans were coming. And now that you are back, Dread Lord, I think we would be wise if we too melted away. There is much hostility to foreigners now, as if somehow we were the ones to bring this trouble upon them; nevertheless, your servant has contrived to make certain preparations—"

"Where will I find Senefru? Just tell me that, Kephalos, and I will trouble you no more."

"It is best, Master, if you forget the Lord Senefru," he answered, putting his hand upon my arm. But in a sudden flash of anger I stood up, shaking him off.

"Just tell me! Tell me where he is, and if it be not already in his tomb, I will kill him."

But Kephalos only waggled his head, beholding me with sad eyes, as though I were a child indulging in a tantrum.

"My Lord, he is not dead, and you cannot kill him. Three days after you set out for Naukratis he departed the city in secret to join the approaching army and only returned when the gates were thrown open in submission. As of this hour he is in Tanis with Pharaoh, or on his way there. It is said that he will be prince now in Nekau's place. You cannot reach him, and it would be your death even to try."

He was right, of course—I saw that at once, for all that I would gladly have traded my own life for Senefru's. I tried to think, to find some path to revenge, but there was none. Grief and impotent rage clouded my mind so that I had to sit down again, not upon the bench with Kephalos but on the flat stones that covered Nodjmanefer's grave. My breast felt choked with tears, yet my eyes burned in their sockets. I did not think I could stand it—once I was dead, he would be safe forever. Senefru's triumph seemed to dig its claws into my flesh, and there was no way I could make it let go.

"Come into the house, Master. It is not entirely safe out here. Come inside and take some food and wine. Then sleep."

I spent the night in my own bed, racked by dreams that did not wait upon sleep but started as soon as I closed my eyes. I watched them murder Nodjmanefer, I listened to her screams and felt the sword in my own bowels when they killed her. Over and over, as if she would be compelled to die forever and I to witness it. In the morning I was feverish and Kephalos gave me some drugged wine that kept off dreams, and I slept into the afternoon.

"I think it best we leave soon," he said. "I know where there is a boat hidden, although the knowledge cost me more silver than I care to remember. If we can reach the harbor we will be safe."

"Why did the soldiers come to my house?"

He began to speak, and then caught himself before he had uttered a sound. The question seemed to take him off his guard, as if it had never occurred to him to wonder.

"I was not here—if they were Pharaoh's soldiers they would have known I was not, because Senefru knew. Did they go to many houses?"

"None." Kephalos frowned, cocking his head to one side as if he were listening for another answer. "They came here and to Senefru's house—I saw his doors standing open the next morning—but I have heard of no other intrusions."

"Is anything missing? Did they loot anything?"

"No. I would not even know they had been here if I hadn't heard them in the entrance hall while I was climbing down the back stairs to the kitchens."

"And they came here first?"

"Yes."

"Perhaps they were looking for the Lady Nodjmanefer. Perhaps Senefru wished to create the impression they were looking for me and only killed her by chance."

"We are unlikely ever to know, Lord."

"No. We will never know."

"We should leave as soon as it is dark, Lord."

"Yes—whatever you say. It is better to do anything than to stay here and . . ."

I did not finished the sentence because I did not know how. And what? I could not imagine.

"I have food, enough for a few days, and there is still a purse or two of silver . . ."

"Why did you stay, Kephalos?"

"Because I knew you would be back, Lord."

Yes. I believed him. Somehow I could no longer bear it. I covered my face with my hands and wept like a child.

I am an old man, and I will not trifle away what time the gods have spared me by making an adventure of our escape from Memphis. If the patrols had caught us we would have been executed as looters— Pharaoh's soldiers enjoyed a monopoly on looting and guarded it jealously—but we reached the harbor without incident, almost as if a path had been cleared for us.

Kephalos' boat was hidden under a pile of dirty straw in an empty grain warehouse, the last place anyone would have thought to look for it, and we carried it down to the water, raised sail, and were three hours downriver before the sun rose.

We had only to float on the bosom of the Nile. Our food would last us until we reached the Delta, and after that we had only to pull in at villages along the way to barter for food and ask directions. We slept on the boat, taking turns with the steering oar, and never stopped anywhere, not even at Naukratis, for more than an hour. Thus we made good time in our flight, a clean journey with no mishaps.

I believe it would have gone better with me if our journey had been filled with hazards, for as things were I had too much time to brood. There were too many long, empty nights, with Kephalos snoring in the stern of the boat, when I had nothing to think about except how I had left Nodjmanefer behind in Memphis, dead and unavenged. A thousand times I had cursed Senefru's name, calling down upon him the gods' retribution, vowing that while I lived he would never be safe, that one day I would find him again and give up his corpse to the delicate feasting of the crows. Yet these were dreams and I knew it. They were all empty boasting, born of my own sense of failure, for I believed Senefru had escaped me forever. Then I knew only that I was fleeing Egypt like a thief, and a man is most shamed by the lies he tells in his own heart.

We arrived in Buto after seventeen days. One morning we simply lowered our sail, coasted up to the wharf, tied up, and walked away from our boat as if it had ceased to exist.

The first thing we did was to find the public baths and wash off the filth of our journey—one does not trust one's body to the Nile, since the crocodiles might consider it disrespectful. Then we went to the bazaar and bought clean clothes. We both had almost a month's growth of hair and beard, but we had decided not to visit a barber since we had both had enough of the Egyptians and had thus decided to be Greeks once more. Then we went in search of Enkidu and Selana.

They were not hard to find—all that was required was to return to the waterfront and ask after the foreign giant with hair the color of wheat.

"He comes here every morning and afternoon," we were told, "with a maiden who is his voice. You have only just missed them."

We went to a tavern and drank wine for two hours, and they were there when we returned.

Enkidu of course offered me no greeting beyond his usual cold glare. What kept you? he seemed to be asking, as if I had only just stepped out of the room—but Selana wept and threw her arms around my knees, and then cursed me for a reckless fool. She asked no questions, then or later, probably because she had already guessed the answers. I had returned without Nodjmanefer; therefore Nodjmanefer could only be dead. We followed them back to their tavern, where rooms had been prepared against our arrival and left waiting the previous ten days. That night we feasted solemnly, in joyless luxury, and I retired early, feeling spent and empty.

For almost a month I had taken what rest I could on the ground or at the bottom of a reed boat, stinking of tar and stale water. I had lived with anxiety and despair, and these from moment to moment, with no space for anything else. Now my bed was a freshly woven mat on a well-swept floor, and there was no one about with a reason to kill me. I was safe, I was clean, I was quiet in my mind and only a little drunk. My passion of grief had worn itself out, leaving only a sullen bitterness, like an old bruise that is still sore to the touch even after its pain is gone. Yet I could not sleep. My mind, released at last from the web of danger and sorrow that had held me fast minute by minute, would not be quiet.

Three years in Egypt—what had it all been about? Nodjmanefer was dead, and I had had some hand in slaying her. I was not blameless. There was enough guilt that Senefru could afford to share it with me. What had I imagined myself to be doing?

"Visit Memphis and gorge on it," Prodikos had advised me, in what seemed now like another existence. "Afterwards, have a good vomit to purge your bowels of such follies and then continue with the rest of your life."

And I had gorged until my belly was rotten. I had been living for my own pleasure, thinking I could call it happiness, as if nothing else mattered. And the god had spared me to see the madness of such a life. That was my punishment.

Why? Why else, except to show me that mine must be another way? "Continue with the rest of your life."

It seemed hard, but no one had ever given me better counsel. The god, I knew, had spoken through Prodikos' mouth.

The next morning, early, I stole into Kephalos' room and shook him awake.

"Go down to the docks," I said, crouching over his sleeping mat. "Find us a ship that will take us away from this place. Do it now, for Egypt burns the soles of my feet."

For a moment he only stared, blinking up at me like an owl that has been stunned by the light.

"My Lord—now?" he asked finally. "By the gods, my head buzzes like a nest of hornets, for I was stiff with wine last night. I have not been in bed these three hours . . ."

"Now. Do it now."

"Seventeen days," he muttered, rubbing his eyes. "Seventeen days we are on the river, trapped in a boat no bigger than a coffin. One night on dry land, where there is food and drink and a clean bed, and now he would be on his travels again. Cursed is the man whose lord the gods have touched with madness—is there any wine hiding still in that jar? Here—hand it to me . . ."

Thus, that very night, as soon as the land winds had risen, we left the black lands of Egypt behind us. The morning found us on the Northern Sea, bound for Sidon.

We sailed on a Phoenician merchant ship bound for her home port in Byblos but trading up and down the coastal cities, so we stopped at Joppa and Tyre before reaching Sidon. We were favored by wind and weather, and the voyage lasted ten days.

Our captain was a friendly, open-hearted man, as I have found is usually the case with sailors, but he was a Phoenician and thus very sharp and cunning in all matters of business. Like so many of his race, he was intelligent, spoke several tongues, and had been everywhere men live within sight of the sea.

The Phoenicians are one of several nations whom the chronicles of the kings of Ashur, referring to all the peoples who lived along the coast of the Northern Sea between Egypt and Lydia, lumped together as "Canaanites," which means, as does the Greek word, "the red people." Except that they trade in the purple dye for which they are famous, I have never discovered why they are so called, but I do know that the

Phoenicians are as different from, say, the Hebrews, who are herders of goats and tenders of vines, as the men of Ashur are from the Elamites or the Chaldeans. The Phoenicians are sea people, as restless as the desert nomads of Arabia. They live for adventure and wealth, which to them are almost the same thing, and they build their cities as if they distrusted the solid land—such a place was Sidon.

The city occupied both an outcropping of the mainland and an island that follows the coast in a lazy curve and is joined to it by a stone causeway. The island was the port and at its northern end offered seagoing vessels safe harbor even in winter, when the waves are held back by a stone embankment, the blocks of which are up to six paces long. Its southern end is a long sandy shoreline perfect for beaching smaller craft. Thus Sidon is everywhere open to the sea, as if to an avenue of escape, whereas the face she presented to the land was that of a mighty fortified citadel.

I write of her as she was that first day, when we tied up along her outer harbor and stepped ashore. It was long ago, and today she may lie in ruins—it would not surprise me, for I saw the hand that would break down her walls and I heard the voice that sentenced her to death. But cities are stronger than men and can come to life again even after you have killed them. Sidon may flourish today, but I think of her as a stone corpse which the sand and sea have reclaimed for their own.

Yet she was not so when I first beheld her. She was bursting with life that first day, and I felt, when I saw her, as if I were stepping out from the darkness into the light.

Sidon was then perhaps the most beautiful city in the world. She was a city of gardens; every rooftop, every spare patch of ground was a blaze of color. Flowering vines crept over the walls of houses and the air was strong with their scent. There was a fruit tree in front of almost every door, carefully pruned and tended—these the Sidonians kept solely to delight their eyes and hearts, caring nothing for the fruit, for the hills just half an hour's walk east of the city walls were rich with orchards.

But if the first thing one noticed was the sheer beauty of the place, it was not long before the ingenuity of its construction made as great an impression. The harbor seemed to be unprotected, since there were no visible fortifications, but along its southern end the water was too shallow for warships and the northern end was protected by a series of artificial islands rendering it necessary for heavier vessels to approach the port singly, thus making attack from the sea almost impossible. Within the city, houses were built to include a system of drains, so that in winter and early spring, when the rains fall, there was hardly a drop that is not caught and held, for the Sidonians put no faith in the wells that lie beyond their gates.

It has been my observation that those peoples who live under the most precarious circumstances tend to become the most enterprising, and that salt water, which will drown a man but which it is madness for him to drink, nurtures the cleverest of races. No nation illustrates this better than the Phoenicians, who control a vast empire around the Northern Sea—an empire which somehow contrives to remain as insubstantial as a spider web. They are not interested in territory, only in wealth, so their cities tend to be no more than trading posts clinging to the edges of the land, and they are found everywhere. Their success can have no greater evidence than the intensity with which they are hated by the Greeks, their only rivals.

We spent our first night ashore in a tavern near the harbor, but as soon as Kephalos made himself known on the exchanges we received an invitation to stay with a timber merchant named Bodashtart, with whom he had deposited some fifty thousand silver shekels to be applied to the cedar trade with Babylon—a trade interrupted of late by the deteriorating relations with the Land of Ashur. Thus the silver had remained in the counting houses of Sidon, uninvested and producing no return, and thus Bodashtart's hospitality was not entirely without guile, for he showed himself most unwilling to surrender so considerable a sum and doubtless wished to keep Kephalos near him in hopes of awakening his interest in some alternate commercial scheme.

"You have heard the proverb, Master," Kephalos said to me, after our first dinner in the house, during which Bodashtart had spoken almost without pause of the riches to be gained from exploiting the dye trade with Libya—the tribesmen there, it seemed, had developed a passion for coloring their ragged garments with the celebrated "Phoenician purple" and paid for their infatuation with precious stones which, we were informed, they could pick up out of the desert sand like acorns from beneath an oak tree. "'Trust an Egyptian before a Greek and a Greek before a Phoenician, but never trust a Phoenician.' This man is without decency and treacherously attacks me where I and all others of my race are most pitifully vulnerable, in my greed."

"Do you believe what he says about Libya?"

Kephalos shook his head, making a contemptuous face.

"If the Libyans could gather up precious stones like nuts in springtime, certainly there would not be so many of them in Pharaoh's army, for who would be a soldier in Egypt if he was not starving? No, he merely wishes to keep our silver. He is annoyed with his king, who has revolted against your brother Esarhaddon and refused to pay the yearly tribute to Nineveh, thus cutting off the lucrative trade with the east. Bodashtart is a cedar merchant—he cannot carry his wood to the lands between the rivers, and now Egypt is in chaos and he cannot be sure he will be paid for what he sells there. Thus his hope is to cover his expected losses by swindling me."

"If his king of Sidon is not more careful, he will have more to worry him than merely the displeasure of his merchants. He will have the army of Ashur camped outside his walls."

But my servant only smiled at me, as if I were a child.

"The king is not concerned, My Lord—he is not concerned."

"If not, then he understands nothing of my brother."

"Even your brother, Lord, would not be such a fool as to attack Sidon, which has stout walls and can withstand the longest siege as long as its sea lines are not cut. Doubtless Abdimilkutte will come to some understanding with the Lord of Ashur."

And so I learned that even the Phoenicians could be fools, for it is a foolish man who believes there is nothing he cannot buy, and the king of Sidon seemed really to imagine that he could defy Esarhaddon and then strike some sort of bargain with him over the tribute money he owed. He might as well have tried to bribe Death.

I was to discover the source of this folly the very next day, when I returned from a visit to the bazaar with Enkidu and Selana to find a royal herald, dressed in a purple robe shot through with silver and carrying the willow staff that was his badge of office, waiting for me in front of Bodashtart's door.

"You are summoned, Lord Tiglath Ashur, Prince of the Eastern Lands and Conqueror of Many Nations. The Lord Abdimilkutte, Star of the World, King of Sidon, sends you his greetings and requests that you enter into his glorious presence."

The man spoke in Aramaic, and Selana, who spoke only her own tongue and the Egyptian of the kitchen slaves, stared at him as if she imagined he must be mad. When she had recovered from her surprise she reached down to remove the new sandals I had bought her and then wiped the dust from her feet.

"What is this?" she asked finally. "He dresses like a harlot and gibbers like an idiot. I like not the look of him—what is he doing here?"

"Inviting me to an audience, it appears."

"An audience—with whom?"

"With the king of this city."

"Well, take my advice and don't go. Kings always mean trouble, especially for you."

I agreed—kings always meant trouble. I could not possibly have explained how much trouble, since this one, it appeared, possessed knowledge of my lineage and history. I had not been in Sidon three days, and yet the secret I had preserved in Egypt for as many years seemed open to everyone.

"Selana, go inside and tell Kephalos what has happened," I said, only to get her out of the way, for I had no doubt Kephalos knew all about the matter. "Enkidu, go with her—I am perfectly safe."

My silent Macedonian, who all this time had been measuring our visitor with his eyes, as if he thought him too tall by about a head and was considering how best to remedy the matter, growled like a dog and then took Selana's hand, dragging her into the house.

When we were alone, I smiled at the man and opened the palms of my hands to him in a gesture of compliance.

"I am at your king's disposal."

The palace of King Abdimilkutte stood at the highest point in the city, adjacent to its outer wall but otherwise unprotected. As a structure it had much to say about the Phoenicians' view of their own position in the world and that of their ruler living amongst them—as a Sidonian, Abdimilkutte needed no protection from foreign aggressors except the city wall; as a king, he was allowed none against his own people.

Neither Esarhaddon nor Pharaoh Taharqa nor even Prince Nekau would have considered that the king of Sidon lived with much outward show, for the palace was no larger than my own house in Memphis. The Sidonians were merchants and their ruler had accustomed himself to a merchant's understanding of wealth and importance. His subjects would have regarded it as both unseemly and absurd if Abdimilkutte had tried to awe them into submission with a great display of regal splendor. As a king his business was to keep public order and to protect the city's commercial interests abroad, and any Phoenician knows that the measure of a man's power is taken in his counting house, not in his receiving hall.

So I was not overwhelmed as I waited with a chamberlain to be admitted to the royal presence. I would not have been overwhelmed in any case, for I had lived my whole life in the shadow of kings and knew they were only men. I was, however, curious to know what this one wanted of me.

"My Lord Tiglath Ashur—the glory of your name is known to us even here, at the edge of the world," he said, in a voice that sounded as if he had a stone lodged in one of his nostrils. "Please, be seated. Have you dined?"

Except for a few women servants to wait upon him, Abdimilkutte was alone in the room, reclining on a couch. It was only the middle of the afternoon, and every appearance suggested that he had already been at table for a few hours at least. The dishes before him were many and of gold, an extravagance even for a king, and most of them were already nearly empty, but the king himself gave the clearest indication of what progress he had made in feasting—his eyes had already taken on that glazed look, as if they might burst from their sockets at any moment, which is often the first hint of drunkenness. The Lord of Sidon, it would appear, was something of a debauchee.

He dipped his hands into a bowl of hot, scented water, drying them on the hair of one of his women. His fingers, even his thumbs, glittered with rings, and his short black beard was shiny with oil and elaborately curled. He was as elegant as any woman and his face showed signs of intelligence, yet his body was soft and heavy, as if he had given over his whole existence to voluptuous delights. Such a life is dangerous for a king, for the constant and easy gratification of the senses nurtures not only weakness but pride, and pride clouds the mind. I did not envy the Sidonians their master.

I bowed and sat down and allowed a cup of wine to be poured for me. I could see that Abdimilkutte was waiting for me to ask his will, and how he had known who I was, but I saw clearly enough that I would have all the answers without asking. He was so looking forward to telling me.

"You have been so many years away from your own land," he said finally. "Everyone imagined that you were dead. And now the gods choose this moment to bring you to my city. It is as clear a sign of their favor as I could have hoped for."

There are instants of time, and this was one such, when a man has the sickening premonition of having stumbled into a disaster.

"Is the king of Sidon in need of providential signs?" I asked, smiling, mocking him just a little, for all that my bowels were turning to water.

"I was speaking of the honor you do us, My Lord. And you of all men, who has come through so much treachery and covered yourself with such glory, should know how to value the favor of the gods. As a friend I welcome you."

As a friend? Yes, of course—why hadn't I guessed sooner? The Arabs had a proverb: "The enemy of my enemy is my friend." And the king of Sidon was in rebellion against the king of Ashur.

There was a pile of figs on a dish just at Abdimilkutte's elbow. He took one and split it open with a small silver knife.

"I offer you my protection as well," he continued, after he had scraped the flesh away from the tough green skin. As I watched him eat I had the impression that he rather resented this intrusion of business upon his pleasures. "We live in a world where a brother's loyalty does not always have its fitting reward, and the favor of the gods can take many forms."

"My Lord, what is it you want of me?"

He appeared startled, as if no one had ever had the effrontery to ask him a direct question before. His eyes widened and he set the little silver knife down on the table in an absent-minded manner that suggested he had forgotten why he was holding it.

"My Lord, I cannot help you in your quarrel with the king of Ashur. My alliance is worth nothing."

He smiled. It seemed I had made a jest.

"I see you have a soldier's directness," he said, opening his hand, palm up, as if to weigh the usefulness of such a virtue—it did not appear to be much.

"I have not been a soldier for many years."

"Perhaps it is time to be one again." He smiled once more, not very pleasantly. "What would you answer, My Lord, if I offered you the command of the army I have garrisoned within these walls?"

"Against what enemy?"

"The one we both share—your brother, the Lord Esarhaddon."

"Then I would say that the people of Sidon should lament, for their king has gone mad."

He laughed at this. At least, he laughed until he saw that I was not laughing with him.

"Am I so mad to resist a despot, then?"

A man reclining on a couch has a difficult time looking martial and defiant, but Abdimilkutte made the attempt. I could almost have pitied him.

"My Lord," I asked finally. "How many men have you under arms?"

"Eight thousand."

"If Esarhaddon comes against you, it will not be with less than fifty thousand, and probably many more."

"He will need them if he attacks this city. You forget the wall."

"The soldiers of Ashur are very skilled in siege warfare. Do not forget, they took Babylon. They can take Sidon if it is their will."

"They could enclose Babylon—Babylon did not face the sea. The men of Ashur are not, I think, a race of sailors."

"These eight thousand, are they mercenaries or citizens?"

"Three thousand Sidonians, the rest hired from Lydia."

"You cannot depend on mercenaries if things begin to go badly."

"It is also possible that not all of Esarhaddon's soldiers will remain loyal to him."

The smile had taken on a fixed quality by this time, as if he imagined he had answered every possible argument—as if everything were understood between us.

"Yes, of course," I said, feeling in but little humor to smile. "You imagine that my presence here will divide the armies of Ashur against themselves. It is a device which others have tried."

"Yes, of course—and perhaps, by this time, the Lord Tiglath Ashur will have learned enough to make it work."

But it was not Abdimilkutte who spoke. I turned toward a curtained doorway, from which the voice seemed to come, and saw there my royal brother, the eunuch Nabusharusur.

XIX

ON THE PLAIN AT KHANIRABBAT, IT IS SAID, THE GRASS grows waist-high, nourished by the corpses of the men who died there. Yet cattle that feed on it sicken. No plow breaks the soil, for the people have all been driven off into the barren night by the wailing of ghosts. So it is said. I have never been back, not since the day of the battle my brother the king fought there against his enemies, but I can believe the ground is under a curse.

Esarhaddon had relieved me of my command, thinking to shame me before the armies of Ashur, yet he did me a kindness. In the years since, I have not had to remember how I raised my sword against the men of my own race, the companions of my young manhood, soldiers who had fought at my side in better times. I merely had to witness the slaughter, for the king's heart was bitter towards those who had rebelled against him.

Among these had been Nabusharusur.

"Did Esarhaddon ever find out that you gave me that horse and let me escape?" he asked in his reedy voice as together we dined in his rooms at the palace of the Lord Abdimilkutte. "Is that the reason he banished you?"

"Had he found out, he would have killed me. I have often wondered why he didn't anyway, since he regards me as even a greater traitor than you."

"Yes, that wound goes deeper. I may have raised the rebellion against him, but he never loved me."

Nabusharusur smiled. As so often with him, looking into his smooth face, on which no beard would ever grow, I could not tell if he mocked me or not.

"How did you come to this place?" I asked.

"Oh, it is not a very exciting story." He shrugged his thin shoulders, as if to dismiss the idea that one such as he could ever pretend to heroism. "I simply rode hard enough to keep ahead of any news of the battle. I told anyone I met that I was a courier in the king's army—I was dressed as a soldier, so they had no reason not to believe me. I sold off my jewelry as I needed money. The horse, by the way, dropped dead on the road to Hamath, but I was able to buy another. I was in hiding here in Sidon when the king renounced his allegiance to Nineveh, so I offered him my services, from which he has been profiting ever since. I have risen very high in favor here, for Abdimilkutte values my counsel. These people are not as clever as they would have the world imagine, or, at least, this one is not."

"I congratulate you, then, on your good fortune in finding this place of refuge. The Sidonians, no matter what you think of them, seem to have timed their defection for your particular convenience."

My words had been spoken partly in jest, but Nabusharusur did not take them so. He shook his head.

"Fortune had little enough to do with it," he said. "There were rebellions in half the states in the empire after Esarhaddon took the throne, and he has spent most of the years since quelling them. It is so with every new king, for these foreigners seem not to bear our yoke lightly. In our father's day it was Tyre that led the revolt of the Phoenician cities. This time Sidon has taken her place while Tyre, out of pique, remains loyal. We have conquered the world, we men of Ashur, but if we hold it at all it is only because each of these little states hates its neighbors even more than it does us."

It was early evening, but Nabusharusur had dismissed all his servants and we were alone together in a large room that had a view of the harbor. We spoke in Akkadian, but my brother was a cautious man and doubtless did not care to have our conversation overhead. He ate a sparing meal, picking disdainfully at the dishes before him, yet he did justice to the wine—this seemed to be a habit he had acquired in exile. We had been friends as children, but much had come in the way since then and I had to keep reminding myself that I hardly knew this man.

"Will the king persist in his rebellion if Esarhaddon takes the field against him?"

"A sensible man would not, but Abdimilkutte is not a sensible man." Nabusharusur smiled again, that smile which spoke so eloquently of his contempt for the whole race of men. "A sensible man would make an arrangement for perhaps a lower rate of tribute and count himself fortunate, but the king of Sidon is not that man. He is not like his subjects, who think only of profit. He dreams of glory, of the old league of Phoenician states, with himself at its head. I, of course, foster these dreams, for if he comes to terms with Esarhaddon, my head will certainly be part of the bargain. But I think I am safe enough for the time being—they are neither of them sensible men. Esarhaddon burns and slaughters wherever he goes and by his own lack of moderation stiffens the resolve of the likes of Abdimilkutte. I am not the only one who fears for his head."

"If Esarhaddon brings an army here, you would both do well to settle your affairs. You know how he is. He will resent the city's defection as a personal affront, and he will not rest until it has been punished."

"This is true—I count on it to be true."

The smile, by this time, had taken on the fixed character of a mask. It revealed nothing now, not even contempt. With great delicacy Nabusha-rusur lifted his wine cup to his mouth and then set it down again. It was like a ritual, a statement of confidence before the gods.

"What game are you playing, brother?" I asked, wondering if I did not already know the answer.

"What game? The same one I have always played."

He offered me a plate of glazed plums and I took one, hardly knowing why. I did not even eat it but set it down on the table in front of me.

"I have come to believe, Tiglath my brother, that truly you must be favored by the gods. The world is an evil and corrupt place and you are an honest man who has never learned guile. Yet you seem to survive every catastrophe. I think, finally, you will outlive all of us. And I believe that your presence here, in this city, at this precise moment, is a sign from heaven that my designs will prosper. For, you see, I intend to destroy Esarhaddon, and I shall use Sidon as my instrument."

"You are mad," I said, with something like awe. "I think perhaps you have always been mad."

"You think so? Perhaps. But life itself is a kind of madness, and thus I am counted as a clever man."

"Then what will you do?"

"Wait—stiffen Abimilkutte in his purpose, and hope that Esarhaddon is as great a fool as I have always believed and swallows the bait."

He raised his arm and made a sweeping gesture through the air, seeming to encompass not only the room where we sat but the whole city.

"You are a soldier, Tiglath, so you know even better than I that a besieged city cannot be taken so long as it is well provisioned. We are not a sailing race. Esarhaddon may be able to hire a few warships to patrol in front of the harbor, but the Sidonians have a vast fleet and will keep themselves supplied no matter what. Let Esarhaddon come—let him camp beneath the walls of Sidon, wearing himself out until the army grows so weary of his obsession that they cut his throat."

"It will not succeed, brother. Esarhaddon may be a fool, but he is a good soldier. He will find a way."

"You had best hope he does not," he answered, leaning towards me, grinning like a demon—yes, of course he was mad. "I have spoken to Abdimilkutte, and you will not be allowed to leave the city until he has settled with Esarhaddon. If Esarhaddon triumphs . . . Well, brother, I leave it to your judgment. How long do you think you will survive once the king of Ashur has you in his hands again?"

"How did he know, so quickly, that you were in the city?"

"Who can tell? Perhaps he saw me. Perhaps he did not need to, for Nabusharusur is the sort of man who will find out anything of interest to him."

Kephalos shook his head in perplexity and alarm. At that hour of the night, and with me summoned away by the king's herald, he was deep in wine. I did not blame him.

"And he can keep us here," he said. "Indeed, he can keep us here. The city is a trap if he chooses to make it one—the harbor is patrolled and there are only three gates through the wall, all of them guarded. He has us sealed inside like wine in a jar."

"He has *me* sealed inside," I corrected him. "Get out while you can, my friend. Take ship to Greece. No one will trouble to stop you and you can do me no good by staying here. Take Selana with you."

"Selana will not go."

I had not seen her standing there in the doorway of my room. She looked pale and shaken—I wondered how much of our conversation she had overheard.

"You do not know what you are saying," I told her, with some asperity, for I was in no temper for girlish heroics. "If the worst happens, and the Assyrians take the city, you will be carried away into slavery—always provided, of course, that you have not starved to death or been massacred first. Go with Kephalos while you have the chance."

"I am your slave already."

"You are my slave only because it is your perverse humor to call yourself such. If you are carried out of Sidon as war booty, you will find it is a very different matter. I should not like to think of you growing old as a tavern harlot in Nineveh."

"Master, is the king of these Assyrians really your brother?" she asked, deliberately changing the subject. I knew these tactics of old.

"Yes, he is my brother. And the man who stands at the right hand of the Sidonian king is also my brother. And both of them hate me as much as they hate each other—I do not expect much benefit from my family connections. Will you go, Selana?"

"No, I will not go. My Lord is a great fool even to think it. A slave's place is with her master."

"A slave's place is to obey, and it is my will that you should go. If need be, I will have Enkidu carry you aboard the ship in a leather sack."

"Enkidu will not go either. You know that."

"Then you must go without them, Kephalos."

But the worthy physician, made melancholy from drowning his fear in too much Lebanese wine, could only raise his hands in a gesture of despairing resignation.

"What am I to do, Lord—am I to be shamed by the courage of a child? No, the little bitch has sealed all our fates. I too will stay. Perhaps, after all, it will all come out right."

He did not believe it himself. There was sweat in the creases of his face and his eyes were damp with panic, but, as he had in all the many crises of my life, he meant to stay and do what he could for me. The gods were kind to grant me so loyal a friend, for I never deserved it.

"Perhaps," he went on, "perhaps the Lord Esarhaddon will not even come."

But we had not been in Sidon half a month when the first reports began to be heard. An army, numbering between eighty and a hundred thousand strong, was on the march down the northern caravan route from Kadesh.

"You see?" Nabusharusur was almost beside himself with triumph. "He comes. Of his own will he sticks his head into the noose. I *knew* this was a temptation Esarhaddon would never be able to resist."

Because, of course, no nation save the Land of Ashur, not even the Egyptians, could have fielded so many men. And if the cities by the Northern Sea were to be brought to heel, Esarhaddon was not the ruler to sit quietly in Nineveh and let his generals steal the glory of it. He was a soldier long before he was a king, and he had waited all his life to command great armies. My eunuch brother was right—he would never be able to resist.

"Yet we shall see, at last, whose head is in the noose."

Nabusharusur only stared at me, as if he hardly believed I could be such a fool. They were both mad, both of them—hatred and the taste of power had turned their wits. Neither of them cared what they did, or how the world suffered for it, so possessed were they by their private demons.

Thus the siege of Sidon began.

I suppose what surprised me the most was the calm with which her people greeted the approach of this the mightiest army on earth. To them it seemed almost a matter of routine—after all, this was not the first time foreign invaders had camped beneath the walls. There was not even a sense of urgency.

The men of Ashur were still four days' march distant when the villagers from the surrounding countryside began streaming through the city gates, the men leading small flocks of goats and the women carrying great bundles balanced on their heads, usually with a child on one hip and another, a few years older, clutching a handful of skirt as they trailed behind. I wondered, as I watched them arriving, how many of Esarhaddon's spies were mixed in with these crowds.

The first effect of this influx was a sharp rise in the price of everything except meat, for the Sidonians were quick to see an opportunity for profit and the refugees had to sell their animals at once to keep from starving.

On the night his patrols had spotted the first scouting parties of cavalry, Abdimilkutte ordered the gates closed and barred. The next day there was nothing except a great cloud of dust on the horizon, but the morning after, standing on the city walls, I could watch the long columns of soldiers fanning out over the plain that spread eastward to the mountains. By midday they had sent out foraging parties and established a series of camps, and by twilight the first lines of earthworks were already in place. The reports had not exaggerated. Esarhaddon's force was at least a hundred thousand men, as large an army as that which had assembled for Khanirabbat.

The next morning, a herald rode up to the main gate bearing the king's terms for accepting Sidon's bloodless surrender. A clay tablet was carried to the palace, but the herald would not be content until anyone who cared to hear knew Esarhaddon's demands: the city must pay thrice over the five years' tribute that was due, and that at once; since his soldiers were not to be cheated of their rightful booty, the citizens must submit to two days of peaceful pillage; a selection of prisoners was to be taken, up to the number of a thousand, and carried back to Nineveh; and Abdimilkutte was to abdicate, since he had proved himself unworthy, and leave the throne to whichever of his sons Ashur's king thought best. In exchange, the people of Sidon would be granted their lives and liberty, and the city would be spared.

It was not an offer to attract much enthusiasm, particularly since the Sidonians did not believe their city could be taken, not even by an army of a hundred thousand men, but I had no doubt, even then, that Esarhaddon intended to have it refused. He was looking for a pretext. He wished to make an example of Sidon, one that would not be forgotten until the world was dust.

"The king, naturally, rejected such terms at once," Nabusharusur reported, with no small satisfaction. "He was frightened, of course—he is always frightened—but it took me only a little time to restore his valor. Is it not wonderful how Esarhaddon makes the way smooth before me?"

After he heard Abdimilkutte's reply, Esarhaddon ordered the aqueducts pulled down, cutting off the supply of fresh water from the mainland. The city itself was too close to sea level for wells to be dug within its walls.

"This is not really a difficulty—we expected it. We can bring water in from the Litani River by ship. We can journey even farther if necessary. Esarhaddon's army can only be in one place at a time. Besides, how long can he provision such an army from the surrounding countryside? He must move on soon. His soldiers will demand it when their bellies begin to grow pinched."

Nabusharusur's confidence seemed general. After the first surge, prices for food began to steady. After the first week, Kephalos told me, it was hard to find anyone prepared to wager the siege would last through the month.

"Then these people understand nothing of the men of Ashur. In my father's time, we camped beneath the walls of Babylon for fifteen months, and finally we took the city. And who is more obstinate by nature than Esarhaddon?"

Kephalos shrugged his shoulders, for he too was not very hopeful.

"These Sidonians will not release the money I deposited with them from Egypt. They say we must wait until the Assyrians have withdrawn. They say the merchants of other cities expect payment in silver now, or they will sell them nothing. We are not only trapped, Lord, but very shortly we will be beggars as well."

"Take heart, my friend," I told him. "No man minds being poor after he is dead."

My former servant did not find this remark particularly amusing. He regarded me with large, injured eyes, as if I had insulted him.

"You may jest as much as you wish, Lord, but not all of us will find escape in the tranquil dignity of death," he said, sighing heavily. "The real misery of a conquered city belongs to its survivors. I know, for was I not captured by your father's army at Tyre? And did I not spend nearly half my life as a slave in a foreign land?"

"Yes, I know it must have been dreadful for you, my friend—especially when one considers that within three or four years you were one of the richest men in Nineveh. The hardships you endured there were no doubt unspeakable."

"Master, you are without proper sympathy."

I began to laugh—I could not help myself—and then Kephalos really was annoyed.

"You have only to wait," he said, eyeing me narrowly. "A month, Lord, or perhaps not even so long as that, should your royal brother decide to make an issue of this siege, and you will witness such scenes of wretchedness as shall make you blanch."

"I know, my friend. I saw Babylon after it was taken."

"Yes, but you did not live in it while it waited to perish."

A month did pass with the army of Ashur camped beyond the gates, yet life in Sidon changed very little. In an attempt to close the harbor and starve the city into submission, Esarhaddon had hired thirty warships from Cyprus, but the harbor entrance was too narrow for them to think of risking a landing and the smaller and faster Sidonian merchant ships had little trouble evading them in open water. Thus the blockade was not successful. Grain, fruit and water were plentiful, meat was only three or four times its usual price, and even wine could still be found. It began to look as if Nabusharusur had been right, that the siege would fail and that Esarhaddon would be forced to accept a humiliating defeat.

One had only to look out over the wall, however, to grasp that the king my brother entertained no such possibility. There had not as yet been any fighting—Abdimilkutte had wisely refused battle, keeping his eight thousand troops safely in their barracks, but the surrounding countryside was completely in Esarhaddon's hands, and the elaborate series of trenches and earthworks that fortified his encampments indicated plainly enough that he meant to stay.

The fortifications began about a quarter of an hour's walk from the city gates, but the soldiers of Ashur always lay out their encampments in the same way, with the commander's tent in the center, so I did not have to strain my eyes to discover where the king met with his officers and put down his head at night. I spend many hours gazing out over the empty plain to where the sentries patrolled and the cooking fires burned bright. It gave me a peculiar, tormented pleasure to watch them, as if I were divided against myself. There were men out there I had known all my life, my enemies now through no wish of theirs or mine. There was my brother, who hated me, yet who had been my friend too long for me to stop loving him. I would have given much to be able to cross the distance and walk among them, to hear their voices and fill my eyes with the sight of their faces, but it would have meant death even to try.

Once, only once, I saw Esarhaddon up close enough to recognize him. One afternoon he and an escort rode out beyond the earthworks, coming almost within bowshot of the walls. He was dressed in the uniform of a *rab shaqe*, with nothing to distinguish him from the eight or ten senior commanders who formed his party, but I knew him at once. My heart twisted within my breast.

He looked tired, but there was nothing of the sullen grimness I had seen so often in his face during those last years. I was too far away to hear his voice, but there was authority in his gesture. He was probably happy, for he had escaped from Nineveh and had an army to lead, which was what he had been born for. Esarhaddon was a soldier. He had never wanted to be king.

Yet he looked like a king now. Perhaps the god had chosen well after all.

Keeping his horse to a walk, he paced off the whole length of the wall. He seemed in no hurry. After a few minutes, he turned and rode back to camp, his officers following at a respectful distance.

The evening of that same day a stranger called at my house, a man dressed in a rough farmer's tunic. He brought me a message.

"If you go to the main gate an hour after the sky is dark over the sea, you will find that a horse has been provided. The guards have been bribed and will open the gate for you. The Lord Esarhaddon will meet you halfway between the city wall and the outer perimeter of the Assyrian camp. He will come alone and he guarantees your life."

He spoke in Aramaic—he was no countryman—and as soon as he had finished speaking he departed. He would not even stay for a cup of wine but crept away into the dusk, for a spy lives every moment of his life in fear.

"Needless to say, you will not go," announced Kephalos, as if quoting that day's price for cooking oil. "You would not be such a fool as to go. If your brother can arrange to have the city gates opened for you, he can arrange to have them closed and bolted at your back."

"And he is not such a fool as that. Do you think he waits outside with a party of soldiers to take me prisoner? Do you think he wants me brought into his camp, either living or dead, that the men of Ashur may look upon my face?" I shook my head, for Kephalos, though wise in many things, understood nothing of this matter. "No one, I would wager, beyond a few of the king's most trusted officers is aware of my presence in the city, and my brother has every motive to keep the secret. I am not some nameless criminal, my friend. I am Tiglath Ashur, a king's son whom all the world knows to have been wronged at his brother's hands. Esarhaddon might have me murdered secretly, but he will not put me to death in public. Unless things have changed very much in the Land of Ashur, he would not dare take the risk."

"Then you will go?"

"Yes, of course. Who can say that some good may not come of it?"

"All that will come of it is that you will end the night a corpse in some ditch," Selana jeered, as if spitting the words at me. "You go only because it is your perverse fancy to go. And because you cannot bear to think that your brother might believe you are afraid of him."

"Yes—there is something of that as well."

I smiled at her, since I knew it would make her even angrier. For this she threw a cooking pot at my head, missing by only the width of a few fingers and almost leaving nothing for Esarhaddon's assassins to do.

Half an hour after sunset I began walking toward Sidon's main gate, making sure as I went along that no one was following me—after all, Esarhaddon was not the only one I had to fear, and the kings of besieged cities are naturally suspicious of those who hold commerce with their besiegers. But I was not followed, and when I reached the gate I found a horse tethered beside the guard station. A door in the gate had been left slightly ajar and no one challenged me when I led the horse through it. What fate awaits the Sidonians, I found myself wondering, when their lives are in the hands of soldiers whose vigilance can be bought as easily as this?

I rode out into the darkness, now knowing what I would find there.

There was the torchlight from the city wall behind me, and in front, three or four hundred paces away, the fires inside Esarhaddon's camp flickered like sparks from a grindstone. Between these all was darkness, but it was a clear night and the moon was close to being full. I had no trouble finding my way.

I had not gone very far before I could make out a faint glimmer of light—someone had set an oil lamp on the ground for me to find. When I approached I saw the outline of a man behind the lamplight. His horse was tethered not far away. I knew it was Esarhaddon even before I heard his voice.

"So you came," he said. "I was beginning to doubt that you would."

I slid down from the back of my horse and dug the point of the javelin I was carrying into the ground.

"I have come. But if you draw your sword or cry out for help, I will kill you, Esarhaddon. This time I will not stay my hand."

"I am your king!"

He stepped forward a little, so that the light fell across his face, and I saw that he was genuinely shocked. Under the circumstances, I could only laugh.

"My king has turned his face against me—I have no king, nor have I country, nor have I brother. And all of this by your will. What claim can any man make to my loyalty, least of all you? Do not speak to me of kings."

My bitter speech died away into a silence that seemed to last forever. We stood facing each other, and then, slowly, a change came over my brother, a small thing, hardly noticeable, something in the way he held himself which stated as clearly as any words that he felt he was safe. I had lied. I would never raise my hand against him, and he knew it.

"Yet I am still your king," he said at last, as if stating a neutral fact.

"What do you want, Esarhaddon?"

"Among other things, to know how you come to be here, Tiglath— here, in this city, at this moment."

"Chance."

"I do not believe you."

"Then because it is my *simtu*—the god's pleasure. Will you believe that?"

With his left hand, Esarhaddon made a contemptuous gesture, as if sweeping away a cobweb.

"Then believe what you like," I said. "It is much the same to me."

"I believe you conspire with Abdimilkutte. I believe you encourage him in his rebellion and traitorously work against me, you and Nabusharusur together—you did not think I knew he was here with you?" He shook his head, as if disappointed in me. "I knew."

"Then, since you are so wise, there is nothing I need tell you."

"You conspire against me! Do you deny it?"

"I deny nothing."

Esarhaddon started to answer and then checked himself. His was not a complicated mind, but he was not a fool and knew that I was baiting him. He also knew I had not conspired with his enemies—this was merely something he wished to believe.

"Yet you encourage this king to resist me," he said at last, narrowing his eyes as if to suggest he could see into my heart.

"I do not need to encourage him. He does not believe you can take his city—no one believes it."

"I will take his city." He bared his teeth in a savage grin. "And when I have taken it, I will tear down its walls and sack its temples. I will lead its people away into bondage, and I will slay Abdimilkutte as if he were a dog caught stealing scraps. I do not care if I wait outside its walls this year."

"You can have the city sooner than that, sparing many lives and much trouble. Let Abdimilkutte keep his throne—he cares for nothing else—and accept tribute."

"Why do you speak thus, Tiglath? You know that if this king surrenders to me he will deliver you into my hands. Have you no fear of death?"

Esarhaddon cocked his head to one side and folded his hands in front of him, as a man will who studies some curious object that has come in his way. Thus he waited in silence, perhaps actually expecting that I would answer him.

"My reasons are my own concern," I said at last. If I can persuade Abdimilkutte to make submission, will you spare the city?"

"I have stated my terms, and they have been refused." His face darkened as he spoke—I do not believe his anger was directed against the Sidonians. "This place will be annihilated so that men will forget it ever existed."

"Then Nabusharusur will be very pleased, for you will have given him all he could ask for. Did you know that I saved his life at Khanirabbat? When the battle was over, I found him hiding in a cleft of rock. I gave him my horse that he might make good his escape."

I do not know why I told Esarhaddon this, but the effect was immediate. His hand went to the hilt of his sword, and he would have drawn it to take my life if I had not pulled the point of my javelin from the earth, reminding him that he lived at my suffrage.

His hand dropped back to his side, but his anger persisted.

"Then you are a traitor," he said, hissing the words. "For all that the army holds your memory in such honor, blaming me that I sent you into exile, you are a traitor to the god and to your own people."

"Because I would not betray one brother to another?" I laughed, yet it was a bitter sound. "If you believe that, then command me, as my king, to open the city gates that the men of Ashur may pour through them and conquer. You have but to give the order, to say 'Do this, out of the loyalty you owe me as your sovereign master, though Abdimilkutte's soldiers will surely kill you for it.' Why do you hesitate? Do you imagine I will not obey? Only speak, Esarhaddon, and I will give over to you the triumph you so crave."

Yet he did not speak. He could not, for he knew that if he spoke it must be as my king and I that would obey, and he could not bring himself to accept victory from my dead hand. He knew that when his own soldiers captured the city gates and found my corpse—men who had fought with me against the Elamites, the Scythians and the Medes—they would know the truth of everything that had happened between us, and he would never be able to trust them again.

At last, baffled, full of wrath he could not utter, he turned from me to mount his horse, riding away into the darkness.

Yet perhaps his silence was no more than pride, the knowledge that he did not need me to breach the walls of Sidon for him. He meant to send the men of Ashur over them, and he would do it without my help.

For Esarhaddon, whatever his other limitations, was a good commander. He was careful. He laid his plans like a builder raising a house. He was a pious man who did not presume on the favor of the gods but made his own good fortune. And he knew what was required to storm a city.

At Babylon we had undermined the outer wall, and Esarhaddon and I together had thrown the great Gate of Ishtar open to our father's army. Sidon was not Babylon—with the sea near, the ground roundabout was too soft to allow for tunneling and, besides, the wall had not been raised to so great a height. Here the wall could be scaled. Men with ladders would stream over it like water over a stick.

But not before the defenders had been reduced almost to starvation. A wise hunter does not make a lion rise from its dinner.

Therefore, Esarhaddon had hit upon a means of closing the harbor. No other conclusion was possible.

Four days later, the Tyrians came in a hundred ships—these the Sidonians could not simply slip between. Only a madman would have dared putting to sea against them. The city now felt my brother's hand around its throat.

XX

HAVING SUFFERED FOR SUCH FOLLY TWENTY YEARS BE-
fore, in the reign of my father the Lord Sennacherib, the worthy citizens
of Tyre had not joined the rebellion against my brother. A siege, as they
had learned, was a troublesome and expensive business and bad for trade.
Besides, the kings of Ashur were not celebrated for their forgiving natures
and could be counted on to take drastic revenge against any second
defection. So instead, like good men of business, they had decided that
the greater profit lay in paying the yearly tribute to Nineveh and, as a
reward for adding their weight toward the destruction of Sidon, being
allowed to inherit her commercial empire.

Thus the Tyrians, who cared only for money, had allied themselves
with my brother, who cared only for conquest and glory, and between
them they would leave Sidon a heap of smoking ruins.

And Esarhaddon had struck this bargain before his first sight of the city
walls. He was a good soldier and understood the value of fear and greed.

The effects of the Tyrian blockade were drastic and immediate. Food
simply disappeared from the bazaar stalls, but men can go longer without
food than without drink, and within three days the price of water had shot
up to ten silver shekels a jar. Within five days the same price only
purchased a cup. By the tenth day people who had been driven mad with
thirst were hurling themselves head-first into the sea.

But it did not take as long as that before angry mobs were throwing
stones at the palace of Abdimilkutte, cursing his name that he had
brought this misery down upon them.

"Listen to them!" he shouted at me—I had been summoned by the
king, and his soldiers had had to fight their way through the crowds to

escort me through the great cedarwood doors. "What do they expect of me that I have not done, My Lord Tiglath? I have sent messengers, bearing offers of surrender, and the king of Ashur sends them back with their tongues cut out. You know him—he must be brought to relent! I will give him gold—anything! He must relent! I will—"

"He will not relent," Nabusharusur said in a placid voice. He even smiled, as if wonderfully satisfied with the fact. Abdimilkutte turned on him like a cornered cat.

"You—all this is your fault! If I had not listened to you . . ."

But he could not even finish, so choked with wrath and terror had he become. Finally he sat down on his throne, slumped over in defeat.

"The Lord Nabusharusur speaks the truth," I said. "Esarhaddon will not relent against you, but he may yet spare the city. Throw open the gates."

"It means your own death as well, Tiglath. And the king's. And mine."

And still my eunuch brother smiled, making one wonder what pleasure he found in the idea.

"No—there can be no thought of that!" Abdimilkutte's eyes bulged from his head. "I will not turn myself over to have the skin stripped from my body. No!"

He waved us away, burying his face in his other hand, and Nabusharusur walked with me to the palace doors.

"Shall you need an escort home?" he asked. "The mob is in an ugly mood."

"No one notices me—all the city's hatred is directed against their king."

"And rightly so, for who could not hate so cowardly and self-indulgent a buffoon?" Nabusharusur's smooth face wrinkled in disgust. "Can you imagine, he still sets aside two hundred jars of water a day for his gardens—in these times? The greatness of kings!"

He laughed, contriving nonetheless to make no sound.

"And Esarhaddon is no better. He is like a little boy, angry because he cannot open a jar of dates. But you hate him as much as I do—I can see it in your face. Perhaps you have even more reason."

"What reason do you have?"

Nabusharusur cocked his head a trifle to one side and smiled, his own peculiar smile of contemptuous amusement that I could be simpleton enough even to ask such a question.

"Ask me rather what reason I have for living. It is not love, for I have been disqualified from that. Therefore it must be hate."

He watched me for a moment, his eyes narrowing slightly, as if inviting me to disagree. But if he expected some answer he would have to be disappointed, for what answer was there? Answers meant nothing to someone like Nabusharusur. Perhaps this was what he wished me to understand.

"Every life must have purpose—mine is the destruction of Esarhaddon. That is why he is here."

"You think so? It is much more likely he will destroy Sidon, and you with it."

"And you, brother. Shall I tell him you are here? He has spies in the city, so it would be a simple enough matter."

He smiled again, and then shook his head. Did he know of my meeting with Esarhaddon? Who could say?

"No, Tiglath, I am not trying to frighten you. A man must have two things before he can be frightened: imagination and something to live for. We two both have the first, but the second is mine alone. Esarhaddon took everything from you when he took the throne—have you wandered so far through the world without discovering that? Make your purpose mine, brother. I can achieve it without you, but why deny yourself the satisfaction? Help me to kill Esarhaddon."

I do not know why I was surprised, yet for a moment I was speechless. My mind raced, asking a thousand questions, turning over a thousand possibilities.

"*I can achieve it without you,*" he had said. "*Help me to kill Esarhaddon—I can achieve it without you.*"

Doubtless he could.

"You have a plan?" I asked finally.

The smile changed slightly, as if he knew he had won.

"I have a plan. Of course I have a plan. With your help, I can save the city, kill Esarhaddon, and put you in his place. But only with your help. Otherwise I will only succeed in killing Esarhaddon, and at the cost of my own life. The army still loves you, Tiglath. They will accept Esarhaddon's death if it is at your hands."

"The army has forgotten me—Esarhaddon is king."

"You could be."

No, I could not. And Nabusharusur knew it. I would perish, and he with me. And the army, in its wrath, would sack the city and put every living creature within its walls to death. But what was any of that to Nabusharusur, provided he achieved his purpose?

"Tell me what you intend," I said.

So he did. We walked down the stone passageways of Abdimilkutte's palace and Nabusharusur described to me how I would kill Esarhaddon. They were both mad, my two brothers, and between them they held me and the whole of Sidon hostage.

"We must act now, Tiglath. We must kill Esarhaddon. Abdimilkutte thinks of nothing but his own safety, so we have no choice. If we hesitate, the whole city will perish."

I left him at the doors, through which, because of the crowd waiting before them and the soldiers' quite understandable fear that the palace might be overrun, I had to squeeze like sap out of a tree.

I walked back towards the harbor district through streets which, almost from one hour to the next, had taken on the stricken appearance of a place from which all hope was fled. The sides of houses were streaked with dirt because people had begun digging up their flower gardens to eat the bulbs. I could not remember how many days it had been since last I had heard a dog bark—they had all been chased down and eaten as soon as the Tyrians blockaded the harbor. The odors of cooking had disappeared, even the smell of excrement. Except to search for food, of which there was none, people stayed indoors and starved quietly.

It was the quiet which was most oppressive. Hunger begins in pain and ends in lethargy, so that even the children stop crying. Abdimilkutte need not have worried—the mob outside his palace would end by returning to their homes and staying in them. And a man whose lips are cracked with thirst has no voice to shout his anger.

What would be the conclusion of all this? Would the soldiers of Ashur storm the wall or would the citizens merely open the gates to them, begging for a last sip of water before offering their throats to be cut?

And was it possible I could prevent such an outcome by so simple an expedient as murdering Esarhaddon?

"The guards will not attempt to prevent your leaving the city," Nabusharusur had said. "I will see to it that you are given a horse, and then you need only ride into camp and kill him. His men, down to the commonest soldier, are sick of him. They will welcome you as their hero and liberator. No one will interfere, for you are still a royal prince and your person is sacred. Even Esarhaddon himself will hesitate. At first he will only want to know what you intend—he will suspect no danger. That is your great advantage, Tiglath. He hates you, but he has never learned not to trust you."

It was all lies. Nabusharusur did not even believe it himself. Esarhaddon was king in the Land of Ashur, and I was forgotten—it had been four years.

And the army would show no mercy if their king was murdered. Their revenge would be terrible. No stone would be left standing upon another, and there would be such slaughter as would make the gods weep. I would not be the only one to perish, merely the first. Sidon and all who dwelt within her walls would become a memory. This is what Nabusharusur was hoping for. He knew he was doomed, but he planned a more general destruction. He wanted the world to be blotted out with him.

But I could not oblige. Even if it had all been true, even if I could have saved Sidon and raised myself to glory as king in the Land of Ashur, Esarhaddon was my brother—whatever else he had become or made himself, he was still my brother, and I could not forget the love I bore him. If he razed Sidon to the ground and put her people to the sword, it was not in me to rob him of his life.

Yet it was for their sake that I had also to stop Nabusharusur from taking it. "*I can achieve it without you,*" he had said. I believed him. No one is safe from the man who despairs of living, who does not care if he lives or not.

Before returning to the tavern where I occupied rooms, I went down to the great stone quay that guarded the entrance to the city's harbor. Perhaps a hundred of the swift little Sidonian merchant ships and many smaller craft were trapped there, lying at anchor, deserted. Across the water, obscured by distance and the dancing sunlight, I could just distinguish the sails of the Tyrian fleet scattered across the horizon. These tiny vessels, seemingly numberless but each guided by its own will, cruised back and forth, back and forth, tacking into the sea breezes to keep from being run aground among the maze of channels nearer to shore. They were the net that held us all inside.

But the net was fragile, for the Tyrians, drifting over the empty water, could not bring their strength to bear on one spot with any speed. A spider's web might be useful to catch a few flies, but before the hawk it breaks like a shadow.

Why had a thing so obvious not occurred to me before?

I hurried back to the tavern and found Kephalos.

"Can you buy a ship?" I asked. For a moment he only stared at me, the expression on his face somewhere between pity and wonder.

"Yes—yes, of course," he stammered out at last. "If a man is fool enough to buy that which is of use to no one, who would refuse to sell it to him? The harbor is full of ships I can buy for a cup of fresh water. Yet—Dread Lord—the Tyrians . . . What would you want with a ship?"

"Buy us a ship, Kephalos. Find one that runs like the wind and is large enough to carry us across the sea to Greece."

He grabbed my arm, his eyes wild with hope.

"Is that what it will do, Master?"

"Perhaps. If the gods favor us."

He needed to hear no more. We went in search of Selana and Enkidu and found them together, sitting in the shade of the withered garden. I explained my intentions.

"We will all go with Kephalos," I told them. "But when I leave, Enkidu, you and Selana must stay with him on board and wait for me to return. I charge you, my friend, let no one else come near. At all costs, stay with the ship and guard it with your life. If you fail in this, by tomorrow we will all be feeding the crows."

He nodded, once. I knew he understood and would show neither weakness nor mercy.

The ship was a merchant craft obviously built to gratify someone's private whim. She was perhaps forty cubits in length and no more than twelve through the waist—too narrow to hold much cargo—and her great square sail could catch enough wind almost to lift her out of the water. I doubted if she had been profitable, but I could not doubt she was fast.

When everyone else was aboard, I untied the ropes that held her to the wharf and set her adrift.

"In two hours we will have the land winds," I said to Kephalos. "Keep away from the wharf, or before very long you may have enough people clambering on board to swamp her. If I am not back when the time comes, leave without me."

He nodded, his heavy face puckered with anxiety. I watched him cast off from the stone pier and then turned and left, heading back towards Abdimilkutte's palace. I had almost broken into a run by the time I reached the end of the wharf. My heart was pounding in my ears like a war drum as I thought, There is just time, before my meeting with Nabusharusur . . .

Thus I did not hear the splash when Selana dived into the harbor, intent on following wherever I went.

My first object was to see the king and, for once, without the presence of Nabusharusur. This, I fancied, would not be difficult—Abdimilkutte had almost ceased to exist for my brother, who thought only of his revenge. By this time, I hoped, Nabusharusur would not even be in the palace.

The guards at the great cedar doors recognized me, and I was admitted without hindrance.

It was always dangerous to share a secret with a king, for every king is surrounded by spies. I had lived most of my life in royal courts and knew their ways. Doubtless Nabusharusur kept himself informed, and it would not have surprised me to learn that more than a few of Abdimilkutte's most loyal retainers had given consideration to how they could survive him and were sending messages to Esarhaddon.

Thus, when I requested admission to his presence, I did not ask to wait upon the king alone—why draw attention to my business? I would find some means when the moment came.

He almost refused to see me, and when I beheld him his distracted condition I could understand why. This was not a man whose mind could tolerate any more bad news. And, besides, he was with his concubines.

"Well, My Lord, and am I to have no refuge from my cares?"

He was lying on a couch, his tunic pushed up around his waist and his loincloth undone—the Phoenicians are the most immodest race the great gods ever fashioned—and an exquisitely made young girl with skin the color of tarnished brass was crouched over him, doing all that she could towards solacing the flesh. I waited with averted eyes until she had quite finished.

"Mighty King," I said, when he had readjusted his garments and sent his women away, "I wondered if you might be kind enough to show me the wonders of your garden—I am informed it is the last patch of green in Sidon with any hope of surviving."

His eyes darted to my face, narrowing suddenly, as if he wished to be quite sure of what he had seen there. Yes, he understood well enough.

"My Lord, with the greatest pleasure . . ."

The roof of Abdimilkutte's palace was a kind of paradise, lush with flowers and pleasantly cool. The wind had died away almost to nothing, so it was more for privacy's sake that we chose the shelter of a vine-covered arbor that allowed a view of the sea. The king had brought with him a pitcher of wine and a pair of golden cups, and with his own hands he filled them.

"Notice, My Lord, how thin the Tyrians have spread themselves," I said, raising an arm to point towards the horizon—at this distance the sails of their ships were almost invisible, so probably Abdimilkutte, who did not possess a hunter's eyes, had to accept my assessment on trust. "They dare not come in too close, for they do not know the channels and fear to run aground. And it is a wide expanse of sea they have chosen to close."

"Yes, but they have done it effectively enough," he answered, sounding faintly annoyed. "In fifteen days, no ship has dared to sail from this harbor."

"Quite true—a ship alone is too easily picked off. But think of a hundred ships, sailing in a mass with the land breezes stiff behind them. Some would be lost, certainly, but the rest would break out like a bull through a wooden fence."

His eyes trained on the horizon as he tried to see the thing in his mind. He leaned forward, resting the palms of his hands on his knees, and I could hear his breath catch. Yes, he understood now.

"It would be a chance at life—for you and some few thousand of your subjects. To stay here is to die, for the king of Ashur will drive pity from his heart once his men are inside the city walls. You know that, My Lord."

"The Lord Nabusharusur says the army of your brother is already maggoty with unrest, that they will go away if we only wait . . ."

"They will not go away. The Lord Nabusharusur knows this, for the king is his brother as well as mine. Leave the Lord Nabusharusur to me. If you listen to him, you are a dead man."

He swallowed, hard, but it would seem that whatever was in his throat refused to go down. Perhaps it was his own heart.

"An hour before dusk would be the best time," I continued, "when the wind is the strongest. I have a fast ship waiting already. I leave it to you and your people to settle who goes with us and who stays behind."

"My soldiers—I will take my soldiers with me." He licked his lips as if they were cracked with thirst. The wine cup, which he held cradled in his hand, was forgotten. "Eight thousand men and perhaps only a hundred ships . . . A great pity, I shall have to leave some behind, and yet . . ."

"You will have no need of soldiers, Lord. You will have need of men to sail your ships—think of your people. War is a soldier's business, and his only virtue is to know how to die. Have a little mercy on those who have trusted you."

"My people—well . . ." He smiled blandly, gazing into empty space. "They hate me now, so . . ."

I might as well have been speaking to the wind. The king of Sidon had no thought for anyone but himself. I needed Abdimilkutte, for without his help no escape was possible, but I did not like him.

"One hour before sunset, then."

I rose and left him there, wondering why I had thought to hang my life by so weak a thread. Because, of course, there had been no other choice.

Not a hundred paces from Abdimilkutte's palace, the door to a baker's shop stood open. The shop was dark and there was no smell of bread—it had been many days since anyone had smelled bread in Sidon. As I passed, I heard the low, sobbing moan of a woman's voice.

She was in the little room that is hidden behind all such shops, where the tradesman lives with his wife. There was no man about, only this woman and her child, an infant lying motionless in its crib, the cord she had used to strangle it still around its neck.

She looked at me with huge, starved eyes, not wondering who I was or what had brought me—she was beyond all that.

"My son," she said, in a voice that was no more than a whisper. "My son . . . No food . . . Five days with no food . . . I could not listen to him cry."

"Yes—I understand. Where is your husband?"

She shrugged her shoulders. She did not know and perhaps did not care.

"Kill me now," she said. "There is nothing now, but I lack the courage to die."

"Yes."

I carried a short dagger in my belt. I gave neither of us time to think. The stroke caught her just under the left breast, and she pitched forward, dead without a murmur. I doubt if she felt a thing, even fear.

I wiped the blade clean on the skirt of her tunic and left.

Death held no novelty for me. This woman I could kill because she was a stranger and required it of me as a kindness. But what of Nabusharusur, my own brother?

"*I can achieve it without you,*" he had said.

We had been children together in the king's house of women, and no one but Esarhaddon himself had been more my friend. And then, when we had come of an age to begin life in the world of men, the castrator's knife had done its bitter work. Esarhaddon and I, having been spared, studied to become soldiers, while Nabusharusur disappeared into the tablet house to learn the arts of a scribe and to nurse his bitterness. I did not hear of him again for many years.

And it had all led to this. He had had a hand in our father's murder, and his had been the voice raised loudest to urge rebellion against Esarhaddon—and not for his own sake, nor for Arad Ninlil's, who had struck the blow that killed the Lord Sennacherib, nor for any abstract love of duty or his native land. Why then? The reasons were hidden from me, and perhaps even from him. Perhaps, by now, reasons no longer mattered.

I was to meet him by the Great Gate, where he would be waiting at the third hour past midday. I was not his brother now, or even his friend—only his instrument. I would do well to remember that.

Perhaps, even now, if I could persuade him . . .

He stood by the gate tower, dressed in a simple soldier's tunic, talking to the officer of the watch. When he glanced up and saw me his eyes tightened, as if he looked into a bright light. More than this, he betrayed not the slightest emotion.

"I see you are here," he said, turning from the officer with a gesture of dismissal. "I was not entirely sure if at last you would come, but perhaps I should not have doubted. Everything is prepared. I even have a fine horse for you, that you might ride into our brother's camp not like a fugitive or a thief but like a prince of Ashur."

He put his hand on my arm, meaning to draw me aside for some private word, but when he saw that I was not prepared to be moved he released me at once.

"That is all there is for you," I said, feeling less anger than a kind of grief. "You and I and Esarhaddon—it is like we three were somehow alone in the world, isn't it. The people of this city, they do not even exist for you."

"What are you talking about, Tiglath?"

His face crumpled in a strange and unnatural way, creating the impression he could not decide between rage and mere perplexity.

"I will not kill Esarhaddon this day, brother. Nor will you. But I have arranged an escape. Forget Esarhaddon. Abandon your revenge. Come with me, and live."

"Forget Esarhaddon? *Forget?* Have you gone mad?"

"It is not me, I think, who has gone mad."

He took a step backwards, as if repelled. He seemed, for the moment, to have lost the power of speech. I could almost see his mind reeling, clutching for anything to seize upon.

"I see how it is," he said finally. "I see! Once again, as when first I invited you to join the rebellion against Esarhaddon, when we might have won so easily, you have no bowels for the thing. I can only wonder what could have made you such a coward."

With a sudden movement he drew the dagger from his belt and cut the air with it, more as a demonstration than a threat.

" 'I am Tiglath Ashur!' " he shouted. " 'My father is Sennacherib, Lord of the Earth, King of Kings! Come near me at your peril!' Did you think I had forgotten? By the gods, what a lion you sounded then! So they spared you. They spared you, and they cut open my scrotum like a green fig.

And now you cannot find even the little courage it takes to push aside a lump of mud like Esarhaddon and take the world for your own! You are less of a man even than I am, *brother.*"

"Come with me, Nabusharusur. Save yourself. To stay here is to invite death."

"You think I fear death? Let me show you how I fear death!"

He took a wild swing at me with his dagger, so close that it cut my tunic even as I dodged out of its way—yes, this time he had meant to kill me.

"You should have obliged me at Khanirabbat," he shouted, beside himself now with rage. "You should have spilled my guts on the hard earth when I asked you to, for life is an endless misery to one such as I. But you shall pay for that mistake, brother—or you shall make it good."

He lunged again, but this time he did not take me by surprise and I parried his arm with a slap of my hand. He stumbled back and I drew my own dagger, hoping he would think better of this folly. Nabusharusur had no skill with weapons, nor even a man's strength, and I had been a soldier all my life. I could have killed him so easily, yet I shuddered to think of it.

"Let it have an end, brother. Stop this before it is too late."

"What troubles you, Tiglath?" His voice trembled and there were tears streaming down his face, so hot was his wrath. "Have you no knees even for this fight?"

Another thrust—he struck out, like a woman, his arm carrying his body with it and thus betraying his whole attack—and I caught his blade on my own, leaning into him to take him off balance. He staggered back, and—

It all happened so quickly that no one had time to intervene. The soldiers of the watch were only now rising to their feet, but it was already too late, The blow that felled Nabusharusur had come not from me nor from one of the guards' spears, but from above.

He snapped up straight for an instant, as if there had been a noose around his neck, and then fell forward directly onto his face. A jar of water that had been standing on the catwalk around the top of the wall had fallen over and struck him on the back of the head before smashing on the ground.

But it had not fallen. It had been pushed. I glanced up and saw Selana crouched above on the wall, staring down in what seemed a paralysis of horror.

"Come down," I shouted, not even knowing why I sounded so angry. "Come down at once."

Nabusharusur stirred, bringing his arms together around his head. I thought perhaps he had only been knocked unconscious, but when I turned him over and looked into his wide, fixed eyes I saw at once that he was dead.

"I never meant . . . I never . . ."

Selana, who now was standing beside me, covered her face with her hands and broke into uncontrolled sobbing. It was not her fault. She had followed me, all this way, and had thought that Nabusharusur, whom she had never seen before, might really have killed me.

I took her in my arms, picking her up like a child.

"I think the gods have at last shown him some mercy," I said quietly, stroking her hair. "But you shouldn't have come. You should have stayed on the ship, as I bade you."

"I couldn't . . ." She pressed her face against my chest, still weeping. "I thought you might never come back."

"I would have come back—haven't I always?"

It was strange how in that moment everything seemed to change between us. She was only fourteen, but a child would never have done what she did. Her childhood had ended with Nabusharusur's life. We would never be the same together again, she and I.

A soldier stumbled toward us. He had been drinking and he looked down at the corpse on the ground with an expression of profound astonishment. The wineskin dangled loosely from his fingers.

I took it from him—he did not even the time to protest—pulled the cork, and poured out the contents over Nabusharusur's broken head. For all the evil he had done, he was my brother and would not go down into the dark realm of Death without a grave offering.

Then, with Selana still clutched in my arms, I started back toward the harbor.

Of all Sidon, the harbor was perhaps the most deserted. For fifteen days now ships had been left at anchor, their hulls knocking against the stone quay with a hallow, haunting sound, as empty and disregarded as forgotten promises. As we crossed the causeway to the port island we could see their naked masts rocking back and forth, ever so slightly, in the first stirrings of the land breeze.

"The man I . . ." Selana said at last, her hand holding mine tightly as we walked along, "who was he?"

"A bad man—you did right to kill him."

She nodded, accepting this on my authority but perhaps not quite believing it. Without even a few words of Akkadian, she had understood nothing of my conversation with Nabusharusur and therefore had no idea that the man she had killed was my brother. It seemed to me best that she should remain in ignorance.

"We will mention nothing of this to Kephalos," I went on, careful not to look at her. "Just tell him you found me at the entrance to the king's palace."

"Is it a secret? I did not think you had any secrets from Kephalos."

"Everyone has secrets, even from Kephalos. This is one."

She was willing enough to abide by my request. She even smiled, for it gave her pleasure to think she shared my confidence where my former slave did not. It was the reaction I had been counting on.

When we neared the quay, Kephalos waved his arm in greeting. The ship was still out in the middle of the harbor, so Selana and I took off our sandals and swam out to her. Enkidu pulled Selana out of the water by the neck of her tunic and shook her the way a dog does a rat.

"All is well," I said to him. "She was with me and out of harm's reach. I have already punished her disobedience."

He glared at me, as if unconvinced that I had shown the proper severity, then he opened his hand and let her drop to the deck like a sack of meal.

Selana crept quietly out of reach of her great protector, conscious that she had escaped lightly and unwilling to tax his restraint.

"What now, Lord?" Kephalos asked, eyeing the horizon nervously. It lacked but little of the last hour before sunset.

"That is up to Abdimilkutte and the immortal gods. If he comes, if he brings with him sufficient men to handle the ships, if he does not create a dangerous panic among those left behind . . . By dark we will either be well out of this place or dead. Are you sure you can sail this thing, Kephalos?"

"Oh yes—there is no difficulty about the ship." He snapped his fingers to show how little he thought of the task. "Two men can take her anywhere. I will work the sails, which is the only part requiring skill, and you can take charge of the rudder. Just keep her on a straight heading and all will be well. I would not trust the Macedonian even with something that simple, for they are not sailing folk, being born with dung between their toes."

No more than a quarter of an hour later, we witnessed a column of soldiers emerging from the city. By the time they crossed the causeway we could see they were about four hundred strong. In their midst was

carried an enclosed sedan chair which doubtless contained King Abdimilkutte. Within ten minutes they were in control of the north end of the
quay.

The curtains of the sedan chair parted and Abdimilkutte alighted, as
daintily as any maiden. He smiled, waving towards where we stood on the
deck of our ship.

"My Lord Tiglath Ashur," he shouted. "As you see, I have not
abandoned you. I have come!"

"No, Mighty King," I said under my breath, "it is not I whom you have
abandoned."

He stepped aboard a small boat, and two of his soldiers began rowing
him towards us.

"By the gods, he means to favor us with his useless presence," Kephalos
exclaimed, with no small vexation. "I have always told you, Lord, that a
man does well to keep clear of kings."

Nevertheless, with my own hands I helped Abdimilkutte aboard. When
one of his soldier escort started to follow, Enkidu blocked the way, resting
the head of his ax against the man's neck. He had only to look at Enkidu
to see what wisdom there was in retreat.

"You honor us, My Lord," I said, turning to Abdimilkutte with a smile
that did not attempt to conceal its menace. "However, you will not
require a bodyguard on this ship."

The king was not pleased.

"The Lord Tiglath Ashur might do well to remember that he is in my
hands now, not I in his."

"Why have you brought so many soldiers, Lord?" I asked, choosing to
disregard so empty a threat. "You would have done better with men from
the town, men who understand the management of ships."

"A king must have an army; otherwise he is not a king. They will do well
enough as sailors, I fancy, since their lives depend on it. The rest, by the
way, are still in their barracks—and happy enough to be there. They
imagine their comrades here to be preparing a reconnaissance in force
outside the walls. Hah!"

The jest, it seemed, set everything right again between us. He
dismissed the two soldiers with a wave of his hand and they rowed back to
shore, glad, no doubt, to have escaped Enkidu's ax.

"However, we will have sailors enough," the king went on. "We will
select as many as we need. See? Already the crowds have followed us
down from the city. The cowards! It is almost as if they can smell escape."

It was almost as if they could. Men, women and even children,
attracted by the movement of so many soldiers and hoping somehow it

might mean their salvation, poured over the narrow causeway, a pathetic mob of the starving and the desperate. Some of them were pushed over into the water by the sheer pressure of so great a multitude, only to scramble back up the stone sides of the embankment and rejoin the crush. I know not how many there were, but they must have numbered in the thousands.

I saw at once what Abdimilkutte had intended by allowing this multitude to collect in his wake. His soldiers would pick and choose among them, selecting who would have a chance at life and who would be abandoned to death according to how many were needed to man the ships in which we would attempt our mass escape. It was as heartless a device as I could imagine, making me wonder how the gods suffered such a man to encumber the earth.

But even more terrible than its success was its failure, and it began to fail almost immediately. Once they grasped what was intended—and the idea of a breakout through the Tyrian fleet was obvious enough that this did not take very long—the crowd of citizens simply went mad.

Starved and defenseless, they would not allow themselves to be thus used and then abandoned. In their rage they seemed to forget they faced four hundred well-fed, well-trained, well-armed men. They threw themselves at the king's soldiers, heedless of life, sometimes impaling themselves on the swords that were raised against them. As if with one mind, in a single great surge they attacked.

Such a battle can have but one outcome, for weapons are useless against a force at once vast and indifferent of death. A soldier can kill only one enemy at a time, and while he opens this man's guts, another, perhaps four or five others, perhaps his victim's wife and children, pull him down and tear him to pieces.

In those few minutes I saw and heard things that will haunt me while there is breath under my ribs: the stone embankment suddenly running with blood as lifeless bodies piled up on the quay or were hurled over into the harbor, the screams of men suffering unimaginable deaths, the mingled cries of terror and of fury. It was worse than war, because in war there is surrender and then, sometimes, mercy. Here there was only slaughter.

But it was not a long struggle. Within a quarter of an hour the quay was carpeted with the dead and the dying, and the soldiers had retreated into the ships that were tied up along the embankment. They tried to cast off, to escape by setting themselves adrift, but there was no escape. Soon the ships too were overrun and the harbor filled with corpses.

People crowded the ships around the quay now until some were in danger of sinking under the weight. Some, many of them children, jostled into the water by the crowd or simply hopeless of being taken aboard anything close to shore, swam for whatever craft they could see anchored in the harbor—ours among them. Enkidu and I began lowering ropes to pull them aboard.

Abdimilkutte was beside himself.

"In the names of all the holy gods, have you gone mad? They are savages—they will kill us if you let them on the ship. This is not mercy, this is suicide!"

"They will kill you, it may be," I shouted back at him. "And let them, for all I care!"

We managed to save perhaps seventy, and then there was simply no more time if we were to have any of the daylight. Kephalos lowered the great sail, and when the wind caught it we lurched forward in the water, leaving the rest behind, our ears still full of their cries for mercy.

And, if many must die while the rest escaped, all of us knew who was to blame. Our passengers prowled around Abdimilkutte like wolves. Most had never seen him before, but they knew who he was. And they hated him. He was the author of their misery. Still, they did not kill him—not yet. It was not yet the time for thinking of revenge.

As if on command, the other ships also got under sail and began filing through the narrow harbor channels to open water. Some ran aground. Some were so overloaded they could hardly move, and there were terrible scenes as people were thrown into the water and then sometimes beaten to death when they tried to cling to the sides. But at last the great mass was underway, bunched together like a swarm of bees, heading into the sun as fast as the wind could carry us.

There was no way to tell when the Tyrians guessed what was happening, but it hardly mattered. By some shared impulse that could not be understood, we picked a point on the horizon and all sailed toward it. We broke through their line almost as easily as a man pushes aside a cobweb—our enemies hardly had time to concentrate their numbers, so all they could do was use their grappling hooks to pick off a few of the more exposed ships.

Many more just foundered, the victims of overcrowding or perhaps only inexperience. All in all, perhaps seventy of our number reached the wide open plain of the sea and scattered in as many directions.

But the Tyrians were not finished with us. Some of them gave chase. One of these, a warship, like a floating mountain, bore down on us.

She was only a few minutes behind us, and the night was coming. She would have torches on board, and we did not. It was a dangerous business to sail at night—surely we would tear our guts out on the rocks, or she would catch us.

"Give them the king!" someone shouted. Another picked up the cry, and then another and another. "Yes, curse him—give them the king!"

I could not have stopped it. I did not even want to stop it. Abdimilkutte, Lord of Sidon, screaming in the high-pitched voice of a frightened child, was hoisted aloft from the deck by twenty sets of hands and carried shoulder-high to the stern of the ship. They threw him overboard, and he hit the water with a great splash.

That was what saved us. We watched as the Tyrian warship stopped, lowered a couple of rope ladders, and sent two men down to pull him from the sea. When they had him they did not continue the pursuit. Perhaps they thought this prize was enough.

Thus is was that Abdimilkutte, a bad king and a worse man, at last saved all our lives.

XXI

MANY MONTHS PASSED BEFORE WORD REACHED ME OF how it had all ended at Sidon. My brother took the city, almost without resistance, and gave it over to pillage and destruction. He had taken an oath to Marduk that he would not leave one stone standing upon another, that Sidon would vanish from the earth, and the king of Ashur was a man who stood in awful fear of the gods. The people were sent into exile, to dwell in distant places far from the sight of the sea. They lamented, but most of them were spared. The soldiers, those who survived, were chained together to live out their short and joyless lives as slaves, and their officers were butchered.

It is only proper that the kings of ruined nations should suffer for the misery their pride and folly inflict upon their innocent subjects. Abdimilkutte died before the broken gates of Sidon. His head was struck off—Esarhaddon, with uncharacteristic generosity, required nothing of him but his life, which he took without the usual embellishments. When I heard, I was not sure that I approved.

But I did not hear for a long time. There was no news yet when we landed at Byblos, and we only stayed long enough to let off our Sidonian passengers and buy water and provisions to continue our journey. Then we left, turning our faces west towards Greece.

"Kephalos, my friend, what shall we do?" I asked, not very concerned for an answer, since the very emptiness of our future filled me with a curious elation. "I suppose, finally, we can sell the boat, but what then? Are there any wars about? Perhaps I can hire myself out as a soldier?"

"My Lord, we are poor, but we are not destitute. So much was I able to salvage from those thieves, the merchant princes of Sidon."

He opened his medicine box and took out a leather bag, casually dropping it on the deck. It made a quite substantial sound, as well it should have, for it was full of silver coins. When I laughed at this, Kephalos only scowled and shook his head, as if I had committed some breach of decency.

"I know you mean no harm," he said, "and that you are merely of a light and careless disposition, having not yet reached an age of sobriety, but give some thought, Master, to the fact that we can no longer afford to live as great men. This is only enough to purchase a start in some profitable venture. We shall have to look about us."

Yet I laughed still—I could not help myself—until, no doubt, my wise friend despaired of me. I felt free. If all the wealth we had in the world could be contained within the sides of a leather bag, then perhaps I had at last fallen beneath the notice of the mighty. Who, after all, among the great kings of the east had ever even heard of the lands beyond the Northern Sea? Thus would not Esarhaddon at last forget me? Thus was I not now at liberty to live as other men? I felt as if I had been given a new beginning.

We sailed north and then west, avoiding Cyprus, whose kings had allied themselves with my brother, always staying within sight of land but putting in at port only when the weather turned bad or our supplies began to run low. There was nothing to hurry us, and we did not pass through the straits of Rhodes until the twentieth day.

Once we passed an island, and I noticed that Kephalos could not take his eyes from it, as if the sight fed some hunger in his soul.

"What is this place?" I asked him.

"Naxos, Lord—where I was born, where perhaps my mother and father live even now."

"Then shall we stop here for a visit?"

He shook his head, and there were tears in his eyes.

"No, Lord," he said at last. "As a boy I was eager enough to leave these shores, and it is now too late to return to them. Some things are best left as they are."

He watched the island slip past us, even until the darkness closed over it. That night he kept silent vigil with his wine jar, and we spoke no more of the matter. Those who have never known the pain of exile cannot understand.

For the next several days we traveled west and north, without particular purpose, through the islands of the sea the Greeks call Aegean. We visited Delos, said to be the birthplace of Apollo and sacred to him, and there I consulted the oracle, who took my silver and told me the god was silent. We also stopped at Cythera, which claims to be the birthplace of Aphrodite, as do Cyprus and half the islands between Caria and the Peloponnesos. The Greeks, I was discovering, are not overly scrupulous concerning their gods.

At last we came to Attica, to the mainland, and we followed its southern shore to Athens.

We stayed there for six months. I have difficulty in describing Athens, for by comparison with the other great cities I have seen it is hardly more than a tawdry little waterfront settlement, and yet it made a considerable impression on me. For one thing, it was a Greek city, and that separated it at once from the rest of the world.

I was struck immediately by the fact that there were no grand palaces or temples, for the Greeks seem to think that buildings are only for sleeping in—they live in their marketplaces, for they are the most sociable of races.

A Greek is always talking, either debating the significance of some piece of news or complaining to anyone who will listen about prices or the general unworthiness of human nature. It is for this reason, I think, that the Greek tongue is so powerful and supple an instrument, for it is in constant use.

There are also no kings, the Athenians having expelled them at least a hundred years before. The government and most of the wealth are controlled by an aristocracy, but this is a very fluid body into which a man may rise if he has gathered enough silver to himself. In the councils of war, a common soldier may argue strategy with a general, and if he carries opinion with him can succeed to the command. An Athenian, like every other Greek, regards himself as being at least as good as any man alive, so they do not tolerate much insolence from their leaders.

Yet, although the kings are gone, one can still see the remains of their citadel. Like many Greek cities, Athens is built around a huge outcropping of rock, the site of an arcopolis surrounded with fortresslike walls. The Athenians use theirs as a temple district and for ritual enactments of the stories of their gods during the Festival of Dionysos, which is a rather frenzied affair. They worship their gods as they do everything else, in public, and they seem to have no priestly caste. Piety is a duty of the citizen and therefore incumbent on all.

The roads leading into the city are lined with linden tress, and I could not but be reminded of the one that grew in the garden in the house of women while I was a boy there. In Nineveh it was rarity, but here they were as common as weeds. My mother came from Athens, and the Greek spoken there always sounded to me as if it could have come from her lips. Thus Athens seemed filled with ghosts, and I found myself much oppressed in spirit.

My mother had spoken to me often of her father, who had sold her into bondage to relieve the debts he had incurred through unwise investments. She bore him no ill will for this, for he had wept as he carried her to the slave ships bound for Cyprus—my mother was a forbearing sort of woman who imagined herself to have little claim on the world; so if her father wept, she forgave and loved him. I spent many hours on the Street of the Sandalmakers inquiring after Melos the cobbler but was able to discover little beyond the fact that he had died in poverty some fifteen or twenty years earlier. No one seemed to know where his grave urn might be.

A thing that struck me about the Athenians—and I am sure it is characteristic enough of the Greeks as a race—is the tolerance they exhibit towards lovers of the same sex. For men to take beardless boys to their sleeping mats seems a common and accepted practice among them. It is even regarded as beneficial, as part of their education, for youths thus to be brought into commerce with those older and more experienced than themselves. In the land of my birth such a thing, had it became known, would have carried with it scorn and even punishment.

I had known for some time that Kephalos shared this taste, but I did not immediately connect it to the change that came over him shortly after we arrived in Athens. I had begun to notice in him a certain bemused preoccupaton—he would often lose the thread of conversations and sometimes stared distractedly into space for long moments, as if he had forgotten where he was. He drank more wine with dinner and often had to be carried to bed. And he had taken to dressing with more than usual care, even to scenting his beard, before going out for a stroll in the afternoon. I was becoming very worried about him until one day, quite by chance, I discovered what was ailing him.

Peiraeus is the harbor area of the city and also a place where much business is done. I was returning from an inspection of our ship when I happened to pass close enough to the slave market to catch a glimpse there of Kephalos, in seemingly casual conversation with a boy who wore the bronze collar that meant he was for sale—it was clear from their demeanor toward one another that this was not their first meeting. I kept out of sight, observing their curious transaction, and watched as a few coins changed hands and the two of them disappeared into a shed.

This explained much. My friend, it seemed, had fallen in love.

It gave me an idea, for I remembered what Selana had once said: "Someday, if you have pity on him, you will go to the slave market and buy him a dark-eyed boy with a face as pretty as a woman's." It seemed a small enough recompense for all that I owed him.

I waited until they came out again and Kephalos, with a fond smile and a final caress, took his leave. Then I approached the slave dealer.

"This one, Your Honor, is just eleven years old and was the body slave of Cleisthenes, the renowned charioteer, until that gentleman was dragged to death by his horses while preparing for the games at Nemea. I bought him when the estate was settled, last month, and have been awaiting a buyer who would appreciate him. Cleisthenes, as you may have heard, had a reputation for being most discriminating in such matters, so I am sure the youth will give satisfaction."

"The youth" had round red cheeks and large dark-brown eyes with the longest lashes I had ever seen on anyone, man or woman—I doubted he would ever grow to proper manhood, for he seemed quite hardened in his effeminacy. Already he had acquired the insinuating smile of a practiced harlot, and I suspected he would probably turn out to be a thief and a troublemaker, but it was not I who had to be pleased. I guessed he would do very well.

"You will observe that his hind parts are remarkably well formed," the slave dealer told me, pulling up the back of the boy's tunic so I might see.

"Yes—most impressive. How much do you want for him?"

"Two hundred drachma, Your Honor."

He cringed slightly, as if afraid lest I might strike him in my outrage. It was not an unreasonable expectation, since the man was obviously attempting to rob me by profiting from the ignorance of a foreigner.

Two hundred drachma was an absurd figure. The slave dealer in Naukratis had asked only one hundred and fifty for Selana and in the end had settled for thirty silver shekels. Besides, this boy had gone unsold for a month.

"I will give you fifty drachma, and no more."

The speed with which my offer was accepted indicated clearly that even at fifty I had overpaid.

"My name is Ganymedes—after the cupbearer of Immortal Zeus," the boy announced in a lisping voice as he followed me back to our lodgings. He smiled, showing his teeth, and allowed his eyelashes to flutter seductively. One did not have to be a soothsayer to observe how extraordinarily vain he was of his beauty. "I know how to make myself approved."

The information was not particularly welcome. Perhaps unfairly, I had already conceived a strong dislike for him.

"It is not I who must approve you," I answered curtly. "You will serve at my table this evening and there meet your new master, if he will have you. If not, then I will apprentice you to a sailmaker or some other craftsman that you may learn to support yourself through a useful trade."

This had the desired effect of ending his flirtatiousness, for it seemed I had guessed correctly that useful trades would be very little to young Ganymedes' taste.

"Then you are not to be . . . ?" he began again, after a short silence.

"No, for my inclinations do not tend toward little boys with remarkably well-formed backsides. You will be the servant of a wise and learned man who has traveled widely and served as physician and counselor to princes."

"He is not by any chance a fat gentleman who perfumes his beard, is he?"

"Yes. You shall be my gift to him."

"Oh, well then!" he exclaimed. "If it is to be Master Kephalos, I shall not disgrace you."

"It would be best for you if you did not."

That evening I presented my gift. Kephalos almost wept for pleasure and retired for the night with what could have been taken for unseemly haste.

The next morning Selana brought me my breakfast.

"I gather you have made the old pederast a happy man," she said, drizzling honey over a piece of bread for herself—lately she had fallen into this habit of eating half my morning meal for me. "Do not expect him out of his bed before noon, for he and that horrible boy were at one another most of the night."

"You were listening?" I asked, less shocked than perhaps I should have been.

"Who could help but listen? The walls are thin, and Master Kephalos is noisy in his ecstasy."

"You are impudent, and you have honey on your chin."

"Why don't you lick it off for me?"

She smiled—a wicked, lecherous enough smile for one who had never felt a man's weight on her belly—but when I answered only with silence her eyes filled with tears.

"Perhaps you too prefer little boys with cheeks like apples," she shouted, rising angrily and throwing down her unfinished piece of bread.

"Unless you have been sneaking off to the brothels, you have not had a woman since we left Egypt. I am grown up now, so what else am I to think if you treat me with such indifference!"

"I am not in the habit of sneaking, Selana—to brothels or anywhere else."

"Then when is it to be *my* turn, Lord?"

She did not wait for an answer but ran from my presence in a storm of humiliated wrath.

Selana was right, of course. This banter between us, which in earlier days had been merely amusing, had gone past a jest. She was a woman grown, and I would soon have to make some decision about her. I must either take her as my concubine or find her a suitable husband and part from her. I could not account, even to myself, for my reluctance to choose.

Perhaps this made some part of my weariness with Athens, for I was becoming more and more convinced that I would not find the end of my quest along her sand-covered streets. Athens was my mother's city, but she was a city of merchants and craftsmen and within her walls there seemed to be no place for me. It was time to leave.

One day I met a man who spoke of an island in the Western Sea, a place called Sicily, where there was rich, well-watered land to be found, with fewer stones in the ground than one encountered in Greece. He said there were colonies of Greeks all over it.

"It seems a likely place," I said to Kephalos. "And I cannot stay in Athens."

He raised his eyebrows at this, for he would have been more than willing to stay in Athens, which was very much to his taste, yet he knew me well enough to understand.

"You are a soldier, Lord. What will you do in Sicily?"

"Farm—aside from war, it is the only work I know."

"Well, I do not know how Ganymedes will fancy the change, since he has had little experience of the rustic life. Yet his jealous nature may find solace in such an isolated place."

"My friend, nothing compels you to follow if it is not your will."

"I have followed you too many years to change now, Lord. And, in any case, the likelihood of its vexing the boy is in itself reason enough to go."

Selana too expressed her willingness.

"I will follow wherever you lead, Master, but if you think to marry me off to some farmer with dung where his brains should be, you will find you have made an error."

When I told Enkidu, I could not even be sure he was listening.

We refitted our ship and set sail in the spring, for no man who is not weary of life sails upon the sea in winter.

It took us four days to make our way around the Peloponnesos to Mount Aegaleos, and on the first of these Ganymedes grew violently ill and spent most of the time with his head over the rails, to the general benefit of the fish. Kephalos gave him a draught, which steadied his belly and took away the greenish pallor from his face, but he continued to complain.

From Mount Aegaleos, so we were led to believe, we had only to sail "straight into the dying sun." After the first day we were out of sight of land, a thing every sailor fears, and on the third a storm, lasting all afternoon, tossed the ship about like a piece of driftwood, so that for a time we despaired of our lives. After that we had smooth weather. It was not until the morning of the fifth day that we saw a plume of smoke on the western horizon, the sign we had been told to look for.

"It is a mountain which burns in its belly," Kephalos explained. "Sometimes, when the giant who lives beneath it is angered enough, it belches forth fire and even molten rock. I did not imagine I would ever live to see such a thing."

He looked very much as if he would have been just as happy not to, but the sight of it greatly delighted Selana.

"It will be like living next to a god," she said.

That afternoon we dropped anchor near a small settlement named, perhaps providentially, after Kephalos' birthplace.

"Naxos!" he declared, throwing up his hands in mock surrender. "So you have caught me again at last. Now I know we have reached the place where I will lay down my bones."

"Then you can have no objection to selling the ship—she should fetch a good price, for the Phoenicians are skillful builders, and it will give us more to invest in land and seed."

Poor Kephalos, he looked as if the cage door had closed on him forever.

"It shall be as you think best, Master."

We were spared the trouble of deciding where to stay, for there was but one tavern in Naxos, a village not any larger than its namesake. I slept soundly that night, glad to be on the solid earth, believing that a new life was opening for me and that I had left the past behind me forever.

The next morning I was up and breakfasted well before sunrise, for I wished to undertake a walking tour of the surrounding countryside and see if this place of exile, chosen almost at random, would answer my hopes for it.

What struck me at once was its great beauty. The bay was shaped like a crab's claw, and immediately behind its white sand beach rose the gently sloping, tree-dappled hills, leveled off here and there to form plateaus and hiding in their midst valleys full of tall grass and wildflowers. And behind them all, vast and solitary, a trail of thin black smoke rising from her summit, was Mount Aetna. Selana had been right—it would be like living next to a god.

And the soil was good. The volcano, I had been told, scattered its fertile ash like a benediction all over this side of the island. I could pick up a handful of the dark, fragrant loam and it would cling to my fingers, almost alive. Anything would grow in this, I thought. A man might have grain, vines, fruit trees, anything.

I had only to look about me and my heart swelled with happiness. The god had brought me to a paradise. That night I made inquiry of the tavern keeper about purchasing land.

"Most of the better sites nearby are occupied," he said, pulling his beard and regarding me mournfully through watery blue eyes. Like most of the Greeks who had settled here, he was from Euboea. "There is plenty of good, well-watered land not two days' journey from here, though you will have to pay something to Ducerius, king of the Sicels, if you want to be left in peace. He is an old thief who has never reconciled himself to our presence here yet is afraid to make open war against us. We find it wisest to offer him token submission and pay the taxes he levels, for neither are we strong enough to drive him out. Look south and you will find what you want. And, while you are about it, consult the sibyl. She will be on your way."

I must have looked puzzled, for he laughed.

"You talk like an Athenian. Have you no sibyls near Athens? This one is mad, mad since childhood. She killed her mother being born and came into the world with her right hand closed in a fist—no one has ever succeeded in getting her to open it. She sits under a chaste tree, talking gibberish to herself, but sometimes, if you leave an offering of food and wait until sunset, she speaks with the voice of Phoebos Apollo. Though mad, she gives good advice when the fit is on her and can be trusted."

"Where will I find her?"

"As I said, on the trail south. If you leave when the sun rises you will find her in plenty of time before it sets again. It is a pretty place she has chosen for herself, and good land, though no one would dare to claim it while she is there."

"I will do as you recommend, my friend. I thank you."

As soon as I had mentioned the sibyl, Selana was eager to come with me. And if Selana went, it meant that Enkidu would follow, and finally even Kephalos agreed to accompany us, which meant that Ganymedes had to come. Thus we decided we would make it into an occasion. We would bring food and wine for five days and sleep in the open like soldiers.

The next morning, while the sky was still a pale gray, we left Naxos and followed the line of hills south. It was an easy walk and the trail was well marked and crossed here and there by small streams the waters of which were always cold and delicious. Every few hours Kephalos would complain most bitterly that he had to sit down and rest, yet in spite of these interruptions we kept to a good pace.

At last, in the middle of the afternoon, we came to a place where a large patch of high, level ground was surrounded on three sides by meadow. Behind it was a long slope leading up to a chain of rocky and forbidding looking mountains. To the east, perhaps a two hours' walk, was the sea.

In the center of the plateau was a tree with at least seven trunks, each twisted about at odd angles like the tentacles of a sea anemone. I was sure I had never seen another like it, and still it seemed strangely familiar.

Beneath the tree sat hunched a filthy creature, fleshless as if from long starvation, half-naked in a tunic of greasy rags, watching our approach through eyes that seemed to burn like embers. She could have been any age between fifteen and fifty—it was difficult even to be sure she was a woman. She was the sibyl.

"She frightens me," Selana murmured, clinging to my arm as if preparing to hide behind me.

"Then she must belong to the gods, for I did not think any mortal creature was able to frighten you."

"*She* does."

We set down our packs at a suitably respectful distance and waited. At last, at sunset, I took out a pair of wooden bowls, filling one with wine and the other with dried meat.

"This I will concede to you, Master." Kephalos relieved me of the open wine jar and lifted it to his lips. "I too dislike the look of her and, besides, you have had more experience than I with these sacred mysteries. I would not dream of interfering."

I took the bowls in my two hands and approached the sibyl. When there were perhaps three paces separating us I knelt on the ground and set the bowls down before her. All the while her gaze never left me—she did not even glance at my offerings. Her clenched hand she carried to her breast. She stared at me through her tangled hair as if somehow she had been expecting this visit but was not sure whether I had come for good or ill. Neither was I.

"Holy One, I am here as a petitioner," I said, opening my hands in supplication. "If you have any word for me, speak it."

Almost at once her eyes went wide, as if with the most appalling terror.

"Ashair!" she shouted breathlessly. "Ashair! ASHair!"

It was the birthmark she saw, the bloody stain on the inside of my right palm. I know she only wanted to call it a star, but in her strange, strangled voice it sounded as if she called the god's name.

"Ashair."

Slowly, the hand came down from her bosom until she seemed to hold it under my gaze. This hand, which had been clenched since birth, then began to open.

Each finger loosened, as if by a separate act of will. If I had pried them apart with the point of a sword I might have been acting in kindness, for the very bones seemed to be breaking under the strain. As her hand opened she whimpered in pain and the tears rolled down her face like drops of blood.

At last the sibyl looked up into my face, half to reproach me and half beseeching my pity, and a gold coin the size of a man's thumb rolled out from between her fingers and fell to the soft earth.

Will this be enough? her eyes seemed to ask. *Is this the task the gods have set for me?*

I picked up the coin, turning it over. On one side was the image of a coiled serpent, and on the other an owl.

And the tree had been the one I had seen in my vision, my waking dream. An owl had perched in its branches and around its base had coiled a serpent. It was all fulfilled now. I had been granted the sign for which I searched.

"Thank you, Holy One—you have answered my every hope."

The coin, since it was a sacred thing, I dropped into her lap. Then I rose and went back to the others.

"We need go no farther," I told Kephalos. "Tomorrow we will return to Naxos, and the next day I shall see King Ducerius and I shall purchase all the land that can be seen from that tree. I will not disturb the sibyl, but it is here that the god intends me to settle."

"It seems you have disturbed her already, Lord," Kephalos answered. "Turn and look."

Sure enough, she had risen to her feet and was making her lame way toward the mountains.

There was a farmer who claimed to have seen her a few days after we did, and local legend has it that she climbed up Mount Aetna and threw herself into the fiery crater. I cannot speak for the truth of these stories. I only know that I never set eyes on her again.

XXII

IN THOSE DAYS SICILY BOASTED MANY KINGS. DUCERIUS, who called himself Master of the Sicels, claimed sovereignty over the eastern half of the island, but other kings ignored his pretensions and he was able to maintain his authority only within the territory between Mount Aetna and the sea, and hardly at all over the Greek settlers who had been arriving in a steady trickle for the last fifty years.

Perhaps to compensate, his rule over his own subjects was rapacious and cruel. So harsh was he that the native peoples often preferred slavery under the Greeks, who hold all other races in great contempt, calling them "barbarians," to liberty under their own lord. The Greeks, they said, at least allowed them bread to eat.

And it was to Ducerius I went to buy the land wherein the god had pledged I was to lay down my bones.

Like the Greek kings of antiquity, he dwelt in an acropolis, a stone-walled fortress atop a bare, rocky hill. It was an ancient structure, perhaps dating from a time when his ancestors could call themselves Masters of the Sicels with a better right, and the soldier in me could not but admire its defenses. Over the main gate was carved a pair of female lions fighting over the carcass of a dead faun. It seemed a fitting enough emblem.

As I crossed the central courtyard I was struck by the noise of the place. It sounded like the Street of Adad back in Nineveh, and I had only to look about me to see why. Between the main watchtowers there were at least six forges scattering sparks over the hard-packed earth, and the beat of the metalsmiths' hammers made the air tremble like the surface of a pond across which the wind blows. Within these walls Ducerius controlled the working of bronze inside his domain, and this was both the source of his power over his own subjects and the reason for his cautious hostility toward the Greeks—the Sicels he could overawe with his weapons, but the Greeks understood the art of working iron.

I walked through the great wooden doors of the palace—so safe did Ducerius feel himself here that they were not even guarded—and, after elbowing my way through the usual mob of courtiers, idling soldiers and favor-seekers, I presented myself to a gray-haired chamberlain who stood absently scratching his bosom with a bony right hand as he stared into space. When I spoke to him he seemed vexed at the interruption, and his eyebrows almost crossed in annoyance.

"You are a petitioner?" he asked, in a voice like a reed flute, his tone suggesting that an answer in the affirmative would justify him in dismissing me from existence. "What is it you wish of the Great King?"

My friend the tavern keeper had explained how matters stood at court, and so I was prepared. The chamberlain had a large pocket in the front of his tunic and into it I dropped a small leather purse containing the prescribed number of silver coins.

"I wish to purchase a tract of land," I said. "I hope to farm it and live there by my own labor."

The chamberlain wrinkled his nose, as if at the offensive odor of sweat.

"You are, of course, a Greek."

I nodded. I even smiled, although doubtless his object had been to insult me—what else could he have imagined I was, since our whole conversation had been carried forward in that tongue?

"I will inquire whether the king will consent to an audience. Be patient, for he is occupied with affairs of state. Doubtless it will be some little time."

He was not mistaken, for I waited for several hours there in that vast and crowded hallway, the walls of which bore the painted images of men in armor and women dancing naked in front of strange and terrible gods, before I was finally admitted into the royal presence. But at last, in the middle of the afternoon, when my legs ached from standing, the gray-haired chamberlain returned and, without a word, beckoned that I should follow him.

The king sat on a wooden throne in a room no wider than ten or twelve paces. He was dressed in a blue robe that looked as if it had come from the loom that morning, but his black hair and beard were matted and greasy-looking. He had the face of man in late middle age who had kept his strength, with a heavy brow and cheekbones that stood out as brown knobs.

His eyes, however, had that haunted look I have seen before in rulers who know no law but their own will and cannot govern even that. They were the eyes of a man who would condemn a peasant to die for holding back five measures of grain to feed his family.

"What is it you want of me?" he asked sulkily. There was a half-empty cup of wine on a table at his right hand and a slave waited behind him with a jar, yet the king it seemed, did not drink to make himself merry. He glowered at me savagely from beneath his eyebrows, as if with the next breath he might order my head struck off.

I had had my foot on the necks of mightier rulers than he and therefore was not overly impressed. "I wish to purchase land, Great King. I have found a place that pleases me and I mean to farm it."

"What place?"

I told him and he blinked suddenly, as if he had been startled awake.

"Have you no respect for your own gods?" he asked. "The sibyl takes her ease there and will not care to be disturbed."

"She has vacated the site for me. It seems it is the gods' will I should have that land and no other."

"Indeed—and are you on such intimate terms with the gods?"

I did not answer, and this appeared to unsettle Ducerius. Kings are not used to silence, and they are cautious around men whom they cannot frighten.

"I have granted you an audience merely from courtesy," he went on at last, quite as if he had never asked his question. "For it is not my will to sell any more land in these domains. If better judgment had been shown in my father's time, we would today be less troubled with foreigners."

He waved his hand, dismissing me.

"Great King," I said, without moving, "I mean to have what the gods have promised me. I take my oath that I will still be here when you have seen fit to grant what I ask."

I raised my hand, and the sight of it made Ducerius open his eyes in wide amazement, as if the stain on the palm had been fresh blood.

But he grew calm quickly enough.

"Then you will have a long wait," he said.

One of his guards made as if to take me by the arm, but I brushed the lout off and went of my own will to take up my vigil again in the hallway, wondering if I had made a foolish boast.

At last, in the evening, the great doors were shut and I was dismissed into the courtyard. There, after the forges had grown quiet and the soldiers had either found their beds or trickled into the village in search of women or a wine jar, I spent the night wrapped in a blanket, sleeping in snatches and sharing a fire with a small group of prisoners, four men still showing the raw marks of the lash across their backs. They were Sicel peasants who had hidden grain from the king's tax gatherers and in the morning would suffer execution by being hurled from the citadel walls to the rocks below.

Knowing the ways of royal courts, where a measure of a king's greatness is the time one wastes waiting for an audience with him, I had brought with me food and a goatskin bag of wine, and this I shared out among the condemned men. They sat shackled together with copper chains, silent, giving the impression that they had grown indifferent to death when most probably their minds had only become numb with terror.

"Food is wasted on such as we," one of them told me in halting Greek. "We have no stomach for it. But I will drink your wine—the gods know none of us will ever have another chance to grow drunk."

"Nor do we have to think how our heads will buzz in the morning," another said. This remark was greeted with a nervous ripple of laughter, dying away almost at once.

There was silence while they passed the goatskin among them, but wine loosens men's tongues while it dulls the sharp edge of fear. Soon one of them turned to me and said, with tears in his voice, "I find it hard to believe that by this time tomorrow my sons shall have collected my ashes into an urn. How will they live when the king has taken my land? Who will feed my wife and take her breasts in his hands? It is a bitter thing to die."

Thus did I pass the night within Ducerius' walls, watching the firelight play over the faces of men who had lost everything except their hunger for life.

In the morning the chamberlain came outside to fetch me. Somehow I was not surprised to see him.

"The king will see you now," he said. I followed him back into the same audience chamber, where Ducerius sat in the same blue robe—he might not have risen from his throne through the whole night.

"It is true that the sibyl has departed," he said, his voice hardly more than a whisper. "I have consulted with my magicians, and they think that, since it seems you bear the mark of some god, perhaps it would be best . . . How much of this land do you have it in mind to claim?"

"From the mountains to the sea, and as far north and south as the eye will carry."

"So much as that?"

"So much as that."

"How much will you pay for it?"

"Three drachma a *plethron*—say, two thousand drachma."

It was a good price and he could not argue with it. I could see he would have liked to, but he could not. I think he would have sold the land at any price I offered, for he was afraid. Thus he would have to find some other way to assert himself.

"It is a large plot for man to farm alone," he said.

"I will not be alone."

"No?" He laughed. I could not imagine why. "Then, since you are a Greek, I will only tax you at the rate of one measure of wheat in five," he said. "And a like proportion of whatever you may harvest in olives or wine."

I shook my head, not so much in refusal as in recognition of the impossibility of meeting such a demand, as if it violated some law of nature.

"It would be better to settle at one measure in ten, Great King, since that is as much as I will be able to afford without rendering the entire scheme pointless."

For a long moment he studied my face, as if trying to puzzle out some answer hidden there—or perhaps only to discover some weakness in me. But I meant to have the land, whether he agreed or not. It is possible he understood as much.

At last he raised his hand and let it fall back to the arm of his throne, a gesture I took to mean he had accepted my terms.

"Since the gods seem to favor you, and since it is as much as you are able to pay—or, more likely, as much as you find it perfectly convenient to pay . . .

"May the gods, who are so much your friends, deliver decent men from the avarice of Greeks!" he shouted all at once, and with startling earnestness. "Settle with my chamberlain . . . What did you say your name was?"

"I did not, Great King, but it is Tiglath Ashur."

"I will remember you, Tiglath Ashur."

We parted then, each knowing he had found an enemy in the other. Outside, in the bright sunshine of morning, I saw that the king's prisoners had already met their punishment.

"You have a gift for antagonizing powerful men," Kephalos said, after I had told him of my meeting with Ducerius. "It is the trait you share with all the nobly born—nothing in life has ever taught you the wisdom of humility. We have not heard the last of this king of the Sicels, for with such a man to look him straight in the face is as good as to insult him. I see trouble, Master."

"Trouble is a thing of which we have had much recent experience, my friend. We will meet it when it comes."

And, indeed, I did not wish to think of Ducerius just then. As I took the winding, narrow path down from his acropolis I had seen the corpses of the peasants he had ordered hurled to their deaths, still twisted by their final agony, left to lie on the stones below as a warning. Perhaps by now their families had been allowed to reclaim them, but in my mind's eye their blood was still fresh.

I was a farmer now, one of them. I felt this injustice as touching myself.

Yet I did not wish to think of it. I wished only to think of my new life in this place, a life without shadows. I still imagined such a thing to be possible.

And so it really seemed. Kephalos let it be known in Naxos that our ship was for sale, and within six days he had duped a local shopkeeper with dreams of becoming a merchant prince into paying four hundred drachma for it. Thus, even after I had paid Ducerius, we still had enough money to buy a few tents to live in, tools, seed, a goat for milk, ducks and chickens and two pair of workhorses, with some left over to keep us in bread and wine until the land might begin to show a profit. We had made a beginning.

We made our camp on the highest piece of level ground we could find. Selana set herself to do the cooking and attend to the livestock, and Kephalos kept accounts and rode back and forth to Naxos to keep us provided with supplies and gossip while Ganymedes loafed about, quarreling with Selana.

Enkidu and I set to work clearing the bottom land. My hands, softened by years of leisure, first bled and then grew callused again, and my body reaccustomed itself to long hours of work. But a man is better for his toil. My mind was at peace and my days filled. It was like being on campaign with my soldiers. I was happy once more, without consciousness of being happy, which is the best way.

Life in my father's army had taught me carpentry and a few other useful skills, but I had never been more than an occasional visitor to my estates in the Land of Ashur. There was much I had to puzzle out for myself—or to learn by watching Enkidu. He labored with the tireless efficiency of a grindstone, and because of his great strength he was capable of three times the work that would have killed me. Yet, more important, he seemed to understand farming with the intimacy of one bred to it. I never learned anything of his history before that moment when I found him in the Wilderness of Sin, yet I am sure that he must have been born on the land.

We felled trees, using the horses to pull out the stumps, and we set fires to burn off the withered grass. We measured off our first field, a hundred paces to the side, and cleared it of stones—here we would plant vegetables to help feed us through the winter. There was a small stream flowing along its northern edge, and we dug irrigation ditches and I constructed a treadmill to raise water to fill them. Within three weeks we had our first seeds in the ground.

I was particularly pleased with the treadmill, modeled after one I had seen in Egypt, a device of no small cunning. It was in the shape of a hollow wheel, and the man inside climbed upwards with his hands and feet and thus turned the wheel, which in turn drove a chain of leather buckets bearing water from the stream to the irrigation ditches.

"Who shall work it?" Kephalos inquired, peering dubiously into the wheel. "It is a small space for a man, even if he is doubled up like a squirrel in its burrow."

"Ganymedes shall work it."

"I . . . ?" Our beautiful youth's cheeks grew even more radiant with alarmed surprise. Apparently he had thought he would be allowed to idle on forever.

"Yes—two hours should be enough to irrigate the entire field. Every morning, before breakfast, while it is still cool. Ganymedes will be just the right size and weight."

Selana was so pleased that she laughed aloud, an indiscretion that earned her a black look and a curse.

The stones Enkidu and I had gathered from clearing the field we carried up to camp, where they quickly began to make an impressive heap. We also saved the larger trees, lopping their branches and stacking the logs until they had dried out enough to be sawed up for lumber. Thus before long we had the material for a house—it was soon time to begin thinking of building it.

There were other farms near ours, some only half a day's walk distant, and from time to time neighbors would come riding over to introduce themselves and see what progress we made. One of these was Epeios, a Thracian who had come to Sicily five years before and was prospering enough to afford a fine brown gelding for his personal pleasure.

"I love this horse," he said, running his hand lovingly along its neck, "more than my wife, who is neither as beautiful nor as companionable.

You do well having a slave girl to share your bed with you, for there is less discord with a slave. I, however, was too poor for such a luxury, and the flesh leaves a man no peace when he sleeps alone. Therefore, I married."

He sighed, grieving over this lost opportunity. He was a tall man with ugly, capable-looking hands and red-brown hair. There were deep creases at the corners of his mouth and his eyes were triangular and a watery blue. I had no doubt that his wife tormented him, for he seemed one of those who always dream of women the like of whom never encumbered the earth with their weight.

The horse pawed at the ground, as impatient as any woman, and Epeios looked up and smiled.

"When do you begin building your house?" he asked.

"In five or six days. We will work on it as we have the time, and we hope to have it finished before the summer ends."

"Nonsense. I will send word around to every farm within a day's walk, and six days hence you will have fifty pairs of hands to help you. The house will be up before the sun sets twice."

"I could not ask such a thing . . ."

But Epeios merely shook his head, as if I were a fool.

"It is the custom here for neighbors to help each other when a house or a barn needs building," he said. "Every Greek in Sicily has a claim on every other, and when the time comes you will travel a day's journey to mortar together stone for me or for someone else. Mind you, we will all expect to be fed, and to have enough wine each night that we may go to our beds well and truly drunk. It will be a holiday for everyone."

As soon as he had gone I told Kephalos to ride into Naxos and purchase sheep, barley, millet, onions, spices, oil and wine enough to keep a hundred men content for five days. He folded his hands across his belly for a moment and considered the wisdom of such an undertaking.

"We will need a wagon in which to carry it all."

"Then you must purchase a wagon too, for we have need of one in any case."

"It is all a great expense," he said mournfully.

"Kephalos, have you not yet tired of sleeping on the ground and eating your meals around a campfire?"

This put a different complexion on the matter and he was on his way within half an hour, taking Selana with him.

Young Ganymedes was not very pleased to have been left behind.

" 'Mind the ducks,' she tells me. 'See to the goats at night.' " He made a face to express his disdain. "You would think the master was taking her on their wedding journey."

"Perhaps he is, for Master Kephalos has parted the legs of more women than you will ever have hairs in your beard."

Hearing this, Ganymedes flew into a frightful rage and uttered a remark so disrespectful of my friend that I felt obliged to give the boy a thrashing and set him an extra hour on the treadmill in which to cool his wrath.

Yet it had occurred to me too to wonder why just lately Kephalos had decided to make up his quarrel with Selana, a thing of so many years' standing that it had taken on almost the character of a tradition. I gave no credit to Ganymedes' suspicions, but I did wonder. I knew of old that the worthy physician could never rest content unless he had underway some new scheme or other with which to exercise his guile. I only wondered what he might be hatching now.

"I do not know how I will ever be able to cook so much for so many," Selana cried as she climbed down from the wagon she and Kephalos had brought back from Naxos. There was a lively little black-and-white puppy, no more than a month old, clutched in her arms, licking her face as if to catch the tears that welled from her eyes, but this, it seemed, did nothing to dispel her misery. "It will all fall to me, and I have not even a proper oven in which to bake bread!"

Indeed, I could hardly fault such anguish, for the wagon looked as if the axletree might break under the weight of so many jars of oil and wine, so many baskets of grain, dried fish, onions, apples and pomegranates. Since the twenty sheep Kephalos had purchased could hardly have been expected to fit, he had been constrained to hire a boy to drive them along behind.

"Twenty sheep?" I asked, hardly able to credit my eyes. "Twenty sheep for five days? It is enough to feed an army on campaign, let alone some few score farmers."

Kephalos dropped a couple of copper coins into the boy's hand and waved him off, all the while glancing nervously about as the sheep began slowly to disperse around us.

"I got them at an excellent price, Master; however, it was a condition of the sale that I take the entire flock. Surely even after the house is built we will have enough remaining to begin breeding them for their wool, which we can weave into cloth. Why, the wool from these alone is worth the ten drachma I paid for them. Ten drachma—think of it!"

"We have neither loom nor spinning wheel. What good is wool to us now?"

"My Lord is clever enough with his hands to make these things. One must think of the future."

"The first thing in my future is building a stockade to hold them," I said, resigned by then, for I could see that Kephalos was in the grip of an enthusiasm. "Otherwise, they will be trampling down our vegetables before nightfall. I have no doubt, by the way, that you must have had some very good reason for bringing home that dog."

"Selana wanted it—she is very maternal. Besides, we will need a dog for the sheep."

"The dog is yet hardly old enough to chase its own tail, let alone herd sheep."

"Trust me, Master. I was born on an island famous for its wool. I understand these matters."

I could see that there was nothing to do except surrender, and by nightfall Enkidu and I had managed to put together a serviceable-enough corral by filling in a split-rail fence with brush. After we had finished, Kephalos came out to inspect our work.

"It will do very well," he said. "Those animals which must be slaughtered to feed our impending guests can be sheared first, and when the wool has had the grease boiled out of it we can roll it up in bales until you have devised the spinning wheel. How long do you think that will take you?"

"Kephalos, I know nothing of spinning wheels."

He raised his hand and waggled it from side to side like a battle flag in the wind, dismissing this as a difficulty.

"I will explain precisely what is needed; have no anxiety on that account. And after you have built a loom I will teach Selana how to weave on it. She is an excellent girl and, just by the way, has attracted much favorable notice in Naxos. 'The Athenian's lovely young concubine'—that is how she is known. Perhaps, if I whisper it around that you have grown weary of her, some young farmer will present himself willing to take her, perhaps even without a dowry."

"How can I have grown weary of her when I have never visited her sleeping mat?" I asked, taken by surprise by the irrelevance of my own question. "Besides, she has said many times that she will not allow herself to be married off to a farmer."

"Yes, but the blood heats quickly at her age. And something must be decided soon. She is almost fifteen."

"Yes . . . Something must be done."

Kephalos showed me a queer smile and changed the subject.

"I heard much talk that the Sicels are having a desperate time of it," he said. "It is said that many have been driven to drowning their girl babies in the sea because they are without means of feeding them."

I shrugged my shoulders in disbelief.

"The earth here is rich," I said, "and the rain falls equally on Greek and Sicel alike. How can they be starving while we live in comfort?"

"We do not feel quite so heavily the weight of King Ducerius' hand." Kephalos smiled again, but this time his expression was easier to read. "He will not even permit his own people bronze for their plowshares for fear they might reforge the blades into weapons. So they must use wood, which breaks at the touch of the first stone. The Greeks understand the art of working iron, which secret the king cannot take from us because we carry it about in our heads. A Greek spends one afternoon plowing the field a Sicel would labor over for five days. Thus they starve. They murder their children because they cannot feed them, or try to hide grain from the tax gatherers and risk death if they are caught, or turn to brigandage and prey on their neighbors."

"I am surprised they do not rise up and slay him."

This made my former slave laugh.

"My Lord, he has four hundred men under arms—trained soldiers with swords of bronze."

I could have laughed myself, but I did not. On this island four hundred men ready to cut throats for him made Ducerius a Great King. The garrison at Nineveh had as many stable boys.

"One does not require an army of thousands to be a despot," Kephalos announced, as if he had read my thoughts. "Four hundred will do very nicely if one has only peasants to fight against, men who have nothing more to defend themselves with than stones and sharpened sticks."

It was the very next day that I had my first taste of that despotism, for we were visited by a squad of the king's soldiers.

"Master—come at once!"

Enkidu and I were clearing stones from a new field when Selana ran to tell us. Her face was flushed, more with excitement than anything else, I fancied, and my first thought, the gods help me, was how pretty she looked.

"Soldiers!"

Enkidu frowned and laid down his pickax.

"Then they are Ducerius' men, and we have no quarrel with him," I said, with perhaps more conviction than I felt, since in my years of exile I too had slowly acquired the conviction, common to the peoples of every nation, that soldiers nearly always mean mischief.

"Are they simply passing or have they business?"

"I know not," Selana answered, shaking her head. "They had hardly dismounted their horses when Kephalos fetched a jar of wine for them and sent me after you."

"How many were there?"

"Three or four—four, I think."

"Did they see you?"

"No."

"Then stay away until they are gone. I am sure they intend no harm, but you have reached an age . . ."

"Yes, Master!"

She blessed me with a radiant, happy smile, as if it was her proudest boast that at last I had noticed.

"Be gone, brat!"

She ran away like a young deer, leaving Enkidu and me to wash the sweat from our faces and consider the situation.

"There is nothing to be done except to see that they want," I said, but the grim Macedonian growled deep in his throat, as if to suggest that it might not all end with a polite inquiry. We headed back to the camp, abandoning our tools where they lay.

As we walked, I happened to glance up and noticed how the wind in the trees made their leaves flash like silver. It was so beautiful a sight that I felt a twinge of something almost like pain. It was the first time, perhaps, that I realized how happy I had been even this short time here in Sicily.

They were sitting beside the largest of our tents, enjoying the shade, passing around the wine jar Kephalos had given them. Their horses were tethered a few feet away. At first I thought Selana had exaggerated, since ther were only three men in sight and, but for the fact that they carried swords, in their greasy blue tunics that hardly reached to their knees they looked little enough like soldiers.

Kephalos was nowhere about, for dealing with armed men was not his province, but I noticed that he had left my javelin leaning just inside the tent flap. I reached inside and took it, wrapping my hand around the tip to conceal its bronze point.

As I approached, one of the soldiers—the leader, I could only assume—climbed slowly to his feet, as if annoyed by this intrusion on his comfort. The same displeasure registered in his face as he started to say something.

"What do you want?" I demanded first, not awaiting his convenience, for it is never wise to suffer impudence patiently. "If you have stopped merely to refresh yourselves and rest, then you and all peaceful men are welcome. If you have some other business, however, you had best state it and be done, for we have our work."

He glanced at the staff I was carrying—for such it must have seemed to him, nothing more than a farmer's staff—and he did not seem much impressed.

"You *are* insolent, even for a Greek. Are you not insolent?"

Grinning with enthusiasm for this witty thrust, he glanced back at his comrades, who were following the dialogue with only casual interest. They laughed briefly, since it was expected of them, and then subsided back into quiet attention to the demands of Kephalos' wine jar. Yet it seemed to be enough. My interrogator turned to me again, still showing his teeth, his confidence apparently strengthened.

"Everyone knows the Greeks are insolent," he went on. "Are you not an insolent beggar?"

Great is the force of habit. The Sicels are not a tall race, being on the average about half a head shorter than the Greeks, yet this one, perfectly sure of himself, faced both me and my companion, who loomed behind me like a wall of stone. Was he not a soldier of the king, and did he not know all about farmers? He was accustomed to overawing his own kind, so why should we be any different? What could there be to fear from a couple of unarmed, sweat-stained dirt scratchers?

He looked out at me through close-set brown eyes that seemed like pieces of broken glass. His hair and beard were cut very short, and it was perhaps this that made his head seem just a little too small for his body. He stood with his narrow shoulders slightly hunched, unimpressive, even slightly ridiculous, but experience had taught him that the sword he carried, and his mandate to use it, should frighten Enkidu and myself into meek submission. Doubtless he imagined himself a terrifying figure.

"What do you want?" I repeated.

He made no reply. Instead, I heard only a high-pitched bleat from the direction of our new sheepfold, and the next moment a fourth soldier approached with a ewe slung over his shoulder, the blood from its freshly cut throat still dribbling onto the ground.

"Want?" The leader actually stamped his foot in an excess of good humor, so amusing did he find my question. "To begin with, a few more jugs of wine, and some bread, and a good supply of firewood—you didn't expect us to eat our mutton raw, did you?"

The soldier who had killed our ewe dropped the carcass on the ground and wiped his hands on the front of his tunic.

"Hey, Fibrenus," he cried—in his villainous Greek, so I would be sure to understand—"tell him to send over that woman of his to cook for us. I saw her scampering away!"

They all laughed at this, little understanding that their comrade had just rendered a peaceful outcome impossible. Behind me, I could almost hear Enkidu's teeth grinding.

"I see. Everything is clear now." I shrugged, as if dismissing even the possibility of a misunderstanding. "You have come to plunder. You come not on your king's business but your own, as thieves."

The one called Fibrenus frowned and look angry.

"He is your king too," he said, "and you are subject to the tax like everyone else. We are tax gatherers."

This too was a great jest. I waited patiently for the laughter to stop. When it did I allowed my hand to slip down, revealing the bronze point of my javelin.

"No, thieves. And I will not suffer myself to be robbed. I settled with the king for one measure in ten of the *produce* of this land. As yet it has produced nothing, and therefore I owe nothing. The sheep you have just killed cost me half a drachma—that is what you owe me for it."

The threat was plain, even to Fibrenus the soldier, who seemed finally to realize that, perhaps for the first time in his life, his bluff had been challenged.

This was not a clever man. Every thought, every impulse registered in his face: first surprise, then anger, then the desire for revenge. No fear, not yet—he was not alert enough to be afraid. He only wanted to re-establish himself by punishing me. It was all so plain, even before his hand touched his sword hilt.

The shaft of my javelin caught him squarely on the cheekbone. His weapon dropped useless to the ground and he let out a wild cry of pain that was cut short by the second blow, just at the joint between neck and shoulder, which came close to crushing his windpipe. After that I had only to kick his legs out from under him, for he had no fight left.

Only the man who had killed my sheep remained standing, and as soon as he saw my javelin leveled against his chest he raised his hands in submission. The other two stayed where they were, safely on the ground—it required no more than a glance from Enkidu to keep them there, and they looked as if their greatest fear was that I might tell him to take the wine jar back. This battle was finished.

Fibrenus the soldier rolled onto his side and coughed up a thin spattering of blood. I reached over and picked up his sword from where it lay beside him, but he was in some private, pain-washed world of his own and seemed hardly to notice.

"I will keep this," I said, holding up the sword to his friends. "He may redeem it whenever he has the money—all he has to do is come back for it."

I allowed myself a villainous grin.

"When he comes back for it, he will put it between your ribs," said the man who had killed my sheep. His voice was heavy with mortified resentment, but it was plain he did not believe his own words.

"He is welcome to try," I answered, not even smiling now.

"The king shall hear of this."

"I certainly hope so. I have half a mind to tell him myself, that he might know how his soldiers abuse his trust."

There was nothing more to be said, but it was several seconds before these louts could bring themselves to acknowledge even so obvious a fact as that. Finally one of the wine drinkers rose from the ground and helped the sheep killer to stand Fibrenus the soldier back up on his feet.

"Take this carcass with you," I said, pointing with the sword at the dead ewe. "You have paid for it, so it is yours."

It was not until they had ridden away that first Selana and then Kephalos came back to camp, followed shortly by Ganymedes, who looked almost sick with apprehension.

"It was wonderful!" she announced, as if she thought I had missed it all and would be pleased to know. She took my forearm in her hands, just below the elbow, and squeezed it hard.

"It was dangerous," Kephalos replied. "Now they are certain to be back."

This made Selana laugh gaily.

"Let them come," she said. Then, for some reason, she stuck out her tongue at Ganymedes.

"They would have come back in any case," I said. "I rather suspect that Ducerius sent them."

I freed my arm from Selana's grasp and, without thinking, put it around her shoulders—she seemed to melt into me almost at once.

"Possibly he is not very happy with his bargain and hopes to see that he can extort something more from us. Either that, or drive us out altogether."

Kephalos shook his head.

"We have not seen the end of this," he said.

"No, we have not."

Things seem sometimes to happen strangely, but all is by the god's design. In the whole of life nothing is random, and Ashur's hand is everywhere. So much I have learned in my years.

On the night following this intrusion I felt restless and could not sleep, so I took my javelin and a jar of wine and went out to sit under the chaste tree, where the sibyl had kept her watch, hoping to find some peace of mind.

For a long time I sat there, drinking wine with the care that it requires at such an hour. There was a faint wind, but it was warm, almost comforting. The stars were blocked out by clouds, and I thought it might begin to rain towards morning. I remember thinking how glad I would be when the house was built and we would no longer have to sleep on the ground.

"Your house will stand here for many generations," I heard someone say—it sounded like my mother's voice. "This must be your reward, that the children of your loins will dwell quietly in this place when Nineveh is a home for foxes, when the owl makes its dwelling in the palace of her kings."

She was there, crouched beside me, a pale figure, her copper-colored hair covered with a linen shawl. I had not seen her since the day I left the garrison at Amat to join Esarhaddon in crushing the rebellion against him.

"How is it you have found me here, Merope? Have I murdered you with grief, and are you dead now in the Land of Ashur?"

"You have done no more than the god's will," she murmured. I felt her hand touching my face, as she had when I was a child. "And Death opens her arms to us all. Even you, one day, shall die."

"Are you dead, my mother?"

"Do not mourn for me, my Lathikados, for I will never leave you now. Build your house of stone and your house of flesh, and fear no king. The glory of this world is no more than a shadow."

"Mother . . ."

Without thinking, I turned my head the better to see her beloved face, and she melted into the darkness, the smile still on her lips.

XXIII

SHE HAD NOT BEEN A DREAM, OR A PHANTOM RISING FROM a wine-fogged brain—my mother's ghost had been real enough. Thus I knew that the last tie holding me to my old life had been broken. Merope was dead.

My mother had been a gentle, harmless creature, an enemy to no living thing, and she had been content to live in my shadow, for I was her only, her much-loved child. And now she had laid down her bones in a foreign land, perhaps with no one to make grave offerings for the peace of her soul. I did not know how she had died; it seemed likely I would never know. And now, in death, she had reclaimed her son. I wept for her that night under the sibyl's tree. I wept until I thought my eyes would melt.

The next morning, I said nothing of what had passed. It was not a secret, yet I did not speak of it.

And two days later my Greek neighbors came to help me build my house of stone, which it was promised would last through numberless generations.

They came in wagons and on horseback and on foot, all that morning and afternoon trickling into camp by twos and threes, speaking the accents of many different places: there were Dorians, Aetolians, Epirians, Euboeans, Thessalians, and people from all the islands of the Cyclades. I was the one "Athenian"—what else could they imagine me to be, a man who had come, it seemed, from nowhere but who spoke the Attic dialect?—and Enkidu was the only Macedonian; yet among us all we embraced nearly all the nations and cities of the Greeks. And now we were residents of this place, the kingdom of Ducerius on the eastern shore of Sicily. By that one accident of fate we had all become countrymen, and I was no more than one of them, no different from any other. I found I preferred it thus, for I was sickened of kings and princes and wished to forget that my life had ever been anything other than what it was now.

Selana need not have worried that she would be unable to manage hot food for so many, for some of our neighbors had brought their wives with them and these set to work at once to help with the cooking. By early in the afternoon they had a long trench fire burning and were busy baking bread over hot stones, grilling the pieces of one of our sheep, and boiling millet porridges in a dozen different iron pots. There was a pleasant buzz of women's voices, and the air was a rich mixture of delectable smells.

Besides myself, Enkidu, Kephalos and Ganymedes, who kept inventing reasons to disappear for long stretches of time and was next to useless even when he was about, there were at least thirty other men to help with the work. By the last hour before sundown a crew laboring under Kephalos' direction—had he not overseen the raising of the walls of the fortress at Amat and built my palace there, and was he not therefore qualified before all others to guide the building of a simple farmhouse?— had leveled the ground and buried the first row of foundation stones while the rest of us sawed tree trunks into boards for the floor and roof. We had all earned our supper by the time it was ready, and there was much laughter as we filled our plates with food and our cups with wine. Most of these my neighbors I had never met before that day, but labor, like war, quickly makes men brothers.

Even on this distant island the Greeks maintained their customs, and for our rustic banquet the men dined separately from the women. Thus no one's modesty was offended when Ganymedes, who apparently had neglected to thin his wine with five parts of water, as was appropriate to his years, performed an obscene dance which even in Nineveh would have earned him a whipping but here only raised such laughter as seemed to shake the darkness. Following this triumph, however, his excesses made themselves felt and, upon emptying his guts behind the sheepfold, he staggered back, curled up on a blanket at Kephalos' feet, and fell into a profound sleep.

Following this, someone chanted a song about a king named Menelaos, who brings his wife home after waging a long war to win her from the man who abducted her and whom, it seemed, she preferred. It was a very humorous song, and everyone laughed all over again. Then someone chanted another song, this time about the heroes who had died in that same war, and the song was noble and beautifully sad. Then I, as the host, was asked for a song, but as I knew none I told the story I had learned as a schoolboy of how Ashur slew Tiamat the Chaos Monster and created the world from her corpse. This narrative was received politely but without much enthusiasm, so that I was embarrassed to have told it. Yet I could not resent their judgment, for the Greeks are better storytellers than the men of any other race. Then another chanted a song about the death of a king named Pentheos, who as a punishment for mocking the god's rites was torn limb from limb by women possessed of Dionysos.

"I would that Ducerius was fool enough to mock the gods," someone said, after the song was finished.

"I think there is little chance of it," came the answer, from my neighbor Epeios, who had grown melancholy with too much wine. "There is a prophecy that his line will rule until one of their number has despoiled some holy place. Thus he is careful to commit every crime except impiety."

"Nevertheless, he is a reckless man," said another. To this there was a general murmur of agreement.

I happened to be sitting near Epeios, so I asked him if indeed there was such a prophecy.

"Oh yes." He nodded several times, with that slow deliberation which marks a certain stage of drunkenness. "The sibyl foretold the end of his house—sitting right over there."

He pointed to the chaste tree, some forty or fifty paces distant, its outlines still visible against the night sky.

"Then it will happen," I said, remembering Ducerius' sudden decision to reverse himself and sell me this land after all—it was *that* against which he could not stand, not me but the sibyl's voice.

"Yes," answered Epeios, nodding again. "Then it will happen."

The evening did not last much longer, for work, food and wine are the ingredients of weariness. Soon each man found his own bed, some to fall at once into heavy sleep and some to labor just a while longer between the legs of their wives. Most had spread their blankets in the open, but darkness seemed to provide cover enough for these decent farm women and I heard many a muted cry of passion as I made my way to my own sleeping mat. I had been several months without a woman—there had been no one since the Lady Nodjmanefer—and so my heart was oppressed.

I sat for a long time in front of my tent, staring down at the sandals on my feet, too tired and dispirited even to take them off.

"Drain off one cup more while I see to those," Selana told me. I had no idea where she had come from, for her step was as light as falling snow—all at once she was simply there, standing with the wine jar clutched in her hand. While I drank she crouched beside me and undid my sandal straps.

"We will have our house in a few days," I said, if only because I was unable to think of anything else. "Tomorrow the floor goes down and, if you like, you can sleep there as soon as we have sanded it smooth."

"I will sleep in My Lord's house when he does." She put her arms around my neck and kissed me on the lips. "When the roof is on, and everyone has gone home, then there will be time enough."

She kissed me again and then departed, disappearing as soundlessly as she had come. It was all I could do to keep from calling after her, for I was deeply stirred.

But at last the night closed her eyes to me.

The next day we did make good progress. My house would be shaped like the three sides of a rectangle, with the kitchen and hall taking up the longest side and two much smaller rooms jutting forward at either end. Under each room we raised a platform about a span above the ground, and over that we nailed down the boards, still smelling of pitch. Then, while the women scoured the new floor smooth with handfuls of wet sand, the men raised the outside stonework all the way to the tops of the doorposts. The next day we would finish the walls and make the frame for the roof. On the fourth day we would cover the roof with shingle and plaster the inside walls, and then my house of stone, which Merope's ghost had promised would still stand when Nineveh was a ruin, would at last be finished. We knew, when the sun began to dim, that we had labored well.

"You must walk to Naxos and take fire from the shrine of Hestia to light your hearth," I was told. "Make an offering of bread and silver, and speak to no one on your journey home. As head of the household, it is your place to perform this rite. Go tomorrow, and when you return we will have completed our work."

I set out the next morning, leaving my sandals behind, since the ritual prescribed that one's feet keep contact with the earth. The whole day, as I followed the wagon track north, with the mountains a gloomy presence to my left and to my right the shining sea just visible, like a ribbon of silver on the horizon, I knew an absurd happiness, as if every wish of my heart had been granted. These few years had transformed me from a conqueror at whose word vast armies moved as one man, a royal prince possessed of unimaginable wealth, to a simple Greek farmer sweating out his bread at the very edge of the world. I had forfeited much, and I had grieved over all that I had lost. Yet now I could not escape the sense that I had profited by the change. A king, it seemed to me, made a pitiful object.

But not so pitiful as some of those over whom he ruled.

At the first hour after midday, near where the road to Naxos is crossed by another which leads inland from a cluster of meadows near the sea, where Greek and Sicel farms lay side by side, I stopped for a time to sit under a fir tree and eat the meal which Selana had packed for my journey. The shade must have concealed me, for I know not how else I ever escaped with my life.

They were heading toward the mountains, four men on horseback, their copper swords glittering in the sun. One of them had a woman riding in front of him—he had one arm around her waist and held the reins in the other. At that distance I could not tell if she was Sicel or Greek, but she was young, hardly more than a child, and she wailed in uncontrolled despair. It was not very difficult to imagine what must have happened.

Everyone spoke of brigands—what else should these be? Whose farm had they raided, and how many had they left dead? And I could do nothing. I was one man against four, and I carried nothing but an iron knife hardly fit to peel an apple. It was foolish even to think of such a thing. If they had chanced so much as to see me, they would have cut my throat for sport.

What would they do with the girl when they grew tired of her, sell her into slavery? Was that how it had been for Selana? For my mother?

I watched and waited, cowering in the shadows, until they were out of sight, and then cursed the evil of this world and continued down the road to Naxos.

In accordance with custom, an hour before dawn I approached the temple of Hestia to accept the sacred fire from her alter. Then, as now, the cult was served entirely by women, so I gave a silver coin to the priestess. I made sacrifice of wine and left an offering of bread at the shrine—it has always been my experience that the gods are pleased with less than are their votaries. I received three living coals from the goddess's hearth, and these I was to carry home in an iron bowl, fueling the fire as I went. The priestess touched her fingers to my lips in token of silence and sent me away.

This time I did not stop for food, and I met no one on the road. When I arrived back I was greeted with a cheer, for the house was finished and my return meant the hearth fire could be kindled and the celebration might begin.

The consecration of a house is one of the few times when men and women mingle freely, and this because the keeping of the household shrine is peculiarly a woman's business. After I had coaxed the sacred fire into a blaze, I gave the iron bowl to Selana and she emptied it out over the bed of faggots she had prepared on the hearth.

Selana was now mistress of my house, and it would be her duty never to let the fire go out—except if someone in the family should die, when it is extinguished in token of mourning and, after five days, when the house has been purified, a new fire is carried home from the temple.

I cannot forget how happy this little ritual made her. She had become a great favorite among the women, and all men love a pretty young girl, so everyone teased her until her face burned as hot as the fire—even Kephalos kissed her and pinched her backside, calling her our "little mother"—but she was as ecstatic as any bride.

She belongs now, I thought. She is among her own people and she has a place in this house which no one challenges, so of course she is happy.

Such blind fools are perhaps all men.

Outside, the evening was warm and three sheep were roasting on spits over the trench fire. Everyone had been to the wine jar, even the women, so everyone was merry. An Achaian named Teucer entertained us with a comic version of the story of Heracles and Eurytus, performing all the parts himself in different voices, and there was much laughter.

It seems a peculiarity of the Greek temperament that at a certain point in any evening's entertainment, usually after everyone's belly holds at least three cups of wine, conversation begins to take on a certain quality of abstraction. Phrases like "to return to first principles" or "to consider the nature of the thing" or "looking at the matter in its essential character" begin to turn up, and very quickly one finds oneself in the midst of a philosophical dispute.

Philosophy—it is a lovely word, native to the Greek tongue and descriptive of a concept for which, so far as I am aware, no other has an equivalent.

On that particular evening the discussion began with various critiques of Teucer's performance and from that proceeded to an analysis of the myth and an argument over whether or not the king had been right to deny Heracles the wife he had won through his prowess in archery, which in turn led, by a chain of reasoning I could not hope to reproduce, to a general discussion of kingship and whether it or oligarchy or even democracy was the most natural and desirable means by which a state might be governed. One or two of the poorer farmers favored democracy; the majority, however, held for the rule of an aristocracy, although even this was not without its detractors:

"To choose oligarchy over democracy is to make a great distinction out of a small one," maintained Teucer, who I think continued to nurse a sense of injury over a few of the things which had been said concerning his performance. "Since all men are selfish, both systems divide men according to their interests and thus create dissension, which is in all societies the enemy of good order. Democracy only achieves this end a trifle faster."

"But by the same line of reasoning a king, who is after all a man and thus will promote his own happiness over that of others, grows divided from his subjects."

This made Teucer smile and nod and lay a finger to the side of his nose.

"Ah yes," he said, "but a king has the power to enforce his will and thus maintains order, and it is order rather than happiness which is the aim of government."

"Someone should inquire of the Sicels whether they prefer the order which Ducerius has brought to their lives over such happiness as they might find without him."

I do not remember who said this, but it had the effect of demolishing Teucer's argument with one sentence and imposing on all of us a profound silence.

"No. No one can prefer kingship under such a man as Ducerius," said my friend Epeios, morose as ever. It was a sentiment with which all concurred, even Teucer.

"Yes, and soon it will be not merely the Sicels who feel the weight of his hand, for he means to drive us out if he can."

"Soon!—hah!" A Boeotian named Cretheos, who owned a farm near the mountains, laughed scornfully. "Already the brigands have raided a neighbor of mine, burning his barn and killing one of his young sons. Ducerius has an army of four hundred soldiers, so why then does he not drive these thieves and murderers from his territories? Because, as everyone knows, they pay him a regular tribute from their spoils. They are an instrument of his power and would not now be attacking Greeks if he had not given his approval."

This too every man present understood to be the truth.

Yet it was not an evening for gloomy reflections, and if the world was a mad place we were still all fine fellows and Greeks in the bargain. There is a saying that the gods will not permit a man to be unhappy when danger is far away and the wine cup is at his elbow. This too is the truth, and thus it was not very long before we had jested our way into a better temper.

When the sheep were well roasted and the meat was almost falling of its own weight from the bone, the women took their knives and cut away great pieces, draping them over plates of boiled millet so that soon every man's beard was shining with fat. Men and women together, we gorged ourselves sober again, packing our bellies so tight that all drunkenness was squeezed out of us—we did not dispute then, not only because the Greeks consider it unseemly to speak of public matters before their wives but because at such a time a man can only lie on the cool ground gasping for breath.

But at last we returned again to our wine jars, and the women entertained us with chanting and dancing such as one sees among no other people. Then Ganymedes danced again, this time with greater propriety, and then the women departed to perform certain rituals over the threshold of my new house which are their sole province and which it is forbidden for any man to witness.

Then Kephalos came and sat down beside me, carrying with him a wine jar from which he refilled my cup.

"I did not notice Selana among the dancers," I said, wondering why, when only the instant before I had been intending to say something else.

"Did you not, My Lord? Then perhaps she was occupied elsewhere." Kephalos smiled cryptically, as he was likely to when he found himself in possession of some secret. "Perhaps her thoughts are not on dancing but on her new duties as mistress of My Lord's house."

He paused for a moment, appearing to savor the discomfort this idea caused me, as if I had at last stepped into a trap against which he had been warning me for years.

"There are many unmarried men here tonight," he went on at last. "Doubtless most of them would be receptive to a reasonable offer, for Greek women are still scarce on this island. Have you noticed any, My Lord, whom Selana seems particularly to favor?"

"No . . . no, I have not."

"Neither have I, so perhaps it shall prove necessary to provide for her in some other way."

"I think, however, that Selana's future can safely wait a little longer."

"So you are continually saying, My Lord." He leaned toward me to refill my wine cup, which had somehow become empty again. "Yet she is like a flower whose petals open wider under each day's sun. She blooms, and the fragrance is sweet in every man's nostrils."

"Then let her choose the man she wants and he shall have her," I snapped, wishing Kephalos would be silent.

Just then Ganymedes approached, staggering under the burden of the wine fumes that clouded his brain. He lay down beside Kephalos, who caressed the boy's tangled, shining hair with the tips of his fingers, and within a few minutes he asleep at his master's feet, snoring like an ox.

"You had best bring him under control," I said, happy to be taking my revenge. "He grows more dissolute and lazy every day."

"He is dissolute and lazy by nature," Kephalos responded, calmly enough. "He knows neither honesty nor modesty nor loyalty. He is full of cunning shifts and will doubtless come to a bad end one day. Yet what am I to do? He is as he is, and I cannot change him. I can only love him, for I too am what I am. A man does well to take the world as he finds it, for he cannot make it or himself any better by pretending to turn aside from his own wants. Our selfish passions are wiser than we know."

We sat together for a long time, and Kephalos kept refilling my cup until, I must own, I was somewhat flush with wine.

Then at last, and in accord with custom, my neighbors came with torches to light my way to my new house. There was much laughter intermixed with the chanting of hymns, for, even though my part in it was over, the celebration would continue until dawn.

It was a fine moment when at last I crossed over the threshold of my house of stone. Everyone cheered loudly. I was given an oil lamp to light my way to bed, and Kephalos stepped forward to close the door behind me.

The fire which only death could quench burned on the hearth. In the morning Selana would rise to replenish it, and the continuity of life within these walls would be affirmed. For generation upon generation, the children of my loins would live here—thus the shade of Merope had promised. The children of my loins . . .

I needed to ease my mind in sleep. I walked through the kitchen to find the bedchamber I had chosen for myself.

When I opened the door I heard something stir. I raised the lamp to see—it was Selana, lying under a blanket on my sleeping mat. She sat up and the blanket slid down to reveal her breasts.

For a moment neither of us either spoke or moved. The expression on her face was fierce, as if I were an intruder to be warned off, but I think it was only that the light had startled her awake.

"Go to your own bed, Selana," I said at last. "what game is this?"

"It is not a game, and I am in my own bed."

"Who has decided that?"

"I have, since you would not."

Suddenly I felt very tired. I knelt down beside the sleeping mat—I could not fight her any longer. She put her arms around me and kissed my lips, and I knew I was lost.

"*Build your house of stone and your house of flesh,*" my mother had said. Selana's flesh seemed to glow in the soft light of the lamp. Her mouth was warm against mine, and I could taste the desire that heated her blood.

"Come into me," she whispered. "I belong to no one but you—I have been yours since the first day, and only because I would have no other. Come into me. Find your rest and the easement of your body. I have lived only for this moment."

The weight of her arms pulled me down. I lay beside her, feeling the whole length of her body against mine. My hands sought her breasts, and I could almost feel her heart beating beneath my fingers.

Her legs opened to receive me, and there was only a short, choking sob of pain as I thrust into her and then a moan of passion that seemed to come from deep within and filled me with the most terrible desire, as if it would burn us both to ashes.

XXIV

THAT NIGHT, AMIDST THE NOISE OF MY NEIGHBORS' revelry, I went into Selana many times, and at last, bathed in sweat, we fell asleep in each other's arms. When I awoke the next morning she had gathered up her sandals and left—the smell of cooking already filled the house.

The hearth fire burned brightly while Selana heated up a pot of barley with pieces of mutton in it. No one else seemed to be awake yet. I stepped out through the door and saw that last night's guests had all crept away with the dawn. There was no mist, and on the eastern horizon the sea looked like polished stone. It would be a fine, warm day. A bird perched just at the edge of the roof looked down at me with wary curiosity.

"Come inside and eat," she said softly.

She was beautiful to behold that morning. Her face appeared to glow with new blood, but she seemed unwilling to meet my eyes. When she brought the food I caught her wrist and pulled her to me for a kiss. She fell into my embrace with a passion that was almost desperate. She was trembling, as if it were not so much my arms that held her as her own fierce longing for them.

It was perhaps only then that I realized how much she loved me—how much she had always loved me. She had never told me so, never actually spoken the words, but for how little did words count against that one moment.

Then, all at once, she freed herself and stepped away from me.

"Eat," she said. "The others will not sleep forever, and I have my work to do."

Since the day I had gone to the house of war to learn how to be a soldier, the women who served at my table had always been slaves. Some of them had found their way into my bed, but none had ever loved me. I had never known a wife.

Selana called herself my slave, but she was not. She slept beside me because it was her will and she kept my house because it was her will. If she had left to follow some other man, I would not have put out my arm to stop her. Nothing compelled her to submission.

That morning, when I took the breakfast bowl from her hand, I knew for the first time what the simplest goatherd knows who has covered with a veil some woman who loves him. I cannot describe it more than that.

This both pleased me and, I must own, left me feeling somewhat ill at ease. I ate quickly and departed for the fields before anyone else was stirring. I think I was somehow a little ashamed to face them. To those who are not accustomed to it, happiness brings as its attendant a peculiar confusion of feeling.

We were clearing another hundred-paces-square patch of ground for our autumn wheat crop, and a few hours of pulling stones out of the earth had a clarifying effect on my state of mind. Sore muscles make a man impatient with a fastidious conscience, even if it is his own—at first, when I sat down for a moment to rest and take a drink of water, the only emotion of which I was capable was a certain irritation over the fact that, for some reason, no one was there to help me. So I was a little relieved when, at the hour before noon, Kephalos appeared at the edge of the new field. He smiled, perhaps a trifle foolishly, and held up a leather pouch for me to see.

"In your inexplicable haste, Lord, you departed this morning without your midday meal. Selana sent me along with it, lest you starve."

He appeared to regard this as something of a jest as he sat down in the shade of an elm tree and began untying the pouch's cord to share out its contents between us. There was no wine, so he had to be satisfied with the contents of my waterskin, at which he wrinkled his nose in disgust.

"I think," he continued, wiping his mouth, "that it cannot be too soon before we begin to plant some vines—I have a spot picked out that offers just the right mixture of sun and shade . . ."

When he looked into my face the sentence died on his lips and he threw up both hands in a mute gesture of resignation, as if he despaired of ever tasting wine again.

"You must not blame yourself, Lord, since before women we are all but guileless children. Besides, we shall all grow accustomed to it—one can grow accustomed to anything. Selana, by the way, is in a very agreeable frame of mind this morning. She does not even scold Ganymedes."

"Then you think I have acted unwisely."

"You?" Kephalos found it impossible to restrain a short fit of laughter. "My Lord, *you* hardly acted at all. In these matters it is not the man but the woman who acts, even if she is only fifteen years old—perhaps particularly if she is only fifteen years old. Selana simply decided that she had waited long enough. In recent months she had expressed this view to me many times. She was very firm in her resolve and I, like you, was at last unable to withhold my consent."

He shrugged his shoulders, denying responsibility, like a servant who has been robbed of his master's cloak.

"You had best be reconciled, Lord, for the thing is done."

We sat beneath the elm tree sharing out cheese and a flat piece of bread from which we tore strips. I ate slowly, as a man will when his own thoughts do not much please him, and Kephalos watched me with worried eyes.

"Where is Enkidu?" I asked finally.

"Enkidu?" For a moment he seemed not to know to whom I referred. "He is with Selana—she has set him to digging her a pantry behind the house that the meat will keep better. Ganymedes sits nearby and supervises, encumbering everyone with his valuable suggestions. Why do you ask?"

And then, of course, he realized why.

"You may dismiss that idea from your mind," he said, with a contemptuous gesture. "He is a brute, but he is wiser than you are, Lord. Whatever is agreeable to Selana is agreeable to him."

"I wonder if it will always be so agreeable to her—in my life I have caused much misery to the women who loved me. And she does love me, Kephalos. That, as much as anything, is what oppresses me."

"I know. But perhaps at last your god, who is as possessive as any woman, has decided to let you go. In any case, to love is to take risks, as Selana is old enough to appreciate—it is only the dead who are safe.

"Think no more of it, my foolish Master, since, as I have come to understand, you have as much need of her as she of you. The thing is done and cannot be undone. I do not believe that now you would wish it undone."

The worthy physician Kephalos spoke, as always, with much wisdom. The gods, who are more generous than men deserve, had offered me not a second but a third chance at contentment and a quiet spirit, and I would have been an even greater fool than my friend imagined me if I had refused it.

An hour later Enkidu joined me in the new field and we spent the rest of the daylight clearing stones. As soon as I saw him I realized how foolish I had been to suspect him of reproaching me—this was not a matter in which he chose to involve himself, it seemed. When the sun set behind the mountains we returned home for dinner.

In the course of the evening Ganymedes entertained himself with a number of coarse jests at Selana's expense, which she found it possible to ignore but which finally moved me to drag the little brute outside and to thrash him soundly, with a warning that any repetition would earn him more than just a raw backside. He limped back into the house feeling himself very ill-used indeed, but after that he contrived to hold his tongue.

I found my bed that night with a still unquiet heart, but Selana opened her arms to me and in her body I could find comfort and peace. She had what she wanted and so did I, so I was not inclined to argue with this new order of things. Perhaps Kephalos was right, I thought, and the god is at last disposed to leave me in peace. Perhaps I can die here after a tranquil life, and this woman who loves me—and she was a woman now—will draw off my last breath with her kiss.

It seemed little enough to hope for.

The next four months brought us the autumn rains and then the long drought of winter and then our first reaping of wheat. We had cleared perhaps half our arable land, but much of it still lay fallow simply because we had no opportunity to bring it under the plow and so it would have to wait until the next planting season.

With the stones we built first a barn in which to store our harvest and stable the horses, and then a permanent enclosure for the sheep. After that we simply piled the stones along the edges of the fields, where they formed long, useless ramparts.

"Someday," I said to Kephalos, only half in jest, "I shall have to build myself another great palace, like the one you raised for me at Amat—the gods know we have all the stone we need."

But there were many more urgent tasks before us in that first year. I constructed a spinning wheel, in accordance with Kephalos' design, and Selana set to work to make thread from the fleece of our sheep. Soon my skills were called upon again, this time to made a loom for turning the thread into cloth, and thus it was not very long before each of us had a new tunic, with enough cloth left over to use in bartering with our neighbors for fruit, honey and wax, none of which we could yet produce for ourselves.

Those days, each with its labor and its rewards, were a time of nearly unblemished happiness, when the past came but seldom to darken my mind.

But if the all-knowing gods touched us with their blessings, many more suffered under the blind, pitiless hands of men. One morning, when I had been at work about two hours, Selana came running to fetch me from the fields.

"Dread Lord, a woman has come with two boys," she announced, almost breathless. "A Sicel woman!"

"What of it? What do they want?"

"They will not go away, Lord."

Her eyes beseeched me to understand what she could not say with words—I had never seen her thus.

I asked no more questions, since clearly they would be useless, but put aside my hoe and followed her back to the house, wondering what Selana, whose knees were stronger than most men's, found so dismaying about these intruders.

When I beheld them for myself it was plain that what had moved her was not fear but pity. Even Kephalos, who stood in the doorway, as if to guard its privacy, seemed to feel himself reproached by such misery.

The woman had not yet known thirty years, but she seemed old, worn out with suffering, weariness and degradation. She was also very dirty. Her skin and hair were streaked with sweat-stained dust, and the tunic she wore, which did not even reach to the middle of her thighs, was matted and stiff with mud, as if she had been rolled in it.

Doubtless this was precisely what had happened, for her arms and legs were bruised and across the left side of her face was a long, purplish-black swelling so heavy that it had nearly closed her eye. There was a spattering of blood just at the hairline, and I think her cheekbone must actually have been broken—someone had struck her with savage, merciless force, probably using the butt of a spear. A little more and certainly he would have killed her. In my mind's eye I saw a soldier . . .

The boys who accompanied her were obviously her sons. They were strongly built and close to each other in age, and the elder was a handsome lad standing on the brink of manhood—Ganymedes certainly found him an interesting object of contemplation. They had also been beaten but not with the same furious thoroughness. There is a certain sort of man who reserves for women the worst that is in him.

She spoke a few words through swollen lips—it was in Sicel, but I would not have grasped it anyway—something low and indistinct, even apologetic, as if she felt obliged to beg my pardon for having the effrontery to be alive. When she saw that I did not understand she seemed to lose heart altogether and fell silent.

"My mother begs that you will take us as slaves," said the elder of the two boys, speaking in clear but heavily accented Greek, his voice trembling with what seemed a subdued, helpless rage. "We are farming folk and know how to work. We ask only enough to preserve us from death."

This was a bitter moment for him—I could see as much in his eyes, which burned with shame, and fear. Yet he did not look away, for there was still pride in him. This, one sensed, was their last hope before they abandoned themselves to the lifeless earth. The gods alone knew how far they had wandered, or for how long.

I had only to glance at Selana to know what she felt. I saw the face I had seen that first day on the dock at Naukratis.

"We will speak of such things later," I said to the boy. "For now, my woman will feed you. And my friend, the Lord Kephalos, who is a physician, will see to your wounds."

Everyone seemed relieved. Now no one would be forced to choose in the face of such wretchedness, where all were at a disadvantage. Selana went into the house to build up the fire and drop a few extra handfuls of meat into the noontime stew. When she came outside again, carrying bread, a wineskin and a basin of heated water, Kephalos was already at work to open the bruise on the woman's face.

"That is a nasty business," he whispered to me. "Left untended for another few days, it might easily have gone putrid and drained off into her brain—first paralysis, then madness, then death. Whoever did such a thing to her is little better than a brute."

The woman was still too sick with pain to take more than a few sips of wine, but the two boys gorged on the bread like famished dogs.

"What happened to bring you to such a condition?" I asked the elder, after he had a little appeased his hunger. "How did you come to be set upon?"

For a moment he looked at me with something almost like astonishment, as if he could not believe in such ignorance.

"We had a farm," he said, after a moment, "a small one, but our ancestors had worked the land there for as long as men could remember. My father could not pay the king's taxes, so he slaughtered the goats and salted their flesh that we should not starve through the winter. The king looked upon this as theft and soldiers took my father away to hurl him from the walls. When he was dead, we claimed his body that we might wash it clean and bury it in the earth. But the soldiers said he must be left on the stones, his flesh feeding the dogs. My mother was much overcome with grief, and she cursed them to their faces, telling them they would die with blood in their mouths, and they beat her. The king said that for our insolence the farm was forfeit, that if we again set foot on our own land he would bury us alive in it. That is what he said. We have been on the road for six days now and without food, since all whom we know are afraid to raise their hand to help us. Thus we thought to sell ourselves among the Greeks that we might live."

It was a stark little narrative, yet all that had been left out of it—and that, no doubt, was much—was visible in the worn, sullen faces of these two boys and their mother. I could see the bitterness of their hatred, which included Ducerius, their neighbors, and even myself. And I did not resent this, though I was innocent of all that had befallen then, for it was natural that they should hate the whole world. When one has been sufficiently wronged, nothing can set it right again.

"What is your name?" I asked of the elder son.

"Tullus, son of Servius."

"And your brother?"

"Icilius."

"And your mother?"

"Tanaquil."

"Then you may sleep in the barn for now, Tullus, son of Servius. It is a poor place, but it will keep the rain off. We will find better for you if you choose to stay. But first you must rest and eat and find your strength again, for you are of no use to anyone the way you are. When that is done, you and your brother will help in the fields, and my woman, whose name is Selana, will find work in the house to occupy your mother. I, by the way, am Tiglath, son of Sennacherib."

Tullus translated my words for his mother, the woman Tanaquil, and when she understood she wept and threw herself to the ground to kiss my feet. This was an embarrassment not only to me but to her sons, who were shamed that their mother should abase herself thus before a stranger. I raised her from her knees and gave her into Selana's care.

"I see that the Lord Kephalos, whom you call a physician, has had his ear notched," said Tullus as he and his brother walked with me to the barn. "Is he your slave?"

"He was once, long ago, but we have been through much together since then. Now he is only my friend."

"And will you notch our ears too?"

"No—and I did not notch his, for he was captured by soldiers in a place called Tyre and it was much later that he came into my possession, when I was myself yet a boy, not any older than you are now."

I looked at him and smiled, but he did not return my smile. His mind turned only on the injustice of all that had befallen him, of which now I was a part.

"I will not mark you as my property," I said. "You and I both know what we have a right to expect from one another, and that is enough. If this farm prospers, then we will all prosper together, and if it fails I will be no less a beggar than yourself. Be at peace with me, Tullus, son of Servius, for I too know what it is to be an exile, to be driven from one's home by the wrath of a king. It is a bitter thing to lose one's birthright."

Our eyes met for an instant, and I could see that he did not understand. How could he have understood? Yet it formed the basis for an eventual bond of sympathy.

Still, things were not immediately easy between us, for the pride of youth does not grow supple all at once. Mother and brother presented no such difficulties—Tanaquil, who felt only gratitude and was, I suspect, by nature a submissive creature, developed an admiration of Selana that was almost worshipful, as if she herself and not the "Domna," the mistress, as she called her, were the younger of the two. Selana, who gave herself no proprietary airs and perhaps had missed the companionship of another of her sex, treated the Sicel woman as an equal. And little Icilius was still only a child, without fear or self-consciousness, and surrendered quickly to a smile and a kind word, even if the word was Greek and he could not understand it.

And in the days that followed, Tullus as well gradually yielded up his hostility and learned once more to take a certain pleasure in life. He understood farming and knew how to work, so I listened to his suggestions and left him to do things in his own way, allowing him to be a man among other men. When he saw that he was treated with respect, he at last forgave us.

"I think they will do well enough," I remarked one day to Kephalos, after they had been with us a time. "All are good workers and the elder is a born farmer."

But Kephalos only shook his head, a look of worry clouding his eyes. I knew what was troubling him, and I could not help but laugh.

"You are jealous of Ganymedes' interest in Tullus," I said. "But you need not concern yourself, for if I read the thing rightly Ganymedes is foredoomed to disappointment—Tullus has no such inclination."

"Still, Lord, I see evil coming from this business. Perhaps you would have been wiser to keep your generous instincts under better control."

I laughed again, not knowing that my friend spoke with the voice of prophecy.

I could not, however, believe that I had misplaced my confidence in these two boys. With their help our second harvest was more than twice as great as our first, and in this Tullus seemed to take as much pride as if the land had been his own and his fathers' before him for a thousand years.

Yet he had been right to have expected evil at our hands and to have dreaded his lot, for the Greeks, I discovered, treated their slaves wretchedly. In the east, where I was born, there is no dishonor if a man, overwhelmed by debt, sells himself into bondage. It is not forgotten that he is a man like other men; he is treated with humanity and enjoys the law's protection no less than if he were free. But to a Greek, a slave is nothing more than a tool with life in it. Tullus and his family would not have come to us except that the only thing even more grievous than slavery was death itself.

I have always thought the Greeks were fools to be so harsh, for it is nothing more than chance that one man is free while another is chattel. I do not hold that it is evil for one man to own another's labor, and doubtless there will always be slaves and masters—each of us must live in the world as we find it. Yet I have always felt it both decent and prudent to treat my own slaves with kindness and to afford them such respect as their natural gifts make them deserve. Thus, because they understand that there are rights and obligations in both directions, I have always commanded their loyalty, and this is worth more than the submission of a brute.

But the Greeks, though they were bad masters, were at least preferable to Ducerius, who trampled over all his people, free and slave, as if they were the very dust. I had not realized how utterly he was hated until I heard Tullus' words against him, each one sharp as the blade of a copper knife. Other stories as well made their way to us—the whole countryside, it seemed, festered like a putrid boil.

And increasingly it was not only the Sicels who complained, but the Greeks as well. Brigands came down from their mountain strongholds and ranged through the flatlands, plundering farms as freely as dogs steal scraps in the bazaar, and the king did nothing to prevent them.

One afternoon, eight days before the Festival of Mounichion, when the trees have found their leaves again, my neighbor Epeios came by leading his fine horse, which was burdened with sacks of food.

"You remember Teucer?" he asked, "the one who spoke so eloquently at your house-building in praise of kingship? He was raided night before last. I am on my way there now."

"I will go with you," I answered. "We can take the wagon—how bad was it?"

"I know nothing more than that Teucer lives."

When the wagon was ready and Epeios had tethered his horse to it and sat beside me on the bench, Selana came out of the house with a large bundle in her arms.

"I will come too," she said, climbing into the back. "His woman may need assistance."

This was so obvious that Epeios and I exchanged a glance, as if to inquire of each other why neither of us had thought of it.

Teucer's farm was some four hours from mine, and it was almost nightfall before we arrived. The wagons of several less distant neighbors stood about in the yard and there were perhaps thirty men and women about, most of whom I knew by then. I did not see Teucer among them.

The farmhouse showed clear evidence of having been put to the torch—one wall was badly scorched and half the roof would have to be replaced. Otherwise there was little to show how much else had been lost in the raid.

Teucer had no reputation as a man of energy, and his farm was a small affair, with no more than five or six *plethra* of land under cultivation and only a few domesticated animals, enough to provide a living for himself and his wife but no more. His house and barns were shabby in appearance, as if the master had neither time nor inclination to keep them up. I could not help but wonder what brigands found in such poverty to tempt them.

It would appear they had not even been tempted by Teucer's woman Ctimene, for she was laid out on a table in the farmhouse kitchen with a ragged wound just above her left breast. Thus, as it turned out, the only assistance Selana could give her was to join with the other women in preparing her for burial.

Teucer crouched on a stool beside the table, tears streaming down his leathery face as he watched them clean the blood from her corpse and wrap it for the fire.

"This will finish him," Epeios murmured to me as we stepped outside again. "Some men are lost without their wives. It has nothing to do with love—even if each hates the other, they cannot function without a push from behind. Teucer is that kind. He will not know what to do with himself now. He will go to pieces. And I believe he was fond of her."

Inquiry revealed that all the brigands had stolen—perhaps all there had been to steal—was one broken-winded old horse, good for nothing except pulling a plow. It seemed an inexplicable piece of mischief. Finally a number of us collected in Teucer's barn to discuss the matter.

"Why did they kill Ctimene?" someone asked. "This farm is not close to the mountains, and no one else in the neighborhood was raided—why go to so much trouble, and spill blood, for nothing but a worthless old horse?"

"Perhaps their dogs were hungry."

Everyone laughed at this, but it was not an answer so much as a comment on the senselessness of this crime.

"Perhaps they believed they would find more."

"No," I said, shaking my head. "Everyone knows that Teucer is poor. Even I knew it, and I have been only a few months on this island. Except to ruin him, I cannot understand what their object could have been."

There was an uncomfortable silence, as if I had unwittingly spoken the truth they had all been struggling hard not to mention.

"Still, something must be done."

Diocles the Spartan stood up from where he had been sitting on an empty harness box. He was a squat man with black hair and a black beard, and his face was as red as if he had been drinking wine all morning—he always looked thus, although he was a man of the most abstemious habits. His hands moved impatiently as he spoke.

"If they will raid Teucer, they will raid any of us—no one is safe now, that is obvious. By the Mouse God's navel, we cannot wait patiently to be looted and murdered at the convenience of these bandits."

He sat down again and looked around at us defiantly, challenging anyone to disagree. This, of course, was impossible.

"Yet these men are many—they have horses and arms, and when they have done their wickedness they vanish back into the mountains like shadows. We are but farmers. What can we do?"

"Even a farmer knows enough to cut the head off a snake," I said. "I keep an iron sword beside my sleeping mat, and I am sure it is not the only weapon in Greek hands. There are lions in the mountains as well as men, or so one hears. Let us hunt one as we would the other."

"Lions do not fight back," Epeios said.

Had I wished to prove him wrong I had only to remove my tunic and show him the scars I carried on my chest and shoulder, but I did not.

In any case, it did not seem to be a popular suggestion.

"This is a matter for the king to settle," said Halitherses the Ithacan, after a long silence. He was nearly seventy and had lived on this island longer than any other Greek. Many thought of him as a wise man. "It is the duty of kings to protect their subjects, and we all acknowledge the sovereignty of Ducerius and pay his taxes."

"He has no love for the Greeks," someone answered. There was a general murmur of agreement.

"Yet he is still king here, and dealing with bandits is a king's province."

"Yes, he deals with them—for a portion of their spoils."

There was much laughter at this and it made Halitherses grow wrathful, as old men will.

"What else would you do?" he shouted. "Follow Tiglath into the mountains and end there with your throats cut? No—I thought not!"

"He is right. Let us appeal to the king before we do anything mad." Epeios glanced at me as he spoke, raising his eyebrows as if to suggest, I am still your friend, though I speak against you when you propose folly.

"Yes, let us appeal to Ducerius," I answered. "Certainly he would consider it an act of defiance if we did not. Kings grow uneasy when their subjects take up arms on their own."

Halitherses was very pleased.

"Then we are in agreement?" he asked, looking from face to face..

We were. I even consented to make one of the delegation. We would ride to the king's citadel the day after next.

But first there was the funeral of Ctimene to be attended to.

A group of us stayed up through the night with Teucer, for there was anxiety that if left alone he might try to harm himself. Thus the men at least were rather sullen with excess of wine the next morning, when in the gray light the murdered woman's corpse, wrapped in linen and purified with wine and spices, was laid upon a pyre which Teucer, as her husband, set to the torch.

The logs were from a fresh-cut beech tree, still full of pitch so they burned hot and fast. It was not even two hours before the ashes were cool enough to allow us to gather up Ctimene's bones for burial in a bronze jar.

Epeios rode back to his own farm by a different route, and thus Selana and I were alone together in the wagon as we drove home in silence.

At last, when she attempted to say something, she began to weep. I put my arms across her trembling shoulders, holding the reins with my free hand.

"You do well to weep," I hold her. "And not only for Ctimene's sake. I am very afraid these may be the last days of peace."

XXV

THE EMBASSY FROM THE GREEKS INCLUDED FIVE OTHERS besides myself, and the Lord of the Sicels kept us waiting in the courtyard of his stronghold for three days. Halitherses, who had been on terms of friendship with Ducerius' father, was almost as much overcome by the insult as by the hardship of being forced at his age to sleep so many nights on the cold ground. When the time came for speaking, the old man could hardly find his voice.

"Great King, we are oppressed," he said, looking up with watery blue eyes to where Ducerius stood, surrounded by retainers, at the top of the stone staircase before the great double doorway of his palace—he would not even admit us to a formal audience but only stopped for a few moments on his way to an afternoon of hunting.

"We are beset by robbers who raid our farms and murder our women and our young children. Now no man feels safe in his own home, and we have nowhere to look for salvation but to you. Drive these brigands from the land, O King. Let us find our protection behind the strength of your sword, and your people will bless you!"

It was a fine speech, but anyone could see that Ducerius was little impressed. He hardly even waited for the old man to finish before dismissing his words with an impatient movement of his arm.

"You are not my people—you are Greeks."

He smiled tightly and glanced about, as if he had made a jest and was waiting to hear the laughter of his retainers. A few of them actually did laugh.

"I have not soldiers enough to guard every farm," he went on, turning suddenly wrathful, scowling around at us as if we had accused him of a weakness. "And, besides, if my people resent foreigners who grow rich at their expense, how am I to restrain them?"

"Show us what we have taken away from any man and he will have restitution from us. How have we diminished the Sicels when we work the land as they do, earning our bread with our sweat? You wrong us, Great King."

Halitherses spoke less in anger than in sorrow and disappointment, for he remembered the father even as he was constrained to listen to the son's bitter words. He lowered his eyes to the ground, quite as though Ducerius' bad faith had been his own.

"My Lord, you misunderstand us," I said, once it appeared that Halitherses had been silenced—I could hardly do otherwise since I happened to be standing beside the old man and the king had fastened his attention on me, almost daring me to answer him, as if this were all a purely private quarrel between myself and him. "We would not have your soldiers wasted in guarding us—we would have you send them into the mountains to root out these brigands . . ."

"Yes!" shouted Diocles, just behind me, raising his fist in a gesture of angry defiance—since he was a Spartan, his friends forgave him these outbursts of intemperance. "Yes, the mountains! No man keeps watch on his chickens when he knows where the fox digs her den."

The king shifted his gaze for perhaps a second—that was all the acknowledgment Diocles was to receive—and then his eyes returned to my face.

"You ask then that I make war on your behalf," he said, in a voice of the deadliest calm.

"Does My Lord's notion of war encompass running to earth a handful of renegades? I should rather have thought that, as a hunter, he might relish a few days of good sport."

Ducerius did not relish the laughter this raised, even among his own men. With an imperious gesture he compelled them to silence.

"It is sport I willingly leave to you, Tiglath Ashur, since you regard it so lightly. I hope the Greeks are pleased to have found such a champion."

He swept down the stone steps and away, surrounded by his entourage, leaving us to gape at each other in frustrated silence.

"I would not have thought it possible," Halitherses muttered, to himself as much as to us. "I never imagined he would have thus turned his face from so plain a duty."

"By the Mouse God's navel, I do not know why you are so surprised, old man. The king's character has never been much of a mystery. The only duty he understands is to himself."

Diocles' words were met with a general murmur of assent.

"Come—let us not stand about here like penitents. We must make our report to the assembly. We must decide what we are to do."

Even in those times the Festival of Mounichion was celebrated in Naxos with games and a market day. The first ceremony of the morning was a procession of young girls in saffron robes who danced before the altar of Artemis, where goats and wild birds were sacrificed in the purifying fire. This everyone attended. Afterwards, since the remaining rites were the natural province of women, who are most particularly devoted to the cult, the men were free to try their prowess against each other in various contests. I took the first prize in both archery and javelin throwing, considered auspicious victories as the goddess is a great patron of hunting, but I finished a miserable sixth in the foot race, and my place in the long jump is perhaps best passed over in silence.

But after we had amused ourselves, and then adjourned to the baths to sweat ourselves clean again, every Greek male over the age of twenty and in possession of more than one hundred drachma in goods or coin met in solemn assembly to settle what was to be done about the raiding brigands—this was the real purpose which had brought us all together.

Since Naxos was too small for each god to be worshiped within his own precincts, most of their festivals were celebrated in the streets. Only the shrine of Dionysos had an amphitheater attached to it, and thus, after the sun had set and darkness covered the world, some four hundred men crowded over its tiers of stone seats, our faces illuminated by the flickering, unearthly light of numberless torches. I sat next to Kephalos, who had that day won enough money dicing to put to rest any doubts concerning his right to be there, and as I looked back at the black hills surrounding this place I could not help but wonder how many spies Ducerius had set to listening out there in the shadows.

Epeios, whom I had not seen since our audience with the king and who now occupied the place just behind me, put his hand on my shoulder and leaned forward until his mouth was almost at my ear.

"Did you hear that Teucer killed himself yesterday?" he asked. "Some neighbors found him this morning, on their way to the festival."

"No, I had not heard," I answered, feeling the chill of mortality.

"He took poison. It could not have been an accident—they said he was stretched out over his wife's grave with the wine cup still clutched in his hands. They said the dregs stank of hemlock."

He leaned back and appeared to forget all about it. I turned away, oddly troubled, feeling as if somehow I had become involved in the guilt for this death, as if Teucer had taken his life in response to some collective failure from which I could not extricate myself.

At last old Halitherses, who had been sitting in the first tier of seats, rose and turned to face us, ready to speak. He raised his hand, craving the indulgence of our attention, and so great was the respect in which he was held that the assembly of the Greeks at once fell silent.

"I am here to report that our embassy was without success," he began, allowing his arm to sink slowly back down to his side. "The king, the Lord Ducerius, has closed his eyes to our necessity. He abandons us to our own defenses. He refuses to take our part against the brigands."

There was so general an outcry at this that Halitherses did not even try to continue. For a moment he stood before us, like a rock against which the storm breaks its force, and then finally he resumed his seat, conceding, in effect, that the problem had exhausted him, that no words of his, no action within his power, could be of any use to us. It was like watching a man resign himself to death.

"What did they expect?" Kephalos murmured to me. "They sent you on a fruitless mission, and now they put the blame on Halitherses."

"They blame him because he hoped for success," I answered.

Suddenly a man I had never seen before, and whose name I later learned was Peisenor, jumped to his feet, waving his arms above his head to command attention.

"The king must be compelled," he shouted. "Let us withhold our taxes from him until he agrees to protect us—*that* will bring him around quickly enough!"

"Oh surely—and if he sends a company of his soldiers to your farm? I prefer to be plundered by only one set of bandits."

"It is a fool who puts himself between the hammer and the anvil."

So then it was Peisenor's turn to be hooted into silence.

There were other suggestions, equally servile and self-defeating, and the debate was long, with many bitter exchanges as we wore away the night. It was even proposed that we bribe Ducerius, offering to pay his soldiers if he kept the peace. I listened in silence, anger gathering in my bowels like the poison in Teucer's wine cup.

Finally Epeios rose and proposed that we send a delegation to the brigands.

"Surely they can be bought off," he said, hooking his thumbs into the belt of his tunic. "Let us discover what terms they will accept, that we may once more live in peace."

I could hear low voices all around me, murmuring assent—the Greeks liked this plan.

"Then do not ask me to be one of this embassy," shouted Diocles. "For it does not take a clever man to know that I and all the rest would come home in pieces. If Ducerius will not grant us peace, what makes anyone think the brigands will?"

"Diocles is a fool!" someone cried out. "Yes, yes," came another voice, and then another and another. "Diocles is a fool!"

There was a general roar of laughter. Diocles, choking with rage, was forced to sit down again. All he said was no more than a great joke. I kept remembering the sense of shame I had felt at the news of Teucer's death.

"Diocles may be a fool, but at least he has not forgotten how to be a man," I bellowed, on my feet before I even realized I had any intention of speaking. "Would you set two masters over yourselves? Is not one bad enough? Would you make treaties with those who have butchered your women and children? And what price do you think they will ask of you? And what price next year, and the year after next? If rabbits get into a man's garden, does he put food out for them? No, by the gods, he turns his dogs loose!"

"His victories today have gone to Tiglath's head. He fancies that because he can throw a javelin he has become a hero of legend."

I turned and saw that it was Peisenor who spoke. He was smiling, as if somehow he had redeemed himself.

A few laughed, but not many—I think finally they had begun to feel ashamed.

"What would you do, Tiglath?" asked Epeios.

"Do?" Now I laughed, although I felt little enough like jesting. "What would I do? I would take a hundred men, or two hundred if that was what the task demanded, and I would hunt the brigands in their dens and kill them there. That is what I would do."

They did not shout me down. I kept my feet, but all around me there was the sound of angry disagreement, like the buzzing of wasps that have been disturbed in their nest.

At last the noise subsided, and I was left to finish.

"Sooner or later—and I pray it will not be too late—you will discover that there is nothing else to do. But if you wait, if you crawl to embrace the knees of these men who will then be so merciful as to cut your throats slowly, so that you bleed to death only a few drops at a time, then you can take this shame upon yourselves alone. I shall wait until the Greeks have grown tired of being women, and on that day they will know where to look for me. But until then I will not lie with my face in the dirt, waiting for thieves and murderers to break my back when it should please them. Believe me when I say that I will not meekly submit to pillage. If they come to me I will know how to deal with them."

I did not linger to hear if they cared to answer, for by then I had had a bellyful of their words. What they shouted after me as I strode down the stone tiers and out of the amphitheater was in my ears as no more than the sound of rushing water.

I have often wondered since if my own final boast did not bring down upon me all that happened next, if perhaps the listening gods, or perhaps only King Ducerius, decided to test my mettle against the bold sound of my words. If that can be so, then I think it must have been Ducerius, for the gods can see into our hearts easily enough and know how to set far more cunning traps for a man's pride.

Yet certainly Kephalos thought that I had tempted fate. All the way home, as he sat in the back of the wagon between Enkidu and the peacefully sleeping Ganymedes, nursing a jar of yellowish local wine, he berated me for my lack of discretion.

"My Lord has a gift for attracting trouble," he said, with more than usual asperity. "In Assyria, among the Chaldeans, in Egypt, in Sidon, and now here, in what must be our final place of refuge, you take upon youself the enmity not only of a king and his bandit henchmen but even of the Greeks, our own countrymen and neighbors. Always you think to stand against trouble like a wall—and you, as a soldier of no small experience, should be familiar enough with the customary fate of walls. When will my Lord Tiglath Ashur forsake his vanity over having once been a prince and learn to exercise a little reasonable caution?"

"I am all gratitude for the tenderness of your concern, Worthy Physician, but you minister to the wrong patient and prescribe the wrong treatment. I will not die of my vanity, but our countrymen and neighbors shall surely die of their caution."

"It is much more likely that *you* shall die of their caution, for it is always the tallest tree which is cut down first."

"Kephalos would do well to keep his wind for belching," Selana hissed, throwing him a glance over her shoulder that should have withered him.

"The Lord Tiglath knows what he is about and needs no advice from sottish cowards whose highest wisdom is to crawl inside a wine jar and name it 'caution.'"

"Heaven preserve my master from heeding the admiration of Doric peasant girls who know no more of life than can be seen from between the back legs of a milking cow."

Selana reached around and would have left the marks of her hard little knuckles deeply impressed in Kephalos' skull had I not caught her by the yoke of her tunic and dragged her back onto the seat next to me, where she had to content herself with sticking her tongue out at him and offering several rude suggestions about his own origins.

It was only the middle of the afternoon when we arrived back at the farm, so Tullus and Icilius were still out laboring. And since the sun would hold above the horizon for at least another two hours, and the daylight is from the openhanded gods, who will not bless a man who spurns their gifts, Enkidu and I did not go into the house but stopped on the porch only long enough to wash our faces in the pan of water Selana brought out for us before we too left for the fields.

As we picked up our mattocks, Enkidu, his eyes narrowing as he shaded them with his hand, looked toward the eastern mountains. What he saw there, or merely sensed, I know not, but when he stepped back over to the wagon to fetch his ax, which he always kept by him, he lifted out my quiver of javelins as well and handed it to me.

I took them, for I knew that he was right and these were not the times for a man to walk about defenseless.

Since the wheat fields and the vegetable garden were by then well established, and the women had taken charge of the livestock, I had decided to yield to Kephalos' advice—if so self-interested a suggestion can be called such—and to clear a patch of land by the river, well watered and with just the right amount of shade, and to plant vines there. We would have no grapes for another two years, and no wine for three, but one has to make a start.

Tullus and Icilius had been busy. A neat pile of stones stood near the water's edge, and the earth was nearly all turned over and ready to receive the rooted plants. In a day or two we would construct long rows of wooden frames to give the tendrils something to climb over, and then, when Kephalos and I had selected and bought the right varieties of vine shoots, we would have to trust to time and careful tending. Vines are like a woman who knows her own value and must be wooed with patient tenderness, but perhaps that is why every farmer loves them above all else that the hard ground yields to him.

We worked until dark, until the smoke from the hearth fires was almost invisible against the evening sky, and then we gathered up our tools and made ready to turn back toward the house.

"I think we would do well to plant a line of trees on the seaward side," Tullus said, running his hand along the eastern horizon. "It will shelter the grapes from the wind. Otherwise their flavor may grow harsh in dry seasons."

"If we plant trees today, it will be ten or fifteen years before they are full enough to do much good," I pointed out.

"Yes, but if the vines take they will still be yielding fruit a hundred years after we are all dead—one must think of the future, Lord, and the generations to follow."

"Then it shall be as you think best, Master Tullus, for you are wiser than I in such matters. When we are both old men and good for nothing except getting drunk on the veranda every afternoon, we shall know if your trees were worth the labor."

He smiled, a willing, open boy's smile, pleased to have been judged right and pleased all the more, I believe, to think of himself as having earned a place here that would last out his life.

It was a warm twilight and I could almost imagine I smelled our dinner cooking, for my appetite was sharp. I had forgiven the Greeks their cowardice, or, more accurately, I had simply forgotten their existence. I was looking forward to dinner, and after that to drinking wine—but not enough wine to dull the senses—and after that, to gathering Selana into my arms and experiencing how the pleasure of the embrace made her breath catch in her throat. I felt life to be a very fine thing indeed.

We had almost reached the edge of the farmyard. I did not guess that anything could be wrong until I heard horses neighing and the door of my house slamming shut.

This was followed almost at once by the high-pitched screams of a woman's terror.

At such times the senses are as quick as fire. Even in that first instant, before a thought or an action formed in my mind, I understood with wonderful precision what was taking place. There were four riders. I had never seen any of them before, but they wore the short-belted tunics of Sicels. One of them had already dismounted before the house and was loudly demanding that everyone come out, and the other three had caught Tanaquil outside and were trying to ride her down before she reached the barn. She was running in a blind panic, her arms stretched out before her as if she had to push her way through the air. They would have her in a few seconds.

"Mother!" Tullus shouted. I had to grab him by the shoulders to keep him from darting out and being trampled to death—what could he, a boy, have done except get himself killed?

"Mother!" he cried again, struggling to free himself from my grasp.

It was Enkidu who saved her.

Twisting from the waist, he swung the great ax in a wide circle over his head, cutting the air with a sound like a gasp of astonishment. His hands parted and the ax tumbled through empty space, end over end, and then with a sickening thud buried itself blade-first in the chest of the first rider, yanking him from his mount as if he had been pulled from behind.

The other two reined in their horses at once, making them rear up and claw at the air with their hooves.

Even over the horses' wild neighing I heard the whisper of metal against leather as swords were drawn from their scabbards.

If they wanted to fight, I thought, well and good. I raised my javelin, waiting for the Sicels to charge, knowing that only then would these shadowy figures offer me a target.

But instead, after a second or two, they seemed to think better of the idea and wheeled about to flee.

"Cowards!" Tullus shouted after them. I let him go to rush into his mother's arms, and Enkidu and I started running toward the house.

The man who had been standing in front of our door turned to look when his friends galloped past. He saw us too, realized that he was outnumbered, and scrambled to climb back on his horse, but he was an instant too late. I let fly, and as he took hold of the reins my javelin caught him somewhere in the left side of his back. It pulled loose and fell to the ground, but I knew from the way he seemed to sway in his seat that I had wounded him badly. He crouched down, holding on to the horse's neck, and rode away.

Suddenly the farmyard was quiet again. The whole incident had lasted only a few minutes, yet nothing was the same now. Safety had vanished.

The door opened and Kephalos timidly stuck his head outside. An oil lamp burned in his hand, and he peered about like an owl blinded by the sunlight.

"Everything is over," I said. "Who is inside with you?"

"Selana and Ganymedes," he answered, after swallowing hard. He looked a trifle ashamed of his own fear. "I heard strangers riding up—no neighbor would call at this hour—and I bolted the door."

"You acted wisely. Everyone is all right then?"

"Yes. Everyone is all right."

He came out and together we looked at the spattering of blood on the ground.

"You killed one of them?"

"No." I shook my head. "At least, he was not dead when he left here."

Selana and Ganymedes came out, clutching at one another for comfort. They followed us to where Tanaquil stood with her two sons gathered around her. Ganymedes looked as if he could hardly restrain himself from throwing himself into Tullus' arms.

A little way away, Enkidu had pulled his ax from the chest of the dead bandit and was busy dragging the corpse out of sight. A few minutes later he came back. He had wiped the ax blade clean and was holding the dead man's severed head by the hair. His expression was like defiance but amounted to no more than a kind of harsh expectancy.

"Yes, there will be other trophies. We will go after them," I said. The idea had just come into my mind, and as a settled matter. I had not decided anything, but only remembered what was required of me. Such men as had done this, who had ventured onto my land in order to rob and murder, could not be suffered to live.

"At first light we will pick up their trail. You need not think they will escape us, Enkidu. This whole island is not big enough for them to hide in."

Nor was it. We found the first one not three hours after sunrise. His eyes wide with that surprise that so often overtakes men in the last instant of life, he lay where he had fallen from his horse, which was peacefully grazing some fifteen or twenty paces farther up the trail. My javelin had gone deep, and then torn a wide gash when it twisted loose. He must have bled to death fairly quickly.

The others we surprised that night around their campfire—I do not think it ever occcurred to them that they would be followed into their own mountains. We slaughtered them like sheep and cut off their heads to take away with us.

We spiked the heads of the four brigands on poles and set them out at the approaches to our farm for the crows to feast upon. Anyone riding down from the mountain and intending mischief would be sure to come upon those grinning faces, with their empty eye sockets and the blackened, rotting flesh peeling away from the skulls, and they would know that intruders could expect harsh treatment.

The warning seemed to have its effect. Many farms were raided over the next few months, and with ever increasing frequency and violence, but my own was left untouched. Even the Greeks saw the lesson in this, for whenever I had visitors, and they passed by the grim trophies that were posted beside the road to my door, they too were reminded that Tiglath the Athenian had purchased immunity for himself at the price of blood.

Thus it was that at last they came to me one hot afternoon while I worked among my vines. I was not expecting callers, and they found me stripped down to my loincloth—a delegation from the Greek council, which, it seemed, had at last agreed on something, for they included in their numbers those two old antagonists Diocles the Spartan and my neighbor Epeios.

"I am embarrassed," I said. "If you will accompany me back to the house I can offer you some wine."

"We have not come to drink wine, Tiglath, but to seek your help." Diocles, stepping forth from the group, spoke with his usual forthright bluntness. "Events have unfolded just as you said they would. We have tried to parley with the brigands—they take our silver and rob us just the same. You said we should hunt them to their dens and kill them there, but to do this we need a man to tell us how. We are but farmers and know not how to answer men riding war horses and armed with bronze weapons. By the Mouse God's navel, we need a soldier."

"I too am a farmer," I said, for in my bowels I shrank from what they proposed.

"Now perhaps, Tiglath, but I think it was not always so." Diocles raised his hand and pointed to my bare chest. "If I understand anything of the world, it was not by tending vines that you received such wounds as you carry upon your body."

"We ask you to accept the office of Tyrant," Epeios broke in, smiling as if at last he had found me out. "For six months you will have absolute authority—for twelve if the situation demands it and the council agrees. Then you must surrender your power and answer to your fellow Greeks for the uses you have made of it."

"I must have time to consider."

"My all means, consider. But do not take too much time, for, Tiglath my friend, time runs against us."

We walked back to the farmhouse together, and Selana broke open a wine jar. An hour later they departed, leaving me with a dark and divided mind.

"You must accept," Kephalos told me, when the evening meal was over and we had stepped outside to enjoy the cool of the sea breezes. "You must, Lord. It would be for our safety as well as theirs, since the brigands will in the end remember that we are few and they are many."

"I would be as powerful as any king—for six months. Kephalos, my friend, have you and I not seen enough of the evil power brings, and most especially to those who hold it?"

"Yes, Lord, but there must always be men who hold authority over others. For in the rule of one over many lies the only safety, the only peace. Our neighbors understand as much, so they turn to you—as men have always turned to you. The greater evil now would be to refuse power."

He shrugged his shoulders and smiled rather lamely, as if to excuse himself for speaking the truth.

"We enter now into a season of war," he went on, "And these men who call upon you to lead them are farmers, not soldiers—I say no more than they acknowledge themselves. You are the soldier. There was a time when men called you the greatest soldier living. A ruler is not wicked if he holds power by consent, and you know there is no one else."

"Yes, I know."

That night I dreamed of my father.

"Do this which they ask of you," he said. "Only do not let them make of you a king, my son. It is a bitter thing to wear a crown, although once that was all I wished for you. Besides, I do not care to think of my son as a king among foreigners—such a thing would be undignified. Yet do this which they ask of you, for you were born to it."

The next morning I sent Kephalos to Naxos with my answer. It seemed the god had not finished with me yet.

XXVI

"HOW MANY FORGES HAVE WE ALTOGETHER FOR WORKING iron?"

"Four—all in Naxos. The king ignores them because they are used only to make farming tools."

"He will not ignore them much longer, not once we have begun hammering out swords under his very nose. We must disassemble them so they can be moved to safer locations. We must work in secret."

"No secret like that can be kept forever."

"We will not need forever. Once we have a sufficient quantity of arms, he will think long and hard before attacking us. If we can keep two forges working for a month, we will be safe enough. What about the supply of iron ore?"

"This side of the island is poor in it, but there is plenty of ore on the mainland, only a few days' sailing from here."

"Then we will begin by melting down our household utensils, even our plowshares if it comes to that. We cannot risk bringing ore in by ship until we are in a position to defend it."

"You sound as if you are planning to make war against Ducerius instead of against merely a handful of brigands."

"It may come to that. Few kings are foolish enough to tolerate the presence of a foreign army in their midst—and that is what we shall become before we are finished, an army. Besides, to strike at the brigands is to strike at Ducerius. We all know it amounts to the same thing.

"We will need to train and equip at least two hundred men, since we will need to keep half that number in reserve lest our enemies decide to attack our homes while we are off in the mountains chasing shadows. Thus I propose a levy of all able-bodied men between the ages of fifteen and thirty. There will be no exceptions. That the burden will be shared out evenly, during harvest time farms where no man is left may claim aid from more fortunate households."

"It shall be as you say, Tiglath, for we have appointed you Tyrant over us."

"For six months, and then I must answer for the results."

"Yes."

We sat beneath the sibyl's chaste tree, within sight of the house my neighbors had helped me to build. There were six of us, including Kephalos and myself: Epeios and Peisenor, representing the Greek council; Diocles, whom I had decided upon as my second-in-command; and a man named Talus, who could speak for the merchants and craftsmen of Naxos. Peisenor had spoken against me at the assembly and perhaps even imagined that therefore we were enemies, yet it is always best to hold such men close. Perhaps I could win him over, but at least I would keep him under my eye.

"There is a wide plain north of the city," I went on. "It is a good spot to drill soldiers. Let all those liable to service gather there in five days' time, with such weapons and horses as they can bring. If men must fight they must be taught the arts of war, for the only thing a rabble can do in battle is die. The sooner we begin, the sooner we will be ready."

"I know that spot—Ducerius will be able to watch us from the walls of his citadel."

"That is true, Peisenor." I smiled, as if pleased that he had guessed my private thoughts. "I never claimed we could hope to keep our intentions a secret. And that which cannot be kept secret, even for a short time, is best done as openly as possible. If we do not behave like conspirators, Ducerius will lack an excuse to move against us as such. And we have only to remind him that he has given us his mandate to solve this problem for ourselves—'It is sport I willingly leave to you,' he said, and before many witnesses. Let it be the king, and not the Greeks, who breaks the peace between us."

Selana had made up a leather corselet for me, sewing strips of copper on the front and back in the childish expectation that these might stop a sword thrust and thus save my life. On a summer day it was hot as a pottery kiln and I felt like a fool in it, but she would not be easy in her mind until I promised to wear it, so for her sake did I go off thus to make war against the brigands.

We assembled on what was called locally the Plain of Clonios, after a farmer who had once had a house and some vineyards there—two hundred and twenty Greek men, not fifty of whom had even served in a city militia, and of these only eight had ever felt the shock of battle. These eight I immediately appointed squad leaders, even though one of them had two fingers missing from his right hand and another looked as if he could hardly stand up under the weight of his dented iron war helmet.

Yet what they lacked in experience and skill they compensated for in enthusiasm. They stumbled like blind men through even the most basic drill and many carried only pruning staffs and wooden swords, but not one among them was not eager to fight the brigands, and anyone else for that matter. For men accustomed to spreading dung over their fields and listening to the endless complaining of their wives, the enterprise of war had almost the welcome character of a holiday. It is always so. It was so with me the first time, when I was but fifteen years old and marched off with my father's army to fight the Elamites—my own heart-swelling dreams of glory lasted right up to our first sight of the enemy.

About ten of my more prosperous neighbors had brought their own horses, and they thus became our cavalry. In the Land of Ashur cavalry were of some importance in war, but the Greeks appeared to be hopeless in this regard. Above a trot, they could not seem to keep their seats unless they held on to the reins with one hand and the horse's mane with the other, and thus occupied they would be of little value in a battle. Even assuming they did learn to fight, they were too few to make a difference. I decided I would use them for reconnaissance and divided them into two companies of five men each, leaving them to spend the whole first day charging up and down one end of the plain at full gallop, that they might at least learn how not to fall off. This was a lesson they would have to master for themselves, and one with which I could not help them very much. Besides, my immediate concern was with the foot soldiers.

"Most of you imagine that a soldier is required to be brave and daring," I told them, that first morning while we sweated under the unforgiving summer sun. "You all hope to distinguish yourselves by some great act of courage, and even if you die for it think you will be numbered among the heroic dead. Allow me to disillusion you: there are no heroic dead. If a soldier dies in battle it is generally because he is unlucky or, more probably, has done something stupid, and the dead are merely dead. If you are killed, your wife will grieve for you for two months and then marry some other man, and your children, by the time they are grown, will have forgotten your name. The fruits of victory belong only to the survivors.

"Now let me tell you how to survive. It is a simple matter, really: one only has to remember that battles are fought not by individuals, one man against one man, but by armies, and that an army exists to protect its members and to crush its enemies. There is no such thing as single combat, not unless both commanders' plans have gone hopelessly wrong, so there is no place for individual prowess. There are no heroes in any army; if you long to be a hero, then compete in the games. An army is made up not of men but of soldiers, and soldiers become an army by submerging themselves in discipline and drill. Follow your training, look out for those who fight to the right and left of you while they look out for you, and remember that the one who breaks and runs is usually the first one killed. If you can hang on to these rules, you have a good chance of living long enough to tell lies to your grandchildren about the glory of war. When all of this is over and we can go home again, you are free to believe whatever you like. But for now, believe what I tell you."

Of course they did not—I could see as much in their faces—but at least they had been warned. Now my task was to drill them until it no longer mattered what they believed, until they had forgotten that they were many rather than one, until thought had been replaced by habit. Then perhaps we would not be utterly abandoned to fate.

I started by forming them up into three battle squares, each eight men deep. They found this a clumsy and comical proceeding, and none of them seemed to believe that armies could possibly wage war thus.

"How can men fight, all bunched up together like this?" they asked with some asperity. "Perhaps, Tiglath, after all you acquired those scars fighting in taverns."

"A man cannot even draw his sword when the next fellow is jammed against his elbow. We will make a lovely target for the brigand horsemen—they will trample us down like spring grass."

I listened, and said nothing, and held them to their drill. We were at it all of the first and most of the second day before they could advance without breaking up their lines. As I watched their progress I picked out the best men and moved them to the front ranks, where their skill and persistence, which two are the only real courage to which a soldier can lay claim, would be of most use.

After the third day, when the basic lessons had sunk in, I set them to fighting mock battles, more like shoving matches, in which two squares would run against one another and try to crack each other's formations. They enjoyed this—it was great sport—and by the end of the fifth day I began to hope these farmers might at last have the makings of an army.

After eight days most of them had exhausted the food they had brought with them and, besides, it was time they learned the use of weapons.

"Go back to your womenfolk," I told them—an order that was greeted with cheering. "And while you are at home, I want each of you to cut a staff from wood fresh enough not to have grown brittle. Make it half again as long as a man is tall, and to a thickness of two fingers. When you return, we will tip them with iron spearheads. Remember, if they are not strong, if they break, it will be your own lives you impale upon them.

"And let every man make himself a shield. Let it be round, and as wide as a man's arm is long. Cover it with as many layers of oxhide as will allow you to carry it through a day's fighting. Let those of you who are skilled with the javelin and the bow bring these weapons as well when you return. We will all assemble here again in five days."

Kephalos met me at the outskirts of Naxos, and we rode home together in the wagon.

"How goes the rest of our plan?" I asked him.

"It is as you would wish, Lord," he answered, smiling to himself as if he had swindled the whole world. "Three of the forges have been dismantled and the sections carried out into the countryside in farm carts—I judged it best to leave one in place, lest the king's watchdogs grow suspicious. The blacksmiths are presently at work, the spearheads are nearly finished, and, since the day after tomorrow is a market day, I thought that would be a convenient moment to smuggle them back into the city for distribution to our soldiers. Each man has only to present himself at the brothel of Melantho the Thessalian woman and he will come away with something crammed into his loincloth a good deal stiffer than anything he ever found there before."

"And what about the import of iron ore?"

"The ore itself is too bulky, so I have arranged for ingots of iron to be smelted on the mainland, in Rhegium. By in large they are Euboeans, countrymen of our neighbors, and they are demanding twice what the ore and their labor is worth, so they will not sell us to Ducerius. The metal is already being landed by night at an isolated spot farther down the coast and carried to our forges to be reworked into weapons. I believe I can promise that the Lord Tiglath, Tyrant of Naxos, will have all he needs within the next five or ten days."

"You have done well, my friend. As always, where cunning and good management are required to achieve a thing, you have done very well."

Kephalos closed his eyes and nodded, acknowledging the justice of my praise, for indeed he possessed a great talent for duplicity and was never so happy as when he had a chance to exercise it.

"It is like the old days, is it not, Master," he said at last. "I might almost believe myself back in Nineveh, when you were almost the lord of the world. Sometimes I miss those days."

He did not seem to require an answer, and I was happy enough to hold my tongue. Yet I could not deny to myself that I too missed the old days—or perhaps, more accurately, I lamented the opportunities I had squandered before I was old enough to judge more wisely. Would I ever know if I had been right to squander them?

And was that not, perhaps, the reason I had agreed to play this precarious game against the Lord of the Sicels? If I could not—or would not—topple one king, then perhaps I would topple another. If not my brother Esarhaddon, then maybe Ducerius, to whom I owed no debt of loyalty or love.

I spent most of the next few days carrying stones to clear a new field. Each evening I felt as if my back had been broken for good and all, and I was glad to have found such weariness, for it freed my mind from all thought of what was to come. At night I buried myself in Selana's arms and prayed that no dreams would find me.

But in the cold black hours before the fifth dawn, I loaded my horse with provisions and weapons, put on my leather corselet, and set out for the Plain of Clonios, there yet again to take up the work I once imagined I had put behind me forever.

Fresh from home, my Greek neighbors were at least beginning to look like soldiers. Drawn up in their battle square, the new iron points on their spears glittering in the sun and their leather shields massed like the stones in a fortress wall, the Naxos militia presented the appearance of a formidable army. They were brave, and willing too, but still I harbored doubts, for I was building this house with green wood. These men had never seen blood spilled in anger—who could say they would not break and run when the moment came?

Ducerius certainly was not impressed.

"Is this the force with which you plan to conquer the world?" he inquired mockingly that third morning after our return, when he rode a fine gray stallion down from his citadel on his way to a day's hunting. "It is a strange manner of fighting, more suited to a festival dance than a war. Have you cobbled together this army to drive me out that you may take my place upon the throne?"

He lowered his gaze to where I stood on the hard-packed earth before him and grinned, and his retainers, their horses jostling each other nervously, laughed at his wit. I even laughed with them.

"No, Great King—I have done no more than assemble a small hunting party, perhaps not so very unlike your own. Perhaps, when we return from our sport, you will accept a trophy."

The Lord of the Sicels was not amused by this suggestion, and the eyes glittered dangerously as they scanned the rows of iron-tipped spears.

"You prepare a disaster for yourself, Tiglath Ashur. What do you imagine can be done with a mob of dung-raking Greeks? In their hands, those spears are only good for lancing boils. Paugh!"

His gaze returned to me, as if he had dismissed my two hundred armed men as no more than a phantom.

"One is either born with a warrior's fire in his belly or he is not, and if I am any judge of men you are not someone who has spent his whole life behind a plow. So I would expect you to know better—even brigands are better fighters than such as these."

I had almost lost interest in what he said. A cart piled to the top with loose hay was drawing toward us over the plain. When it stopped, Diocles looked to me for a signal and I nodded. At once several men climbed onto the cart and began throwing its contents to the ground—mixed in with the hay were over a hundred new-forged swords, their blades so bright it hurt one's eyes to look at them.

I turned back to Ducerius, my very silence a challenge.

Suddenly he laughed, as if he had only just seen the jest.

"Yes, Tiglath Ashur—play with your new toys. We will have good sport, you and I, before we are done."

With a vicious yank on the reins, he turned his horse about and rode away, his retainers close behind. The pounding of their hooves died away slowly across the wind-swept plain.

I waited until the king was out of sight and then stalked over to the wagon, my legs feeling as stiff as though I had spent the whole day with my knees locked straight.

"By the Mouse God's navel, what was that about?" Diocles asked, making a gesture toward the still-visible spiral of dust from the king's riders.

"He is pleased with us," I answered. "He is pleased that we prepare for war. He looks forward to meeting us in battle, although in his view it will hardly be a battle at all. We are only 'dung-raking Greeks,' weak in numbers and unprepared to face a seasoned army like his own. He is happy because now he will have the pretext to destroy us."

"But is he right?"

What could I do except shrug my shoulders?

"The gods know, my friend. We are in their hands now."

"This is the hardest time, when everything is still to come. It is worse for you than for me."

"Are you then not afraid?"

"Yes, I am afraid. But I know that when the moment comes my fear will desert me. If it were not so, no man could ever bring himself to raise his hand against another."

"Perhaps that would be better."

"Perhaps—but that is not how the world was made. The brigands have declared themselves our enemies and we must fight them."

"Will it end there, this wickedness?"

"I am not wise enough to know."

In the darkness, as we lay together on our sleeping mat, Selana pressed her hands against my chest, as if to assure herself that I had not vanished. The house was quiet around us. There was not even an oil lamp burning in our room. Tomorrow, in the morning, Enkidu and I would depart to join our neighbors and she would lose me to "this wickedness," as she called it. I would become the Tyrant of Naxos, leading an untried army into the mountains to test the will of the gods. But for what was left of that last night, I was only hers.

I felt her lips against my throat and heard her weep.

"It is terrible," she whispered through her tears.

"Yes, it is terrible. But it is the same for everyone. In every Greek household tonight, a man lies in his woman's arms. It is no different for them. It has always been just so, whenever men have had to go away to fight."

"That makes it no less terrible."

"No, it doesn't."

"If you let yourself be killed, I will not forgive you."

"I will not forgive myself."

"How am I to stand this?"

"You will find a way."

"Come into me, My Lord, my beloved. Burn me to ashes."

And at last, even as the black night moved across the sky, we found sleep, and forgetfulness.

XXVII

MOVING SINGLE-FILE OVER THE SWITCHBACK TRAILS THAT wind through marshy valleys from one chain of mountains to another, hampered by the persistent, haunting threat of ambush, even an army of only a hundred men travels as slowly as a wounded snake. We were five days reaching the flatlands watered by the Salito River—a man alone, with no enemy patrols counting his steps, might have covered the same terrain in less than three.

Yet at last we found ourselves able to look back on the western slope of Mount Aetna. We had reached the interior of the island, and so far the brigands who were supposed to control this whole region had not thought to attack us. I wondered why.

And then, when we reached the Salito Plain, I understood. It was level country, where men on horseback would feel themselves to hold the advantage. In the mountains they could only harass us, wear us down and perhaps make us lose heart and turn back. But a series of inconclusive skirmishes was not what they hoped for. They wanted to settle this quarrel forever. They wanted a pitched battle. They wanted to catch us in the open and destroy us.

Thus as soon as we descended from the mountain, while we still had those walls of sheer and ragged rock at our backs, I gave orders that an encampment be laid out and earthworks dug to protect our exposed flanks.

"The men are tired, Tiglath. They need a night's rest before they will be ready for such a task."

"Is this such a fair place that you would care to lie here forever? They will likely rest a good deal longer than just one night if the brigands choose to strike before dawn."

Thus, with much grumbling, the thing was done. Great fires were lit that the men might see to work and trenches were dug thirty paces long on each side, the earthworks behind bristling with sharpened stakes. By morning it was possible for at least some of us to sleep in safety.

"Now we are at liberty to look about us and decide what to do. Their plans are clear enough—it is time we made a few of our own."

With the first gray light of dawn I left Epeios in command and borrowed his horse to scout the surrounding area alone.

"Keep them at work," I told him. "And I will try to bring your precious gelding back still fit to pull a cart."

"Be sure you bring yourself back. Just try to remember, Tiglath, we will be in a fine mess here if anything should happen to you."

"I promise to remember."

As I rode away from the encampment, I could not but experience a certain sense of escape, as if I had broken the tether that held me back. I hadn't realized how much I needed to be alone for a time. I gave the horse its head to gallop off in whatever direction it chose.

Although it did not look as if a plow had ever broken the earth here, this was rich country. The sun-yellowed grass reached as high as a man's knees, and clumps of trees here and there indicated the presence of water if a man would only take the trouble to dig for it. The Sicels appeared to understand almost nothing of irrigation, for otherwise they would be a rich people instead of a nation of beggars and these plains would be waist-deep in grain.

I was aware, of course, that I was being watched. Two riders followed at a discreet distance but made no move to approach or challenge me. I had expected something of the sort, nor did it alarm me particularly, since our arrival was not a secret—the brigands could hardly be expected to ignore the presence of a force like ours, and the movements of our scouts would be of interest to them.

The Salito River, from which the region took its name, was not more than an hour's march from our encampment. It was swift-flowing and wide enough to constitute a formidable barrier, yet I found two or three places where foot soldiers could cross safely.

It divided the plain into north and south, and the other side, I gathered, was less sparsely populated—I could see thin trails of smoke on the northern horizon, probably from cooking fires, and, once I had gained the opposite bank, even a few huts made of rough-hewn stone and hardly big enough for a man to stand up in.

I rode into the farmyard of one of these and came upon an old man in the process of feeding his geese. He was remarkably surprised to see me—or perhaps only frightened—and stared openmouthed, as if I had come wrapped in a mantle of fire like one of the deathless gods.

"Good morning to you," I said, without dismounting from my horse. My Sicel was in those days awkward at best, so while I waited through his long silence for some reply I wondered if perhaps he hadn't understood me at all.

"Is Your Honor one of the Lord Collatinus' men?" he finally inquired. "My woman is old, dried up with years, and we have hardly enough to feed us. There is nothing here anyone would want, yet if Your Honor will show us mercy I will kill one of my geese and cook it in milk for you to breakfast on."

"I want nothing from you, my friend. I mean you no harm. I am Tiglath the Greek, and I owe service to no one. Who is the Lord Collatinus?"

"You say you are a Greek?" The old man clawed at his beard with blackened fingernails—he seemed to be trying to remember if he had ever heard what a Greek might be. "The great lord's horsemen raid across the mountains, where it is said strangers dwell. Are you from across the mountains?"

"Yes," I answered, glimpsing a possibility. "I have come with a mighty army of my neighbors. We are here to take revenge for the murders of our children and the plundering of our farms and women."

"The great lord has weapons of bronze, and many horses. He is powerful and cruel. He is without pity, and if any speak against him he burns their crops in the fields and crucifies them on the very doors of their houses, taking their women as slaves."

All the while he spoke he seemed to be assessing me, measuring my chances of success against this Collatinus who filled him with such terror. From time to time he would glance toward the horizon, for doubtless he too had seen the riders watching from a distance—a distance that now appeared to shorten every minute.

"A man who is wise enough to stay alive does not challenge those who are stronger than himself," he went on, his eyes on the spiral of dust that was coming ever closer. "He is prudent, and keeps his nose pressed against the earth. Or, if he has a horse, as none here do except the great lord's men, he runs away."

"I thank you for your timely warning, my friend, but sometimes a man is wiser still when he stands and fights."

I reined my horse about and drew a javelin from the quiver I was carrying slung behind my back. The two riders who had been following me all morning were now no more than a hundred or so paces away and closing at a trot.

Why they had chosen this moment to confront me, I will never know. Perhaps merely to give the old man a lesson. There are those who must forever be displaying their might, afraid that any restraint will be seen as weakness. These two were so sure of themselves, I almost could have found it in me to pity them.

I prodded Epeios' horse to a canter and then to a full gallop, not allowing myself to wonder what this gelding was made of, if he would stand the shock of battle. With my javelin couched under my arm like a lance, I bore down on the two riders, making straight for the man in the lead.

It was not what they had expected. For an instant they drew to a complete stop and then, when they saw what I intended, the man in the lead tried to rein his horse to the side, out of my way, while the other drew his sword. But they had already waited too long.

This style of combat I had first seen among the Medes, against whom I made war in my father's name. Their leader, the brave and noble Daiaukka, a man possessed of every excellence and whom it was an honor to have killed, almost stripped me of my life fighting with a lance from the back of a horse, and on that day I had learned from him that momentum was everything. Thus these Sicel brigands were already food for the dogs.

Epeios' horse was no plow beast—gelding that he was, he had a stallion's heart. He did not shy or falter, but stretched out his neck and burned the earth with his furious charge.

The first man's horse panicked, trying at once to escape a collision and to buck off its now unwelcome master—it succeeded at the first, if only by the space of a few fingers, but it was I who tore the rider from its back, my point catching him just below the rib cage so that he fell to the ground with his guts spilling out onto the dust.

The second man, his sword in his hand, could not seem to decide between flight and attack, so I decided for him. I drew my own sword and went for him.

Our horses slammed together, shoulder to shoulder, and my sword caught the edge of his. We stumbled apart, both of us still on our mounts, still within reach of each other's swords.

I never fancied myself as more than just adequate with a sword. In the house of war, where I learned the soldier's trade, there were many who excelled me with that weapon, and I never improved upon the skills I learned there.

This poor fool, however, cut and sawed as if he thought we did battle with kitchen knives. At only his third or fourth thrust he overreached himself so badly that I was able to grab him by the sleeve with my free hand and pull him straight off his seat—he fell into my point, which buried itself in his heart, and he was dead before he touched the ground.

The fighting done, I collected the two horses and slung the corpses of their riders over their backs, tying them down with the reins. A slap on the rump with the flat of my hand sent each in turn galloping off over the level landscape. After a time they would find their way back to their own stables, and Collatinus, this king of brigands, seeing their burdens, would be free to draw what conclusions he wished.

I rode back to the old man, who waited on the same spot where I had left him, except that now his wife had joined him and was standing by his side.

"What will you do, Your Honor, if you kill the great lord?" he asked. "Will you rule here in his place?"

I shook my head.

"Rulers are a burden to all men," I said, "and there is nothing here I want. I will take the Lord Collatinus' head and carry it home to mount on a stake. I will leave his body for the crows to feast on."

"And his riders, with their bronze weapons?"

"I will scatter them to the winds like chaff. I will make of them an example, that others will not be tempted to plunder their neighbors."

The man glanced at his wife, who answered him with a nod. Then he turned back to me.

"Your Honor, these men, or ones like them, murdered our only son before his parents' eyes—not for any offense of his, but only for their own cruel sport. I am but a farmer, defenseless and old, and to seek revenge against such as these was merely to embrace death, yet I am not so meager in spirit as not to know a father's grief, and his shame. The grief I will feel while there is breath under my ribs, but today, perhaps, I may wipe out some small measure of the shame. My name is Maelius, Your Honor, and I am old and poor and good for little. Yet tell me, if you will, what gift or tribute might a humble man like myself offer to one such as you?"

"The gift of his counsel," I answered. "And the tribute of his blessing."

For half an hour, while his wife prepared us breakfast, I squatted with Maelius in the doorway of his hut, and he told me much of this man

Collatinus, who some five years before had sprung up as if from the earth, attracting to himself every cutthroat and malcontent in the region until he seemed to transcend his position as a leader of thieves and murderers to rule on the Salito Plain like a king in his own right. He was by reputation clever, brave, and utterly without scruple or feeling—one might say that he had all the virtues of a great prince and thus was necessarily among the worst of men.

Maelius had never heard of the Lord Ducerius, but he did know that Collatinus occasionally sent payments of treasure "to some great king in the east," who could have been no one else. I had no trouble understanding how such an arrangement would be convenient for both men, since Ducerius commanded a vastly superior force but could not have moved against the brigands without leaving himself dangerously exposed at home. Thus he was content to collect tribute and claim nominal sovereignty while suffering Collatinus to enjoy unmolested the fruits of his thievery.

That the brigands were regularly sending parties of raiders over the mountains was, apparently, a recent development. Maelius had assumed that the "great king in the east" made war against some neighboring peoples and that Collatinus was acting as his ally, and in this he had not been far wrong.

He was very precise about the brigands' strength and disposition, telling me that Collatinus had a force of about two hundred horsemen and that they occupied a stronghold less than two hours' walk to the north. And, as soon as I had discharged my duty as a guest by eating a bowl of barley and milk curds Maelius' wife had prepared for me, it was in that direction I rode.

Collatinus' "stronghold" consisted of a log stockade with some earthworks thrown up outside the walls—in its very air of casualness it demonstrated how safe the brigands felt themselves, how little they looked for any armed resistance within their own territories. I was able to ride all the way around it, at a distance of no more than five hundred paces, without ever being challenged or even encountering a patrol. I doubt if they even saw me.

I had led a hundred men on a five days' campaign to besiege a fortification in which the soldiers of Ashur would not have descended to corralling their pack animals. How my brother Esarhaddon would laugh now, I thought, to see the paltry scale on which I fight my wars.

At about an hour past midday, the two horses, with their slain riders still tied to their backs, at last stalked up to the stockade gates. I watched from a clump of trees, invisible in the shade, and I could hear the cries as the sentries sent up their alarm. Since this was a provocation not even villains careless as these could overlook, I started back toward our own encampment.

"By the gods, Tiglath, where were you hiding yourself? We began despairing of your life these three hours ago . . ."

They crowded around me, my hundred citizen-warrior Greeks, like children who had thought themselves abandoned by their mother. I climbed off Epeios' horse, and someone handed me a cup of wine.

"Their riders have been everywhere—we thought sure they would attack. What would we have done then, Tiglath, with you face down in the mud somewhere?"

"These brigand horsemen are easily evaded," I told them. "A few gave chase along the way, but those who came close enough to offer battle have not lived to regret it. Believe me when I tell you, my friends, that we have nothing to fear. Our enemies are perhaps just good enough to raid farmhouses, but they are no army."

"Neither are we, really. What if they had attacked during your absence?"

"They will not attack as long as we stay within our earthworks—horsemen are useless against a fortified position. That is why we will leave here tomorrow and force a battle upon them on their own ground."

"Tiglath, the sun must have baked your brains!"

The soldiers of Ashur would never have spoken thus to me when I was *rab shaqe* of my father's northern army, but the Greeks were the Greeks and no respecters of rank. That night, after the evening meal, for all that the assembly in Naxos had elected me Tyrant, I had to explain my plans to these farmers-turned-soldiers and to listen with patience to all their objections and complaints, all their nagging fears that the style of warfare I had taught them could not possibly prevail against even such a force as Collatinus and his rogues. I listened, and tried as best I could to explain away their fears, for had they not been satisfied with my leadership they doubtless would have elected themselves another commander and I would have found myself fighting in the ranks.

"They have horses, Tiglath—all of them! How are men on foot to stand against horsemen?"

"A horseman is still nothing but a man on a horse, and cavalry are no better than a mob that can run fast. The only advantage their horses will confer upon Collatinus' band of thieves is that, once we have defeated them in the field, the survivors will find it easier to escape. Believe me, for I have never seen horsemen prevail against foot soldiers, not even when I fought against the Scythians, who are the best riders and the bravest warriors the gods ever made."

"Yet if we lose, we perish; while if they lose, they can leave us with nothing gained except the field of battle. What is the point of fighting them at all if, even when we defeat them, they have only to run away?"

"My friends, where will they run except to their stronghold? We will know where to look when we want them."

"They will be safe there."

"No, they will be trapped."

"That is foolish, since you claim we are safe from attack behind these earthworks—how is it different for them?"

"Cavalry cannot attack a fortified position, but foot soldiers can. Once we have defeated them in the field, their stronghold will serve for nothing except their tomb."

"Yet we must defeat them first, and they outnumber us two to one."

"Smaller forces than ours have prevailed against greater. We will defeat them."

Thus it went, through half the night. I think that the only reason they at last decided to accept my plan was that no one had another. For this I did not fault them—I was much less sure of victory than I sounded.

The gray light of dawn found me sitting atop the crest of our earthworks, watching the brigand scouts as they cantered bank and forth, back and forth, across the plain, some six or seven hundred paces distant. I saw four riders, but there were probably more—they could not know if we would be prepared to offer battle today or if we would wait, but Collatinus would want to hear as soon as we broke out of our encampment.

Epeios came and joined me, bringing with him a bowl of dried meat for my breakfast.

"The men have all eaten," he said. "So should you."

"The river is an hour's march from here," I answered, setting the bowl aside—somehow I could never seem to keep anything on my stomach at such times. "We must be on the other shore before word reaches Collatinus that we have started to move. If they gain control of the north bank ahead of us, and we are caught on this side, then there will be no battle and he will have won by default. If they surprise us while we are still fording the river, it will be a disaster. He does not know where we intend to cross, so he must wait for his scouts to bring him notice—that is something. And his stronghold on the other side is twice as far from the river as is our encampment. We are entitled to hope that time is with us.

In his place, I would bring my forces closer in, within sight of the bank, and wait with them there even if it took a month, but I do not think Collatinus has done that."

"Why do you think he has not?"

"Because I do not think he can keep his men under that kind of discipline—no one likes to sit in his armor on the cold ground. We do not fight an army, remember, but a band of thieves."

"I hope you are right."

"So do I."

We watched the brigand scouts a while longer, consoled by our own silence.

"Assemble the men," I told him at last. "Give me five minutes after I have taken them over the earthworks, then come out with your horsemen. Some of you will provide Collatinus' riders with someone to chase, and the rest will fan out toward the river to see if anything is moving there. Keep me informed."

"Where will you be?"

"In the second rank of the left-hand battle square, with the javelin throwers."

"Should you not stay in the center? It is not wise to expose yourself like that—what if you are killed?"

"I must be where I can keep our lines in order. Besides, who will follow a leader who will not share the common danger? Our neighbors would think me a coward, and they would be right."

"It shall be as you order, Tiglath."

The men stamped their sandaled feet against the earth and looked about them nervously as they adjusted spears and leather shields, the unaccustomed implements of battle. Hardly anyone spoke, and each did what he could to hide his growing fear. I knew how they felt, for I remembered what it was to face an enemy for the first time. It was not so very different with me now.

"We will go over the earthworks at quick march," I told them. "We will all call the pace together—right, left, right, left. Do not be tempted to break into a run, or your lines will go to pieces. Remember, survival in battle depends on keeping together and maintaining a decent order. Do not be afraid of the brigand horsemen, but depend upon the archers and the javelin throwers to deal with them. As long as we keep our squares tight and our spears level, they can do nothing against us—after all, not even a horse is stupid enough to try eating a hedgehog."

This made them laugh, which was good. Men who can still laugh are proof against any sudden panic.

I took my place in the left-hand battle square. Enkidu was in the right-hand square, in the center of the first rank. He was like a wall, and he feared nothing—as I had known they would, men drew confidence from the mere sight of him.

"Over the top, then!"

We breasted our earthworks one rank at a time, slowing when we reached level ground that the rank behind could pull up. It took us five or six minutes for everyone to reach the plain, but by the time Collatinus' scouts had begun to react we had reformed our squares and were back in good order.

I shouted a command and both squares wheeled to the right and began moving north at a quick trot.

For several minutes, while their horses snorted with impatience and pawed at the ground, the brigand scouts simply watched us, as if they did not quite know what to do. Then two of them broke toward the river at a dead gallop. The remaining three, more foolish than the others, started toward us.

I cannot guess what sport they expected, but they thundered down on us waving their swords over their heads. I called a halt, told the first two rows of archers in both squares to make ready, and waited the quarter of a minute it required to be sure the riders were within range before I gave the order to shoot.

There was a harsh twang of thirty bowstrings singing together and a cloud of arrows took off, sailed though the empty air, and then dropped on their targets. Two of the brigands fell limply from their seats, dead before they touched the ground, and the third alive and apparently unhurt, was pitched off by his wounded horse. He scrambled to his feet and ran like a rabbit.

The Greeks cheered, but there was no time to celebrate a victory. We took up our trotting pace again, and a quarter of an hour later the first of our riders returned.

"Clear to the river, Tiglath!" he shouted. "Callias went across to climb the bank for a look—he shouted back that he could see nothing."

Half an hour later we were there to judge for ourselves.

There are few undertakings so frightful to a commander as leading an army across a river and into hostile territory. To be surprised at such a time is to be annihilated, for soldiers can do little to defend themselves while they are still waist-deep in swirling water. We were forty minutes getting the last man over, and I died inside every time a scout rode up to report if Collatinus' horsemen had been sighted.

And indeed we had hardly dried our sandals when Epeios rode up to announce that the enemy would be on us in a quarter of an hour.

"It is all right," I said to him, loud enough that everyone might hear. "We have made the bank, so we have level ground to fight upon. And we will have no need of a retreat."

I did not give them time to think—no man is better for thinking when he is face to face with his first battle. Our riders, as they came in, one after the other, with the same news, abandoned their horses and joined the ranks of the two battle squares.

"Remember—stay tight! Let their charge break over us like the sea over a rock. Let them die before our arrows and impale their lives upon the iron points of our spears!"

They shouted their answer, for they were defying their own fear as much as any enemy. We trotted forward at the same steady rate until the river was some hundred paces behind us. We could already see the clouds of dust raised by the brigand horsemen.

How many were there? A hundred and fifty? Two hundred? Such things freeze a soldier's bowels with terror. Soon the pounding of their hooves against the earth was like summer thunder, and here and there the pale morning light flashed from their bronze swords. War cries like the shrieking of hawks trembled in our ears—these were not men but demons, pouring toward us to deal out cruel death, to leave our corpses to rot unmourned in the pitiless sun. Thus our fears would have it. There seemed nothing to do except to wait.

Yet a soldier lives not to die but to fight, and these were not demons but men. I delayed only until they came within range.

"Draw your bows!—let fly!"

Massed arrows are as indiscriminate as rain, but they kill at a great distance. I know not how many of Collatinus' robber warriors fell dead in that one instant, but we could see their horses tumbling over into the dust like wine jugs toppled from a shelf. Suddenly there was a new sound, the screams of the maimed and dying rending the air.

A second flight dropped hissing down upon them to bury their points in the flesh of men and animals. Collatinus lost fully one in six of his horsemen before they even came within seventy paces of our lines. And then it was time for the javelins to do their work.

There were twenty of us, ten each in the second and third ranks of both squares, and the men behind fell back to give us space for throwing. The brigands were almost upon us now, and they were still many, so each of us had to measure our aim and only the quick had any chance for a second dart.

War has its own ecstasy, and the frenzy of battle possesses one like the lover's passion. I forgot in that moment that I was anything except a Greek with a javelin in my hand. I might have been alone there before the horsemen of Collatinus—I had eyes now only for the mark in front of me, the men whom I would carry down to death with the strength of my hand.

One took my stroke in the root of his neck, so that he spattered the air with bright blood even as his soul fled screeching off into the dark realms. The other fell with his belly torn open; I watched him go down, knowing before he did, I think, that his life was ended.

Then there was no more time. The men in the front ranks locked their knees and dropped their spear points to the level, waiting for the shock of impact.

Perhaps they imagined we were bluffing—perhaps they simply did not know what else to do—but several of the brigands rode straight into us. For a few moments it was a scene of carnage and chaos such as I hope never to witness again as horses impaled themselves, breaking off the points of our spears as they screamed as only a horse can scream and then folded at the knees and rolled into our lines, sending their riders flying. More than one Greek was kicked in the head or had a horse roll over him. The man in front of me was pulled under and had his ribs crushed. His face was black; he could not even cry out in his pain. Someone handed me a spear and I jumped forward to take his place in the front line.

Yet the line held. We advanced over the bodies of the fallen, men and beasts, our own dead and the enemy's, and when we came to a halt we were as impenetrable as ever. The brigand horsemen could do nothing against us.

They were not all so mad as to throw themselves against our bristling squares. Many pulled up short when they saw what was happening, and after the first charge they simply milled aimlessly around, as if they did not know quite what to do next.

What will happen now? they seemed to be asking themselves.

We answered with another volley of arrows, and another. More men dropped lifeless from their mounts, and finally the brigands saw that it was hopeless and rode back the way they had come, leaving us in undisputed possession of the field.

When they saw the brigands fleeing, the Greeks raised a cheer that seemed to shatter the heavens. Relief and mad joy swept over us as we realized that we had won. We broke our voices calling upon the gods to witness our victory.

I could hardly believe it myself. As easily as that, we had won.

I knelt down for a moment to catch my breath, and in my heart I gave thanks yet again to the Lord Ashur for preserving me in the jaws of battle.

"Count the dead," I ordered, as soon as I could find my words again. "Theirs and ours."

The tally was quickly made: we had lost eight men, but the brigands had left seventy-two behind, dead or crippled. A few of us who had sustained wounds were tended by their neighbors, but if the Greeks found any of Collatinus' men alive but too injured to have managed an escape, they cut their throats.

"It is a great victory," Epeios stated in his matter-of-fact way. "Yet it was not so complete that the enemy does not still outnumber us by better than five to four, and they have retreated to their stronghold."

I could only laugh, shaking my head, for there are those who can never be schooled in the obvious.

"Yes, but they are defeated men," I said at last. "And once a man is beaten—defeated in the core of his soul—nothing can save him. If need be, we will pull them from their 'stronghold' by the hair."

XXVIII

THE OUTER PERIMETER OF COLLATINUS' STOCKADE formed a square no more than one hundred and fifty paces to the side and consisted of earthworks raised to perhaps the height of a man within a shallow ditch. At the corners of the inner walls, which rose about five paces back from the earthworks and were some thirty cubits high and constructed of notched logs, there stood watchtowers, and the one gate seemed to have a catwalk over it, but these were the only strong points. The Lord of Thieves clearly had never given much thought to the possibility of a siege.

I intended to make the brigands understand that their log walls were not a sanctuary but a trap and, when at last this idea had seeped into their brains, certainly their initial thought would be to attempt an escape. They would think to try a mass breakout on horseback—and therefore my first task was to deny them this possibility of flight.

It was an hour after noon when at last we came within sight of the stockade, and even before we made camp I set men to work building a light wooden frame, ten paces by fifteen, upon which they might hang their shields and be protected while they dug horsetraps in a semicircle around the one access through the earthworks to the main gate. Thus now the only way in or out was by foot.

The brigands watched all this from their catwalk—perhaps for fear of opening their gates to us, they did not even attempt to drive us off—and shortly before dusk they called down that they desired a truce in which to discuss terms.

"Send out four men," I shouted back. "Let them come unarmed and on foot. We will receive them peacefully, and they will be free to return to you whenever they wish, unharmed."

It was already dark when four rather grand figures rode into the light of our campfires, but it seemed they had come to negotiate our surrender rather than their own.

One, clearly the leader, a man well past his middle years yet of undiminished strength, was perhaps half a span taller than the others. He wore the usual knee-length Sicel tunic, but dyed a vivid red, and the chain around his neck was of massive gold. His beard just touched his breast and was cut straight across, which somehow managed to give the appearance of great severity of character—I would not have cared to be his dependent.

"You have won a victory," he began, as if addressing himself to the darkness. "But consider what must come after. We allowed you to come over the mountains unmolested because, to speak the truth, we expected to make short work of you in open combat, but sooner or later you must return whence you came. The journey home, you may trust my words, will not be so agreeable. We know the mountains better than you, and you cannot march all the way back to Naxos in your hedgehog formations. While you are strung out along the trails, we will harry you again and again, until you will think yourself fortunate if one in four of you lives to smell once more the wind from the salt sea."

He looked around at us, glancing from one man to the next, as if he pitied us our rashness in ever venturing into the territory of the Lord Collatinus. And one could read in the faces of the Greeks the impression his words had made—and if he did not believe them himself, then he was a more talented liar than most men.

"Thus it seems you leave us with only one choice," I answered, breaking a silence that was beginning to be oppressive. "We shall have to destroy you before we leave, and so we shall have less to fear from your wrath."

His eyes fastened on me, and I grinned impudently.

"You then are Tiglath Ashur, whom the Greeks have named their Tyrant," he said matter-of-factly—thus it seemed that each of us had recognized the other, for I had no doubt it was Collatinus himself who stood before me.

"You have done well for yourself, but there is no honor in the way you have taught the Greeks to wage war. A man who will not fight except from behind the protection of other men is a coward and no true warrior."

"On the contrary, My Lord, for it is the business of a warrior to conquer. When we have left the last Sicel bandit a corpse upon the ground, I will be happy to cede all the honor to the slain."

"Yet since you will not fight like gentlemen, there will be no one to conquer. We will wait inside our own walls until you tire of this game and depart. And then we will destroy you."

He turned away from me, as if there could be nothing more for us to say to one another.

"Still, I have not come here simply to pronounce sentence upon you," he went on, speaking once again to the whole assembly. "For it is true that you have won a victory—and a victory should not be without its reward. We are prepared to reach a settlement. If the Greeks will leave as soon as they are reprovisioned, then we will grant them safe conduct back to their own homes. Beyond this, we will make a treaty with them, guaranteeing that their lands will never again be plundered from across the mountains. There will even be a distribution of silver, ten pieces for each man, lest any complain that the Lord Collatinus is ungenerous.

"Consider well, for the alternative is death. I will expect an answer by tomorrow, at first light."

He swept out of camp, his three colleagues trailing behind him, and after he had gone the Greeks sat about glumly, exchanging baleful glances, the firelight playing over their faces like sullen laughter.

"Perhaps we should accept," Epeios said at last, and it was clear he spoke the thoughts of many. "After all, we would achieve everything for which we came. We will have taught this rogue a lesson . . ."

I laughed aloud—men stared at me as if they suspected I had gone mad.

"Epeios, you seem to learn nothing from experience." I shook my head, as if the joke were still with me. "You have tried already to strike a bargain with these thieves—what came of that? If Collatinus can harry our journey home as he claims, what makes you imagine he will refrain simply because we have accepted his assurances and his silver? He will butcher us, and then take the coins from our purses as we lay dead on the ground."

"How can you know this, Tiglath?"

"I know it because it is in his interest to betray us. His only safety lies in our destruction—otherwise those whom he holds in subjection will fear him less, for we have dealt him a fearful blow. Therefore, he will allow us to withdraw from the level plain, where he now sees that all the advantages are ours, and his horsemen will try to cut us to pieces on the narrow mountain trails where we cannot group for defense."

My neighbors, the men with whom, that very morning, I had won a great victory, whose voices had grown hoarse shouting their triumph, they sat with their faces clouded in uneasiness, for they knew what I said was the truth. The knowledge was not pleasing to them, but they recognized it for what it was.

"Then what are we to do?"

This was the question they asked of me—what were they to do?

The next morning, while the mist still rose from the ground, I rode almost to within throwing range of the stockade walls and gave my answer to Collatinus and his men.

"We call upon you to surrender!" I shouted, my voice echoing in the still morning air. "We offer you no terms except your lives, and Collatinus we will take back in chains to stand his trial before the assembly at Naxos. Yet if you force us to lay siege to you, and one drop of Greek blood is spilled, then there will be no quarter given and men shall live or die as it is our whim. This is the choice we give you: surrender and be spared the cruelty of death, or fight and perish!"

There was a long silence, so long that I began to wonder if the brigands had not begun to comprehend the danger that faced them and were preparing to accept my bleak offer. And then, at last, I heard the throbbing of bowstrings and a flight of arrows shot from the catwalk over the stockade gate to bury their points in the ground almost at my feet.

Maelius listened to me in silence, his cloudy old eyes opening and shutting as if he struggled to stay awake. It was impossible to know what he thought.

"If the Sicels wish to pull their necks from beneath Collatinus' yoke, then they must help me now," I said. "I ask no man to die, or even to bleed, only to sweat a little that he and his sons and his sons' sons may live in this place as free men and not as slaves. I need the labor of two or three hundred men for perhaps five days. Let them bring tools for digging and for hewing wood. And I need food for my soldiers—flour, cooking oil and meat, all of which will be paid for out of the plunder from the brigand stronghold. And I will need timber. You have told me how you craved revenge, my friend—now is the time to take it."

He tugged at his beard with his ragged fingernails and sighed. He is not a warrior, I thought, and he and his neighbors must live here even if I do not destroy Collatinus. Of course he is afraid—a man would have to be a fool not to be afraid. Probably he is trying to find some tactful way to refuse.

"Give me three days," he said at last. "The settlements here are widely scattered and I have no horse to ride. In three days I will come to you with whatever this weak tongue of mine can persuade the Sicels to hazard. I do not know how much that will be. They are not all old men like me, with nothing left to fear from death."

I rode back to the Greek encampment, shutting my heart to the voices of doubt. If their victims willed it, those whom they had brought to misery and despair, then the brigands could be brought low, but men do not always have the will to act together.

Three days—three days of sullen grumbling. As a race the Greeks have many virtues, but patience is not among them.

"The brigands are blockaded behind their logs walls, and we are out here," they said. "What miracle is it you wait for which will change that fact, Tiglath? And all the while our supplies dwindle."

"Perhaps even now Collatinus will keep to his bargain."

"We wish to go home. What are we to do, wait out the winter here?"

And at night the smoke from the stockade cooking fires would blow across our encampment, and we could smell burned mutton.

"No doubt they have wine to drink—wine that lingers on the tongue like a harlot's kiss. None of us has tasted wine these ten days. Perhaps some of us never will again"

And then, halfway through the morning of the third day, Maelius came. And with him were his neighbors, six hundred strong.

They carried their tools slung over their shoulders, along with sacks of grain. Women balanced clay jugs upon their heads, dragging babies with them who could hardly walk, and little boys of six and seven tended herds of goats. Oxen drew wagons loaded with rough-hewn logs. I had never seen such a sight. Even the Greeks took new heart.

"They needed no eloquence of mine," Maelius exclaimed, smiling with pride. "They have counted the corpses your soldiers left for the crows to feast upon, and nothing could keep them away. Say what you would have us do, Your Honor, and it shall be done."

The brigands, when they watched from their towers, must have wondered what we were about. We began by sinking a great hole, seventy paces from the stockade's outer perimeter, as far across at the mouth as a man's outstretched arms and twenty cubits deep. It was the first of four we would dig, and I sat at the bottom of it with the man whom the Sicels had chosen to be overseer of their work crews, explaining what was needed.

"I want tunnels," I said, "cut high enough that a man may walk hunched over, and from this point to the wall. The ground is good clay here, but keep the ceilings propped up with beams or they will come down on you."

"Your Honor has it in his mind to dig tunnels through into the brigand compound and surprise them by night?" he asked. He was a big man with a massive, bony face and eyebrows that formed a single heavy line the ends of which almost grew into his beard. Although a good worker, he was not the sort to impress anyone with his intelligence, and yet, for all that he was too tactful to say so, this struck even him as a foolish plan.

"No, such is not my intention. We will go no farther than the wall, and then we will branch to the sides and connect the four shafts. That phase I will supervise myself, for it must be done with the greatest care. How long will it take you to reach the earthworks?"

"With three men digging at once in each tunnel, and we change shifts every two hours, I think we can move thirty cubits of earth between sunrise and sunset. If we work through the night we can be there two days hence. Will that serve?"

"Yes, that will serve very well."

And so the crews of Sicel laborers bent their backs to the task I had set them. They worked tirelessly, all day and into the moonwashed night, and deep underground where the only light came from flickering torches. The piles of damp, clay-soaked earth rose on the flat Salito Plain.

The brigands watched from their towers, but I think they were only curious, for they made no attempt to interfere. Such was their faith in their own impregnability that I do not believe they had an inkling what awaited them.

And then at last I estimated we were directly under the stockade's western side. With my own hands I dug a narrow shaft straight up, a space hardly wide enough for my own body, where I clung to footholds I cut for myself in the sides and the dirt I pulled away from above my head poured down over me and fell to the tunnel below. The air was dead in my lungs and my face and body were bathed in cold sweat. I had no light save the little that reflected from beneath me. This toil, the most difficult of my life, which left me with skinned arms and shoulders and muscles that felt as if they would break if ever I had the impudence to move again, lasted through six long hours, but at the end of it I could reach up with my hand and touch the end of one of the logs, sharpened to a point and then driven into the earth, that made up the outer walls of the brigand stronghold.

My calculations had been correct. I had not missed my mark even by so much as a cubit. It seemed that even here, in this place at the edge of the world, the god of my fathers still cradled me in the hollow of his hand.

The strength left me. My own weight dragged me slowly down the shaft and into the tunnel below. As I lay there on the sodden earth, the Sicel overseer held me up by my shoulders and gave me water to drink.

"What have you found, Your Honor?"

"What I sought," I told him. I pointed up toward the shaft. "I need ten of your best diggers and your most skillful carpenters, careful men all of them, for this is work that is unforgiving of mistakes and he who takes a false step will carry many with him down to the dark worlds. We must scrape out a high vault here, supported with timbers that it does not collapse under the weight of the stockade wall—at least, not before we will it to."

I could just manage a grin as gradually it came to the overseer what I intended.

"Yes," I said. "We will bring down their house around them."

We were three days finishing our great vaulted chamber under the earth, and I died twenty deaths when with every small earthfall the whole seemed about to come crashing down upon us. Yet when it was finished it was beautiful. Three men standing on each other's shoulders still could not have touched the ceiling, and all was held in place by a careful latticework of struts and crosspieces that finally found their support in only three beams—I could have brought the whole down with a single well-placed kick.

I ordered the chamber filled with brush and jars of oil, for it would be in fire that it all ended.

In the days of my youth, when I still cherished dreams of being a great man in my own country, my father the Lord Sennacherib, Terror of Nations, King of the Earth's Four Corners, made war against the city of Babylon, famous for her sun-burned walls which had defied many conquerors. Yet these same walls were breached and the city taken and pillaged, and this because the men of Ashur had no equal in the arts of siege warfare.

It was the work of many months, but the walls of Babylon were brought low, undermined by the method that now I employed against these log ramparts. But logs must be bound together with stout ropes, and they lean against one another for support. It is different with brick, for when brick fails it breaks away clean and leaves the rest standing. Thus where my father had collapsed only a section at a time, I hoped to fold in the walls of Collatinus' stronghold like a leather tent.

That evening I opened my mind to the Greeks and let them know what I had planned.

"All this night we will send flaming arrows into the brigand stockade, that Collatinus and his men shall be visited by countless fires that seem to spring up from nowhere. Fire is a great spreader of confusion, for those who are occupied with a hundred small emergencies have trouble organizing to repel an attack.

"Two hours before dawn I will light the tunnel fires. I hope they will burn quickly so the walls will collapse before dawn—it is best if this disaster overwhelms them while it is still dark. As soon as the wall is down, we will rush the stockade. Stay together in groups of five or six that your attack remains coherent and thus we may take full advantage of surprise. Remember that we are outnumbered, so take no unnecessary risk and show no mercy. Sweep through. Comb the brigands out and kill all you can find. Forget that they are men and imagine yourselves hunting rats in a barn."

"Will it succeed, Tiglath?"

"Those of you who are alive by noon tomorrow will know how to answer that question."

So, we waited. As soon as we had the cover of darkness, archers began running to within ten or twenty paces of the brigand earthworks and shooting arrows with oil-soaked rags tied round them over the stockade wall. We could not see the fires they started, but we could hear the shouting.

I lit the underground fire with my own hand, since I would trust it to no other. I started back through the southern tunnel as soon as I was sure the beams were burning, for I was afraid of being overwhelmed by the smoke. The wind below ground, when once the fire began drawing air to itself, was like the god's own breath.

We waited in the darkness, Greek and Sicel together. No one spoke. I could almost hear the pounding of men's hearts.

And then, in the gray light just before dawn, it happened. Just as I had seen it with the eyes of hope, it happened.

There was a low rumbling, as if the earth were clearing its throat, and then, along the whole west side, first in the center and then gradually spreading towards the watchtowers at the corners, the stockade wall seemed to sag at the knees, pause for a moment, and then simply fall back upon itself.

I could hear the men in the watchtower screaming as that too collapsed and fell inward, and then one section after another, with gathering speed, peeled off the south wall and came crashing down. The noise was appalling as logs as thick as a man's waist snapped in two like rotten kindling. Everywhere the wall was pulling itself down.

"Seize the moment!" I shouted. "Attack!"

We ran, our feet hardly brushing against the ground, our lungs full of fire. It seemed hardly an instant before we were climbing over the tangle of fallen logs, and then the terrible carnage began.

There was smoke everywhere—the fires had done more damage than I could have guessed—and the brigands, most of them, simply stood about, as if trying to grasp what had happened to them. Some did not even have their swords, and those who did seemed to have forgotten the use of them. The air was rent with screaming. I cut down men that day as if I were harvesting wheat.

All of us, we were like demons, our arms smeared with dirt and gore, the lust of slaughter upon us. There was no place for fear. We killed until our arms ached.

And then, in perhaps less than half an hour, it was over. Somehow we simply lost the taste for bloodshed, and quiet swept over the ruined stronghold like cold wind.

The surviving brigands, those twenty or so who had been lucky enough to be allowed to surrender, were herded out onto the plain and left there, sitting on the ground under a light guard. They would cause no one any further trouble.

As we searched the stockade we found the body of Collatinus. It was Enkidu who found him, lying crushed to death under a fallen log. True to my word, I took his head and left his body for the crows.

We also found boxes filled with gold and silver coins, and women.

One of these, dark-haired and young, I recognized as the girl whom I had seen being led away the day I had walked to Naxos to fetch fire for the consecration of my hearth. She stared at me with large, terrified eyes, as if she expected nothing better at my hands than she had known among the brigands.

"Are you Greek or Sicel, child?" I asked. For a long moment she could not speak at all, and then she nodded.

"Greek, Master."

"Do your parents live, or did the brigands kill them?"

"I know not."

"Well, if they live we will return you to them, and if they are dead we will find a place for you among your own people. You are safe now. You will return with us."

She wept. She could not control the tears. She tore at her face with her nails and wept.

An hour later I saw her again. She was drinking wine from a clay cup and talking with two or three young men. She could smile by then.

"The brigand prisoners, Tiglath—what shall we do with them?" It was Epeios who asked.

"We will ask Maelius. What would you do with them, my friend?"

The old man's brow darkened.

"Kill them—kill them all."

"No, that is too much," I said. "But you will see justice done, I promise you."

I sent for Enkidu, and his ax.

"We will take the head of every fourth man—let them draw lots among themselves to see who will live and who will perish. The others will have their rights hands struck off, that they may be marked as thieves and shunned."

Men too cowed even to struggle against death knelt on the ground to give their necks to the ax. While the corpses of these were still twitching, we took the rest and with our swords we hacked through their wrists. The air stank with blood and the only sound was the low moan of helpless fear, yet they stretched out their arms upon the block, not daring to resist.

At last the thing was done, and the severed heads and hands were presented as trophies to Maelius, in payment for his son's life, and the surviving brigands, after their bleeding stumps had been seared shut in the fire, were whipped out of camp.

The Greeks who had died numbered only twelve men. We collected their bodies for burning and put their ashes in copper jars to be carried back for burial in their own lands. We collected plunder from the stockade, paid the Sicels for the food they had brought us, and divided the rest equally among ourselves, no man's share greater than any other's.

That day and the next we feasted and held games in honor of our fallen friends. All doubts were banished. We had achieved a great victory. All was well with us.

At noon, on the day we had chosen to begin our journey home, we saw an eagle dropping down towards us from the sun, flying east. I held up my hand to shade my eyes from the sun and, just as the eagle's shadow passed over me, a drop of blood fell and struck me on the palm.

I looked at it, and my bowels went cold. The blood on my palm covered perfectly the mark that the gods had left there in the hour of my birth—the blood star was now blood indeed.

Men gathered around me to see, and the sight filled them with fear.

"What does it mean, Tiglath—is it an omen?"

"It is an omen, but I do not know what it means. I will not know until the time for remedy is past."

"Are the gods angered against us? Have we committed some offense?"

"No. The Greeks are without crime or impurity. This was meant for me alone."

XXIX

BUT WHAT DO FOREBODINGS OF EVIL MEAN TO THOSE drunk with their own glory? The eagle had hardly disappeared over the horizon, nor I washed its blood from my hand, before this strange omen was forgotten in the general triumph of men who now, and for the first time in their lives, knew the sweetness of victory.

It was better so, for this dark business concerned not them but myself alone. I cannot say how I knew as much, but I knew. I could hear the god's voice whispering in the wind's very stillness.

I could hear his voice, but the words were lost in silence. Yet again he had given me a sign and kept its meaning hidden. There had been five eagles in my dream, each with a severed talon dripping blood—five assassins sent from Nineveh to be the means of my death. Four had met their own instead, and thus one remained. Was his coming now foretold? Then why had this eagle flown out of the sun and east, seeming thus to return to the Land of Ashur? And why had his blood dripped on the stain of my birthmark?

I knew not—I could not even guess. Once again, the god's warning would remain a riddle until the time had passed to profit from it. Thus did he jest with me.

Besides, I too was a Greek and had tasted the heady wine of victory, and I was as drunk with it as the rest. Once more, when I had thought all that behind me forever, I had known what it was to be a soldier, to feel the swelling exultation at the nearness of danger, to have cheated death yet again and to have ended by carrying the lives of my enemies on the point of my sword. It was easy enough to surrender myself to this, and to let my lingering fears die away like the sunset. It was easy enough.

So we made our way back over the mountains to Naxos and our homes, where we could expect the reception due to conquerors. In our train walked twelve Greek women whom the brigands had carried off, and like us they were going home. On our shoulders we bore the urns holding the ashes of our fallen comrades—this was our only burden, but even this was lightened by the knowledge that the family of each dead man would receive a four-fold share of our booty, which was not inconsiderable. We had much to be cheerful about.

The mountains of eastern Sicily are beautiful and, although we kept a good pace—it is always so on the way home from a successful campaign—the march back was like a holiday idyll. We had no sense of danger, so we sent out no advance patrols. I can only reproach myself for such blind folly, for I had been trained up as a soldier and should have known better. Yet as the mercy of the gods would have it, we came within sight of Naxos before encountering a hint of trouble, for we did not deserve such luck.

We were already on the long sloping foothills that led down to the sea, perhaps a three hours' march from the harbor, when Callias trotted back through the lines on his fine gray stallion to tell me that he had seen a pair of horsemen riding toward us.

"They are holding almost to a gallop," he said. "Uphill like this, their mounts will be broken-winded by the time they arrive. It is a cruel and senseless thing to push a horse like that."

"How far away are they?" I asked.

"Half an hour—no more."

He shook his head disapprovingly and then rode back to meet the approaching horsemen, doubtless rehearsing to himself how he would reprove them for their lack of proper consideration. Callias had once raced in the games at Nemea and treated his animal as another man might his bride.

"Half an hour then," I said, glancing at Enkidu, who walked at my side. "Doubtless they are sent by the assembly for news of how we fared against the brigands."

It was a reasonable enough assumption, but Enkidu only growled, as if somehow he could smell the truth.

And, as always, that instinct for danger served him well, for by the time I could hear the pounding of horses' hooves against the hard earth I recognized the lead rider as Diocles. And he did not look as if he came to congratulate us.

"By the Mouse God's navel, I thought you would never get back," he cried, sliding from his horse to crouch on the ground, gasping for breath. "What kept you? We expected you days ago. Why have you stayed away?"

"We won."

He only stared, as if he could not understand what I was talking about.

"We won," I repeated. "The brigands are utterly defeated, and Collatinus is—"

"Yes, yes—we know all that!" He shook his head with impatience. "A rider came to Ducerius' citadel twelve days ago, and by sundown word had reached every house in Naxos that the Greeks had conquered. Ducerius is in a great rage and takes his revenge on us every hour."

"What do you mean, Ducerius takes his revenge?"

"He is sending patrols of his soldiers out to raid Greeks farms, quite as the brigands did. He boasts that Collatinus may be defeated but we will hardly notice the change. He means to destroy us now, Tiglath. Did you say that Collatinus is dead?"

"Enkidu, show him."

Enkidu carried a leather sack tied to his belt. He opened it and dumped out the contents. Collatinus' head struck the ground with a thump—his eyes were still open, and he looked as if he felt the insult.

"By the Mouse God's navel . . ."

"You had half the militia in reserve," I said, perhaps a little impatiently, for, until Enkidu picked up his trophy and returned it to its leather sack, Diocles seemed to have attention for nothing else. "Has nothing been done?"

"What could be done? The men were anxious to be home that they might protect their families and property—I could not hold them. Besides, what are a hundred men to do? We could not fight Ducerius, not by ourselves. Not without you. What *kept* you?"

I told him, in as few words as I could, all that had happened on the Salito Plain, and at the end of my narrative he nodded.

"Indeed," he said, "you have conquered. Yet I fear now you will need to again. Ducerius expected the brigands to do his work for him—he laughed at us, calling us dung-rakers. And how he does not dare to let matters rest as they are, for we are a challenge to his power. He thinks to goad us into facing his army straight on. It is an army, Tiglath, not a band of brigands. And he has two men for every one of ours. He means to crush us forever."

"Was my farm attacked?" I asked—I was a man and selfish, and I had to know.

"Yes."

"Was anyone killed?"

"I know nothing of it, Tiglath. I only heard this morning. One man tells another, who tells another—you know how it is."

"Yes, I know."

I thought of Selana. If she was dead . . .

A glance at Enkidu was enough to settle the matter as far as it concerned us.

"I am going home now," I said, speaking to Diocles but conscious that others were listening as well. "But if Ducerius longs for a war, it seems wisest to give it to him. My six months as Tyrant are nearly over—the Greeks must decide for themselves what they want. They know where they will find me."

I did not accompany the militia into Naxos—there would be no victory celebration, no cheers for the conquerors, since, it seemed, we had conquered one enemy only to raise up another. In any case, I found I had no taste for glory.

Enkidu and I broke off from the rest and followed the line of hills south, heading for home.

We were five hours on the trails, and through every minute I could feel my heart lodged in my throat like a fox caught in a hollow log. If Selana was dead . . .

What a fool I had been to abandon her thus unprotected—could I not have seen that Ducerius would single me out above all others for his revenge? Yet I had to go off like a little boy with his playmates, intent on nothing but his childish little game. I would never leave her again, if only . . .

I thought of every way I would kill Ducerius, how I would strip his life from him the way the skin is peeled from an apple. Yet I did not care—he had my permission to live forever if only Selana could be safe and I could fold her in my embrace once more.

When at last we came within sight of the farmhouse, I saw that no smoke rose from the hearth vent.

She is dead, I thought. The hearth fire was her special charge—if it is dead, then so is she.

But she was not. I found her on the porch, waiting for me, her eyes wide with anxiety, as if she could not be sure I was real.

And then she was in my arms, sobbing.

"I thought you had been killed," she whispered at last, her voice still ragged with tears. "You were so long—I thought the brigands had won and you had all been killed."

"You heard no news of our victory?"

"Nothing—and then, eight days ago, the soldiers came . . ."

She seemed so small, caught thus in my arms, as if she were still the child I had found on the wharf at Naukratis. What terrors had she known while I was gone? What had happened?

"Was anyone killed?" I took her by the shoulders, for she seemed suddenly unwilling to look at me. "Selana, if the hearth fire is dead . . . Was anyone . . .?"

"Yes, one, Master."

It was Kephalos' voice. He was standing in the doorway—I had not even noticed him. He looked gray and haggard, as if many nights had left him sleepless.

"Who then?"

"Your servant's servant, Lord. The boy Ganymedes."

"Know, Master, that I bear the youth Tullus no ill will over this, for all that happened was not his fault, since the threads of all our lives are caught up in the same web, and my poor boy was never pleasing to the Lady Nemesis. You will do me the justice, however, to remember that even when the woman Tanaquil came with her two sons I said things would end badly."

We sat together on the porch, sharing a third jar of wine—there are times when nothing else will serve. It was almost dark, but no one had thought of food. Kephalos had grown quite drunk, and in this I had kept him company, which was no more than a friend's office.

"The poets who sing of love as the gods' curse upon a man have hit upon a great and mysterious truth," he continued, his eyes damp with more than just surfeit of wine, for his grief was profound. "And the most cursed sort of love is that which lavishes itself upon an unworthy object—for know, Lord, that I was never blind to the depravity of Ganymedes' nature. I loved him with clear eyes, which is a torment fools are spared."

"How did he die?"

"Worthily, if you can credit such a thing. I suppose I ought even to be grateful to Tullus, for in the manner of his death my poor boy showed himself not entirely wicked. Do you suppose, Lord, that it is possible, in one final act of perfect nobility, to redeem a lifetime of selfishness?"

"I have no doubt of it. A man needs but a single occasion to show his true character."

"Or, at least, the possibility of what he might have been?"

"Yes."

"Then I am somewhat consoled. I mixed silver coins with the ashes in his funeral urn, that he might want for nothing on his journey to the Dark Realms. Promise me, Lord, that when I am dead you will bury me beside him."

And then he wept, long and bitterly. I put my arm over his shoulders to comfort him, even as one might a child, for the passion of his sorrow was like a child's, untempered and consuming.

It was only slowly, like the painful unwrapping of a wound, that I heard the full story.

"That was not a night for sleeping within four walls, Lord, for the air was as thick as millet gruel and it was so hot that only the black sky overhead showed that the sun had ever set. All of us had taken our sleeping mats outside that we might live in hope of some faint breeze from the sea. Thus it was we heard the king's soldiers approaching, the neighing of their horses and the sound of many hooves against the hard-packed earth. There would have been time for everyone to escape into the covering darkness.

"I had thought to hide myself in the vine arbor, and Ganymedes and I were retreating in that direction even as the soldiers entered our farmyard. I had seen Tullus and his brother running into the barn, which struck me as a foolish choice since the king's men, meaning to do mischief in your absence, would surely burn it. I confess I never guessed he . . .

"Then I heard Tullus' voice—he had come back out of the barn carrying a mattock, of all things, and he was shouting the most fearful curses: 'Your mothers mated with donkeys, you gelded bastards,' he yelled, 'I will kill you, all of you, murderers of my father.' There was more, although I hardly remember all of it. The boy was beside himself with rage.

"The soldiers, still on their horses, only laughed. Perhaps they would not even have harmed him, but who can ever know now? Yet the danger seemed real enough.

"It all happened without any warning—I do not believe there was anything I could have done to stop it. All at once Ganymedes began to wail in a high-pitched voice I had never heard before. I turned around to see what had possessed him, and he broke from me and began running back toward the farmyard. I shouted after him, but he paid no heed. He had already gone too far to be called back, for the soldiers had seen him.

"I suppose they must have imagined themselves attacked from two directions, if one can rightly speak of being 'attacked' by a pair of boys, one of whom is perfectly defenseless while the other wields nothing but a turnip digger. Yet men under such circumstances will panic at the slightest thing.

"By the time Ganymedes had reached Tullus to throw his arms about him—that seemed to be his only intention, to shield him with his own body—one of the horsemen was almost on top of them, bearing down at a gallop. He trampled over them both. I could see their bodies rolling under the horse's hooves.

"If there had been time or space even to frame the idea, I would have imagined them both dead, but my mind was filled with that horror which overtakes one at such moments. There was nothing else, only the shock that seemed to fill me with emptiness.

"And then, when I began to come a little back to myself, it was as if the god himself—your lonely, unforgiving god, who watches over you with such jealous eyes . . . I could almost have believed that Holy Ashur found a voice for everything that was in me.

"One of the soldiers was carrying a torch and had been attempting to set the farmhouse ablaze. The roof, it seemed, refused to catch fire, and at last, in simple frustration, he threw the torch from him. It landed at the foot of the chaste tree, which did not wait an instant before it began to burn furiously.

"I tell you truthfully, Master, had I not seen the thing for myself I would not have believed what happened then. I would not have believed it could happen."

He paused for a moment to take a swallow of wine and to wipe his mouth. His eyes glistened as the memory of all he had seen and felt in that terrible moment crowded back into his mind.

"The burning chaste tree seemed to light up the world, but only for an instant, as with the sudden flaring of a spark. There was hardly time to open one's eyes to the sight before the night's stillness was broken by the howling of a sudden, terrible wind that broke upon us as if it had been kicked down from the heavens and had struck the earth still rolling.

"It seemed to suck the very breath out of one's lungs, and the sound was like the howling of a wolf with a brass throat, only the wolf that could make such a sound would sleep in the bowels of Mount Aetna as if it were a fox hole. My Lord, I have never heard such a sound as that, and the wind that made it blew out the fire that nested in the chaste tree's branches as you or I might blow out an oil lamp.

"Surely it was a sign from the gods—and surely the soldiers took it for one, for they turned their horses and fled for their lives. We could hear the pounding of their hooves as they galloped away, for the instant they were gone the wind dropped to nothing and the night was once more still.

"When the wonder of it had left me a little, I remembered my poor boy. I ran to where he lay, but in my heart I already knew what I would find.

"The horse's hoof had broken open his skull as easily as if it had been the rind of a melon. His face was covered in blood so that his open eyes peered through it as one might through the slits in a mask. He seemed so surprised by death. I do not think it was at all what he had expected.

"Yet he had achieved his object, for Tullus was only a trifle bruised about the chest—in another ten or twelve days Tullus will not even carry the marks of what happened. As I have said, I do not begrudge him his life."

Kephalos at last stumbled off to bed, clutching the wine jar to his breast as if it were the corpse of his beloved Ganymedes. I stayed outside on the porch, turning over in my mind all that he had told me of the events of that fatal night, until Selana, who had tactfully stayed away all evening, came to sit by my side.

"He is much affected," she murmured, glancing back over her shoulder to the darkened house. "Every night he goes to bed stiff with wine, and every night he weeps until at last sleep releases him. One cannot withhold one's pity."

"What he said about a great wind putting out the fire—was that truth?"

"The fire in the chaste tree? Yes, it was like the gods' blind rage. And then it was over—why?"

Why indeed? The king's soldiers, in a careless moment, had set fire to the chaste tree, beneath which the sibyl used to speak with the god's own voice, a spot made sacred by her presence, and the gods had answered this impiety. I remembered what Epeios had once said of the Lord of the Sicels: *"There is a prophecy that his line will rule until one of their number has despoiled some holy place."*

XXX

"THE KING HAS AN ARMY TO DO HIS BIDDING. NOT A BAND of brigands good for nothing except raiding farmhouses, but real army. And not only is his force twice the size of ours, but many of his soldiers fought in the wars against Quertus, king of Gela. If one discounts the recent adventure against Collatinus—and I think we must discount it, for thieves will be chased away by a barking watchdog—there is only one among us who has had any actual experience of war. Or at least he claims as much for himself. So far, I am personally unconvinced that Tiglath has proved that he is anything except lucky."

It was Peisenor who spoke. His words were reasonable enough, but he seemed to spit them out as if they tasted of poison, and thus he betrayed himself. Sometimes men make themselves your enemy on the merest whim.

The leaders of the Greek assembly, those whose voices made themselves heard in debate, looked to me, their eyes full of questions. My prestige as a commander stood high, for Collatinus' head was on a stake before the city gates, but at such times only a word can fill the mind with doubt.

"We too are now an army," I said. "Men who have been blooded on the field of battle are not barking dogs. I have no misgivings about leading the Naxos militia against Ducerius, and I do not care if he has three times our numbers. I believe the gods favor us, and I know that the Greeks can fight. I think the time has come to bring an end to this petty despot."

"Tiglath is right—only look about you!" Diocles waved his heavy fist in the air, as if inviting us to inspect that instead. "The king's soldiers roam the countryside, plundering and murdering us at their will. *His* soldiers, no longer brigands but his own men. The mask is off. By the Mouse God's navel, what choice does the king give us when it is *he* who declares war?"

Peisenor gave him a look that would have withered grass, and then turned aside with a contemptuous sniff.

"Diocles will start a quarrel over a spilled cup of wine, and a man who is always as sore as the boils on his backside makes a bad counselor. I say the king only wishes us to disband this foolish militia and return to our plows."

"Oh yes—he wishes that, no doubt. Let us disband the militia, and then he will crush us at once!"

"You dull clod of a Spartan . . ."

"Cease this!"

Old Halitherses stepped between the two men. I think, had he not, there might have been the shedding of blood.

"Cease at once! If we fight each other, we do the king's work for him. Peisenor, you have the manners of a Hittite, yet perhaps it is wisest to be careful. What do you say, Epeios? In the past you have opposed Tiglath's ideas of meeting violence with violence, yet you were with him at the Salito Plain—what is your advice?"

Epeios smiled lamely and shrugged his shoulders, as if to disclaim any opinion worth listening to.

"I am done opposing Tiglath," he said. "He has been right too often, and if the gods are not with us, as he claims, they certainly seem to be with him. If Tiglath says we will be victorious against Ducerius, I am prepared to take his word for it."

"Yes, victorious . . ." Peisenor made a sour face. "Soldiers always talk of victory, as if that were all that mattered. But at what cost will this victory be achieved? How many good men, Tiglath, will you leave dead on the field? How many Greek widows will your victory produce?"

"How many widows will surrender produce? Would you prefer to abandon this place and return to wherever you came from, or will you fight—and take the chance of dying—that you, or at least your sons, can live here in peace?"

We had been standing on the porch of Halitherses' house, from which it was possible to look east over the hills all the way to the curling sea. So many of the Greeks had built their houses to face the sea that sometimes I wondered if perhaps, like the Phoenicians, they did not a little distrust the solid land and long always to be moving across the smooth, empty water to the temptations of some new place.

Yet not I. Fate had decided that I was to lay down my bones in Sicily, and I could not find it in me to wish for anything else.

Thus there could be no compromise with Ducerius.

"But these things are not for me to decide," I went on, turning my eyes from the shoreline, against which the white waves soundlessly rolled. "My six months as Tyrant are nearly finished, and I am ready to answer for all that I have done in that time. What happens now is a matter you must settle among yourselves. You know my opinion, so there is nothing left for me to say on the matter."

When I went home that afternoon, nothing had yet been settled. I turned my mind to other things, but always I was like a man who waits to hear his child crying in the night.

Three days later a messenger came from Naxos. The assembly had voted to renew me as Tyrant for another six months.

Peisenor spoke bitterly against the appointment, so I was told. And after the vote was taken he went straight to Ducerius' citadel and threw himself upon the king's protection. Thus were the sides chosen in this war.

Naxos was not a defensible position, and I had no intention of allowing the militia to be trapped inside her walls the way we had trapped Collatinus, so I gave orders that all men under arms, along with their families, were to withdraw to the Plain of Clonios, from which we would at least be free to retreat if Ducerius should move against us before we were ready to force battle. Predictably, this caused a considerable outcry.

"The king's soldiers will be left free to loot our homes and shops," I was told. "What is the point of our having an army if we leave everything we intended to defend at the mercy of our enemies?"

"You have your lives, and those of your women and children. At the moment, they are all we can be concerned with defending."

"Even if we win, we will be beggars. Ducerius will burn our houses."

"That he will probably do in any case, but at least you will not be in them."

"We will starve even before we have a chance to be killed in battle."

"When Ducerius is dead, and we occupy his citadel, you can eat his food at his table. Believe me, he will not object."

I spoke many such brave words. And brave words are very fine, yet wars usually have more cautious beginnings than one would gather from listening to the commander's speeches, and opponents try each other's strengths many times in furtive, whispered exchanges before ever sword rings against sword in the fierce dissonance of combat. It is almost as if the two sides must first agree between themselves who will be the victor and who the vanquished, and only later is this accord sealed in blood.

Thus, even as the Plain of Clonios filled with Greeks in flight from Ducerius' soldiers, neither we nor the Sicel king were so eager to commit ourselves to war that first we did not at least try to reach some settlement—or, to speak true, his ministers tried, for Ducerius himself seemed abandoned to his wrath.

"I will agree to anything that does not compromise the safety or well-being of my neighbors," I told the gray-bearded Sicel nobleman who rode down under flag of truce from his master's citadel to see if there was any way of avoiding open conflict. "Thus I will not disband the militia, for your king is not a man to be trusted."

"He must consider his honor. He will never agree to terms until the Greeks lay down their weapons."

"Then he will have no need to agree to anything—he will simply massacre us. Do you really imagine I am such a fool as that?"

He smiled tightly, as if to say, "Perhaps not, but the king seems to."

"Your force is small compared to ours," he said, perhaps instead of saying something else. "You cannot hope for anything more than defeat."

"So Collatinus thought—perhaps you have seen his head where I left it for the world's admiration, spiked by the city gate."

"Our citadel is not a stockade of wood. No one has ever taken it."

"I will remind you of that when you are caught inside her stone walls, beaten and starving."

This made an impression, if only because he saw that I meant it. He was silent for a moment, as if listening to some inner voice.

"What would you accept as a guarantee of safety?" he asked at last.

"Ducerius' life."

"Nothing less?"

"Nothing less. Abandon him—the Greeks and the Sicels had no quarrel before he made one.

He did not answer. Instead he turned his horse and rode back to the citadel, but the seed was planted. It is always wise to let an enemy know he has a way out if he can bring himself to take it.

Selana, Kephalos and all our household had joined the general migration and so were with me on the Plain of Clonios. Like all the others in flight from the king's soldiers, they pitched a tent and cooked our meals over an open fire and complained that they had been abandoned by the gods—all, strangely enough, except Kephalos, who still remained in a trance of grief, who looked about at the bustle of camp life with weary, tear-filled eyes as if searching for some escape from himself. He had even given up drinking wine. I began to be seriously worried about him.

"He would have been well enough at home," Selana told me. "He could have tended Ganymedes' grave and at last found consolation. It is being here—he feels abandoned by life in all this bustle where he finds no place for himself. I know how it is with him, for am I much the same myself. Do you think, Master, that we shall ever see our home again?"

"Yes. When this is over, then we will go home."

"But will it still be there for us? Or will the Sicel king have burned it down and laid all that we made there waste?"

"I think we can hope not. With us camped here under his very walls, I think he will feel but little inclination to send his men off raiding farmhouses. He is not that confident of his strength. He will want to concentrate his forces in this one place and wait to see what we will do."

"Then why do you not say this to the others? They all believe that they have lost everything."

"Because they will fight better for believing thus. They will think not of compromise but of revenge. Every man is braver for imagining that he has nothing left to lose."

She stared at me for a moment, as if she no longer knew who I was, and then at last she let her eyes drop to the ground.

"Try not to dwell on it," I told her, putting my arm across her shoulders. "If I am ruthless and deceiving it is only because I must be. I have all our lives in my hands and I must think only of victory, for it was to this end that they elected me Tyrant. When we are all safe again, then I shall be as I was."

I did not know whether she believed me, for she said nothing.

We started with a farm wagon. We kept the tongue and front wheels, lightening them for speed, and mounted an armored platform over the axle. When we had harness for two horses, we had a chariot. I do not think the royal stables at Nineveh would have been impressed, but it would do well enough against Ducerius.

"We will need body armor for the horses," I told Diocles. "And we will need to find a pair that will run together and not grow skittish at the sound of battle."

"Tiglath, you are a fool," he answered. "You are going to drive this thing into a formation of armed men? They will kill you before you have completed your first pass."

"I have done it before. Besides, I did not claim it was without risk."

He shook his head and I grinned at him, trying to forget that this was only a farm wagon we had fitted up, that I would be driving horses unused to running together, remembering only that Ducerius had at least two men for every one of ours and that we had to do something.

"The hammer weighs less than the building stone, but the hammer is harder and can smash it to pieces—particularly if the stone already has a few cracks in it. That is what I propose to do: crack the Sicel lines so that our own men can break through."

"I will see to it that your funeral games are properly splendid," Diocles said, frowning.

Callias was no more enthusiastic when I called on him to lend me his stallion.

"He is not a cart horse," he told me, with some asperity. "He has never been in halter. Besides, this scheme of yours does not fill me with confidence that I will ever get him back."

"We all must make sacrifices, Callias—some of us will be sacrificing our lives."

He regarded me in resentful silence, for he knew I would not have asked if I had been prepared to accept a refusal.

"You will not find another to pair him with," he said finally.

"Pylades the Theban has a horse he claims can outrun any in Sicily."

"They will fight—my Xanthos will not tolerate another stallion. He will kick until the chest of Pylades' nag looks like a crushed eggshell."

The thought of what awaited Pylades' stallion seemed to satisfy him, and he fetched his pampered Xanthos for me. After a little initial friction, which Pylades' Chiron concluded by biting Xanthos on the neck, they worked together quite harmoniously. By the middle of the afternoon I had accustomed the two horses to pulling in tandem and to turning, which is the real difficulty in driving chariots.

There was nothing left to do, except to goad Ducerius into taking the field.

The noose was tightening. Tomorrow, or the next day, the king's soldiers would come down from their citadel and everything would be settled between Greeks and Sicels, perhaps for as long as men lived on this island. I knew this, if no one else did, for I knew that the Greeks could not wait much longer without losing heart for this fight. Time was with the enemy—perhaps Ducerius knew this too.

I sat beside Selana's fire, eating her lamb and millet with my fingers, looking at the faces around me and wondering if I had not been a vain fool to take up this quarrel. But perhaps tomorrow, or the next day, my head would be on a stake alongside Collatinus', and then I would care no more than he did.

Tullus worked at his dinner with sullen concentration. I had watched him watching the Greeks at their drill, and I knew what was in his mind. He thought of his murdered father, and he dreamed of fighting in this battle that must come and of taking his vengeance. Such thoughts were dangerous in one so young.

When the meal was over I summoned him to me.

"I wish you to do me a service."

"Lord, I am yours to command," he answered, almost resentfully.

"Yes, but this is not a service that one man may command of another. And, besides, you are not a Greek and nothing obliges you to make our quarrel your own."

His eyes brightened at once.

"You would have me fight?" He drew himself up very straight, but still he was only a boy, hardly reaching my breast. "I will gladly fight, and you will find me no coward."

"Any fool can be a soldier," I said, "but if you do as I ask, and succeed, you will move Ducerius closer to his destruction than any man in the front line of battle."

He was disappointed, yet he said nothing, waiting.

"You know the chief men among the Sicel peasants, those to whom the others will listen. Go to them. Persuade them to withhold their support from Ducerius, or at least to wait and see how things go with him. Carry this message to them: that Tiglath Ashur, Tyrant of Naxos, wishes only that Greek and Sicel might live together in peace, that after Ducerius there will be no king over them, nor will the Greeks oppress them."

"Only this, Lord? Only to speak your words? This is nothing."

"It is not nothing, Tullus. I need at least the neutrality of the Sicels, for this war may not end with a single battle. And you must be very careful—if the king's soldiers find you, they will certainly kill you."

This made him happy. I had made the thing dangerous for him, and so he was pleased. He nodded his acceptance.

"Go tonight, under the cover of darkness. Travel by foot and stay away from the main roads. Do not return here. I will know whether you have succeeded by how things fare with Ducerius."

He was gone as soon as the moon rose, and I had the pleasure of thinking that there was one at least who would be alive when the world had been won or lost.

"You have sent him away?" Kephalos asked. "That is wise. It would not, however, be wise to send me away as well."

I had not even heard him approach. I turned around to find him standing behind me, clutching a rolled-up blanket in his arms. When he saw he had my attention he knelt down on the ground and unrolled the blanket. Inside were a leather corselet and a sword.

"I purchased these in Naxos, the morning of the same day I went to the temple of Hestia to take fire to relight the hearth after Ganymedes' death. I mean to fight with the rest when we meet the king's army. I will not run away or shame you in any way—do not deny me this, Master, for it is a thing I must do."

"You have no experience of war, Kephalos. Nor have you trained."

"You forget that I was conscripted as a soldier at Tyre when your father's armies besieged the city, and I still remember a few things. Besides, I have for many years served one whom many call the greatest soldier living. No man will put himself at risk by standing beside me in battle."

"I would not have you killed then," I said. "You are my oldest friend, Kephalos, and I cannot do without you."

"I cannot do without this, Lord. I must do something to avenge my dear boy's death. I cannot stand apart."

His eyes pleaded with me. I knew it was a wicked thing to do, but I knew just as well that he would never be whole again if I refused him this chance.

"Very well—but if you let yourself be slain, Kephalos, I will never forgive you."

He began to say something, but a sob caught in his throat so he merely embraced me, gathered up his war gear, and went back into the tent to find his rest.

Perhaps tonight he will be quiet in his heart, I thought.

It was long past midnight when I lay down myself. Selana had been waiting for me, knowing how I would need her, and even as I lay in her arms, even as sleep closed over my mind, I thought I could hear Death flapping her black wings.

XXXI

EVERY MORNING DUCERIUS SENT OUT AN ARMED PATROL
of ten or twelve riders to survey the perimeter of our camp, this as much
as a display of strength, to intimidate the Greeks and to show that he did
not regard himself as being under siege, as for any tactical reason. And
every morning we had let these patrols go uncontested, for until we were
ready to engage the Sicel army directly I saw no point in wearing away
our strength with pointless skirmishes.

Today, however, was to be another matter. Today I intended to
provoke the king into battle. And, since the gods always oblige those who
court danger, I succeeded better than I could have hoped.

It was not more than a quarter of an hour past dawn, while the ground
was still covered with mist, that the Sicels, twelve men in splendid war
gear and mounted on twelve matched black stallions—not common
soldiers these, so who could they be who rode out like the king's guard on
parade?—cantered down the road from the citadel gate and onto the
Plain of Clonios. The lead horseman, clearly their officer, was a
particularly grand specimen, for his leather corselet sparkled with a
hundred little silver disks and his beard was elaborately curled and
glistened with so much scented oil that a dead man could have smelled it
at fifty paces.

"By the Mouse God's navel, what a peacock!" exclaimed Diocles. "It is
easy to see that he fancies himself, and who can blame him?"

"I only hope he is quarrelsome as well as vain."

For our problem was to provoke a fight. We needed an incident to force
Ducerius into taking the field, something that his self-esteem would not
allow him to ignore. We needed to shame him into battle.

We had eight riders of our own and thirty-five foot soldiers arranged in one small battle square. Diocles and I stood next to each other in the second rank, and I took the outside position so that I could remain in contact with our cavalry, who, since they would be no match for the enemy horsemen, were under orders to stay to the rear unless things went very badly. Thus we could challenge the Sicels, taunting them with our presence, but we could not force them to engage if they were not inclined to it, since they only had to ride away. Nothing would serve if Ducerius was a prudent man, willing to wait, but I did not have that impression of him.

Every morning the Sicel patrols followed the same route, around the base of the great stone hill upon which Ducerius' citadel was built and across a kind of no-man's-land separated from the Greek encampment by a ravine that had held no water within living memory. At the edge of this ravine they would stop and peer across at us as if trying to decide which among our women they would take as their share of the booty after they had killed all the men—this, needless to say, had a very unsettling effect, which was doubtless their intention.

We were waiting for them on the far side of the ravine, and it was from there that we trotted out to try provoking the Sicel horsemen into a fight. Thus we reversed their accustomed route so that the wide track of hoofmarks they had etched into the dust over so many days was partially obliterated by our sandalprints.

After some two hundred paces we stopped. They were just beginning to make their wide turn onto the plain and we would be directly in their way. Now they had either to face us or to go around.

They began to trot straight for us. I kept expecting their horses to break into a gallop, but they did not. It was as if they were merely curious to inspect some harmless, inanimate object they had found unexpectedly in their path.

"Are they really such fools?" I found myself asking—a trifle surprised at the sound of my own voice. It had been a mistake to speak thus, for I could sense a flutter of apprehension passing through the men. Now I had no choice but to take the offensive.

"Well—if they are in such a hurry to die, let them. Archers ready!"

We waited until they were within range, then I dropped my arm and a throbbing of bowstrings filled the air with arrows. Two of the enemy riders fell from their horses, dead or wounded. There was a moment of confusion, and then the rest, chastened, retreated to a safe distance.

At last the Sicel patrol gathered in a little knot. From a distance they seemed to be debating among themselves what they should do next. The two groups stood facing each other. We seemed to have reached an impasse.

And then—and it was a remarkable piece of folly, the sort of defiant gesture one might expect from a child—the Sicel officer drew a little forward of his companions, drew his sword and flourished it in the air.

"It is well known the Greeks make war like women, hiding behind each other's skirts," he shouted. "There is more honor to be had in spanking a saucy harlot than in killing the whole lot of you."

What was this about? I wondered. Did he imagine this to be a game?

"Not one among you has scrotum enough to come out of hiding and fight like a man."

He laughed, mightily pleased with himself, and he flourished his sword a few more times above his head. I doubt he ever imagined that anyone would accept his challenge.

There were ugly mutterings among my Greeks, but for myself I was highly pleased. I took three javelins from my quiver and handed the rest to Diocles.

"What ails you, Tiglath?" he whispered through his teeth, grabbing me by the tunic when he saw what I intended. "Have you suddenly gone stupid?"

I only smiled. Diocles was always worrying that I would get myself killed. His face crumpled with something like grief, and he released me.

I stepped out from the battle square and into the open, feeling almost naked.

"You had best put that sword away, little boy, before you cut yourself!" I shouted. "Or perhaps your mother dulled the edge before she let her baby play with it."

A few of his soldiers, apparently understanding a word or two of Greek, laughed, and the officer's face darkened with anger. Since he had been fool enough to have picked this quarrel, he wouldn't have the sense to back away now.

I ran seventy-five or eighty paces to the side, far enough that I was no longer covered by my own men's weapons but still close enough to get back if the Sicels charged me in a body—I did not, however, think they would do that.

"I am waiting, Pretty One."

He needed no further encouragement. Goading his stallion first to a trot and then to a canter, he began angling toward me, cutting this way and that, trying to get in close before he charged and made himself a target for my dart.

I waited. I had played this game before.

As I had thought he would, he crouched down by his stallion's neck as he urged him to a gallop, letting his sword swing back to front so that it would catch me like a hook. I suppose he imagined I would wait there patiently until he killed me.

A spring to one side saved my life. I scrambled to my feet, and as the Sicel officer, realizing that I had evaded him, started to bridle in his horse, I set myself for a throw.

An old soldier would have kept his horse to a run until he was well clear. He would not have straightened up to look back at me. But this one, clearly, had fought all his battles on the training field—it simply hadn't occurred to him that the initiative was not entirely his own.

I let myself uncoil like a snake. The javelin left my hand, arching through the air, and then fell. Its point went straight through the Sicel officer's bowels.

He slid from his horse's back as if his legs had gone dead, but he was still alive when I walked up on him, clutching with both hands the javelin that was sticking out just below his belt, as if he might have been trying to keep it from moving. As I stood over him he looked up at me with glistening, pain-filled eyes, his face bathed in sweat. His lips formed some word that he no longer had breath to speak, and then, suddenly, he was a corpse.

Their horses nervously stamping the dusty earth, the Sicels watched and argued among themselves in excited words which, at that distance, faded away to nothing. There was no predicting what they would do now—they hardly seemed to know themselves—but it was not a moment to be left exposed on open ground. I gave a signal and in an instant our own horsemen surrounded me, and Diocles led the foot soldiers over until we all stood about staring at the body of my vanquished adversary.

"In the name of the deathless gods, Tiglath, do you have any idea who this is you have killed?" It was the Boeotian Cretheos who spoke.

"Enlighten me."

"By the Mouse God's navel, he's right, Tiglath!"

Diocles pushed his way forward and peered down into the dead man's face.

"I saw him not a year ago, when Ducerius came down to Naxos harbor to welcome some Italian ambassador—this is Volesus, the king's son, his sole heir!"

"You mean, he *was*. Hah!"

I shook my head, but little inclined to laugh at Cretheos' wit, as I remembered the burning of the chaste tree and marveled at the god's cunning.

"That means the line of succession is broken," I said, almost to myself. "Already Ducerius has begun to pay for his impiety."

We carried Volesus' body back to camp with us, and the sun was still two hours from its zenith when an emissary came down from the citadel bearing a flowering tree branch in token of truce. I met him outside my tent, with the black stallion, my rightful prize, tethered only a few paces away. I knew what the man sought, and I had already considered what answer I would make.

"The king my master wishes to know what ransom you will accept for the corpse of his son," he said. He was an elderly chamberlain dressed in the black tunic of a mourner, and he regarded me with doglike eyes as if he expected a kick.

"You may tell your master that I will take no ransom, that he will not have his son's corpse back, not if he offered me the whole of Sicily for it. Tell him that I regard Volesus as having sought this death, for no one but a man sick of his life would have hazarded it against Tiglath Ashur, the son and grandson of kings who would have put a ring through Ducerius' nose and fed him on scraps from the tables of their slaves. Tell him further that Greeks do not offend the eyes of the immortal gods with a suicide's funeral rites, and thus Volesus' corpse will be burned at night and his ashes will be scattered over the sea."

The old man was so horrified at this that for a long moment he altogether seemed to lose his power of speech. Finally he reached up and dragged his hands over his beard, giving the impression he needed to be reassured it was still there.

"That which you contemplate is an offense against all decency," he said at last. "The Sicels do not burn their dead, and for a thousand years their kings have been buried in the royal crypt. Would you deny the Lord King his right to pour out offerings of wine and honey over the body of his only son? Is not your vengeance satisfied that my master will now be the last of his line?"

"My vengeance is satisfied, but that of the gods is like the dry sand that will drink tears forever and know no end."

"Then at least might I be allowed to see the prince's corpse, that his father may know the manner of his death?"

"Of course."

I had already ordered the funeral pyre built, at a spot not far from a gully that was being used as the camp's refuse pit—a fact which was not lost on the king's emissary. The dead prince, stripped down to his loincloth, lay on a bed of logs, ready to receive the torch. His belly was still bathed in blood, and the wound under his rib cage was large enough that a man might have slipped three fingers into it.

"An hour after sunset," I said, "I will light the fire with my own hand. Then Ducerius will never know if the dust the sightless wind blows in his face might not have mixed in it the ashes of his own son."

"Is there no way then my master can reclaim the Lord Volesus' corpse?"

The old man's voice was full of tears—the gods knew what wrath he faced when he returned—and I pitied him. Yet one to whom the lives of many have been entrusted must learn a certain shamelessness.

"There is one."

We could still see the walls of Ducerius' citadel from where we stood, and as I glanced up at them I found myself wondering if the king might not even now be watching us from his battlements. I found the idea strangely distasteful.

It was almost with relief that I turned back to his emissary.

"As I have said, I will stay my torch through this day. The Lord Ducerius has that long to win back his son's corpse by the might of his hand."

As I watched the old man ride back to report to his master all that I had said, I thought, It is decided. He cannot refuse now, or he will be shamed forever. Before the sun sets, the deathless gods will have chosen between us.

It was three hours before sunset as we ranged for battle across the empty plain. Every man knew what we risked on this one throw of the lots. Save for the wind, whispering through the dry grass like the voice of prophecy, there was hardly a sound.

The horses seemed aware that something was about to happen. They snorted tensely and changed their footing, making the chariot rock back and forth, back and forth, so that I had to hold them in check with the reins. We all waited, men and animals alike.

And then, at last, the great gate to the citadel opened out and columns of men began to file through and down the road to the plain. Very quickly we could see that this was not a patrol in force but an army. Ducerius had taken the bait.

They came down in rows of four abreast, and the first had almost reached the plain before we saw the end. At the very least four hundred men, about fifty of them mounted and the rest on foot. In his determination to crush us, the king held nothing back.

There is little enough that one can tell from the mere appearance of soldiers, and a commander watching his enemy must always beware of seeing only what he most wishes or fears to see. I saw an army of seasoned men, confident, even arrogant, expecting to make quick work of us and to be back in their barracks for supper. This might be good or bad, depending on how the Greeks stood the first shock of battle.

They carried few spears but trusted to their short swords, for combat to them was but a series of personal duels. Their arms were of bronze and thus we had the advantage of them in weaponry, yet a man can die upon the point of a wooden stake if he lacks either skill or luck. I did not think that iron or bronze would make the difference.

And they had no chariots, this being a style of warfare unknown to them. We had one, of indifferent construction, driven by a pair of horses that until the day before had never pulled together. It was a questionable asset.

If the Greeks held, how much blood would these Sicels be willing to spill on the contest field? How badly did they wish to triumph?

The whole art of war is the application of strength against an opponent's weakness—what was their weakness? I had little enough time to discover it.

I wheeled the chariot out in front of the five battle squares into which the Greek militia was arranged. Back and forth I rode, back and forth, encouraging them while we waited for Ducerius' army to draw up into ranks.

"Hold it in your minds that this army has but one neck—we have only to hack it through and we will triumph, no matter how many soldiers they field. Drive for the center. Break them without being broken. Only have the bowels to conquer and by sunset their women will be howling like beaten dogs. Ducerius the king thinks he will make a meal of us, but so did the bandit Collatinus and we brought his head home in a leather bag. Be stubborn—take them by the throat and do not let go until your jaws close."

"We will be dog soldiers," someone called out from the ranks, making everyone laugh.

"And, Tiglath, you thief, mind you take good care of my horse," I heard Callias shout after me. The men were in high spirits—frightened, as was only reasonable, but cheerful.

All the time, as the Greeks bandied jests with me and with each other, I had one eye for Ducerius' army, watching as they formed their lines for battle.

And that was all they were—merely lines, five rows of men, one after the other, separated by eight or ten paces. They thought they could overwhelm us with sheer numbers. We would have to see.

It is not an easy thing to face so many men across perhaps a hundred paces of empty plain. The waiting is what makes it hard.

Then, quite suddenly, it began. As if startled awake, the Sicel horsemen charged, screaming wildly as they brandished their swords overhead. It was beautiful, in its way.

My men had forgotten nothing since the campaign against the brigands. When the enemy riders had crossed half the distance to our lines, the five battle squares launched their arrows, in five waves following one upon the other. I think perhaps as many as twelve of the Sicels dropped lifeless from their saddles or had their horses killed under them—of itself it was almost enough to break their charge. A second volley, and then a third, and no more than twenty of the enemy horsemen reached our lines.

And of these, many perished on the spears of our first line, but the rest—those who broke in on men who had not fought on the Salito Plain, or had not learned its cruel lessons—before they were driven off, those few brought a terrible slaughter to the Greeks. In war men pay with their blood when they forget to angle their spears properly, or suffer an instant of failing courage, and many were crushed beneath the hooves of the Sicel horses, even as those horses stumbled and died, spilling their guts onto the parched ground.

Yet that one charge, bitter and costly though it was, was the last Ducerius' cavalry could mount against us. When it had spent itself, the king's horsemen could only mill aimlessly about, hacking at spearmen here and there, reduced to a nuisance rather than a threat.

From then on it was a foot soldier's war.

And it was only after the cavalry charge that the battle began for me. I had driven the chariot out, hoping to distract the Sicels a little and to help blunt their attack, but they seemed not to know what to make of me and, being more agile, declined my challenge and kept away. But when Ducerius unleashed the first two waves of his infantry, men who had only their own legs to carry them, then my moment came.

There is nothing like a chariot for spreading terror. And terror is the mother of confusion, whose child is defeat. I cannot claim I killed so many Sicels that day, although more than a few bodies were broken beneath my wheels, but I made the king's soldiers know that fear which burns on the tongue like the taste of copper. They learned there was no safety in their lines of attack and their short swords. I scattered them like the dust.

When first they beheld me driving down upon them, their mouths dropped open with astonishment. They seemed unable to move, as if they could hardly believe that I actually intended to ride over them. And at the last second they parted before me—those who were quick enough—like standing grain before the charge of a wild boar. As I passed I gave out death with a generous hand, stabbing many with my javelin.

There is an excitement in battle that is like no other. Men hacked at me with their swords. Arrows flew past me, yet I heeded them no more than the buzzing of flies. I did not think of danger. I felt as if my skin were gray iron that nothing could pierce. I was not so much brave as, I think, a little mad.

But I taught the Sicels fear. Their lines weakened, they had no time to reform them, and when they charged our battle squares they broke as does the sea against an outcropping of rock.

And my valiant Greeks, how they fought! Theirs was not the witless frenzy of war but the true, steady courage of men who face death with cold hearts. And many did die, for the Sicels were true soldiers and understood the arts of killing. But the Greeks never faltered. They kept their squares tight, and when a man in the first rank fell, another stood in his place before his spear could touch the ground. Where the Sicels each fought bravely, each one alone, the Greeks fought bravely together, making of themselves an engine of slaughter.

Ducerius released wave after wave of his soldiers, but as the Sicel attack began to weaken, the five battle squares began to advance. The middle square pushed ahead of the others so that the whole was like a wedge, splitting the enemy in two, and those unlucky enough to be caught between our formations were ground as under a millstone.

It was a time of great carnage, and many men died on both sides. I tore back and forth across the field until at last my chariot lost a wheel and I had to cut the horses free and fight my way back to the Greek lines, killing four men before I reached them.

No one even greeted me as I took my place in the front line—there was no time. We were all covered with sweat and bloody dirt. There was no glory now, only the hard, hazardous work of war as we fought to live and conquer.

I caught a glimpse of Ducerius only at the end. I saw him riding away on his fine stallion, back up to his citadel, followed by a group of officers. It was a clear sign he knew the day was lost.

I was not the only one who witnessed Ducerius' flight, and men will not fight when they have been deserted by their leaders. Defeat spread among the king's soldiers like a contagion. Just as they had made war as individuals, as individuals, first one and then another, they decided they were beaten. As with one who suddenly realizes that his hand is in the bear's mouth, they started to pull back, and soon they were running away in a mob. Theirs was not a withdrawal, but a rout.

What followed was little less than a massacre. With a wave of my hand I called in our horsemen, who had been waiting until that moment, and they swooped down upon the scattering army like hawks after mice. In their panicked flight the Sicels left behind them a wide trail of corpses.

At last, exhausted, we gave up our pursuit. Ducerius' army was in full retreat, streaming back toward his citadel, leaving fully two thirds of his men dead or dying on the field. We looked about us, feeling like butchers. None of us had any more taste for killing.

The sun was already on the horizon. In a quarter of an hour it would be dark. As the battle ended, the Greek women took possession of the field their men had won. Some looted corpses, the rest tended the wounded and the dying.

But most of us walked away from this battle. We looked about us, a little astonished to be alive, none more so than Kephalos, who had sustained a cut about three fingers wide just above the elbow. It was bleeding copiously but did not look dangerous—indeed, he seemed very pleased with it.

"We won," he exclaimed, so breathless that the words were hardly more than a murmur. "Master, we have conquered."

His eyes were wet, whether from joy or simple fatigue it was impossible to say, but he was a happy man.

"Yes—now all debts are paid."

"Yes." He nodded, several times, as if the significance of the fact were only just the beginning to sink in. "Yes, now all debts are paid."

"Have that wound cleaned out," I told him. "Have one of the women—"

"I shall see to it myself, Lord," he said, taking his hand away to examine the blood on his fingers. "I am, after all, a physician, and the pain is nothing."

I watched him trudge back to our camp, weary but satisfied. He would be all right now. There would be a limit to his grief, for he had avenged

Ganymedes and was at peace with himself. And he would have a fine scar to prove it. That was all, just a scar.

Not everyone, however, had been so fortunate.

"Tiglath?"

I heard a weak voice and glanced down. It was Diocles, lying on the ground, half covered by his shield and with a sword cut in his side—the hand that held it together was caked with blood. I knelt down beside him. He smiled.

"We won," he murmured. His joy was the same as Kephalos', as that of all the others, a mixture of astonishment and relief. It did not seem to matter that he had sacrificed his life to achieve it.

"By the Mouse God's . . ."

And then death darkened his eyes.

I rose to my feet, black anger welling up in me once more, as if this battle were still to be fought.

But we had won. Diocles had at least seen us victorious, although his life was only one of many this victory had cost us. In all, some thirty-two Greeks perished on the Plain of Clonios, a heavy toll in a force of less than two hundred men, yet our own losses were small compared to the enemy's. The next morning, when it was light enough to survey the field, we counted over three hundred Sicel corpses. The army of Ducerius had been bled white.

When we gathered up our dead, and their ashes were in copper urns for their families to bury, it was time to think what must come next. It was time to turn our eyes to the stone walls of Ducerius' citadel and to consider how we might end this war.

And no more did I need to worry that the Greeks would lose heart, for victory had turned their courage into recklessness.

"We should press our initiative. Let us attack the acropolis at once!"

"And will you run it through the belly with your sword?" I would ask. "It is not a man—you cannot slay it. The problem is not so simple as that. Ducerius will not come out, so how will you get in?"

This forced them to think, which was at least a beginning. They raised their heads to gaze at the sheer rock faces that surrounded the only road up, trying to imagine what it would be like to storm such a heavily fortified position, and a little of their bravado left them.

"Can it be done?"

"Can what be done?"

"Can the acropolis be taken?"

"Possibly—provided everyone is willing to pay the price. I am speaking of at least three months of hazardous, back-breaking labor to make a breach in the walls and then an assault in which perhaps one out of every three of us will be killed. And the attack, of course, might be repulsed. There are no guarantees of success, but the thing can be attempted."

"Perhaps they can be starved out!"

"Does any one us know for certain how much food they may have in storage? Enough for four months? Six? And how are we to feed ourselves while we keep them under siege? We cannot simply slink back to our farms and expect them to wait quietly up there until we have finished our harvest. And if we plunder the Sicel peasants of their grain and livestock, we will have an enemy at our backs as well as ahead of us. I do not believe that way holds much promise of success. I do not believe our people are prepared to be that patient."

"Then what you say is that we are beaten."

"No. That is not what I say."

"Then what, Tiglath?"

Then what, Tiglath? This was the gods' punishment upon my arrogance, for in honesty I was forced to admit—at least to myself—that I had no idea.

"I will consider this matter," I told them.

And this I did. And the more I considered it, the more entangling the problem seemed to become.

Had I been in command of one of my father's armies, there would have been no difficulty. The soldiers of Ashur fought for the glory of their king and their god, and thus they did not question if a thing should or should not be done, or if the prize was worth the labor and risk of seizing it. They had camped for fifteen months outside the walls of Babylon, painstakingly undermining the walls and waiting for the order to attack, and all because the Lord Sennacherib, King of the Earth's Four Corners, had willed it thus.

The Greeks were not so. They had no king, and the sense that they were now a community to which each man owed allegiance, even unto death, had as yet shallow roots. And, of course, their gods were lazy, pleasure-loving creatures, too indifferent to the affairs of men to be concerned with the outcome of one little war fought out on a distant island. No sensible Greek ever went to war for the glory of *his* gods.

Thus I feared to begin this siege of Ducerius' citadel, for when the walls did not come down after half a month my neighbors would start quarreling among themselves, and soon the men who had conquered a mighty enemy on the field of battle would simply melt away, leaving final victory behind them as their thoughts turned to their farms and their accustomed lives. I did not want the Sicel king left thus unpunished. I felt I still owed that debt to the men who had perished here on the Plain of Clonios.

But sometimes when a man cannot see to do a thing for himself, luck and the bright gods will do it for him.

Three days after the battle, at first light, a rider came down from the citadel under token of truce. He dismounted and led his horse to the center of the battlefield, where I and other members of the Greek council walked out to meet him. He was the same man whom Ducerius had sent once before.

"I would speak with the Lord Tiglath Ashur," he said as his first words, glaring around at my colleagues as if he thought each of them concealed a dagger in his cloak.

"There is nothing you can say which these men are not privileged to hear," I answered.

Nevertheless, he only shook his head, maintaining a grim silence.

"Oh, very well then," said Epeios, dismissing the matter with a wave. "Tiglath, I suppose we can depend on you not to sell us to this villain?"

The others laughed and started back toward the camp. I had the impression they were even a little relieved. I heard Callias laugh, as if at some jest.

The Sicel nobleman seemed to peer into their backs as we watched them go. Then, at last, when the only sound we could hear was the wind in the dry grass, he turned to me.

"You are not like them," he said, breaking the long silence. "You would not be wise, I think, to trust them as completely as they do you."

"I am exactly like them."

He smiled tightly, as a man does when he hears a lie he is too polite to contradict.

"The question is, what will you do now?" he said. "You have won a victory, of sorts. You cannot hope to win anything more."

"You told me once that I could not hope for anything more than defeat."

"In the long view, that is still the case."

"You no longer even believe that yourself," I said. "You cannot hope to make me believe it."

"The walls of the king's citadel have never been breached."

We both glanced up at those walls, those huge blocks of granite that seemed fitted together as tightly as the scales on a snake's back. I had no doubt he was telling me the truth.

"With fortresses, as with maidens, there is always a first time. I will not pretend the thing would not be difficult, but it can be done. It will cost many lives, but in the end we will rend open those walls like a bride's wedding tunic, and then there will be no mercy."

Once again, and for a long time, we listened to the silence of the wind. Did he believe me? Did I believe myself? I had no confidence about either.

"We would fight you for every handspan of wall," he said, as if it were a conclusion he had just reached. He did not look at me as he spoke. He never took his eyes from the gray stones of his master's citadel. "Men would die for every foothold. It would be an expensive victory."

"I have no doubt of it. Do you think, after what this ground witnessed three days ago, that any of us imagine the Sicels are women? Of course many would die—I have said so. Many Greeks, and your own forces to the last man. I would prevent it if I could; however, the power to do so lies not with me but with you."

"What would you have of us, Tiglath Ashur?"

The question was asked in the most offhand manner, almost as if he were posing me a riddle. I found myself wondering if he did not perhaps see through the emptiness of my threat.

"The same as before, my Lord. I would have Ducerius."

From the expression on his face I might have asked him for the life of his first-born child, for it is no trifling matter to abandon one's sovereign king to death. Yet I think we both understood that nothing else would serve.

"He has become a burden to us all," I went on, hardly knowing if he heard me—hardly knowing why I troubled him with reasons he must have understood as well as I did. "The Greeks and the Sicels had no quarrel before he made one. This war is his alone, and there will be no safety for anyone so long as he lives and rules."

But the Sicel nobleman only shook his head. His face was almost as ashen as his beard.

"My ancestors have served his since the days when gods walked the earth with men," he said. "What you ask is a monstrous thing. A monstrous thing."

"I will wait until tomorrow, Lord. And then I will know whether this war will have ended or only just begun. If it ends, then all save one may feel safe of their lives. If it does not, the gods will not visit our heads with the blame for the slaughter that must surely follow."

He did not reply—I do not think he had the bowels for it. He merely mounted his horse again and rode away. I waited until he had disappeared inside the citadel gates before turning my own steps back to camp.

Once, during the Babylonian wars, I told my brother Esarhaddon that no city had even been taken by bluff. Yet the Greeks have a story about a city in the east called "Ilios" which was sacked by men who had hidden themselves inside a wooden horse. One cannot credit such a thing, for the Greeks are a people full of lies, yet the story contains a kind of truth. Perhaps, living among them, I had become more a Greek than I knew.

At any rate, upon my return to camp I said nothing about what terms I had offered the Sicel nobleman—I merely told them that by the next day I would lay before them my plans for ending the war against Ducerius. It was only to Kephalos that I confided the truth.

"I would feel safer gambling with another's man dice than playing this game of yours, Lord." He shook his head. "You risk much on a slender hope—we all risk much. What will we do if the Sicels defy you?"

"I have not the shadow of an idea, my friend. Yet I know not what other course I could follow."

"Then we can only wait to see if your *sedu* has at last deserted you."

"Yes, we can only wait."

That night I did not sleep until the blackest part of the night, just before sunrise, and it seemed I had hardly closed my eyes before Selana, who had been out gathering wood for the breakfast fire, pulled me by the beard to awaken me.

"My Lord—hasten!"

Even as I scrambled to my feet I could hear the murmur of many voices and the dull sound of footfalls against the hard-packed earth. I was only one of many who assembled by the camp's edge to look up and see in the gray light of dawn that the gates of the citadel had been thrown open.

"What can it mean?" How many times did I hear that question: "What can it mean?"

We saw soon enough. A single gray horse—did I know it, or was my mind playing tricks?—trotted out onto the road and began making its hesitant way down to the plain. It had nothing to direct it save its own will, for it bore no rider, only a burden.

Even at such a distance we could make out that that which was tied across its back was a corpse.

"Callias, ride up and catch its bridle—bring it down here that we may see."

He returned in a few minutes, leading the horse, shouting as he rode. "By the gods, it is Ducerius!"

The horse was skittish and its flank was stained with blood. I walked up carefully on its left side and took hold of the dead man's hair to have a took at his face. It was Ducerius right enough, and they had cut his throat.

"What can it mean, Tiglath?"

I turned to my neighbors, feeling as if a weight had been lifted from my heart. I even smiled.

"It means that the Sicels have decided to make peace."

XXXII

DUCERIUS' ARMY, IT APPEARED, HAD SIMPLY NO MORE bowels for a fight. When we marched in to take possession of their citadel, they lingered about in aimless little groups, too cowed even to look us in the face, like men who stood condemned.

I inquired after the nobleman with whom I had negotiated their surrender and was told that he had died by his own hand in remorse over concurring in his king's death. I was shown his body—his fingers were stained with blood and were still clutched around the hilt of the dagger that had searched his breast. The Sicels asked permission to bury Ducerius and, at last, his son in the royal vault, and I allowed this on condition that the nobleman, whose name I never learned, might be buried with them. So it was done.

There was some feeling that these defeated soldiers, guilty of so much evil in the land, should have their ears notched and live out the rest of their lives as slaves. Yet I had given my word that they would be spared, and slavery is as bitter as death, so I would not consent. I did, however, put certain conditions upon their liberty, and these were: first, that they must tear down Ducerius' citadel so that no stone rested upon another and no king would ever think to reign from there again; and second, that after their release if any man among them was ever found bearing weapons, he should be put to death.

In the four days after the battle, when anything was still possible, perhaps the greatest danger had been that the Sicel peasants might rally to the defense of their king and we would find ourselves, the besiegers, besieged. This had not happened. Tullus had done his work well, and the Sicels had stood outside their lord's quarrel with the Greeks; but after the surrender their headman came to me, asking what was to become of them now.

"No, you will not have Greeks for masters," I told them. "We are all simple farmers and the land is fertile enough to feed us all. Let us live together as neighbors, each people keeping to its own laws. You have the word of Tiglath Ashur, Tyrant of Naxos, that every man's rights will be respected."

Ten days later the Greek assembly met and voted to abide by my promise. I then resigned my authority as Tyrant.

"Let us have Tiglath as our king," someone shouted—a cry that was taken up by many voices. "Let Tiglath make of us a great nation that all may fear us and we may live in this land with safety."

I rose to speak, holding up my hand for silence.

"Our safety lies not in the strength of one but of many," I said. "You won this victory for yourselves, and my share in it is no greater than any other's. I would not be another Ducerius, and you will not purchase greatness at the price of advancing Tiglath Ashur's pride. Besides, it is not our way to set one man above another except by the consent of all. As I am a Greek, I disdain to be a king."

There was much debate, but at last, when my neighbors saw that I would not be moved, they relented and awarded me instead a pension of ten jars of wine and ten baskets of barley, to be paid every year for the remainder of my life. I was also granted the right to sit in the first row of seats at all meetings of the assembly and at religious celebrations. These were small things, but they were meant as honors and I accepted them as such.

"Do not let them make of you a king," my father had said, speaking to me in a dream. "I do not care to think of my son as a king among foreigners—such a thing would be undignified."

Was it truly his ghost or only some fancy of my own mind? Was there any difference? Nevertheless, I would honor his wish as if he had spoken with his living voice. I was now a man living as other men, happy to have put all thought of greatness from me, but I was still the son of Sennacherib the Mighty, Lord of the Earth's Four Corners, King of Kings, and I still had the pride of a prince. I had not refused the Throne of Ashur to be a king at the world's edge. "Such a thing would be undignified."

But men listened when I spoke in the assembly. I had only to rise to my feet to command silence and attention, for my victory over Ducerius had earned me respect. I will not claim that I always carried my point, but I was the first among equals, which is as much as even a king can claim if he is a Greek, for there are limits to how much the Greeks, who have never learned the habit of obedience, will honor any man. It is better thus, and I was right to decline a crown. Those who are truly free have no need of kings.

So I returned to my farm and was a farmer again.

And in truth the next year of my life was full of happiness. Our harvests were rich, and mine was the satisfaction wealth brings when it is wrested from the earth by one's own labor. I had the respect of my neighbors, and I had Selana, who gave me that which no woman had ever given me, a love I could enjoy without self-reproach, a love I could acknowledge to the world, conscious that I offended against no man or god.

Selana, the peasant girl I had bought on the wharf at Naukratis when she was no more than a child, and yet I valued her above any noblewoman with perfumed breasts who had lured me to her bed with promises of golden pleasure. In her love there were no dark secrets, no hidden place of treachery. All was as it appeared. With her I was more than happy—I was content.

But if I fancied myself safely beneath the god's notice I was mistaken, for the Lord Ashur has a long reach. I knew this the evening Epeios stopped by my house on his way back from Naxos to tell me "of a stranger who has come, a man who speaks a tongue no one has ever heard before, who asked through his interpreter if there was one among us who carried the mark of the blood star on his hand.

"It seemed to me that you should know, Tiglath. He does not make an encouraging impression, so no one has thought to betray you to him, but he has clearly come a long way and he knew where to look for you—I think he will find you out here soon enough."

He was still mounted on his horse, while I stood on my porch. I had not even offered him a cup of wine yet. I was glad no one else was about to hear him.

"Did you see him yourself?"

"Yes."

"Has he a finger missing?"

"I do not think so. I am sure not, for that is the sort of thing one notices."

He was longing to ask the inevitable questions—Who is he? What business could such a one have with you?—but he did not. So many among the Greeks of Sicily had things in their pasts they preferred to leave undisturbed that it was not considered polite to make such inquiries.

"Then let him find me," I said. I even managed a thin smile, as if the matter were something indifferent. "Perhaps I am not the one he looks for—I am not the only man alive who carries a red birthmark upon his hand."

I did not expect him to be deceived, but I was past caring what Epeios thought of the matter.

"Come down from your horse and break the seal on a jar with me. Think no more of this other matter, for it is of no importance."

When he was gone I ate my evening meal, listening in silence as Kephalos offered his nightly description of his exploits during the battle on the Plain of Clonios. I listened, glancing about me, all the time thinking to myself, all of this, this life I have made for myself, this happiness which is so a part of every hour that I am hardly conscious of it, it was all no more than a shadow, a thing that vanishes with the sun, of no substance.

And I remembered the eagle whose shadow had fallen across me after the defeat of Collatinus—an eagle, flying east, staining my palm an even darker red with his blood. The god's purpose, it seemed, was about to be revealed.

The next morning, without a word to anyone, I hitched up our cart and drove it into Naxos. There seemed little point in delaying the inevitable.

It happened to be market day, and even during the last few hours of daylight the square was crowded. Voices, like coins clattering against the paving stones, cut the silence into little pieces, and the air was rich with the smell of life. The wineshops were doing a brisk business and I traded greetings with old friends and comrades in arms and even men whose faces were unknown to me.

Everyone, it seemed, was ready to take my hand and to offer me a taste from his jar, and more than a few told me again of the barbarian who inquired after one marked with the blood star, confiding it to me in whispers like a secret.

Yet the man himself appeared not to be there.

And then, quite suddenly, he was. As I stood beneath the awning of a wineshop I did not see him at first—I only heard the growing silence as men nudged one another and pointed, letting their conversations die away. I turned, and my heart almost froze within my breast.

He was one in the middle of life, and by the standards that would apply among the Greeks he was an exotic enough sight. His beard, which reached to the middle of his chest, was carefully plaited, and he wore the elaborate, richly embroidered court robes of a royal chamberlain in the Land of Ashur. In his hand was his staff of office, and from this dangled the silver ribbons which meant his message was for a prince of the king's own blood.

I knew him, of course, by sight if not by name. As soon as our eyes met, he bowed from the waist.

"My Lord Tiglath Ashur," he said, in a voice that carried to every corner of the square—my friends and neighbors, it seemed, were to be treated to a spectacle—"son and grandson of kings, Prince in the Land of Ashur, attend me, for I bring you the words of your royal brother the Lord Esarhaddon, Lord of the World, King of the Earth's Four Corners."

It was a shock. Whatever I had expected, it had not been this. Even the sound of my native tongue, which I had not heard in years, rolled in my head like distant thunder. For a moment I could only stand and stare.

"I have no brother who is a king," I said, when at last I found my voice again. "The Lord Esarhaddon has said I am his brother no more. He has turned his face from me, and he and I can have no business."

"Then it is the king who speaks, and it will be the subject who listens. Or do you deny that bond as well, O son of the Lord Sennacherib?"

I studied his face with bitter eyes, hating him, feeling like a fox in a wooden cage. Did he dare to mock me, this one?

"Speak then."

"Look about you, Lord. The king's words are not for the ears of common men."

I did look about, at the staring faces of the Greeks, and all at once, and of its own will, a fit of laughter broke from my lips.

"Be at ease, Chamberlain," I said, still laughing. "The king's secrets are safe enough. The king bid me hide myself in the dark lands beyond the sun, and I have made a reasonable enough effort to oblige him—there is not another within five days' journey of this place who can understand a word we speak."

"Still, my Lord . . ."

It was then that I noticed the man who stood beside him, a short, dark, compact figure in the costume of an Edomite. His interpreter, doubtless—but perhaps not entirely trusted.

"As you wish," I answered, gesturing toward the entrance of the wineshop. "I am sure the proprietor will oblige us."

We were met in the doorway by Timon the Arcadian, the owner, still in his leather apron, who had been just on his way outside to see what the stir was about.

"Can you oblige us with a little privacy?" I asked him, smiling. He had fought at the Plain of Clonios and was a good fellow.

"Of course, Tiglath, of course! Take whatever room pleases you," he said, pointing up the stairs to the second story, where the harlots entertained their customers. "And if any of my girls are still asleep up there, just kick them out."

He laughed at this.

When we had four walls around us and the door was closed, the chamberlain turned to face me, his lips closed as if he would never speak again. He bowed once more.

"The king summons you home," he said. "He demands your attendance upon him at Nineveh."

I do not know why I should have been so surprised. Perhaps anything he said would have had the same effect. Perhaps I had simply not recovered from my initial astonishment. Yet I found I had to repeat the sentence to myself before I could even grasp its meaning.

". . . Summons me home?" I shook my head. "It is my death if I return to the Land of Ashur—it was his judgment against me. I cannot go home."

"Nevertheless, he summons you."

"No doubt, that he might once again put me within reach of his assassins," I said.

"The Lord Esarhaddon guarantees your life, in token of which . . ."

There was a small linen bag hanging from his belt. He undid it and placed it on a table beside the room's only window, stepping away, inviting me to examine its contents.

Inside was a human hand, severed at the wrist and dried in salt until the flesh was the color of harness leather. It was a left hand, and the smallest finger was missing.

I felt a thrill of horror, without even knowing why, for I had seen many worse things in my life. Perhaps it was merely the nearness of my escape. And also there was in this something of the secret which had been betrayed.

So the last one was now accounted for.

"The king cannot make me come," I said, almost to myself—the words seemed in place of others that remained unspoken. "His power, even his name, is nothing here. I am beyond his reach."

"Yes. Nothing compels you except duty."

"I have no duty to Esarhaddon."

"But to the king . . ."

I could have struck him, but instead I turned my back that he might not see how his words twisted my heart.

"Leave me, Chamberlain. Your duty is done. Return to Nineveh and say you received only silence for an answer."

He bowed yet again and turned away. I could hear his footfalls on the stairs. I did not see him again.

The hand remained on the table where he had left it.

As I drove the wagon home, I thought how it would please Esarhaddon to see me thus, a dusty farmer jostling along a rutted country road, on an island the name of which he had probably never even heard. I wondered why he was not content to leave me so, as I was content to be left. I was no danger to him here. It appeared he simply could not bear the idea of having me in the same world with him.

I put no faith in his guarantee. A severed hand meant little enough, and Esarhaddon had already broken his word on this account—I had fled his realm and still he had sent men to murder me. It might be that the five assassins which my dream had foretold were at last accounted for, but perhaps my brother now felt safe enough on his throne that he had decided he preferred to enjoy his revenge in person.

And he had the impudence to send for me thus, as if he were recalling one of his provincial governors.

And that because he knew I would come.

I was trapped. It was such a jest on me that I felt almost like laughing. Yes, Esarhaddon's messenger had seen through me—as had his master. I might dress like a Greek, but this incident had been all the god required to remind me that I remained a man of Ashur. I had been an exile for many years now, yet I could not break the habit of obedience—Esarhaddon was still my king.

Each of us must have something at the core of his soul, some final loyalty, to deny which would be to deny his own nature. I was the son and grandson of kings, and the king spoke with the authority of Holy Ashur himself. I could not join the rebellion against Esarhaddon when our father was murdered; I could not stand aside and let Nabusharusur kill him at Sidon. Even on the other end of the earth, I was still the *quradu*, the soldier of the royal bodyguard, sworn to lay down my life at the king's word. To be such had been the pride and glory of my youth. To be such had been, to me, more than to be prince or conqueror, more even than to be king. The time for breaking faith with all that had long since passed.

Thus I knew I would return, simply because it was the king's will. And Esarhaddon had known it too.

Thus I looked upon myself as a dead man.

Kephalos bustled out to greet me as I pulled into our farmyard. I tried to smile as we unbridled the horse, but from the way he stared I gathered I was not very convincing.

"What afflicts you, Lord? You look as if you have seen an evil spirit."

"Perhaps I have. A messenger has come from Nineveh. I am bid to return."

He stood silent for a moment, the horse's bridle hanging unregarded from his hand. At first he seemed relieved, even expectant, and then gradually his face began to register that tension of a man waiting to have his worst fears confirmed.

"You would not return, would you? Not even if the message should be that Esarhaddon is dead . . ."

"He is not dead—no, my friend, I am not being recalled to the throne. Quite the opposite, I fear."

"Then you will not go. Master, tell me you will not go."

I did not answer. I could not. Perhaps I did not need to.

He shook his head.

"Esarhaddon will have you killed. He cannot risk allowing you to come so close as Nineveh—you will be assassinated as soon as you set foot within his domains."

"He sends a guarantee of my life," I said. I opened the linen bag and showed him the severed hand.

Kephalos spat upon the ground. "At such a rate you should value his guarantee, Lord."

What was I to say? That I was of his opinion? That I too held my life as worthless if ever it came again under my brother's power? So I said nothing.

"You will return, then." He shook his head, as if at a piece of folly that could not be prevented. "You will go back."

"Yes."

We walked to the house together.

"Give this to me," he said, taking the linen bag out of my hand. "I will see that it is cleansed and then burned—it is an unholy thing in the sight of the gods."

"Say nothing of this matter to Selana," I said, as if he had not spoken. "I will tell her in my own time."

"As you wish."

No, not as I wished, for here too I was a coward. At night, with her arms around my neck, I could not seem to pronounce the words. And in the daylight it struck me as nearly an impurity.

But at last I did speak. In the middle of the morning I simply laid down my hoe and walked back to the house.

I think she knew something was wrong the moment she saw my face.

"I must go on a journey," I said. "I do not know when I will come back—probably I will never come back."

"Then I will go with you," she said, without hesitating a moment. "Where my lord leads, I will follow."

"I am returning to the Land of Ashur. You cannot follow me there."

Her eyes narrowed, although I believe she understood well enough what I meant.

"You can try stopping me, but you will not have much success."

"I will not deliver you to your death, Selana. Or, perhaps, what is worse than death. You will remain here—you, Kephalos, even Enkidu; you will all remain here."

"You have said I am not a slave, Lord." She smiled, like a cunning child. "And if I am free I will go where I choose. You cannot stop me."

"You will not come with me, Selana," I said with some heat. "And we will not discuss this matter again."

But that evening, when I returned from the fields, I found Enkidu sitting on the porch, sharpening the blades of his ax. When he lifted his sullen eyes to my face, I knew.

"He will accompany us," Selana announced, stepping outside into the soft light of sunset. "You will not dissuade him either."

Even now I am not sure why, but the tears started in my eyes.

"I am not sure what I have done to deserve either of you," I said.

In the east they say that love, power and revenge are the three great sources of happiness. I have known all three, and only love endures.

Or perhaps it is enough simply to be loved. Selana loved me, enough to accept any risk rather than be parted from me. How was I to put a high enough value on that?

So I decided I would make of her my wife.

Our wedding was a hurried affair—a trip to the sacred spring to purify ourselves in its waters, a few honey cakes burned in the sacred fire of our hearth, and a feast for as many of our neighbors as could be gathered together on two days' notice. I do not think that anyone was particularly surprised by the sudden invitation. Everyone seemed to have grasped that there was a connection with the visit of the mysterious barbarian. Everyone seemed to know that I was returning to the east.

As was the custom, we ate our banquet out-of-doors, the bride's party separate from the husband's. Thus I do not know if it was the same for Selana and her women friends, but among the men we seemed no so much to be celebrating a marriage as mourning a departure, even a death.

They were my friends, and I felt I owed them so much explanation as was in my power. They listened in silence, and for a time after I had finished, the silence remained. Then Callias, whose horse I had driven at the battle of Clonios, set aside his wine cup, shaking his head.

"Who is this King Esarhaddon and what is this place Nineveh that we should regard them?" he asked. "No foreigner who sits beside a muddy river shall take you from us, Tiglath—not if you do not choose to go."

"He is my brother and my lord. It is not a thing a Greek can be made to understand, but I must go, no matter what I might choose."

No one cared to debate the point—the Greeks, it seemed, disputed only for their amusement, so we drank wine together and tried, haltingly, to speak of other things.

And at last, just before sunset, my friends led me back to the house, where Selana and a company of women were waiting. I took my new wife inside while men and women sang wedding songs, and I went into her once more, as if it had been the first time. There was so much of grief mixed in with our joy that neither of us seemed to know which was the greater.

Morning came. We walked down together, hand in hand, to the point where the wine-dark sea spread itself before us in the distance. Ashur's holy sun seemed to stain the water with blood.

"There is already a ship in the port at Naxos," I said. "When she is ready to sail again, we will be on her. I cannot explain, but I am impatient to be gone."

"To embrace death?" she asked. There was that in her voice to make one almost think she spoke of a rival.

"No. But whatever follows, even if it be death, when it is over, I will be free."

Even as we spoke, the sun rose and the sea washed itself clean again.

XXXIII

AS THE FIRST OF THE LAND BREEZES FILLED HER SAILS, the ship that was to carry me away from Sicily crouched in the water like a runner at the start of a race. The sailors dropped their lines and we pulled away from the dock where Kephalos, my trusted friend and servant, watched my face with silent, tear-swollen eyes.

"My property I leave with you, to treat it as your own," I had told him. "Be good to my slaves and leave the management of the land to the boy Tullus, who understands farming. If I do not return, then surely I have found death in the Land of Ashur, and in my will, which is deposited at the shrine of Hestia, you are named as my heir. When you die, the farm goes to Tullus and his descendants."

"You do a wicked thing to put yourself once more within your brother's reach," he answered me, as if my words had been no more than the buzzing of flies. "I wish you were not such a fool and would allow your servant to come with you, for you will have need of my cunning."

"If the king wants my life, no cunning can save me, and I am not so base that I can allow you to embrace death to no purpose. No, Kephalos, you must stay behind and be my faithful steward, as always, robbing me only a little, that if someday the god allows me to return I will not then find myself a beggar."

I smiled, as if uttering a harmless pleasantry, and took his hand, but he could not meet my eyes. Neither of us expected that I would ever return.

Selana, my bride of less than three days, and the huge, speechless Macedonian whom I called Enkidu waited aboard the ship. The wind was rising. It was time to depart.

Thus Kephalos stood silently on the dock and watched us drift out into the bay. He was still there when our ship rounded the point of the harbor and Naxos disappeared from sight.

"This ship takes us to Pílos," I said, more to break the silence than anything else. "From there we can take passage to Crete, or to Cyprus, and from there to anywhere. With luck and a fair wind, we can be on the coast of Asia in twelve or fifteen days."

"My Lord is pleased to jest," answered Selana—she was but sixteen and had dogged my steps since a child, yet she had a sharp tongue. "It is never a fair wind that will carry us to Asia."

She huddled beside our baggage, covered by Enkidu's vast shadow as he leaned against a bale of wool, sharpening his great two-headed ax, precisely as if he were alone in the world. The sound of his whetstone against the iron blades seemed to scrape away at a raw place on her nerves, for, sitting there on the deck with her arms wrapped around her knees, she hunched her thin shoulders in an attitude of misery.

"You say your brother claims to be master of all Asia, and you speak of fair winds!"

She held my gaze for an instant and then looked away, for her eyes were filling with tears. The sunlight on her bronze-colored hair seemed to blaze with helpless anger.

Your brother. What a monster of wickedness Esarhaddon must seem to her, I thought. Esarhaddon, whom she had never even seen. Whom she knew only as a kind of personal legend, like a ghost in a story meant to frighten children. What could Selana possibly understand of this quarrel between us, of my reasons for returning now, under such circumstances, to the land of my birth? What reasons could count for anything with her against the terrible name of my brother Esarhaddon?

We had an uneventful passage, and for three days we stayed in Pílos, once the seat of great kings but now little more than a village, until we found a ship to carry us to Byblos, which, like all Phoenician cities, is beautiful and rich. However, I was not charmed by it.

Byblos had grown more prosperous than ever since the destruction of Sidon, and her king, a wise man who had profited from the unhappy example of Abdimilkutte, paid his tribute to Nineveh on time and in gold. It was there that I first felt myself to be under my brother's eyes.

We had not been in the city an hour—we had not even found a place to sleep for the night—when Enkidu growled and stretched out his arm to indicate a man, dressed like a porter, leaning against the corner of a building. He did not so much as glance in our direction, but the instant Enkidu pointed him out he scrambled off like a spider that feels the sun on its back.

"Yes, I saw him. He was on the docks when we arrived. But we must expect to be watched from now on."

Enkidu did not seem reconciled. I think he counted it a weakness in me that I did not send him to bring back Esarhaddon's spy by the heels for some painful questioning.

"There is nothing he can tell me that I do not already know, so let us forget this intrusion and find rooms for ourselves. We will have a good dinner tonight, and soon we will be on the wide road to the East."

I was all the next afternoon trying to buy us suitable horses, and most particularly one that could bear Enkidu's weight without collapsing after an hour. When at last I had found them, the merchant, who dealt in all manner of animals, even to exotic green birds from Africa that could be taught to speak, did not even attempt to bargain me into paying a higher price. I had the impression he did not care for the beasts and was glad to be rid of them. The Phoenicians are sharp traders, yet, being a sailing race, they understand nothing of horses and stand in something like dread of anyone who does.

The next morning we were on the caravan trail north and east to Carchemish, which had borne the yoke of Ashur since the time of my grandfather the Great Sargon, and the Euphrates beyond.

We tarried more than a month covering that distance—we did not travel every day; Selana was not accustomed to riding and at first could not keep her seat for more than a few hours. Besides, as we approached my native land I felt once more the pull of old habits and I began to honor the custom of my ancestors and stayed in my tent on all evil days, dressing in rags, eating nothing that had been cooked in a pot, and abstaining from the embraces of my wife. Selana was unimpressed by this display of piety and fancied herself neglected, declaring it her opinion that eastern men must all be eunuchs and pederasts and haters of women. I bore this with what patience I could, for she was a Greek woman and could know nothing of the exacting god whose presence I felt more strongly with every step we took.

It was the height of the summer when we entered the plain of the Euphrates, a long, slow, smooth descent where the mud laid down by the spring floods of a thousand times a thousand years was baked hard as brick, and the sun had long since withered the grass to nothing. Here and there we would find a village where we could buy beer and bread and perhaps a little fresh meat. The people spoke Aramaic, for the kings of Ashur, though they had ruled here for five hundred years, were far away, a race of conquerors destined one day to disappear like all the other conquerors who had thought to claim this land as their own. The headmen, when they spoke to me, were guarded in their answers and kept their women out of sight. I did not have to ask myself why.

We could see them too—sometimes only the dust raised by their horses' hooves, but they had been with us, just at the edge of the horizon, for several days. They never came closer, but I had the impression it was a fairly large patrol, perhaps as many as twenty men, and that they sent riders ahead to report on our progress. Esarhaddon, it seemed, wished to be sure that this time I did not slip away from him.

We stopped in Carchemish for two nights and crossed the Euphrates by raft on the fourth day of the month of Elul. We traveled east for twenty days, stopping for only five of those, before I knew that at last I had returned to the land of my birth.

On the twenty-fifty day of Elul, just an hour after we had left our beds, I saw an old man waiting by the side of the road. He was still only a tiny figure in the distance, but I knew he was old, just as I knew he wore the yellow robes of a priest and that his eyes were blind to the things of this world. I discovered I was not even surprised. In some part of my soul I seemed to have been expecting him.

Something must have registered in my face, because Selana looked at me with a queer, puzzled expression. Yet she held her tongue.

As we approached, I let my horse drift to a halt. It was he, unchanged since the first time I had met him almost twenty years before, in my green youth. His skin, darkened by the sun to the color of leather, was stretched tight over his old bones, and the dead eyes looked at nothing.

"So, Prince, you have come home at last," he said, turning to me, and seeming to see beyond me as if I were a shadow. "You have not feared to answer the king's summons—and the god's."

"Is it the god who calls me back, Holy One?"

"Can you doubt it? Has he not revealed a hundred times how he cradles you in his hand?"

He shook his head, as if I were a child who would not be taught.

"Have I something to fear then?" I asked. At first he only smiled, as if my question, upon the answer to which my life hung as from a thread, merely amused him.

"O Tiglath Ashur," he said at last, "Son of Sennacherib, when have you ever truly known fear, the fear that is worse than death? The fear that is the wrath of heaven? It is not you but your brother Esarhaddon whose bowels turn to water. He calls you back, for all that he dreads to meet you. Yet he must call you back, for it is Holy Ashur's will. He does the god's work, though unwittingly. He is worthy of your pity."

"Then what is the god's work for me, Holy One? Am I to live my life in darkness, or will you speak the god's voice?"

"All that is to come you have seen already, Prince—you need no word from me, for the god speaks with his own voice. Go now, Prince. You will not always be as blind as you are now."

He had finished we me, so I pulled the reins about and goaded my horse on. Selana and Enkidu followed in my wake, as if I pulled them after me in my haste. I did not look back. I did not dare to look back.

"Why did you not give him something, Lord?" Selana asked, when we were well away. "It is not like you to be so pitiless to a blind old beggar."

"Is that what you imagined him to be?" I laughed, perhaps a trifle hysterically. "Believe me, he has no need of anything *I* could give him."

"*He is worthy of your pity*," the *maxxu* had said. The words rang in my ears. Long ago, in what seemed like another life, I had asked my mother what I was to do about my brother Esarhaddon, whose old love for me had grown all twisted with jealousy and hatred, and she told me, "*Only pity him, and be his friend—no matter what.*"

Everyone, it seemed, spoke of pity. Esarhaddon was now the king, and he had called me back from exile, perhaps only to death. Yet somehow I was to find it in me to pity him.

We rode on through the rest of that day in silence. My thoughts were full of the past, so that nothing else seemed real. Memories that were like pangs of conscience rose unbidden in my mind, and Selana, understanding perhaps only that I was troubled in some way past remedy, did not speak.

Just before nightfall we reached a village. Children gathered about us with the usual mixture of anticipation and dread. Somewhere I heard a dog barking. And at last the headman, whose old legs, sticking out beneath his plain woolen tunic, seemed carved from a thorn tree, came out to meet us.

"We are unaccustomed to strangers here," he said in Akkadian—it was the first time I had heard my native tongue since returning to Asia, and the sound of it made my heart pound in my breast. "We are poor people. The harvests have been bad these seven years. What do you want of us?"

"Is this what a traveler must expect from the men of Ashur?" I allowed my face to fill with a wrath I did not feel, for indeed I had only to look around me to behold the cold cooking fires, the dust and the flies, sure signs of want. "We ask a place to sleep and food, and we will pay for these things in silver, for we are not thieves."

When he realized I was not a foreigner, the old man was abashed and lowered his eyes in shame.

We were given an empty hut, and the villagers slaughtered a goat and held a feast for us. There were still a few jars of beer, hardly enough that everyone had a full cup for himself, yet men who have not tasted beer in many months can grow drunk enough on that to become careless. Thus it was, perhaps, that the headman admitted me to his confidence.

The conversation began harmlessly enough, growing out of the curiosity that all men feel in the presence of travelers.

"You have come some distance then," be began, stating it as a fact as he cradled his empty cup in his hands, as if treasuring the memory of it. We sat together in front of the great fire, now hardly more than embers, over which the village women had cooked our goat. "Farther, I think, than even the Great Salt, where my brother died on campaign with the old king."

"Yes. We have journeyed from as far beyond the Northern Sea as we are distant from it now."

"Ah." He nodded. "I thought as much. I heard you speaking to your slave woman, and it was like no tongue known to me."

"She is an Ionian, and she is my wife."

The headman's brow furrowed in concern, but I smiled and waggled my hand to show that I had not taken offense.

"She does not wear the bridal veil because it is not the custom among that nation."

He would not say so to a guest, but I could see that he thought it strange of me to permit such impropriety in a wife, even if she was a foreigner. Indeed, it was not until that moment that it occurred to me to reflect on how the matter must look to the eyes of my countrymen.

"You have been long away from home, then?" he asked, perhaps not intending the question to sound like a reproach.

"Long enough—too long, for I feel almost as if I am nowhere at home. A man picks up foreign habits when he travels over the wide earth, so that at last he seems to see even familiar things through the eyes of a stranger."

He laughed, slapping his knee as though I had made a joke. His laughter had a peculiar, hollow sound.

"One need never have left it to feel a stranger now in the Land of Ashur," he said. "Things are not as they were. We have fallen upon evil days since the old king was slain, and the god curses us."

"Yet the king his son reigns, and the murderers of the Lord Sennacherib were put to flight."

"Yes, but the new king is not beloved of heaven. He sent his own brother into exile, whom Ashur loved and all knew to be a blameless man, and the god will not forgive him. Thus the new king, in his terror of Ashur's wrath, hearkens after the unclean gods of the black-headed folk. But the god punishes him, denying him victory over his enemies and leading him into disaster in strange lands. We starve at home and our sons go off to die in foolish wars—thus does the god seek vengeance against his people for the king's sins."

He glanced about him, as if suddenly afraid someone might have heard his words.

"The king is at war then?" I asked, for I had heard no news of home in many years.

"I have said enough. These days, no man may speak his mind in safety."

I did not press him. We talked of other matters, and finally I excused myself and retired to my bed. I did not sleep, however, for my mind was full of many things and they permitted me no rest.

In the morning I gave a bag containing twenty silver coins into the headman's keeping—I could see how he weighed it in his hand, for doubtless never in his life had he been possessed of so great a treasure. A man does little enough in this life to have earned the mercy of heaven, and it pleased me to think that at least from this village I had lifted the curse of poverty.

The next morning we saw a rider on the horizon, the first in many days. He was alone this time, not part of a patrol, so perhaps Esarhaddon felt more secure of me now.

Two days later we reached a town—hardly more than a village really, since there was no fortified wall around it. Yet it could boast of a bazaar. There I purchased for Selana a veil of purple linen, fringed at the bottom with tiny silver coins. When I presented her with it that evening she did not seem pleased with the gift.

"What am I to do with this?" she asked, holding it up as if to examine it for dirt.

"You will cover your hair with it, and your face up to the eyes," I said. "That way everyone will know that you are my wife and not my concubine or a harlot I have picked up for one night's amusement. No respectable married woman in this part of the world would dream of appearing in public without one."

"I am a Greek woman. I am not *from* Assyria."

"Yes, but you are *in* Assyria now, and you will abide by its customs."

"You were not ashamed to own me as your concubine in Sicily," she declared hotly. "I will not wear it."

She wadded the veil up into a ball and threw it at my feet.

"You will wear it," I said, picking it up. "I will not have it thought that you came out of a brothel. You will wear it because it is my pleasure that you should."

"Yes, *Lord*."

She snatched it from my hand and shook it out with such violence that one of the coins came loose and tinkled against the brick floor.

"I wish now I had let you marry me off to some pig farmer."

I did not reply, but I could see it in her face that she regretted her words. She fell silent and would not look at me.

"There is the law to be considered," I said at last. "A wife is entitled to the law's protection, Selana, no matter what becomes of her husband. My fate grows more uncertain every day, and I would shield you any way I can. You will wear the veil."

"Yes, Lord."

She threw herself into my arms and wept, and then I understood. How could I blame her for being afraid?

For five days after crossing the Khabur River we traveled along the southern foothills of the Sinjar Mountain Range. We had come within two or three days of Rasappa, most western of the great cities of Ashur, when, about two hours after midday, the rider who had been following us for so long, staying always just at the horizon—had there been one man all along or had they dogged us in relays? I would never know—turned his horse and began to approach at a canter.

I had known all along that, sooner or later, something like this must happen. It was almost with a sense of relief that I stopped my horse to wait for him. I could hear Enkidu growling behind my back.

"He is nearly an hour away," I said, without looking around, "and he is alone. What harm can he intend us? Without doubt he is only a messenger.

"Yes, but for whom?" Selana brought her horse up beside mine, so that our legs nearly touched. "And to what purpose?"

I threw back my head and laughed—I could not help myself.

"Concerning the first of these I have no doubts. Would that I could feel as sure of the second."

"Look!"

Selana raised her arm and pointed. She had seen the tiny pulses of light that appeared over the rider's right shoulder, so that we seemed to see the beat of his horse's hooves rather than hear it.

"He is carrying something!" She turned to me with an excitement in which fear seemed to have no place. "What . . . ?"

"It is his staff of office," I said, feeling nothing except a dreary sense of inevitability, as if the past had reached forward to reclaim me forever. "He is a royal *ekalli*—a messenger, as I had thought—and the silver ribbon tied to his javelin is in token of the fact the he bears the king's words to a prince of his own blood. My brother means me to know that the moment has come."

We waited in silence, as there was nothing more to be said. We kept our horses there under the roasting summer sun while fate rode briskly toward us, its ribbons flashing in the harsh light.

When the *ekalli* had narrowed the distance down to perhaps fifty paces, he allowed himself to slow. He was younger than I had expected, and he did not have the appearance of a man who had spent many days on the road. His uniform, which declared him to be a *rab kisir*, looked as if it had only just come from the loom. Some great lord's son, I thought, one who wishes him to make a career for himself as a barrack soldier. Such men cluster around the person of a king like flies about a stinking carcass.

He stopped, and then, at last, he dismounted and, to my utter surprise, dropped to his knees, his hand closed around his chamberlain's staff, bowing before the royal prince whose existence I had almost forgotten.

"Tiglath Ashur, Dread Lord," he said, in the accents of Nineveh—it was plain this was a man of the court—"Son of Sennacherib the Mighty, Great Prince . . ."

He raised his eyes to my face, waiting for me to acknowledge his salutation. I could not escape the impression that his words were addressed to someone else, the ghost of a man long dead. I could not have answered him, for my throat had squeezed shut. At last I contrived to nod.

"Great Prince, harken to the words of the Lord Esarhaddon, Master of the World, Lord of the Earth's Four Quarters, King in the Land of Ashur, whose wrath is terrible . . ."

"I am well acquainted with the king's wrath," I said at last, for anger had found its way back into my heart, and anger conquers even despair and the certainty of death. "Speak, man, and be done—what is the Lord Esarhaddon's will of me?"

Whatever he had expected, it was not this. For a moment he looked at me through eyes filled with wonder, as if I had committed some dreadful sacrilege and he waited for the gods to strike me with fire.

Finally, in the manner of one concentrating his whole will into a single gesture, he placed his right hand, with the fingers spread, over his breast.

"Great Prince, you are to follow me—alone."

I looked back over my shoulder at Enkidu, who of course understood not a syllable of our conversation, and wondered if he would be content to allow me out of his sight. He did not seem to care for Esarhaddon's *ekalli*. His eyes were fixed on the man as if measuring him for his grave.

I dismounted and gathered up the reins of Selana's horse, leading her and it back to where Enkidu waited in his impenetrable silence.

"The two of you will go on to Rasappa without me . . ."

"If you think for a moment . . ."

"Hold your tongue, woman," I shouted, without so much as glancing at her.

"You will take her there, Enkidu, whether she will or no. If I do not join you within five days, then assume that I have met the fate from which no one can save me. There is a purse of silver coins hidden in Selana's sleeping roll—use it to escape from this place and find your way back to Sicily. If anyone comes saying he brings word of me, know that he is lying and kill him."

I turned to Selana, whose face was streaked with hot tears. There was only one word left between us, and so I spoke that one.

"Good-bye."

She shook her head violently, as if she would not hear me.

"I will not let you leave me as easily as that," she said, in a voice that was like a sob of rage. "I will not let you . . ."

"If she resists, tie her across her horse," I said to Enkidu, my eyes on Selana's face. "This is why you came, my friend, to preserve her life where you could not preserve mine."

He nodded. He understood and would do as I bid him.

"Then I will go now."

I mounted my horse and followed the king's *ekalli* south. I did not look back—I was not brave enough for that. For what seemed an eternity I could still hear Selana's voice, shouting after me, "I will wait for you, Lord. No death can touch you while I wait. I will wait for you in Rasappa, if I wait my life through."

For two hours the *ekalli* and I rode together in perfect silence. I did not even look at him. I wished only to forget that I was not alone. He, for his own reasons, seemed content that it should be so.

A man's mind plays strange tricks with him when he believes he is about to die—I amused myself by forming speculations as to how it would happen. Would this one kill me, drawing up beside me and then, suddenly and without warning, pulling a dagger from his cloak? It seemed unlikely, if only because the outcome must be so uncertain. I would be waiting for something of the sort, and I traveled armed. Perhaps I would strike first. Esarhaddon had not summoned me all this way to have the work bungled at the last moment.

Or perhaps there was a patrol of soldiers ahead and, when they had me in their midst, they would simply cut me down. They would carry my head back to Nineveh for their reward, and no one would ever know what had become at last of Prince Tiglath Ashur, Dread Lord, Son of Sennacherib the Mighty.

On the whole I rather favored this idea, although I could not understand why they had waited until now. Why not a quick raid while we were camped for the night somewhere? They might have caught us asleep and unprepared. It might even have been safer to attack two men in their bedrolls than one while he is alert and filled with apprehension. Even a dying man can have a sharp edge to his sword.

Of course, what one finds in such cases is what one least expects.

It was barren country just there, far from any river. In those two hours the *ekalli* and I crossed several irrigation ditches that looked as if they had not held water in living memory—from how many mouths, since coming home, had I heard the tale of the drought that had descended upon the Land of Ashur in recent years? Not once did we see signs of life.

Memory. One cannot be forever thinking of death. Or perhaps it was my sense of the nearness of death that turned my mind back to the past. In my mind's eye I saw the palace of my father, the Lord Sennacherib—the rooms were filled with ghosts, living and dead, and the shadows of my own youth.

I remembered the night Esarhaddon and I, with a bag of silver supplied by Kephalos, had gone prowling the streets of Nineveh in search of wickedness, finding only a tavern slut. I remembered our father, sunk in confusion and old age. I remembered Esharhamat, still bright with hope—Esharhamat, whom I loved more than life yet not quite enough.

And Shaditu, my wicked half-sister, whose body burned like fire. She had loved me, so she said, and yet somehow—just how, it seemed likely, I would never know—had shattered my every hope.

And now I was coming home again, if only to die.

At last we came to a ruined farmhouse, the walls broken and the mud bricks worn smooth by the wind. Beside it was pitched an officer's tent, and beside that a single horse was tethered.

"I am to leave you here," the *ekalli* said, his voice sounding rusty from disuse.

"What happens now?" I asked. "Am I to wait? Will another meet me? Speak!"

"I have no instructions, except to leave you here."

He glanced about him—there was fear in his eyes—and then he goaded his horse into a gallop. I listened to the beat of its hooves fading into the distance.

I did not dismount. There was no sound but the low whisper of the wind. I seemed to be alone in this place.

And then the tent flap opened, and my brother Esarhaddon stepped out into the light. He was unarmed, and in his hand he held a wine jar. I felt the blood run cold in my veins.

"Come down from your horse," he said, just as if we had last seen each other only that morning. "By the gods, it is hot in this doghole. Come down and have a cup of wine."

XXXIV

THERE WAS A LITTLE MORE GRAY IN HIS BEARD, BUT otherwise no change in him—his hard, compact body had all the solidity of a wall, as if nothing could ever move him from that spot, as if he were one with the earth beneath his feet. Yet I, who knew him, knew better. My brother Esarhaddon, who had been born to be a soldier, for whom life should have held no doubts, looked at me through haunted eyes.

I dismounted and went down on my knees, lowering my gaze to the ground before the Esarhaddon who was my king, who must be my lord while there was yet breath in my body.

"Get up, Tiglath—you know you only do this to mock me. Get up at once. I never could stand to see you thus."

"I am a subject," I said, speaking the words from behind clenched teeth. "I am also a proscribed fugitive. How else am I to greet the king of Ashur?"

"Why do you insist on making this as difficult for me as you can?" He wiped his beard with the back of his hand, in the manner of one making a painful confession.

"The king of Ashur is not here," he went on. "The king of Ashur, as everyone knows, is in Egypt, fighting a fruitless and costly war. Presently he will be back in Nineveh, drunk as a pig, making a fool of himself with his women and his magicians—you think I do not know what they say of me behind my back? There is no one here except you and me, Tiglath Ashur and his brother, that clod of mud Esarhaddon."

"That, of course, is a different matter."

I rose to my feet, striding across those few paces that separated us while I knitted my hands together. As soon as I was close enough, I swung them over my head and brought them down with a slanting blow across Esarhaddon's face.

He was caught completely by surprise and went straight over backwards, the jar flying from his hands and its contents staining the ground like fresh-spilled blood. For a moment I thought I had knocked him unconscious—it even went through my mind that in my heedless rage I might have killed him—and then he sat up, holding his head in his hands. A thin trickle of blood, this time quite genuine, ran down his fingers.

"Ough! You needn't have hit so hard." He reached into his mouth with finger and thumb to assess the damage. "By the Sixty Great Gods, I think you have broken a tooth."

"I certainly hope so."

He looked up at me woefully, and then shook his head.

"Well, naturally you're angry—I can't really claim to be surprised," he said finally. "I suppose you have a right to be."

"You banished me!" I shouted, my fists clenched, only just able to overcome the impulse to kick him. "And, not content with that, you set assassins on me, hounding me to the ends of the earth! Do you know how many times they came within a hair's breadth of murdering me? 'Well, naturally you're angry.' I ought to gut you, Esarhaddon. I ought to squash you under a rock like a frog."

Yet my brother merely blinked, as if the sunlight bothered his eyes, and wiped the blood off his hand with the hem of his tunic. Then he stood up, went into his tent, and fetched out another jug of wine, breaking the seal with his thumb. When he had quenched his thirst, he offered the jar to me—I snatched it away from him and, after taking a long swallow, dashed it against the wall of the ruined farmhouse.

Esarhaddon regarded the wet smear on the dusty, wind-worn bricks with dispassionate interest and then returned to me.

"I hope this tantrum of yours is over," he said calmly. "For one thing it is a sin against the immortal gods to waste wine in this heat, and for another I have heard all of this from you before. That night at Sidon—remember? You would not have believed me then, but believe me now. I never sent assassins after you."

I could not possibly have said why, but I did believe him. I knew at once that he was speaking the truth.

"Of course. I suppose they had no idea at all of a reward for carrying my head back to Nineveh." I answered, unwilling to part with any share of my wrath. "I suppose they simply appeared of their own will."

"Hardly that."

Esarhaddon threw back his head and laughed, which seemed to remind him that his head hurt and that he was thirsty. He fetched another jar of wine and sat down in the shade of his tent to drink it. This time he did not offer me any.

"My mother sent them," he continued, quite at his leisure now. "She mentioned nothing of the matter to me—she simply sent them. You will recall she has done that sort of thing before."

"Are you not the king then? Do you still find it so difficult to keep a leash on the Lady Naq'ia?"

"Oh, please, Tiglath! Since when have you grown so very unreasonable?" It was odd, but he seemed genuinely vexed with me. "I can rule the world, or I can rule my mother. It is a bit absurd to expect me to manage both."

He took a long swallow of wine and then sat back with his arms resting on his knees, as if he had explained the matter to his own perfect satisfaction.

"I have taken steps to contain her, however," he went on, seeming to address no one in particular. "I have ordered her confined to my house of women . . ."

"Which will do little enough good—you will recall how many years she was confined there during the reign of our father, and how much mischief she was still able to achieve."

Esarhaddon glared at me for a moment, and then seemed to dismiss his annoyance with a shrug.

"I am also moving my court to Calah. My mother, as you might assume, will not be included in the move."

"Then the Land of Ashur will merely have two capitals."

"You seem to have remarkably little faith in my ability to govern my own house, Tiglath."

"It is merely that I have known your mother all my life."

"Yes—there is something in that. What would you have me do? Have her throat cut?"

He took another long swallow of wine, swilled the last of it around in his mouth, and then spat it out.

"At least I have learned one thing," he began, after a long pause. "I have learned that I can never trust her, not in the smallest particular. It was not only this business of the assassins, but there have been other matters . . ."

His voice trailed off, and the haunted look returned to his eyes.

"I can trust no one." His head turned slightly and he met my questioning gaze—in that instant he reminded me of our father, so old did he seem. "No one except you, Tiglath my brother. You alone, in all the world, will never betray me. I have learned that too."

"'Tiglath my brother.'" The words had a bitter taste in my mouth. "I seem to remember a time when you said you had no brother of that name."

"Yes—yes, I know what I said, and I repent of it . . ."

"And besides," I broke in on him, unwilling to let his head out of the noose, "besides, as you will recall, ties of blood count for very little in our family. Son murders father. Brother makes war against brother. Brother banishes brother . . ."

"Yes, yes, I know . . ."

"Brother insults brother, in front of his own soldiers, stripping him of honor and command." I walked over and grabbed him by the collar of his tunic, shaking him as a dog shakes a dead rat. My own wrath nearly choked me. "Brother locks brother in a tiny iron cage, leaving him there to feed on his fear for over a month, and then brother banishes brother, and for no just cause!"

"Enough!"

Esarhaddon took hold of my wrists—even as a child, he was always the stronger—and forced me to release him. Our eyes met in the most fierce anger.

"Enough," he went on, more calmly. "It was a mistake . . . a bad time, when my mind had grown maggoty with suspicion. Everyone—my mother—pouring lies into my ears . . . I repent of it. Damn you, I repent of it!"

He let go of my wrists, and I sat down beside him in the shade of his tent. Quarreling makes a man thirsty, and for a long time we sat together, passing the jug back and forth until we were both comfortably fuddled. For the moment at least, we seemed to have forgotten the bitterness between us.

"You have been in Egypt?" I asked finally.

"Yes—in Egypt." He made a face, as if the memory of the place was distasteful to him. "I managed to garrison a town at one of the mouths of their great river and I would have taken the attack straight up to Memphis, but then a storm . . . Conquest is not as easy as we imagined when we were boys, Tiglath. I have been plagued with all manner of ill fortune. I could have used you this last season."

"Is that why you have repented?"

"Of what?"

"Your brains are made of mud, Esarhaddon. What am I doing here? Why have you recalled me from banishment?"

"Oh—that! Why did I . . . ? I am not sure. Perhaps I am not drunk enough to remember."

He took another swallow of wine.

"Yes. Now it all comes back to me." He shook his head, as if something inside had gotten out of place. "Sidon. You killed Nabusharusur."

"I did not kill him."

"Did you not, by the Sixty Great Gods! Then I have been robbed, for I paid the spy who told me of it one hundred silver shekels. Well, it hardly matters. He is dead—someone must have killed him."

"The woman who is now my wife killed him. She did not know who he was. She did it to save my life."

"You have taken a wife?"

"Yes. An Ionian woman."

"The one who is traveling with you?"

"Yes."

He laughed. "Esharhamat will be disappointed to hear of it."

Esharhamat.

I cannot well describe how the sound of that name clenched my heart. I had not seen her in nearly ten years . . .

"But if it was your wife, then you as good as killed him," he went on, precisely as if we had never strayed from the subject—Esarhaddon was not a man to notice when he had inflicted a wound. "In any case, by the time I heard of it you had already escaped. It was good of you, by the way, to leave Abdimilkutte behind for me. It would have been humiliating if he had slipped through the net."

On this point at least I thought it better not to disabuse my brother, so I said nothing.

"I would have pardoned you then, you know." He turned to look at me, and his eyes were full of the sadness of wasted chances. "I would have pardoned you that night when we met outside the walls if your pride had let you bend a little. You cannot know, Tiglath, how I have missed you all these years."

"Do not speak to me of pardon."

I stood up—the illusion was shattered. We were not children again, Esarhaddon and I, and there was no forgetting all that had happened between us.

"Do not use that word to me!" I shouted, for I had found my wrath again. "Would that you had left me where I was, for I will not hear you speak of 'pardon.' It was never I who betrayed you, My Lord King, my thick-headed fool of a brother, for if I had I would be sitting on the throne of Ashur this day, and you would be a corpse whose bones the birds had picked clean these many bitter years I have spent wandering the edges of the earth. Never say you will 'pardon' me, Esarhaddon, or I will give you the word to eat at the point of my sword!"

"What a temper you have now, brother! Is this what comes of living among foreigners?"

He laughed, as if he had made a jest, and took another swallow of wine, for he was very drunk now.

And then, in an instant, his face darkened with melancholy.

"I have said I repent. For pity's sake ask no more of me, Tiglath, for I am a king and I have my pride. Let it be enough that I have restored to you all your property and honors."

Now he too stood up, but he had to reach out his hand to my shoulder lest he fall.

"I will never understand why you must always have the last word," he went on. "You must always carry your point, mustn't you. You must persuade our father to make war against the Medes so that you can go off to become a great hero while I am forced to stay at home to grow drunk each night and rut on Esharhamat that she may bring forth sons who may as easily be yours as mine . . ."

In that moment, with his hand still on my shoulder, I could easily have drawn my sword and killed him—he almost looked as if he would have wished me to, so black was his mood. Instead, I merely brushed away his arm.

"I think it best we do not speak of Esharhamat," I said quietly, for I was past all anger.

"As you wish." He reached down to pick up his wine jar, as if the matter were of no importance to him. "What, then, am I to tell her?"

"Tell her . . . ?"

"Yes, of course. I have promised her I would make it right between us again, and I do not like to disappoint her. She is not well, you know."

"What—what is wrong with her?"

"The gods alone know." He shrugged his shoulders. "Some woman's complaint. She has not been right since the birth of her last child. I believe I shall miss her when she dies."

I wished to hear no more. I took the reins of my horse and jumped up on its back, longing to be as far from this place as I could.

"Where will you go?" Esarhaddon asked, looking up at me like a child who knows he is about to be abandoned.

"To Three Lions, now that it is mine again. And then—I know not."

"You will not find your mother there, Tiglath, for she is dead."

"I knew."

"You knew?" It was as if I had struck him between the eyes with my closed fist. "How could you have known?"

"I knew—that is enough." I pulled the horse around sharp and he snorted loudly, as eager to be away as I was.

"Then come to Nineveh when you are finished grieving. Your king awaits you in Nineveh. When will you come?"

"Who can say? Perhaps never."

He shouted something after me, but I did not hear what it was. I heard only the wild beating of the horse's hooves, like the sound of my own heart.

Half an hour after I left Esarhaddon the sun was quenched behind the western horizon like an ember dropped into the sea. It was rough country and, so far from the main caravan trail, treacherous. I did not care to lose my way under the moonless night sky, so I decided I would not try to go on before morning. I found a low bluff to shelter against, tethered my horse and wrapped myself in a blanket, hoping for the release of a little sleep.

It was a doomed enterprise—too much had happened too quickly and I could not sort it out. My mind felt numb, helpless against the tides of feeling and memory that flooded over it unbidden.

"Esharhamat will be disappointed to hear of it." I had taken a wife, and Esharhamat would be disappointed to hear of it. She was my brother's wife and the mother of his children—many children, so I gathered—and I cannot describe how I shrank from the idea that she must now hear of my marriage.

"I do not care how you spend your seed," she had told me once, *"so long as I have your heart."* Now, after all this time, would she still whisper those same words to her soul? Did I wish it? Selana did not deserve this of me. It seemed that I could keep faith with nothing.

I had been away, wandering the earth, these seven years—had I changed so much? Or, perhaps, I had not changed at all. I did not know which was worse.

And what of Esarhaddon? He was my brother and yet my king. Did it matter if I loved or hated him? Did I know which, or could the two exist together? *"I have repented of it,"* he said. Did I believe him? Did I care? *"Your king waits for you in Nineveh,"* he said. Let him wait, I thought.

Nothing was settled. I was now once more a great man in the Land of

Ashur, so the king said. I was returned to favor, so the king said. He might even believe it, yet it meant nothing. There was no safety.

I spent that night in a kind of giddy despair, waiting for the sleep that never came, waiting for dawn.

At the first hint of daylight I started on my way again. I found the main road quickly enough, but Selana and Enkidu were at least six hours ahead of me. I did not catch up with them before I reached the gates of Rasappa, two days later.

In the days when my father still imagined he could bully the gods into making me king after him, I had visited Rasappa to pray at the temples and win the garrison to my cause. That had been nearly fifteen years before, and I had not been back since, but the place was little changed. There is such a sameness about provincial capitals, with their mud-brick walls and their corner towers, that I think I could be set down in one I had never seen before and find my way about quite easily. I entered through the main gate just an hour before sunset, a little against the tide of farmers returning home after a day at the bazaars. The two guards looked as if they were already half asleep.

"Did you notice a man and a woman enter the city this morning?" I asked one of them. "Foreigners—the man has wheat-colored hair and is the size of three. He carries an ax slung over his shoulder. If you saw him you would remember."

"We only came on duty at noon," he answered. Yet he looked at me strangely, so I thought it possible he might be lying. "Friends of yours, these foreigners?"

"Yes, friends. Due to an accident we became separated on the road."

"Well, we saw no one like that. Try the wineshops."

I thanked him and went on through. A moment later I happened to glance back and noticed that he and his colleague were engaged in what had every appearance of being an argument.

It has nothing to do with me, I thought. To them, doubtless one dust-stained traveler is like another.

I made other inquiries and quickly discovered the stable where Selana and Enkidu had left their horses.

"A foreign woman? Young?" The ostler seemed to brighten at the recollection. "She wears a marriage veil but lets it hang open as if she has forgotten that it is there?"

"I fear so, yes."

"She gave me a piece of silver. She babbled at me in a tongue that sounded like birds chirping, but her coin spoke clearly enough."

He laughed at the recollection, or perhaps only at his own joke.

"Where did they go when they left here?" I asked.

"To the tavern just opposite," he answered, indicating the direction with a short, chopping motion of his hand. Then, as if some thought had just come into his mind, he tilted his head and regarded me through narrowed eyes.

"But pardon me, Your Honor—do I not know you from somewhere?"

"It is unlikely. I have been away for several years."

He accepted this as an answer without seeming to believe it, and I bade him a good evening. It is strange how the habits of a fugitive stay with one, for I had a dread of being recognized.

At the tavern I was shown to an upstairs room, where I surprised my friends at their dinner. The impenetrable Macedonian merely grunted and turned back to his food, but Selana, looking up at the sound of the door curtain being pushed aside, dropped a bowl of millet and onions into her lap and let out a shriek to awaken the dust of my ancestors.

"I have been visiting with the king," I announced pleasantly. "I found him in a forgiving mood—I am welcomed back as his friend and brother."

First she wept, and then, almost immediately, she was of course furious with me.

"My lord frightens everyone and then, after three days of suspense, turns up again as if he had just stepped outside to empty his bladder!" she shouted, hot tears streaming down her face as I held her, her little fists beating at my chest as if she intended to break my collarbone. When this did not avail, she pulled herself loose from my embrace and kicked at me so that I was hard-pressed to preserve my shins from injury. "You knew all along there was never any peril—you have thought of this game merely to torment me!"

"Be quiet, Selana, and bring me some wine, for the last thing to pass my lips was a handful of water from an irrigation ditch, and that this morning. Knowing how the landlord would doubtless cheat foreigners by giving them worthless food, I have ordered up bread and melon and the roasted hindquarters of a goat."

I sat down and began eating her millet with greedy fingers, for I was hungry past imagining.

"And do not imagine that we are out of all jeopardy just because Esarhaddon did not have my throat slit on the road—we are not. The king says he loves me again and may believe it, but he was never the real danger. The king has a mother who is as cunning as an adder and hates me worse than death."

>> 467 <<

"What will happen now?" Selana asked, lying by my side in the darkness. It was yet an hour or two before dawn, but sleep had fled from both of us.

"I cannot say. The king expects me and I must go, but perhaps it would be just as well to let him wait a while yet. One of my farms is about half a day's ride from Nineveh—it appears to be mine still, since my properties have all been returned to me. We will stop there."

"One of . . . ? You have more?" Even in the dark I could see her eyes grow wide with wonder.

"Yes—of course. In this land your husband is a royal prince and rich beyond avarice. I own vast estates, most of which I have never even seen. I have a palace in Nineveh. You will have the finest garments and jewelry of gold, copper and silver. You will have servants past counting, Selana. Will it please you to live as a great lady?"

"How can I know? I . . . I am a peasant girl, Lord. I was born in a stone hut to parents who knew nothing all their lives except work, sleep, food and rutting. I never even owned a pair of sandals until you found me. Oh, I wish we could go back to Sicily!"

"That I fear we cannot do. Yet you will like Three Lions—that is the name of the place. If I have a home on this earth, it is Three Lions."

"I thought the farm in Sicily had become your home."

I did not answer, but poured myself a cup of wine from the jar beside our sleeping mat.

"Do you think we shall ever go back there?" she asked, after a long silence. "Do you even want to go back?"

"We must wait and see. It is not in my hands." We both understood that I had not answered the question.

"Yet surely the king will let you go if you wish it—he would not hold you against your will."

"It is not in the king's hands either."

She did not understand—how could I have explained to her that Esarhaddon and I, even Naq'ia, though she acknowledged no will but her own, could only wait upon the pleasure of heaven? The Lord Ashur was wise, but he kept his purposes hidden.

She did not understand, but she was clever enough to hold her tongue.

As dawn approached I began to be aware of a curious silence that had settled around us.

Even at this hour, while the sky was still a pale gray, I would have expected to hear the rumble of farm carts on their way to the market stalls. There should have been the sounds of voices in the street below us, the shouts of revelers going home at last to their beds, and the muttered conversations of respectable tradesmen who had risen early to open shop for the day.

And the tavern itself seemed empty. Where was the smell of wood-smoke as the landlord's wife made breakfast? Where were the footfalls of the household slaves, and the chatter of ceaseless quarreling that is part of every tavern's life? Had the world died around us as we slept?

I was not the only one who had noticed it. Selana had fallen asleep again, but I saw the light from the doorway darken as Enkidu stepped soundlessly into the room. He was dressed, and he carried his ax in his hand.

He motioned for me to stand and attend, and then pointed back the way he had come. I saw at once what he meant, for the stairway was as silent as if it led down into the bowels of the earth.

Our rooms were in the back of the house, so the only window looked out upon an alley, which was also deserted. The only way to discover what had happened was to go out into the street.

I went back to my sleeping mat and held Selana's foot until she woke up.

"What is . . . ?"

And then she heard it—the silence.

"Get dressed," I told her. "Be quick."

By the time I had buckled on my sword, she was ready. We made our careful way down the stairs. The tavern door stood open. I had only to go outside.

And there they waited. It looked as if the whole city had risen from their beds to keep this vigil outside the tavern door. They filled the street in every direction. Common soldiers, merchants and craftsmen, porters and harlots and dirt-smeared farming folk, great and humble together, men and women, even children, standing in perfect stillness. I could not help but wonder how long they had been there.

The instant I appeared the knelt. In their hundreds they went down on their knees before me, in waves, like the sea parting. Their eyes never left my face as they paid me this silent homage.

They have remembered me, I thought. After seven years I come among them as a nameless traveler, and still they know me. How in one lifetime shall I ever merit such an honor?

XXXV

THERE IS NO SOUND ON EARTH STRANGER THAN THE SI-
lence of a multitude. I stood in the doorway of the tavern, the focus of a
thousand wills, as if by that single act I had answered the dearest wish of
their hearts. I did not speak—they did not wish me to speak. There was
no place for words.

I do not know how long we continued thus, and at last I became aware
that Enkidu and Selana were standing behind me.

"What do they want, Lord?" she asked, in a voice that was no more
than a breath. "They make me afraid."

"They make me afraid as well," I answered. "Just not in the same way."

I made a gesture with my hand, holding it out and turning the palm up,
and the people of Rasappa knew they had permission to rise. They came
to their feel slowly, as if their joints had grown stiff, yet even now they did
not break their silence.

"Selana, put your veil on—now. Enkidu, fetch the horses."

We were suffered to go. The crowds did not hinder us but stood aside,
and Enkidu crossed over to the stable and came back leading our three
horses by the bridles.

All the way to the city gates, the streets were filled with people. They
made way for us and knelt in silence.

"Why do they not speak?"

I turned back to Selana, who, out of some instinctive caution, rode a
little behind me, and smiled.

"I can only guess," I said. "Perhaps they do not know that Esarhaddon
has recalled me from exile. If this is so, then to speak would be to defy the

king's sentence against me, and they would not insult the king. They honor me in the only way left to them."

Neither of us spoke again until the city was far behind us—until we no longer felt those hundreds of eyes on our backs.

"Is it because you are a prince? Who are you to them?"

I did not answer. Instead, I thought of Tabshar Sin, my second father, my old *rab shaqe*, who had taken a raw boy and made him into a soldier. What had he said? *"You are praised all the more because you are not Esarhaddon."*

I noticed, with some irritation, that Selana had once more removed her veil.

Five days later, we crossed a pass through the Sinjar Mountains and looked down to see the Tigris, Mother of Rivers. When I wet my mouth with her waters, I wondered how I had lived these seven years without dying of thirst.

On the second morning after we crossed the river we found the boundary stone bearing the winged disk of Ashur that meant I was now passing across my own land. We would sleep that night at Three Lions.

At that season of the year the village people, my own tenants, were already busy with their first harvest. We rode through fields where the wheat was waist-high—it seemed as if my own lands had remained untouched by the famine and drought I had seen elsewhere—and as we passed, men and women would look up at us from their labor and their eyes would grow wide with speechless wonder.

And then the cry would break from their throats—"The Lord Tiglath has come back, the lord is home again!"—and they would gather around, reaching up to touch me that they could confirm to themselves that I was a living man and not a spirit let loose into the daylight. And then the men would offer me their beer jars, as if they thought that a journey as long as mine, all the way back from the earth's end, must have been a thirsty business.

"Shall we send a runner to inform the overseer, Lord?"

I laughed and shook my head. "If I know Tahu Ishtar, he is probably already well aware of my presence. I hope I will find him well."

"He is dead, Lord—he died two years ago. He broke his neck when his horse threw him."

The news came as an unpleasant shock, which must have shown itself in my face because quite suddenly the man seemed embarrassed, as if he had revealed a secret.

"His son is overseer now," he went on, after only the briefest pause. "Qurdi."

"Yes—of course."

"Shall we send him word, Lord?"

"No."

We rode on. Tahu Ishtar had been an able overseer and a man of dignity. To be respected by such a man as his master was an honor, and I had felt it as such. Now he had vanished into the emptiness of death. The world was forever diminished.

We reached the farmhouse just an hour or so before dark. As we approached I saw that a small crowd of house servants were already waiting to greet us. Among them was Qurdi, along with his wife and their six children. I noted that Naiba's belly was round with a seventh—she was even more beautiful than the last time I had seen her, and she seemed happy. Perhaps that was why. When our eyes met she blushed and lowered her gaze.

Qurdi, his staff of office in his hand, bowed. Then everyone else bowed, as if they had been waiting for his signal. Qurdi's beard was quite full now and he had acquired something of Tahu Ishtar's bearing. The first time I had seen him he was no more than a boy, to be lifted up with one arm to ride behind his father.

His obeisance made, he smiled with pleasure, showing strong white teeth.

"Welcome, Lord—welcome home!"

I slid off my horse and took his hand. "It is good to be home," I answered. "And from what I can see, you have served me well as overseer, as I would have expected from your father's son."

I felt a tug and looked down to behold Naiba knealing down to kiss the hem of my tunic. I tried to lift her up again, but she took my hand and pressed it against her forehead.

"My lord, my lord," she cried, her voice trailing off into a sob. I risked a quick glance at Qurdi to see how he took this display, but there was a grin on his lips and his eyes shone with obvious pride in his wife.

"A fresh-killed goat is already on the fire, Lord," he said. "And the stones are well heated in the sweating house."

After I had greeted each of the servants in turn—most of them had been trained by my mother and were old acquaintances—all I wanted to do was to clean off the dust of my long journey. The first breath of steam from the sweating house was like the perfume from an orchard that is in flower.

"Who is the woman?" Selana asked, as she scrubbed my back with the green leaves of a tree branch. Enkidu, crouched naked in a corner of the tiny building, looked as if he wished himself somewhere else.

"She was formerly my concubine," I answered, seeing no reason to lie. "I took her as booty when once I made war against the tribes of the eastern mountains. In time she came to love the boy Qurdi, so I gave her to him as his wife."

I was sitting on a stool, and she put her hands on my shoulders and leaned around to look at my face.

"You tolerated this insult?"

"What insult?"

"That she should raise her eyes to another man while you still took her to your sleeping mat?"

"A woman cannot help where she loves, no more than can a man. I was not touched in the matter, not even in my vanity, so why speak of an insult?" I shrugged. "Selana, for all that you were born free, you have retained the outlook of a slave. She wished to be his wife—why should I make her life a misery by denying her this?"

"You had grown weary of her."

"No. I did not want to be the cause of her suffering."

She asked me no more questions about Naiba, but what conjectures she formed on her own I cannot answer for.

That night at dinner I drank no wine, only the beer that had been brewed out of my own grain. I ate alone, and the woman who served me had been one of my mother's favorites.

"How long ago did your mistress die?" I asked her, for I wished to hear of Merope.

"Nearly three years ago, Lord," she answered, shaking her head as the tears welled at the recollection. I do not doubt that her grief was real, for my mother had been an easy woman to love. "I remember it well, for it was the winter after the king first returned from campaigning in the west—I am not likely to forget that."

"Why?"

"Why, Lord?" She looked into my face as if she thought I must be having a jest at her expense. "Because that was the first time he came here. I had never expected to live to serve bread and beer to the king!"

"He came *here*?" I could hardly believe it.

"Oh yes—twice that autumn. He came to see the Lady Merope. To bring her the news."

"What news?"

"That he had seen you during his travels, Lord. That you were still alive."

I cannot describe the effect these words had on me. That Esarhaddon should have delayed his triumph in Nineveh to stop here and bring a few words of comfort to my mother was a kindness I would not have expected of him.

"You say he came twice?"

"Yes. He traveled up from Nineveh with only a light escort and stayed for three days. He hunted during the days and took supper with my lady in the evenings—they would talk far into the night . . . Do not grieve, My Lord, for she lived each day expecting your return and died quietly in her sleep."

"Leave me now, Shulmunaid."

I stayed upon a long time that night, with no company but a wine jar and the soft light from the brazier fire. My mother was the gentlest spirit I had ever known, and she had died without her only son there to close her eyes. I was not the one to blame for this, yet I felt as if I had wronged her. She was buried, I knew, under the floor of that very room, according to the practice of my people. Yet had I been here I could have burned her body first and sealed up her bones in a silver urn. Did her soul rest quietly in this foreign earth, so far from her home? I could only hope.

The next morning I came outside and found Qurdi waiting for me.

"Will it please My Lord to ride out with his servant and look over the condition of the estate?" he asked, as with his right hand he made a sweeping gesture that seemed to take in even the mountains in the distance. "I have a horse ready for you."

My overseer was still a young man, no more than four or five and twenty years old, and there was a twinkle of mischief in his eye as he spoke. I wondered what he could be about.

We walked over to the stable, and even before Qurdi opened the door I could hear the sound of hooves beating against the stall gate.

Ghost! I thought. But no, it was not possible. I had ridden Ghost during my campaign against the Medes, and that had been ten years ago. A horse, even such a one as my Ghost, does not live so long as that and still break down the stall gate of a morning.

And yet the fine silver stallion I found inside might have been he, by some magic returned to youth and strength. The only difference my eye could find was the absence of the crescent-shaped scars on his chest, put there by the hooves of the Lord Daiaukka's horse when we fought our death duel, and Ghost, braver than his master, had refused to accept defeat and saved my life. This was not Ghost, but it might have been.

"His foal," Qurdi announced, running his hand over the stallion's neck to quiet him. "Ghost was found dead in his pasture last year, and we buried him as if he had been a man, with offerings of wine, because we knew you honored him—but he left this behind."

"He is fine," I said, filled with wonder, for such a horse is nobler than any man.

"And ready for campaign!" My overseer grinned, as if this jest had been kept in waiting for me. "The king had him brought to the royal stables in Nineveh to be trained up as a war stallion. He was sent back twenty days ago—that is how we knew you would be home soon. He answers to his sire's name."

"Ghost," I whispered, for I felt choked with emotion. I reached out to him and the horse accepted the touch of my hand. If Esarhaddon had studied to please me, he had found the right instrument. "Yes, by all means—let us ride out and look over the condition of the estate!"

That first day home was perhaps the happiest of my life.

And the happiness continued, so that I was not eager to depart from Three Lions. I found I preferred the life of a farmer to that of a prince, and there was little enough to draw me to Nineveh. We stayed the better part of two months.

Selana, as soon as she had learned some twenty or thirty Akkadian words, enough to make her will understood among the servants, took over the management of my house as seamlessly as if she had lived within its walls all her life. There is perhaps more wisdom than we imagine in the universal prohibition against teaching the military arts to women, for some of them would make fine commanders and turn the world into an even more quarrelsome place than it is. Or perhaps not, for she and Naiba soon became close companions, so much so that, when Naiba's time came upon her, Selana was there to help with the birth of a daughter, named Selana Ishtar to do her honor.

I cannot claim that I did not look with a certain uneasiness upon this friendship between my wife and my former concubine. There were things about my old life I would have kept from Selana's ear, and no secret is safe between two women who have known the same man.

But in all else this was a season of unblemished peace. The farm had prospered in my absence, and I delighted to see the plow open the black earth and to break in my hand the wheat that had grown in my own fields. This was wealth beyond the dreams of kings, I thought. This is glory to make the mightiest conqueror weep with envy. If I could but contrive to stay here until the end of my life . . .

Yet it was not to be. I kept remembering Esarhaddon's words—"*Your king awaits you in Nineveh."* I must go. It was not something I could evade forever.

So one day I gave orders that Ghost was to be ready in the morning. I would leave the next day.

"I think it best you remain here," I told Selana. "You will be happier here than in Nineveh."

I smiled when I saw the expression on her face, wondering why I even bothered to make the effort.

"What is there in Nineveh that should keep me from my lord? Or perhaps my lord thinks that there he will have no need of a wife."

Her eyes narrowed—yes, of course, she had heard something. Perhaps, I thought, she is even right not to trust me. So little did I know my own mind.

"Then come if it is your will. In Nineveh you can be a court lady and live in luxury. I will even buy you a slave girl, a child even younger than yourself, that she may torment you as you do me."

It was an old jest between us, and it made her laugh and forget her suspicions. And I laughed too, and felt as if I had somehow betrayed her already. And then I remembered Esharhamat, and my mind darkened.

We left the next morning, before sunrise, while the sky was still the color of tarnished silver. It was a journey of no more than half a day, yet Selana was filled with anxious impatience, as if it would never end. The closer we came to our destination, the more it seemed to trouble her.

"Is it far now?" Selana asked, for the twentieth time. She glanced about at the empty countryside as if expecting a trap.

"Be patient another quarter of an hour, and you will see a sight to take the breath from beneath your ribs."

I had traveled this road a hundred times in my life and knew it the way a man knows his wife's body. For most of its length it followed the river and then, at a point just ahead, veered away to sweep around a low hill, rising halfway up its side. I knew that as soon as the road broke its climb and leveled out we should see Mother Tigris again, stretched out in a great glistening curve, and, beyond that, less than an hour's ride before us, the walls of Nineveh.

We saw all that, as well as the crowds that waited along the approaches to the Ambasi Gate. It was like the Festival of Akkitu, when the whole city turns out to welcome the birth of the new year. It was like the day my father brought home his armies from the conquest of Babylon, and the people of the god lined the roads to celebrate Ashur's triumph . . .

We were still more than half a *beru* from the first guard tower, and already I could hear the trembling sound that is the mingling of a thousand voices into one. The very air seemed to shake as their cry reached us—"Ashur is king!" they shouted. "Ashur is king! Ashur is king! Ashur is king!"

We descended the hill onto the broad plain that led to the city, and still they shouted "Ashur is king! Ashur is king!"

"What does it mean, Lord?" The question carried with it a certain edge of panic that drew my gaze to Selana's face.

"I do not know what it means. I have no . . ."

But by then we had come close enough to see their faces—and they ours. They surged forward along the road, and all doubt ended when the cry broke from their throats.

"Tiglath! Tiglath! TigLATH! TigLATH!"

I knew then.

"Selana, stay back. Enkidu, keep her back, or they may tear you both to pieces. A mob such as this is as dangerous and unpredictable as a jealous woman."

I goaded my horse into a canter and met the crowd perhaps a quarter of an hour's walk from the city gate. In an instant they engulfed me, their faces full of adoration as they reached out their hands to me, holding up bread and fruit and cups of wine, women holding up their children that my shadow might touch them like a benediction. My horse was nearly mad with fear, and it was all I could do to hold him.

I looked back and saw that Enkidu had his hand on the bridle of Selana's horse. They were well behind me, following at the rear of the crowd, which hardly noticed their existence. They were safe.

It was more than an hour before I passed beneath the Ambasi Gate and entered the city. I passed up the Street of Adad, still deaf from the shouting, hardly able to move at all of my own volition, driven slowly ahead by nothing save the weight of the multitude that pushed forward to be near me. I lost all sense of time, of place, of my own identity except as the object of a whole people's love.

I cannot describe what it was like. The people of Nineveh threw flowers in my path, and even gold and silver coins. Many cheered—a sound full of wild joy—and some even wept, but most kept up the chant. "TigLATH! TigLATH! TigLATH!" The clamor of their voices beat at my ears like a hammer. The air left my lungs and my throat tightened as tears filled my eyes.

And still, always, in some quiet place in my heart, I heard the words, *"You have known all this before—this has all happened before and it did not protect you then. There is no safety in the worship of a mob."* Yet how could I not be moved? How could I not belong to them in that moment, who had made me their soul?

At last we reached the steps of the palace from which my father had ruled the four corners of the earth. It now belonged, with all else in the land, to my brother Esarhaddon, who even at that moment stood before the great cedar doors, resplendent in his golden robes, in his hand the golden sword of Ashur's kings.

I reined in my horse, who stamped with his stone-hard hooves and snorted like a demon. The crowd fell silent in the presence of their lord and judge. I dismounted and knelt, dropped my gaze to the cobbled street, waiting until the only sound I heard was the breath in my own nostrils. We all waited together: I the outcast prince returned from exile; Esarhaddon the king who had issued the sentence of banishment; and the mobs of Nineveh, our witness and our judge.

I stood up and raised my eyes to Esarhaddon's face. The drama has gone on long enough, I thought. Have we not been through all this before?

Our glances met. Esarhaddon was as impassive as an idol. He neither moved nor spoke.

Then I will make you choose, I thought. I will not humble myself yet again, for you have forced this upon me.

The palace steps rose before me like a mountain. I began to climb them, a step at a time, slowly. The whole city seemed to hold its breath.

And then, quite suddenly, Esarhaddon handed his sword of office to a chamberlain and started down the stairway toward me. His pace quickened as he went, as did my own, and we met in the middle and embraced, for the first time in many years, as brothers.

The crowd found its voice again, and their cheers crashed over us like the waves of an angry sea.

"I see you have learned to be clever," I whispered in his ear, even as we held each other in our arms. "You arranged this, to bind me to you."

"I? I did nothing, except to have the road watched, and to send heralds through the city to proclaim the return of the Lord Tiglath Ashur, the king's beloved brother. I did nothing—well, hardly anything.

"You see?" He held me away from him for a moment and smiled, a bitter smile as his eyes turned toward his exulting subjects. "I am only their king—nothing more. I have their obedience, but it is to you they have given their heart."

XXXVI

I SLEPT THAT NIGHT IN THE PALACE I HAD INHERITED from my uncle the Lord Sinahiusur, *turtanu* in the reign of my father and a wise and good man who had been dust in his tomb for more than ten years. Most of the household slaves had been his, and thus I felt there was perhaps a little less chance that I would find poison in the wine or be murdered in my bed before the dawn broke on my first day home. This was Nineveh, I reminded myself, where Esarhaddon was only the king and treachery ruled.

"I do not know how I shall manage such a place," Selana exclaimed, looking about in wonder—we were in the great hall, where the walls were covered with painted friezes and a plot of land the size of the floor would have fed a large family. "It dwarfs the palace in Memphis, where I was only a kitchen servant."

"You will not have to manage anything. The steward has been with my family for more than twenty years and knows his work. Here you are not a farmer's wife but a great lady."

"What does a great lady do?"

"She plots the ruin of her husband. She breeds up sons that she may rule through them when he is dead."

"My lord is pleased to jest."

"Am I? You have never met Esarhaddon's mother."

"What then will I do?"

"Only love me—and pray that we may someday contrive to leave this place alive."

I embraced her, wishing I could have left her in Sicily, yet glad to have her here.

"Are we not safe then?" she asked, clinging to me as if afraid she might drown in the strangeness of this evil city. "The crowds today . . . These people love you as if you were a god."

"The last time I passed under the gates of Nineveh, it was just the same. The mob cheered me because they thought I would save them from my brother, and then Esarhaddon had me locked away in an iron cage, where I thought I would probably die, and then he drove me from the land as if I had been a dog caught stealing table scraps. And now I am back, and they cheer me again. Who can say what they expect of me this time? But probably they will be disappointed, and then, if it should be the god's pleasure, they will stand passively aside and watch me be destroyed."

"When you speak thus, though you are here with your arms about me, you make me more afraid than I was when you left me alone to fight against the bandits."

"When I speak thus, I am more afraid than ever I was then."

The next morning I went back to the king's palace to take breakfast with Esarhaddon.

If my father had had anyone whom he could truly have described as his friend—and kings, it has been my experience, do not usually have friends, for friendship implies trust—then that person was my uncle the Lord Sinahiusur. They had known each other since infancy, and in all the years that the Lord Sennacherib reigned as Master of the Earth's Four Corners he never made a decision without first discussing it with his brother. When the king was away on campaign the *turtanu* ruled in Nineveh as if he were king himself, and when the king was home the two men saw each other every day.

Thus, when I went to visit my brother that morning, there was no necessity for me to venture out into the street. The two palaces were connected by a series of courtyards and enclosed gardens leading from my private apartment to Esarhaddon's. In one of these, sitting on a small stone bench beneath a wall covered with vines, I found the Lady Naq'ia.

She was probably fifty years old, yet she was still handsome and her hair remained smoothly black, whereas her son's was patched with gray. I had not seen her in seven years, but it might have been the hour before, so little had she changed—such women do not age; they merely harden with time. She raised her eyes to me and smiled with closed lips, not even pretending to be surprised.

"Well, Tiglath, shall I welcome you home?" she asked, looking down to adjust the folds of her tunic—black and shot through with silver threads, the only color I had ever seen her wear. "It seems your victory over me is quite complete. Shall I congratulate you?"

"I had rather you did not, Lady, since we both know that you can afford to lose many times and I not even once."

Her smile tightened slightly in acknowledgment of the compliment, if that was how she chose to interpret it.

"I despair of finding the instrument that could vanquish you, for you seem to be endlessly resourceful at saving yourself."

She shrugged her thin shoulders—a graceful movement that somehow reminded me of a spider walking across its web. Did she mean to imply that I was now to consider myself proof against the hand of another assassin? It was not an assurance in which I was prepared to put any great trust.

"Or perhaps it is true that you live under the protection of the gods. Do you believe that heaven intervenes in the affairs of men, Tiglath, that we are hostages to their will? Or perhaps we are beneath their notice?"

"I believe what I have seen, Lady."

Naq'ia, whose blood was colder than the winter wind, laughed at this. The sound was like the tinkling of little copper bells, like no human laugh. It made my bowels turn to water.

"Yet it is good to remember, Tiglath Ashur, that heaven sometimes preserves a man only to make him wretched. Your god perhaps has drawn a magic circle around you, but it extends no wider than your own footprints."

"I understand you, Lady," I said, for the threat was plain enough. "I have a wife, and you think to make me afraid through her. But she too has a protector."

"The giant with wheat-colored hair?" She nodded, as if nothing could have mattered less. "He appears a simpleton. Yes—I have seen him."

"He is not a simpleton, but something both less than a man and more. Do not misjudge, Lady, for if any accident should befall my wife he will seek you out. There will be nowhere to hide yourself from his wrath, and with the great ax he carries he will split you open like a rabbit. It will avail you nothing then that your son is a king. He will not care."

Was she frightened? If she was it did not show, but she understood well enough. Once more the shoulders moved under her black tunic.

"You must think me a very wicked creature, Tiglath."

"I do, Lady—the most wicked I have ever known."

I suspect that in her own strange way she was flattered, but who could ever hope to look into Naq'ia's dark soul?

"Yet it is some virtue, at least, that we can speak so frankly to each other," she said at last. "Who is there else in the wide world to whom I can reveal my mind, Tiglath? My son? No, not he. Only you, who holds me in such scant honor."

"On the contrary, Lady—if fear is a kind of honor, I honor you. I am not likely to slight your claims to respect."

"Sit down beside me, Tiglath." She moved a little aside on the stone bench, making room. "Esarhaddon has waited seven years and can wait a while longer. Sit with me for a time and bear an old woman company."

Stirred in with my earliest memories is the fear of Naq'ia. No man has ever inspired such dread in me, perhaps because men are not gifted at dissembling—not that Naq'ia attempted to conceal her hatred for me, but even as her tongue spoke of my destruction her manner was soft, almost motherly, as if I were nothing more than Esarhaddon's boyhood friend, known to her since infancy, almost a second son. Thus it had become a matter of habit to treat her with courtesy. I did as she asked and took my place beside her on the bench. Besides, Naq'ia did not gossip idly. If there was something she wished to tell me, I thought it best to know what it was.

She spoke to me of all that had befallen the land of Ashur since I left it, of Esarhaddon and her disappointment in him, of many things besides. More than this, she told me of Ashurbanipal, the son whom I could never acknowledge as my own, Esharhamat's child.

"He is very intelligent—he would make a better scribe than king, I fancy, for he does not relish his training in the house of war. But of course what else can one expect when his mother spoiled him so? By that, if by nothing else, I would have known him for your son rather than Esarhaddon's. Esharhamat is not so fond of her other children."

"Who else knows then?"

"Oh, the secret is safe enough." Naq'ia made a loose gesture with her hand, as if to wave away any thought of disclosure. "Esarhaddon suspects—more than suspects—but only you and I and Esharhamat know for certain. The boy himself, of course, hasn't an inkling. He calls me Grandmother and I treat him as if he were my heart's darling, preferring him even over his brothers."

"And that because he will rule one day, and they will not."

Naq'ia glanced at me quickly, out of the corner of her eye, and smiled.

"So you say, and the omen readers, but Esarhaddon insists that the child of his loins shall sit upon a throne and be called king. He favors the boy Shamash Shumukin, and why should he not? They are alike as a pair of hands, those two. I too am fond of him—his mother never loved him, so I have been called upon to fill her place."

Yes, I saw clearly enough now. Perhaps she could not help herself, I thought. I could almost have pitied her. Naq'ia, who lived for power, to whom intrigue was as natural as breathing, saw plainly that she had lost her chance with Esarhaddon and was plotting to be great in the next reign. She might be dead by then, or too old to care, but she must weave her web or lose all pleasure in life.

In my blind stupidity, I imagined it was no more than that.

"Esharhamat is not well, you know," she said, as if she thought I might not have heard. "Will you see her?"

"I think not, Lady," I answered, lying to her and to myself.

"Ah—you feel some scruple about it, but that was ever your way, Tiglath. Do not concern yourself, for Esarhaddon will not mind. They have softened toward one another in recent years, so much so that my son would not deny his wife anything that could ease her mind. In any case, there will be no more children, so there can be no harm done. Or perhaps it is because of the pretty foreign girl you have taken to wife . . ."

"I will not see her, Lady," I said, rising—this had gone on long enough, I had decided. "I will not because it is not my will."

"Yes, I see that it is not." She smiled, offering me her hand to kiss. "The will of Tiglath Ashur, which, like the will of heaven, is unknowable, even to himself."

"Where have you been? I thought perhaps you had left again on your travels."

Esarhaddon enjoyed his own jest enormously, laughing and slapping his thigh hard enough almost to raise a bruise.

"I have been sitting in the garden with your mother," I answered, not particularly amused—in my heart I had forgiven my brother, but he could still nettle me. "She complains that her son is a fool and a bad king and lies under the gods' curse."

"That only means she is angry because I have grown up and slipped the leash."

Nevertheless, his face blackened with something between wrath and dread. Esarhaddon was lying naked on a couch, playing with a small bowl of dates while one of his women—an Elamite from the look of her, with breasts like melons and skin the color of wood smoke—was rubbing oil into his legs. He kicked her away, hard enough that she pitched over onto the tile floor to land backside first with a loud smack, and then he stood up and wrapped a sheet around himself, knotting it at the waist with quite unnecessary violence.

"She said I was cursed by the gods, did she?" he went on, glowering, looking around as if for someone else to punish. "And if I am, it is no one's doing but hers—you will do well to stay away from my mother, Tiglath. She will poison you if you are fool enough to give her the chance."

"Then I promise not to accept any dinner invitations."

"That is wise of you."

He seemed to grow a little more cheerful. The Elamite woman was still lying on the floor with her face hidden in her hands, crouched in supplication before her master's displeasure. Esarhaddon looked down at her as if he had momentarily forgotten her existence, and then he laughed and put his hand on her naked back, patting her as he might pat one of his hunting dogs. When she had summoned courage enough to rise to her knees, he took her right breast in his hand, seeming to measure its weight.

"She is not a bad one, this," he said, smiling down at her with the pride of ownership. "Her husband was a tavern keeper in Kish. I gave him a hundred silver shekels for her and forgave him his taxes for five years, but one cannot expect a tavern keeper to put a proper value on such a woman. She can press the seed out of you like a millstone. Her name is Keturah. By the gods, I believe will make you a present of her, simply because I love you so well."

I was about to refuse—Selana's reaction, if I began collecting women to be run in teams, like chariot horses, was something I would rather imagine than witness—but my brother was a king, and the gifts of a king are not to be despised. Besides, Esarhaddon had meant the offer kindly, and he was not the sort of man to appreciate my wife's objections, or even to imagine she could have any. I did not like to hurt his feelings.

"She may not relish the change," I said, thinking . . . I know not what I thought.

"Nonsense. Unless you met with some accident while you dwelt among the foreigners, you will do well enough for Keturah. Like a wise harlot, she measures a man strictly by the contents of his loincloth—in handfuls. Hah, hah, hah!"

He did not even notice that I failed to laugh with him. He was too occupied with looking about him for his wine jar.

"Keturah, you worthless slut," he shouted, honoring her with another kick, "fetch us more wine. And bread, and cheese, and some lamb boiled in millet. Can't you see that we are hungry? Be quick, or your new master will think I have merely grown tired of your sloth. Go!"

An hour later, our bellies full and our heads buzzing with wine, we sat outside together in the shade of a courtyard wall. Esarhaddon looked half asleep.

"Do you remember when we were boys in the house of war?" he asked suddenly, after a long silence. "Do you remember the night old Tabshar Sin sent me up to the barrack roof without my supper as a punishment for fighting, and you stole bread for me, and a jug of beer? Do you remember how drunk we got that night, how we almost fell off the roof we were so drunk?"

"We were very young then," I answered, for I did remember. "You have to be *very* young to get drunk on half a jar of beer."

"What went wrong, do you suppose? We trusted each other then."

"We were boys then, Esarhaddon. We are men now, and much has happened in the meantime."

"Yes." He sighed and leaned forward to rest his arms on his knees. "The gods decided I would be king—or, rather, my mother decided it for them—and then I decided that you wished the throne of Ashur for yourself."

"I did, only I did not want it badly enough."

"Because if you had, you would be king now, and I would be dead."

"Yes—that was the price I was not willing to pay. Your death."

"Yes. I believe it. No one wanted me to be king." Esarhaddon straightened up and wiped his face with his hands, as if waking up after a long debauch. "Not our father, not the army, not even I. No one except my mother."

"Your mother, and the eternal gods."

"You believe that, do you?

He looked at me with a kind of amused scorn—Esarhaddon, who all his life had lived in the most dreadful fear of the Unseen. That look should have told me everything.

But it was Ashur's pleasure that I would never know the truth until it was too late.

"You believe that fat priests can read the gods' will written in the entrails of a goat?" he went on. "Do you really, brother?"

"Yes. No less than you yourself. That is how the kings of Ashur have been chosen for a thousand years, and we are all still here, still masters of the earth. We must trust that the gods have chosen wisely this time as well."

"The gods, then, keep their purposes hidden—or perhaps they simply are not so clever as my mother. Remember, Tiglath, that I warned you."

When the sun began to approach its zenith, a chamberlain was sent to remind the king that his ministers required him. Esarhaddon threw an empty wine jug at his head and chased him away with a string of hideous curses.

"The Land of Ashur will not rule itself," I reminded him when he had caught his breath again.

"No, nor be ruled by a drunken fool, you might add." He shrugged his shoulders, as if dismissing all hope. "My servants tell me lies and do what they like—I am a soldier, Tiglath, not a mud-scratching scribe. The tax rolls are a riddle to me, and the speeches of foreign envoys tie my poor brain in knots."

"You have a *turtanu*. Leave these matters to him."

"Sha Nabushu?"

My brother laughed. He laughed until he had to wipe his eyes.

"Sha Nabushu?" he went on, when he could speak again with tolerable calm. "That empty melon? That daub of unfired clay? He is so frightened of my mother that he will not even loosen his loincloth to piss without her express permission. Sha Nabushu?—have you ever met the man?"

"Yes, I have met the man," I answered coldly. "It was he you sent to relieve me of my command before Khanirabbat."

But Esarhaddon, far from being abashed at this reminder, turned to look me in the face, quite as if I had said something brilliant.

"Yes—that is true. I did, didn't I."

For a moment there was no sound except the tinkling of water in the courtyard fountain next to which we happened to be standing. I was taller than my brother by more than a head, so he had to reach up to put his hand on my shoulder. He almost seemed to be pulling me down to his level, as if he wished to whisper something in my ear.

"Then here is your opportunity to return the compliment," he murmured. He seemed infinitely pleased with himself. "Go to him. Strip him of his title and rank. Become *turtanu* in his place and rule the Land of Ashur as king in all but name. Only leave me the army and I will be happy enough—free at last of this burden, I will conquer what is left of the world and make a name that will live forever. If you like, you can set Sha Nabushu to molding bricks for the city wall."

"I will serve you in any way you wish, Esarhaddon. I will put on a soldier's cloak and fight in any war, in any distant, god-cursed place you name. You have only to say 'do this,' and I will do it. Yet I will not be your *turtanu*, for if the god had meant me to rule, he would have made me king in your place."

My brother pushed himself away from me, as quickly as if my arm had turned all at once to molten bronze. His eyes blazed—he might have struck me had he dared, but somehow I knew he did not dare.

"With you it is always pride!" he shouted. "Pride, and nothing else. You will be second to no man living. If you cannot be king in name, even when I offer you a king's authority, you will not humble yourself to be anything. You are too great a man in your own eyes to accept honor at any man's hand. And most particularly not at mine!"

It might even have been true. I did not know. I only knew that something inside would not allow me to be Esarhaddon's *turtanu*.

"I might command it, you know."

His voice was lower now, yet the rage still quavered in every word.

"Yet you will not, Esarhaddon my brother—you will not."

"No. I will not."

Standing a little apart from me, he turned that I might not see his face. Thus I know not what passion it was, whether grief or rage or something which was neither, that made his shoulders tremble so.

"If you wish," I began, after a silence that seemed endless, "if you wish, I will depart into exile again. I will leave the Land of Ashur and never come back. It shall be as if the earth had swallowed me up."

"That you must not do. You must stay with me, Tiglath, until one or both of us have found death."

And then he turned to me and smiled broadly, as if his soul had been cleansed of wrath. It was not a smile one could trust.

"In any case, I have a use for you."

The sun crossed its zenith like a breathless, beaten runner, as if it too was glad to have left this morning behind it. Esarhaddon and I had drunk too much wine, and in the heat wine makes men quarrelsome. I decided that I would return to my own residence and steam the poison out. I would not leave the sweating house until my skin had grown as soft and wrinkled as goat cheese.

I did not see Selana again until dinner. By then she too was grim as death.

"Your new plaything has arrived," she said, sitting glumly at my feet while I ate—she had chased my servants away, and it had occurred to me to wonder for what crime I was being punished that she would not break bread with me like a wife but insisted on playing the kitchen girl. "I had not realized it, but there appears to be a whole wing of this palace set aside to house my lord's concubines. There must be room for fifty or sixty women. You eastern nobles certainly know how to keep yourselves amused."

At first I had no notion of what she could be talking about, and then I remembered Keturah.

"She is a gift from the king and one does not refuse gifts from a king, particularly not when one has been wronged by him."

Selana uttered a short, joyless syllable of laughter, expressive of her conviction that I was a bad liar.

"Well, it is little enough to me," she said, rising to her knees to fill my wine cup. "My lord is rich now, and a prince, and there is nothing that obliges him to restrict himself to one woman."

"Esarhaddon collects women. They are merely an appetite, and he loves novelty. I am not my brother, Selana. One woman at a time has always been sufficient for me."

For a long time she did not answer. She would not meet my gaze but stared at nothing as she seemed to consider the matter. At last it appeared that she was prepared to excuse me.

"In any case, keep her," she replied at last. "As you say, Lord, it is not wise to offend a king and—who can say?—you may chance to find her useful later on."

She favored me with a cryptic little smile, which said as plainly as any words that I would be wasting my time to inquire further into her meaning.

"What else of interest did your brother have to say?"

"Only that he will never part with me a second time during his life, so I think it likely we will not see Sicily again."

She made a little sidewise motion with her chin, as if to say, "Who imagined anything else?"

"You expected as much?"

"Half a month ago, you thought your brother would have you killed. Am I to grieve now that he raises you to glory in your own land?"

I wondered what Selana would think if she knew that Esarhaddon had offered me supreme power, but I judged it best not to ask.

"We were happy in Sicily," I said. "I had expected you would miss it."

"I would miss life even more. Did he say anything else besides?"

"Yes. In four months he will make war against Shupria. For this he needs quiet along his eastern borders, where the Medes and the Scythians have lately shown signs of forming an alliance. Such an alliance can have only one purpose. I am to collect an army from the northern garrisons and enforce the peace."

I had long since discovered that my wife, although hardly more than a girl, was a shrewd judge of affairs. I saw her eyes narrow slightly and knew she understood that all was not as it seemed.

"Why does the king send you?" she asked. "Why must it be you?"

"Because I once fought a long war against the Medes. They are an enemy I undersand."

"But if the king fights in one place and you in another, he will take the bulk of the soldiers."

"Yes."

"Can you have enough?"

"Not to win a war, but perhaps Esarhaddon does not mean me to win. I do not believe he would grieve overmuch if I failed. But to secure peace I will need only a very small force."

"How many soldiers?"

"Only one—myself."

XXXVII

ESARHADDON, I HAVE COME TO BELIEVE, WAS AFRAID that my presence in Nineveh was a danger to him. He wanted me gone while he moved his capital to Calah, where he had ruled as *marsarru* during our father's lifetime and was therefore more popular. He hated Nineveh and thought I might become a focus of unrest there. In any case, the king gave me only seven days' grace before my departure to the northern garrison at Amat.

"See Esharhamat before you go," he said. "She is ailing and longs for the sight of you. Have a little pity."

Coming from anyone else, it might have seemed an odd request for a man to make of his wife's old lover, but jealousy over women was not numbered among my brother's vices. I think he only meant to do her a kindness.

Yet I shook my head and declined.

"I am sorry that she is not well, yet for both of us there would be nothing but pain in such a meeting. That time is past."

Yet I did see her, even if it was only by chance—if it *was* by chance. As I returned from a meeting with Esarhaddon, my way passed through one of the king's private gardens. I found her there, resting on a divan, surrounded by her ladies.

Though she was still beautiful, the illness had left its mark. Her face looked wasted, making her dark, lustrous eyes appear even larger. When she saw me, a strange shadow seemed to come over her features. I do not think she had even the strength to rise. From the poles lashed to her divan it was clear that she had had to be carried out-of-doors.

The sight of her was like the fingers of an iron hand closing about my heart. I stopped and waited for her to speak, but she did not. My own voice seemed dead within me. She looked for an instant as if she would speak—her lips seemed to move, but there was no sound. If she had spoken I know not what I would have done. At last, knowing not what else to do, I bowed and turned back the way I had come.

Esharhamat. In the days of my exile, when I believed I would never see her again, I had wondered sometimes what it would be like to fill my eyes once more with the sight of her, to feel her presence like the gods' blessing. Would she have the same power over me, or had time done its work? Love for a woman, it is said, withers with the spring grass.

Yet it was not so. Even as a boy I had loved Esharhamat, and I knew that moment, seeing her again after so many years, that I would love her as long as she lived, and even when she was dust, until the last moment of my life. Once, long ago, she had cursed me, saying she wished my love for her would haunt me until I died, driving me mad. The Greeks say that love itself is madness, and if it is so, then Esharhamat's curse has been fulfilled.

Esharhamat. Her name sounds in my brain with the thrill of youth and hope and reckless passion. I am cursed. I am driven mad. Yet to pluck this nettle from my breast I have neither the power nor the will.

The Lady Ishtar, Goddess of Fleshly Love, Giver of Delight, She Who is Wrapped in Loveliness, is a magician, a worker of wonders. Esharhamat, once I had seen her again, filled my heart to bursting, yet it was only then that I grasped how much I had come to love Selana. Two things may not occupy the same space together, as every schoolboy knows; nonetheless, it was just so with Selana and Esharhamat—I found I could love each as if there was not strength left in my soul for another thought, and yet love the other no less.

Those last few days in Nineveh were torture, from which I longed to escape to the tranquillity of war.

The evening before I was to leave for the north, the king gave a banquet to honor the occasion. It was, after the fashion of all such affairs, a rough, soldierly sort of entertainment during which everyone grew drunk and tumultuous and the harlots and dancing girls had a hazardous time of it. I became bored very quickly and left as early as decency permitted. When I returned home I found that Selana had waited up for me.

"Since you must rise early tomorrow, I have prepared an herb drink to clear your head," she told me. "But I see you are still passingly sober."

"No, I did not drink much," I answered. I found myself wondering why she seemed disappointed.

"Have you at last reached an age when debauchery is no longer amusing? Or perhaps it was simply that she was there."

Esharhamat's name had never been mentioned between us, nor had Selana ever before indicated that she knew of her existence, but I would not now insult my wife by pretending I did not know who *she* was.

"No, she was not there, since it is not the custom for court ladies to attend. The only women present were entertainers."

I kept my gaze steady on her face as I spoke, and when I had finished she lowered her eyes.

"I know my lord has done nothing of which he need be ashamed," she said at last. "He cannot help that he loves another—I always knew as much, though I thought until we came here that it was the Egyptian woman—and I cannot help that I am full of jealousy. Therefore he need not look at me thus."

"You have no reason to be jealous, for there is safety in love. You are my wife, and it would not be so if I had known no love for you. The past is dead."

"But the Lady Esharhamat is not."

"Selana, I wish never to speak of this matter again."

She began to say something—doubtless, something full of fire and defiance, for she was a passionate creature, in both love and hatred—but that instinct by which women know their danger checked her, and she held her tongue.

"As my Lord wishes," she said, seeming to choke on the words.

That night I went into her, and there was nothing she held back from me. I had all of her passion, as if her very soul were flesh and that mine to do with as I liked. Her love was perfect, she seemed to say, even if my own was divided.

Two hours before dawn I rose and went out to the sweating house to wash myself. I imagined I had left Selana still asleep, but when I returned to my bedroom I found breakfast ready and the uniform of a *rab shaqe* already laid out for me. I dressed and ate in silence.

"How long will you be away?" she asked.

"Five months, perhaps six," I answered. "The king expects me to join him once I have completed my task. I will lead half the garrison at Amat into Shupria and meet him there, but that is high country and even Esarhaddon will have no taste for campaigning once the snow begins."

"Six months then." She smiled with a kind of radiant happiness, as if her dearest wish had been answered. "So you will be back in time for the birth of our child."

I carry on my body many scars received in battle and know the shock of a great wound, like a sheet of lightning that blinds the world, when an arrow point or lance has torn at my flesh. These few simple words, *in time for the birth of our child*, were just such. I was a moment just finding their import—*our child?*—and longer than that finding my tongue again.

"Are you sure?" I asked, stupidly, gathering her into my arms. "Are you quite sure?"

"I am quite sure." She smiled again, and this time I could see the tears shining in her eyes. "Yes—yes, I am very sure."

I left the city at first light with an escort of twenty soldiers from the Nineveh garrison. The road into the mountain provinces covers rough country, so perhaps they wondered what there could be in these northern wastes that I pushed them so hard to reach it. Between sunrise and sunset, and for ten days, I hardly allowed them to climb down from their horses.

This was my first real journey with Ghost for a mount, and I was anxious to see if he had the stamina for campaigning. I needn't have been concerned. Like his sire before him, he seemed never to weary.

We reached Amat just before noon of the eleventh day, and the *ekalli* in command of the watch—a boy almost, with hardly enough beard to hide his face—rode out to challenge our approach.

"Who goes there and what is your business?" he roared, pulling up smartly like a man perfectly prepared to draw his sword against the whole lot of us. He made an excellent impression.

"The Lord Tiglath Ashur," I answered, "prince of the royal house and *rab shaqe* in the king's army, and my business is with the garrison commander."

"Ti—Ti——?" The first syllable of my name came out of his mouth as little more than a clicking sound. I cannot remember when I have ever seen anyone's eyes open so wide.

He did not try to speak again but pulled his horse around with a jerk and galloped back through the fortress gate as if a demon had risen up before him in broad day—perhaps he thought one had.

Five minutes later he came back, on foot, bringing the garrison commander with him. Now it was my turn to be surprised, for the *rab abru*, who almost dragged me down from my horse that he might throw his arms around me in welcome, was my old comrade-in-arms Lushakin.

"Prince, is it really you?" he exclaimed, when his voice came back to him. "So you are not dead, and the king found you at last—may the gods be thanked!"

An army is like a family, and men who have suffered the hazards of battle together grow closer than brothers. Lushakin had been my *ekalli* in my first battle and had fought at my side against the Uqukadi, the Babylonians, the Scythians, and the Medes. When first I had come to Amat to take command of the garrison as *shaknu* of the northern provinces, Lushakin had been in my bodyguard. We embraced and wept.

As we walked across the parade ground together, crowds of old soldiers, men who had been with me in the wars against the northern tribes, crowded around us. I looked upon them, men whose faces I had not seen in seven years, and their names sprang of their own accord to my lips. They had not forgotten me, nor I them. I was home again and among my own.

That night Lushakin and I, sitting together in the garden of the commander's residence, broke open many a jar of good soldier's beer and grew pleasantly drunk.

"I was surprised to find you in command here," I said and then, thinking how such words must sound, "I mean, I did not expect that the officers of the northern army would prosper much after Khanirabbat."

"You mistake your brother then, Prince. No man suffered for having served under you. Indeed, we have been much preferred, and many went on his western campaign with him—I, alas, had to stay behind to keep the tribesmen in good order and thus missed the fun."

"Then you will be pleased to hear that the king proposes to make war against the Shuprians this autumn. We will join him in three months."

"Is that why you have returned, Prince?" he asked, grasping my arm in his eagerness. "Will you assume command again? Oh, it will be like the old days!"

"I will be there, Lushakin, but I do not think I will command the northern armies—I am not here for that. The king wishes me to secure his back against attack from the east. I am to pacify the Scythians and the Medes, who threaten to form an alliance."

My old *ekalli* seemed to consider the matter for a time, and his face began to grow dark with anger. Finally he picked up an empty beer jar and threw it against the flagstones with such violence that it seemed to shatter into dust.

"This is madness!" he declared hotly. "The last time it took us two years of campaigning to render the Medes harmless, and we needed an army three times the size of the force I have presently under my command, together with the Scythians as allies—and, as you doubtless remember, it was a very close thing. Now, with the Scythians allied to the Medes, the king expects us to do the same work in two months? My Lord Prince, you have been sent upon a fool's errand!"

"I know all this, my friend. That is why I will not lead the garrison at Amat into the steppes of the Zagros. I would only be throwing away the lives of your soldiers to no purpose, and perhaps supplying the Medes with just the provocation they have been seeking."

"Then what will you do? If the king . . ."

"The king commands that I pacify the tribes—nothing else. This I believe I can best achieve on my own."

Lushakin stared at me in disbelief.

"My Lord Tiglath Ashur is a madman," he said at last, in the tone of one making a profound discovery. "I have seen you do many foolish things, Prince, and always your *sedu*, which all men know is mighty, has protected you from your own folly. But do not tempt the god's favor too far. Do not even think about venturing into the Zagros without an army at your back, or you will never come out again."

I smiled, for I would not have Lushakin imagine that I feared death.

"Then only one will be dead, instead of many," I said. "A man's *simtu* is written on the day of his birth—he cannot evade it. And the king will not leave the murder of a royal prince unavenged. Perhaps it will not be a bad thing if we have our final reckoning with the Medes now rather than twenty or forty or sixty years hence."

The commander of the Amat garrison broke the seal on another beer jar and drained off the contents almost in one swallow. Then he set the jar back down on the flagstones, very gently. I knew he was about to say something dangerous.

"Prince, you know I am loyal to the king," he began, holding up a hand to prevent any interruption. "All the officers of the king's army reverence him, for he is the god's choice to rule over the Land of Ashur. Yet things are said when men feel themselves in the company of friends—the truth will always find a voice. I have spoken to many who have served under your brother in his campaigns, officers whose judgment I respect, and the king, while an able soldier, is by no means brilliant. He imagines everything can be achieved by brute force and the stubbornness of his own will. He has neither your cold clarity of thought nor your genius for the unexpected. He is not the man to trust against an enemy as wily as the Medes. If he had been in command ten years ago, we would all have laid down our bones in the tall grass and Daiaukka would today be reigning in Nineveh."

"Lushakin, I must tell you that what you say is very close to treason."

"It is no less true for being so."

"Then I think it best we all pray that I come back from Media alive."

Lushakin, when he discovered that I could not be turned from my purpose, insisted on accompanying me with a force of three hundred men at least as far as our eastern borderstone.

"You are a great fool, Prince," he said to me as we parted beside the stile my grandfather had put up to mark the limit of his empire and to warn away barbarians. "Think again what the Medes do to enemies unlucky enough to fall into their hands alive."

"I think of it constantly—I hardly think of anything else. Yet there is no turning back."

I smiled, perhaps a little foolishly, and Lushakin offered me a final salute, even as he shook his head in disgust.

"You are a fool, My Lord Tiglath Ashur, but no man living has the right to call you a coward. May the god be with you."

He turned his horse and rode back the way we had come, his three companies of cavalry behind him. I waited there a long time beneath the frowning stone image of the Great Sargon, until I could see nothing except the dust raised by my departing bodyguard, and then I struck out for the foothills of the Zagros Mountains and whatever fate awaited me in the wilderness of the east. I cannot remember a time when I was ever so conscious of being alone.

Besides Ghost, I had a pack horse bearing provisions for a month. This was good country for hunting, so I knew I would not starve, even after three months. The hazard lay elsewhere.

I reached the steppes after six days. The sun was fierce, burning yellow grass that reached sometimes as high as my chest. In all that time I never saw a living man, yet I knew I was being watched. Now and then I would see horse droppings that could not have been more than a few hours old and, besides, an old soldier develops a sense for these things. Sometimes I could almost feel their gaze upon me.

The Zagros are a wild place. In the mountains, which from a distance seem all sharp stone, lifeless as any desert, there are valleys astonishing in their lushness and canyons, hidden to the eyes of strangers, where a thousand men could hide while an army passed by outside. I kept to the plains, for this was not my home and I did not care to be ambushed.

On the eleventh day, just at noon, I saw three horsemen at the crest of a foothill. They were perhaps half an hour's ride distant, but I had no difficulty making them out. They intended to be seen.

I stopped and, as if that were the signal for which they had been waiting, they started down the hill towards me. From their dress I knew them to be Medes.

The ground just there was fairly clear, which was a blessing. I dismounted and, since I did not yet know how Ghost would stand the shock of battle, tethered the horses where they would have good grazing and be out of the way. I took my sword and a quiver with some eight or ten javelins in it and found myself a good spot to wait. The three riders thus far had kept their horses to a walk, but if they urged them to a gallop I knew I would have a fight on my hands.

At first they kept bunched together, but gradually, keeping abreast, they began to spread out in a line. This I took for a bad sign, since horsemen know to keep clear of one another in a charge. I took out a javelin, tested its bronze point against my thumb, and decided this was as good a day as any for men to die in combat.

They did not disappoint me. When they were some hundred paces distant they began to gather speed. First one drew his sword and then another—I could see the blades flashing in the sunlight.

Any sudden attempt to turn a horse at full gallop is an enterprise full of danger, so in battle a cavalryman has no more control over his destiny than if he were riding a comet. Thus the first Mede was a dead man long before his corpse hit the ground—I had only to measure the distance, compensate for his speed, and throw. My javelin arched through the air and fell on him like a clap of thunder.

My second throw was not so elegant, for I had little time. I killed the horse instead of the rider, but the dying animal pitched him over its neck and when he went down he did not get up again, so I thought perhaps the fall had done for him. I was not really at leisure to consider the matter.

The last Mede was almost upon me now. There was no time for a throw—the only use I could make of my javelin was to parry the slash of his long curved sword. My javelin splintered under the blow and the impact dashed me to the ground, but at least my head was still on my shoulders.

He pulled his horse to a gradual stop and turned to look back at me. It was almost insulting, as if he thought he had the rest of his life to kill me at his convenience. I drew two more javelins from my quiver, stuck one of them point-first in the ground and balanced the other in my hand, ready for any mistake my opponent thought fit to make.

Suddenly he charged. Perhaps he imagined the range was too short to allow me another throw, and he was almost right. There was no time even to aim. My javelin followed a low arc and bounched off his horse's shoulder, leaving an ugly, blood-soaked tear behind it. Yet even this was enough. The horse screamed with pain and terror and stopped. The Mede struck it cruelly on the flank with the flat of his sword, but the horse would not go forward. For the moment at least, it would have no more of fighting.

"Get down," I said, reaching back ten years to the few words of Farsi I had learned while making war against these people. "Get down, and fight or die like a man."

I drew my sword. The Mede considered the matter for a moment and then smiled—why should he not smile, when his sword was easily two handspans longer than mine? He was young, with a beautifully curled black beard, and he knew no better. He threw his leg over the horse's neck and slid to the ground as carelessly as if he were crawling out of bed. I knew I had him.

The javelin and the bow were my weapons, in the management of which I had few rivals, but by the standards of the Nineveh barrack I was not much of a swordsman. Esarhaddon was much better. This Mede, however, was not Esarhaddon and had never been closer to the Nineveh barrack than a twenty day's journey. I did not care if his sword was long enough to stir the stars with.

Cavalrymen only know how to slash, and this he did with terrifying energy. Yet I only had to keep out of his way and wait until he tired enough to grow careless and overreach himself. This he did and very quickly. He cut at me with too wide a swing. I parried, throwing his blade even farther out of reach, and stepped inside its arc. One quick thrust up under his rib cage finished him. He did not even have time to cry out, for he discovered his error and died in the same instant.

I cleaned the blood from my sword with the skirt of his tunic and sat down beside the corpse to rest for a moment. I did not look at his face, for I had learned long ago that there was no sense of triumph in contemplating one's dead enemies. At that moment all I could think of was how much I would have given for a few sips of beer.

The dead Mede's horse was grazing nearby and seemed to have forgotten all about the wound in its shoulder, which was already closing under a heavy scab of dried blood. I had no trouble catching its reins, and it was willing enough to be led provided I did not urge it above a walk.

The second Mede, whose horse was lying dead beside him, was alive after all. The fall had knocked him out, but he came to himself quickly enough and had suffered nothing worse than a broken ankle. He was only a boy, hardly more than fifteen. He watched me with large, frightened eyes—I fancied there was something familiar about his face, but I could not have said what it was. I had been myself just fifteen the first time I went to war. I found I did not have it in my bowels to kill him.

"Is Khshathrita still *shah* over the Medes?" I asked, crouching beside him on the ground. "Or have his people, who are as treacherous as serpents, turned against him and left his corpse to the delicate feasting of crows?"

He made an answer, most of which I could not understand but the import of which was that Khshathrita still lived and ruled.

I opened my right hand and held it up before the young Mede's face.

"Then tell him you have met the man who carries the mark of the blood star on his palm."

Ten years before, this boy with his downy beard would have been a mere child, following his mother about, clutching at her skirt with his tiny hand. Yet he understood now who I was. I could see it in his eyes, which were filled with more than the terror of mere death. It seemed that I had not been forgotten in the villages of the Zagros.

"Go now. Accept your life as a gift of the Lord Tiglath Ashur."

I had to help him onto his dead comrade's horse, for his ankle would bear no weight. As he rode away, as fast as his wounded mount would allow, he kept glancing back over his shoulder, as if he expected that I would turn into a pillar of fire.

I knew the Medes would be back, if only to collect their dead for burial according to their own barbaric rites, and I had no desire to risk another confrontation before Khshathrita had been made aware of my presence in his domain. Thus I departed the scene of battle at once, camping toward sunset on a bluff several *beru* distant, from which I would have some notice of any approach of strangers.

I did not light a fire that night, but I had no illusions that I could keep myself concealed for very long. It would be just as well if tempers had a few days to cool, but in the end I had come here to be found.

Yet for five days no one ventured near me—I even lost the sense of being watched from a distance. I might have been alone in this vast landscape.

I had not seen Khshathrita since he was a boy, not since that summer, nearly ten years before, when my armies had held him hostage while I recovered from the wounds I had received in mortal combat against his father. We had grown to be good friends then, but the boy was now a man and the leader of his people, and anyone who counts on the friendship of kings to save him has mud where his brains should be. It would be necessary to wait upon events.

There was nothing to make me pursue one direction over another, so I followed the hunting, which was good. I dined on fresh meat every night, and in the morning whatever was left on the blackened bones, plus a little cooked millet, did me very well for breakfast. The nights were warm and I slept well. It was a luxurious existence, made uncomfortable only by the knowledge that it continued at the sufferance of my enemies.

Would they come swooping down one night, a hundred strong, and butcher me in my sleep? Would I be taken alive and staked out on the ground to have my skin peeled off? Lushakin had been right, for the Medes are cruel to their prisoners. If it came to the point, I resolved to die by my own hand before allowing myself to be captured.

But even fear loses its edge with time. After the second day I stopped thinking about death. I let my mind go empty and achieved something like peace.

I thought of Selana and the child she carried in her womb—it might be a son for all I knew, to be born after his father's death. A son is like immortality, or as good as any man can hope for.

I thought of Esharhamat, who had borne me a son, a child conceived in guilty love, one I could never name as my own.

I thought of the child Nodjmanefer had not lived to bear, and my bowels went cold. It was well that Enkidu had remained in Nineveh to guard my family, for the world was an evil and uncertain place.

At the end of the sixth day, near sunset, I saw a lone rider approaching over the grassy steppes. I could not see his face, for it was covered up to the eyes with the end of his turban, as is the custom in that part of the world, for the dust can be terrible, yet he was not dressed like a Mede. He carried a bow across his back and a quiver of arrows. When he came closer I saw a short curved dagger stuck in his belt.

At last we were no more than twenty paces apart. He stopped his horse, and I could see from the way his eyes narrowed to slits—they were the eyes of a cat—that he was smiling.

Then he took down the cloth covering his face and I knew him.

"Brother!" he exclaimed, in Aramaic, "have I aged more than you that you stare so? It is Tabiti, son of Argimpasa, headman of the Sacan tribe of the Scoloti."

XXXVIII

"THIS AHURA OF THE MEDES IS NOT A GOD MUCH GIVEN to hospitality. Each time I visit young Khshathrita in Ekbatana I must camp outside the city walls, for I am an unbeliever and therefore impure. When first we contemplated this alliance, I offered him the elder of my two daughters for a wife and he refused her. Well, I thought, perhaps she is not to his taste, so I offered her sister as well, and still he persisted in his refusal, for it seems he will not risk defilement by taking women of other races to his sleeping mat. Can you imagine such a thing? Where would the world be if all of us were so fastidious? Clearly, the man is a barbarian."

We sat under the bright stars while Tabiti stirred the fire with the point of his dagger. He had brought with him a goatskin full of *safid atesh*, a wine the Scythians make from horses' milk—the name means something like "white lightning" and is a reasonable description. I was by then drunk enough that I no longer minded that it tasted worse than ox piss that has been left standing in the sun.

"Then this alliance cannot last long," I suggested, but Tabiti, ever the practical man, shook his head.

"This is not marriage but statecraft, and our mutual distaste will not keep us a part. It serves the interests of my people that I should join Khshathrita if he makes war against Esarhaddon, for otherwise we will be left out of the spoils. That I do not love him is beside the point. I love you, my friend Tiglath Ashur, no less than if you were my own brother, yet, had I not sworn an oath to you that day at the Bohtan River, when your soldiers had conquered the Sacan, spilling our blood as punishment for having entered the Land of Ashur, I would this minute be cutting your throat."

This struck me as a rare jest, no less because I knew he spoke the truth, and I laughed.

"It is good to be among friends again," I said, and laughed still more.

"And I am glad to see you, My Lord, for I had thought you long dead and my liver was afflicted that you should suffer so at the hands of your own king and brother. Still, it is a grief to me that now the Scoloti may not fall like wolves upon the Land of Ashur. For years now visions of her plundered cities have filled my dreams."

We spoke no more of such matters but remembered, as warriors will, the old days. We drank to the brave men, his and mine, who had drenched the earth with each other's blood when we fought against one other beside the Bohtan River. We lived again our war against the Medes, for memories of ancient battles are full of sweetness.

"I still think you were a fool not to have killed Daiaukka the moment he came into your hands," Tabiti said. "As it was, he nearly killed you. I do not know what it is in you, brother, that makes you take such risks."

"Perhaps, if I had listened to you and had the father strangled, I would not have had to come back to this place to make peace with the son."

But the headman of the Sacan waved this aside as mere giddy talk, worthy of women.

"Daiaukka was a brave man and a great leader, but leaders are less important than you imagine and war is the common condition of life. The Medes will fight the Assyrians until they have poured over your borders and laid your land waste—or until you have butchered them to the last sucking babe. It does not depend on any of us, not on you nor me nor that ill-mannered brat of Daiaukka's who now calls himself 'king of kings.' It is the way things are."

"Then Daiaukka was right: it will never end."

"No, it will never end, and that is just as well"—he nudged me with his elbow, as if telling me something in confidence—"for you and I are warriors, My Lord, and there is no one more to be pitied than a warrior who knows he will never again see battle."

"How did you know I was here, brother?"

I found I did not entirely trust Tabiti in this reflective mood, for when a man such as he, a savage accustomed to living each day as if it held his whole life, begins to brood darkly over the meaning of things, it is usually a sign that his conscience is not clear.

And I knew I was right the instant he looked at me. The reddish color of burned brick, with narrow, catlike eyes and only a few wisps of beard framing his mouth, Tabiti's was not a face to show much range of feeling, yet I knew he was holding something back.

"I happened to be with Khshathrita when his younger brother returned," he answered, implying that this was a sufficient reply.

"His brother?"

"Yes—his brother. It is well you spared his life, yet this is still a messy business, My Lord. The two you killed were cousins."

He made a gesture with his hand as if it were loose on his wrist and the wind moved it.

"At this moment the Medes are struggling among themselves over who is to lead them," Tabiti continued. "Khshathrita is the true *shah*, but he is young and he has an uncle who fancies himself a great man—you, the son of a king, will know the sort of thing I mean. It can only end one way, for at last Khshathrita will crush his uncle and gather all power to himself, yet it may not end soon. Do you understand me, Lord? Your life is threatened now, while a foolish and vain man grieves over the deaths of his sons and perhaps has the power to demand that they be avenged."

"Where is Khshathrita now?"

"In a village about four days from here."

The direction he indicated lay over a line of rocky foothills, so I knew the sort of place he meant. The Medes often built their villages straight into the face of a mountain, like fortresses, with only a goat path leading down to the plain.

"I am on my way back north." Tabiti glanced away, as if the admission shamed him. "There is nothing I can do to help you, my friend, and it is better that I do not become involved."

"I understand your position. You must act for your people, and it is always better not to take sides in another family's quarrels."

"You are wise, brother. But take heart, and do not imagine I will forget you. No alliance can endure forever, so be sure that one day, should the Medes chance to strip you of your life, I shall exact from them a fitting blood price."

Tabiti rode away the next morning. I waited two more days, and still the Medes did not intrude upon my solitude.

Why? What held them back? I was an old enemy, a trespasser in a land they held sacred to their unforgiving god, and I had recently killed two cousins of their *shah*. Why did they stay their revenge?

I thought perhaps I knew.

Ten years before, when I first came into the Zagros with a vast army at my back to make war against the Medes, their sorcerers had told them that I was the spirit of the Great Sargon made flesh again. There had been many who still remembered him from the days of his own campaign in their mountains, when he had taken their first *shah*, one Ukshatar, father of Daiaukka and grandfather of Khshathrita, a captive that he might wear out his life under the yoke of Ashur. They fancied a resemblance, and it had filled their hearts with terror, for they are a superstitious people. I had used this as a weapon, invoking the magic of my grandfather's name and leading my army under the banner of the blood star which had blazed in the eastern sky the night of his death. I defeated the Medes and then, in answer to his challenge, killed Daiaukka in single combat, nearly losing my own life as well but greatly impressing the Medes. From that day there had been peace.

Daiaukka, on the night before his death, had told his son that if I prevailed against him it could only mean that I lived under the protection of Ahura, the Median god who is lord of all truth and power. Thus he made the boy swear an oath that there would be no war between his people and mine as long as I stood at my king's right hand.

The Medes do not lie, not even to their enemies, so Khshathrita would never have broken that oath had not my banishment released him from it. Yet now, like the taint of some ancient curse, I had returned to spoil his plans for an alliance with the Scythians and an attack upon the Land of Ashur.

Ten years, however, was not a moment, and none among the Medes except their *shah* would feel bound to keep the peace only because an unclean foreigner had returned as if from the dead.

Still, they would hesitate. They would remember the fate of Daiaukka. They would remember that the man who killed him might be something else besides a man, and they would not be anxious to test his magic. Perhaps they would be just as pleased if I slinked quietly away, for they were afraid—the fact that I was still alive was testimony to their fear.

I would have to stake my life, and the success of my mission, on that fear. My only hope lay in boldness. If the Medes would not come to me, then I would have to force myself upon them.

I had had enough of waiting. I mounted Ghost and rode in the direction that Tabiti had indicated led to Khshathrita's headquarters.

My sense of utter isolation returned, and with it a cold, unforgiving fear that settled in my bowels like a piece of jagged ice. I was alone in this land where once I had earned for myself the enmity of a conquered people—a people who might now be watching my every movement, whose moment for revenge had now come if only they chose to take it. They were many and I was alone. How should I contrive to leave this place with the flesh still on my bones?

Yet long ago I had delivered myself into the hands of my god, and he had thus far kept me from death. If he had indeed given me a *sedu* to watch over my life, then I could only pray that it had not deserted me.

On the third day there was a frightful lightning storm such as sometimes happens in those mountains. In the middle of the afternoon the sky was black as night yet torn by ghastly sheets of fire that burned a man's eyes. I thought the thunder would shatter my head, for it made the very breath in my nostrils tremble. There was no wind, and the air was dry as sand. My horses were terrified, but I judged it best to keep them moving ahead, for a horse is like a man and will panic the sooner if tethered to one spot.

I rode over the summit of a line of low hills and saw a village, much as I had imagined I would find, spread over against the face of a cliff.

Perhaps I have been here before, I thought. Perhaps I have spent a night in one of those stone houses after my advancing armies had sent the inhabitants fleeing into the mountains. Yet there were so many in those days, who can know?

At the base of the mountain was grassland. I could have crossed it and been in that village in an hour, except that spread out across the plain was a line of horsemen, fifty at least. They seemed to be waiting for me.

In their center, mounted on a black horse that could have been the great stallion his father rode on that last day, was Khshathrita. He was some distance from me and I had not seen him since he was a boy, yet I picked him out from the rest as easily as one might pick a lion cub from among a litter of kittens. After all, he was Daiaukka's son.

At precisely that moment, when I first looked across and saw the Medes, the storm ended abruptly. It might have been a sign from the gods—I hoped Khshathrita and his followers would interpret it as such. The thunder died away in an echo, and a light wind stirred the grass on the plain below. I rode down the rocky hillside to meet whatever destiny the Lord Ashur had prepared for me.

When perhaps no more than forty paces separated us, I reined in Ghost and stopped to contemplate the faces of the men who seemed to make of themselves a wall against my approach. Many of them, I discovered, I knew by sight; they were the *parsua*, as the Medes call their tribal leaders, who had gone down on their knees to me after Daiaukka's final defeat. They meant nothing, for they had tasted subjection once and, of their own, would never dare to raise their hands against me a second time. They were beaten men who could not even meet my glance.

Then there was Khshathrita himself, a young man now, perhaps not yet twenty years old but already a king in his bearing, the image of his father. He could be restrained, I thought, but never by fear. At his left hand was the youth whose life I had spared, whom Tabiti had designated Khshathrita's younger brother. He kept his gaze down, as if conscious that he had made a fool of himself once already.

And at Khshathrita's right hand, on a dappled stallion that seemed to totter under his weight, was my real enemy. A huge man, as tall as myself yet built on a broader scale, with thick-fingered hands that made the reins they held look like threads. I knew him at once from the expression of hatred that seemed to have stamped itself permanently around his eyes, which were just a trifle too close together. This was not a clever man—I could see as much at once—but he was dangerous the way a bull is dangerous, by virtue of its mindless ferocity. This was Arashtua, *parsua* of the Miyaneh and younger brother of Daiaukka. And not twenty days before I had slain his two eldest sons.

Yet my fear had deserted me, as it always did at such moments. The great merit of danger that it does not leave a man leisure to be afraid. I could look this man in the face and feel nothing but a certain impatience to be finished with him, one way or the other.

"So it is you in truth, My Lord Tiglath Ashur. I will not claim that I am not disappointed."

I had to force my attention back to Khshathrita, for it was he who had broken the silence. I looked at him and smiled.

"A king should learn to be less candid," I answered. "Yet you were always so, My Lord *Shah*, even as a boy. Still, I see you are a boy no longer."

An expression crossed Khshathrita's face like a shadow, and I saw that he did not relish this interview, conducted in the presence of so many of his vassals. I could only guess what had constrained him to arrange it so.

"Why have you come back, My Lord?" He glanced quickly from side to side, as if to tell me that it was not he whom I must satisfy with my answer, that the question, though spoken with his voice, had passed already through many other lips.

I allowed myself one more faint smile before speaking, that he might know I understood my part in this recital.

"I have come, My Lord Khshathrita, Son of Daiaukka, *Shah-ye-shah* among the Medes, to remind you of your oath, made not to me but to your noble father—may the glory of his name survive forever—that there must be peace between your nation and mine so long as I live as a servant of my king. I remind you of this because it is folly to challenge the might of Ashur and because I would not have your people's blood on my hands a second time."

"O Worshiper of Fiends, you need have no fear of more blood on your hands!" shouted Arashtua, his horse stamping the ground with its hooves, as if it shared his impatience for my life. "Your conscience will be clear while you live, for that will not be long!"

His words died away into silence, leaving behind a terrible suspense as palpably real as the ache that gathers in a man's wounds to tell him of an approaching storm. I could see it in the faces of the Medes, that longing that a hasty word might be taken back, that dread of what must follow because it cannot.

Yet the fact still remained that I was one and they were many, so why would they be afraid when I was not?

And then, of course, I understood: I faced only death, whereas they . . . I threw my head back and gave myself to the luxury of laughter.

"It is not a jest, My Lord," exclaimed Khshathrita—I believe he was not angry but shocked. "You have slain two of this man's sons, for all that no one can hold you guilty of their deaths. . . ."

"I hold him guilty." Arashtua's horse cantered a few steps forward and then was reined back. "He is here, speaking and breathing, while they lie in the towers of silence, their flesh picked over by carrion birds. He gave them no more chance that he did the Lord Daiaukka, whom all men know he murdered with treachery and foul magic."

"My magic lay in the strength of my arm and the favor of the bright gods!" I snapped. Let them see my anger, I thought. I will gain nothing by abasing myself. "It is my proudest boast that I carry on my body the scars from Daiaukka's lance—magic did not hold back his point when it tore into my bowels. Daiaukka issued his challenge and I accepted it, for Daiaukka was a great man whom even his enemies respected, and whom it was an honor to have killed in equal combat! Yet I can see the same generation can bring forth both a hero and a buffoon."

Arashtua's neck seemed to sink into his shoulders. His eyes bulged and the muscles in his whole body tensed and trembled with wrath. I think it likely he would have gone for me that instant if Khshathrita had not laid a restraining hand upon his uncle's arm.

"Yes, it is well that there be a limit to your grief and anger, *parsua*," one of the gray-bearded elders said to him. "You saw yourself how he came among us not as a man but mantled in a cloak of fire."

The lightning—was it that? Or had the god, with his protective hand, covered me with a *melammu*, what the Greeks call a nimbus?

I was never to know. Perhaps it did not matter, for I felt myself guarded by the Lord Ashur's divine strength. Perhaps that was enough.

"I do not care if he came cradled in the hand of his unclean god," Arashtua shouted. "I will not swallow his insults, for he is only a man after all and he butchered my sons like cattle."

Nothing would stop him now, I thought, for his wrath has blinded him to everything else. And not simply because I had killed his sons, but for some other reason I could only guess at. Just so. I decided to make the most of the advantage this fool offered me.

"If they are dead, then the guilt is yours," I said, grinning at him, showing my teeth in mockery. "Who sent them if not you? Who else would send boys to do battle against one he had not the bowels to face himself?"

Had I guessed right? Close enough, it seemed, for with a growl of hatred Arashtua shook off his nephew's hand. His dappled stallion bolted forward as he drew the long curved dagger from his belt.

He was on me almost before I had drawn my sword—I had just time, as our horses jolted together, nearly toppling us both to the ground, to catch his blade on mine and turn it harmlessly aside.

Arashtua yanked back on the reins to put himself beyond my reach, but not before his stallion had a chance to bite Ghost on the throat, just under the jaw, making him scream in pain and wrath. Ghost reared and struck out with his hooves, but his enemy, like mine, had withdrawn to a safe distance.

"Unclean dog, I will kill you!" Arashtua's face was nearly black with rage. Still, I had lived through his first charge, and that had taught him caution. He kept the reins pulled tight. "I will spill your guts onto the ground for crows to eat!"

"As I did your sons'? But even before they died they were already shriveled with womanish terror—I think the maggots could hardly make a meal of them."

Thus we circled one another, hurling insults, hardly ten paces apart, as the Medes waited in silence to see who would make the first mistake.

Arashtua charged again, and I pulled out of his way so that his curved sword cut with a whistle at the emptiness. He rode past and wheeled about, cursing. Ghost showed no signs of panic; I was beginning to feel a certain confidence that he would keep his courage.

"Fight, why don't you? Fight!"

The dappled stallion stamped the ground, as eager, it seemed, as his master.

I flourished my sword in the air.

"Are you so impatient to die then? Very well. As you wish."

I touched Ghost's flanks with my heels and he bolted forward in a furious gallop, as if he hated the earth beneath his hooves. Arashtua, who thought the initiative all his own, had not expected this, which gave me the advantage of a moment's surprise.

What happens almost too quickly for the eye to follow can sometimes seem to unfold with excruciating clarity. Thus it was when we came together—I can still remember the sickening whine of metal against metal, the way the horses snorted for breath, the little cry of astonishment as my sword slipped down the blade of Arashtua's dagger, caught for an instant at the hilt, and then, meeting the clenched fist, cut away two of the fingers and half the hand, all the way down to the wrist.

It should have been finished—for me, it was finished. This was no more than a lucky accident, yet it would have been the work of a moment to swing Ghost about and fall on my adversary, killing him while he was still stunned and helpless. Yet, like a fool, I did not.

Let him live, I thought. This fight is over.

Arashtua sagged for a moment, almost falling to the ground. He let his horse carry him back among the Medes as the blood poured down over its flanks.

"You are vanquished, Uncle," I heard Khshathrita say. "He has beaten you, and still he has spared you your life. Let it end here."

But Arashtua only glared at me as he wrapped his severed hand in a strip of cloth. This man, I saw at once, was no rabbit.

"It does not end here!" he shouted. He snatched a lance from someone and, gripping it in his left hand, broke free of the Medes surrounding him. "I will kill this unbeliever, lower than any beast. I will not suffer him to live!"

I drew a javelin from my quiver—it was not as long as a Median lance, but it would serve.

Yet again Arashtua charged. There was no difficulty about turning his point away, for he managed the lance awkwardly. My javelin slid inside his defense and caught him just under the ribs, tearing a great hole and pulling him down from his horse. I circled around slowly, but he did not even attempt to rise. This time he really was finished.

And I would see to it—I would leave no such enemy alive to trouble me again. I dismounted, sword in hand, and walked over to where he was lying. His face was twisted with pain as he held the wound in his belly, the blood pouring out over his hands. He did not even resist when I grabbed him by his long hair and prepared to hack through his neck.

A moment later, covered with blood, I stood and held up the severed head for the Medes to see.

"Now it will end," I said, suddenly filled with a wrath that, until that moment, had not possessed me. "I would have shown him mercy, as I would have shown mercy to the Lord Daiaukka, but neither would accept it from my hand and now both are dead.

"Thus have I learned my own folly, and you shall see how I put the lesson to use: if ever I find the hoofprint of a single Median pony on the sacred soil of Ashur, then there will be no more mercy. I will come back to this place, bringing fire and sword, and I will not depart from it until the last of your nation, even to the sucking babes, are left as corpses to rot under the summer sun. And for this you have my oath."

I threw Arashtua's head from me, so that it rolled between the legs of the Medes' horses, making them snort with terror.

"Go now!" I shouted. "Leave me before the ground has more blood to drink!"

I raised my gore-spattered sword and the Medes started as if at the sight of a ghost—all save one.

Khshathrita, son of Daiaukka, *shah-ye-shah* of the Medes, raised his arm to command silence and obedience.

"Depart then, my brothers," he said, never taking his eyes from my face. "I would speak with the Lord Tiglath Ashur, and alone."

The sound of horses' hooves died away, leaving only the whisper of the wind. Across what seemed all at once the emptiest place the gods had made, Khshathrita and I stood facing one another.

At last, with the air of one who never doubts, the Lord of Media dismounted and walked over to where his uncle's head lay in the dust. Using the point of his lance, he picked it up and dropped it beside the corpse.

"Are you as pleased as I am with this day's work, My Lord?"

He looked at me, his face without expression—in his passionless fixity of purpose he reminded me most unpleasantly of his father.

"I am pleased if it means peace," I answered, wondering why I suddenly felt as if I had walked into a trap this boy had set for me.

"It means peace for a time, and then the certainty of war. The Medes are not ready now to challenge the might of Ashur, and you have saved them from committing that error."

He stood there, absent-mindedly cleaning his lance tip on the long grass, as if he had forgotten I was there. And then he glanced up, frowned, and shook his head.

"My uncle was a rash man," he went on, "but in his rashness was that which would have carried many with him. Who can say if he might not have made it impossible for me to keep my people from the folly into which he would have led them? Now they, and I, have time to prepare and the last check on my own power has been removed, yet no blood guilt stains my hands. You have served the Ahura well, Lord Tiglath Ashur."

My hand still held the sword with which I had killed Arashtua, and Khshathrita was not more than four or five paces away. I had been fond of him as a child, and it would have pained me to kill him . . .

"Will you keep your oath, My Lord *Shah*, or will you break it?"

The question seemed actually to take him by surprise.

"I will keep my oath, My Lord." Looking into my face, he blinked like an owl dazzled by the sun. "How can you doubt it? Yet it can matter but little, for you will be long gone by the time I am ready to strike. No king could bear forever having one such as you by his side, for kings are vain creatures and the favor of your god shines about you all too brightly. Your brother, if he lives, will one day repent of calling you back from exile."

"If he lives . . . ?"

But the *shah-ye-shah*, who was hardly more than a boy, merely smiled, as if he pitied me my simplicity. What did he know, or guess, that was hidden from me?

"By the way, I thank you for my brother's life," he said. "He acted basely to join his cousins against you, and his punishment is that he knows it. Return home now, My Lord Tiglath Ashur, for you have secured the peace you sought."

I rode away, knowing I would never see him again.

XXXIX

THAT NIGHT, LYING UNDER THE MEDIAN STARS, I dreamed of Nineveh. I saw her as I had seen her before in dreams—her walls in ruins, the wind blowing dust over her silent, broken dwellings. She was a dead city, her very name forgotten by the tongues of men.

"Look to Nineveh," the maxxu had told me once, long ago. "Its streets will become the hunting ground of foxes, and owls will make their nests in the palace of the great king."

And then I awoke, and my doubts lefts me. And as I cooked breakfast over a fire of thorn-tree branches, I saw a horseman approaching. He was alone, like myself. He was Tabiti. It was good there was food enough for two, for he had not eaten.

"Halfway home, I was overtaken with shame," he said. "Statecraft makes a man into a coward, I decided. So I came back to see if the Medes had killed you. I gather they did not."

"No—instead, I killed Arashtua."

"Did you, by the gods! Khshathrita was no doubt relieved, although over the years you have reaped a great harvest of his kinsmen."

"What would you have done if the Medes had killed me?"

Tabiti shrugged, the eyes narrowing to slits in his catlike face as he smiled with embarrassment.

"I would have killed Khshathrita, and then, after his kinsmen had killed me, my eldest son, as the new headman of the Sacan, would have declared a blood feud against the Medes. When one considers it carefully, this would not have been a bad thing, for my people have been at peace too long. A few years of warfare would have reminded them that it is not dignified for a Scoloti to die in his bedroll."

I laughed, for I knew he meant everything he had said, and we shared out the millet gruel and the dregs from my wineskin.

"I do not know how a man can take pleasure in drinking such trash," he said when the wine was gone. "It tastes like stale horse piss and it only makes a man drunk enough to rob him of his courage."

"Whereas on *safid atesh* a man can grow drunk enough that he can ride into the midst of battle and never even notice the enemy."

We laughed together at this and then, suddenly, Tabiti became very serious.

"Now that you have ruined all my plans by securing peace with the Medes, I will take my people back to the grasslands west of the Shaking Sea," he said, staring sullenly at the last smoking embers of my campfire. "Perhaps the Urartians will care to dispute our presence in their territory, although I doubt it. Their mad king Argistis is dead, you know, and his brother, by whose hand he died, is a weakling. Or perhaps we can pick over the corpses of the Shuprians after your brother makes his war against them this winter—everyone knows of his intentions, My Lord Tiglath, so you can save yourself the trouble of lying to me about them. In any case, you see the shifts to which I am brought to provide the Sacan with a little excitement."

He looked up to study my face with narrow, speculative eyes.

"I will not move my people for several months, not until after the snows have melted, for the mountains above the Shaking Sea are treacherous in winter and I have given my word not to enter the Land of Ashur. The grasslands north of the Bohtan River are good, so we may stay there for several years—remember this, My Lord, if ever you should chance to need a place of refuge."

Tabiti rode with me for two days and then struck off toward the main Scythian encampment on the western shores of Lake Urmia. He was a savage and a vagabond, by the standards of civilized peoples perhaps no better than a common thief, and yet I would rather my life were in his hands before any other man's. We parted as brothers.

Not five hours after passing the borderstone set up by my grandfather, I encountered a rider from Amat.

"We did not expect you back so quickly, *Rab Shaqe,*" he said. "Did you subdue the Medes all by yourself then?"

I laughed, as much with relief as anything else, since I could read it in his face that he had not expected me back at all—danger never seems so close as when it has finally passed forever.

"There was only one who mattered, and now he is dead. We will have no more trouble with the Medes for a few years at least."

He was young, and my answer pleased him enormously. He galloped away, eager to win glory by bringing first word of my return.

By evening of the next day I found I had a patrol of twenty men to conduct me back to the garrison. Lushakin had come himself to command my escort.

"You are harder to kill than the great gods themselves, Prince. But as a practical man I have brought you a jar of beer to clear your throat of all that foreign dust."

He held it out to me and I broke the seal with my thumb, drinking as if I thought I might die of thrist.

"You see, Prince? It is still cold—that is how fast we have been riding. Hold! You might save a drop for me!"

But there was more beer in Amat, and the garrison did it ample justice celebrating my return. This, I must own, was not solely out of love for my person, since for most of these men I hardly existed except as a name in the barrack stories of the northern army. Rather, it testified to the general relief that the soldiers of Ashur would not now be required to fight another war against the Medes. And this was only right, for the sufferings of those terrible years were more vivid in their memories than was that poor shadow, the glory of Prince Tiglath Ashur.

Shupria, however, seemed to be another matter.

"We fought two campaigns against the Medes," Lushakin explained, his face crinkling with disgust, "and hardly a man of us brought back enough pillage to buy an hour between a tavern harlot's legs. It is all very well for a king's son to win himself a great name by going off into the mountains to slay bandits, and doubtless the Lord Sennacherib had his good reasons for wanting Daiaukka put down, but for a humble soldier who lives all the winter on garrison bread and cares nothing for statecraft or honor, what is the point of doing battle against people as poor as himself? And the Medes, like all poor men, know how to fight. The Shuprians, on the other hand, are a soft, city-dwelling people, and my soldiers are sick of peace. They dream of ravaging the perfumed daughters of wealthy merchants—and of winning enough plunder to buy a wife and a plot of farmland when they leave the army. As soon as they hear of this war they will bless the king's name."

And so it was. When I received word that Esarhaddon had already taken the field I issued orders that fifteen companies were to prepare to join the main army on the northern bank of the Tigris, just a day's march from Sairt, and the men who found they were to be left behind imagined themselves to be no end of unlucky.

It was the twenty-ninth day of the month of Elul when we left the fortress at Amat and turned our faces west, and the summer heat had already broken. I had exercised a decent care in the choice of my officers, but the ranks were filled with raw youths, most not a year from their fathers' farms, whose experience of combat was confined to the drill fields. This was to be their first taste of war. I hoped it would not be too bitter in their mouths.

I marched them hard, so that by the seventh day of Tisri, which is an evil day, when even soldiers stay beside their dead campfires, we were close enough to our rendezvous meeting that we had already encountered the king's outriders. On the eleventh day we saw the tents of his army.

"Very well then, you are here," said Esarhaddon. "My magicians said you would not tarry long with the Medes. I am glad of it, for the Shuprians, who are all women, with a king who is little better than a cutpurse, will not take the field against us. I feared lest you miss all the sport."

He had driven out alone in his war chariot, whipping his horses until their sides were lathered with sweat. He reached down to pull me in beside him, smiling like a boy—he was always happiest while on campaign.

"You take the reins. Tell me about the Medes—how large a force did you take?"

"I went alone."

"You what?"

My brother stared at me with such incredulity that I was forced to laugh. When I touched the lead horse with the whip, Esarhaddon was almost thrown out onto the ground.

"What did you . . . ?"

But his words were overwhelmed by the jolting of the wheels over the hard, rock-strewn earth. The horses, accustomed to their master's heavy hand, ran like demons, and we did not stop until we pulled to a halt before the king's tent.

"You didn't really—you couldn't have gone alone!"

"My advice is to take it a little more gently with your animals, brother, or you will break their wind. Yes, of course I went alone. What did you expect?"

"Then I will have my chief necromancer's tongue cut out, for he told me he had raised the ghost of old Shalmaneser, who said you would conquer with fire and sword."

All at once my bowels seemed to turn to water, for I remembered the lightning storm that had ceased so suddenly the moment I saw Khshathrita and his nobles—"*He came among us not as a man, but mantled in a cloak of fire*," the old Mede had said. And Arashtua had bled out his life on the point of my sword. The god's favor was as terrible as death itself.

"Let him live, for he spoke no more than the truth."

Esarhaddon glanced at me for a moment and then grunted his consent. He gave the impression that this was not a subject into which he wished to look too closely.

"Then I will not send you to treat with the Shuprians," he said finally, "for they are appalling cowards and you would probably persuade them to surrender. That would not meet my purposes. We will march on Uppume, which they fancy as impregnable a citadel as was ever fashioned by the hand of man. I mean to take it. I mean to set these people an example."

He stepped down from the chariot and handed his whip to a chamberlain, all the time his eyes restlessly searching. When he looked up at me his mouth was set with hatred. Yet it was not me he hated.

"This king—this brigand—not only does he withhold the tribute he owes, not only does he write me insulting letters, telling me 'reckon it not a sin if I seek not the king's peace,' but he gives sanctuary to traitors, men who have fled the Land of Ashur like thieves. Yes—I mean to set these people an example they will remember until the world is dust!"

I had only to see the expression on his face to realize there was nothing to be gained by arguing with him—he had set his ferocious heart on this conquest, and he was not to be denied.

So I contented myself with a warning.

"Just remember there is a time limit. These mountains are not Babylonia, and when the snows come it will not be the Shuprians who are trapped, but us."

"Fear not." He grinned at me with the serenity of perfect confidence. "I shall be holding my triumph in Calah before the end of Marcheswan."

But the month of Marcheswan came and went, and Kislef found us still camped on the plains beneath Uppume, an army close to eighty thousand strong besieging a city that held no more than twice that number, while Anhite, their king, sat within his walls and waited for winter.

Uppume was a hill city, what the Greeks would have called an acropolis, built upon a crown of rock. Its walls were made of heavy logs laid end to end—no great defense, if one could reach them, yet who could reach them above those sheer stone cliff faces? To do this would not be the work of a day. This had been the city's protection for a thousand years: that no invader could hope to breach her defenses before freezing to death in the deep snows.

But the king my brother was building a great ramp, straight up the face of the hill. Men in their thousands carried stones and great logs and baskets of earth. They worked through every day—every day except the month's five evil days, for the king lived in great fear of the gods—and every day, it seemed, the ramp rose another cubit, until soon it would reach the foundations of the city itself. When it topped the wall, and there was only the empty air separating it from the Shuprian battlements, the soldiers of Ashur would throw a great bridge across that chasm and then pour over the wall like a rain-swollen river over a mud turtle.

There was nothing wrong with the plan, for we excelled all other nations in this sort of siege warfare. The only question was whether the month or so that remained to us would be enough.

And each afternoon the king and his officers, myself among them, rode out to observe the progress of this great work. Esarhaddon would stare up at the silent walls of Uppume, his face hardening with wrath, and then we would return to camp and my brother would spend the rest of the day sitting before his tent, drinking plain soldiers' beer, speaking to no one.

It would have been better if the Anhite and his nobles, on the first day of the siege, had presented themselves before the king of Ashur dressed in rags, kneeling before him and baring their necks for his sword. Perhaps then some few would have been spared. But now they had doomed themselves utterly and condemned the common people of their city to a great slaughter. Each hour my brother's mind grew one shade darker against them and all mercy fled his soul. He no longer cared what this siege cost. He would let his army freeze and starve, he would perish here himself upon the broad Shuprian plain, but he would lay this city waste and put its inhabitants to the sword.

And this was how the god had cursed the Land of Ashur, by giving her a king whose soul had stiffened with bitterness until he no longer felt the same wind that chilled the bones of common men.

Since I retained command over the fifteen companies of men I had brought from Amat, I put Lushakin in charge of supply. He went out on patrol almost daily, and he when he returned our wagons would always be loaded with grain, salt, cooking oil and beer, and hanging beside the wheels, tied by the feet, would be scores of live ducks. In the wagons' wake would follow cattle and whole flocks of goats. I did not ask how he came by these things, and I tried not to think of the Shuprian villages where there would be starvation that winter.

I told myself that the Shuprians were the enemies of my king and that an army in a hostile land must of necessity feed itself by the sufferings of her people. I knew what Esarhaddon would have said: "Let Anhite look to his own subjects—he should have considered them when he threw off the yoke of Ashur and gave refuge to my enemies. If the Shuprians are in want, let their curses fall upon the head of their king."

Always thus have kings and the sons of kings explained to themselves the evil they do in the name of pride and power. Yet once, in a far-distant place, I had put aside the dignity of a prince and lived as other men, so my mind was troubled and I knew the evil I did for what it was.

So we waited, we men of Ashur, while Esarhaddon's ramp rose ever higher beside the battlements of Uppume. We plundered the countryside until we had stripped her bare, and then we starved. And the cold wind blew like needles of iron, and we huddled together. And the king turned his eyes to the walls of the city and nursed his dark wrath.

I had begun to believe we would perish like dogs left out in the storm. I had begun to imagine that the bright gods had turned their faces from us. And then the glory of Ashur made itself manifest and we were saved from our own folly.

It was the twenty-first day of the month of Kislef, when the men of Ashur dressed in rags, ate no food cooked in a pot, and abstained from labor, which the gods would only curse, for it was an evil day. Esarhaddon would see no one but his magicians and soothsayers. He kept to his tent, for he feared to let the sun of such a day shine on his face.

In the evening, beside a campfire that had been lit to keep demons away, Lushakin and I shared out a meal of bread, dried meat and beer.

"When we marched against the Scythians, do you remember what you told the men who wished to keep the evil days in quiet?"

"No, I do not remember," I said, shaking my head. What difference could it make what I told them?

"You said that we lived under the protection of the god Ashur, who could forgive any sin—I think you were more afraid that the winter would catch us than of the heavens' wrath."

We looked up at the great ramp, now nearly finished, and I dare believe the same thought was in both our minds.

"Will we live to use it, do you think, Prince? Or will the dead snow cover it and us together?"

I did not know what to answer, so I said nothing. Instead, I watched the last glow of sunset descending behind the ramp.

Except, as I suddenly realized, it was not the sun, for the sun does not send forth a pall of smoke, black as the night sky.

The ramp was on fire.

"By the gods . . . !"

The words died on Lushakin's lips, for now he saw as well as I. Shouts began to rise from the camp as the ramp quickly became engulfed by flames that spread all the faster in the wind which had been blowing since the middle of the afternoon. I could hear voices of panic everywhere.

Why were there no sentries posted? I thought. Damn Esarhaddon and his imbecile piety!

And then, out loud: "We must fetch the king."

The blood beating in my head like a hammer, I ran back through the clusters of tents to my brother's, where the guard, a young officer armed with a javelin, stepped into my path.

"The king has given orders, Prince. He is not to be disturbed."

By then the flames from the burning ramp lit up the western sky like a torch—was the man blind? There was no time for this. I waved him aside without speaking and, when he tried to block my way, I drew my sword and hacked his javelin through, no less than if it had been a twig. I was in a blind fury. I think in the next instant I would have had his life.

"Hold! What is this?"

It was Esarhaddon himself, drawn by the sound of angry voices. He looked at me, and at my naked sword, and his eyes went large. Did he think I had come at last to kill him?

Instead, the sword swung in an arc to the flame-red sky.

"There!" I shouted. "It burns!"

He turned and saw, and never have I seen such an expression of anguish upon a man's face. This he feared even more than the blade of an assassin. This, it seemed, was the final confirmation of all his darkest terrors.

"I am cursed," he said, his voice full of wretched awe. "I have sinned against the gods' majesty and they have turned their faces from me."

His person was sacred, but there was no time to waste on ceremony. I took him by the collar of his tunic and shook him as a dog shakes a rat.

"It is a fire—nothing more. Your soldiers need you now if they are to save themselves. Look at me, Esarhaddon! Recall that you are the king!"

For a moment I was not sure he even understood me. I released my hold on him and he stumbled back. Then, in an instant, he came to himself.

"We will need water," he said, calmly enough. "There is a horse pond close to the ramp."

"And put everyone under arms who is not needed to fight the fire. It should be no surprise if the Shuprians choose this moment to counter-attack."

"Why—have you seen something?" Once more he seemed ready to slip into his nameless panic.

"No, but it is what we ourselves would do."

"Yes. What we would do . . . " He laughed. It was a hopeful sign. "Damn Anhite and his race of cutpurse rogues! Akim Teshub, you lazy son of a crossroads harlot—where is my horse!"

Esarhaddon, mounted on his horse, the wind tugging at his robes, really looked the part of a king as he rode about issuing commands and putting the heart back into his soldiers. Men with buckets of water climbed the ramp like ants swarming over the corpse. There was shouting everywhere. For a furious half an hour I thought we might somehow win through by our own labor, but man is a little thing under the eyes of heaven and the flames that were quenched in one place sprang to life in another—it was soon apparent that we could not stop the fire quickly enough to save the ramp.

And then the Lord Ashur, Master of Destiny, spoke the words of our salvation, and his voice, that filled all men's minds with terror, was the wild screaming of the wind.

Never have I felt such a blast. It was a fight simply to remain standing, and more than one of the king's soldiers, caught near the top of the ramp, was swept off and cast down to his death. There was not a cloud nor a drop of rain, only the burning wind, a wind that would have torn the eyes out of a man's head had he dared to face into it, a wind that howled like a soul lost in darkness. It was as if the heavens had gone mad with despair.

"Look!" someone shouted—or perhaps the shout came from a hundred throats, for I could hardly hear even my own voice—"Look! The wall! It's set the wall on fire!"

I could hardly believe what I saw. The shower of burning embers from the ramp had blown across to the high walls of Uppume, and her battlements were already in flames. We watched, transfixed. In what seemed hardly a moment, that whole face of the wall was a sheet of fire, and then, slowly, the great logs began to tear loose from one another and to tumble down. The city's defenses were crumbling before our eyes.

And then, just before midnight, the wind died away to nothing. We were able to put out the last fires on the ramp, which was still almost intact, but the Shuprians, who had not our easy access to water, were not so fortunate; their wall burned out of all control.

But there were still fires everywhere, large and small, so that even in the black belly of the night it was almost like day.

"We will wait a few hours more," said Esarhaddon—I had not even noticed his approach. "And then, when the wall is utterly broken, I will give orders for an attack. The city will be ours by morning."

"Wait. Let us keep the advantage of our massed strength and not have our number cut to pieces in narrow, unfamiliar streets. Let them come to us."

Esarhaddon waved his arm in a gesture of extreme impatience, and yet he was a good enough commander to see the advantages of meeting the Shuprians on the open plain.

"They are cowards," he said at last. "They will not come out to fight like men. Now or later, we shall have to clear them out of their dens like foxes."

"Esarhaddon, my brother and king, they know as well as we that there must be a battle now. If you were they, and your wives and children were behind that wall, where would you rather do your fighting?"

"Tiglath Ashur, whom Lady Ishtar, Queen of Battles, loves as her own son, your heart is as cold as a serpent's. It shall be as you say."

And the Shuprians did not keep us waiting long. Thinking perhaps to strike before we could prepare, they poured over their ruined wall to meet our swords. They must have known they were dead men, for they fought with the courage of desperation, but their valor was of no use to them. We were ready and the battle was short and one-sided. Dawn found the plain littered with their dead—hardly a man among them survived to witness the sun's glory.

Esarhaddon ordered that the corpses be collected and hung from his great ramp like bunches of grapes, that the people of Uppume might see all was lost. They made a ghastly enough sight, and before noon the city sent envoys, Anhite's own sons, to sue for peace.

They carried before them an effigy of their king and father, an image of wood, dressed in a suppliant's rags and its hands fettered with chains. They begged for his life, but Esarhaddon was deaf to all pleading.

"There has been too much death here," he said. "How can the king who carries the guilt of so many lives be spared? Open the city gates or fight on until you are all slain. The king of Ashur offers you no terms for surrender."

They accepted, knowing they had no choice. The city gates were thrown open and Esarhaddon entered it with his army at his back.

Anhite was already dead by his own hand—he had cut his throat—and Esarhaddon was so furious at having been cheated of the pleasure of killing him that he handed Uppume over to his soldiers, who plundered, raped and murdered for three days and nights. Esarhaddon ordered the chief nobles of the city executed and made a great pile of their bleeding heads. Those of his own officials who had fled the Land of Ashur, taking refuge with King Anhite, lost their eyes and ears. Their hands were cut off and their noses slit, and blind and bleeding they were driven into the wilderness, there to live or perish as the god decreed.

And when the soldiers of Ashur had finished, so there was not a mouthful of wine left undrunk nor a gold coin unplundered nor a woman unravaged, the king had them flogged back into order. The few Shuprian men who still survived were organized into labor gangs and with their own hands tore down what remained of the city's fortifications. This was enough. Esarhaddon's taste for vengeance was now sated.

"I will leave them as they are," he said. "Your Scoloti friend, this bandit who plans to lead his people here next spring, he can do with them as he sees fit. We need a strong ally on our northern border. Perhaps I will give him one of my daughters for a wife."

"Then which of your daughters do you love the least? A Scoloti wife is strangled when her husband dies, and buried in his tomb."

Esarhaddon laughed at this. He really did send Tabiti one of his daughters, the child of a Hebrew concubine, a girl he perhaps did not even know by name. The Scythians are secretive about their women, so what became of her I never did find out.

The day we left on the march home, I rode out and had a last look at the ruined city of Uppume. Would anyone ever live here again, I wondered, or would her very name disappear?

This will be our fate, I thought to myself as I gazed at the blackened buildings and the corpses left still unburied, a meal for the crows that had grown so fat on carrion they could no longer fly. The dust will drift over the ashes of our dead cities. The very graves of our fathers will be plundered, and their bones left scattered about. Someday Nineveh will be like this.

XL

ESARHADDON CELEBRATED HIS TRIUMPH IN CALAH, whence he had moved his capital before entering on the Shuprian campaign. He had ruled there as *marsarru* during the Lord Sennacherib's lifetime, and so the citizens, who imagined themselves in rivalry with Nineveh, looked upon him with great favor—it was possibly the only city in all the Land of Ashur where he might claim to be loved.

And so it was a glorious day when the king led his conquering army through the great gate. The war drums beat and people shouted until their voices cracked, offered bread and wine to the parading soldiers and threw flowers under our horses' hooves. Esarhaddon wore the golden robes of the priest-king of Ashur, and even his chariot was covered with hammered gold and glowed like the setting sun. That night the streets were a riot of drunken celebration as men who had lived for three months on millet cake and dried goat flesh made merry with the booty they had won from the vanquished Shuprians. It was like the sack of Uppume all over again, except that this time the women and the shopkeepers plundered the soldiers.

And the king too held his revels. He feasted his principal officers with great splendor at a banquet that would have made even our father blush with astonishment. Esarhaddon had brought back with him a hundred Shuprian women, of which he planned to keep the ten or twenty best as slaves for his harem. Part of the evening's entertainment was the selection of these, a task which he left to his guests, who were free to make any trial of them they cared to. The women, for their part, knew that life among the king's concubines would be better than any other fate they could expect, and this knowledge made them eager to please the men who had slaughtered their husbands and fathers at Uppume. It was a lively evening. Esarhaddon, who had sated himself earlier, sat back and watched, drinking spiced wine and laughing.

I left early, as soon as I could be sure the king was too drunk to notice. It was the first time I had been allowed out of Esarhaddon's sight, and I wanted to find my wife. I could not even be sure she was in the city.

I owned a house in Calah. My father had always loathed the place, never referring to it except as "that doghole Calah," nor had he ever entered it once Esarhaddon, whom he despised, had been named by the god to succeed him. But I had inherited property there from my uncle the Lord Sinahiusur, the old king's *turtanu* who had died sonless and left me his heir. Selana would be there if she was not still in Nineveh—the only difficulty was that I had never seen the place and had no idea where it might be found.

This problem was solved almost at once. Esarhaddon's banqueting hall opened onto a central courtyard. I looked about me and saw that the darkness was pierced by blocks of light from a web of torchlit corridors that ran to every corner of the palace. One of these went suddenly black, as if someone had shut a door on it. But it was not a door. It was Enkidu.

He gestured for me to follow and turned back into the corridor. Soon I found myself outside again, not in the crowded street, as I had expected, but on a pathway through what seemed a long private garden with a mud-brick wall on one side and a canal on the other. There was no light but the moon and no sound but the quiet lapping of the water and the crunch of our sandals against the graveled walk.

Enkidu opened a wooden door in the wall—he had to stoop to pass through it—and we were in another courtyard. When we entered the house, servants I had never seen before bowed to me as to their acknowledged master.

"Where is the Lady Selana?" I asked.

"She is here."

I turned and saw her. She smiled, and I saw that the belly under her tunic was already as round as a melon. Our child—I had almost forgotten. Something inside my breast seemed to melt and I could feel tears in my eyes. She ran to my arms. I caught her up hungrily and she covered my face with kisses.

"Are you all right?" I asked.

She smiled again, this time with a hint of mischief.

"Yes, My Lord, I am very well. And I will not break if you touch me."

It was a strange thing to go into this woman big with my own child. There was great passion yet there was a great tenderness that clawed at my heart and almost unmanned me. Perhaps it was only my long absence from her, but I think not. I felt as if we really were one flesh, as if she and I had become so intermingled that I might see with her eyes and touch with her hands. Thus I discovered that love is not the limit of human feeling, for this was more than love.

"When will . . . ?"

"In the spring," she answered—she seemed strangely confident, as if she had strength enough for anything. "Your son will be born in the spring. I know he will be a boy. Sometimes at night I can feel him kicking."

I rested my hand on her belly just below the navel, but of course there was nothing. I must have looked disappointed, because she laughed.

"In a month or two you will be able to feel him too, but not yet. Now he is only mine."

A month, or two. The spring was four months away. So much could go amiss before then. It seemed an eternity.

"What happened while I was away?"

"Very little—we came here." Selana moved her narrow shoulders. She was lying with her back to me, and the touch of her naked flesh against mine stirred me deeply. "I worried at first, but once I heard that you were safe I was tranquil and content to wait."

"How did you hear?"

"The Lady Naq'ia. She seems to know everything."

"She is here? In Calah?" I could hardly believe it.

"Yes—she has been very kind to me. Yet there is something about her . . ."

So Naq'ia had defied her son yet again and followed him to his new capital. I wondered if Esarhaddon knew yet, or if he had known already in Shupria. What would he do? Nothing, probably. What could he do? What would he dare to do?

"Yes. There is something about her." There was a cup of wine, still unfinished, that I had brought with me to our sleeping mat. I sat up and took a swallow. It seemed to burn my throat.

"Listen, Selana, and promise me. Do not let the Lady Naq'ia become your friend. Promise me on the life of our son that you will never trust her."

"Is she so wicked then?"

"Yes, she is wicked. She is wicked past your powers of imagining. Never allow yourself to fall into her hands, for she is without pity."

"Then I will not trust her."

She turned to face me, reaching out to draw me down to her, finding my lips with her own.

"I would not in any case," she went on, "for I do not trust any of these Assyrians—they are all barbarians. I trust only you, My Lord."

"Yet I too am an Assyrian."

"No, you are not. Once, you might have been, but not now."

The next morning, an hour before the sun rose, I was awakened by a servant. She was in such a high state of excitement that it almost amounted to terror, and she told me that the king was sitting outside in the garden, with no company but a jar of wine and an oil lamp, hurling curses at anyone who attempted to come near him.

I went out to see for myself and found Esarhaddon wrapped in his cloak, crouched on the bare stones, the wine jar between his knees. The lamp had gone out, but I could see enough to know that he had drunk himself into a black fury. I sat down beside him.

"She is here," he said, in a low, flat voice. "She has followed me here, against my express command, all the way from Nineveh. I am the king, and yet she disregards my will as if I were still a child."

For a moment I thought he was about to rage or weep, or both, but he did neither. He only stared at his feet as if he couldn't remember where he had seen them before.

"What am I to do, Tiglath? What am I to do?"

"Come inside and have breakfast," I told him. "Drink cold pomegranate juice until your head clears."

I was not even sure he had heard me, but then he nodded.

"This is excellent advice," he said. I helped him to his feet, and he clutched me as if afraid of falling.

"I have no friend but you, brother." And now he really did weep. "I have no one to trust except you."

There was no time for a reply, for quite suddenly he doubled up at the waist and emptied his belly into a flower bed. The smell of rotten wine was very strong, and Esarhaddon's face was as pale as a frog's belly. I had to lead him away.

We went into the small room just off my sleeping chamber, and Selana brought us bread, herbs, cold meat and beer. After one cold, appraising look at my brother, she returned to the kitchen and brought back a cup of something that looked exactly like fresh blood, set it down before him, and left without uttering a word.

"You taste it first," he said. He watched, with an appalled curiosity, and then asked, "Is it bad?"

"Yes, it is very bad. Nevertheless, drink it."

He drank it, and then made a face as if he would retch again.

"You are right, it is very bad. Yet I feel better—or will, once the taste is out of my mouth. Perhaps that is its magic, that it makes all other discomforts seem so trivial. Who was that woman? Will you sell her to me after she has whelped her child?"

"She is my wife."

"Yes—I had forgotten. But if she is your wife, why does she not wear a veil?"

"She forgets sometimes."

"Oh." He shrugged his shoulders, as if such mysteries were beyond him. "In any case, perhaps it is just as well you will not sell her, for I have the impression she does not like me."

"Her father, who beat her and sold her for a slave, was an Ionian pig farmer. Doubtless she fancies a resemblance."

Esarhaddon threw back his head and laughed. Then he ate a great quantity of bread and drank most of a pitcher of beer, without speaking.

"What should I do about Naq'ia?" he asked finally, leaning back from the table and holding his belly, as if afraid it might burst. "What if I had her poisoned?"

"Are you serious?"

"Yes." And then, almost immediately, he shook his head mournfully. "Except that it could not possibly succeed. She is too clever for any poisoner. And then she would find out that I had ordered it—she always finds out everything—and I would never again be able to drink a cup of wine without wondering if I was not filling my bowels with venom."

"Why not send twenty soldiers to take her back to Nineveh under armed guard? Seal her up in your old palace, make sure she has plenty of servants to bully, and let her live out her days in impotent splendor. Then you can sleep at night."

"I will never be able to sleep at night as long as she is alive." And the expression on his face made it plain that he was merely speaking the truth. "She knows too many secrets, Tiglath. If I try her too far, she will fill the world's ear with stories about how I . . . No, I will never be safe until she is rotting in her tomb and, pathetic coward that I am, I have not the courage to kill her."

"Then ignore her. You are king, not she—live and rule as if she did not exist."

Esarhaddon put his hand on my shoulder, like a man pitying the ignorance of a child.

"Be glad that Merope was a gentle soul," he said, "since not having had a scorpion for a mother has allowed you to keep your innocence. How am I to rule as if she did not exist when my ministers and servants are even more terrified of her than I am myself? That is why it is you alone I can trust, brother—because you alone have never been afraid of Naq'ia."

"Do not talk like a fool, brother. I am afraid of Naq'ia. Anyone with sense enough to shut his mouth in a rainstorm would be afraid of her."

"Yes—as one is properly afraid of a scorpion, because it is a bad omen and evil. But you have never known what it is to fall under the spell of that evil. She does not own you, brother."

I understood what he meant, for ever since he was a child Esarhaddon had lived in the most terrible dread of his mother. He had never had the will to defy her, for she held him as a net holds a fish. Why this should be, perhaps not even Esarhaddon knew.

He finished the last of the beer and then allowed the jar to roll away across the floor until it stopped of its own.

"One crushes a scorpion under one's heel," he went on, his voice filled with hopelessness. "That is why Naq'ia hates you, Tiglath. Because she knows that you alone in the wide world might someday crush her."

We went back outside, and the King of the Earth's Four Corners lifted up the hem of his tunic to relieve himself against the wall of my house. It was cold that morning, but Esarhaddon did not seem to notice. He asked for more beer.

"You left early last night," he said, breaking the jar's seal with his thumb. "You thought I was too drunk to notice."

"How did the selection go?"

"Ah!"

He sat down on a stone bench, took a long swallow of the beer and handed it to me. He seemed to have forgotten about Naq'ia.

"You remember the one with the wart on her belly? It appears to be gone now—I think they rubbed it off."

This struck him as so amusing that I had to catch him by the beard to keep him from falling over backwards.

"I will keep her. And the one with the pretty breasts. And the one who did such interesting things with her backside. I haven't decided about the rest."

"I thought it was all to be settled by acclaim."

"My officers are all pigs, without the least particle of discrimination," he answered with a kind of benign contempt. "Each cried up the two or three he had mounted while still sober enough to remember and damned all the rest. There were even fights over it. The whole idea was a mistake."

He laughed again, shaking his head.

"Do you recall the little brown one with the long nipples? I will keep her as well. Did you go into her? No—you didn't. You did not go into any of them. Someday, Tiglath, I will take it as an insult that you no longer accept the favors of my women when I offer them. It was not always so. I can remember . . ."

But the recollection did not seem to please him, and he scowled and fell silent.

I found myself wondering if he thought of Esharhamat.

"I am grieved that you no longer have a brother's love for me," he said at last. "Yet I suppose I have forfeited my right to expect it. When we were boys . . ."

"When we were boys, Esarhaddon, we were boys. We are men now. Yet I do not nurse any anger against you for having banished me."

I sat down beside him and put my arm across his shoulders, for I did not wish to wound his spirit. I knew I could never make him understand that it was a question not of love but of trust.

"I am afraid, Tiglath. And it is not only just my mother. I never have a quiet night."

"Yes—I know. I remember our father, and the haunted look that used to come into his eyes sometimes. Perhaps it is simply a king's fate to live with that nameless fear."

That winter was a bitter time. Water froze in the canals, and the Tigris turned so cold that it grew to the color of iron. The snow that fell was as hard as crushed stone.

Esarhaddon was always restless and increasingly left the business of rule to his scribes while he went hunting. Wild pigs were plentiful in the open country around Calah, and he preferred that style of sport to the great hunts, almost like military expeditions, involving scores of men to act as beaters and dog handlers. On good days the two of us would go out alone, sometimes on horseback and sometimes in a single chariot. We would stay out sometimes until it was dark, perhaps taking our dinner in some peasant's hut, his wife serving us boiled goatflesh and onions out of an iron pot, and then return to drink heated wine and purge ourselves of the cold in the king's sweating house. At such times Esarhaddon could forget himself enough to be happy, but it was not like the days of our youth, when we had lived in a careless boys' world that we imagined would go on forever. I understood this, if Esarhaddon did not.

And, I must own, my mind was filled with other things. I had seen Esharhamat again.

Nothing in this life is innocent, although whom I injured by this one act of remembrance for an old passion I cannot say. Esarhaddon, caring only for his own pleasure, was not of a jealous temperament when it came to women and was unconcerned if his wife had given her heart elsewhere. And Selana, as her time approached, was turning inward to the child she carried and hardly noticed what I did. Occasionally, when her burden made such things uncomfortable for her, she preferred that I lie with one or another of the women servants. Yet this with Esharhamat was not of the senses but of the soul, and I think Selana would not have been so indifferent had she known. I took pains that she should not know, and in this concealment, if in nothing else, I knew I wronged her.

It happened almost as soon as I returned from the north. One morning, as I was on my way to go hunting with Esarhaddon, a slave, one of Esharhamat's women, stopped me.

"Each afternoon my lady sits in the sun and waits," she said. That was all she said, and then she turned and ran away.

For several days I did nothing. It all belongs to the past, I told myself. She and I are not even the same people we were then. What could come of it, if we were to meet again? What could it bring to either of us except misery?

So I told myself not to think of Esharhamat, discovering only that trying not to think of her was like trying not to breathe. By the simple expedient of reminding me that she was alive she had made the world seem an empty place, as if I had been abandoned in the midst of a desert.

Finally one day, shortly after noon, I found myself in her garden. I hardly even knew how I had come there.

"Have I grown so old and faded that you stare at me thus?" she asked. She was alone, lying on a couch, and indeed I felt my eyes filling with tears to see what time and illness had done to her.

"You are still beautiful—you are . . ."

But she stook her head. "I know what I have become, Tiglath. You needn't sweeten your words to me. I have grown into an old woman, and my last days are near."

"You are younger than I am," I said. I do not know why I said it, for even on my lips it sounded like the remark of an idiot.

Perhaps Esharhamat thought so too, for she smiled.

"A woman ages faster than a man, and you have not brought nine children into the daylight. They have taken their toll, especially the last. My physicians tell me to come out here and breathe the cold air that I may be restored to health, but they and I know I am past all hope. I am bleeding to death, Tiglath, but slowly, so that I may live through another year. Sit down here beside me—please?"

I sat down beside her on the couch and she rested her hand on my arm. There was hardly any pressure from her touch, as if she had already been released from her dying flesh. For a long moment neither of us spoke.

"Have you seen our son?" she asked finally, I think only to break the silence.

"No, I have not seen him."

"Do they keep him from you then, our little Ashurbanipal? I am not surprised, for it is a great secret that he is not Esarhaddon's child—only you and I and Esarhaddon and Naq'ia and the whole court and nation know of it." She laughed joylessly, and her fingers tightened on my arm. "That is what a secret is, the thing everyone knows but no one speaks of, except in private. I do feel pity for Esarhaddon, though, for it grieves him that the god favors your son over his own."

Perhaps she saw something in my face, for her eyes narrowed.

"You do not believe me?" she asked, with perhaps a little scorn. "You doubt that I can pity Esarhaddon? I do pity him, for I have wronged him. You and I, both of us, have wronged him, though he hardly feels it. Our breeding of sons was a duty to the god, in which he knew no more pleasure than I did myself, but over the years we have become friends in spite of it.

"Do you know how? I will tell you, Tiglath, if only to burden your heart. After he sent you away, when he began to realize how much he missed you, he turned to me as the only one who could understand the weight of his loss."

I cannot easily describe the impression her words made on me. I felt suddenly as if all along I had understood nothing, as if the whole of my life had been nothing but a selfish dream. Esarhaddon, Esharhamat and myself: this strange ritual of betrayal in which somehow we had become entrapped. I had fancied myself the only victim, yet it was not so. How had we all gone so wrong? If truly Esharhamat had meant to wound me, she had found the way.

"Then you still have not forgiven me," I said. And even as I spoke her dark eyes, in which a man might lose himself forever, clouded over with pain and she put her arms about my neck.

"I never meant . . . No, Tiglath, my darling, my love, I never meant . . ."

I held her to me as she wept, and all my old love for her swept through me like the sea through the timbers of a foundering ship. I understood then, as I held her, that she would die soon but that death would release neither of us. Death seemed as helpless as we ourselves.

And at last she was quiet.

"They tell me you have a wife now," she whispered, in the voice of one who has never known jealousy—why should she care if I loved another? What was that love measured against her own?

"Yes, I have a wife."

"And she is with child?"

"Yes."

"And you have found happiness with this woman?"

"Yes."

These words passed my lips, even as I held Esharhamat in my arms, loving her as I had in the days of our hopeful youth, and they were no more than the truth. Strange are the ways of passion, stranger still of love, and yet it was impossible to lie. I believe Esharhamat, who saw with a woman's cunning and had suffered enough to learn wisdom, understood.

"I am to go to Uruk." She reached up to touch my face, as if this were already the time of parting. "I will pray there to the Lady Ishtar that my health might return—Esarhaddon has restored her shrine lavishly, hoping she will show me a little mercy, but I fear the gods' just wrath cannot be turned aside so easily."

"Tell me of Ashurbanipal," I said, believing in that moment that my heart might burst. "Tell me of our son."

Esharhamat smiled with her eyes. Yes, of course, she had understood everything.

"They train him to be a soldier," she answered. "Yet I think he does not much love the life. He is clever, Tiglath. Like his father."

"Will he make a good king?"

She shook her head. "I will not live to see it. I am only his mother—I leave all that to the god."

Her arms tightened about my neck.

"Was I wrong, Tiglath? I longed to see you, if only just once more. I

>> 532 <<

have done so much wickedness in this life that I will be glad when it ends at last. Was I wrong to draw you here one last time?"

Because of course she knew, as I knew, that we would never see each other again.

And then one evening, not many days after the Akitu Festival, when the Tigris, swollen with cold water, announces the rebirth of the world, I was sitting at dinner with my wife when, all at once, she put her hand on her belly and a strange expression crossed her face.

"I feel something," she said. She started to rise from her chair and I jumped forward to help her up. "My water broke two days ago, so I think this must be the beginning. Help me to my bed, Lord, and I think I will be well enough. Peasant women like me bear their children in the fields and live to smile about it. No, do not carry me. It is better, I think, if I walk."

I sent a servant to fetch the midwife and sat beside Selana's bed, holding her hand—more, I suspect, for my comfort than for hers.

"Do not be concerned, Lord. It will be over by morning, and I am not afraid. My mother had six live children and her labors never lasted more than a few hours."

And truly I could not but marvel at her calm. I was as frightened as before my first battle, but Selana only stroked my fingers and smiled. A man's courage is nothing against a woman's.

At last the midwife came. By then Selana was having pains every quarter of an hour, but the midwife felt her belly, pronounced herself satisfied, and ordered me from the room.

"Go away, Lord, for this is woman's work. Stay out of earshot and drink wine mixed with very little water. It would not be a bad thing if you took a concubine to your sleeping mat tonight, just to ease your mind. The child will be brought to you as soon as it is born."

Thus was I dismissed. I waited in the next room for a time, listening to Selana's cries. I felt as if my own bowels were being pulled out, a coil at a time. Finally I could no longer stand my own sense of helplessness and I went outside to sit in the garden.

Keturah, the Elamite woman who had been a gift from my brother, brought me a jar of wine and lifted her tunic over her head to offer me the consolations of her wood-smoke-colored flesh—this, I think, Selana had arranged in advance, for she was ever attentive to my little comforts—but the mere sight of her round breasts filled me with horror and I chased her away. I kept the wine, however,

An hour later I was just breaking the seal of a second jar when Esarhaddon turned up.

"What are you doing out here?" he asked. "You will catch something getting drunk out-of-doors like this. There are too many evil spirits out at night."

"My wife is in her travail," I answered bleakly.

"I see." Esarhaddon nodded several times and sat down beside me.

"What brought you here?"

"I am escaping from a banquet my ministers have forced on me to honor the Urartian ambassador. Besides, there was something I wished to discuss with you."

"What *something*?"

"It can wait—you are hardly in a suitable frame of mind now. Are you going to give me any of that wine?"

My servants, who had long since lost their awe of Ashur's king, brought out two more jars of wine and a brazier, for it was a cool night.

"When did she start?" Esarhaddon asked, holding the soles of his feet up to the glowing coals.

"Just at dinner."

"Oh, well then! We can expect to be out here all night. Why not steal back to my house of women, just to pass the time?"

"It is death for any man save the king to enter there."

Esarhaddon considered this for a moment and then laughed. "Well, if you won't tell, I won't," he said, and then laughed even louder.

I had a blinding headache by then, so I only glared at him.

"It was only a thought."

For a long time we sat in silence, passing the wine jar back and forth between us. I kept thinking that I heard Selana's screams, but that was merely my own morbid imagination.

What is taking so long? I wondered. Something must have gone amiss that no one has brought me any word.

The time passed as slowly as sap dripping from a broken tree limb.

I will never touch her again, I thought. If the god grant that she be returned to me alive, I will never inflict myself on her again.

"I never had anything to do with any of this," Esarhaddon said finally—I actually started at the sound of his voice. "I can't stand the sight of women with their bellies stretched tight. Whenever any of mine were far enough along that it began to show, I always had them taken away somewhere. I never wanted to hear anything about it until after the child was delivered."

"With all respect, My Lord King is an appalling, selfish brute. And a coward in the bargain."

"Yes, I suspect so," he answered.

In the last hour before dawn, when the world seems about to stop forever, a servant woman approached and silently bade me come in. As soon as I was inside the house she put a bundle into my arms. I hardly glanced at it.

"My Lady is . . . ?"

"Quite well, Lord. Asleep now. This is your son."

I looked down and found my gaze caught by a pair of large, dark blue eyes. Exactly my mother's eyes.

"My son," I whispered.

Esarhaddon had wandered in, disregarded by everyone, and looked at the child.

"He looks like an Ionian," he said. "Of course, that shouldn't surprise anyone."

"Then he shall be called Theseus Ashur—the god shall share the honor of his name with an Ionian king."

"No one will be able to pronounce it."

"They will learn."

"Let me take him again, Lord, and I shall give him back to his mother," the servant woman said. "It is too cold for him here."

I relinquished up my son to her, and when she had left Esarhaddon touched me on the arm.

"It would be wisest to go back outside and open another jar to the health of young—whatever his name is."

"Theseus Ashur."

"Yes, quite. And then I will tell you all about my new plans for the conquest of Egypt."

XLI

THE HOUSE OF WAR WAS THE GARRISON OF THE *QURADU*, the king's own bodyguard, who shielded his sacred person in battle. They always fought in the front ranks and always took heavy losses. They were the best soldiers in the army of Ashur and it was the pride of my life that I was one of their number, for I counted the honor of being a *quradu* far greater than that of being a prince.

The house of war also included the royal barrack, where those of the king's own blood were trained up to be soldiers. My brother and I had both spent our youth on the parade grounds at Nineveh, where our father had had his capital. Esarhaddon's sons were here in Calah, but it would be just the same for them as it had been for us. And little Theseus—provided that I did not fall victim to some palace intrigue— would in his turn join his royal cousins to learn the soldier's trade.

My son cried lustily when he was born, and the midwife declared that he would be tall like his father and have powerful limbs when he grew to be a man. Perhaps she said this of every male child she helped to bring into the world, but just the same it filled me with pleasure to hear it. For the first several days of his young life I spent as much time as I could in the nursery, being generally in the way. I had had no notion of how much I would love this child. I would watch his mother nurse him, and afterwards I would be allowed to hold him in my arms and feel his tiny fingers clutched around my thumb. I dreaded every moment that required me to be absent, for in his smallness he seemed so fragile that I was tormented by a thousand fears for his life. Yet he did live. Selana assured me that he was healthy and strong. Gradually I learned to believe her.

The birth of a son turns a man's mind back to his own childhood. Memories of my mother filled me with sorrow that she had died while I was in exile, that at the end I had not been there to close her eyes. I remembered Esarhaddon when our friendship was still unshadowed. I remembered the house of war.

I was a *rab shaqe* in the king's army and my campaigns against the northern tribes were the stuff of fable. No one questioned my right to enter the garrison of the *quradu*. No one, perhaps, except myself.

As my eyes swept across the parade grounds, I was struck at once by their strangeness and their utter familiarily. As a boy I had never driven my teams of horses across this dark-packed earth, endlessly practicing the sharp turns at full gallop that are the charioteer's highest art. That had all been in Nineveh. Yet the youth who held the reins that morning, who made the ground shake and sent up plumes of dust from under his wheels, might have been myself at his age. He was in fact Ashurbanipal, who would be *marsarru* one day and then, when Esarhaddon died, king in his place. He was as well, if I could give credit to Esharhamat's word, the son of my own loins.

I watched him for a long time. He was still only a boy, for the tufts of beard that were visible here and there on his face were hardly more than baby hair, but he handled the horses with a man's skill. His mother said he had little taste for a soldier's life—it might even be true. Others said that he was clever, that he collected clay tablets for the sake of the old learning on them, that he was arrogant, that he was too much under the sway of his grandmother, the Lady Naq'ia. Many stories, most of them vicious, collect around the boy who will one day hold the world in his hands.

"Your pardon, My Lord, but are you not the Lord Tiglath Ashur?"

I glanced around and saw a youth of about thirteen standing behind me. He wore the uniform of a royal cadet.

"I am he," I said.

"Then you are he who crushed the Medes, who killed the mighty Daiaukka with your own hands and in single combat?"

"I am that one also."

"Then I am your nephew, Lord, for I am Shamash Shumukin."

Yes, I could believe this was Esarhaddon's son, for he looked just as his father had at that age, with the same open face and the same wide, solid stance, making him appear as impenetrable as a mud-brick wall.

I offered him my hand and he took it, pumping my arm as if he wanted to tear it loose and take it home with him for a trophy.

"And it is your ambition to be a soldier?" I asked, merely out of politeness, since the answer was obvious enough.

"Yes, Lord. To be *rab shaqe* of the king's armies and lead conquered nations under the yoke of Ashur."

He spoke with such ardor that I was touched, remembering the glamour that war had held for me at that age—when I had never seen it.

"And is it the same for all the royal cadets? Is the next reign to be the scene of so much carnage?"

We both looked toward the figure in the chariot, who at last was bringing his team to a walk.

"It is not the same for Ashurbanipal," Shamash Shumukin announced, watching his brother with unself-conscious pride. "He will be the king. He is too clever to care much for soldiering."

I found myself wondering whose words these were, his own or Ashurbanipal's. And if he was aware that there was a difference.

"We have worked it out between us," he went on. "He will be the king and I will be his sword."

"Then you are friends?"

"Yes, Lord—friends and brothers."

The words sent a shiver down my back.

All this time Ashurbanipal's horses had been marking out a wide circle in the dust, which they now left to pull up beside us. The boy whom the god had chosen as the next king of Ashur did not step down from his chariot, and thus he retained the advantage of forcing us to look up to him.

"You are the Lord Tiglath Ashur," he said coldly, as if he thought I might like to know. "I am Ashurbanipal, son of the Lord Esarhaddon, Ruler of the Wide World."

For a moment I actually had the impression he expected me to bow. Then his gaze turned to his brother and he smiled.

"Come, Shumukin. There are still at least four hours of daylight left—we can go hunting."

I watched the two drive off together and then, as I turned to leave, saw that another pair of eyes had been watching me. Esarhaddon stepped out of the shadow of a doorway, grinning. I bowed to him.

"Stop that, Tiglath," he said, punctuating the command with an irritated wave of his hand. "There is no one about to be impressed, and you know you only do it to annoy me. What are you doing here, anyway? Come to get away from the smell of milk and excrement?"

He grinned, as if he had said something enormously clever.

"No. I have been looking into the future."

"Ah, the boys." The Ruler of the Wide World shrugged his shoulders, as if to indicate that his concern for the future did not stretch so far as into the next generation. "Ashurbanipal would make a better scribe than a king. He despises me for a dull hunk of brown clay, so that sometimes I wonder if he doesn't suspect . . . But Shamash Shumukin will make a very proper soldier—I have plans for him. They are great friends, you know. They are like we were at their age."

"Like us, you say? Then one can only wonder which of them, in the end, will first betray the other."

I still remember how the light changed in Esarhaddon's eyes.

Egypt. All that summer, I hardly heard of anything else. Was there a soul in Calah, or in the world beyond it, who escaped knowing that the king of Ashur was planning a second attack on Egypt?

"The tribes are crawling around the northern borders like flies over a dead horse, and you want to take an army to Egypt?" I asked him, for I thought the whole idea mad. "You will need at least a hundred and fifty thousand men, and if you succeed you will need to leave half that number behind to garrison the country. What is there in Egypt that is worth stripping our defenses naked in order to get?"

"You have settled with the northern tribes, Tiglath—or had you forgotten? As long as you are alive, there will be no war with the Medes, and none of the others count."

"I could be thrown from a horse tomorrow, or your mother might finally find a way to have me poisoned. You hang a great deal on the life of one man."

"My soothsayers tell me you will live into extreme old age. So we are all safe enough."

Esarhaddon grinned, as if the last possible objection had been answered.

"What is your real objection to this venture?" he asked me, quite as if he thought he was being excluded from some secret. "I will not make the same mistake as before—this time we shall attack from the east, where they are not so well guarded."

"What do you know of Egypt?" I asked him in turn.

"That it is rich." He shrugged his shoulders in disdain. "You seem to forget that I have already seen one season of campaigning in the Delta—the place is not unknown to me."

"But that was the Delta, as you say. You saw garrison duty in the west during our father's reign. How close did you ever come to her eastern borders?"

"I was stationed in the Land of Bashan." Esarhaddon laughed. "You remember Leah, the woman I brought home from there, who had a ring put through her nose because there was no other way to keep her in order? It was there I—"

"Egypt, brother!"

"Yes, Egypt—after Sidon was destroyed, we went as far south as the Great Salt Sea in which nothing lives, into the lands of the Hebrews."

"But did you know that between there and Egypt there is a great desert?"

"What of it?" he asked, as if he had seen something of the sort on a map and was not impressed.

"To take an army across that desert will be a fearful thing."

"Why should it be? A desert is merely a patch of waste ground—we are not women, you know."

What could I do but shake my head at such ignorant folly?

"I have crossed that desert, brother. It is a place more terrible than anything you can imagine. I am lucky that my bones are not still there."

"You have been to the western desert?" Esarhaddon's face shone like a lamp, and he reached across the table where we were having breakfast to put his arm about my neck and pull me to him. "You have truly been there? Tiglath my brother, I *knew* I was right to bring you home!"

"By the merciful gods . . . !"

For I had sealed my own fate—now he would insist that I come with him on this mad adventure.

Yet mine was probably the only voice Esarhaddon heard that did not encourage him in his Egyptian enterprise. It is always the same when a new campaign is proposed; everyone sees in it some road to personal advancement. The soldiers, who were weary of garrison life and excited by the prospect of plunder, spoke to him of the conqueror's glory; and the courtiers, who dreamed of power and place and a chance to undo their rivals, worked hard to smooth away every doubt and at the same time whispered into the king's ear how Pharaoh was stirring rebellion among the western vassal states—which was true, but had been just as true every day since the reign of our great-grandfather.

The whole of Calah seemed united in conspiracy, and even Naq'ia, although she said nothing directly to her son, let it be known that this Egyptian scheme had her approval—why should she not approve, when every day that Esarhaddon was away from his capital strengthened her own hold, both on the present government and on the heirs to the next?

"Suppose then that you succeed," I told him. "You have driven Pharaoh's armies into the desert, where they will have nothing to eat except the grave offerings left for their ancestors. The Nile Valley is yours, from the Delta to the gates of Karnak. What will you do then?"

"I will sack Memphis, which you claim is such a prize. I will strip the temples of their gold. I will rape the women and carry away the best. I will put an iron ring around Pharaoh's neck and drag him back to Calah behind my chariot."

"And then what?"

Esarhaddon stared at me as if he did not understand the question, so I repeated it.

"And then what will you do?"

"Do? What else is there to do?"

"A conquered nation must be governed, and Egypt is like an anthill. If you kick it to pieces you will have a hard time putting it back together again."

But the King of the Earth's Four Corners dismissed that difficulty with a contemptuous lifting of his eyebrows.

"What does it matter then? I will put the double crown on the brow of some local idiot, and my garrison commanders will rule in his name."

He grinned with mischief.

"Or perhaps I will make *you* Pharaoh, and you can shave your face and put on a little false beard made of lacquered wood. Think of how surprised all your old friends would be."

At last I gave up and let Esarhaddon have his way, reconciling myself to it with the thought that, by accompanying him, I might be able to open his eyes before it was too late. I should have known then that it was already too late.

"When will you go?" Selana asked. We sat together on the floor of our bedroom, which was now covered with a thick reed mat, watching our son, who was five months old, display his latest accomplishment—sitting up with no other support than his mother's steadying hand on his backside. He seemed almost as pleased as his parents at this new ability and smiled broadly, showing two glistening slivers of front tooth that had recently broken through the gum.

"Not until after the end of next year's floods," I answered, as young Theseus stealthily guided my finger into his mouth and then bit down hard enough to make me wonder if he would relish the taste of blood. "Nothing on such a scale can be done in haste."

"And how long will you be gone?"

"Six months, or perhaps eight." The finger, as I was glad to discover when I got it back again, was deeply indented but intact. "It depends most on what we will find in Egypt. Esarhaddon expects a quick campaign, but I fear he will be disappointed."

Whether weary of the effort involved in holding himself straight or annoyed at a conversation not directed at him, my son made a loud, inarticulate sound and raised his arms to indicate that he wanted to be picked up. I obliged him, and he expressed his appreciation by reaching across my face and putting his thumb in my eye. Selana remained silent, looking down at her hands in her lap.

"I will be perfectly safe." I said. "This will be nothing like Sicily—I will go as a *rab shaqe* in an army numbering at least a hundred thousand men. Soldiers die in battle, but commanders generally perish in their beds."

This seemed to ease her mind a little, yet I continued to suspect that she regarded the whole venture as a fool's errand. I refrained from telling her how closely I agreed with her assessment.

"Little Theseus must be fed," she announced tonelessly, reaching out to take him from me. She opened her tunic to expose a breast, rubbing the nipple with her thumb.

"Soon you will have to give that up," I told her. "He is not yet old enough to eat meat."

She smiled a tight, brief smile and dropped her head to kiss the child that milked her—things had not been well between us of late, although she had said nothing.

I got up to leave.

"Will you be sorry to be gone so long?"

I had almost reached the doorway. I turned around to answer, and the sight of her there, with our boy in her arms, made my voice catch in my throat. I left without speaking.

Shamash Shumukin was much to be pitied. His mother had never cared for him, giving him up to the care of nurses from the hour of his birth, and his father was that remote and awful being the king of Ashur.

He had the companionship of his brother, but at that age a boy needs something more. I had had my uncle the Lord Sinahiusur, who had treated me with kindness when I was a youth and had made me his heir, and Tabshar Sin, the old soldier who had taught me to be a man. They had given me the guidance I needed, along with the sense of being approved. And thus, when in his loneliness Esarhaddon's forsaken son attached himself to me, I remembered the debt I owed to others and tried to be his friend.

And, more than anything in this life, Shamash Shumukin wanted to take part in the Egyptian campaign. Thinking this might not be the worst thing, I promised him I would raise the matter with the king.

"Ashurbanipal, of course, cannot go," I said to Esarhaddon. "He will be the *marsarru* in a year or two and, in any case, he is too young; but Shamash Shumukin is a different matter. Eight months on campaign would be worth three years in the royal barrack. Only think, brother, what you or I at his age would have given for such a chance."

But the king of Ashur was hardly listening. His face was flushed and he glared at me with exhausted rage. There were broken clay tablets all over the floor of his study and his scribes were nowhere about. Apparently I had only just missed a scene.

"I am the victim of my servants," Esarhaddon declared, stamping his sandaled foot against the floor. "The Land of Ashur is not ruled by her king but by eunuchs who scratch lies into mud as soft as their own flabby bellies. They know nothing of war—all they ever think of is money."

He sat down behind a table half covered with the contents of a spilled wine cup, looked at another tablet, and then abruptly threw it too to the floor. Then he refilled the wine cup and looked up at me as if he were trying to remember why I was in the room.

"Now—what is this about Shamash Shumukin?"

"He wants to join the expedition to Egypt. I think it would be a good thing."

"That is impossible. He will be in Babylon by then."

"And why by the god's mercy would you send him to Babylon?"

"To be viceroy. And the Babylonians had better grow accustomed to him, because after I die he will be their king."

The announcement was made in a flat, passionless voice, but I must own I would not have been more amazed if I had found it written across the sky in letters of fire. It took my breath away. Esarhaddon, I knew, was not the wisest head ever to wear the crown of Ashur, but I never would have credited even him with such a monstrous piece of folly.

"Whom else have you told of this?" I asked.

"No one else." He grinned at me savagely. "You are the first whom I have honored with my confidence."

"Then all is well. Just forget all about it, and we will take Shamash Shumukin with us to Egypt."

But Esarhaddon only stared at me with a dangerous look in his eyes.

"You cannot bear it, can you," he said at last. "You could not be king yourself, so everything must go to Ashurbanipal."

He rose abruptly and started pacing about the room. As he walked, the wine in his cup splashed over his fingers and onto the floor.

"I will make my son a king!" he shouted. "It is not enough that you have rutted upon my wife, that the god has put *your bastard* next to the throne of Ashur, but you must rob me of everything. You are not my friend, Tiglath. You do not love me at all."

The wine jar was still on the table. I picked it up and found that it was still half full. There was no second cup, so Esarhaddon handed me his.

"I did not remember that you were so jealous of Esharhamat's affections," I said coldly—really, there were times when I had no patience with my brother.

"I am *not* jealous." He stopped pacing long enough to take back the cup, drink it off, and hand it back to me. "I have always been openhanded with you. When have I ever said, 'This one among my women I prize so much that I will not share her with my brother Tiglath'? And as for Esharhamat, I have grown fond of her over the years—in a friendly way, you know—but I never made so much of her as you did. *I* never cared what you did with her!"

"Then has being king meant so very much to you?"

Esarhaddon answered with a scowl and a contemptuous noise like an ox passing wind.

"I thought not," I went on, making a face at the taste of the wine, which was terrible. "Then have a little pity for your son, for he is the very image of yourself at his age and will find no more joy in kingship than you have. He wants to be a soldier, just as you and I wanted to be soldiers. Let him have his wish. Besides, it will cause trouble to set up a king in Babylon, even if he is the king's own brother. When the time comes, let Ashurbanipal take the hands of Marduk, or let him appoint a governor, that the Babylonians do not forget that the Lord of Ashur is their king."

"Our father made *his* son king of Babylon," replied Esarhaddon, his eyes narrowing with suspicion.

"That was a father and his eldest son, who, had he lived, would have been king one day in his place. Ashurbanipal and Shamash Shumukin are brothers."

"And close friends, just as we were friends. They will do very well together."

"Yes—just as we were friends."

The king's face hardened, and I knew he would listen no more.

"I will make my son a king," he said. "You cannot stop me, Tiglath."

"No, I cannot stop you."

When I told Shamash Shumukin, he wept. And well he might weep. As I tried to comfort him I remembered what Esharhamat had told me while she still carried him in her womb. "*I dream of fire—everywhere fire, red and gold flames like the tongues of serpents. The walls of a great palace are burning around me. And I have set the torch myself. I die by my own hand, yet it is not I. I see it all, as if through the eyes of another.*"

The future was full of nameless dangers. Without knowing what it might mean, somehow I could think of nothing else except Esharhamat's dream of fire.

XLII

WHEN ESARHADDON ANNOUNCED THAT HE WOULD DESIG-
nate his eldest living son viceroy of Babylon, there was almost no
reaction. It is true that one Adad Shumusur, a counselor to the old king
our father and reputed a man of wisdom, wrote a letter warning him
against committing an act of folly which would be offensive to the
gods—Esarhaddon showed me the letter; he was not pleased and had to
be dissuaded from having the old man's life—but hardly anyone else
seemed even to notice. Thus dazzled was the king's court by the prospect
of Egypt.

And so it came to pass that within a month Ashurbanipal was installed
in the house of succession as *marsarru*. The ceremony was carried out
with splendid pomp, and all the great men of Ashur who had collected in
Calah for the event were required to swear that upon Esarhaddon's death
they would abide by his arrangements for the succession. This was a
matter of tradition—the Lord Sennacherib had exacted the same pledge
from his nobles and kinsmen when Esarhaddon became the *marsarru*, yet
it had not prevented civil war when my brother came to the throne—and
so, when my turn came, I presented myself to the king prepared to put
my name to the oath.

"This will not be required of you," Esarhaddon told me. He offered no
explanation, yet there was about his eyes a strange, haunted look. I was
surprised, but at the time I thought little more about it.

Shamash Shumukin was packed off to Babylon. I never saw him again.

Naq'ia, who claimed to love the boy, accepted his departure with her
usual calm—the very next day I received an invitation to attend upon

her, apparently only that I might witness how well she had accepted this latest of Esarhaddon's caprices.

I was shown to her private quarters and found her sitting on a sofa with her black tunic rolled up to her knees, soaking her feet in a copper water basin. A man whom I assumed to be a physician knelt beside her and kneaded the calf of her right leg with his delicate, feminine hands. He had a heavy nose in a face that was almost perfectly triangular, and his eyes were small and glittering with apprehension. He glanced at me and then dropped his gaze, as if I had caught him in something shameful.

There was a cane resting against the sofa, although I had never seen Naq'ia use such a thing. I bowed and she looked up and smiled, as if we were sharing a jest at her expense.

"My legs trouble me during the cold weather," she said with a shrug. "This close to the mountains, the winter air seems filled with ice."

"Perhaps my Lady should spend her winters with Shamash Shumukin in the south, where the weather is warmer."

This made her laugh. I can hardly remember another time when I heard her laughter—it was an odd, inhuman sound, like the cry of some bird of prey. She lifted her left foot out of the basin and kicked across at the man who was massaging her other leg, spattering the floor with water and causing him to withdraw, crawling backwards a few paces before he summoned the courage to rise and bow himself out of her presence.

"He is a clever physician," she said, when he was gone. "From Tushpah, in the kingdom of the Urartians—a place, I believe, you know. But at my time of life . . . The infirmity of age, Tiglath. It will come to you one day too."

"It is a relief to hear my lady expects me to live that long."

She laughed again, and one of her women came with a cloth to dry her feet. I took the opportunity to study Naq'ia's face. She seemed to have aged so little that she might have been Esarhaddon's sister rather than his mother. To me she did not appear to have grown an hour older than my childhood memories of her—merely, in some indefinable way, harder.

I decided that all this nonsense with the cane and the complaints about the northern winters was merely some sort of device. Perhaps she even expected me to see through it. A lie does not have to be credited in order to have its anticipated effect.

"You will never believe anything good of me, will you, Tiglath. Well, I am not surprised, for we have had our bad days, you and I."

I said nothing, and after a few seconds she seemed to dismiss the thought.

"You will see," she said abruptly, "Esarhaddon will bide his time, and then he will allow Shamash Shumukin to take the hands of Marduk and be king in Sumer." She shook her head, in which there was less gray than in her son's beard, pretending to disapprove.

"And yet, lady, this at least has forced the king to declare Ashurbanipal *marsarru*."

"Yes, Tiglath—it has achieved that."

She looked at me in an odd, speculative way, as if weighing the possibility that I might at last find some place in her plans. The next king, through whom she hoped to achieve the power that Esarhaddon had so long denied her, was my son, not his. Did that make me a rival, or an ally?

"And since the *turtanu* the Lord Sha Nabushu will be accompanying his master to Egypt, Ashurbanipal must be named viceroy."

"Yes, Tiglath. That also is true." The Lady Naq'ia smiled. I never knew what she meant to convey by her smiles, but they always turned my bowels into ice. "I am surprised you have not persuaded my son to let you stay behind to advise him."

"The king requires me in Egypt. And the *marsarru* will have you, My Lady."

This woman, whom I had feared all my life, nodded in acknowledgment of the compliment.

Because, of course, it was her hand which had moved events to this point. Now everything was as she would have willed it, and I did not believe in chance. Just how she had played on Esarhaddon's fears and jealousies I did not know, but all that had happened was through her contrivance. No, it was not her capacity to govern to which I paid my poor tribute, but to her cunning.

The spider, spinning her web over the mouth of an unfinished jar, knows not that all her toil, perhaps even her own frail body, are fated for the destroying fire. She goes on, tenacious in her labor, blindly patient, as if the snare she sets could trap the sun.

War is a great relief to the troubled mind. A soldier's life is simplicity itself—there is drill, there is campaign, there is courage and danger and death. It is difficult without being complicated. It is an escape from the maze of ordinary existence. There is nothing wonderful in the fact that men are so often anxious to flee to the comparative safety of battle.

Thus I was actually beginning to look forward to Esarhaddon's

Egyptian expedition, if only because it would take us both away from the toils of his court.

Selana, of course, sensed all this and retreated farther and farther into silence.

Once, and only once, I awoke in the darkest part of the night and found her sitting up on our sleeping mat, her naked back bathed by the moonlight from a half-open window, shuddering with whispered sobs. I tried to take her in my arms, but she turned her head away.

"What is wrong?" I asked stupidly. "Are you ill?"

"I am not ill."

"Then what vexes you?"

"Nothing, Lord—go back to sleep."

I took her chin in my hand and compelled her to look at me. Her face was stained with tears, as if she had been weeping for hours.

"Do not tell me it is nothing." I let her go and used a flint to light the oil lamp we kept beside our bed. "You are not a woman to crack your heart in the middle of the night if there is no reason. Tell me what it is, or I will send a servant for a physician."

There was wine on a table near the door. I poured her out a cup and made her drink it, and presently she brushed the tears from her eyes with the back of her hand.

"What is it?" I asked again. "What has made you unhappy?"

"Nothing. I dreamed of Sicily, that was all."

"And a dream brought down this torrent? Are you so wretched then?"

"We were happier there," she said, as if stating the obvious.

"Have things changed so much for the worse? In Sicily you were a farmer's concubine. Here you are the wife of a prince. We have a fine son who will take his place beside the mighty of the earth."

She merely shrugged, as if to suggest that all these things were shadows.

"Have *I* changed so much then?"

"It is not for a slave to question the ways of her master," she answered quietly.

It was only then, I think, that I understood how deeply I had somehow managed to hurt her.

"Then I have changed," I said, drawing her to me—this time she did not resist, but seemed to disappear into my arms. "Yet I have not changed toward you."

"Have you not? Is a man's soul not all of one piece? In Sicily I thought I understood you, but here . . ."

"Nothing is different here, except that I am home. Go to the city walls and listen to the swift sound of the river—on the day I was born, they washed me in its water. I breathed this air with my first breath. Whatever I was in some other place, the Land of Ashur made me."

"That, perhaps, is what I do not understand. You are bound to all this with chains no eye can see. Your brother, your pitiless god, this woman of whom you never speak—what is there here that . . . ?"

I did not answer. I only held her in my arms until at last she fell asleep again. In the morning, after she had left me to feed our son, I hitched a pair of horses to a light hunting chariot and drove out onto the plain until I could look around to all points of the compass and not see another living thing. Until the city of Calah, and all she held, was no more than a ragged patch on the horizon.

It was like Selana that she did not seem to be jealous in the usual way of women. Of course she knew about Esharhamat—how could she not know when there were so many only too willing to fill her ears with everything that was known or guessed by the good ladies of my brother's court? Yet it was not a rival she feared, for Selana had never feared anything for herself. It was the burden of the past she feared. She was like someone who has broken in on a ritual that is only just being completed. She sees the dagger raised and hears the incantation of the priest and knows how it will all end without knowing what it means.

And I was as helpless as she, for it was not in my power to make her understand.

So I churned up the dust under my chariot wheels, taxing both the stamina and the patience of my horses and greatly annoying the wild deer with my fruitless attempts to run them down. By the day's end, with my team lathered with sweat and gasping like a pair of broken bellows, I had achieved nothing, not even the temporary peace of mind that goes with sore muscles and spent strength, so I turned my face back to Calah and passed beneath the gates to the house of war just as the sun touched the western skyline.

When I returned to my house I was met by a royal chamberlain waiting for me with the king's command that I attend him at dinner.

I found Esarhaddon in his private apartments. Sha Nabushu was there, whom I had not seen since he relieved me of my command at Khanirabbat, but apparently he had not been invited to dine. He stood, almost at attention, while his royal master sat behind a table and drank wine.

"My *turtanu* has come back from the south," Esarhaddon said, without visible enthusiasm. "Perhaps more to the point, he has brought thirty companies of soldiers from the garrisons at Amara and Lagash."

"I trust he has left behind at least a few old men and boys to frighten the Elamites."

My brother glared at me, not at all amused.

"I cannot undertake to conquer Egypt by myself," he said finally. "Besides, the old king is dead and Urtaki, who is my vassal, has taken his place. He is a fool and a lunatic, as have been all the kings of Elam since the world was born, but he knows that the crown is his only because I plotted and paid bribes to put it on his weak head. We will have no trouble from him."

Then he turned to Sha Nabushu as if surprised to find him still in the room.

"My Lord King will excuse me," the *turtanu* murmured, bowing nearly double. He turned next in my direction and bowed again. From the expression on his face, one might almost have thought the sight of me hurt his eyes.

"He dislikes you," Esarhaddon said, as soon as Sha Nabushu was out of the room. His tone was that of a man stating an indifferent fact. "He has spent most of the last hour trying to persuade me to leave you behind when we go on campaign."

"Yet this is the office of a friend," I answered, smiling no doubt a trifle wanly. "Perhaps it is just his way of apologizing for having insulted me at our last meeting."

Once again the Lord of the Earth's Four Corners regarded me from beneath lowered eyebrows.

"I can do without the bitter jests, Tiglath—I have not had a remarkably cheerful day. Come, sit down. You had better start with unwatered wine, for I have an hour's start on you and it is unseemly to be less drunk than your king."

And indeed he did appear as if the weight of his cares might at last crush him. My brother, who was even a few days younger than myself, had begun to bear the look of an old man.

"You should give more thought to your health," I said, for his appearance really was shocking.

"You sound like my mother." He laughed, and then shrugged his shoulders dismissively. "She is always complaining that I live a debauched life and will end by killing myself with my excesses—she has even sent me her physician."

"The Urartian? Perhaps he can massage your feet too."

But Esarhaddon shook his head.

"There are some things, Tiglath, my mother understands very well, and one of them is the way to a long life. I trust her judgment in physicians. This one will do me good. You will see."

"You are ill?"

"I am quite well."

"What troubles you then?"

"This is not the moment for talk," he said. "It is best now to fog the brain with strong drink."

Esarhaddon's servant women brought in dinner, but when they saw that their master was not interested in food they took the dishes away. They sat crouched about the room, silent and watchful, as if this fit of royal melancholy had been making their lives difficult for some time. When Esarhaddon at last noticed their presence he chased them away with curses.

We were both very drunk when, without warning, the king buried his face in his hands and began to weep.

"She is dead," he whispered, after the first spasm of grief waned a little. "She died six days ago in Uruk—the messenger arrived this morning. Esharhamat is dead."

"She is dead," I repeated. At first the words seemed to make no impression on me. Then my heart felt as if it were turning to stone. Then I understood.

Suddenly I no longer wished to be in Esarhaddon's presence. I stood up, though because of the wine or for some other reason I had to steady myself against the table for a moment before I could think to move further.

"Where are you going?" he asked.

"Home—to bed," I told him. In fact I had no particular intention except to get away.

"You are drunk. I had better send someone with a torch to light your way."

"Leave me in peace, damn you!"

I was instantly sorry, for it was not Esarhaddon's fault that his wife was dead. Nothing, really, had ever been his fault.

"I will find my own way," I said, no longer shouting. "Good night to you."

"Good night."

I left, taking a half-empty jar of wine with me. I did not go to bed but sat in my garden, beneath the faint, flickering light that shone through the shutters of my son's nursery—an oil lamp burned on a table there all through the night because Selana thought little Theseus Ashur might be frightened if he awakened in the darkness.

It was the month of Nisan and the air was cold, yet I felt nothing. I merely sat there, watching the light in the window, wishing all of this world's shadows could be so easily dispelled.

"He cried, and I saw you out here . . ."

It was Selana. She put her arms around my shoulders and touched her cheek to mine.

"So my Lord has heard about the Lady Esharhamat."

Only then did the tears well in my eyes.

"I have loved her since we were children," I said, my voice no more than a thick whisper. "All these years I have loved her, and now she is dead and I feel . . . Really, I have no idea what I feel."

"I know."

"The gods play with us, Selana." I reached up to touch her arm—strangely, in all our time together I had never felt as close to my wife as in that moment, grieving for another woman. "They mock us."

"I know. I know."

By ancient custom the king can take no part in any ceremony of mourning, not even for members of his own family. The *marsarru* was still hardly more than a boy, and thus it fell to me, as Esharhamat's eldest living relative, to accompany Ashurbanipal to the holy city of Ashur, there to receive his mother's corpse for burial in the royal vault.

We traveled by barge and the journey occupied us for one full day, from sunrise to sunset. It was the first time I had ever spent more than a few minutes together in Ashurbanipal's presence, yet when we reached the wharf at Ashur I found I understood this young man, who would one day rule the Earth's Four Corners and who was probably my own son, no better than when we had first stepped on board.

He was proud and silent, as I knew already, and he kept his own counsel—these were perhaps admirable qualities for a king, but they did not make him an agreeable companion. If he grieved for his mother's death, if he knew or guessed that I was anything more to him than merely his father's half-brother, he gave no sign of it. During the two days we were obliged to wait before the funeral cortege arrived from Uruk he amused himself with hunting.

And then, on a wagon drawn by six black oxen, Esharhamat's iron casket passed under the city gates. On pain of mutilation, the people of Ashur were commanded to remain in their houses while the procession made its slow way over streets that had been covered with straw to muffle the sound of the wheels. No one spoke, not even in whispers, as Ashurbanipal and I followed the casket through the doors of the god's great shrine and down into the royal vault where my father, my uncle the Lord Sinahiusur, and the dust of a hundred generations of kings and princes slept in the darkness. We laid Esharhamat in her crypt, where one day the king her husband would rest beside her. The stone lid settled into place and was sealed with bronze. Thus did we consign her forever to the shadowed past.

Not only the flesh is mortal. There is a sense in which that day some part of me died and was buried with Esharhamat, and something else found at last a means of struggling into life.

XLIII

IT IS TIME NOW FOR MY PEN TO SPEAK OF OTHER THINGS—
of war and the ringing of weapons in battle, of slaughter and unimaginable suffering and the heroism of ordinary soldiers, of defeat that is victory and victory which becomes defeat. I have now to tell of Esarhaddon's campaign into Egypt.

Just as I had refused to be his *turtanu,* I refused my brother's offer to be sole commander of his army—that honor therefore fell to Sha Nabushu, who I am sure spent many days puzzling his brain to discover what sort of trap I must be laying for his unwary feet. Instead I went as *rab shaqe* of the left wing, with some forty thousand men, many of them from Amat, under my orders. Lushakin, my onetime *ekalli* and my comrade in a score of great battles, all the way back to Khalule, when we were both green boys, had marched two hundred and fifty companies down from the northern garrisons and put aside the chance of an independent command in this great undertaking that he might serve as my lieutenant. It was quite like the old days.

On the third day of the month of Iyyar, almost a week before Esarhaddon, his principal officers and most of the royal garrison enjoyed their triumphal departure from Calah, I bade farewell to my wife and son and rode off to the city of Nisibis, which was to be the assembly point for the entire army. I would meet the northern forces there and ensure that all was in order and the whole expedition would be properly provisioned. The king wished to be certain there were no lapses, for he was in a hurry to feel the sands of Egypt under his feet.

At Selana's insistence I took Enkidu with me. "I will not send you off again into that nest of scorpions without his great shadow to cover your back," she said. "Little Theseus and I will be safe enough alone, for the Lady Naq'ia knows well the value of all her hostages."

Nisibis was only a provincial capital, with no resources to feed and shelter the host that was about to descend on it, so I called out the local garrison and set them to work building a camp that would soon hold an army over a hundred thousand strong. I chose a spot some half a *beru* from the city walls—discipline is not improved when soldiers who are soon to face the enemy have too easy access to the comforts of town life—and set men to digging earthworks and laying out defensive perimeters, just as if the Egyptians were about to attack us rather than the other way about. From the local merchants I requisitioned all their available stocks of grain, oil, beer and livestock, and I sent out foraging patrols to see what could be purchased from the local farmers. These measures caused very little grumbling because everyone was paid for his goods in silver. It is the custom of all nations to plunder their enemies, but a good soldier does not steal bread from the mouths of his own people.

Thus within ten days, when the first companies began to arrive from the northern garrisons, we were prepared to receive them. By the middle of the month, when I welcomed the king, there was a city of white tents where before there had been nothing but an empty plain.

"Hah! They begin to look like an army!" Esarhaddon exclaimed, climbing down from his horse—being a practical soldier, he had abandoned his royal chariot as soon as he was out of sight of Calah's walls. "By the Sixty Great Gods, we will throw a fright into the Egyptian king when he sees us."

"Perhaps, but Taharqa does not have the look of a man whose knees are much given to buckling."

"You have seen him then? How I envy you your travels, brother! What is he like? I have heard he is as black as a monkey."

Esarhaddon accepted a cup of beer from one of his orderlies and put his hand on my shoulder.

"He is from the Land of Kush," I said. "He is not an Egyptian, which in my experience is not to his discredit. I saw him only once, but he has a reputation as a man of vigor."

"When we capture his women, we will see what they have to say of the matter—hah, hah, hah!"

And so it went, straight through supper. My brother was a born warrior and, like this, in the midst of his armies, far from the intrigues of the court, he was always in fine spirits. It was only the burden of kingship which oppressed him.

Esarhaddon was sufficiently pleased with all that I had done in preparation for his arrival that he began referring all matters of supply and disposition to me.

"You see what a useful thing it is to be possessed of a brother who is half an Ionian?" he would say. "Perhaps, when we get to Egypt, instead of fighting for it we will simply send Tiglath out with a bag of copper shekels and let him buy the place for us."

But when one of his officers ventured to laugh, Esarhaddon struck him in the face so hard that the man almost lost his right eye.

"Do not mock my brother, cur." He picked the poor unfortunate up by the front of his tunic and shook him like a dog would a water rat. He had been drinking, which always made him quick to anger. "I jest with him because I love him, but he carries the scars of many battles and I will not have him mocked by one such as you."

"Doubtless he intended no insult," I said, stepping between them and helping the man to his feet—I preferred to make my own enemies. I got him out of Esarhaddon's sight as quickly as I could and took him to my own tent to close the gash in his face with a salve of mud and wood pitch, a recipe I had learned from Kephalos. A few cups of wine numbed the pain. His name was Samnu Apsu. He was very young, and he sat with his head in his hands as if he had forfeited the right to live.

"Do not be distressed," I told him. "By tomorrow the king will have forgotten the whole incident. He will probably ask you how you came to cut your face."

"I meant no disrespect, Lord," he said. He looked as if any moment he might begin to weep.

"I know it—probably the king knew it. It is probable that display was for my benefit. As you doubtless know, we have not always been on the best of terms."

He nodded. Almost at once he seemed to feel better, as young men will when they feel they have been admitted into a confidence.

The next day we broke camp and set out for the west.

"May the gods curse him!" shouted Esarhaddon. "May his seed be cursed to the tenth generation! May his loins wither and his heart rise in his throat and swell until it chokes him! The cowardly, deceitful, effeminate, double-dealing swindler—I treat him as a friend, giving him all of Sidon's trade routes, and my thanks is to be betrayed to the Egyptians. I will have his life for this!"

The king was understandably upset, for Ba'alu, prince of Tyre, had hearkened to the words of Pharaoh and joined the revolt of vassal states that seemed to be spreading across the coast of the Northern Sea like rainwater on a flat roof. Now he had closed the gates of his island city in our faces, and the soldiers of Ashur were digging siege trenches all around the walls. It was Sidon all over again.

"I will starve him out. I will undermine the walls and sack the city. The Tyrians will follow Abdimilkutte's subjects into exile while their houses burn at their backs. These Phoenicians—you would think they might learn."

"You cannot starve them out because you cannot cut them off from the sea," I said. "This time you have no allies."

"I am entering into negotiations with the seven kings of Cyprus," Esarhaddon grumbled. I could only shake my head.

"Then you will negotiate until we are all old men," I told him. "The Cypriots are cautious men . . ."

"You mean, they are Ionians—hah!"

"Yes, they are Ionians. They will not take sides until they see who prevails, you or Taharqa. You cannot take Tyre in less than five months, and if you wait around here much longer you will find yourself trying to cross the Egyptian desert in the middle of summer. This is madness."

"It is not madness to punish traitors," he replied stiffly. Yet he knew I was right.

"If you conquer Egypt, Ba'ala will come crawling to lick the dust from your sandals. If you do not, it will not matter. We can ill afford this, brother."

Still, we waited on the Tyrian plain for the better part of a month. Every morning the king and I would ride out to watch the progress of the earthworks being dug to undermine the city walls, and every morning I told him the same thing.

"This is folly. Do you want Pharaoh's double crown, or do you want to chase after every copper shekel that rolls away into the gutter?"

And above us the watchtowers of Tyre glittered against the bright blue sky.

"They will laugh," Esarhaddon would say. "They will rejoice when we slink away like beaten dogs. Ba'ala will mock at the glory of Ashur."

"Let him laugh. He will stop when we return from Egypt—if we return."

But at last my brother allowed himself to be persuaded. We struck camp and turned our faces to the south, to the land of the Samaritans, to Israel and Judah. Always we stayed within sight of the sea. We did not venture near Jerusalem, although her king Manasseh was in revolt against the Lord Ashur and had even given one of his sons the name of Amon, after the greatest of the Nile gods. Esarhaddon listened to reason and did not allow himself to be distracted by quarrels with petty rulers who would abandon their impudent rebellion as soon as Pharaoh was crushed.

The garrison at Ashkelon was another matter. We did not relish the prospect of crossing the Egyptian desert with thirty thousand of Taharqa's Libyan soldiers at our backs.

We stopped our march and made camp about two *beru* from the garrison walls. We had seen their patrols, but thus far the Egyptians had not seen fit to challenge us. As soon as a defensive perimeter had been thrown up, the king and his principal officers—myself among them, with Enkidu as my constant shadow—rode out to have a look.

Ashkelon was a stone fortress with its back to the sea. It had stout walls, and the ground around it had been cleared for an hour's walk in every direction. It would not be easy.

"We shall have to take it," Sha Nabushu announced, with the air of stating the obvious. "Tyre was one thing, and this is another. We have no choice."

Ghost started at something, and I climbed down to see what it was. I touched a flat stone with the point of my javelin and a scorpion the size of a man's hand scurried off to find itself another bit of shade. The sand under my feet was so blistering that I could have cooked an egg simply by burying it under a few handfuls.

"Feel the heat?" I asked, looking up at Esarhaddon—the sun was almost directly behind his head, so I had to shade my eyes. I could not see his expression. "We are already near the end of Siwan, and next month the desert will be like the inside of a pottery kiln. We can reduce this fortress or we can invade Egypt, but we cannot do both. Perhaps the garrison commander will be convinced of the wisdom of staying within his walls.

"Why should he do that?" Sha Nabushu asked contemptuously. "he will say anything, but once we are in the desert, he will be on us."

There was a buzz of agreement from the other officers, but the king, I noticed, kept silent.

"Yes, brother," he said at last, "why should he do that?"

"Because we have five men to his one, and because the Lord of Ashur is not noted for his forgiving temper."

Esarhaddon laughed. Then he nodded in agreement.

"Go talk to them," he said. "You know these Egyptian rogues—if they let you out alive, and if it smells right to you, we will make a truce with them. If they kill you, brother, I give my oath to avenge your death."

He laughed again and yanked the reins around to return to camp. In a moment, as the sound of hoofbeats died away, only Enkidu and I were left. Enkidu glared at the garrison walls as if he would have liked to pull them down with his bare hands.

"You think all of this is mad," I said, but my mute companion did not even glance at me. "Doubtless you are right."

I climbed back on my horse and we started toward the fortress. I found myself wondering if the Egyptians would favor me with a cup of wine before they cut my throat.

The watch patrol offered no challenge until we were some five or six hundred paces from the main gate. Four cavalrymen rode out to meet us. All four had that sullen, sun-hardened look one associates with Libyan mercenaries, and none carried an officer's whip. They stopped their horses about thirty paces in front of us. No one drew his sword.

"I would speak with your commander," I said in my villainous Egyptian.

At first there was no reaction. The Libyans kept their eyes on Enkidu whom, doubtless with perfect justice, they must have thought the more serious danger.

"Who wishes it?" one of them asked finally. I remember he bore three parallel scars on each cheek—the Libyans are a primitive, brutish people, and these wounds had probably been intended as enhancements to his manly beauty.

"An officer in the service of the king of Ashur, Lord of the Earth's Four Corners, Master of the World." I grinned contemptuously, showing my teeth, on the theory that nothing would make a stronger impression on this lout than a display of impudence. "His camp is not two hours' ride from here, as doubtless you know. I have come because the king has seen fit to grant you a chance for your lives."

Whether this speech had produced the desired effect I was left to guess, since the four Libyans turned their horses and rode back to the protection of their walls. There was no choice but to wait outside in the sun.

Within a quarter of an hour another rider came out through the main gate, an Egyptian this time. By the time he was close enough for me to see it, his face was registering an expression of the most profound astonishment.

"The Lord Tiglath Ashur, is it not?" he said, sounding a little awed by his discovery. "Nefu, son of Hardadaf, prince of Siut—I was once a guest at one of your famous dinner parties. I had heard you were dead."

"As you see, I am not."

Did I remember this smooth-faced youth? No, I thought not, but people had come and gone in my house in Memphis, making themselves at home as if they were in a brothel. He could have visited a score of times without my ever noticing him.

"I might never have recognized you with that beard, but your servant is another matter. Come within, Lord, and let us drink such wine as this doghole can offer and talk of happier times . . ."

Nefu's father, it seemed, had somehow run afoul of Pharaoh.

"And, as you see," he told me, gesturing around with a hand that held one of the dried apricots that had been served with dinner—I cannot fault his efforts at hospitality in that forsaken place. "As you see, the disgrace extended to the whole family. I have been out here a year, and it shouldn't surprise me if I die as commander of this garrison. Such is the wrath of the Living God."

He grinned, a trifle foolishly. We had been at table not half an hour and already he was considerably the worse for wine.

"You may die here sooner than you expect," I said. "That is what I have come to discuss."

The temperature in that dark, stuffy little room seemed to drop markedly. Nefu of Siut looked at me through narrowed eyes, as if I were guilty of some lapse in etiquette.

"Whose soldiers are those out there?" he asked finally. "One hears so little news in a wilderness like this."

"The king of Ashur—he is in personal command of his army, which is some hundred and fifty thousand strong, and he means to cross the desert into Egypt. The only question is whether he will have to delay here the brief time it would require to crush this garrison. You may be sure, should you so inconvenience him, that he will make his resentment felt."

"And what is he to you then, Lord Tiglath?"

"My brother."

At first, Nefu's only response was a slow whistle as his wine-dulled mind struggled to take in this astounding new fact. Then he laughed.

"I am astonished, then, that the king of Ashur would put you so conveniently within reach," he said, refilling my cup.

"If you have some thought of using me as a hostage, I would caution you to discard it," I told him. I did not even glance at my wine cup. "My brother loves me—not enough to abandon the conquest of Egypt for my sake, but enough to visit the most terrible revenge against the man who would presume to take my life. You would not, I think, enjoy having your skin, from your eyebrows down to the soles of your feet, stripped off in a single piece. I have seen this done for lesser offenses and, trust me, it does not improve one's appearance. On the other hand, if you require the king to stop here for a while, I think he will be content merely to kill you."

"You say he plans to invade Egypt through the desert?"

"Yes."

"Have you any idea, My Lord, what it is like in the desert at this time of year?"

"Yes. And so has the king."

"Is he mad then, or have all you eastern barbarians bellies of iron?"

He shook his head in wonder at such folly, and I knew at once that the garrison at Ashkelon would not impede us.

"I would not go into that desert," he said—there was a note of real horror in his voice, as if the terrors of the place were starkly visible in his mind's eyes. "I would not, for what you will find there is not the double crown of Pharaoh, but death."

"Which you will find here, should you attempt to interfere with us." I picked up my wine cup and drank, as if we had already struck our bargain.

"Then it seems I have no choice," Nefu answered, even as his fingers closed around the neck of his wine jug. He refilled first my cup and then his own. "Who do you imagine will thank me if I throw my life away trying to stop you? Besides, the desert will kill more of you than all the armies in Egypt. If any of you do come out on the other side, Pharaoh's soldiers will have to compete with the vultures for the honor of stripping your bones."

He even smiled, as if at some harmless jest.

"Go in peace, Lord Tiglath. I would not dream of detaining you."

As I rode back to Esarhaddon's camp, many things kept turning over in my mind. I was not afraid of any treachery from Nefu. I had kept my eyes open while I was within his walls and had noted the general laxness of discipline. For officers and men alike, assignment to such a place is usually a form of punishment and, from the commander on down, these were bad soldiers. Besides, years of duty in this forgotten outpost had rendered them too dispirited to pose any threat to us—most likely, if he ordered them to pursue us into the desert, they would turn straight around and cut his throat for him. And most likely, he knew it. No, there was nothing to fear from the garrison at Ashkelon.

Nefu had, after his fashion, even offered himself as an ally.

"If, by some miracle, you should prevail . . ." He shrugged his shoulders, giving the impression he was embarrassed even to entertain such an idea. "If somehow you should conquer both the desert and Pharaoh's armies . . ."

"But you have declared that to be impossible."

"Yes, I know it, but you were reported dead after the disturbances in Memphis, and here you are. You seem an uncommonly durable man, My Lord." He laughed—it was like a woman's giggle and was beginning to prey on my nerves. "Even Lord Senefru . . ."

"Lord Senefru! Is he still living?"

"Oh yes," Nefu answered, nodding vigorously. "He is alive and prospers. He is Pharaoh's governor of Memphis."

It seemed to give him pleasure that he could report such a thing of one whom all the world had taken to be my intimate friend.

"I heard it from his own lips that you had been murdered by some foreign villain in Naukratis. He seemed much affected by the news."

"One can imagine."

So—I had not missed my chance after all. Senefru would be waiting for me in Memphis. Somehow this one fact seemed to make the whole enterprise worthwhile.

"What favor would you have of Egypt's new rulers?" I asked, for suddenly I felt myself very much in Nefu's debt.

And the commander of the Ashkelon garrison did not hesitate.

"Escape," he said simply. "If you triumph, send some other poor soul to guard the gateway to paradise, and let me come home."

If we reached the Nile, I told him, I would intercede for him with Esarhaddon and he might count on spending the winter in whatever fleshpot he chose. There was only the one trifling condition: that both I and Ashur's king live to see his dream of conquest fulfilled.

But between us and the Nile were the armies of Taharqa and, still worse, that nightmare of heat and emptiness I had once called in my heart the wilderness of the god Sin.

Still, my brother was pleased enough, as if by arranging a truce with this frontier outpost I had handed him Egypt on a trencher.

"Tiglath, it is for such things I love you so. If ever an empire is won with nothing but charm and guile, the glory will be all your own. Your words are like poison mixed with honey—you could talk the teeth out of a serpent's mouth."

We became very drunk that night, as soldiers will when they have escaped a dangerous and difficult task. Esarhaddon put aside the majesty of his kingship and sang an Aramaic song about a donkey and an innkeeper's daughter that was breathtaking in its obscenity. We played lots, gambling over the spoils we would win in Egypt, and I won eleven cities in the Delta, plus my pick of Taharqa's harem, which I traded to Esarhaddon for next year's date harvest—it was but a game we played, a kind of elaborate jest. Only Sha Nabushu did not laugh, but he had already fallen asleep by then and had to be carried back to his tent.

The next day was soon enough to think of business. We were camped, the gods be praised, near a large oasis, and I saw to it that even the large jars that held our cooking oil were cleaned out with sand and filled with water from the wells.

"You make too much of this desert," Esarhaddon said. "Only look at the map. There are hardly more than twenty *beru* between us and the city of Ishhupri, where we will have everything we need for the drive to the Nile. Twenty *beru*—what is that? Not more than a two days' march."

"I have been there. You have not. What is a two days' march in another place can be ten days, or even more, in that hideous waste. Besides, our soldiers must not only survive this march but at the end of it they must be in proper condition to fight. Taharqa will certainly be waiting for us at Ishhupri."

"How do you know that?"

"Because Ishhupri is within easy reach of the Nile but far enough from Memphis that he will have room to fall back if he does not stop us at once. Because at Ishhupri his troops will be fresh and ours will have just come off the desert. Because Ishhupri is where I would be waiting if I were Pharaoh of Egypt."

The king did not answer, but neither did he interfere with my hoarding of water.

"And we had best give a thought to the horses," I told him. "A horse drinks as such as three men—more if they are used as pack animals. We will have to unload them and simply lead them across."

"I have given some thought to that," Esarhaddon said, laying his finger against the side of his nose like an Amorite blanket merchant. "Wait until we reach the oasis at Ruhebeh."

And, sure enough, at Ruhebeh we were met by agents of King Lale of the Bazu, a nation of wanderers over the northern reaches of Arabia.

They had nearly five hundred camels, which they sold to us for four silver shekels apiece.

"This I arranged before we left Calah. You see, brother? I am not so great a fool as I seem."

The Arabs taught us how to induce a camel to kneel and how to load its back. They tried to teach a few of the officers how to ride one, but this lesson was less successful. As it turned out, I was the only man in the armies of Ashur who had ever ridden a camel, and even I preferred to walk. Esarhaddon made one attempt and became so sick that he emptied his guts as soon as his feet were back on the ground.

"Filthy brute," he growled, as he sat under a date palm washing his mouth out with wine. "When we reach Egypt I will personally feed that one to the dogs—piece by piece."

"The Arabs say that the camel you love the best is the one you only hate a little."

He laughed at this. It was the last time I was to hear anyone laugh for many days.

The next afternoon we reached the Brook of Egypt.

"Brook of Egypt," Esarhaddon hissed with bitter contempt, kicking angrily at the stone-hard riverbed with his sandaled foot. "How many centuries has it been, do you suppose, since any water passed through here?"

"This might have been a torrent only last winter," I told him. "It is said there are sudden floods in the desert, which dry up in a day or two so that they leave no trace."

We both looked out over the flat western landscape—the desert stretched before us, empty and pitiless, like a warning that is content not to be heard.

XLIV

THE LAST TIME I HAD WANDERED OVER THIS DESERT WE had been three men, alone and without direction. Yet the passage of Esarhaddon's army was more terrible even than I could have imagined. In our thousands we seemed a weight around each other's necks, and the sufferings of one were compounded by the hardships of many.

The first day, while we were still fresh, the ground was covered with tiny, sharp, white stones that turned out to be alum and, since most of our soldiers were unsandaled, it was not long before many could hardly walk—they said it was like having the soles of one's feet covered with bee stings. We managed only four *beru* that day, and we were not to do so well again for many that followed.

That first night on the desert, the moon shone with a clear, cold light that seemed to illumine the world like a heatless sun. I had seen it before, but it filled the soldiers of Ashur with dread.

"I feel as if the air is swimming with ghosts," Esarhaddon confided. There was not a breath of wind, and the ground was still warm from the burning day, but he shuddered as if with cold. "Is it always like this?"

"Yes—the moon seems to love this barren ground, and so I have always thought of it as the Place of the God Sin."

He looked at me as if I had just uttered prophecy, for my brother lived in mighty fear of the gods.

"Then let it be called that," he said. "Let it be known as such until the end of time. Let it be the Sinai."

And so it became.

The second day was worse than the first, for the sun was hotter and the rock-strewn ground, bad as it was, gave way to sand into which with every step a man sank up his ankles. It was like walking with weights. Besides, the rocks had cut us, but the blistering sand ground at the soles of our feet like a millstone. By the end of two hours we were so exhausted that there was nothing left to do except to find a little shade to hide under and conserve our waning strength.

"It would be best if we marched at night," I told Esarhaddon.

"A hundred and fifty thousand men cannot march at night—there would be chaos."

"Then we had better wake them two hours before dawn and keep to the few cool hours of the morning. They cannot march in this heat either."

And so it was. All the way through that caldron of stone and sand, where no living thing dares tempt the sun's wrath, we never managed more than two hours' march a day. The rest of the time we rested, in whatever shade we could make or find, and prayed that we might live once more to see the green grass.

It was not long before men began to feel the effects of thirst. Enkidu, who never tired, showed me how in places the very stones themselves were covered in heavy, crude, evil-tasting salt. This a man might collect and take with his ration of water, which increased his power to fight off weakness. I do not know how many lives thus may have been saved, but not enough. There were quarrels already on the second day, and by the third morning a few men were found dead in their sleeping rolls. Of what they died I cannot begin to guess.

On the morning of the fourth day we awoke to find the camp filled with serpents—hundreds of them, many twice the length of a man's arm, had apparently crawled in from the cold desert night. Men discovered them in their bedrolls, wrapped around their legs, and many were bitten in this way. More suffered trying to drive the serpents away, for these were Egyptian cobras and became aggressive when disturbed. They would raise themselves up, spread their hoods, and attack anyone who ventured near them.

"By the bright gods," Lushakin exclaimed, "if this place the king wishes to conquer has many more such fearsome creatures dwelling in it, I think he would do well to take us home. Is there nothing that can be done?"

"Only tell the men to be careful, to keep clear when they can and to assume that anything lying on the ground may have a serpent under it. The Egyptians, if memory serves, recommend a poultice made from the scrapings of crocodile teeth, but we have nothing like that. I fear most who have been bitten will perish."

And so it was. Cobra venom is fast-acting and deadly, but not without mercy. Those who were bitten grew first heavy-eyed and then began to drool. There was no pain, and even the fear of death seemed blunted. Finally, after a few hours, they would lie down and simply stop breathing. A few tried to cure themselves by drinking strong wine mixed with pepper, but this had no effect. We lost some fifty or sixty men before midday.

One seemed to recover. For a while he was sick like the others, but then, quite suddenly, he got better. By the middle of the afternoon he seemed to have nothing to show for his ordeal except some discoloration of the skin around his wound. This, however, turned putrid after two days. His arm swelled so that he could not even move his fingers, he became delirious and died.

Inevitably, all of this had a dispiriting effect. Some believed the cobras were not mere beasts but two-headed demons, for the menacing hood display was unlike anything they had encountered before, and who expects a mere serpent to be so belligerent? No one was more frightened than the king himself, for Esarhaddon always lived in the most exquisite terror of the supernatural.

"Egypt is full of cobras," I told him. "Magicians and charmers carry them about in baskets, and they are no more than they seem— dangerous, evil-tempered brutes best left to themselves. They are sacred to the Egyptians, and the Pharaohs themselves have taken them as their emblem. Be comforted, brother. If one bites you, you will have offended no god or spirit. You will merely die."

Esarhaddon, who did not find this in the least amusing, nevertheless consulted his necromancers and his priests. They employed all manner of charms, incantations and spells to keep the Lord of Ashur safe. Perhaps they availed him something, for we were plagued with serpents all the way across the desert, but none ever had the effrontery to bite the king.

But the main horrors of the Sinai were not murderous serpents or the scorpions with the habit of dropping into one's lap from every overhanging rock that seemed to offer a little shade. The desert itself was our most dreadful enemy, and its weapons were heat and thirst.

Soldiers were dying at a rate of two or three hundred a day. Some died in their sleep—in the morning we would find a corpse lying in its bedroll, its knees drawn up almost to its chin—but more often than not men perished during our short but unbearable marches. It happened over and over again, in just the same way: all at once a man who had seemed fit enough only the hour before would just sit down, unable to go on. His comrades would offer him water and salt, and if he accepted them he might get to his feet again and be all right. But most of the time he would shake his head, giving the impression he had lost interest in life. Then we had no choice but to leave him behind because he would be dead within a few hours, no matter what we did for him. After a while, one could simply look at a man and know if he was finished.

On the eighth day, when our water was nearly gone, we found an oasis with about fifty wells. Esarhaddon wisely gave orders that no one was to drink from these until first our jars had been refilled and then the horses, most of whom had shriveled bellies and were almost unable to stand, had been watered. We spent most of one whole afternoon at this, by which time more than half of the wells had gone completely dry. Some men waited until the middle of the night for nothing more than as much sweet water as he could hold in his cupped hands, and many did without. This was the last oasis we would see until the desert was nearly behind us. What we suffered over the next seven days is hardly to be imagined.

There is no extremity like thirst, for it shrivels up the vigor in a man's bowels and leaves him unable to think of anything except how he hates the taste of sand. By the end of the eleventh day I found that my mouth had grown so habitually dry that I could no longer even spit. Rations had been reduced to a single cup of stale, cloudy water, which most of us saved until the evening meal because it was almost impossible to swallow anything until we had rinsed our mouths. To his great credit must it be said that Esarhaddon allowed himself no more than anyone else. He gave away his wine to be drunk by common soldiers and endured with the rest of us. This silenced most of the grumbling, since men were ashamed to be heard complaining over what the king himself bore in silence.

The heat raised dust storms that blotted out the distinction between earth and sky so that we seemed sometimes to wander aimlessly in a gritty, burning cloud. We covered our faces and marched on, hardly believing that one direction could be better than another, and sometimes even the camels simply sat down and refused to take another step. When one of them could not be raised, we cut its throat, drained the water from its belly—water that smelled and tasted like a rotting corpse, but which no man was by then too proud to drink—and left the carcass for the vultures that had been circling above us almost since we crossed the Brook of Egypt.

Yet we went on, not because we believed there was anything ahead of us except the emptiness of the desert but because it was impossible to go back and the only alternative was to fall down and wait for death. Esarhaddon offered prayers to the gods—and most particularly to Marduk, whom he regarded as his special patron—and the rest of us cursed into the darkness which seemed to swirl with evil. I thought to myself that if we reached Egypt we must conquer, for men who can endure this will never perish by the sword.

And at last, when our water jars were nearly empty and we had abandoned ourselves to death, on the sixteenth day after entering this terrible wilderness, we raised our eyes and beheld the settlement at Magan. It seemed, after all, that the gods had shown some pity.

Although perhaps fifty or sixty Egyptian soldiers were posted at Magan, it could not with any accuracy be described as a garrison. The soldiers were no more than wardens to the poor wretches who had been condemned by Pharaoh's justice to work the silver mine there, and they fled almost as soon as they saw our dust on the horizon. What we found were an oasis, a score of deserted buildings, and some hundred or so gaunt, earless, sun-dazzled prisoners in copper chains who could not understand why they had suddenly been left unguarded.

"By Adad's thunder, these fellows must be villians," Esarhaddon commented. "What crimes they must have committed to be sent to wear out their lives in such a place."

I made a few inquiries and discovered that most were farmers who had suffered during bad harvests and not been able to pay their taxes. Even my brother, who had sentenced many a traitor and rebel to a cruel death, could not understand such harshness.

"This Taharqa must be the most savage of rulers. I believe I do the Egyptians a great service to liberate them from such a monster."

"Yet I doubt they will thank you for it," I told him.

There was water at Magan, which made it seem a paradise to our exhausted soldiers. We were now less than twenty hours from the Nile Valley and the sand dunes had given way to ground as hard as stone, which was hardly wet grass under a man's feet but which made marching easier. The king decided we would try to reach Ishhupri in one final dash, before Pharaoh's army, which doubtless knew something of what our progress had been like, would be expecting us.

"We will allow one day of rest, and then it will be forced march. I will give orders to slaughter the camels, since we no longer need them and the men will appreciate the fresh meat."

Esarhaddon was a harsh commander, but war is a harsh business. I could not bring myself to make any objection to his plans.

"It would be well to find out if there are any recent arrivals among the Egyptian prisoners," I told him. "They might be able to tell us something worth the trouble of finding out."

"As you wish." Esarhaddon made a gesture with his hand as if waving away a fly. "As you understand their chatter, I leave it to you."

I had the prisoners' chains struck off and ordered them fed and given beer from the stores their jailers had left behind—gratitude loosens a man's tongue, and beer keeps it from swelling with lies.

Most of these men had been in the labor gangs for years and therefore knew nothing of interest, but I did find one who still had scabs where his ears had been cropped. He had been brought through Ishhupri only the month before. The city, he said, was almost unfortified, but the streets were full of Libyan soldiers. Pharaoh had not yet arrived from Memphis, whither he had shifted his capital after Esarhaddon's attacks on the Delta cities two years before, but he had been expected any moment. I went immediately and told all of this to my brother.

"Then you were right—he means to stop us now, before we have had a chance to recover from the desert." Esarhaddon grinned, as if the idea pleased him. "We will have to show him that the men of Ashur do not faint like women at the first touch of the sun."

We rested through the next day, but the morning of the eighteenth day since we had entered the Sinai we were all up three hours before sunrise and had already marched seven *beru* before noon. By nightfall our outriders were already reporting back that they had seen the lights of Ishhupri.

"Five more hours tomorrow, and then we will see what this fellow Taharqa is made of," said Esarhaddon.

The next day, an hour before noon, we reached cultivated land and had once more the pleasure of feeling the mud from irrigation ditches between our toes. That afternoon we made camp within sight of the city walls.

I had half expected Taharqa to have his soldiers already drawn up in battle array and ready to engage us at once—this is what I would have done in his place, refuse us even an hour in which to rest from our forced march from Magan—yet, aside from a few mounted patrols that watched us for a while and then rode away, we never saw an enemy soldier.

Perhaps we really had caught them by surprise. Perhaps they really had thought they would have at least another day or two before we were upon them. I must own I began to entertain a new respect for Esarhaddon's talents as a strategist.

We camped half a *beru* from Ishhupri's main gate. As the sun set the wind rose, raising clouds of dust over the empty no-man's-land between our trenches and the city walls. The ground which tomorrow would be so crowded and full of death was that night naked and silent, like a bride who fears the unknown violence of her husband's lust.

Soldiers everywhere are the same on the eve of battle. Those who had work, reassembling the chariots that had had to be carried across the desert sands or deepening the trenches that would be useless in a few hours, were lucky because they had no liberty for helpless dread. Otherwise, men kept to themselves or collected in little groups and spoke in hushed voices. The tension is almost unendurable, yet everyone is kind and patient. There were no quarrels, for personal grievances seem unimportant in the face of the vast slaughter that waits behind only a few more hours of darkness. I went to visit Esarhaddon in his tent.

"How is the army?" he asked me. When I told him he nodded in approval. "Good. If tonight they are not too weary to be frightened, tomorrow they will not be too weary to fight. Come—I will share my last jar of wine with you. I have been hoarding it against this very hour."

We had marched almost ten hours a day for two days, but no one slept that night. We were all tired, but if we won tomorrow we would sleep the next night in Ishhupri, and if we lost we would probably sleep forever, so it did not matter that we were tired. I spent the hours before dawn with my staff officers, planning in detail how our wing of the army would face an enemy we had not seen and could not even number. We only knew we had not come all this way to find death on our knees.

In the last few minutes before sunrise Ghost was brought to me with the bit already in his mouth. I took my own good time renewing the acquaintance, stroking his nose and talking to him in the low voice that horses find so calming—this was to be his first battle, but his sire's heart beat under his ribs and I wished I could be as confident of victory as I was of him. A warrior projects much of himself onto the animal he trusts with his life. Perhaps I only wanted, for a moment or two at least, to escape from the thought of all that was coming.

I would fight with my cavalry that day. I was not the king and therefore could be spared, and, regardless of the lies I had told Selana, the men of Ashur have no respect for a field officer who cowers behind his own lines.

At first light, with a wild beating of war drums, the gates of Ishhupri were thrown open and Pharaoh's army began pouring out onto the plain. I lost count after a hundred chariots, and the foot soldiers, who moved at a brisk trot, seemed to take hours to fill out their lines. I think it possible there might have been something like two hundred thousand men facing us.

Lushakin was in command of the infantry. I rode up and exchanged a few final words with him, then we watched in silence as the enemy marshaled his forces. We did not speak of it—one simply does not at such a moment—but we exchanged a glance. No, neither of us had expected anything like this.

Yet somehow I found it impossible to be afraid. I beheld the long lines of Pharaoh's soldiers and with the eye of memory I saw the streets of Memphis as they had looked after troops like these, perhaps some of these same men, had surfeited themselves on pillage, rape and murder. I remembered Nodjmanefer, left to rot in her own house. My heart, I found, had turned to iron and was as insensible to fear as to pity. My brother, I knew, wanted glory, and the soldiers of Ashur dreamed of their share of plunder. I wanted only revenge.

Finally the war drums were quiet. It was that terrible moment before the order comes down to engage. It was like watching the door to death swing open.

The red flag rose by the king's chariot. "Advance!"

In a battle of this kind it is always the horsemen who make the first contact. I drew a javelin from my quiver and let Ghost feel the touch of my heels—he needed no urging; he was as eager as I.

As I galloped out onto the empty plain between the two armies, I had no anxieties about being left in peace. There were Libyain cavalry everywhere, it seemed, swarming out through the lines of infantry like ants out of a burrow. The Libyans are skilled riders, and suddenly I saw one of them bearing down on me, his curved sword flashing in the morning sunlight. This was what I had been hoping for. I locked my javelin under my arm, leveled the point, and charged. I caught him just below the rib cage, just as his sword slashed at me—it split the javelin in two but too late to save him, for as I rode past he was already falling backwards over his horse's rump.

He was lying on the ground, vainly trying to turn over on his side, one hand strengthlessly holding the broken shaft that had pierced his belly. I cantered back, reached down, and yanked the javelin loose. He screamed as I did this, and then was silent. I rode back to our lines, carrying the javelin with me as a trophy.

"You see how easily they die?" I shouted, waving the bloody point in the air as I rode back and forth before the ranks of our infantry. "You, whom heat and thirst cannot kill, whom the terrors of the desert have hardened into men of stone, you will trample them down like the very grass!"

"Ashur is king!" they shouted back. "Ashur is king! Ashur is king! Ashur is king!"

I turned back to the fight, and for a time the cavalry skirmishes raged like a fire. The ground was quickly covered with dead and dying men, but neither side seemed able to break through to attack the opposing ranks of foot soldiers, and time was running out as our armies swelled towards one another—this, it appeared, was a battle that the infantry of the two sides would have to settle between themselves.

Yet cavalry soldiers are much too vain ever to admit they will not turn the tide of the fighting with their own valor, and on neither side were horsemen threatened with indolence. We engaged the Libyans in several pitched and bloody skirmishes, and I felled two more of the enemy before my own carelessness and one of Pharaoh's charioteers almost ended my life.

The Egyptians sometimes use Fowlers' nets to entangle men and drag them from their horses. I knew this and had therefore kept a respectful distance from their light, agile war chariots, but in the heat of battle one sometimes grows heedless. It took no more than the instant I stopped to catch my breath.

I hardly even knew what had happened except that I heard Ghost neighing in panic and then, in the next instant, found myself trapped in the coils of the net. That was my first sensation, of trying to fight my way clear of this snare, which at first seemed as insubstantial as smoke. Then I felt the tug of the rope, and the blind terror that comes with being yanked helpless from a horse's back. One of the lead throwing weights had caught me above the ear, so I was too stunned even to try freeing myself. I remember the sensation of falling—very slowly, it seemed, for the ground took forever to reach me—and then the sickening shock of pain when it did.

And then . . . nothing. I was in too much pain to be afraid. As I lay there in the dirt, I became the disinterested observer of my own extremity. There was dust everywhere and I couldn't see much beyond the chariot that had brought me down turning to finish the work.

I'm as good as dead, I thought. I'll be under his wheels in half a minute. Strangely, this didn't make much of an impression on me. It simply didn't seem to matter.

Certainly I would have been killed if not for Ghost. Like his sire, he refused to acknowledge defeat and, when the Egyptian chariot started to roll down on me, charged the horses, lashing out with his hooves and knocking one of them down so that the whole team became ensnared in its own lines. The driver was thrown and had to run for his life, so for the moment I was safe.

All I recollect is feeling a certain smug satisfaction in the ownership of such an animal. He is fine, I thought. He is braver than any ten men.

I must have fainted. I have no idea how long it was, whether five minutes or an hour, before someone noticed that the commander of the left wing was down. Finally a team of stretcher-bearers carried me from the field, and by then my wounds were painful enough that I almost hoped I would die.

"This campaign's fighting is over for you," the physician told me as he washed out the gash along my rib cage with heated wine. An assistant was already heating the blade of a knife with which to sear the edges.

"It can't be that bad," I said, feeling sick with dread—I had had this done to me often enough before to know what to expect. "Just be quick, and I will be quite fit again in a few days."

"A few months perhaps. Your arm is broken in two places. I shall have to reset the bone, and you will like that far less than the touch of a hot knife."

The physician was right. When he had finished, and was stitching a wound in my leg closed with a silver fishing hook and a piece of catgut, I no longer felt so warlike. I could not even move the fingers of my right hand.

"Prince, you are a capon," I whispered to myself. "You are as worthless as a woman."

A few minutes later Esarhaddon rode over to see whether it was true, as he had heard reported, that I was dead.

"I knew they were lying," he said. "No Egyptian will ever kill my brother, who has been favored with the *sedu* of Great Sargon—you will have nothing more than a few scars about which you can tell outrageous stories."

He laughed loudly at this, for the Lord of the Earth's Four Corners was in a fine, excited temper. It seemed the battle was already turning against Taharqa.

And perhaps it really was true that some change had happened to us on our journey here, for the soldiers of Ashur fought as if the desert's own relentlessness had entered their souls. We were outnumbered, but that somehow did not seem to matter. Wave upon wave of the enemy pushed against their lines and then broke into pieces. Slowly we advanced on the walls of Ishhupri. This army which had crossed the Wilderness of Sin was like a grindstone crushing all beneath its weight.

It was shortly after noon that Pharaoh's men, first in one place and then another, made the collective decision that they were beaten and turned to run for their lives. The slaughter that followed was terrible to witness. Those who fled back through the city gates were hunted down and butchered. The rest, the bulk of them, retreated west toward the Nile valley. Our cavalry pursued them, but most made good their escape. By twilight, the field was ours.

"We have vanquished them!" Esarhaddon boasted. He mounted his chariot, for in a few moments, to the cheers of his army, he would ride in triumph through the gates of Ishhupri. "We have vanquished Egypt."

From the wagon on which they had stretched me out, I raised my head and looked around at the field where, although I did not know it then, I had seen my last day as a warrior. It was covered with the dead and made my heart stick.

"We have vanquished an Ethiopian Pharaoh and his army of Libyan mercenaries," I told him. "Egypt still lies ahead."

XLV

THE MEN OF ASHUR ENTERTAIN NO GREAT HOPES FOR the life after death, yet it is a fearful thing for a man's soul to become lost in the darkness, to wander forever in the night winds. Thus before the sun set we buried our fallen comrades on the battlefield they had won with their blood, appeasing each man's ghost with offerings of bread and wine that he might not know want in the Land of Spirits. The enemy we left to the feasting of dogs and carrion birds.

We had lost some nine or ten thousand men, which was not many in a host of perhaps a hundred and forty thousand after so terrible a battle. We counted nearly seventy thousand enemy corpses strewn over the plain, and our soldiers killed numberless others who had thrown aside their weapons and taken refuge within the city walls—the people of Ishhupri, who wished to ingratiate themselves with the victor and, in any case, had no love for Taharqa's Libyan mercenaries, were quick to betray them to us. In this single morning, Pharaoh had been bled almost white.

Ishhupri was no great city, but after the desert it seemed to hold every luxury. Esarhaddon wisely forbade looting but ordered the citizens to turn over all their stocks of beer as the price of being allowed to submit. Egyptian beer is not the like beer of Sumer, yet provided a man is thirsty enough he will not disdain to wash out his mouth with it and the soldiers of Ashur blessed their king for permitting them the indulgence of a single night's drunkenness. The next day we set out in pursuit of Taharqa's army, on the road that led to Memphis.

It is a measure of how badly Pharaoh's soldiers had been mauled that they left behind them a trail of corpses. In any withdrawing army many of the wounded die along the way, but the Egyptians, and even the Libyans, are usually scrupulous about carrying away their fallen for later burial, for to them the grave is the entrance to paradise—the body must be preserved against decay or a man forfeits his hope of immortality. Yet our enemy appeared too occupied with preserving himself in this world to think of the next. In their haste to escape, it appeared, decency had been hurled to the winds, for the route of their flight was marked by their abandoned dead.

Pharaoh was retreating towards his capital. He had to know that Esarhaddon would declare himself master of Egypt as soon as he had captured this greatest of prizes, so we expected him to turn and make another stand somewhere along the road to Memphis. Thus we faced the dilemma of whether by swift pursuit to maintain our pressure on the enemy or to proceed cautiously and perhaps avoid falling into a trap. The momentum of victory was ours, our path was unobstructed, and my brother was eager for his final, glorious triumph, but in the end the issue was decided by common sense and the weather.

It was already late into the month of Tammuz and the heat was terrible. Our soldiers were not yet fully recovered from their ordeal in the wilderness of Sin. A rapid advance would leave them dangerously near exhaustion if suddenly they were called upon to do battle. Besides, Esarhaddon had campaigned against this foe before and had learned a sobering respect for Taharqa's tenacity and cunning. We would be careful. In the end, this proved to be the wisest choice.

Three days' march from Ishhupri we found what the Egyptians call the Bitter Lakes, salt-laden and lifeless, stretching north to south across our path from the Red Sea to the Delta. We could not go around them— Esarhaddon had tried fighting his way through the Delta two years before, and the expedition had ended in failure—and the only break through which it would be possible to lead an army of any size was heavily fortified. A vast wall of limestone blocks ran across our path. There were watchtowers and great gates built like traps for the unwary. These had guarded the road to Egypt for a thousand years.

Yet it was here that Pharaoh committed his first and greatest blunder, for it seemed he had thought of these fortified positions as a mere check to us, as a covering for his retreat. If he had stopped here and defended the wall with all the strength that remained to him, he might yet have stopped us altogether.

As it was, the garrison troops stationed here had seen the condition of the army as it fled west, listened to the stories of the fighting at Ishhupri, and drawn the inescapable conclusion that they were being left behind as sacrifical offerings to gain Pharaoh a few days' breathing space. Naturally, they had fled.

We found the walls deserted and the watchtowers empty. The gates had been left standing open and our riders passed through them unchallenged. When these came back to report, Esarhaddon decided to see for himself.

"Come with me," he said, although I had not been on a horse since Ishhupri and my arm was bound to my side with leather straps. "The exercise will do your wounds good."

So I accompanied my king, feeling giddy with pain each time Ghost's hooves hit the ground. Inside the fortress, we found the embers in some of the cooking fires were still warm.

We also found that the Egyptians, in their haste, had even left a few of their women behind. The minute we rode into the fortress's main courtyard, four or five of them came running out, pulling their tunics up over their heads that we might see they were not soldiers, and abased themselves in front of our horses' hooves, kneeling in the sand with their hands held above their heads in token of submission. When we did not kill them at once, others followed. Soon we had some fifteen or twenty collected around us. Esarhaddon looked down at their naked backs and grinned.

"Truly Pharoah must have been in a hurry," he said. "Find out what you can from them, brother. But first find out if there is any beer to be had."

He climbed down from his horse, took the woman who knelt closest to him by her long black hair, and gave her a little shove to indicate that she had better find herself a soft place to lie down because she was soon to feel his weight on her belly. They disappeared into what looked like a grain storehouse.

"What has happened here?" I asked, in my halting Egyptian. "Where are your menfolk? Look at me. Do not be afraid, for I mean you no harm."

They raised their eyes, perhaps not yet quite convinced I did not at last intend to eat them, and told me how the garrison soldiers had run away. They knew little else—how could they?—but one of them had heard that Pharaoh was wounded.

"When the king comes back, he will be thirsty," I said.

A few of them ran off to fetch a couple of jars of beer. I could see the relief in their faces, for Esarhaddon and I had put off our fearful strangeness and they could see we were merely men. One cools a man's lust with one's body and his throat with beer. One turns aside his wrath with a smile. They were soldier's women and would know how to behave now. I do not know whether they believed or even understood me when I called Esarhaddon a king.

I kept to my horse, trying not to notice the expectation with which they watched me. Any one of them would have wept with gratitude if I had gone into her, but, even without the discouraging pain of my wounds, the sight of these women oppressed me and I was filled with longing for Selana. A Doric peasant girl had ruined me forever for the sort of careless lechery in which my brother was at that moment easing his liver. I wanted only to see my son and to hold my wife once more in my arms. My thoughts returned to Sicily, where we had been so happy, where our little Theseus might have grown up to tend vines and break the black earth under his plow, and all at once the glory of conquest seemed an empty thing.

About a quarter of an hour later Esarhaddon came outside again, one hand clamped affectionately over the back of the woman's neck while the other adjusted the contents of his loincloth. The woman was blushing even down to her dust-colored breasts, and Esarhaddon looked very well pleased with the quality of his entertainment. I welcomed him to a small table and a couple of stools that had been set up for us in the shade. There was beer and dried fruit, and his new favorite crouched at his knee like a pet cat.

"I like this one. I think I'll keep her," he said. "There isn't time now to see about the rest, but we can take them with us. You can have first pick."

"I'll wait until Memphis—just remember that you owe me a favor."

He looked around him, and his lecherous greed was so obvious that a few of the women started to giggle.

"Egyptian women have pretty eyes," he said. "And they are as predatory as falcons. I thank you, brother, for you are generous to a man's weaknesses. When we have taken Memphis you shall have any that pleases you, even if she is Pharaoh's own queen."

"That is not what I meant."

But he might not even have heard me, for his attentions were elsewhere. After a while he went back to the grain storehouse, taking with him the same woman he had had before, and yet another. It was an hour later, and not before a patrol had come looking for us, that he was at last prepared to resume command of his army.

"What do you think, brother? Will we have to fight again before we reach Memphis? If Pharaoh is wounded, perhaps he will make everyone's lot easier by dying."

Esarhaddon laughed, but with a certain nervousness, as if he sensed that the subjugation of this ancient empire would never be that easy.

"Taharqa will fight," I said. "What else is he to do, crawl back to the Land of Kush and measure his tribute in handfuls of sand? His wounds may have prevented him from taking his stand against us here, but he will have to offer us battle again before we reach Memphis."

"Then so be it."

I glanced at my brother, lord of Asia and soon, doubtless, conqueror of Memphis, and saw the way his eyes narrowed. I had seen that look before, and I knew that soon the Egyptians would know the weight of his heel upon their necks.

Yet Pharaoh did not disappoint us. Eleven days later, on the first day of the month of Ab, under a pitiless sun and within fifteen *beru* of the Nile herself, we found ourselves confronted with an army even greater than the one we had faced at Ishhupri. By what prodigies of labor he had achieved it we were never to know, but Taharqa seemed to have gathered to him every man under arms in the whole of Egypt. We could not have faced fewer than three hundred thousand men.

Yet in war numbers are not all. These were green troops, or men who had gone stale from too many years of garrison duty, and there was no heart in them. Soldiers who want only to live will never be among the victors. They will break and run, and the ground will grow soft with their blood. So it was with Pharaoh's great horde. The battle was the work of a single morning. The men of Ashur butchered them like sheep.

And still this black Ethiopian, whose very heart must have been made of brass, would not yield to us. Somehow, only two days later, he found the courage to fight yet again. He must have known it was a hopeless business, but some men simply cannot bring themselves to say, "This is enough," and lie down to die.

Yet his soldiers did not have the tenacity of their commander, and our third battle against the Egyptians only served to cover us in the blood of our enemies. When it was over, what remained of Pharaoh's army simply melted away like frost in the desert. We no longer had anyone left to fight.

Save that one morning, so long ago, when I had seen him carried as a god to the temple of Ptah, I never looked upon Taharqa's face, yet there have been few men I have admired so much.

Three days later the sun rose to find us beneath the walls of Memphis.

Certain flowers will close their petals at a touch. Memphis was like that—she shut her gates against us out of simple reflex, a fear that does not see that perhaps submission is the only possible defense.

"These idiots," Esarhaddon bellowed, stamping his foot like the little boy with whom I had grown up in the old king's house of women. "Don't they see how hopeless their position is? Look at those walls—just look!"

I looked. The last time I had seen them, they had been decorated with hanging corpses. The sky had been black with the smoke of a thousand fires as whole districts burned. Libyan soldiers had been everywhere, looting and murdering at will—and all this by command of Pharaoh himself. I found it possible to forgive the people of Memphis their distrust.

"We will crack them open in four or five days, and *then* what do these fool Egyptians think they can expect? It is not my wish to be cruel, but have they no idea what happens to a besieged city after it falls?"

"Then let us hope they come to their senses before we are obliged to resort to force of arms."

My brother shrugged. His was not a complex character, and he saw the matter entirely from a soldier's point of view. Besides, he wished only to celebrate his triumph, and this delay annoyed him.

"Yes—well . . . I will give them until noon. If they make me wait longer, I shall have to execute some ten or twenty of their leading nobles, if only to set an example. If the gates have not opened by tomorrow, then I will sack the city and lead its people away in chains."

And in the meantime, our soldiers began digging trenches in preparation for undermining the walls. The heat was intense and tempers were short, so that many actually hoped Memphis would not surrender that they might have the pleasure of avenging themselves upon her.

Yet reason did at last prevail. By the middle of the afternoon the main gate swung open and a delegation of some fifty or sixty of the city nobility came out to prostrate themselves before the king of Ashur. Esarhaddon sat on a camp stool, glowering like a man with a troublesome stomach, and I stood at his right hand, only one more among his many officers.

I saw many familiar faces among the nobles of Memphis, but no one seemed to recognize me. One of them, I noted with pleasure, was the Lord Senefru.

Esarhaddon remained silent, and the suppliants did not dare rise from their knees. At last one of them—the poet Siwadj, who had dined in my house many times and who, I noticed, had put on weight over the last five years—took a papyrus scroll from his bosom and began to read an address in Greek, which the Egyptians, in their ignorance, believe must be the tongue of all foreigners. It was a very long address.

"What is this gibberish?" the king asked, pulling at my sleeve. "What is he talking about?"

"He wishes to surrender the city," I replied.

"I should certainly think so!"

Then he turned to the Egyptians, frowning like a bull.

"You have made me wait," he said in Akkadian—he would concede them nothing, it appeared. "I, Esarhaddon, Lord of the World, King of the Earth's Four Corners, I who have swept Pharaoh's armies before me as if they were no more than dust upon the threshold stone of my house, I will not be insulted and kept to wait like a peddler from the street. You must draw lots among yourselves, and twenty of your number will answer for this impertinence with your lives."

I translated his words for the Egyptians, who were too appalled by what they heard even to gasp. They did not even glance at me but had eyes only for this foreign king who seemed such a demon.

I knelt down beside Esarhaddon and whispered into his ear.

"You owe me a favor for the Egyptian women," I said.

"And for much else besides—what of it?"

"Be merciful. Let your wrath fall on one and one only, and let me be its instrument."

My brother turned to me and he smiled thinly, as if he suspected I was playing a jest on him.

"Very well. Do what you like with these. Yet know that now I will not let you have Taharqa's queen for your house of women."

"Then I shall have to learn to do without her."

He laughed and stood up, walking away to leave the Egyptians puzzling over their fate.

"The king of Ashur has been persuaded to show you some compassion," I told them. "All shall be spared save one, and that one . . ."

I strode through the mob of supplicants, who were still on their knees and thus had to scramble on all fours to get out of my way, until I came to the Lord Senefru, who looked at me with incredulous horror as I crouched down beside him. I raised my right hand before his face and opened it that he might see the birthmark on my palm. Only then, I think, did he recognize that he had fallen into the grasp of the one man from whom he could expect no pity.

"That one, My Lord, is you."

I did not speak to the Lord Senefru again that day. I gave orders that he be chained and left out in the open overnight—I would give him that time to contemplate what death I might have waiting for him—and I went into the city, whose gates were now thrown open to receive her conquerors, and paid a call at the mortuary of the Temple of Amon. The chief priest, who was so fat that he had breasts like a woman, prostrated himself before me inside the temple door as if afraid I meant to pull the walls down around him.

"Get up," I told him in Greek. "Fetch a casket and whomever among your embalmers are the most skilled. I have need of your art."

The priest scrambled to his feet and disappeared. Before my eyes had time to adjust to the dim light of that great stone shrine, he returned with a retinue of workmen—grave diggers whose ears had been cropped for some long-forgotten offense, mortuary workers with blackened fingernails, smelling of death, and an old man wearing a skullcap who looked about him, blinking like an owl, as if he had forgotten what the world outside his workshop looked like.

"You will follow me to the house of the Lord Senefru," I told them. "There, and in accord with your ancient rites, you will prepare a body for tomb burial."

"The Lord Senefru has died then?" the priest inquired timidly. His smile flickered on and off, as if he could not be sure whether such a thing would be pleasing to me or not.

"The Lord Senefru lives—for the moment. Your work does not involve him."

They followed me through the city streets, the empty, unpainted casket bouncing on the shoulders of the grave diggers, until we came to Senefru's house. I beat on the door with the hilt of my sword until a servant girl opened it and then, as soon as she saw me, fled like a rabbit, disappearing down a corridor. We encountered no other servants, so they must have cleared out almost as quickly. I led my entourage out into the garden, to the flagstones around the fountain, which was still dry, and clogged with sand, as if it had not known a drop of water since the last time I had stood upon this spot.

"This stone, and this one, and this," I said, kneeling down to touch them with the flat of my hand. I spoke in Egyptian, for I would have them all understand. "You will pick them up—you will do this with great care—and beneath them, buried at no great depth, you will find the corpse of a woman. It is she, if there is anything left of her, whom you will prepare for the eternal life which your gods promise."

"And how long, Your Honor, has she been here?"

It was the old man who spoke. His voice was so thin that he might not have used it in decades, yet he commanded complete attention, for his was the authority of a skilled craftsman.

"Five years."

"As long as that, and the stones have not collapsed over her! Then there is hope."

He nodded, and then gestured to the mortuary workers to begin uncovering the grave.

"I will wait inside," I said.

An hour later the priest sought me out.

"They have finished," he almost whispered. I followed him back outside. The flagstones were piled beside the fountain. There was a trench dug in the sand they had covered, perhaps a cubit deep. The casket was open, and in it, beneath a linen cloth, I could see the outlines of a human figure.

"These gardens grow baking hot in the sun," the old man told me. "The sand must have drawn all the water from her body very quickly, for she is well preserved. Ra, in his mercy, has left very little for us to do. Would you like to see her?"

He reached down, and was about to lift the cloth that covered her face, but I shook my head.

"No—I would prefer to remember her as she was."

The old man raised his eyebrows a little, as if trying to account to himself for so singular an attitude, and then bowed.

"As Your Honor wishes. In ten days she will be ready for eternity. She shall be anointed and wrapped for burial, so that she shall be preserved to the end of time. If Your Honor will but tell us her name, that it may be written into the prayers that will seal her bandages . . ."

"Her name was Nodjmanefer."

That night I suffered from unquiet sleep, and the next morning I went to the patch of barren earth where Senefru was staked out like a dog. He was remarkably composed, but perhaps his dreams had been no more restful than mine.

"You escaped then," he said, in his usual level voice. "I had thought you dead."

"No, I did not die. I came back. I went to your house, and we both know what I found there."

He nodded. There was a copper ring around his neck, through which ran the chain that held him to the ground. The chain was not long enough to allow him to stand, and it rattled as he moved his head.

"I was in Tanis, with Pharaoh," he said.

"You murdered her."

"I ordered her killed. That is not the same." He looked up at me, and on his face was the expression of a man who knows he is within his rights.

"If you wish to avenge yourself because I conspired with that assassin . . ."

"I forgive you for plotting against my life, since once you saved me from death. It is for the Lady Nodjmanefer that you will be punished."

"That was entirely a private matter—a man is entitled to deal with his faithless wife as he sees fit."

"She had been faithless for years, and you did nothing."

"It is still not your affair."

"She was carrying my child. For that, if for nothing else, it is my affair."

"Did you love her?"

"Does it matter?"

He threw back his head and laughed. It was the wild laughter of the mad. And then, quite suddenly, he was calm again.

"She was mine," he said. "Whether you loved her or not, she was always mine.

"There were so many dead in Memphis that year that they threw the corpses into the river," he said. He smiled, mocking me. "If you loved her or not, she was carrion. The crocodiles had her at last."

"No, they did not. I buried her with my own hands, and now she will sleep forever in the City of Death."

Senefru looked as if I had just struck him. He was appalled, as if at the desecration of his own grave. Perhaps that was how he saw it.

"And, My Lord, the fate that you had intended for her shall be your own."

"What will you do to me?" he asked. He was afraid now, perhaps for the first time.

"You have been condemned by the word of the Lord Esarhaddon," I told him. "And when the kings of Ashur wish to punish a man, they strip the skin from his body and nail it to the city gates. This I will see done to you—except that I will leave you in your skin, for I wish you to witness the Lady Nodjmanefer's departure into eternal life. One you will not share, My Lord, for when the rotten flesh is falling from your bones, and you stink in the very nostrils of the gods, I will have your corpse taken down and fed piece by piece to the crocodiles, that the last trace of you may sink into the soft mud and disappear forever."

The king meanwhile had established himself in Pharaoh's palace, which in my time had been the residence of Prince Nekau. It seemed there had been little expectation that we would ever reach Memphis, for Taharqa had not even troubled to evacuate his family—his queen, his women, and even his eldest son had been trapped in the city and had thus fallen into our hands. The Lady Merneith, who was an Egyptian and very beautiful, Esarhaddon now led about naked on the end of a silver chain, and she served his bed beside the garrison harlot he had picked up at the Bitter Lakes as simply one more of his concubines. Taharqa's children would be carried back to Calah to live out their lives in iron cages beside the city gates.

"Do you want her?" he asked me one evening, at a banquet for his officers. The queen of Egypt was kneeling beside his chair, and he reached down to put his hand on her round brown belly. "This one will let you do whatever you like with her, for I have taught her that she is no better than any harlot I could have purchased in the bazaars for half a silver shekel, and even your wife would agree that it is not healthy to abstain from women for as long as you have done. I know I said you should not have her, but you are my beloved brother and, besides, beautiful as she is, her weeping annoys me."

I looked at her, crouched there beside her new master, all her great pride crushed forever, and I could see from the expression of her eyes that she knew now what her life must be henceforth. Pharaoh had fled into the Land of Kush, and she would never see him again. No son of hers would ever wear the double crown, and she would die disregarded and forgotten in Esarhaddon's house of women. Were it offered to her, she would embrace death as a blessing. Indeed, she was dead already.

"Presently she will stop weeping. And she will still be beautiful. If you give her to me, after a time you will regret it and want her back again."

"You insult me, brother. You disdain my gifts."

I smiled at him and put my hand on his shoulder, for nothing would ever make him understand.

"I simply have no wish to deny you your rightful pleasures," I said. "You are king, not I. I am but your servant. It is your place to humble your enemies by making of their women the slaves of your bed. That is what it means to be a king."

He was very pleased with this answer and never guessed what I meant by it.

Indeed, for those first few days as master of Egypt, Esarhaddon was much too well content with life to puzzle himself with riddles. From all the great cities up and down the length of the Nile, the great men of the land came to place their necks beneath the foot of Ashur's king.

Even Mentumehet, Fourth Prophet of Amun and Prince of Thebes, ruler of Upper Egypt in all but name, sent an emissary to Memphis to inquire what terms might be offered in exchange for submission. That emissary, a fat, cunning priest who wore a hood of leopard skin to cover his shaven head, cursed the false Pharaoh Taharqa and called the Lord of the Earth's Four Corners a brother to the deathless gods. Esarhaddon, I believe, grew more than a little drunk with his own glory and could not see that these compliments had no meaning.

I might have spared my brother much and guided him to a wiser policy if I had not been so preoccupied with my own fantasies of atonement and revenge. Esarhaddon's weakness was pride, and my own was shame. I do not presume to know which was worse.

On the tenth day after the capitulation of Memphis, I went to the Temple of Amun and was told that Nodjmanefer's body was prepared for reburial. I had given into the hands of the priests five hundred mina of silver that they might offer up the requisite prayers and assemble such grave goods as was fitting for a lady of rank. All was ready for the funeral, and the master embalmer and his assistants brought up the corpse from the mortuary.

I gasped when I saw the face that was painted on the lid of the casket—it was Nodjmanefer as she had been in life. When I asked the old man how he had managed it, he shook his head and smiled.

"It is my art to undertand these things," he said. "Life and death are a seamless web."

"What reward can I give you for this miracle? Name whatever price you will."

"Of what value is wealth in the house of the dead?" he asked me.

The casket was loaded onto a wagon, and the chief priest and some five or six grave diggers and I set out for the City of Death, which lay about five hours into the desert. We made one stop along the way, and that was at the Great Gate of Memphis, where Senefru was awaiting execution.

I had not seen him for ten days, but in that time he seemed to have aged as many years. He looked near death. When I inquired the reason of one of his guards—there are such men in every army, set aside for the handling of the condemned and despised by their fellow soldiers—I was told that Senefru had been beaten and starved through the whole of his captivity.

"It is customary," the guard told me. "In this case it is even a mercy, for the gods alone know how long a healthy man might have to suffer after being nailed up. Are you sure you do not want him flayed first, *Rab Shaqe?*"

I did not even answer him, but went to the spot where Senefru was waiting chained to the ground and there crouched down beside him.

"You will have no mercy then?" he asked me.

"No—I will have no mercy."

He hardly seemed to be listening. He pointed to the wagon.

"Is that her body? Where have you kept it hidden all these years?"

"Under the flagstones, in your garden."

"Ah."

He nodded, without looking at me, as if he wondered how he had missed anything so obvious.

"I am not afraid of death," he said—I did not believe him, for I saw that he was afraid. "But I dread extinction. Have some pity on my corpse, Lord Tiglath."

"There will be no pity. You had no pity for her. Now she will live forever in the Field of Offerings, while you face nothing except a vast emptiness, a void that will fill eternity."

He buried his face in his hands and wept, and as I watched I tried to take some satisfaction from his grief. But there was none. At last I rose and walked away, this to keep myself from speaking the words of pardon.

"Carry out the sentence," I told the officer of the watch.

As I walked behind the wagon that carried Nodjmanefer's casket, I looked back only once. They were already hoisting Senefru up by a rope about his waist in preparation for nailing him to the city gate.

At the time of his marriage Senefru had already purchased a tomb for himself and his wife. It was a vault carved from the side of a cliff, with great stone doors that stood open to receive him. I knew where it was because he had once shown it to me—it is a custom among the Egyptians sometimes to hold feasts in the City of Death, even at the very foot of their own graves. He had been proud to have me see that he would spend eternity in so fine a place. This was where I took Nodjmanefer.

I carried a torch, and the priest and I entered the tomb. Inside there were two great stone sarcophagi, each with a lid that two men working together could never have lifted. On one was carved the face of Senefru as he must have looked when a young man—on the other, which the grave diggers labored hard to move aside, Nodjmanefer, still but a girl. They slid the casket inside and let the lid settle back into place. The priest chanted prayers, and the grave diggers brought in the ornamental furniture, the clay figurines and the jars of wine and preserved fruit that were meant to comfort the lady's spirit until the world was dust.

It was only a trick of the light, which threw the shadowed stone profiles of Senefru and his wife against the back of the tomb wall, yet I had the sense that those two were here with us, watching as the priest invoked the mercy of his deathless gods. I remembered something Nodjmanefer had told me once—the words seemed to ring in my ears like a judgment: "A *woman is tied to her husband by other things than love*," she had said. "*I cannot leave my lord, even for you, if he will not let me go*."

"*Did you love her?*" Senefru had asked me. "*Whether you loved her or not, she was always mine*."

In that moment, and with the perfect clarity of the obvious, I realized that I was an intruder here, that the wrong for which I had been trying to atone was not Senefru's but my own. I had not loved Nodjmanefer, not as she would have had a right to expect, and that was my offense against her. Had Senefru loved her? Yes, probably. Senefru had merely taken her life—in this world and the next, or at least so he imagined—yet I doubt she would have understood that as so dark a sin as mine.

Certainly he deserved death, but not from my hand.

"I have been a great fool," I whispered. In its way, this too was a prayer for the dead.

The priest was finished, and we sealed the tomb's great stone doors. I kept wondering how long a man might live hanging by his nail-pierced arms. Memphis was five hours across the desert. The sun would have set by the time we reached the city gates.

On the way back the priest sat in the wagon that had borne Nodjmanefer's casket. He carried a large, leaf-shaped fan made out of straw and held it above his head to shield himself from the sun, and from time to time he would address no one in particular with his complaints about the inconveniences of making such a journey in the heat of summer. The grave diggers and I walked behind in silence.

The soldiers in Senefru's execution party were sitting in a ring playing lots by torchlight. They scrambled to their feet when they saw me.

"Is he still alive?" I asked.

The officer held up a torch to see. Senefru's feet dangled perhaps two cubits above our head as we stood by the wooden gate. His head hung at an odd angle, and the trails of blood from where the nails had been driven through his wrists ran down his sides all the way to his waist.

"Difficult to say, *Rab Shaqe*. I heard him groan perhaps half an hour since."

"Climb up there and see."

The officer put a ladder against the gate and scrambled up. He put his fingers against Senefru's neck, and I told myself not to hope. I did not believe the god would allow me to lighten my conscience so easily.

"Yes, he is dead, *Rab Shaqe*."

"Then have his corpse taken down."

"But, *Rab Shaqe*, your orders were . . ."

"You heard me!" I shouted—strangely, I felt as if I were about to choke. "I do not care what my orders were. Take him down!"

I turned to the priest, who stared at me as if he thought I might have gone mad in the sun.

"You will carry the Lord Senefru's body to the temple mortuary. You will have the old man who is so skilled prepare him as he did the Lady Nodjmanefer. Then, when all is ready, you will entomb him beside his wife."

"But, Your Honor, he has been executed as a common criminal."

"By us and not by the Egyptians," I said, feeling calmer, almost drained. "He is guiltless in the eyes of his own people, and therefore let him dwell throughout eternity in the Field of Offerings. I will answer to my king for all that is done. See but to this and your reward will not be insignificant."

A man, if he be given the power of life and death over others, will commit many acts the memory of which must shame him all his days. Senefru had murdered his wife because she had loved another and in this had offended against his honor, and I murdered Senefru because I could not tell the difference between justice and remorse.

XLVI

THE NEXT NIGHT, WHEN I WENT TO PHARAOH'S PALACE TO dine with the king, I discovered that Prince Nekau, who had once ruled Memphis from within those same walls, had returned from exile in Upper Egypt and was busy making himself agreeable. He sat at Esarhaddon's table and, with the aid of a Hittite slave woman who could recast his words into Aramaic, he was describing to my brother how in Thebes he had suffered and starved on the pitiful allowance given him by the Prophet Mentumehet—surprisingly, he looked as plump and sleek as in the days of his prosperity—and how Taharqa had made himself hated by all men, so that the armies of Ashur were seen almost as liberators. I do not know how much of these fantasies Esarhaddon believed, but he liked the Hittite woman's smoldering eyes and the trick she had of moving her naked shoulders as she spoke, and therefore he was willing enough to listen. Nekau, who saw this and well understood the weaknesses of great men, did not leave without making the new master of Egypt a present of her fair flesh.

When the banquet was finished, he wasted no time in seeking me out as an old friend.

"I hear from everyone that you put the Lord Senefru to death," he told me—he had a way of leaning toward one, as if imparting a confidence, that I found extremely distasteful. "I applaud you, for he was an evil man."

"We are all evil men, My Lord."

The answer did not seem to please him, and he moved away.

"What do you think of this Nekau?" my brother asked me, after his guest had left. "Did you know him well?"

"I knew him well. He cares for nothing except his own interest. He is corrupt and without principles of any kind. The aristocrats do not trust him and the common people hate him."

"Just so." Esarhaddon smiled, as if about to say something very wise. "Yet he strikes me as clever enough always to side with the strong against the weak, and there might be advantages to leaving a man in power here who has no support except our favor."

"That is a wicked idea. I can only wonder who put it into your head."

"Sometimes my wickedness is my own, brother. Besides, more often than not wickedness is the first virtue of kings. Good night."

He retired to his own rooms, by all appearances well pleased with himself, no doubt to test if the Hittite woman could make a virtue of wickedness.

Yet by the end of our first month in Memphis Esarhaddon was no longer so very pleased. He was an excellent soldier; on the field of battle he knew with the instinct of a born warrior exactly what to do. But Egypt, that land of shadows, was teaching him that conquest was not the same as rule.

"This priest who calls himself Prince of Thebes," he said to me one morning, "Nekau says he is a dangerous man whom no one trusts."

"That is rather like the viper's warning against the lion. Who is fool enough to trust Nekau?"

"Nevertheless, why does a priest send an envoy, as if he would treat with me as an equal? Was he not Pharaoh's subject? Then he is mine now and should prostrate himself like a slave and not imagine he can bargain with me for terms."

"He was never Pharaoh's subject in more than name, brother. You are master where Pharaoh was master, but Upper Egypt is a different place. There Mentumehet rules as the Pharaohs have not ruled in the north for four hundred years."

"Have you been there?"

"No."

"Perhaps you should go." Esarhaddon smiled fiercely, as he did when he imagined he was a great king before whom all the world trembled like a reed. "Perhaps you should take a great army there and teach this priest obedience."

"Pharaoh had an army—he never went. Perhaps there was a reason why not."

"You are afraid?"

"I am cautious. You have conquered a rich land, and I know of nothing in the south which is worth hazarding the wealth of the Delta. If you like,

I will go to Thebes. But I will take only a hundred soldiers, enough to support the dignity of one who speaks with the Lord of Ashur's voice. We will see what Mentumehet answers when I tell him he has a new master."

My embassy to the Prophet of Amun had to wait, however, for the next night, after a banquet of conspicuous debauchery, Esarhaddon woke up feverish and nauseated and went out into the palace garden to empty his guts, thinking this would make him feel better. It did not—once he started he could not seem to stop retching. When his vomit began showing streaks of blood, his physicians grew alarmed for his life and sent for me.

As soon as I saw him I knew that he was dangerously ill. He was sweating heavily and his face was the color of dead grass.

"By the Sixty Great Gods, I feel sick," he said, grasping my hand when I sat down beside his bed. "My bowels feel like they are full of maggots."

"You look dreadful."

He managed to smile thinly. "That is why I love to have you near me, brother," he murmured. "You always have something comforting to say."

Then he was seized with another fit of retching. I held his head in my lap and tried to force a little water down him whenever he could catch his breath. After a time he grew calmer and, at last, fell asleep from sheer exhaustion.

"I think, My Lord, it is perhaps simply a consequence of overindulgence," said Menuas, the physician I had last seen massaging the Lady Naq'ia's feet, and who, unique among his colleagues, remained reasonably calm. "The lord king is, as you know, an intemperate man, and the food and wine of this country are strange to him."

"You don't think there is any chance he has been poisoned?"

"Poisoned?" He looked genuinely surprised at the suggestion. "I think not, My Lord—except if he ate a piece of tainted fish or something of the sort. I see no *human* agency in this."

For all that his eyes glittered fearfully, which seemed to be something over which he had no more control than a man does over the shape of his ears, the Urartian, I had the impression, was humoring me, as if, were it not for my rank, he might have laughed in my face for advancing such an idea. Nevertheless, I did not find myself able to share his faith in the innocence of mankind.

Half an hour later, Esarhaddon woke. He was frightened and almost delirious, casting his eyes about like a lost child.

"Tiglath?" he cried weakly. When he found my hand again he was calmer. "Don't let them kill me, Tiglath. These fools will kill me if they have the chance—promise you won't let them."

"I promise."

I stayed beside my brother, watching him drift in and out of consciousness, until morning, when two of his senior physicians presented themselves like a delegation. The rest stayed in the back of the room, and I noticed that Menuas held himself a little apart from them.

"My lord, we think . . . that is, we are of the opinion . . ."

"Yes? What?"

They exchanged a worried glance, as if their confidence had begun to falter, and I had a sickening suspicion I knew why.

"Yes? What?"

"The king, we feel sure, has offended some local demon. Perhaps if he were bled, and then sacrifice were made . . ."

I looked at my brother's face. His lips worked silently as he slept, and his mouth was almost gray. I drew my sword and laid it across my lap.

"If you wish to make sacrifice, that is your affair," I said. "But if blood is to be spilled, it will not be the king's. Do I make myself clear?"

"My Lord . . ."

"Get out."

I let my hand drop back down to the hilt of my sword, and they bowed themselves out of my presence.

Menuas, I noticed, dared raise his eyes before he left, and even nodded slightly, as if to signal his approval.

Then I sent for Esarhaddon's new Hittite slave woman.

"Do you dream of a life of luxury in the king's harem?" I asked her. "Then go make a cooking fire in the garden and brew up a pot of thin millet gruel. My lord must have something with which to keep his stomach lined. Have a care how you make it and be sure the water is clean, for if the king dies I will cut your throat myself."

She understood that I meant it—I could see the fear in her eyes, so I had no anxiety about her—and an hour later, when Esarhaddon was awake again, I could offer him breakfast.

"What is this stuff?" he asked. "It's disgusting."

"They feed it to babies. Just eat it, and save your strength."

Suddenly he laughed.

"I am always one or two steps behind you, aren't I, Tiglath," he said. "You are wounded in battle, and the best I can do is to get sick and vomit my guts out. You collect scars and are the admiration of the world, and I will die in my bed, puking like a dog that's been feeding on rotten meat."

"You won't die," I told him.

"No?"

"No."

"You promise?"

"I promise."

And he did not die, for all that the local demons were deprived of their blood sacrifice. Kephalos, who, though a scoundrel, was a skilled physician, always said, "When the gods mean to kill a man, they kill him. Otherwise, they do not interfere much in our infirmities, so prayers are of little help, and physicians, alas, are not much better. If you are troubled in your stomach, the best thing you can do is to stay quiet and eat simple, bland food. That, and a little water, will do you more good than all the supplications to all the gods in heaven."

By following this recipe I was able by the third day to see Esarhaddon sitting up in bed and bellowing for wine.

"Go to Thebes," he said. "I am recovered."

"You must give me your promise that you will mind your diet and keep your bowels clear."

"I promise. And I have told my physicians that you will hang their corpses from the city walls if I die—that, I think, is more to the point."

He laughed at this, and I thought, Perhaps it was merely his own intemperance. In Egypt, one sees conspiracies everywhere.

May my dead brother's ghost forgive me such confident folly.

Thebes is nearly a hundred *beru* from Memphis. Moreover, it is upriver and the Nile has a strong current. I had Pharaoh's own barge at my disposal, which was a hundred cubits long and had a huge sail of reed matting, yet in the heat of summer there is hardly a stirring of wind. Even with a crew of fifty oarsmen, we had a tedious journey lasting more than twenty days.

I took Lushakin and a company from the Amat garrison. The men of Ashur are not sailors. For the first few days nearly all refused to eat, instead fortifying themselves with beer to keep off the green sickness. I was not affected, since I am half a Greek and during my exile had become accustomed to water travel. Myself aside, however, only Lushakin, whose father had been a boatman, remained active and cheerful.

"Look at them," he would say, pointing at his soldiers, who huddled miserably at the center of the barge, afraid of falling overboard and being eaten by the crocodiles that basked on the shoreline like pieces of driftwood. "They would cheerfully follow you into the mouth of death, but they sit there, their guts churning with dread, cursing the day they were born because they cannot feel the earth between their toes. If there is an army of a hundred thousand men sharpening their swords for us in Thebes, these farm boys will hurl themselves into the midst of battle with nothing but the most profound relief, content to die on dry land."

Enkidu, who also came with us, spent the whole time sitting at the prow of the barge as if it were a rock in the middle of a desert, endlessly sharpening his ax.

The captain of the barge was a man named Senenmut, who had spent his life in Pharaoh's service, as had his ancestors, so he told me, from the time of the Great Horemhab, almost seven hundred years before, and whose attitude towards his new masters was therefore predictably unenthusiastic. Yet there is something about a long journey which seems to free us from the constraints of ordinary life and to make us willing to speak of things which might not otherwise cross our lips.

Senenmut knew no tongue but his own, and I gathered it pleased him that I could give him my orders in Egyptian rather than having to rely on an interpreter. This perhaps disposed him to think well of me, and thus gradually we began to talk of other things than the currents and where we might tie up for the night. He was an intelligent man, and it did not take me long to understand that a life lived traveling up and down this vast river had made its impression on him. In common with many sailors, he seemed of a contemplative disposition. Besides, he had been born on the Nile's banks and therefore tended to see all existence as an orderly and repetitive process.

We passed many small villages, and the peasants working their water wheels and moving back and forth on their way to their fields became a common sight, so that after a few days one hardly seemed to see them at all. Yet once Senenmut took the trouble to point them out to me, as if he found something about them amusing.

"Do you know the age of that scene?" he asked, indicating a farmer in a linen tunic that reached perhaps to his knees leading a pair of yoked oxen along the top of the high bluff. "Had you passed here four thousand years ago, you would have seen the same man with the same two beasts— possibly, if we were close enough to hear it, he would be singing the same song. This is not a land where anything really changes."

"Yes," I said, for I too had been born on the shores of a great and nourishing river and understood what he meant. "Yet things do change. Is not my presence here proof of that?"

He looked at me and smiled, as if at the credulity of an infant.

"We have been conquered before—by Hyksos and Libyans and the men of Kush, and now by you." He shook his head. "We abide. We make our conquerors like ourselves, or at last we drive them out. Which, do you imagine, will be your fate? In any case, Pharaoh is eternally Pharaoh, and Egypt herself does not change, because she cannot."

"Then you believe Pharaoh will come back?" I asked, aware that it was a question Senenmut might prefer not to answer. He shrugged his shoulders, as if at some imponderable mystery.

"In the life of one man, everything is chance. Yet every spring brings the Nile's flood."

He left me to attend to his crew, and I stood wondering why the god had chosen this particular man as the instrument of his warning.

Thebes is not one city but two, divided by the river into east and west. The east city is quite near the shore, but the west city is parted from the Nile by a wide belt of marshy farmland, part of which is actually an island—one looks up from the shore and, over the palm trees, cut into the sand-colored mountains, one sees the great temples built over the graves of kings who have been dead for centuries. The west city, I knew, in the great temple complex called the Medinet Habu, was where the Fourth Prophet of Amun and Prince of Thebes had his court.

Mentumehet of course knew we were coming. For days I had seen the riders watching us from the riverbank and then galloping south, no doubt to report on our progress. Thus, the afternoon we reached the pier—in the harbor of the east city, for there was where the old palace of the Pharaohs stood—he was there to meet us, a shadowy figure sitting in a sedan chair beneath an awning of leopard skin, like Pharaoh himself come down to bless the waters.

Even before we had tied up I could see that the docks had been cleared. There were only soldiers about, and a few priests, and even these kept at a distance. Beyond these, I might have imagined that Mentumehet, and the few slaves who crouched around his chair, were the sole inhabitants of the city.

As I prepared to leave the barge, the Prophet rose to his feet and stepped out into the sunlight. He wore only a pleated linen skirt and a heavy necklace of enameled gold—only the lacquered shepherd's crook he held in his right hand suggested his office—but he was nonetheless an impressive figure. He was tall and, unlike most priests in this country, slender, the ideal image of a prince as they like to appear in their public monuments. His handsome face was as impassive as if it had been carved from red granite. Only his eyes seemed truly alive, full of dark fire, as restless as those of a predatory animal. I sensed at once that this was a dangerous man, a man whose real life was lived buried within himself, a man at once unpredictable and capable of anything.

My foot touched the wooden dock, and Mentumehet held out his hands and bowed deeply in token of submission. I had conquered Thebes merely by appearing on her shores, it seemed. I had the power of life and death over the whole city, and my word was as the eternal law. This I did not believe, even for an instant.

"Lord Tiglath Ashur," he said in Greek, with a voice that might have been used to invoke the power of a god. "I, Mentumehet, Fourth Prophet of Amun and Prince of Thebes, both bid you welcome and implore your mercy on my poor people and myself. All Egypt lies prostrate before you."

He straightened his back and looked me in the face, and his gaze was cold and without fear or humility, as if he would give the lie to his own words.

"Not before me, but before the armies of Ashur and her dread king the Lord Esarhaddon," I replied, for I wished this priest to know that I would not be mocked. "I come in his name, for he is not without justice or clemency, but his wrath is the right hand of death."

His answer was a thin, joyless smile. We understood one another, it said. Now neither of us would be so incautious as to mistake the other for a fool.

After a brief pause he raised his arm and made a sweeping gesture toward the city behind him.

"It is a tedious journey from Memphis—doubtless My Lord would welcome some refreshment. Suitable entertainment has been arranged for your soldiers."

"My soldiers will be garrisoned within the palace grounds, and their officer will see to their needs. As perhaps My Lord knows, I am not a stranger to Egypt."

The smile was drawn a shade tighter, and Mentumehet bowed again. But at least he knew that I meant to keep control of my men and was not about to have them seduced by foreign luxury.

That night there was a great banquet given at Pharaoh's palace, and the river twinkled with lantern lights as the pleasure boats of the Theban aristocracy crossed over from the west city to the east to behold and be feasted by their new master. My arrival, it seemed, was a cause for celebration—which suggested nothing about their loyalties because these people had no loyalties. They did not care who ruled in Memphis, whether

Pharaoh or someone else, since for all they knew of it the world beyond Thebes might have been a story from the myths of an extinct race. I was merely something different, a kind of treat. I felt rather like some exotic animal put on display.

But their lack of familiarity with foreign ways only made them the more Egyptian, and what they lacked in sophistication they made up for in triviality. Mentumehet knew his subjects and had provided them with entertainment suitable to their temperament. Men and women in jewels and pleated linen threw candied plums at each other and giggled like children as naked girls danced to the strangely tuneless music which has not changed probably in four thousand years, which doubtless will never change, and can be heard anywhere between the Nile's Delta and its first cataract. Mentumehet and I sat together and exchanged meaningless pleasantries. I noticed he hardly touched his wine and never so much as glanced at his guests. He was not very entertaining company and, as I found the banquet wearisome—how many exactly like it had I seen during my years in Memphis?—I retired as early as I decently could.

The Prophet, who was nothing if not a considerate host, had ensured that my quarters were adequately provided with pretty slave girls who went about as noiselessly as deer on their bare feet. Enkidu, who followed at my heels like a particularly ill-tempered dog, did not even have to growl to send them fleeing, for he glared at them as if he planned to tear the flesh from their bones with his teeth.

"Then am I to spent every night in Egypt alone?" I asked him. "If Selana knew she would scold, saying that you endanger my health by thus forcing me to store up seed until it turns putrid."

He did not seem impressed with this argument, so I shrugged my shoulders and went to bed. Enkidu, as was his custom, disappeared to take up his nightly watch in some antechamber. I quickly fell asleep.

Dreams are strange things, the whisperings of the god or of one's unacknowledged intuitions or both, always shadowy and indistinct, the truth impenetrably disguised as itself.

All of Mentumehet's pretty courtesans are old women—in fact, half-decayed corpses without the decency to lie down and be still—and it is Selana who chases them away. Selana, wielding the broom with which she had swept our hearth in Sicily. When they have fled, she turns to me and shakes her head.

"Come home and play with your own harlots," she says to me. "Is there anything here for you except death?"

I woke up. And then I head a dull sound, such as a sword might make striking a pillow, and then, immediately afterwards, a half-strangled scream. To this day I am sure I was already awake when I heard these things.

Ever since returning to the east, I had slept with my javelin beside my bed. I picked it up now, along with an oil lamp that was nearly extinguished, and went to investigate.

Almost directly outside my door I found Enkidu and the man he had killed, though perhaps the man was not quite dead yet. He seemed to have some little sentient power left, albeit how anyone could survive such a blow, even for an instant, is beyond my powers to understand.

He was dressed in a priest's robes and his face, although still twisted with the agony of finding death, was young. Enkidu's ax had caught him just under the rib cage, and it had bit straight through him so that he was pinned to one of the thick wooden pillars in the wall of the antechamber, his spine severed, blood pouring down over his limp, nerveless legs, his feet not even quite touching the ground. If he was still alive it was only from the waist up. For a few seconds he gave the impression of struggling to pull the ax head loose from his bowels—at least, his hands were moving slowly back and forth over the blood-smeared blade—then he raised his eyes and seemed to stare at me with a look of uncomprehending bitterness. Then, quite suddenly, as if death came to him as a revelation, his head dropped and he slumped forward.

It was not until then that I noticed the dagger, lying on the floor at Enkidu's feet. He kicked it over to me and I picked it up. The blade was hardly longer than one of my fingers—had he really thought to kill me with such a toy? It was almost insulting.

I was perfectly calm. Nothing surprised me so much as my own lack of surprise, for it was almost as if I had expected something of the sort. In fact, the thing itself had almost the quality of a disappointment.

Was this somehow the Lady Naq'ia's doing? Had she finally decided that, so far from home, it would be safe to have me murdered? Was her reach so long? I would never know.

By then one of the eunuch chamberlains had come in, attracted like myself by the noise. When he saw what had happened he shrieked like a parrot, and soon the room was filled with servants. Some of them spoke in murmuring voices and the women stood about weeping. It was almost as if they had discovered the murder of a beloved master.

"Does anyone know this man?" I asked in Egyptian.

No, of course not. No one could possibly identify such a man—or would admit to it if they could.

"Then, since he is a priest, he is the Prophet's concern. Let his body be taken to the Lord Mentumehet."

With a sickening sound and a mighty yank that spattered blood everywhere, Enkidu pulled his ax free and the corpse pitched over and collapsed.

"You and you, attend to this. Everyone else go back to bed."

When the servants were gone, and there was nothing left to show what had happened except a heavy smear of blood on the tiled floor, Enkidu and I stood alone in the room. He was waiting for something, although it was certainly not the thanks that I offered him. He glared at me, as if he thought I had committed a stupid mistake.

"Yes, I know," I said. "It is an evil place. We will leave it as soon as we can."

But that could not be too soon, for it would do no good to create the impression that I could be frightened off by assassins.

The next morning, after breakfast, Mentumehet appeared without announcement and invited me for a walk.

"I thought you might like to see our great temple complex," he said, putting his hand on my arm in a way most uncharacteristic of the Egyptians—this was perhaps the only thing in his manner to suggest he had heard about the events of the previous night.

We went out and found the streets deserted, as if they had been cleared. All the way to the entrance to the great Temple of Luxor we met not a living person.

The temple precinct was a vast place, full of open courts framed around with vast pillars and the statues of long-dead pharaohs. Everywhere there was the dull hum of prayer. I saw much and there was much I did not see, for, as Mentumehet said, the very name "Amun" means "that which is hidden."

"Who built all this?" I asked, which made my guide smile.

"It is the work of many," he said. "The building we have just left was begun by Pharaoh Amenophis but not finished until the time of the Great Rameses, who raised it all to splendor. And the work goes on to this day—you see that little chapel there? It is the sanctuary of the goddess Hathor and was erected only a few years ago, the gift of Pharaoh Taharqa."

He glanced in my direction as he said this, but I thought it best to offer no reaction. For several seconds neither of us spoke.

"You are remarkably tranquil, My Lord Tiglath Ashur, for one who has so recently faced the assassin's dagger," he said at last, in the tone of one commenting on the mildness of the weather.

"He was stopped before he reached me. In fact, he was already dead by the time I saw him. Besides, it is not the first time an attempt has been made against my life—one can grow hardened to anything."

"I trust that you do not imagine *I* had any hand in . . ."

"No, I do not, My Lord," I said, interrupting him with a wave of my hand. "Somehow I cannot believe if you wished to have me killed you would send some fool with a knife fit only for peeling apples."

He laughed at this. His laughter sounded rusty, like an instrument hardly ever used.

"And what could I hope to gain, My Lord? What would be likely to bring the Lord Esarhaddon here faster, bearing fire and sword, than the news that his own brother had been murdered? Yet the man was one of my priests—as you might have gathered, passions are high and my authority is not without its limits."

Was it? I wondered. Perhaps, I found myself thinking, perhaps he had sent this assassin, knowing that the attempt could not succeed. Perhaps he had intended it all along as a kind of warning, an example of the risks foreigners ran when they thrust their interfering hands into the vipers' nest of Egypt. Mentumehet struck me as a man capable of anything that served his ends.

"That indeed is to be regretted," I said. "For the king's wrath is not something that bears trifling with."

We went outside and turned into a long alleyway lined on both sides with statues of crouched lions bearing the heads of men. Then, finally, after a sharp turn in the path, the heads on the statues were no longer those of men but of rams. Mentumehet did not see fit to explain the significance of any of this. For a quarter of an hour we walked between these strange figures, hardly a word being spoken.

At last we came to a tiny gateway through a vast mud-brick wall. Mentumehet put his hand upon the wooden door, and it opened soundlessly at his touch.

"This is the Great Temple of Amun," he said, in a voice which, after decades spent in this place, still betrayed a thrill of awe. "This is the soul of Egypt, where the god dwells, breathing life into the whole land."

Yet it was not the mysteries of his religion that the Prophet showed me. What I remember most vividly from that place were the huge statues of the Pharaohs, gods themselves now and more majestic than any god, and the wall paintings showing the wars they had fought in Asia. Horemhab and Rameses and Seti and Tuthmosis—names that were spoken with

respect even as far away as the Land of Ashur. This was what Mentumehet had wished me to see, this reminder that Egypt had not always
been a crippled snake.

"It has been over two thousand years since the kings of Thebes sailed
down the Nile to conquer the land all the way to the sea," he said. "They
made themselves Pharaoh and wore the double crown of Upper and
Lower Egypt, but they had their beginnings here.

"Since then we have had twenty-five dynasties of Pharaohs—some, in
recent centuries, have been foreigners, but they have honored the old
gods of Thebes and ruled in their names. So it will go on until the end of
time, for Egypt belongs to its gods or it belongs to no one.

"You lived in Memphis while you were among us, did you not?" He
turned to me and smiled his thin, faintly menacing smile. "Memphis is
not Egypt. Memphis is a brothel. This is Egypt."

He pointed back to the fresco of Rameses overcoming the Hittites at
Kedesh—I did not have the bad manners to point out to him how much
less decisive the actual battle had been.

"This is Egypt," he repeated. "And that."

His eyes moved to the opposite wall, and to the massive double door in
its center, a door as tall as five men and covered with gold, before which
priests prostrated themselves as they went by. I realized suddenly that
whatever lay behind it must be at the very center of this vast complex, its
secret heart.

"All the power of this land is behind that door," he said, in the manner
of one stating a fact. "That is the sanctuary of Amun, King of the Gods,
whose will is fate. What is Pharaoh before him? What is the Lord
Esarhaddon?"

And he believed it—I could read as much in his face. It was all
nonsense, temple incense clouding a priest's brains until he begins to
have faith in his own magic, but, looking at him, I half believed it myself.
I knew then that Mentumehet was that most dangerous of all enemies,
the man who has no doubts.

Whatever else, I thought, I must never allow my poor superstitious
brother to meet this man. The spell he would weave around Esarhaddon . . .

"I will make my submission to your king," he went on tonelessly, as if
he had lost interest in the subject. "I will send him gifts of gold and
treasure and women—I hear he has a taste for women—and I will make
no objection if he makes himself Pharaoh or names someone else to rule
in his place. Yet it is best if he understands that if he threatens the ancient
order of things, the gods will put might into the hands of some great man

who will sweep him away. It may be Taharqa, or it may be another, but it will happen."

The royal barge, when I left Thebes, was loaded with booty. And I had promised nothing beyond what Esarhaddon and I had agreed to in advance: that Mentumehet should be confirmed as lord of Upper Egypt, subject only to his obedience in all matters touching our interests and the regular payment of tribute. This, after all, was the way our ancestors had always governed their empire—leave the actual administration in the hands of local rulers who could be trusted. Mentumehet could not be trusted, but neither could anyone else.

Yet this was still the safest course. Mentumehet, if pressed, could raise an army of a hundred thousand men in a matter of days. And these would not be Libyan mercenaries fighting for pay, but Egyptians prepared to die for the honor of their ancient gods. Such a force could be crushed, but not easily. Upper Egypt was like a cobra sunning itself on a warm rock, best left in peace.

It was all too easy, I thought. What disaster would come from our having pushed our way into this land of spendthrift nobles and mad priests? What revenge would be visited upon us?

Upon returning to Memphis I was a little surprised to see that Esarhaddon still did not look well. He was up and active, but there was something . . .

I told the king all that had happened. He did not display much interest, except to make a jest about the attempt to assassinate me—"This fellow, Tiglath, was he missing a finger? Hah, hah, hah."

Then I showed him the chests of treasure, the presents of rare art and the dusty-skinned women with melting eyes that the Prophet of Amun had sent as offerings to his new lord. Esarhaddon, who delighted in all such toys, was very pleased.

"You are wise and cunning, brother," he said. "You conquer cities with nothing but your smooth tongue."

And then he grinned, and I knew he would tell me something I did not wish to hear.

"What would you think if I made Prince Nekau the new lord of Egypt? I know that you do not like him, and that he is weak and corrupt and hated by nearly everyone, but for these very reasons he will depend all the more on us. What think you? Will he not do very well as Pharaoh?"

I felt something cold in my bowels, like an intimation of death, yet I smiled and shook my head, for I had lost all hope.

"And why, brother," I asked him, "do you imagine it can make any difference?"

XLVII

AFTER FIVE MONTHS IN MEMPHIS, EVEN ESARHADDON WAS ready to go home. We would leave a garrison of forty thousand men there, and the force at Sha-amelie, which had kept our foothold in the Delta through the three years since the first Egyptian campaign, would be brought up to strength.

Would these be enough to hold the country? It seemed doubtful, particularly if Taharqa decided to gather another army and push up from the south, but Esarhaddon really had no choice. He had stripped the northern borders bare to fight this war, and peace there hung on one man's word to another. Khshathrita was not immortal, and neither was I. The homeland had to be properly defended.

But we did not allow such anxious thoughts to mar the joy of our triumphant departure from the land of Egypt. We had come out of the desert like a tribe of nomadic marauders, but we would leave as conquerors, carried down the Nile on Pharaoh's own troop barges. The men of Ashur are not good sailors, yet no one complained of this journey by water—no one looked forward with much enthusiasm to a second march through the Wilderness of Sin.

This was really Esarhaddon's first good look at the nation he had won with his sword, and he was bent on enjoying it, and on memorializing his own glory. In every city we entered, after the local nobles had abased themselves before the king and offered him entertainment and tribute, he insisted on placing in every temple of Amun an image of the Lord Ashur, inscribed with his own name and his boast of having subdued his enemies by grace of the god's favor. At the time I thought this behavior a most childish display of vanity and an unwise, pointless provocation—I wouldn't have been surprised to learn that the Egyptians took these idols down as soon as we had departed and threw them in the river. I confess, may his ghost forgive me, I had no inkling that my brother might have some other motive for these acts of devotion.

And for the rest, as we were carried along by the Nile's current, he would look out over the green fields of his new realm and his face would glow with gratified pride. Sometimes the peasants, walking along the riverbank, would catch sight of the royal barge and fall to their knees, and this really pleased him.

"You see?" he said to me once when this happened. "You may think I am a donkey, Tiglath, but the Egyptians pay their homage to me as a great king."

"Don't be a fool. Those are farming folk who probably have never heard of Esarhaddon, much less of your victory over Taharqa. They see the barge and think their Pharaoh is on it, that is all."

He gave me a savage look and left the deck. For two days he would not even come out of his cabin.

Yet at length I was forgiven. I even persuaded Esarhaddon to stop at Naukratis by suggesting that the Greeks might, in exchange for certain trade concessions, be prepared to arrange a loan for Prince Nekau's new government—Pharaoh, it seemed, had had the foresight to move his treasury to Napata, his capital in exile on the southern border and well out of reach, and the prince, ever the despair of his creditors, was as usual embarrassed for funds. Such a loan, I suggested, would save us the ill feeling among the Egyptians that must inevitably be aroused if our soldiers were used to collect new taxes. The king liked this idea, since it solved a problem and cost him nothing, so he gave me his blessing to see what I could arrange.

The docks were crowded when he landed, for Greeks and Egyptians alike had thought it wise to greet their new master with enthusiasm. Esarhaddon, when he stepped ashore to receive the people's homage, was the center of attention—no one paid the slightest heed when, a few minutes later, one of his staff officers quietly slipped away.

The city had changed very little in the years I had been gone. Only I had changed. I was no longer a fugitive now, but a conqueror. Yet this perhaps was merely an appearance. Where before it had felt strange to me to be a Greek among Greeks, now I wore the uniform of a *rab shaqe* in the army of Ashur as if it were a disguise. Since I was a child, friends and enemies alike had sometimes mocked me as a foreigner, calling me "the Ionian," yet until I was forced to flee my own land I had never known a doubt of who I was. I was Tiglath Ashur, son of Sennacherib—did not that make me a man of Ashur? Exile had taught me there was another self.

Never more than as I walked the streets of Naukratis that day, in the eyes of all who saw me the very image of an Assyrian, had I felt more divided within my own soul. Perhaps I had been too many years away from home ever truly to go back.

I found the home of my old acquaintance Glaukon. He was not there—doubtless he was on the docks, welcoming the king—but I knew he would be back soon enough. I told his servants, who did not know me and were understandably frightened of a strange foreign soldier, that I had come to see their master on a question of business and that I would wait. They brought me a cup of wine and disappeared.

An hour passed, and then two, and then Glaukon returned. There was more silver in his beard than I remembered, but otherwise he was little different. I was a stranger to him. He greeted me with the worried eyes of a man who fears trouble.

"Am I so altered then that you do not know me?" I asked, smiling and offering him my hand.

The eyes narrowed and then registered an astonished recognition.

"Tiglath, is it really you?" he cried. "I thought you were dead. And what are you doing in this uniform? Have you come then with the Assyrian king?"

I laughed—I could not help myself. I wanted to embrace him as my oldest friend, although we had known each other but slightly.

"Yes, it is I, and I am not dead. And yes, I have come with the Assyrian king."

"Then that at least solves one mystery." He took my hand, as if only just noticing it. "Someone told me once that you had left your own country after quarreling with your family. Are you an Assyrian then?"

"Yes. And my brother and I have made up our differences."

"Is he with you now, or have you come away on another adventure?"

"He is the king," I said.

I do not know what effect I had expected to produce with this remark—certainly not the numbed silence that followed it. Glaukon's hand seemed to turn cold and lifeless in my own, and he stood looking at me as if his powers of speech and movement had vanished.

"Your brother is . . . ?" he managed at last. Without finishing the sentence, he shook his head in astonishment.

"Yes. My brother Esarhaddon. My half-brother, actually, for we had different mothers. We were raised together. When he came to the throne he banished me for a time, and that was when I came to Egypt."

I felt like an idiot. So bald a history of our family quarrel sounded meaningless.

Yet Glaukon, who appeared to have recovered from the shock, did not seem of the same opinion. He was a Greek, and opportunities for profit were beginning to occur to him. He extracted his hand from mine and placed it delicately on my shoulder.

"Tiglath, my friend," he said, "let us go upstairs, where it is more comfortable, and my servants can bring us something to eat . . ."

An hour later, after wine and honeyed figs and salt-water fish served on a bed of grape leaves, it became possible to turn our attention to business. I outlined to Glaukon my hopes of raising a loan for Prince Nekau.

"It seems to me that you had a similar project in mind the last time we met, Tiglath. Pray explain to me what fascination does that extravagant, capricious little villain hold for you that you are always trying to squeeze more money out of me for him to squander?"

Yet he smiled as he said it, for he realized as well as I did how small a place Nekau occupied in this calculation.

"I asked for five million emmer before," I replied. "If we conceded to the Greeks a monopoly in the importation of wood, how quickly could you earn it back?"

He pursed his lips and cocked his head a little to one side, pretending to consider the matter.

"Five years," he said finally, regarding me with ill-concealed curiosity, as if wondering if I could be brought to believe anything so preposterous. "Five years, provided there is not another war in the Lebanon."

"I would have put it nearer to two, but of course I am only a simple soldier, unused to the intricacies of commerce."

"You have lied to me about your birth, Tiglath, for you are no less a Greek than I am myself."

He laughed at his own jest and then leaned forward, as if to whisper some secret.

"Yet you know as well as I that Nekau is a slender reed to bear the weight of Egypt," he said. "The Assyrians are going home, leaving only a few garrisons of soldiers behind. What if in the spring Taharqa comes out of the land of Kush with a new army? What then?"

"Then he will be driven back." I shrugged my shoulders, pretending a confidence I did not feel. "The king my brother is no fool, and he did not come here merely for the sake of a few months' plunder. Yes, of course Nekau may fall. Or his dynasty may last for the next five hundred years—in which case the Greeks of Naukratis could become the richest men in the world. How is profit to be made without risk?"

Glaukon considered this—or pretended to consider it, for we both knew he was not so feeble in his wits as to let an opportunity like this slip away—and then he reached across the table with his wine jar and refilled my cup.

"Nekau is still a slender reed," he said at last. "He is nothing without the Assyrian king. We will need some special demonstration of favor—do you think if we gave a banquet in his honor he would come? Here, to this house?"

"Yes, if I ask it of him." I could not help but laugh at the prospect. "If the wine is plentiful and the harlots are pretty, yes, he will come."

But I had a price for persuading the king of Ashur to come break bread with the Greeks of Naukratis.

"What is it?" Glaukon asked me, his eyes narrowing as he tried to calculate how much silver it would take to bribe a royal prince.

"Only this. If I give you a letter, can you see that it is delivered to my friend Kephalos? He is in Sicily, on a farm near the Greek colony of Naxos."

"Yes, of course. Is that all?" I could see at a glance how I had fallen in his good opinion, since the man must be a fool who will have so little when he could have had so much. "It will take a month or two to reach him, but there is no difficulty about it."

"Then I will bring the letter when next we meet."

Yet what was I to tell Kephalos that could have any chance of making him understand? "I am alive and well, my friend. I prosper, for Esarhaddon repents. I am his brother once more, and he reposes all his trust in my loyalty and love." "The king's mind is poisoned with a strange fear, so he keeps me close to him as if I were his talisman against the god's wrath. While he lives I am a prisoner in my own land." These were two sides of the same truth.

At last I despaired of giving any reasonable account of the atmosphere in which I now lived my life—Kephalos would guess more than I could tell him. So I wrote of Selana and our child, of the death of Esharhamat, and of the great war Esarhaddon had fought in Egypt. On Naq'ia I was silent. "Nothing has changed," I concluded, "except that where once the king was my enemy it pleases him, for reasons which are unclear, now to be my friend. Do not despair of my life, but know that I have little hope of ever seeing you and Sicily again."

Perhaps not until that moment, when I penned those words, did I grasp what a paradox my existence had become. When I was a fugitive I had longed for home and yet felt free. Now, reinstated in my princely rank, the king once more my brother and friend, I seemed only just to have begun my exile.

"What is that you write?"

Esarhaddon had come in without announcing himself, as he was in the habit of doing, as if the cabins of Pharaoh's barge were our rooms back in the officers' barrack when we were hardly more than boys.

"It is a letter to my old servant Kephalos," I answered, without looking up. "I am describing to him your crimes and impieties."

"Well, put it aside for the moment. The ambassador from the prince of Tyre is outside on the dock, and I have refused to see him."

"Why should I interrupt my letter because you refuse to see an ambassador?"

"Because I want to know what he came here to say—what are you really telling that fat pederast about me? Why would you be writing to him?"

"I thought he might be interested to know that you have not had me killed," I said, laying down my writing stylus as a lost cause. "I would be dead now if it weren't for him. And you would have that on your conscience, so do not speak slightingly of him simply because he has a taste for little boys."

"Will you see this ambassador, or not?"

"Why can't you see him and save everyone a great deal of inconvenience?"

Esarhaddon assumed to pose of wounded dignity that was all the more ridiculous for being perfectly sincere.

"I cannot see him—his master is a traitor! It would be much more fitting for you to talk to him."

"As one traitor to another?"

"You are very unforgiving for a brother, Tiglath."

"Yes—very well then," I said, getting up from my desk. "Since such is the acknowledged function of royal princes, I will spare your pride by finding out what message this lackey brings from Ba'alu."

"Good. I will wait here. I will take a nap in preparation for this evening."

Esarhaddon threw himself on my bed and was asleep almost before I had closed the door.

It was evening, but in the Delta there is no relief from the late-summer heat. The air was heavy and stagnant, almost unbreathable, seeming to mix with the river water in a gray haze. I thought for a moment of the sea breezes along the coast of Sicily and wondered how the grape arbors I had planted with Tullus were faring. Perhaps they were already bearing fruit—perhaps Kephalos had already pressed some of it into wine. Perhaps he was already drunk on it. It seemed an evil hour for any man to be sober, and to be meeting with the ambassador of the prince of Tyre.

He could have been no one else, for he was dressed after the Phoenician manner and his tunic was striped with the purple dye of which the people of that race are so proud. The instant he saw me he threw himself down and touched his forehead to the dock. Ambassadors are creatures without pride, so probably he would have thus abased himself before a common harlot if he thought she might belong to the Lord Esarhaddon.

"What does the traitor Ba'alu want that he sends around his dogs to lick the ground?" I asked, speaking in the accepted parlance of diplomacy. I made a point of not looking the man in the face.

"Great and Benevolent Lord . . ."

Half an hour later I sent the fellow away with a kick, telling him to wait upon the king's pleasure another day, but that probably his master should consider the merits of hanging himself.

Then I went back down to my cabin and woke up Esarhaddon.

"Get up and wash your face," I told him. "The Greeks consider it impolite to be late to dinner."

Sitting on the edge of the bed, he shrugged and then made a face, as if there was a bad taste in his mouth. Out of pity I gave him a cup of wine, and then he seemed to feel better.

"What did Ba'alu's ambassador want?" he asked.

"A treaty—peace. Doubtless he finds it inconvenient that you have chased Taharqa out of Egypt. You will confirm him in his vassalage and he will kiss the royal feet and beg your pardon. He will also pay all the tribute he has withheld, plus an indemnity of two million silver shekels. I treated his offer with contempt, which is doubtless what Ba'alu expected. I think we can settle on six million without any difficulty."

You have the soul of a horse trader," Esarhaddon growled. He was always irritable after a nap. "It is my pleasure that this treacherous dog be taught a lesson. I will march back to Tyre, capture the city, and nail Ba'alu's skin to the walls."

I took the wine cup away from him.

"By the time you have garrisoned Egypt, you will have fewer than thirty thousand men," I said. "The campaigning season is nearly finished, and the problems of taking a city which can keep itself supplied by sea are the same as they were six months ago."

"I can use Egyptian ships to cut them off in their harbors."

"Who will sail them? The Egyptians are terrified of salt water. Stop talking like a bellicose fool and accept Ba'alu's offer."

"He would not have made it if he did not think me a bellicose fool," Esarhaddon said, grinning. He was perfectly right. His reputation for vindictiveness was sometimes worth more than his prowess as a commander.

"Wash your face," I repeated. "And see that you don't get so drunk tonight that I am required to have you carried home. These men are my friends and I would prefer that you did not disgrace yourself in front of them."

"I am a king, and a king cannot disgrace himself."

"You can. Besides, the Ionians are not great respecters of kings."

"The Ionians are a race of effeminate, perfumed merchants—just like you."

"Yet you want them to loan Nekau money, don't you? Unless you prefer paying his debts yourself, you had best hold your tongue about effeminate, perfumed merchants. Not everyone has a brother's tolerance of your bad manners."

Esarhaddon conducted himself with reasonable dignity at Glaukon's banquet. Several there spoke some Aramaic, and my brother seemed to enjoy the company of men in front of whom he did not have to assume the majesty of a king. In fact, he was more truly kingly that evening than I had ever seen him.

On the walk back to the royal barge, at almost the last hour of darkness, Esarhaddon said that he was glad he had gone, that he almost envied me for being half an Ionian.

"They are a peculiar people," he said. "I am not surprised they drove their kings out, and I will leave in peace all the lands where they dwell, for I would not inflict upon myself the vexation of ruling them. It seems the Ionians hold no one in reverence. Still, I understand now why it is that I trust you above all other men, for you must love me or you would have killed me long ago. I put a higher price on such love than on the submission of an empire."

It was, in that moment, as if all the suspicion and anger that had accumulated between us over the years had vanished like morning frost, and we had found again the perfect confidence in one another we had known as boys. When had I ever loved my brother as much as on that dark morning in Egypt?

We stayed in Naukratis two more days—time enough to settle all the details of Nekau's loan and even to reach an understanding on the terms of Ba'alu's submission. That prince, it seemed, was even more frightened of the king's wrath than I had assumed, for his ambassador agreed to an indemnity of seven and a half million silver shekels and seemed to count his master blessed to have escaped so lightly.

When we reached the place where the second mouth of the Nile empties into the Northern Sea, we took ship for Acre—not Tyre, as the Tyrian ambassador had hoped, for my brother was determined that Ba'alu should be shown to be not an ally but a vassal, that the prince should be forced to come to him and to kiss the royal feet before all the world. And thus it happened, for Ba'alu was waiting for us at Acre, and he abased himself in the dust before the king of Ashur as only a Phoenician knows how.

From Acre we began the long march back to Calah.

In the Phoenician lands, along the Dog River, and again in the foothills of the Kashiari Mountains and about a day's march from the city of Eluhat, just inside the homeland of Ashur, Esarhaddon caused stelae to be erected to record for all time his triumphs in this campaign. One of these, I remember, showed Taharqa and Ba'alu kneeling in subjection before the king, with rings through their lips such as are used to break the wills of bull oxen and render them docile. Taharqa, of course, was enjoying a comfortable exile in Napata, well beyond our reach, and Ba'alu, though humbled, remained prince of Tyre, but kings are little interested in the accuracy of their victory boasts. There was also some nonsense about being attacked by green flying snakes during our march across the Wilderness of Sin—it was all very childish, and it pleased my brother immensely. Through lies carved into the rock face of a mountain my brother was at last able to see himself as a great king, the god's champion and a fitting successor to our grandfather, Mighty Sargon, whose name is immortal.

I spoke no word against those memorials to an empty glory and, since no one else would have dared, the lies went unchallenged and have remained so to this hour, and will perhaps for all time. I would be pleased if it were so, for what is truth that men should prize it so highly? And who is there still living who has a right to care? I am glad I said nothing, for those bragging stones provided the last moments of unclouded happiness Esarhaddon was to know in his life.

XLVIII

IT BEGAN IN A NAMELESS VILLAGE NEAR WHERE THE RE-
turning army had camped for the night beside one of the tributaries to the
Khabur River. Esarhaddon was sitting in the shadow of his tent, drinking
beer from a jar, when he looked up and saw a delegation waiting to attend
upon him, bowing as he raised his eyes.

There was nothing unusual about the local elders coming to pay
homage to their king. It happened everywhere we stopped. Yet this was
somehow different. Esarhaddon knew at once. I was with him at the time
and saw the way his face changed.

The headman, a grim-looking old peasant with a beard the color of
tarnished silver, stepped forward and bowed again. In his arms was a
bundle, which he laid upon the ground at Esarhaddon's feet. He opened
the bundle to reveal a dead child, a male infant with a red, swollen face
and the right ear gone, as neatly as if someone had cropped it with a
knife.

"It was born this morning, Lord," the headman said. "And it died
within the quarter hour. We felt, as you were nearby, you should see for
yourself. It seems a fearful omen."

"The ear . . . Was it born so?"

"Yes, Lord. Just so."

"What of the mother?"

"The mother has always been half an idiot, Lord—good for nothing.
Now she is near mad with grief and may die herself. No one knows who
the father might have been."

The headman covered the dead child's face again, and Esarhaddon
stood up.

"You did well to bring this to me," he said. "When I return to Calah I shall consult the priests. They will be able to tell what the god means by this."

He turned away and went into his tent, looking stricken, as if he already knew.

Ten days later, Esarhaddon celebrated his triumphal return to his capital.

Calah was mad with joy. Banners hung from her walls. For hours before we reached the city gates the road was lined with people who cheered until their voices cracked and threw flowers under the feet of our soldiers. The king, arrayed in a tunic so shot through with gold that it hurt one's eyes to look at him, rode in his chariot, and behind him, dragged along by chains fettered to the iron collars around their necks, walking on bare feet, came Pharaoh's whole family—his queen, his crown prince, even his brother.

Next came the wagons loaded with the spoils of conquest. Gold and silver and precious stones almost past imagining. Strange idols looted from the temples of the gods. Statuary with enameled eyes. Weapons and armor, shining in the sun. It was quite glorious. The king had not only conquered Egypt, but he seemed to have carried off all its wealth.

I saw it all, for I had entered the city the night before, in secret, and could watch the procession from behind a shuttered window in my house, holding up my little son that he too might see, my other arm about my wife's shoulders. This was the only homecoming that mattered to me.

My son could talk now—he spoke his mother's Greek and called me Father, for, though after so many months I was almost a stranger to him, Selana had kept my memory alive in his mind. I promised myself I would never part from them again.

That night, in her arms, had been like the first time all over. I had an animal's hunger for her that would give me no peace until my groin felt as withered as a pressed date.

"Well, at least you have not forgotten how," she said, wiping sweat from her breasts with the bedsheet, "but perhaps in Egypt you kept in practice."

"Selana, there were no—"

But her silvery laughter cut me short—she did not care, as long as I had come back.

"What was it like in Egypt?"

"An easy war, and a bad peace," I said. "One can conquer the Egyptians without them seeming to notice. I know not what good can come of it."

"And Memphis?"

"Memphis was Memphis. You have been there and know what it is like."

She did not ask about Senefru, and I did not tell her. Perhaps she did not need to ask.

"And what of Calah?"

"What is there to say? With the king gone, Naq'ia rules. Even with the king back, it may be just the same. She is an evil woman."

"Has she . . . ?"

"To me? No. She pretends she could not love me more if I were her own daughter, for she is afraid of you. Yet I do not think little Theseus and I would have lived another hour if word had come back that you were dead in some battle. She is like a spider, and Calah is her web. When the king is dead . . ."

"Perhaps she will die first."

"She will not die," Selana answered, shaking her head. "If her own venom cannot kill her, nothing else will."

She kissed my chest and playfully bit at my shoulder.

"Come into me again, Lord," she whispered. "You have left me alone too long."

"I fear there is no more."

"There is always more—see? There is always a little more."

She climbed over onto me and laughed deep in her throat when I entered her. I ached like an old wound in the cold, but even that was a pleasure.

She was right. There was always a little more.

While the king is young and full of vigor, and the *marsarru* is yet a boy, all is well in the Land of Ashur. Yet let the king begin to falter and, if the *marsarru* is old enough to begin asserting himself, then the nation becomes like a dog with two masters, nervously turning its eyes from one to the other, never sure which to obey.

So it had been in the last years of my father's reign and so it was now, after Esarhaddon's return from Egypt. My brother, who was even a little younger than myself, began to seem like an old man, uncertain and full of fear. The change was like day darkening into night, and almost as swift. Men saw, and averted their gaze in shame, and began to look to Ashurbanipal.

Ashurbanipal—my son. What of him?

I hardly knew him, since my own position in the shifting pattern of rule was difficult. The world might not know that Ashurbanipal had sprung from my loins, but Esarhaddon did, and thus I could not be brother to one and father to the other. I was saved the difficulty of choice, however, by the fact that Ashurbanipal did not know, or perhaps did not wish to know, that I was anything beyond an uncle, a trusted confidant of the "old king." To him, I was in the camp of his enemies, and no one would profit if I enlightened him.

In any case, there were few enough avenues into his character. The *marsarru* is sacred, like the king, and the hours of his life are almost as hedged around by ritual and custom. Esarhaddon, after he was named to succeed our father, had hated the empty ceremony, the shadow of royal glory, but Esarhaddon had never desired to be more than a soldier. Ashurbanipal, it seemed, desired only to be a king, and thus was contented enough. He seemed to wrap himself in the ambiguity of his office, leaving no trace of the man he was becoming. In due course a bride was found for him, a plump, pretty creature named Sharrat. She disappeared into his house of women, and after her wedding day no one ever seemed to see her—she was rumored to have been Naq'ia's choice, which I did not find incredible. What other pleasures beguiled away the young prince's time, who can say?

Esarhaddon disliked the boy, or, more truthfully, regarded him with a superstitious dread. They met only on formal occasions, when the behavior of each was dictated by ancient tradition. For the rest, the king had his circle, and the *marsarru* his. Esarhaddon lived surrounded by old soldiers, priests, soothsayers and magicians, and Ashurbanipal by scholars and librarians. The link between them—and of what that link consisted, whether of fear or favor or something else entirely, it was not in any man's power to tell—was the Lady Naq'ia.

More and more, she was the center around which events turned like a millstone on its axis. What did Ashurbanipal matter—or even the king himself—beside Naq'ia? She began even to give herself the airs of a ruling queen, holding court in her own palace, where the chief ministers of the state felt obliged to consult her about everything. Thus I was more than a little puzzled when, one cold winter morning, I found myself with an invitation, almost an entreaty, to come into her presence that same afternoon.

I found her in her garden, quite alone.

"How does your little son?" she asked, looking up and smiling.

"Very well, I thank you, Lady." I admit I was a little startled by her manner toward me, which was almost warm. "At the moment he cares for nothing except horses. I take him out to the parade ground to see the cavalry train, and he watches in a kind of ecstasy."

"And have you taken him for a ride yet?"

"No, Lady—he prefers to enjoy them at a distance. When I took him into the stalls, thinking he might like to stroke my war horse Ghost's nose, he grew quite frightened and clung to my beard like a little monkey."

She smiled again, expressing the bond of sympathy that exists among all who have known the pleasure of raising up a child.

"Yes," she answered, nodding. "I remember it was just so with Esarhaddon and the little pet deer we had in the house of women. Do you remember the little deer, Tiglath?"

"Yes, I remember those days quite well."

"Yes . . ."

She seemed to drift off into a kind of reverie for a few minutes, and then shook it off with the air of one dismissing a weakness.

"It is the curse of old age to be forever recalling the past," she said, with a certain edge in her voice. "Memory is too seductively kind, making us imagine we never suffered a moment's disquiet until the present hour. It makes one too devoted to old attachments. Beware it, Tiglath. The best thing is to live as if you and the world had no past, as if everyone we meet is a stranger."

She looked up at me in an odd, challenging way. Yes, her eyes seemed to say, *I believe everything I have said, yet perhaps I do not mean it in quite the way you imagine. But that is my secret.*

"I wonder, Tiglath, if you would consider accompanying the *marsarru* on a tour of the outlying garrisons. He is no soldier, as you know, and it would be good for him. Besides, he needs to be more popular with the army. We must think of the succession."

"And you think my going with him will raise his popularity?"

"Yes." Her face, as she spoke, revealed nothing. She could even have been offended. It was simply impossible to know. "You are the army's great hero. The common soldiers love you more than anyone—more even than the king. If you seem to think well of Ashurbanipal it cannot but raise him in their esteem. This time, at least, let the crown be passed without a civil war."

"There is no one who would challenge Ashurbanipal's right to succeed. Besides, the king is young enough that he should rule for many more years yet."

"The king—hah!"

With a shrug that could have been either contempt or despair, she seemed to consign her only son, around whom her every ambition had once been centered, to oblivion.

"It is a hard thing for a mother to say—you now are a parent yourself, Tiglath, so you will have some inkling just how hard it is—but the king seems to be failing from day to day. You must have noticed. He has not been really well since his return from Egypt."

"This is true—he seems to have turned in upon himself . . ."

The thought died in my mind as I studied Naq'ia's face. What really would her son's death be to her? A grief? A mere complication is her pursuit of power? Perhaps even an opportunity? All of these possibilities seemed to find expression in her eyes, which were like those of some savage animal.

And why, suddenly, did I believe with such conviction of certainty that the demons that were haunting Esarhaddon—whether the illness fretting him was of the body or the mind—somehow found their origin in the dark, swirling, haunted place that was his mother's soul?

And I knew in that instant what perhaps I had suspected all my life: that Naq'ia was mad. A lunatic gibbering beside the city gates was not more mad than she, except that hers was the cool, reasonable madness of untempered evil.

"Yes." She nodded, and for a wretched moment I thought she had seen into my mind—perhaps she had. "Yes, you understand how it will be. My son will not live to sit upon the throne of Ashur for all the years that the flatteries of the omen readers have promised him. And you and I, for the sake of our family, who have ruled in this land for a thousand years, for the sake of our subjects, who depend upon that rule for their safety and peace, must give thought to what will follow when he is no longer here."

She looked up at me, carefully placing one hand palm-down on the sofa beside her, watching me with eyes that seemed both to plead and to mock. Naq'ia the patriot, the guardian of the dynasty and her adopted land—it really was too much.

"I will take up the matter with the king," I said, perhaps a little coldly. "If he does not object, then there is no harm in the idea. Ashurbanipal shall have his tour."

"And it will be well," she answered. "A thing pleasing in the sight of the gods."

In the end the plan came to nothing, not because Esarhaddon made any difficulty but because the *marsarru* proclaimed no interest in making himself agreeable to garrison soldiers.

"I think perhaps he is wise in this," I told the king. "He is wary of sponsorship. He does not wish to be seen as the little boy who must be supported on his uncle's arm."

"Yes—he is most clever as he anticipates the day when I will be safely rotting in my tomb."

He actually trembled as he spoke the words, for Esarhaddon, all that winter, was growing more and more afraid—not of death, I think, but of the future he would never see but could imagine, and of the present that seemed to enclose him so that he could hardly breathe.

It was as if his life had been revealed to him as an appalling failure, a trap into which he had been led, never imagining that he could be so credulous.

And he was declining in his health as well, although he hardly seemed to care. His face was growing almost as gray as his beard and, like his mother, he complained of the cold.

He sat huddled on a bench in my reception hall, a brazier at his feet, wrapped up to his eyes in his heavy officer's cloak. My son, who had no notion what a king might be, was kneeling on the stone floor beside him, playing with his Uncle Esarhaddon's turban. My brother watched him for a moment, and then a wan smiled crossed his face.

"I would give him my sword of office," he said, "except he might cut himself and then Selana would scold. Do you know, Tiglath, that this house is the only place on earth where I know any peace?"

"*Only pity him, and be his friend,*" my mother had told me once. Had Merope somehow guessed that, in the end, it would come down to this?

"You simply aren't drunk enough."

I refilled his wine cup, setting it down on the bench beside him.

"No—probably not."

So it went, all that winter and into the early spring, when the mountains began to drip with melting snow and the rivers grew swollen. We all seemed to live with the secret knowledge that things were ending.

And then, when the floods were past and the summer heat baked the city like a brick in the kiln, the king began to hear reports of unrest in Egypt.

"It is that scoundrel Taharqa," he said. "His agents stir up the nobles and the common people alike, inciting them to resist Nekau's tax gatherers—do they imagine Pharaoh will tax them any less if he returns? And now, I am told, my soldiers are set upon so that they are afraid to stray outside their barracks after dark. I broke his armies on the battlefield, and now he hopes to win back with intrigue and treachery what he lost by force of arms. The man is a consciousless villain."

Yet he made no move to ready the army for another campaign. He waited, in a mood of what seemed the most dreadful suspension, as if he hoped that this threat would glide away, like a cloud driven by the wind, without his having to lift his hand.

So the summer passed. And while Esarhaddon waited—for what, even he could not have said, except merely for the time of waiting at last to end—he drank wine, and amused himself with his harlots, and came to my house to hide from the world. And little by little the power of government gathered itself in Naq'ia's hands.

"If I leave to fight in Egypt, she will rule," he said.

"She rules already."

"That is true."

And then at last the time for waiting was over. Taharqa came out of his exile in Napata, marching north with a great army. Everywhere he was hailed as a liberator, and the men whose submission Esarhaddon had accepted, confirming them in their wealth and offices, threw themselves at Pharaoh's feet. Within days he had retaken Memphis, putting the entire garrison to the sword.

"This is my punishment for cowering like a woman here in Calah," my brother said. "Now I will give the Egyptians a lesson they will not forget for a thousand years."

Thus preparations began for another war.

I was not to accompany Esarhaddon on this campaign.

"There is no one else I can trust here," he told me. "All the others are too afraid of my mother, so I have no choice but to leave you behind. You will have full powers, as if you were king yourself—do not be reluctant to use them."

I was not sorry. I wanted no more to do with this Egyptian venture, for the smell of death hung around it like a swarm of flies over a rotting carcass.

On the morning he was about to leave, I stood beside the wheel of Esarhaddon's chariot in the courtyard of the house of war. Soon he would drive through the gates and out into the city, to be cheered by her citizens as he led the army of Ashur to fight in a distant land. Just before he stepped aboard, at absolutely the last moment, he put his hand on my shoulder and smiled. I shall never forget that smile, for it told of a despair beyond all comfort.

"You remember the dead child, born with its right ear cropped?" he asked. "Do you know what my omen readers tell me it meant?"

"No, I do not know," I answered, certain I did not want to hear.

"It meant that we have entered a time when the nation shall be ruled by a madwoman."

XLIX

WITH THE KING OUT OF THE WAY, THERE WAS AN UNNAT-
ural serenity about Calah. Perhaps it is only time playing tricks with my
memory, but I believe I felt even then that Esarhaddon's court seemed to
be waiting for something, waiting with the untroubled confidence of the
heirs at an old man's deathbed, knowing that that for which they
waited—for which they longed—was inevitable and, now, very close at
hand.

I was the king's viceroy and ruled the city and the nation in his name
and with the full weight of his power. My commands were obeyed but, it
seemed to me, with a sly, half-suppressed smile, as if each of Esarhaddon's nobles and servants was thinking to himself, Let him enjoy his
little moment of glory. I will still be here when he is forgotten. It is already
nearly over for him.

I knew something was wrong. Everyone knew it, even Selana.

"I hate this place," she said one evening, while we were waiting for
dinner to be served. "I wish I were back in Sicily, sanding the floors. Is
anyone there taking proper care of my poultry? I feel as if we were at a
banquet where all the food is poisoned."

And then, uncharacteristically, she burst into tears, gathered up little
Theseus in her arms, and ran from the room.

Women are not so lost to all understanding as men tend to think. I
grasped precisely what she meant, yet what could I say that would still her
forebodings, especially since they were mine as well? That night I ate my
dinner alone, and in wretched silence.

Warnings never come singly. On the evening of the eighteenth day
after Esarhaddon's departure, a messenger arrived from Niveneh with

news of a kinswoman—a reminder, if I needed one, that all our griefs are rooted in ancient sins, that the past holds us in its cold, dead hands from which there is no escape.

"My Lord, the Lady Shaditu is dead."

Shaditu, my half-sister, wicked and beautiful, a woman to make one's body burn with lust and hatred—in her time she had made me burn, and Esarhaddon too.

"When did she die?" I asked. "And how?"

"She was found this morning, when she had already been dead many hours. It is believed she took her own life."

I thought of the priest, Rimani Ashur, who had read the entrails of the *ginu* and declared it the god's will that my brother and not I should be king in the Land of Ashur. He, it was rumored, had been one of Shaditu's lovers, and he had died by his own hand, hanging himself in the temple sanctuary, under the very eyes of the Lord Shamash.

"How?"

"Poison, My Lord. There was an empty wine cup beside her sleeping mat. They opened her belly and found her guts were black with henbane."

I did not believe it for an instant. Yes, certainly, if driven to it, Shaditu would have been perfectly capable of such an act—yet why now? Why just now?

Because Shaditu had known a secret, one that some might prefer died with her. And the king was far away, and . . .

What as Naq'ia preparing?

"What should be done with the corpse, My Lord?"

"Bury it," I answered, my heart still cold from the shock. "Bury it before it rots—what else, throw it to the dogs? Bury the Lady Shaditu in the royal vault at Ashur, for she was a king's daughter, and her father, the Lord Sennacherib, loved her."

"Yes, My Lord."

He bowed himself out of my presence and, one assumes, took horse back to Nineveh with the surprising news that there was to be no further investigation. No slaves were to be questioned under torture, no old lovers need fear for their guilty secrets, and the Lady Shaditu, who had been an evil woman and had died such a death as stinks in the nostrils of the gods, was to be laid to rest among her ancestors like some elderly virgin claimed at last by the accumulated infirmities of a harmless life.

That night she came to me in my dreams. Yet I hardly thought it a dream, for it remains in my mind as substantial as the memory of a real event.

She looked as she had in the days of our youth, clear-skinned and sleek, her breasts firm beneath her fine linen tunic. She smiled with mischief as she sat down beside me on a bench in our father's garden in Nineveh—why there, I cannot begin to guess.

"You raped me once," she said, and the memory brought with it a ripple of throaty laughter. "You beat me like a tavern harlot and then forced yourself on me."

"As I recall, you didn't require very much forcing."

This made her laugh again, and she shook her head so that I could hear the hair rustle like dry leaves.

"I would tease you into doing it again, but there are no such embraces among the dead." With her pink tongue she licked her nether lip and brought her face close to mine. I could feel her warm breath as she spoke. "Still, kiss me, Tiglath my brother, if only to show you have forgiven me."

"No, Shaditu. You are dead, remember? Even now, you are lying in your casket somewhere. Try to behave with appropriate dignity."

"You are unkind," she said, pulling away as she dropped her eyes and pretended to pout. Then she looked up at me again and grinned, showing lovely, even, white teeth.

"I will always love you, Tiglath, though you are a brute and do not deserve it. Who else could I ever have loved, for who else understood me as you did?"

"Understood that you were a wanton slut? Many understood that."

"Not as you did." Another rich little throb of laughter. "Still, it was sweet of you to let me be buried in the royal vault. I should have missed being near the family. Esarhaddon would probably have told them merely to dig a hole in the mud."

"What do you want, Shaditu?"

"Only to warn you—and to be avenged."

She sat there, turned slightly towards me, her small hands resting on her thigh, and I could see a hardness come into her eyes, as if the pupils had turned to iron. Yes, of course. My sister would always insist on the final word, even in death.

"It was Naq'ia, wasn't it," I said at last.

"Yes, of course." She shrugged her fine shoulders playfully. "Who else? My servants are all her spies, and at last she had one of them poison me. In recent years I have taken to drinking myself into a stupor almost every night, so I did not even notice the taste of henbane in my wine. Everyone thought I had killed myself, out of boredom, I suppose. But not you, my clever brother."

The smile she turned on me was enough to freeze the blood.

"I cannot have Naq'ia killed."

"There are many things worse than death. You will find a way to punish her."

"And the warning?"

"Do not try to change things," she said, after a moment—it was almost as if she were delivering a message, for the words did not seem to be hers. "There is no place for you in a future which cannot be unwritten, and no labor of yours can avail against the god's will. Do not step into the trap that awaits so many others."

"Only that?"

"Only that."

"Shaditu, what did Rimani Ashur see when he examined the *ginu?*"

"Can a man read another's destiny in the entrails of a sacrificial goat?" She smiled her teasing smile, but even as she spoke her image faded. "You will know all in good time."

And then, of course, I woke up to find the sun steaming over my face. Yet the dream stayed in my mind.

Not an hour later a rider came from Harran with news that the king had fallen ill.

"He has been ill almost since we left Calah. At first he only complained of stomach pains, and even when he could no longer travel it seemed to be nothing, yet now . . ."

"He is very bad. Six days ago, he could not even stand. His physicians do not know what is wrong, but the king himself believes he is dying. He insisted you be sent for, My Lord."

"Then I must go to him."

I did not trouble to appoint a deputy who would govern in my absence, since I knew all such arrangements would be in vain—if I left Calah, Naq'ia would rule, no matter what I did. The king had known as much, which was why I had not accompanied him on this campaign. He knew it now, lying on what might be his deathbed. Thus, if he called me to him, it was for no trivial reason.

I gave orders that Ghost was to be bridled and waiting within the half hour. I sent no word to the royal garrison. There was no time left to squander if I wanted to see my brother alive, and I would travel faster without an escort. If Esarhaddon thought he was dying, I had to believe him.

"Since I know you will not stop along the way to eat, this will keep you from starving," Selana told me, putting a leather satchel into my arms. "It holds enough bread and dried meat to last two men four days. There is even a small jar of wine."

"Two men?"

"Yes, two. You will take Enkidu with you, if only for your wife's peace of mind. Will you send word of the king's illness to the Lady Naq'ia?"

"No. She will hear quickly enough. It would not surprise me if she knew already."

When I came down to the courtyard Enkidu was already waiting, mounted on his horse and ready. I kissed Selana and our son good-bye, the future a blank wall before us. She only smiled and said, "Take care." She asked no questions because she knew I had no answers for her.

The ride to Harran took six days. Horses must be rested and fed and watered, but otherwise we never stopped. For six days I hardly closed my eyes or looked at anything except the road ahead of us. I tried to force myself not to think, since the only idea my mind seemed able to contain was that Esarhaddon might even then be dead—I could not even think as far as what the world would hold for me and mine if Ashurbanipal became king. I simply did not want my brother to die in the presence of strangers, with no loving hand to close his eyes. It is therefore hardly surprising that the journey has left hardly any trace on my memory.

We encountered outriders half a day from the city walls, and they gave us fresh horses. Others met us at the main gate, and I was taken directly to the provincial governor's house, which, in this emergency, had become both army headquarters and royal palace. I had not even wiped the dust from my face when I was shown into the king's presence.

Esarhaddon was lying on a couch, asleep. His face was wasted and gray. From the way his lips worked it was clear his dreams tormented him. His officers and physicians stood about in silence—and among these I saw Menuas watching me with his small, frightened eyes.

Sha Nabushu, the king's *turtanu*, came up and touched me obsequiously on the arm, glancing down at his master's tortured rest.

"He is thus much of the time," he said, this in a voice that just missed being a whisper. "Presently he will wake, and his mind will be clear enough. His strength is waning fast, however. He asks for you constantly."

I made no reply. I did not trust myself to speak.

After perhaps an hour Esarhaddon woke up. His eyes wandered about the room and then fastened on my face and then widened with recognition. I believe he was too exhausted even to be surprised.

Then he turned his gaze to Sha Nabushu.

"Get out," he said, breathing out the words. "Get out, all of you. I wish to speak to my brother alone."

When they were gone, he motioned to me to come and sit beside him.

"I haven't come very far, have I," he said. "I suppose this means we will lose Egypt, and it will all have been for nothing. Ah, well."

Yes—I could believe he was dying. If he could give up his dearest wish so easily . . .

With what seemed a great effort, he closed his eyes for a moment. When he opened them again they seemed almost drained of life.

"I may not have much time." Esarhaddon moved his hand enough to lay it on my arm. "There is something I must tell you."

"It can wait, brother. You will recover and can tell me then."

He shook his head—he knew that I was merely being a coward, that I did not want to hear whatever secret burdened his heart.

"Sometimes the gods are merciful and give a man warning," he said. "I will not recover, Tiglath, and you must know the truth or you will not be able to save yourself after I am gone. I know you, and your conscience will paralyze you."

His fingers slipped down and grasped my wrist, turning my hand over. The mark I had carried there on the palm all my life glowed like a drop of fresh blood.

"When Rimani Ashur read the omens to know if it was the god's will that I should be king, he found a blemish on the *ginu*." Even as he spoke, Esarhaddon's eyes widened with horror. "A hemorrhage, just under the surface, stained the goat's liver. It had the shape of a bloody star."

He told me the whole story, some of which I had already guessed. Shaditu had seduced Rimani Ashur, and Naq'ia, who knew of it, had threatened to tell the king if her son was not confirmed as *marsarru*. The chief priest feared for his life—everyone knew of the doting love the Lord Sennacherib lavished on his daughter, how he was blind to her wickedness—and so he concealed the truth and proclaimed it the will of heaven that Esarhaddon should rule as the next king. But Rimani Ashur was a pious man, for all that he was weak in his flesh, and in the end his remorse drove him to take his own life.

"There could be but one interpretation to so fearful an omen, for the god had marked you in the same way, in the hour of your birth, when our grandfather Sargon was finding his *simtu* at the hands of savages and heaven mourned the death of so great a king by burning the night sky with a star the color of blood. Once more, Tiglath my brother, you were favored over me. It was the Lord Ashur's will that you and not I should succeed our father as king."

I could guess what it cost Esarhaddon to tell me these things.

"I knew nothing," he told me. "I promise you I had no inkling, not until I returned from the campaign against Abdimilkutte. Naq'ia wanted to stop me from giving the order to call you back from exile. That was the one thing she feared—not the judgment of the gods, not my pitiful anger, only your return. She had failed in her attempts to have you murdered, and she could no longer harden my heart against you, so she told me the truth, thinking it would tie me to her even more closely."

"Yet you called me back."

"Yes. You do not know how I missed you, Tiglath, even from the moment I banished you. I would have called you back when we met at Sidon, but you were so stiff-necked and taunting . . . I was still too proud to humble myself, yet I knew, even before I got back to Nineveh, that I had no one else in the world to trust except you. Then Naq'ia told me about the omen, but the story had the opposite effect from what she had intended—I was terrified. By the grace of the Lord Shamash, I had never wanted to be king, and I understood then why the gods had blighted my reign. I needed you to save me from their vengeance, and my mother."

"You could have abdicated."

"No." He shook his head slowly, like a man resigned to fate. "I did not dare, for who would believe that I had not been a party to Naq'ia's plottings? So I thought to bring you home and make it all up to you, heaping you with power and honor—except that you seemed to have lost your taste for power and honor. And I would make it up to the gods by conquering Egypt. I would lay a kingdom at Ashur's feet in atonement for my unwitting sin against his will. The offering, it appears, has not been accepted. Egypt is lost, and I remain unforgiven. Tiglath my brother, do you, at least, forgive me?"

"I forgave you long ago. We have both suffered through Naq'ia's treachery—you, I think, more than I. Esarhaddon my brother, you are not to blame because you have an evil mother."

We both wept and embraced each other, and it seemed we had found once more the perfect love and trust we had felt for each other as boys. Our long estrangement was at last at an end.

"I am weary," he said at last. "By the Sixty Great Gods, I think I can sleep quietly now. Stay with me, brother, and when I am awake again we will talk more."

He drifted off, as easily as any child. And I sat beside him, holding his hand.

I did not want my brother to die. Now less than ever did I want him to be gathered into the Lady Ereshkigal's cruel arms. What was it that worked against his life with such slow cruelty?

I thought perhaps I could guess. I had guessed even in Egypt, but had allowed myself to dismiss the suspicion when Esarhaddon seemed to recover. I had been a fool . . .

"You are a king's son and live surrounded by enemies," Kephalos had told me once. "If your dreams of greatness are to be fulfilled, and if you would survive to be mighty and prosperous, you must learn to keep yourself out of harm's reach."

He had then proceeded to teach me everything he knew of the poisoner's art, and that turned out to be a great deal.

"The Greeks are less gifted in these matters than the eastern peoples," he said. "Yet I have traveled widely, both in the pursuit of knowledge and through the vicissitudes of fortune, and I have learned much from the physicians of many nations. Believe me, Lord, when I say there is little safety in the world. A man may cut an apple in half and share it with you. You will die while he will live, because only one side of the knife's blade was coated with venom."

Esarhaddon's health had been declining for some time—since that episode in Egypt, in fact. Had someone been weakening him, little by little, for so long a period?

"Poisons vary in their effect," Kephalos had explained. "Some are more subtle than others, but each leaves its characteristic mark. One has only to look for it."

I did not have to look very far. I found it on the hand I held in mine. Obscure but visible, showing through the fingernails, tiny flecks of pale brown, like traces of long-dried blood.

"Aphantos. Little known and difficult to obtain in sufficient quantities. It comes from the seeds of a drab little flower called the Philozoös, found in only a few places in the world because it needs heavy brine to thrive—even the sea is not rich enough in salt to sustain it.

"It is not an efficient poison, for it must accumulate in the body over a long period, and thus its administration is a tedious business. Yet it has the virtue of being indetectable, save for those spots under the nails, which hardly anyone would even notice."

Esarhaddon's sleep was deep and untroubled. I left him for a moment and stepped out into the hallway, where a guard was posted. I called him to me with a silent gesture.

"The king's physician, the Urartian Menuas. Do you know where he is at this moment?"

"Yes, *Rab Shaqe*. Shall I send for him?"

"No. Have him placed under close arrest. Take him by surprise, and be sure he has nothing secreted on his person—I will hold you responsible for his life, so be sure he has no opportunity to take it himself. Have his medicine box brought to me."

I went back to the couch where Esarhaddon slept and sat down again, having decided to say nothing to him until I was sure, and perhaps not even then. I did not entertain much hope.

Salt-laden water where the Philozoös might grow—how many such places were there in the world? The Bitter Lakes in the Sinai, at the threshold of Egypt. The Great Salt Lake, called the Dead Sea by the Moabites. And, greatest of all, the Shaking Sea in the kingdom of the Urartians—I had been there, and the waters were as harsh as death.

Who would know better of the properties of the Philozoös flower than a physician from Tushpah? Who indeed.

When Esarhaddon woke up, we spoke again and he was able to eat a little something. Then he drifted back to sleep. I took the opportunity to bathe and catch a few hours' rest. I would leave Menuas to sweat at least that long. He would be all the better for the wait.

When I awoke it was already late into the night. The physician's medicine box was a on table in my room. It contained a collection of surgical instruments, carefully wrapped in linen, and several small pottery jars sealed with wax and with the name of the substance each contained scratched on the side. Some of these I could identify, others not. One jar was marked "*Siburu*," which I knew from Kephalos, who used it on himself as a treatment for thinning hair, a dark powder taken in beer or sweet milk. Yet the powder in the jar was a pale brown—almost precisely the color of the flecks in Esarhaddon's nailbeds. I tried a little on my tongue and found it tasteless. *Siburu* is almost unpalatable.

I went to Esarhaddon's room and questioned the officer in command of the watch.

"Does the king still sleep?"

"Yes, *Rab Shaqe*."

"That is well. Take me to where you are holding the physician Menuas."

My orders had been carried out scrupulously. I found the prisoner, stripped naked and chained by the hands, feet and neck so that he could not even stand up, in a windowless room not much larger than a baker's oven. The expression of his face when I opened the door was one of sheer terror, although, after so many hours in the dark, he may merely have been dazzled by the light of my oil lamp.

I crouched on the floor beside him, setting the lamp down between us, and the guard closed the door from the outside. Menuas and I might have been alone in the universe.

"By the great gods, Lord, I have done—"

"Do not lie, Physician," I said, interrputing him. "Do not add perjury to your sins, and do not insult me by implying that I can be deceived. I have examined your medicine box and found the Aphantos with which you have been poisoning the king."

For a moment he said nothing. He merely whimpered abjectly, as if his sufferings had robbed him of his wits. And in truth I found it impossible to feel any anger against this wretched man. Who could say what threats or promises Naq'ia had marshaled to make him do her bidding.

And yet the murder of a king is a fearful thing.

"It—it is a remedy for impotence," he said finally, perhaps not even daring to hope he would be believed. "It is a remedy . . . It is . . ."

I smiled at him wolfishly.

"I have known the king since we were boys together," I answered. "I have never known him to lack force in his loins, although his passions are cool enough now. I have neither the will nor the power to save your life, Physician. Yet if there is to be any mercy for you, you must speak only the truth.

"Is there an antidote?"

He said nothing. He merely stared at me with his small, frightened eyes, not yet ready to accept that there was no hope for him.

"Do you know what punishment is reserved for crimes such as yours?" I went on at last. "You have raised your hand against the Servant of Ashur—do you know what will be done to you? You will have the hide stripped off your body while you still live. Can you imagine what that is like? I have seen it done, and it is terrible even to watch. The men who do it are greatly skilled, and they take their time, since they want their victim to remain alive and sensible to the very end. Thus they begin at the palm of the hand, you see, and they peel away the skin in a single piece, even taking the fingernails, and then they cut up the inside of the arm . . ."

He opened his mouth as if to scream, but no sound came out.

"Can you imagine, Physician, what it must be like to be no more than a piece of raw, bleeding meat, rolling around helplessly in the dust, unable even to close your eyes because your face has been flayed off, and your eyelids with it? Finally they will feed you to the dogs, and you may be still alive even for that last indignity. Think of it, Physician—you might die only when the king's hunting dogs have torn you to pieces. You might even live to hear them snarling at one another over the bloody scraps."

I paused, to give him time to imagine it all, to let his mind fill with expectations of pain and horror. That is the point of torture, to focus a man's attention on his suffering, and thus make it unbearable.

I could not save him from his fate—no one could. Yet it served my purpose to let him think so, if only for a while.

"Spare yourself," I said, breaking the silence. "If you can, spare yourself this death. Is there an antidote?"

For a few seconds he seemed capable of nothing except little choking sounds, as if the words had caught in the back of his throat. Then he swallowed and looked away from a moment, trying to compose himself enough to allow him to speak.

"There is no antidote," he whispered, without raising his eyes. "In the beginning, if the poison is stopped, the effects will pass off of their own. But by this stage there is nothing to be done."

So it was finished. Nothing could stop the slow ebbing of my brother's life. I had not really expected otherwise, but the heart seemed to turn to stone within my breast.

"Was it poison in Egypt?" I heard myself asking. Menuas hesitated and then nodded his head. "The same?"

"No—another. A stronger poison called—"

"I do not care what it is called. Why did he not die then?"

"When you started to suspect, I was too frightened to administer the fatal second dose. The Aphantos was more like the normal progress of disease, so I have been giving him small amounts ever since the end of the last campaign. The Lady—"

"Do not speak her name, dog!" I grabbed the iron ring around his neck and pulled him to his feet so that it almost strangled him. "Never speak her name—neither to me nor to anyone else!"

I released my grip and he dropped back to his knees, almost gagging as he tried to catch his breath. He was a pitiful villain to have committed so great a crime.

"How long, then, can the king live?"

"Perhaps two or three days—no more."

He raised his pleading, tear-filled eyes to me, his lips shaping the first words of a soundless prayer that I might give him at least a crumb of hope, but I rose and tapped the door to let the guard know to open it. I was finished with this man.

"Two or three days," I repeated. "So be it then, Physician. You have sealed his fate and yours."

"Lord—pity . . . !" He tried to throw himself at my feet, but his chains would not let him and he merely toppled clumsily to the floor. "Lord! What am I to do?"

"Do? Prepare for death." The door opened, and I snuffed out my oil lamp. "Turn to the gods for mercy, Physician, for you will find it nowhere else."

Esarhaddon slept until morning, and I waited by his bedside, trying to decide what to tell him. He was the king, from whom the truth must not be hidden, yet he was also my brother, and how could I steal all hope from him by revealing that he had been poisoned, and that he was past all cure? And how could I darken his last hours by telling him that the poisoner who had robbed him of his life had been sent by his own mother?

In the end I told him nothing—the ties of blood and love meant more than the duty of a subject. Yet when he awoke he seemed to know all without being told.

"Call my officers," he said to me, almost as soon as he had opened his eyes.

"It can wait. Take a little something to eat first."

"No, Tiglath. Call my officers. There is little time left—I can feel it. And soon enough I will have no need of food. Call them."

I did so, and soon the room seemed crowded as the *rab shaqe* of the army filed in and took their silent places around Esarhaddon's sofa. There were perhaps twenty-five of them, not merely the leaders of this expedition but commanders from every garrison within a week's ride. Some of these men I had known since boyhood; others had been my comrades-in-arms at Khalule and Babylon, and in the Zagros when we waged war against the Medes. A few had risen up during my years of exile, but I had marched at their side through the Wilderness of Sin and taken their measure in battle against the Egyptians. These were soldiers, men who could be trusted.

And all had been brought hither by news of the king's illness, ready to do their master's bidding while he lived and, should he die, to secure the peace of the empire according to his will. It seemed as if all the armed might in the world was focused in that tiny space.

I helped Esarhaddon to sit up, arranging some cushions to support his back, since he was too weak to do it for himself—he had spoken no more than the truth when he said he could feel his end coming, for he was failing rapidly.

"I am close to death," he said, in the voice he might have used to discuss his plans for a battle. "I have made certain decisions touching on the next reign, and I wish to know if you will support them. I will be gone, gentlemen, so the matter will be in your hands."

He closed his eyes for a moment, as if gathering strength, and then opened them and looked about him, turning his gaze from one face to the next. No one spoke.

"The *marsarru* is young and without experience," he went on. "We are entering a time that will be full of war, and I do not believe he is ready for the burden of rule—he may never be ready, but this is a thing which only time can reveal. Until then it is my will that my brother, with whom you are all acquainted and who needs no words from me to make his glory known, shall act as *turtanu*. The boy Ashurbanipal shall have the name and honor of kingship, but all power, in peace and war, shall rest with the Lord Tiglath Ashur."

I felt a cold shock go through me, for nothing had prepared me against this. I tried to keep all expression out of my face and to avoid the eyes of the men who all at once were studying me as if I were a stranger to them.

"Well?" Esarhaddon glanced about him challengingly. "How is it to be? Will you abide by this? Have none of you anything to say?"

There was a brief buzz of conversation as the commanders of the king's army exchanged whispers, and then Kisri Adad, *rab shaqe* of the *quradu*, an old soldier whose loyalty and integrity were beyond question, stepped forward.

"So long as the life and honor of the *marsarru* are respected, and his right of succession, which each of us has sworn to uphold, then no one here will withhold his obedience from the Lord Tiglath Ashur, whom every man honors."

He turned his gaze from the king to me, seeming to demand an answer to his unspoken question. Yet for the moment I was silent—I seemed to have lost the power of speech.

"What say you, Tiglath?" Esarhaddon asked finally. "Will you respect young Ashurbanipal's rights, or will you use your power to push him aside and make yourself king in name as well as in fact?"

No doubt the form of his question was a kind of jest, but at least it had the effect of rousing me to something like anger, and I found my voice did not fail me when I made my answer.

"What man here can say he has ever known me to break faith with my king?"

Kisri Adad nodded, and behind him rose a murmur of approval.

"That is enough for me," he said.

"Then take your oath upon it," Esarhaddon answered, holding out his right hand. "Swear your obedience to the Lord Tiglath Ashur, the king's *turtanu.*"

Kisri Adad knelt beside the couch and touched his forehead to the king's hand.

"I swear it," he said.

He rose, and after him each man in turn knelt by the dying king and swore to obey me as master of the world.

"I had to do it, Tiglath. There was no other way. This is why I would not let you take the oath of succession, for you are the true king and I would not have you bound to the son who usurps your place."

We were alone again. I sat beside Esarhaddon, and he clutched my hand in his as if nothing else held him to life.

"You know I will not be able to hold such power long," I said, my voice hardly more than whisper. "Ashurbanipal is no pliable simpleton—soon I would have either to put him under virtual arrest or have him killed. I can do neither."

"Yes, but he does not know that. As you say, he is no simpleton, so he will be too cautious at first to dare challenge you. Thus you will have time enough to find a way to escape."

"Escape from what?" I asked, already knowing the answer. The real question was if Esarhaddon did.

"From my mother."

His grasp tightened around my hand—the increase in pressure was hardly noticeable, but it seemed all the strength he had left.

"Promise me, Tiglath, that you will not have my mother killed," he said, with all the fervor of a prayer. "She is an evil woman, I am well aware. She has committed many crimes, yet she remains my mother. I know you must do something if you are to save yourself, but find a way to spare her life."

"You spared my mother when you thought me a traitor against you. I will spare yours. Much as I would like to see the Lady Naq'ia with her head between her feet, I will do nothing against her. You knew that, without asking."

His hand relaxed again in mine.

"Yes, I knew it. Still, I had to ask."

He was quiet for a moment, and then, suddenly, he laughed.

"Do you remember, Tiglath, when we were boys, and we got leave from the house of war to go into Nineveh and have dinner with that scoundrel Kephalos? He gave you a purse of silver, remember? And we divided it between us by the light from the open door of a tailor's shop and went off in search of harlots."

"Yes, I remember." My eyes seemed to brim with tears as I spoke. "You found one, in that wretched little wineshop, but my shyness unmanned me."

"Yes."

Esarhaddon grew quiet for a moment, so that I thought he might not speak again.

"We might have divided the world between us, Tiglath—just like that purse of silver. We should have. Where did it all go wrong?"

"We grew up, and found the world a more complicated place than a boy's trust can imagine."

"It was my fault," he said, his voice hardly more than a breath.

"It was both our faults, yours and mine together. And the world's. And no one's, for the god willed that it should be so."

When I glanced down at him I saw that he was asleep. Perhaps he had not even heard me.

When I was sure he was resting quietly, I went out onto the balcony to breathe a little clean air and be alone. The sun was not more than an hour over the eastern horizon, and the morning sky was still stained a bloody red. I was in despair, as if the trap that had been waiting all my life had finally closed.

"What must I do now?" I murmured, hardly knowing to whom my words were addressed. "What would you have of me?"

And out of the sun, soaring on the day's first breeze as if he meant to conquer the very air that held him, rose an eagle. I watched him pass overhead. I saw the shadow of his spreading wings sweep over the dull earth. And then he disappeared into the western distance.

"There is no place for you in a future that cannot be unwritten." Shaditu had said. And what was this if not a second warning, whispered across the voiceless sky?

I went back inside, my very soul quaking with dread. I felt as if I had seen the god's own face.

Esarhaddon was still asleep. He never woke up from that sleep. The next morning, just before dawn, Death claimed him for her own.

L

WITHIN HOURS OF ESARHADDON'S DEATH, I PRESIDED
over the punishment of his assassin. I had no choice, since by arresting
the physician I had declared his guilt, and the soldiers of Ashur would
misinterpret any show of clemency toward one who had taken the life of
their sacred king. Thus, since I had accused Menuas, and set his penalty,
it was my duty to witness the execution of the sentence.

I had loved my brother, and never more than in those last few hours,
when we seemed at last to have recovered our trust in one another, and
my heart was black with grief. I had held his dead hand and wept like a
woman. My eyes were still stained with tears when I took my seat before
the great gate at Harran, when the prisoner naked and trembling, sobbing
for mercy in a voice that had grown hoarse with despair, was brought
before me to hear his fate. How I hated him at that moment—hated him
all the more because I knew that the real murderer was not here but in
Calah, forever beyond my reach.

So be it, I thought. Menuas alone would feel the full weight of my
revenge.

"There can be no pity for you," I told him—had I really convinced
myself that I might find some comfort in this dreadful act? I know not.
"You have set yourself against gods and men by the enormity of your
crime. When at last it comes, you will welcome the emptiness of death."

I nodded to the executioners that they should begin their work, and I
watched while, amidst the screaming and the stench of blood, a man's
skin was meticulously stripped from his body.

The only other time I had seen a man put to death in this particular
manner had been during the lifetime of the king my father. Marduknasir,

prince of Ushnur, had refused the chance for a peaceful surrender, and so the Lord Sennacherib had leveled his city and driven its subjects away with scourges. Marduknasir himself was flayed alive and his hide nailed to the door of his ruined palace. The king, well fortified with wine, had presided, keeping his face impassive.

I tried to do the same now. Perhaps I succeeded, yet I had only to glance around to see the effect this grisly scene had on others. It held them, for such things have their own appalling fascination, and each man's eyes registered his horror. Only Enkidu seemed hardly to notice, as if he lived outside the circle of human sympathy. But who ever knew what he thought or felt?

As last the wretched work was done, and when the raw carcass that was all that remained of Menuas the physician lay twitching in the dust, and no man, perhaps not even he, could have said whether he yet lived or not, I rose from my chair.

"Someone have the goodness to cut his throat," I said, my voice perhaps a trifle thick, for I felt as if an invisible hand were clutching my windpipe. "This has gone on long enough."

"And what of the skin, *Rab Shaqe?*" one of the executioners asked, holding it up for me to see—he was spattered with blood and seemed to be inviting me to admire his handiwork, for the skin was all of a piece, even to the beard and the face with its empty eyelids. It made me sick to look at it. Sick with shame at the evil men do in the name of justice and revenge.

"What shall be done with it, *Rab Shaqe?*"

"Tan it," I answered. "Have it tanned and cured as if it were the hide of a slaughtered ox. Bring it to me when you have finished. Perhaps I can put it to some use."

I retired to Esarhaddon's rooms, taking a jar of date wine with me and giving strict instructions that I was not to be disturbed. I then began a serious effort to drink myself into insensibility.

It was useless, of course. When a man's nerves are stretched tight enough he can find no repose in anything. I could not even get properly drunk, for the wine seemed perversely to give a sharper focus to my thoughts.

Esarhaddon's body had been removed and was at that moment in the hands of the embalmers, who would prepare the King of the Earth's Four Corners for his final journey to the royal vault in Ashur. Except that Esarhaddon had never been the true king—I had been the god's choice, after all.

How much might have been different if Naq'ia's ambition had been stilled a little and the will of heaven had been left to its fulfullment. Esarhaddon would have remained a soldier, to pursue a soldier's glory, which would have pleased him better. How he would have loved leading armies across the border into Media. His life would have one long campaign. He would probably be alive now and happy, or perhaps he would have found an honorable death in battle, and in that too he would have felt satisfaction.

And I would have become king. I would have married Esharhamat and fathered a line of kings—which last it appeared I had done in any case. Esharhamat! How my heart had ached for her through all these years.

I would never have known the bitterness of exile. I would have become a different man.

Any how many times, perhaps, would I have presided over the sort of gruesome justice I had seen today? A king's word is life and death to his subjects, and even to his enemies, and would my king's conscience, like a soldier's hands when he first learns to use the instruments of war, have bled and then at last grown callused?

It struck me, suddenly, that I was glad not to be the king I might have become. What in the life I had lived did I really regret? Very little. I thought of Selana and our little Theseus, and I thought that were it now in my power to go back and change my destiny, perhaps I could not have brought myself to do it.

The Lord Ashur had led me on a long journey and had at last placed in my hands the mastery of the world, for I was king now, in fact if not in name, and Ashurbanipal, my own son, would stand in my shadow until I chose to lift it.

Yet the gift had come too late and was not wanted. The majesty of power seemed an empty thing, a prison from which my only thought was to escape.

Yet the will of heaven is never really thwarted—perhaps, after all, the god had shown me a kind of mercy.

"Do not try to change things." Such had been the warning from my sister Shaditu's ghost—for in dreams there is truth. *"There is no place for you in a future which cannot be unwritten, and no labor of yours can avail against the god's will. Do not step into the trap that awaits so many others."*

The duties of command wait upon neither grief nor self-pity. If I wished it or not, I was at the head of a vast army, arrested on the way to the reconquest of Egypt. One hundred and fifty thousand men needed to know what I planned to do with their lives.

"Send riders to Calah and Nineveh, and let them inform the nation that her king is dead. Assemble an honor guard of a thousand men to escort the Lord Esarhaddon's body to Ashur. Put the border garrisons on alert, lest our enemies imagine they have found a weakness that bears probing."

"And what of Egypt, Lord?"

This, of course, was what the king's officers, men accustomed to obeying my brother's orders, now suddenly hanging on mine, really wished to know. They attended me in council the morning after the king's death, full of apprehension over how the world might change now that it was in another's hands.

"Egypt must wait," I told them. "There can be no thought of Egypt while there is the likelihood of unrest at home, for there are many who will claim I usurp the rightful king's power. Before all else, I must speak to the Lord Ashurbanipal."

"The decision must rest with you, and not with the Lord Ashurbanipal," said Kisri Adad, absently combing his beard with the fingers of one hand. He was a soldier, and considerations of state made him profoundly uneasy. "It is as the king said, the *marsarru* is yet a boy and not ready to rule."

"He is not the *marsarru* now—he is the king. He has a right to be consulted. Besides, he is fifteen. I was not much older than that when I first commanded an army."

Kisri Adad was on the verge of making some reply, and then seemed to think better of it. I thought it best not to question him.

"If you consult with the king, it will only give encouragement to those who would rally around him to oppose you."

It was Sha Nabushu who spoke. He smiled faintly, as if he might relish my dilemma. But, as I knew already, he was Naq'ia's creature.

"And they will be right to oppose me if I fail to treat the king with the respect that is his due," I answered, uncomfortably conscious that every word I spoke would find its way into the next dispatch pouch to Calah. "Besides, it is not the king who will oppose me, for I am his servant. Things are sometimes done in a king's name which he is powerless to prevent."

It was as close to a declaration of open war against Naq'ia as I could possibly make. I wondered how she would like it.

"Then we are simply to wait here?" Kisri Adad punctuated the question with a wave of his hand that eloquently conveyed his disgust at the idea.

"There is no point in waiting at Harran. There is nothing in Harran, and Egypt can wait until the next campaigning season. We will return to Calah."

Kisri Adad frowned. He would have marched on to Egypt because that had been his late master's wish, but the others, I suspected, were relieved.

"Do not step into the trap that awaits so many others." Shaditu had been wicked enough to understand all these matters. And she had known that the spider who had spun this web still waited at its center, ready to strike.

Well, I had laid my own trap now, and it was only left to see if the Lady Naq'ia would take the bait.

Esarhaddon's corpse was sealed in its casket, and the casket was loaded onto the traditional oxcart that would convey it to the royal tomb at Ashur. I waited with his other officers to see our king and master carried out through the great gate of Harran and into the waiting embrace of eternity.

He had been a bad king—jealous, erratic, dogged in the pursuit of trifles, heedless of real danger. Yet he had never wanted to be king at all. I did not care what kind of king he had been, for I loved him, even now that he was dust, and his weaknesses had been imposed on him by his mother's ambition, an ambition that had finally obliged her to have her own son poisoned.

In my memory he was once again the shining, confident youth with whom I had gone swimming in the canals around Babylon, with whom, the next day, I had led a patrol into the besieged, hostile city to throw open its gates for our father's waiting army.

"Ashur is king! Ashur is king!" we had shouted, our hearts near to bursting with our own glory, thoughtless of peril—immortal. Would that death could have found him then, when his courage was perfect, instead of lying in wait for the frightened, desperate man he became, sinking beneath the weight of an unwanted crown.

No, the tears that wet my face as I watched the oxcart carry him away were not for any king. It was for a brother I grieved, and a friend. I seemed almost to be mourning myself.

Esarhaddon had been the last link binding me to the past. I was at liberty—I had a life still before me, and I was at last free to live it. I knew all this, yet at the moment it seemed to have no meaning.

I had yet one final debt to pay to my murdered brother's ghost.

An army breaking camp is like an old man getting up in the middle of the night, feeling his way in the dark and grumbling quietly. Soldiers never understand why they should disturb themselves to move and, with nothing ahead of them except the prospect of returning to their wives, they were in no hurry. Half a month after the king's death, we were still two days' march from Calah.

I had my own reasons for encouraging delay. Esarhaddon could make whatever arrangements he liked for the succession, but the nation still had to accept them. Upon ascending the throne of Ashur, my grandfather, my father and my brother had all faced rebellions. I was not even the king, so it seemed certain that my right to assume power would be contested somewhere. I was even courting that challenge, yet I did not wish to appear to provoke it.

Still, if it was possible, I wanted to avoid civil war. And it seemed I might succeed, for every day garrison commanders from all over the empire sent me pledges of loyalty—after all, they knew nothing of Ashurbanipal, and I was a soldier, one of them. If it was the late king's will that I should rule, that was enough. Some even came in person. One of the earliest of these was Lushakin, with a bodyguard of five hundred men.

"The north is secure for you," he said. "There was cheering in the barracks when the men heard you had been named *turtanu*, but even those who do not love you will seal their lips and obey. This is like Khanirabbat. Everyone has seen which way the water is running, and no one wants to be left with an empty cup."

"Except that I don't intend to conclude the deliberations with a massacre. And Ashurbanipal is no Arad Malik, but the rightful king."

"Never fear—if you decide you want to be king, the priests will find a way to make you the voice of heaven."

He grinned, for, like most officers, "the voice of heaven" did not sound very loud in his ear. Ideas of that sort were for omen readers and castrated scribes—loyalty, such as a soldier understands, was a more personal matter.

What was the voice of heaven to me? It did not seem to speak. And then, on the nineteenth day of the month of Kislef, when we awoke in the morning to find the first frost on the ground, I heard it. It came in a message from Calah, that the city garrison had declared its loyalty to the new king and was in open rebellion.

"The king is a young fool—what can he hope to gain by this?"

"The king has nothing to do with it," I answered. "It is entirely the Lady Naq'ia's doing."

Of course. I wondered why I should have been surprised. It was impossible not to admire her daring—had I really expected her to accept defeat so quietly? It was hopeless this rebellion, doomed and hopeless, but every animal is most dangerous when it is cornered. And if she was desperate enough for this, she was capable of anything.

When had Naq'ia not been capable of anything? The spider still has venom enough to kill, even as her web burns around her.

We camped half a *beru* from the city gates, which were closed against us. My wife and son were within those walls—what was I to do? But if Naq'ia knew the value of hostages, so did I.

I called Enkidu into my tent, dismissing the guard that we might be alone.

"I must have Selana and the boy out," I told him. "You must go in and get them back for me, since I cannot. I would not ask this of you, but if I once fell into her hands she would certainly kill them, if only out of spite."

He merely glanced at the city walls, as if he expected to push them over with the weight of his hand.

"No, my friend—one man cannot take them by force, not even such a man as you. You must buy them out, and here is the Lady Naq'ia's price."

I took two objects out of a chest and put them on my writing table. The first was a clay tablet wrapped in a piece of leather. The second was the skin of the physician Menuas, rolled up like a carpet and tied with a piece of hemp.

"You will put these into her hands—and into no other's—and if she does not agree to my terms at once, slay her."

He nodded. Yes, he would do it, even though surely it would mean his death. This was the true reason I could send no one but Enkidu, since only he would dare such a thing.

I was not prepared to keep my word to Esarhaddon at the cost of my own family's lives.

"You had best hear what I have written."

Enkidu merely turned his eyes away, as if to show he was prepared to indulge my whim—what did he care what was scratched on a slab of dried mud, since words would settle nothing? I unfolded the leather wrapping.

"Lady, I will not bargain with you," I read, translating the Akkadian into Greek. "I know not what threats or promises you used against them, but the officers you have seduced into this rebellion are not utter fools. They know the city cannot hold out for more than a few days, and there will be no mercy, for them or for you, unless my family are returned to me, in safety, before nightfall. Give them into the keeping of my servant, and at once. Afterwards, and on any terms he chooses to name, I will meet with the king and we will settle all things between us, after the manner of men. There are no more secrets, Lady. I know all that you have done, now and in the past. I harbor no wish for vengeance, but I am not your son, and if you trifle with me I will teach you a lesson in savagery from which you will not survive to profit."

All I could do was shrug my shoulders.

"Perhaps one is entitled to hope that she will know this is not a bluff," I said.

Enkidu's only answer was a kind of snarl.

The next few hours were the most tortured of my life. I mounted Ghost and rode out to wait within sight of Calah's great gate, my mind seething with grief and fear. As the sun fell slowly toward the horizon, and the western sky grew stained with red, it seemed an omen of disaster.

I did not care then for any pledge I had ever made, whether to my brother or to the gods themselves—if Naq'ia harmed my wife and child, I would have her life. I would strip her old body naked and nail her to the city gates, where she would hang until the flesh fell from her wicked bones. I would leave the city in ruins and plow the land with salt. And if Ashurbanipal raised his hand to stop me, I would take his life was well, for all that he was the king and even my own son. I would have neither mercy or pity, for my heart would be dead within my breast.

At such times does a man learn what it is he truly loves and what that love has made of him. Eighteen years before, I had abandoned the woman for whom my bowels ached; I had turned my back on life and had ridden off to lose myself in the serenity of war, and all to do the Lord Ashur's will—but not now. I wanted Selana and our little son back, and I did not care what sacrilege I committed if they were denied to me.

Thus was my mind darkened as I waited, knowing that if I still waited into the night, that night would never end for me.

And at last, as I stood alone on the plain, my shadow seeming to lengthen out into oblivion, the city gate opened, just a little, and I saw Enkidu, leading Selana by the hand, little Theseus straddled on his great shoulders, stepping out into the faded light.

I had to wait there. It was the most exquisite torment to watch them walking across that great emptiness toward me, but I could not venture within arrow shot of the walls or, careless of Naq'ia's unsearchable capacity for treachery, I might throw everything away.

Yet at last I had Selana in my arms once more—we both wept with relief and joy.

"*Pati, Pati!*"

It was my son, calling to his father in his infant Greek, holding his arms out to me from the great height of Enkidu's neck. I reached up and took him, almost crushing him in my embrace.

"Let me ride, Pati! I am not afraid now!"

"Yes—very well!"

I put him up on my horse's back and, as I held his legs to keep him from sliding off, he took Ghost's mane in both hands. By the time we were back at my tent, the only light came from soldiers' campfires.

I will never know what happened when the Lady Naq'ia received my message—my messages, for the hide of her chosen assassin spread out on the floor like a sleeping mat may have been the more persuasive of the two. Only she and Enkidu were there, and neither would ever tell me. I did not even wish to guess.

"What will happen to us now?" Selana asked, after she had put Theseus to bed. He was wrapped aginst the cold in a soldier's blanket and very pleased with himself for being there. "I know nothing of what has been happening—for days now we have not even been allowed to leave our rooms. How will all this end, Lord?"

"That is in the king's hands now."

LI

THE NEXT MORNING THE GATES OF CALAH WERE THROWN open. No one ventured into the city, nor did anyone come out. Our soldiers stood about in little knots, staring across the plain at the open gates, arguing quietly among themselves what this could mean. I knew what it meant—Ashurbanipal was not so much surrendering as inviting me to surrender.

"Since the way is now clear, I will go pay my respects to the new king."

"Then take a bodyguard large enough to allow you to fight your way out if you have to," Lushakin answered. "A thousand men might be enough."

"That would amount to an insult," I answered.

"The *rab shaqe's* elegant manners will get his throat cut for him. You go alone, and your life won't be worth an hour's purchase."

"What would you do if I were killed in there?"

Lushakin's face hardened. "Calah would be a smoking ruin before evening," he said.

"And you think the king does not know that?" I smiled and put my hand on his shoulder, for the man had been my friend for twenty years and I loved him. "Fear nothing, my old *ekalli*, and put your trust in the wisdom of your new king."

I did not say so, but I was putting my trust not so much in Ashurbanipal as in an intuition that Naq'ia had finally lost control of events.

It did not seem so unreasonable, I told myself as I mounted my horse. Whatever her motives in staging this rebellion, if she even knew them herself, Naq'ia had understood that her only chance of making it work was to keep the king and myself apart. And if I entered the city publicly, the king's *turtanu* making his submission, she would not dare raise a hand against me. Therefore, since the gates were open, the officers of the Calah garrison were listening to another voice.

I could only hope that it was Ashurbanipal's, and that he was wise enough to realize how weak his position might be.

I rode across the empty field that separated our camp from the city walls, letting Ghost keep his own pace, as I was in no hurry for whatever waited me within. There was an unearthly silence. Calah seemed deserted—I looked up and could not even make out the faces of the guards looking down from the watchtowers.

And then, as I passed under the shadow of the great gate, I saw them. The whole city seemed to be crowded into the main street. At first they merely stood there, staring at me stupidly, as if a man on horseback was something beyond their comprehension.

No one spoke. There were soldiers mixed in with the crowd, but the expression on all their faces was just the same. I had seen it before, on the faces of the conquered, that mixture of doubt and hope, the uncertainty that afflicts people when suddenly the next few hours of their lives come to seem like a wilderness in which anything might happen.

Here and there, someone to the front of the crowd would drop to his knees, then a few more, then many. Sometimes there were tears in their eyes. Some reached out their hands to touch me as I passed. The unnatural silence persisted.

When it began, it seemed at first to come from some distance, muffled and indistinct, almost like an echo. Yet quickly it grew in strength, and I recognized my own name, shouted by a thousand voices so that the walls themselves seemed to tremble.

"Tiglath! Tiglath! Tiglath! Tiglath!"

The crowd surged around me so that both my horse and I seemed carried forward more by their collective will than by our own motion. It was like being at the center of a boiling caldron, and the shouting never stopped so that it seemed to beat against me in waves.

"Tiglath! Tiglath! Tiglath! Tiglath!"

Thus it was, every step of the way, until I found myself in the great square before the king's palace. Then, once more, there was silence.

The crowd withdrew to a respectful distance, and I was allowed to dismount. A royal groom took the reins from my hand. I glanced up at the palace doors, half expecting to see Ashurbanipal waiting for me at the top of the staircase, but he was not there.

"Good," I remember thinking. "He is either too proud or too clever to associate himself with the favor of an undisciplined mob. Whatever the reason, it is the kingly way to mark a distinction between ruler and ruled."

I mounted the great central stairway alone. The doors opened to receive me and then closed behind my back, and I felt myself enclosed in a separate reality. I was no more the popular hero. I had become another kind of man entirely, the subject and servant of my king.

At least, that was the impression Ashurbanipal was striving hard to create. Had Esarhaddon never made his deathbed confession, and had this king been other than my own son—a thing known to me but perhaps not to him—it might even have succeeded.

I waited several minutes, quite alone, in the great hall of the palace. At last a chamberlain approached me.

"The king will receive you in his garden," he said, as if he hardly had enough air in his lungs to pronounce the words—he was an elderly eunuch who had been in the royal service even during my father's lifetime, and the grandeur of his position so near the throne seemed to have made an early and indelible impression on him.

"Thank you. I know the way."

Ashurbanipal sat on a stone bench next to a pool that had probably contained fish during the summer months but was now drained. It was a cold morning, but he did not seem to notice. He was reading a clay tablet, from which he looked up when I approached, acknowledging my bow with a slight nod.

"Well, Uncle," he said, "I could hear the tumult in the street, even from here. It seems we are all delivered over to your mercy."

Only then did I notice that the tablet he had been reading, and which he still held cradled in his hand, was the one I had sent to Naq'ia.

"If that is the case, Lord, I would venture you have little enough to fear."

"But is it the case?"

"No."

He smiled thinly. I had to remind myself that I was speaking with a fifteen-year-old boy, for he was tall and had already acquired a remarkable self-possession.

"Grandmother, I gather, is in a terrible state," he said, as if he merely wanted to change the subject. "She has retired to her rooms and refuses to see anyone, so that at last the garrison commander was forced to come to me. Poor man—if he hadn't grown so accustomed to taking his orders from Grandmother he might have thought to declare himself *turtanu* and carry on without her. My youth, you see, Uncle, puts me at a disadvantage. Everyone assumes they should act for me."

He paused for a moment and glanced at me speculatively, perhaps wondering if I believed him. But of course it did not matter if I believed him, because I did not care whether he was telling the truth or not. He had dissociated himself from the rebellion, and that was enough. It freed me from any suggestion of treason.

"Who was the man?" he asked finally.

"What man?"

"The man whose skin . . . Oh, do pardon me, Uncle. I am being rude—please sit down."

I sat down next to him on the bench, although I would have preferred to stand. I would have preferred to be inside, drinking wine in front of a brazier, but Ashurbanipal looked quite comfortable where he was. I found myself wondering what point he was attempting to make by receiving me here.

"The man was the Lady Naq'ia's physician. He poisoned the king."

"Ah, well, then perhaps the less said . . . Is that the 'secret' to which you refer?" To indicate his reference, he balanced the tablet in his hand as if trying to guess its weight.

"No, it is not."

"And this secret, whatever it is—you intend to keep it?"

"I think that is best."

He was still just young enough to be unable to conceal completely the fact that he was relieved.

"Do you suppose, Uncle, there are many families with as many secrets as ours?"

"For the peace of mankind, let us hope not."

For just an instant, as our eyes met, I was quite sure he knew everything. Then the impression weakened and I was no longer sure. I would never be sure.

"What are we to do, Uncle?"

"We are to decide whether you can yet be trusted to be king."

He was proud, and he did not care for this answer, but he was also shrewd and therefore did not say so.

"You have a price, Uncle?"

"Yes, I have a price."

"And that is . . . ?"

"The Lady Naq'ia—you must put her aside. She must never again be allowed to meddle in the affairs of this house."

"I thought for a moment you were requiring that she be put to death."

"For her, that will be worse than death."

He seemed to consider the matter for a few seconds, but I knew at once that he had already made up his mind, perhaps even before I spoke, Perhaps, in trying to rule this boy as she had her son, Naq'ia had at last overreached herself.

"Very well," he said finally. "Let her be sent into a luxurious exile in Babylon. We must not be too cruel—let her torment my brother Shamash Shumukin with her advice."

"Even this may one day prove to have been not far enough, but let it be as the king of Ashur wills."

He smiled another of his pale smiles, which was all the acknowledgment this victory of his was to receive.

"Yet Grandmother is not the only one who must go into retirement, Uncle, for a king is not a king if there is one among his subjects more mighty than he, whose voice alone can humble the crowd to dust."

I could not account for the shock I felt at these words, since I had expected something of the sort. He was right, of course. This boy and I could never share the same world—as he had pointed out himself, there were simply too many secrets in our family.

Yet the prospect of another exile, from which, this time, there would be no return, was no easier for that.

"I understand," I said, after a pause no longer than the time required for drawing breath. "You wish to rule alone, and that you cannot do as long as I . . ."

"Uncle, while Prince Tiglath Ashur is at my side, all eyes are drawn to him alone. Every soldier in my army worships you almost as one of the bright gods. Common people cheer you in the street, and peasants in the remotest villages give their male children your name and tell the stories of your wars and your magic courage. In their hearts, you are the king they would have. I cannot hope to stand against the measure of such glory—not yet. I must have my chance to try."

I could feel the tears standing in my eyes, unshed but blinding. For the first time I felt a father's love for his boy whom I must never own as mine. It was bitter to lose a son even in the instant of finding him, yet I knew that the only father's blessing I could ever give him was the one for which he now entreated me.

"Yes, I really do understand." I put my hand on his arm, allowing myself that one gesture of affection, and his pride did not impel him to pull away, so perhaps he comprehended something of what was in my heart. "I will go. And not to some distant garrison town where, even against my will, I would always be a focus of resistance to your rule. I shall seem to disappear, and forever. It shall be as if I had died."

"As if you had never lived," he answered, a strange hardness coming into his voice.

And I knew what he would do, for this king would not share his crown even with a shadow. And so, like kings before him, he would cause the histories of my father's and my brother's reigns to be rewritten, lest they seem more glorious than his own. My very name would vanish from the annals, which in any case is only a collection of triumphant lies. He meant to destroy the past—or, at least, my past.

And even this, I knew, was for the best. He had a sliver of ice through the heart, this son of mine, and that is not a bad thing for a king, although in other men it stands as a fault. Esarhaddon had not had it, and only knew to be cruel where he should have been merely ruthless. It was perhaps what I also lacked, and why the Lord Ashur at last saw fit to deny me the throne of my fathers. I did not regret the lack in myself, but I was glad for Ashurbanipal.

"As if I had never lived."

We spoke then of many things, for even a king is willing to share his thoughts with a ghost. He promised that no one on either side would suffer for his part in the late rebellion, and I knew he was wise enough to keep his word.

"I will reconquer Egypt," he said. "Not this year, but as soon as the floods are past I will assemble an army and drive this Taharqa so far up the Nile that he will never find his way back. "It is a matter of prestige now, so I have no choice."

"A war of conquest is not a bad way to begin a reign," I told him. "But invade through the Delta—do not attempt another desert crossing, because Taharqa will expect that. And do not underestimate him, for he is brave and clever."

"Yet once the war is won, I think it best to collect tribute for a few years and then let the matter tactfully drop. Egypt is a broken reed. She will never trouble us again, so why waste soldiers trying to hold her?"

"This is wise. And remember, My King, as yet you have no knowledge of war, so listen to your commanders and follow their advice. The men who took Egypt once can take her again, if only you will let them. There will be enough glory for everyone."

"It shall be as you say, Uncle."

When I left the city, by a side gate leading from the palace compound, it was already the middle of the afternoon. I rode back to camp both pleased and sorrowful, and these in about equal measure, for I had accomplished all that I had set myself to do, but now the future had no place for me. Not here, at least.

"Would it pain you so very much to give up a husband who is a prince of Ashur for one who is merely a Sicilian farmer?" I asked Selana, even as a groom took my horse away.

"Are we going back?" she asked, and I knew from the light in her eyes that it was all she wanted.

"Yes—and this time forever."

"Then I shall try to bear it," she said, and laughed.

But mine was not to be an abrupt departure, for it could not be allowed to seem that the king was driving me out. I stayed in Calah for over a month, retaining the title and power of *turtanu*, and I helped in the planning of the next Egyptian campaign, approving the commanders who would be its real leaders. The king and I appeared together in public, and he distinguished me with many signs of favor. At the same time I made it known to the leaders of the army that I planned to return to my place of exile, far beyond the shores of the Northern Sea.

"Why must you go?" they asked. "The king is only a boy, and it was the Lord Esarhaddon's will that you should hold power as *turtanu*."

"I am weary of power—now I seek only obscurity and peace of mind. I came back only because it was the king my brother's will, and now I have permission to return. Trust the new king. He is young, but his mind is quick and he knows how to listen. He will do quite well without me."

I do not know if they believed these assurances, but at last they came to accept that I left by my own wish.

And ten days after our first conversation, Ashurbanipal sealed the agreement between us by sending the Lady Naq'ia into exile. I saw her depart the city, in a wagon drawn by royal oxen, as if she were already a corpse on her way to burial.

We did not speak, but I have not forgotten the expression on her face.

She knew she would never be back, and that a lifetime of treachery and murder had ended in failure. She looked as if she envied her victims.

I could not find it in my heart to pity her.

And at last it was time for me too to leave. The king made me many presents of gold and silver, but great wealth would be of little use to the man I was to become, so most of these I distributed among the bodyguard chosen to conduct me to the northern border. Lushakin insisted on commanding my escort himself.

My last night in Calah, I summoned a scribe and resigned to the king's possession most of my property, my houses and my great estates, arranging that the document be delivered into his hands only after I had departed. These things belong to Prince Tiglath Ashur, and I was not he. Let the king find favorites of his own to make rich, I thought. He will need them.

The one exception was to be the estate at Three Lions, which I would give to Qurdi, my overseer there, and his wife Naiba. I would not deny myself the pleasure of raising them to unimagined prosperity.

A man's final journey out of the land that nurtured him always follows a long road. We did not stop in the cities, but from a distance, windswept and already dusted with snow, I saw the walls of Nineveh, where I had been born, where I had once imagined I would live in glory, leaving her only to fill a royal tomb in Ashur, and I remembered the warning I had heard as a youth: "*Look to Nineveh, Tiglath Ashur. Its streets will become the hunting ground of foxes, and owls will make their nests in the palace of the great king. Do not think that happiness and glory await you here, Prince, for the god reserves you to another way. Here all things will be bitter—love, power, friendship. Sweet at first, but, in the end, bitter.*"

He was waiting for me, sitting by the marker stone at Three Lions. I had known I would see him once more, and I left Selana and my escort at a distance and rode to meet him.

If a man is mortal, time must wear him away like a stone left in running water, but the *maxxu*, the holy one of Ashur, was unchanged from the first time I had seen him, more than twenty years before. The same gaunt, sun-darkened face, the same prominent brow, the same white hair and beard, the same dead and sightless eyes that seemed to look past one and into some hidden reality.

"You have come at last," he said. "One of us has had a long wait."

"And this, I think, will be our final meeting."

"Yes, Tiglath Ashur—our final meeting. You have served the god's purposes well, and now he is finished with you. Find your reward."

"Have the prophecies then been fulfilled, Holy One?"

"Not yet, Tiglath Ashur, but you will know when they have."

"And what is to come now?"

He smiled, mocking me, as if to ask, *Do you really wish to know?*

"What of my son, Holy One? What of the king?"

"Oh, him." He shrugged his thin shoulders. "Ashurbanipal will have the glorious reign that should have been yours, but after him the empire of your fathers will wither and rot away like an apple left in the sun. In time all will disappear, leaving hardly a trace upon the wind-swept earth. The gods will depart. The splendid cities will vanish until they are not even a memory. Their very names will perish from the tongues of men. Nothing will remain except silence. Such is Sacred Ashur's judgment against the land and its people."

"You speak of dark things," I said. "Holy One, you fill me with darkness."

"Do I?" He smiled at me, as if at a child who is frightened of his own shadow. "Then know that the sun spreads its light to many places, and there is always another dawn. Go now, Tiglath Ashur, whom the god loves. Go and live your life."

I turned my horse and rode away, for I had heard enough.

At last we reached the banks of the Bohtan River. When I crossed it, I would be out of the Land of Ashur. I said good-bye to Lushakin, embracing him like a brother. Then I tied Ghost to the back of the wagon that carried Selana and our child and drove it into the water. Waiting on the other side was Tabiti, headman of the Sacan, grinning like a cat.

"My scouts have been following you for days," he shouted. "You have made slow progress."

"We will do better now," I shouted back.

"For the god reserves you to another way," the *maxxu* had told me, so long ago. Now, I thought, perhaps I am to find it.

When we reached the middle of the river, Selana tore off her veil and threw it away. Almost at once the swirling waters dragged it under and it disappeared forever.

EPILOGUE

IF ONE IS SPARED TO GROW OLD ENOUGH, THE PAST assumes a clarity that is denied to the present, and the future disappears like a phantom. I was thirty-seven when I crossed the Bohtan River and left behind forever the land of my birth. That was nearly sixty years ago. It has taken me all my long lifetime to see even dimly into the riddle of those days, of what Esarhaddon and Naq'ia and all the rest of us set into motion while we followed blindly the pattern of the god's great design, thinking it all the movement of our own little wills. I alone have been spared to see the ends of things, only to grasp that these are not the ends, that the Lord Ashur recognizes no completion to his purpose, which is known only to him, and thus the final meaning of all we did and suffered remains hidden.

And perhaps I only deceive myself that I have learned anything at all. Deianira, child of my youngest grandson, is endlessly pleased with herself that at last she is mistress of all the Greek letters in which this long story of my youth is written—she can point to them, one after another, as they appear on the vellum page, speaking the name of each and fancying that thus the whole secret of writing is open to her. Perhaps my understanding is like hers, composed of random fragments of the truth, useless because without a clue to the controlling intention.

So here it sits on my writing desk, scroll after scroll, the product of many days' labor, meant for eyes that can see more clearly than mine. There is only a very little more to add.

We wintered that year with Tabiti and his people, and the following spring we moved west with them as far as Lydia, where the Sacan, along with tribes of the Cimmerians, raided many border villages and seemed able—such was the weakness and turmoil of that kingdom—to come and go as they liked. At the coastal city of Myrina the son of Argimpasa and I threw our arms around each other's necks and through our tears vowed eternal friendship, knowing we would never meet again. Selana, Theseus, Enkidu, and I took passage on a Phoenician ship bound for Lesbos, and from there we traveled to Corinth and on to Sicily, arriving home late in the summer after an absence of seven years.

Our return caused considerable excitement in Naxos, where old friends hurried to welcome us back, to tell us all that had happened while we were gone, and to hear of our adventures in strange lands. We stayed in the town overnight, and then in the morning I hired a wagon and we drove to our farm, where an astonished Kephalos greeted us as if we had dropped from the sky in a shower of fire.

"Dread Lord!" he bellowed, weeping furiously, "oh, bless the gods that they have spared me to see this day. It is as if you've returned from the dead!"

"Not quite, you fat scoundrel. Did you not receive the letter I had sent to you from Naukratis?"

"Yes, Lord, but distance is like eternity and a scrap of papyrus is not a living man. I despaired that you would ever find your way back—yet I gather, since you are here, that the Lord Esarhaddon has met his death?"

I told him all that had happened. It was a long story, lasting far into the night, and by the time it was finished we were both too drunk to find our beds. Such was our reunion.

The farm was much improved in our absence, which was entirely due to the careful management of young Tullus, who had taken a wife and already had a son just Theseus' age. His mother had died, but his brother, as yet unmarried, still lived with him. With some of my little remaining gold I gave Icilius the price of a bride and bought the two families a plot adjacent to my own land, on condition that Tullus remain as my overseer. The rest I laid out on the purchase of another farm, for I meant to prosper in my new life.

The years that followed brought increase and loss, as is the common lot of all men. Selana was with child again even before we left Asia, and a second son, named Patroklus, was born to us soon after our return. He was followed by daughter the very next year and then by two more sons. Selana and I lived together in happiness and as much peace as is possible with such a woman, and she died in her seventieth year, surrounded by a family that extended to the fourth generation. I have never ceased to mourn her loss.

Kephalos died ten years after our return, after dining too well one night on Selana's roast lamb. As I had promised him, I buried his ashes in the same urn with his beloved Ganymedes.

Enkidu died in his sleep. His hair had turned white by then, but his great strength never left him until the hour of death. His ashes lie beside my wife's, as is only his due.

As for myself, I have lived into the extremity of age, fortunate not to have survived any of Selana's and my children, all of whom now have children and grandchildren of their own.

Yet what of my other son? What of Ashurbanipal? Some twelve summers ago I heard that he had died full of years and glory. I cannot describe what I felt, for it was almost as if a part of myself had died.

A traveler told me the news, and from him and others over the years I have heard almost all that I know of events in the land of my fathers. They have no idea who I am, for the name of Tiglath Ashur has been long forgotten in the eastern nations, so what they tell me is perhaps even the truth.

Yet I had some tidings of Ashurbanipal even before I left the Greek mainland, for that same summer he kept his word and returned to Egypt with a large army, this time carrying fire and sword all the way to Thebes itself and making himself absolute master of the entire country. Thus the child of my loins proved himself a soldier after all. Taharqa retreated into the Land of Kush and was never heard from again. Egypt, so I believe, is ruled to this day by the descendants of Prince Nekau, who, with the king his master's permission, made himself Pharaoh.

Then Ashurbanipal made war against the Elamites, destroying that nation forever—I have heard that he had the king's head cut off and hung from a tree branch in his garden. The Assyrian victory, though complete, was by no means a blessing, however, for the collapse of Elam provided an opening for the Medes, who quickly overran the country and proved a far more dangerous neighbor.

The arrangement by which Esarhaddon gave the throne of Babylon to his son Shamash Shumukin lasted for more than ten years, but in the end, as I had feared, peace between the royal brothers was destroyed. Shamash Shumukin, by what agency and for what reasons I have never been able to learn, was persuaded to rebel against the king of Ashur, raising the whole of Sumer against him. Ashurbanipal crushed the rebellion and Shamash Shumukin died, perhaps by his own hand, as his palace in Babylon burned around him—thus was the prophecy of death by fire, which haunted Esharhamat's dreams even as she carried the boy in her womb, fulfilled at last.

I have often wondered if Naq'ia's hand was behind these things, but I will never know. I have heard nothing of her over the years, although she must be long dead.

Of the kings who ruled after Ashurbanipal, whether these were his descendants or others, I know nothing. It has been many years since I have heard the name of my native land on any man's lips, but of her fate I am nonetheless certain.

I have listened to tales of a great king who has arisen among the Chaldeans, a conqueror who has made himself king of Babylon, and the Medes I know wait for any sign of weakness that they may fall upon the Land of Ashur like a wolf raiding a flock of sheep—like Esharhamat while she was big with her doomed son, my sleeping mat is a place of fire and slaughter.

Every night I dream of Nineveh. I see her deserted and in ruins, her gods carried off into slavery, the ground sodden with the blood of her people. I hear the foxes barking in her streets, and the cries of owls that have made their nests in her temples. Soon, I know, some traveler will make his way here with news that the east has given birth to a new strain of conquerors, that the empire of my fathers has perished under the swords of another race. I pray only that death will find me first.

Yet until then I sit here in my garden, shaded by a plane tree I planted with my own hands, within sight of the wine-dark sea, and it is possible to believe that life is a blessing. Nations that have known uncounted centuries of triumph vanish in an instant of defeat, yet men live on without them. Some purpose is served in this, though we may never know what it is, for the god is full of mercy and his holy light washes the world clean with each new day. I see the sun rise over the glistening water and feel its heat against my face, like the warmth of love, and I know that the Lord Ashur has not deserted his creation. It is as the *maxxu* told me, though I hardly believed him all those years ago—there is always another dawn.

NICHOLAS GUILD is the author of several novels, including *The Assyrian, The Berlin Warning,* and *The Linz Tattoo.* He lives in Connecticut with his wife and son.

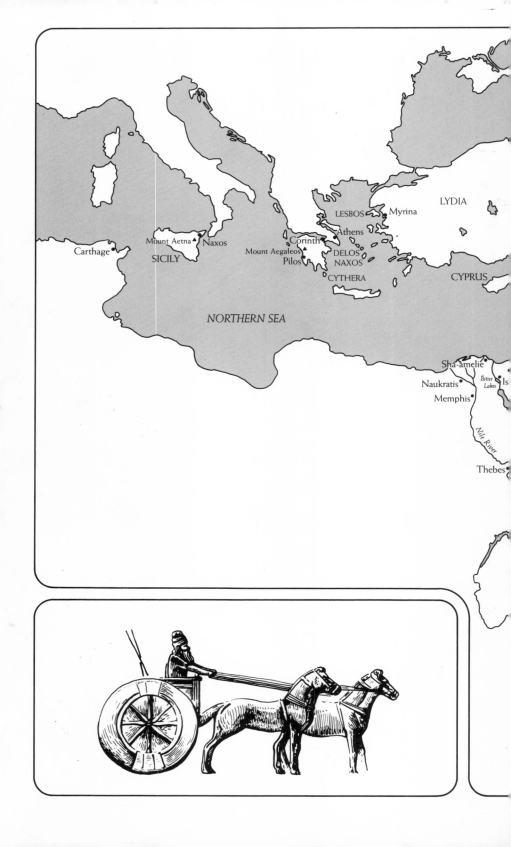

LYDIA

LESBOS

Myrina

Athens

Corinth

Mount Aegaleos

DELOS

Carthage

Mount Aetna

Naxos

SICILY

Pilos

NAXOS

CYPRUS

CYTHERA

NORTHERN SEA

Sha-amelie

Bitter
Lakes

Is

Naukratis

Memphis

Nile River

Thebes